Pilgrim

⌁ BOOK FIVE OF ⌁
THE WAYFARER REDEMPTION

Sara Douglass

TOR®
fantasy

A TOM DOHERTY ASSOCIATES BOOK
NEW YORK

This is a work of fiction. All the characters and events portrayed in this book are either products of the author's imagination or are used fictitiously.

PILGRIM: BOOK FIVE OF THE WAYFARER REDEMPTION

Copyright © 1997 by Sara Douglass
Teaser copyright © 2006 by Sara Douglass

Originally published in 1997 by Voyager, an imprint of HarperCollins Publishers, Australia.

A Tor Book
Published by Tom Doherty Associates, LLC
175 Fifth Avenue
New York, NY 10010

www.tor.com
Tor® is a registered trademark of Tom Doherty Associates, LLC.

ISBN 0-765-34279-0
EAN 978-0-765-34279-9

First Tor edition: September 2005
First mass market edition: May 2006

Printed in the United States of America

0 9 8 7 6 5 4 3 2 1

Author's Note

I wrote this book while replanting and laying out the century-old gardens of Ashcotte, and their thousands of lilies and cornflowers and peonies and poppies and violets somehow found their way through the open spring windows onto these pages. Thus, *Pilgrim* is in part the re-creation of the field of flowers which surrounds Ashcotte.

Acknowledgments

Over the past two years many readers have written in with suggestions, ideas, and frequent pleas for Faraday's life (I always intended to kill her off in *Enchanter*, but no one would allow me to). I thank you all (and Faraday sends her heartfelt relief at being hauled back from the brink of a thousand deaths), but I would particularly like to thank Kylie Coutts, who reminded me about Faraday's enchanted wooden bowl. If the Sacred Groves go up in flames, Kylie, you must bear the responsibility!

Acknowledgments

Over the past two years many readers have written in with suggestions, ideas, and frequent pleas for Faraday's life (I always intended to kill her off in *Enchanter*, but no one would allow me to). I thank you all (and Faraday sends her heartfelt relief at being hauled back from the brink of a thousand deaths), but I would particularly like to thank Kylie Coutts, who reminded me about Faraday's enchanted wooden bowl. If the Sacred Groves go up in flames, Kylie, you must bear the responsibility!

Contents

Contents

Pilgrim

BOOK FIVE OF

THE WAYFARER REDEMPTION

Contents

Contents

Pilgrim

BOOK FIVE OF

The Wayfarer Redemption

Prologue

The lieutenant pushed his fork back and forth across the table, back and forth, back and forth, his eyes vacant, his mind and heart a thousand galaxies away.

Scrape . . . scrape . . . scrape.

"For heaven's sake, Chris, will you stop that? It's driving me crazy!"

The lieutenant gripped the fork in his fist, and his companion tensed, thinking Chris would fling it across the dull, black metal table toward him.

But Chris' hand suddenly relaxed, and he managed a tight, half-apologetic smile. "Sorry. It's just that this . . . this . . ."

"We only have another two day spans, mate, and then we wake the next shift for their stint at uselessness."

Chris' fingers traced gently over the surface of the table. It vibrated. *Everything* on the ship vibrated.

"I can't bloody wait for another stretch of deep sleep," he said quietly, his eyes flickering over to Commander Devereaux sitting at a keyboard by the room's only porthole. "Unlike *him.*"

His fellow officer nodded. Perhaps thirty-five rotations ago, waking from their allotted span of deep sleep, the retiring crew had reported a strange vibration within the ship. No mechanical or structural problem . . . the ship was just *vibrating*.

And then . . . then they'd found that the ship was becoming a little sluggish in responding to commands, and after five or six day spans it refused to respond to their commands at all.

The other three ships in the fleet had similar problems—at least, that's what their last communiques had reported. *The Ark* crew was aware of the faint phosphorescent outlines in the wake of the other ships, but that was all now. So here we were, hurtling through deep space, in ships that responded to no command, and with cargo that the crews preferred not to think about. When they volunteered for this mission, hadn't they been told that once they'd found somewhere to "dispose" of the cargo they could come home?

But now, the crew of *The Ark* wondered, *what* would be disposed of? The cargo? Or them?

It might have helped if the commander had come up with something helpful. But Devereaux seemed peculiarly unconcerned, saying only that the vibrations soothed his soul and that the ships, if they no longer responded to human command, at least seemed to know what they were doing.

And now here he was, tapping at that keyboard as if he actually had a purpose in life. None of them had a purpose anymore. They were as good as dead. Everyone knew that. Why not Devereaux?

"What are you doing, sir?" Chris asked. He had picked up the fork again, and it quivered in his overtight grip.

"I . . ." Devereaux frowned as if listening intently to something, then his fingers rattled over the keys. "I am just writing this down."

"Writing *what* down, sir?" the other officer asked, his voice tight.

Devereaux turned slightly to look at them, his eyes wide. "Don't you hear it? Lovely music . . . enchanted music . . . listen, it vibrates through the ship. Don't you *feel* it?"

"No," Chris said. He paused, uncomfortable. "Why write it down, sir? For *who?* What is the bloody *point* of writing it down?"

Devereaux smiled. "I'm writing it down for Katie, Chris. A songbook for Katie."

Chris stared at him, almost hating the man. "Katie is *dead,* sir. She has been dead at least twelve thousand years. I repeat, what is the fucking *point?*"

Devereaux's smile did not falter. He lifted a hand and placed it over his heart. "She lives here, Chris. She always will. And in writing down these melodies, I hope that one day she will live to enjoy the music as much as I do."

It was then that *The Ark,* in silent communion with the others, decided to let Devereaux live.

1

Questions of Conveyance

The speckled blue eagle clung to rocks under the overhang of the river cliffs a league south of Carlon. He shuddered. Nothing in life made sense anymore. He had been drifting the thermals, digesting his noonday meal of rats, when a thin gray mist had enveloped him and sent despair stringing through his veins.

He could not fight it, and had not wanted to. His wings crippled with melancholy, he'd plummeted from the sky, uncaring about his inevitable death.

It had seemed the best solution to his useless life.

Chasing rats? Ingesting them. *Why?*

In his mad, uncaring tumble out of control, the eagle struck the cliff face. The impact drove the breath from him, and he thought it may also have broken one of his breast bones, but even in the midst of despair, the eagle's talons scrabbled automatically for purchase among the rocks.

And then . . . then the despair had gone. Evaporated.

The eagle blinked and looked about.

It was cold here in the shadow of the rocks, and he wanted to warm himself in the sun again—but he feared the gray-fingered enemy that awaited him within the thermals. In the open air.

What was this gray miasma? What had caused it?

He cocked his head to one side, his eyes unblinking, considering. Gryphon? Was this their mischief?

No. The Gryphon had long gone, and *their* evil he would have felt ripping into him, not seeping in with this gray mist's many-fingered coldness. No, this was something very different.

Something worse.

The sun was sinking now, only an hour or two left until dusk, and the eagle did not want to spend the night clinging to this cliff face.

He cocked his head—the gray haze had evaporated.

With fear—a new sensation for this most ancient and wise of birds—he cast himself into the air. He rose over the Nordra, expecting any minute to be seized again by that consuming despair.

But there was nothing.

Nothing but the rays of the sun glinting from his feathers and the company of the sky.

Relieved, the eagle tilted his wings and headed for his roost under the eaves of one of the towers of Carlon.

He thought he would rest there a day or two. Watch. Discover if the evil would strike again, and, if so, how best to survive it.

The yards of the slaughterhouse situated a half-league west of Tare were in chaos. Two of the slaughtermen had been outside when Sheol's midafternoon despair struck. Now they were dead, trampled beneath the hooves of a thousand crazed livestock. The fourteen other men were still safe, for they had been inside and protected when the TimeKeepers had burst through the Ancient Barrows.

Even though midafternoon had passed, and the world was once more left to its own devices, the men did not dare leave the safety of the slaughterhouse.

Animals ringed the building. Sheep, a few pigs, seven old plow horses, and innumerable cattle—all once destined for death and butchery. All staring implacably, unblinkingly, at the doors and windows.

One of the pigs nudged at the door with his snout, and then squealed.

Instantly pandemonium broke out. A horse screamed, and threw itself at the door. The wooden planks cracked, but did not break.

Imitating the horse's lead, cattle hurled themselves against the door and walls.

The slaughtermen inside grabbed whatever they could to defend themselves.

The walls began to shake under the onslaught. Sheep bit savagely at any protuberance, pulling nails from boards with their teeth, and horses rent at walls with their hooves. All the animals wailed, one continuous thin screech that forced the men inside to drop their weapons and clasp hands to ears, screaming themselves.

The door cracked once more, then split. A brown steer shouldered his way through. He was plump and healthy, bred and fattened to feed the robust appetites of the Tarean citizens. Now he had an appetite himself.

Behind him many score cattle trampled into the slaughterhouse, pigs and sheep squeezing among the legs of their bovine cousins as best they could.

The invasion was many bodied, but it acted with one mind.

The slaughtermen did not die well.

The creatures used only their teeth to kill, not their hooves, and those teeth were grinders, not biters, and so those men were ground into the grave, and it was not a fast nor pleasant descent.

Of all the creatures once destined for slaughter, only the horses did not enter the slaughterhouse and partake of the meal.

They lingered outside in the first of the collecting yards, nervous, unsure, their heads high, their skin twitching. One snorted, then pranced about a few paces. He'd not had this much energy since he'd been a yearling.

A shadow flickered over one of the far fences, then raced across the trampled dirt toward the group of horses. They bunched together, turning to watch the shadow, and then it swept over them and the horses screamed, jerked, and then stampeded, breaking through the fence in their panic.

High above, the flock of Hawkchilds veered to the east and turned their eyes once more to the Ancient Barrows.

Their masters called.

The horses fled, running east with all the strength left in their hearts.

At the slaughterhouse, a brown and cream badger ambled into the bloodied building and stood surveying the carnage.

You have done well, he spoke to those inside. *Would you like to exact yet more vengeance?*

Sheol tipped back her head and exposed her slim white throat to the afternoon sun. Her fingers spasmed and dug into the rocky soil of the ruined Barrow she sat on, her body arched, and she moaned and shuddered.

A residual wisp of gray miasma still clung to a corner of her lip.

"Sheol?" Raspu murmured and reached out a hand. "Sheol?" At the soft touch of his hand, Sheol's sapphire eyes jerked open and she bared her teeth in a snarl.

Raspu did not flinch. "Sheol? Did you feast well?"

The entire group of TimeKeeper Demons regarded her curiously, as did StarLaughter sitting slightly to one side with a breast bared, its useless nipple hanging from her undead child's mouth.

Sheol blinked, and then her snarl widened into a smile, and the reddened tip of her tongue probed slowly at the corners of her lips.

She gobbled down the remaining trace of mist.

"I fed *well!*" she cried, and leaped to her feet, spinning about in a circle. "Well!"

Her companions stared at her, noting the new flush of strength and power in her cheeks and eyes, and they howled with anticipation. Sheol began an ecstatic caper, and the Demons joined her in dance, holding hands and circling in tight formation through the rubble of earth and rocks that had once been the Barrow. They screamed and shrieked, intoxicated with success.

The Minstrelsea forest, encircling the ruined spaces of the Ancient Barrows, was silent. Listening. Watching.

StarLaughter pulled the material of her gown over her breast and smiled for her friends. It had been eons since they had fed, and she could well understand their excitement. They had sat still and silent as Sheol's demonic influence had issued from her nostrils and mouth in a steady effluence of misty gray contagion. The haze had coalesced about her head for a moment, blurring her features, and had then rippled forth with the speed of thought over the entire land of Tencendor.

Every soul it touched—Icarii, human, bird or animal— had been infected, and Sheol had fed generously on each one of them.

Now how well Sheol looked! The veins of her neck throbbed with life, and her teeth were whiter and her mouth redder than StarLaughter had ever seen. Stars, but the others must be beside themselves in the wait for their turn!

StarLaughter rose slowly to her feet, her child clasped protectively in her hands. "When?" she said.

The Demons stopped and stared at her.

"We need to wait a few days," Raspu finally replied.

"What?" StarLaughter cried. "My son—"

"*Not* before then," Sheol said, and took a step toward Star-Laughter. "We all need to feed, and once we have grown the stronger for the feeding we can dare the forest paths."

She cast her eyes over the distant trees and her lip curled. "We will move during *our* time, and on *our* terms."

"You don't like the forest?" StarLaughter said.

"It is not dead," Barzula responded. "And it is far, far too gloomy."

"But—" StarLaughter began.

"Hush," Rox said, and he turned flat eyes her way. "You ask too many questions."

StarLaughter closed her mouth, but she hugged her baby tightly to her, and stared angrily at the Demons. Sheol smiled, and patted StarLaughter on the shoulder. "We are tense, Queen of Heaven. Pardon our ill manners."

StarLaughter nodded, but Sheol's apology had done little to appease her anger.

"Why travel the forest if you do not like it?" she said. "Surely the waterways would be the safest and fastest way to reach Cauldron Lake."

"No," Sheol said. "Not the waterways. We do not like the waterways."

"Why not?" StarLaughter asked, shooting Rox a defiant look.

"Because the waterways are the Enemy's construct, and they will have set traps for us," Sheol said. "Even if they are long dead, their traps are not. The waterways are too closely allied with—"

"*Them*," Barzula said.

"—their voyager craft," Sheol continued through the interruption, "to be safe for us. No matter. We will dare the forests . . . and survive. After Cauldron Lake the way will be easier. Not only will we be stronger, we will be in the open."

All of the Demons relaxed at the thought of open territory.

"Soon my babe will live and breathe and cry my name," StarLaughter whispered, her eyes unfocused and her hands digging into the babe's cool, damp flesh.

"Oh, assuredly," Sheol said, and shared a secret wink with her companion Demons. She laughed. "Assuredly!"

The other Demons howled in shared merriment, and StarLaughter smiled, thinking she understood.

Then as one the Demons quietened, their faces falling still.

Rox turned slowly to the west. "Hark," he said. "What is that?"

"Conveyance," said Mot.

If the TimeKeeper Demons did not like to use the waterways, then WolfStar had no such compunction. When he'd slipped away from the Chamber of the Star Gate, he'd not gone to the surface, as had everyone else. Instead, WolfStar had faded back into the waterways. They would protect him as nothing else could; the pack of resurrected children would not be able to find him down here. And WolfStar did not want to be found, not for a long time.

He had something very important to do.

Under one arm he carried a sack with as much tenderness and care as StarLaughter carried her undead infant. The sack's linen was slightly stained, as if with effluent, and it left an unpleasant odor in WolfStar's wake.

Niah, or what was left of her.

Niah . . . WolfStar's face softened very slightly. She had been so desirable, so strong, when she'd been the First Priestess on the Isle of Mist and Memory. She'd carried through her task—to bear Azhure in the hateful household of Hagen, the Plow Keeper of Smyrton—with courage and sweetness, and had passed that courage and sweetness to their enchanted daughter.

For that courage WolfStar had promised Niah rebirth and his love, and he'd meant to give her both.

Except things hadn't turned out quite so well as planned. Niah's manner of death (and even WolfStar shuddered whenever he thought of it) had warped her soul so brutally that she'd been reborn a vindictive, hard woman. So determined to reseize life that she cared not what her determination might do to the other lives she touched.

Not the woman WolfStar had thought to love. True, the reborn Niah had been pleasing enough, and eager enough, and WolfStar had adored her quickness in conceiving of an heir, but . . .

. . . but the fact was she'd failed. Failed WolfStar and failed Tencendor at the critical moment. WolfStar had thought of little else in the long hours he'd wandered the dank and dark halls of the waterways. Niah had distracted him when his full concentration should have been elsewhere (*could* he have stopped Drago if he hadn't been so determined to bed Niah?), and her inability to keep her hold on the body she'd gained meant that WolfStar had again been distracted—with *grief!* damn it!—just when his full power and attention was needed to help ward the Star Gate.

Niah had failed because Zenith had proved too strong. Who would have thought it? Truc, Zenith had the aid of Faraday, and an earthworm could accomplish miracles if it had Faraday to help it, but even so . . . Zenith had been the stronger, and WolfStar had always been the one to be impressed by strength.

Ah! He had far more vital matters to think of than pondering Zenith's sudden determination. Besides, with what he planned, he could get back the woman he'd always meant to have. Alive. Vibrant. And very, very powerful.

His fingers unconsciously tightened about the sack.

This time Niah would *not* fail.

WolfStar grinned, feral and confident in the darkness.

"Here," he muttered, and ducked into a dark opening no more than head height.

It was an ancient drain, and it led to the bowels of the Keep on the shores of Cauldron Lake.

WolfStar knew *exactly* what he had to do.

* * *

The horses ran, and their crippled limbs ate up the leagues with astonishing ease. Directly above them flew the Hawkchilds, so completely in unison that as one lifted his wings, so all lifted, and as another swept hers down, so all swept theirs down.

Each stroke of their wings corresponded exactly with a stride of the horses.

And with each stroke of the Hawkchilds' wings, the horses felt as if they were lifted slightly into the air, and their strides lengthened so that they floated a score of paces with each stride. When their hooves beat earthward again, they barely grazed the ground before they powered effortlessly forward into their next stride.

And with each stride, the horses felt life surge through their veins and tired muscles. Necks thickened and arched, nostrils flared crimson, swaybacks straightened and flowed strong into newly muscled haunches. Hair and skin darkened and fined, until they glowed a silky ebony.

Strange things twisted inside their bodies, but of those changes there was, as yet, no outward sign.

Once fit only for the slaughterhouse, great black warhorses raced across the plains, heading for the Ancient Barrows.

2

The Dreamer

The bones had lain there for almost twenty years, picked clean by scavengers and the passing winds of time. They had been a neat pile when the tired old soul had lain down for the final time; now they were scattered over a half-dozen paces, some resting in the glare of the sun, others piled under the gloom of a thorn bush.

Footsteps disturbed the peace of the grave site. A tall and willowy woman, dressed in a clinging pale gray robe. Iron-gray hair, streaked with silver, cascaded down her back. On the ring finger of her left hand she wore a circle of stars. She had very deep blue eyes and a red mouth, with blood trailing from one corner and down her chin.

As she neared the largest pile of bones the woman crouched, and snarled, her hands tensed into tight claws.

"Fool way to die!" she hissed. "Alone and forgotten! Did you think, *I* forgot? Did you think to escape *me* so easily?"

She snarled again, and grabbed a portion of the rib cage, flinging it behind her. She snatched at another bone, and threw that with the ribs. She scurried a little further away, reached under the thorn bush and hauled out its desiccated treasury of bones, also throwing them on the pile.

She continued to snap and snarl, as if she had the rabid fever of wild dogs, scurrying from spot to spot, picking up a knuckle here, a vertebrae there, a cracked femur bone from somewhere else.

The pile of bones grew.

"I want to *hunt,*" she whispered, "and yet what must I do? Find your useless framework, and knit something out of it! Why must *I* be left to do it all?"

She finally stood, surveying the skeletal pile before her. "Something is missing," she mumbled, and swept her hands back through her hair, combing it out of her eyes.

Her tongue had long since licked clean the tasty morsel draining down her chin.

"Missing," she continued to mumble, wandering in circles about the desolate site. "Missing . . . where . . . where . . . ah!"

She snatched at a long white hair that clung to the outer reaches of the thorn bush and hurried back to the pile of bones with it. She carefully laid it across the top.

Then she stood back, standing very still, her dark blue eyes staring at the bones.

Very slowly she raised her left hand, and the circle of light about its ring finger flared.

"Of what use is bone to me?" she whispered. "I need *flesh!*"

She dropped her hand, and the light flared from ring to bones.

The pile burst into flame.

Without fear the woman stepped close and reached into the conflagration with both hands. She grabbed hold of something, grunted with effort, then finally, gradually, hauled it free.

Her own shape changed slightly during her efforts, as if her muscles had to rearrange themselves to manage to drag the large object free of the fire, and in the flickering light she seemed something far larger and bulkier than human, and more dangerous. Yet when she finally stood straight again, she had regained her womanly features.

She looked happily at the result of her endeavor. *Her* magic had not dimmed in these past hours! But she shook her head slightly. Look what had become of *him!*

He stood, limbs akimbo, potbelly drooping, and he returned her scrutiny blankly, no gratitude in his face at all.

"You are of this land," she said, "and there is still service it demands of you. Go south, and wait."

He stared, unblinking, uncaring, and then he gave a mighty yawn. The languor of death had not yet left him, and all *he* wanted to do was to sleep.

"Oh!" she said, irritated. "Go!"

She waved her hand again, the light flared, and when it had died, she stood alone in the stony gully of the Urqhart Hills.

Grinning again at the pleasantness of solitude, she turned and ran for the north, and as she did so her shape changed, and her limbs loped, and her tongue hung red from her mouth, and she felt the need to sink her teeth into the back of prey, very, very soon.

Scrawny limbs trembling, potbelly hanging from gaunt ribs, he stood on the plain just north of the Rhaetian Hills.

Beside him the Nordra roared.

He was desperate for sleep, and so he hung his head, and he dreamed.

He dreamed. He dreamed of days so far distant he did not know if they were memory or myth. He dreamed of great battles, defeats and victories both, and he dreamed of the one who had loved him, and who he'd loved beyond expression.

Then he'd been crippled, and the one who loved him had shown him the door, and so he'd wandered disconsolate— save for the odd loving the boy showed him—until his life had trickled to a conclusion in blessed, blessed death.

Then why was he back?

3

The Feathered Lizard

Faraday kept her arm tight about the man as they walked toward where she'd left Zenith and the donkeys. He'd grown tired in the past hour, as if the effort of surviving the Star Gate and then watching the effects of the Demons flow over the land had finally exhausted him both physically and mentally.

Faraday did not feel much better. This past day had drained her: fighting to repel the horror of the Demons' passage through the Star Gate and fighting to save Drago from the collapsing chamber, then emerging from the tunnel to find Tencendor wrapped in such horrific despair had left its mark on her soul. For hours she'd had to fight off the bleak certainty that there was nothing anyone could do against the TimeKeepers.

"Drago," she murmured. "Just a little further. See? There is Zenith!"

Zenith, who had been waiting with growing anxiety, ran forward from where she'd been pacing by the cart. A corner of her cloak caught in the exposed root of a tree, and she ripped it free in her haste.

"Faraday! Drago! *Drago?*" Zenith wrapped her arms about her brother, taking the load from Faraday. "Is he all right, Faraday? And you . . . you look dreadful!"

The staff Drago had been clutching now fell from his fingers and rolled a few paces away.

"He needs some rest," Faraday said. She tried to smile, and failed. "We both do."

Zenith looked between both of them. Her relief that Faraday was well, and had managed to ensure Drago's safe return, was overwhelmed by her concern at how debilitated both were. Drago was a heavy weight in her arms, his eyes closed, his breathing shallow, while the only color in Faraday's ashen face were the rings of exhaustion under her eyes. She had clasped her arms about herself in an effort to stop them shaking.

What happened? Zenith longed to ask.

"The cart," she said, and half-dragged, half-lifted Drago toward it.

"Let me help," Faraday said, and took the weight of his legs.

Between them they managed to lift Drago into the tray of the cart, then Zenith helped Faraday in.

"Sleep," she said, pulling a blanket over them. "Sleep."

Drago and Faraday shared the bed of the cart, and shared the sleep of the exhausted; and they shared a dream, although neither would remember it when they woke.

But over the next few days, as they wandered the forest, the scent of a flowering bush occasionally made one or the other lift a head and pause, and fight for the memory the scent evoked.

Zenith watched them for a long time. She was torn between relief at their return—thank the Stars Drago was alive!—and concern for both Faraday and Drago's state. What both had endured, either with the Demons, or within the Star Gate Chamber itself, must have been close to unbearable. Even though she had been protected by the trees of Minstrelsea, Zenith had felt a trickle of the despair that had overwhelmed Tencendor when the Demons had broken through, and she could only imagine what Faraday had gone through so close to the Star Gate.

But Faraday and Drago were not Zenith's only concerns. She wished she knew what had happened to StarDrifter. He'd been at the Star Gate toward the end, trying to help her parents to ward it against the Demons.

Would she see him again?

It didn't occur to Zenith that she hardly thought about her parents. Now that she knew Faraday and Drago were safe, she needed to know that StarDrifter was as well. To think that he was dead . . . or somehow under the Demons' thrall . . .

Zenith shivered and pulled her cloak closer about her. She could feel how deeply disturbed the forest was. . . . Were the Demons secreted within its trees? Were they even now creeping closer to where Zenith stood watch over Faraday and Drago?

Zenith's head jerked at a movement in the shadows. Something was there . . . something . . . There was another movement, more distinct this time, and Zenith felt her chest constrict in horror. There! Something lurking behind the ghost oak.

She stumbled toward the donkeys' heads, thinking to try and pull them forward, get herself and her sleeping companions away from whatever it was . . . escape . . . but when she tugged at the nearest donkey's halter it refused to budge.

"Damn you!" Zenith hissed, and leaned all her weight into the effort. Why in the world did Faraday travel with these obstinate creatures when she could have chosen a well-trained and obliging horse?

Zenith tugged again, and wondered if she should take a stick to the damned creatures.

The donkey snorted irritably and yanked her head out of Zenith's grasp.

Just as Zenith again reached for the halter, something emerged from the gloom behind the nearest tree.

Zenith's heart lurched. She dropped her hand, stared about for a stick that she could defend Faraday and Drago with . . . and then breathed a sigh of relief, wiping trembling hands down her robe.

It was just one of the fey creatures of the forest, no doubt so disturbed by the presence of the Demons that it cared not that it wandered so close to Zenith and the donkeys.

It was a strange mixture of lizard and bird. About the size of a small dog, it had the body of a large iguana, covered with bright blue body feathers, and with a vivid emerald and scarlet crest. It had impossibly deep black eyes that absorbed the light about it. What it used the light for Zenith could not say, perhaps as food, but once absorbed, the lizard apparently channeled the light through some furnace within its body, for it reemerged from its diamond-like talons in glinting shafts that shimmered about the forest.

Zenith smiled, for the feathered lizard was a thing of great beauty.

Watching Zenith carefully, the lizard crawled the distance between the tree and the cart, giving both donkeys and Zenith a wide berth. It sniffed briefly about the wheels of the cart, then, in an abrupt movement, jumped into the tray.

Zenith moved very slowly so she could see what the lizard was doing—and then stopped, stunned.

The lizard was sitting close to Drago's head, gently running its talons through his loose hair, almost . . . almost as if it were combing it, or weaving a cradle of light about his head.

Zenith was vividly reminded of the way the courtyard cats in Sigholt had taken every opportunity they could to snuggle up to Drago.

Zenith's eyes widened, and suddenly the lizard decided to take exception to her presence. It narrowed its eyes and hissed at her, then leaped to the ground and scuttled away into the trees.

Zenith stared at the place where it had disappeared, then looked back to Drago. She smoothed the loose strands of his coppery hair (was it brighter now than it had been previously?) away from his face, studying him carefully. He looked the same—and yet different. His face was still thin and lined, but the lines were stronger, more clearly defined, as if they had been created through purpose rather than through resentment and bitterness. And even though he was asleep, there was a strange "quiet" about him. It was the only way Zenith could describe it to herself. A quiet that in itself gave purpose—and hope.

His eyelids flickered open at her touch, and his mouth moved as if to smile.

But he was clearly too exhausted even for that effort.

"Zenith," he whispered. "Are you well?"

Zenith's eyes filled with tears. Had he been worried for her all this time? The last time he'd seen her had been in Niah's

Grove in the far north of the forest, battling the Niah-soul within her.

She smiled, and took his hand. "I am well," she said. "Go back to sleep."

Now his mouth did flicker in a faint smile, but his eyes were closed and he was asleep again even before it faded.

Zenith stood and watched him for some time, cradling his hand gently in hers, then she looked at Faraday. The woman was deeply asleep, peaceful and unmoving, and Zenith finally set down Drago's hand and moved away from the cart.

Unsure what to do, and unsettled by the continuing agitation she could feel from the trees, Zenith remembered the staff that Drago had dropped. She walked about until she found where it had rolled, and she picked it up, studying it curiously.

It was made of a beautiful deep red wood that felt warm in her hands. It was intricately carved in a pattern that Zenith could not understand. There was a line of characters that wound about the entire length of the staff, strange characters, made up of what appeared to be small black circles with short hooked lines attached to them.

The top of the staff was curled over like a shepherd's crook, but the knob was carved into the shape of a lily.

Zenith had never seen anything like it. She hefted the staff, and laid it down next to Drago.

Then she sighed and walked away, sitting down under a tree. She let her thoughts meander until they became loose and meaningless, and her head drooped in sleep.

She dreamed she was falling through the sky, but in the instant before she hit the ground StarDrifter was there, laughing, his arms held out for her.

I will always be there to catch you, I'll always be there for you.

And Zenith smiled, and dreamed on.

A hand touched her shoulder, and Zenith awoke with a start.

It was Faraday, looking well and rested.

"Faraday?" Zenith said. "How are you? Is Drago still in the cart? What happened at—"

"Shush," Faraday said, and sat down beside Zenith. "I have slept the night through, and Drago still sleeps. Now," she took a deep breath, and her body tensed, "let me tell you what happened in the Chamber of the Star Gate."

Zenith sat quietly, listening to the horror of the emergence of the children—but children no longer, more like birds—and of StarLaughter and the undead child she carried, and then of the appalling evil of the Demons.

"Oh, Zenith," Faraday said in a voice barely above a whisper. "They were more than dreadful. Anyone caught outside of shelter during the times when they hunt will suffer an appalling death—and a worse life if they are spared death."

She stopped, and took Zenith's hand, unable to look her in the face.

"Zenith, the Demons destroyed the Star Gate."

Zenith stared at Faraday, for a moment unable to comprehend the enormity of what she'd just heard.

"Destroyed the Star Gate?" she repeated, frowning. "But they can't. I mean . . . that would mean . . ."

Zenith trailed off. If the Star Gate was destroyed that would mean the sound of the Star Dance would *never* filter through Tencendor, even if the TimeKeeper Demons could be stopped.

"No," Zenith said. "I cannot believe that. The Star Gate can't be destroyed. It can't. It *can't!*"

Faraday was weeping now. "I'm sorry, Zenith. I . . ."

Zenith grabbed at her, hugging her tight, and now both wept. Although Zenith had known that the approach of the Demons meant that the Star Dance would be blocked, she had not even imagined that the Demons would actually *destroy* the Star Gate on their way through.

There was not even a hope for the Dance to ever resume.

"Our entire lives without the Dance?" Zenith whispered. "Even if we can best these Demons, we will never again have the Star Dance?"

Faraday wiped her eyes and sat up straight. "I don't know, Zenith. I just don't."

"Faraday . . . did you see StarDrifter at the Star Gate?"

"No. I am sorry, Zenith. I don't know where he is . . . but I am *sure* he is safe."

"Oh." Zenith's face went expressionless for a moment. "And the Scepter?" she finally said.

"That, at least, is safe." Faraday looked back to the cart. "But transformed, as is everything that comes through the Star Gate. Come. It is time to wake Drago up. There are some clothes for him in the box under the seat of the cart, and we all need to eat."

"And then?"

"Then we go find Zared, make sure he is well."

"And *then?*"

Faraday smiled, and stood, holding out her hand for Zenith. "And then we begin to search for a hope. Come."

Despair and then, as night settled upon the land, terror swept over Tencendor, but it left him unscathed. He was lost in his dreams, and the Demons could not touch him. He shuffled from leg to leg, trying to ease his arthritic weight, but none of it helped. He wished death would come back and take him once more.

His head drooped. He'd thought to have escaped both the sadnesses of life and the crippling pains of the body. If he hoped hard enough, would death come back?

4

What to Do?

The might of Tencendor's once proud army now stood in groups of five or six under the trees of the northern Silent Woman Woods, eyes shifting nervously. Some members of the Icarii Strike Force preferred to huddle in the lower branches of the trees, as if that way they could be slightly closer to the stars they lost contact with. Thirty thousand men and Icarii adrift in a world they no longer understood.

Their leader, StarSon Caelum, walked slowly about, the fingers of one hand rubbing at his chin and cheek, his eyes sliding away from the fear in his men's faces, thinking that now he knew how Drago must have felt when his Icarii powers had been quashed.

There was nothing left. No Star Dance. No enchantment. Nothing. Just an emptiness. And a sense of uselessness so profound that Caelum thought he would go mad if he had to live beyond a day with it.

"Faraday said she would join us here," Zared said, watching Caelum pace to and fro. He sat on a log, his hands dangling down between his knees, his face impassive.

"And you think she can help us against this . . . this . . . ?" Caelum drifted to a halt, not sure quite what to call this calamity that had enveloped them.

"Can *you?*"

Caelum spun about on his heel and walked a few paces away.

"We can do little, Caelum, until we hear from Faraday."

"Or my parents."

"Or your parents," Zared agreed. He paused, watching Caelum pace about. He did not care for the loss that Caelum—and every other Enchanter—had suffered. They relied so deeply on their powers and their beloved Star Dance, that Zared did not know if they could continue to function effectively without it. Caelum was StarSon, the man who must pull them through this crisis—but could he do it if he was essentially not the same man he had been a few weeks ago? How could *anyone* who had previously relied on the Star Dance remain effective?

Maybe Axis. Axis had been BattleAxe, and a *good* BattleAxe, for years before he'd known anything about the Star Dance.

And yet hadn't Axis said that even when he'd thought himself human, mortal, he'd still subconsciously drawn on the Star Dance? Still used its power and aid?

Well, time would tell if Icarii blood was worth anything without the music of the Star Dance.

At the moment, Zared had his doubts. He would gladly trade Tencendor's entire stock of useless Enchanters and SunSoars for the hope Faraday offered.

Suddenly sick of watching Caelum pacing uselessly to and fro, Zared stood and walked over to where Herme, Theod, DareWing FullHeart and Leagh were engaged in a lackluster game of ghemt.

Leagh looked up and smiled for him as he approached, and Zared squatted down by her, a hand on her shoulder.

"How goes it, Leagh?"

"She wins," Herme replied, "for how can we," his hand indicated his two companions, "allow such a beautiful woman to lose?"

Leagh grinned. "My 'beauty' has nothing to do with the fact, my good Earl Herme, that I am far more skilled than you."

All the men laughed, and threw their gaming sticks into the center of the circle scratched into the dirt before them.

Zared touched Leagh's cheek softly, then looked to Dare-Wing. "My friend, I wonder if I might ask something of you?"

The Strike Leader inclined his head. "Speak."

"Faraday told us that there were certain times of the day when it would be dangerous to go outside, times when the Demons would spread their evil. DareWing, I need to know when exactly these times are."

"Dawn, dusk, midmorning and midafternoon, and night," Theod said. "This we know."

"Yes, but we need to know more specifically. If we know *exactly* when it is safe for us to roam abroad, then we will have a better idea of how to counter these Demons . . . or at least, when we can try to do so. Besides, somehow we will have to rebuild life around," he paused, his mouth working as if he chewed something distasteful, "our newfound restrictions. We need to know when it is safe to live."

DareWing nodded. "I agree . . . but how?"

"Can you station members of your Strike Force, perhaps twenty at any one time, along the southwest borders of the Silent Woman Woods? They will be safe enough if they remain among the trees, and perhaps they can observe . . . observe the behavior of those still trapped in the open."

DareWing nodded, agreeing with the location. The southwest border of the Woods would be close to Tare, an area more highly populated than the northern or southern borders of the Woods. If they needed to observe, that would give them their best possible chance.

"The more we learn," he said, "the more hope we have."

"You do not want any of *our* men stationed there?" Herme asked quietly.

"My friend," Zared said. "I ask only the Icarii because they can move between the border and back to our placement faster than can human or horse legs." He stood up. "I profess myself sick at not knowing how to react, or what to do next. Until Faraday returns we must do what we can."

DareWing rose to his feet, nodded at Zared, and faded into the gloom of the forest.

Fifteen paces away Askam sat with his back against a small sapling, his eyes narrow and unreadable as he watched Zared move to talk quietly with Caelum.

His mouth thinned as he saw Caelum nod at Zared's words and place a hand briefly on the king's shoulder.

After three days of observation, they had a better idea of the span of the Demonic Hours. From dusk to the time when the sun was well above the horizon was a time of horror, the time when first Raspu, then Rox and finally Mot ruled the land. Pestilence, terror and hunger roamed, and those few who were caught outside succumbed to the infection of whichever Demon had caught them. After the dawn hour there were three hours of peace, a time of recovery, before Barzula, tempest, struck at midmorning.

Although the occasional storm rolled across the landscape during Barzula's time—whirlwinds of ice or of fire—the scouts reported that the primary influence of the tempest appeared to occur within the minds of those caught outside. Once Barzula's hour had passed and he had fed, there was again a time of peace (or, rather, a time of frightful anticipation) for some four hours until Sheol struck at midafternoon. Again, an interval of three hours when it was safe to venture outside, then the long hours of pestilence and terror through dusk and night.

The precise time span of the Demonic Hours were marked by a thin gray haze that slid over the land from a point to the east, probably the location of the Demons themselves. It was a sickening miasma that carried the demonic contagion with it, lying over the land in a drifting curtain of madness until it dissipated at the end of the appointed time.

"And those caught outside?" Zared asked softly of the first group of scouts to report back.

"Some die," one of the scouts said, "but most live, although their horror is dreadful to watch."

"Live?"

The scout took a moment to answer. "They live," he finally said, "but in a state of madness. Sometimes they eat dirt, or chew on their own excrement. I have seen some try to couple with boulders, and others stuff pebbles into every orifice they can find until their bodies burst. But many who live past their first infection—and those dangerous few hours post-infection when they might kill themselves in their madness—wander westward, sometimes northwest."

The scout paused again, locking eyes with his fellows. Then he turned back to Zared and Caelum. "It is as if they have been infused with a purpose."

At that Zared had shuddered. A purpose? To what end? *What were the Demons planning?*

But the scouts had yet more to report. One group had also seen seven black shapes running eastward across the Plains of Tare toward the Ancient Barrows. Horses they thought, but were not sure. Above them had flown a great dark cloud . . . that whispered.

No one knew quite what to make of it.

"We have roughly three hours after dawn, four hours between midmorning and midafternoon, and then another three hours before dusk," Zared said to Caelum and Askam on the third morning since they had taken shelter in the Woods.

"Time enough for an army to scamper from shelter to shelter?" Caelum said, his frustration clearly showing in his voice. "And what can an army *do?* Challenge Despair to one-on-one combat? Demand that Pestilence meet us on the battlefield, weapons of his choosing? What am *I* supposed to do?"

"Be patient, Caelum," Zared said. "We must wait for Faraday and—"

"I am *sick* of waiting for this fairy woman!" Askam said. "We must move, and move now. I suggest that—"

"Faraday?" put in a voice to one side of the clearing. "Faraday?"

They all spun around.

Axis and Azhure stepped out from the gloom of a tree. Just

behind them StarDrifter leaned against the trunk of the tree, his wings and arms folded, his face devoid of any expression.

And, yet further behind him, pale shapes moved in and out of sight. Massive hounds—Azhure's Alaunt. Most settled down out of sight, but one, Sicarius, their leader, walked forward to sit by Azhure's side. Her hand touched the top of his head briefly, as if for reassurance.

"Father!" Caelum hugged his parents tightly, relieved beyond measure that they'd arrived. All three had to blink tears from their eyes. They were alive, and for the moment they were safe, and that meant there was still some hope left. There *must* be.

Caelum nodded at StarDrifter, who raised a tired hand in greeting, then returned his attention to his parents. "You were in the Star Gate Chamber? What happened? Did you see the Demons step through? And Drago? What of him?"

"Caelum, enough questions!" Axis said, but his tone was warm, and it took the sting out of his words. "Give me a moment to catch my breath and I will answer them."

He swept his eyes about the clearing, taking in Zared, Askam and DareWing. Together? This group that had only days previously been committed to civil war? For the first time in days Axis felt a glimmer of true optimism. He looked Zared in the eye, remembering the last time they'd met—the heated words, the hatred—but now all he saw was the son of Rivkah and Magariz, his brother, and a man he would have to relearn to trust.

Caelum had obviously done it, and so could he—and Axis knew it would not be hard. This brother was one that, despite all the arguments and differences, he knew he could lean on when they faced a common enemy.

"We left the Chamber before the Demons broke through," Axis said. "We didn't see them—or Drago—although I imagine he came through with his demonic companions in treachery."

Axis paused, and his voice and eyes hardened. "I hope he is satisfied with what he has accomplished. His revenge was harder than I ever imagined it could have been."

"None of us know what was in Drago's heart or mind when he fled Sigholt," Zared said. Like Axis, all Zared's ill-feeling for his brother had vanished. Their personal problems and ambitions were petty in the face of the disaster that had enveloped them. "And we do not know if he was the instigator or just another victim of this disaster. Perhaps we should not judge him too harshly until we have heard what he has to say."

Axis' face hardened, and Zared decided to leave the subject of Drago well enough alone for the time being. "Axis," he said, and stepped closer to him. He hesitated, then took one of Axis' hands between his. "How are you? And Azhure?"

In truth, Zared did not have to ask, for both Axis and Azhure, and StarDrifter who still lingered in the shadows, looked as did every Icarii Enchanter Zared had seen in the past few days. They looked . . . ordinary.

"How am I?" Axis said, and, stunningly, quirked his mouth in a lopsided grin. "I am Axis, and that is *all* I am."

Zared stared at him, holding his gaze, still holding his hand. "Is 'just Axis' going to be enough, brother?"

"It is all we have," Azhure put in softly, and Zared shifted his gaze to her. There was still spirit in her eyes, and determination in her face. "Just Axis" and "just Azhure" might still be enough to stop the sky from falling in. Might.

Zared dropped Axis' hand and nodded. "What do you know?"

"First," Axis said, "I need to know what *you* have here. Zared and Caelum . . . together, in the one camp. And with no knives to each other's throats. Have you made peace? And you mentioned Faraday. Have you seen her?"

Caelum hesitated, glanced at Zared, then spoke. "Father, we fought—"

"And I lost," Zared put in, and grimaced.

"I had the advantage," Caelum said, glancing again at Zared. "We agreed to unite against the threat of the Demons. We were riding to meet you at the Ancient Barrows when . . . when . . . Zared, you finish. She spoke to you, not me."

"On the night before the Demons broke through," Zared said, "we were camped some four leagues above these Woods. I'd been to talk with Caelum, and when I returned I found Faraday and Zenith seated at my campfire."

"Zenith?" Azhure said. "Are you sure it was she?"

Behind her StarDrifter finally straightened from the tree trunk and showed more interest in the conversation.

Zared frowned, at her. "Yes, I am sure it was her. Why wouldn't I be?"

Azhure turned her head aside. Axis had been right then. Niah—her mother—was truly dead. Yet one more grief to examine in the dead of night.

"Faraday and Zenith had just walked out of the night," Leagh said, joining the group. She linked her arm with her husband's, and shared a brief smile with him. "They were well, and more cheerful than any I had seen for weeks previously, or since."

"She said that we had to flee for the Woods," Zared said, "and that we'd be no more use than lambs in a slaughterhouse if we continued on to the Barrows."

"In that she was right," Axis said. "*None* of us were of any use."

Unnoticed, StarDrifter had moved to linger at the outside of the group, listening.

"After some persuasion," Caelum said, "I agreed to divert the army here. If we had been caught outside . . ."

"At least we have an army," Axis said, "although Stars knows what use it will be to us. And Faraday and Zenith. Where are they now?"

"She said she and Zenith were going to the Star Gate," Zared said. "They said they had someone to meet there. I thought it was you."

Axis shook his head. "No. And if they were in the Chamber when the Demons broke through, then they would both be dead. No one has the power to resist them."

"Maybe." StarDrifter now spoke up. "And maybe not. Faraday has changed, and who knows now what enchantment she draws upon. Besides," he indicated the trees, "the forest's power, as the Avar's, has been wounded, but not mortally. There is hope."

StarDrifter knew who it was they had gone to meet. He did not know what kind of a hope Drago provided, but if Faraday believed in him, then StarDrifter thought he might have the courage to do likewise. Stars, but he hoped they'd survived the Demons' arrival. Faraday might well have the power to cope with them . . . but Zenith? StarDrifter prayed Faraday had shown the sense to keep Zenith well back. They'd not fought so long to save her from Niah to lose her now.

"There must always be hope," Axis said quietly. "Fate always leaves a hope somewhere. And I intend to find it."

"And Faraday," StarDrifter said. "Did she say where she and Zenith would—"

"She said that we should wait for her here, and she would eventually rejoin us," Zared said. "She said we were not to go near Cauldron Lake, for that was where the Demons would strike first."

StarDrifter nodded, and tried to relax. Faraday would keep them all well. She must. He suddenly realized how deeply worried he was about Zenith, and he frowned slightly.

"How does she know that?" Azhure said. "Is she somehow in league with them?"

"Faraday has *always* put this land before her own needs and desires," StarDrifter said sharply. "And you, Azhure, should know that better than anyone else here. Have you forgotten she died so you could live?"

Azhure's cheeks reddened, and she dropped her eyes.

"Enough," Axis said. "Caelum, *you* are our hope."

"Me?"

Axis looked about. "Caelum, my friends, can we sit? We all have information to share, and my legs have lost their godlike endurance."

Leagh took his arm, and then Azhure's, and led them toward a fire set mid-distance between two trees where it could do no harm. "Sit down, and rest those legs."

"What do you mean, *I* am your hope?" Caelum said, watching his parents. He had refused food, and had waited impatiently until Axis, Azhure and StarDrifter had eaten. They had very obviously had little in the past few days.

"Not only our hope, my son, but Tencendor's." Axis stalled for time, wiping his fingers carefully on a napkin that Leagh handed him. He hesitated, then looked his son in the eye.

"There is much I did not tell you while you were so entwined in hostilities with Zared. But now that I see you both sit side by side, in peace, it gives me the strength to say what I hesitated to speak previously.

"Caelum, I cannot say all the details, but for now listen to me well. *All* of you listen to me well. Beneath each of the Sacred Lakes lie Repositories, all heavily warded and defended, and in each of these Repositories lies the various life parts of the Midday Demon, Qeteb."

Axis continued on in a low voice, telling of the Maze Gate, and of its age-old message that the Crusader was the only one capable of defeating the Demons. Forty years ago it had named the Crusader as StarSon.

"It waited for a year after you were born, Caelum. It watched and waited until it was sure, and then it named you, StarSon, as Tencendor's hope."

"The hope of many worlds," StarDrifter said reflectively, "if these TimeKeepers can so effortlessly move through the stars."

"But how?" Caelum's eyes flickered between his parents and then about the rest of the group. "*How?* I have no power left! Nothing! How can I meet—"

"Caelum, be still . . . and believe." Azhure rested her hand on Caelum's knee. "There *is* hope, and there is a weapon you can wield."

Caelum said nothing. He dropped his eyes to where his hands fiddled with a length of leather tack.

"The Rainbow Scepter," Azhure said. "It contains the power of this world *and* the power of the Repositories . . . the power that currently still traps Qeteb."

"Unfortunately, Mother," Caelum said, his voice heavy with sarcasm, "Drago stole the Scepter. Took it to the Demons. Should we just ask for it back?"

"The Scepter has ever had its own agenda," said yet another voice to the side of the clearing, "and to blame Drago for its machinations is surely pointless."

Everyone stared, voiceless.

Across the clearing stood Faraday, Zenith slightly behind her left shoulder, Drago standing by her right, his entire body tense and watchful.

Just behind them were the pale shapes of the two donkeys, their long ears pricked forward curiously.

"Zenith!" StarDrifter breathed, locking eyes with the woman, but before he could move, Axis rose to his feet.

5

The Prodigal Son's Welcome

Axis stared, and—in a single flash of thought—remembered. He remembered the years of pain and suffering that had been needed to defeat both Borneheld and Gorgrael. The men and women who had died in order to reunite Tencendor. The lives that had been ruined by those who had thought to seize power illegally. He remembered how he and Azhure had fought to rebuild a life, not only for themselves and their family, but for an entire nation.

He remembered how they had thought themselves free of grief and treachery.

But here before him stood the son who had spent his time in Azhure's womb plotting how best to kill both elder brother and father. Here was the son who'd conspired with Gorgrael, who had murdered RiverStar, and who had single-handedly wrought the complete destruction of all Axis had fought so long and hard for.

Here. Before him. Standing as if he thought to ask for a place among them.

And beside him, Faraday and Zenith. Had both been corrupted by his evil, both seduced into supporting his treachery? His lover and his daughter—had they no loyalty for Axis either?

"You vile bastard," Axis said, very quietly but with such hatred that Faraday instinctively took a half-step in front of Drago. "How dare you present yourself to me?"

And then he leaped forward.

Herme stepped forward to stop him, but Axis spun about and slammed a fist into his face, knocking him to the ground.

As Herme fell, Axis grabbed a knife from the Earl's weapons belt and strode forward again.

Zared jumped to his feet, but was pulled back by Caelum, and both tumbled to the ground.

"No!" Faraday cried, taking another step forward, but Axis shoved her to one side. Faraday stumbled back against Zenith who had to wrap both arms about her to prevent her falling.

Before anyone else had time to move, or even cry out, Axis seized Drago, slammed him back against a tree, and buried the knife a half-finger's depth into the junction of Drago's neck and shoulder.

One of the donkeys brayed, and both pranced nervously.

"I should have done this forty years ago!" Axis cried, and he stabbed the dagger as deep into Drago's neck as he could.

Drago gagged, uttered a low, choking cry, then sagged against the tree trunk as his father wrenched the knife out.

Axis drew it back for the final, killing blow.

Blood pumped out of Drago's neck.

Faraday jerked out of Zenith's arms and tried to grab Axis' hand or arm, but he was too strong for her, and threw her to the ground, overbalancing himself.

"Axis!" Zared yelled, scrambling to his feet again, but this time both Askam and Caelum grabbed him and wrestled him back a pace or two.

"For the Stars' sakes, Zared," Caelum cried, *"let my father end this now!"* He hooked a foot under Zared's leg, and toppled him to the ground.

Leagh dropped to her husband's side, shooting Caelum a hard look. At the same time Zenith knelt by Drago, her joy at seeing StarDrifter alive completely forgotten in her concern for her brother. She grabbed at the hem of her cloak, tearing a section free, and folded the material into a thick square, using it to try to stifle the blood seeping from Drago's throat.

Everyone else stood, helpless and unsure, wondering who was right, wondering what could be done, wondering whether or not another death would truly help.

Axis recovered his balance from Faraday's attempt to push him over, drew his arm back—and found it seized from behind in sharp, murderous teeth.

Sicarius. The leader of Azhure's Alaunt.

No one had seen him move, and no one knew where he'd come from, but now the hound pulled Axis to the ground, and stood over him, snarling and snapping.

"Sicarius!" Azhure buried her hands in the loose skin of the hound's neck and tried to pull him off, but the hound would not budge.

Azhure tugged desperately, unable to believe Sicarius' savage assault. What was the hound doing? To attack *Axis?*

"Drop the knife, Axis!" StarDrifter yelled. *"Drop the damned knife or that dog is going to kill you!"*

Then, ignoring Axis completely, he fell to his knees beside Drago, adding the weight of his hands to those of Zenith to try and stop the bleeding. He locked eyes briefly with Zenith, then turned slightly to Faraday who was now at Drago's side also.

"What were you thinking of to enter this glade with Drago at your side?" StarDrifter hissed. "Didn't you even *think* that Axis might not welcome his son home with open arms?"

Faraday shook her head helplessly, and StarDrifter made a small sound of disgust. She should have known better.

Zenith, absolutely shaken at the violence, drew comfort from the weight of StarDrifter's hands over hers, and hoped they would staunch the bleeding enough to give Drago a chance of life.

StarDrifter lifted his eyes to hers and, although he did not smile, the lines about his eyes crinkled slightly in warmth.

"I am more than pleased to see you again, beloved Zenith," StarDrifter murmured. "You are well?"

She nodded, and StarDrifter looked back to Drago. The bleeding was slowing—Axis' knife must have struck his son's clavicle rather than one of the neck veins. If he'd managed that, Drago would be dead already, for even the pressure of a thousand hands at his throat could not have stemmed the damage.

He gestured to Faraday to help Zenith apply pressure to the wound, touched Zenith's cheek briefly in reassurance, then slowly stood and walked over to Axis.

His son had dropped the knife, and Sicarius had retreated to sit tense and watchful several paces away. His golden eyes flickered between Axis and Drago.

Everyone else was absolutely still, as watchful as the hound.

Azhure was down by her husband, her arms about him, supporting him into a sitting position. "StarDrifter," she began, "what—"

StarDrifter ignored her. He thrust his right hand forward into Axis' face. It was smeared with Drago's blood. "Look at this!" he said. "Your son's blood, Axis, by your hand!"

"Did you never see the wounds on Caelum's body once Azhure rescued him from Gorgrael?" Axis said quietly. "Did you never see *his* blood? And now, look upon the blood smeared across this land, StarDrifter, and tell me that my 'son,'" he spat the word, "does not deserve to die for it."

Drago cleared his throat. "I have come back to help," he said in a hoarse whisper.

"Then die!" Axis threw back at him, pushing Azhure's arms aside and rising to his feet. "*That* would help considerably."

The wound in Drago's neck had now almost stopped bleeding, and Faraday left Drago's care to Zenith. She rose and walked slowly forward. "There has been too much death in this world, Axis, for you to want to add to it."

"Have you ever thought that by killing Drago *now* we might stop further death?" he snarled back.

In response, Faraday lifted her head and stared about at each and every person present. "I want you all to know, and this I pledge on the blood that *I* shed for Tencendor, and for you, Axis and Azhure, that I will stand responsible for Drago's actions. I trust him, and I ask that you give him the benefit of the doubt. Drago wants to help, he *can* help. Let him."

"He murdered RiverStar!" Caelum said, stabbing a finger at Drago. "And stole the Scepter and provided the means whereby this land now stands decimated. *Trust him?*"

Faraday looked at him, then turned to StarDrifter standing beside her. "StarDrifter? I—"

"And I," Zenith put in fiercely from where she knelt by Drago's side.

"We both," Faraday corrected herself, "believe Drago deserves a chance to prove his worth, and his loyalty. He did not murder RiverStar, and if he fled with the Scepter, then that was at the Scepter's doing, not his. It needed to go to the

Demons and so it manipulated Drago's mind to get there. Drago has done regrettable things in the past, but he deserves a chance to redeem himself."

"Redeem himself?" Axis said. "Stars, Faraday! How can you stand there, protecting this misbegotten evil? No doubt he has regained his Icarii powers in return for aiding the Demons—how else could he have manipulated Sicarius into defending him? Does he now covet the Throne of the Stars itself? Has he promised you a place beside him? Is that why you aid him?"

"Believe me, Father," Drago said, his voice a little stronger now, "all my Icarii power has been burned completely away. I have nothing left save my need to help right the wrongs I have done."

Axis ignored him. He stepped forward to stand belligerently in front of Faraday. "How can you aid him?" he repeated.

Sicarius shifted forward slightly, and noticeably tensed.

"You go too far, Axis!" StarDrifter put his hand on his son's shoulder, and wrenched him back a pace. Faraday had suffered too much violence in her life to have more visited upon her now.

"How can you accuse *this* woman, of all people, of aligning herself with the Demons?" StarDrifter continued. "Must I remind you that she died for you?"

He whipped about and stared now at Azhure, her face as cold as Axis'. "And you, Azhure. Have you forgotten?"

StarDrifter turned back and looked at Drago. "If Faraday walked in here with Qeteb himself and said that a spark of goodness rested in his breast, and that she would support him, then that would be enough for me. Drago, do you truly repent for what you did to Caelum?"

"Yes." Drago's eyes were on Caelum standing rigid eight or nine paces away, not StarDrifter. "I am not the hunter you fear, Caelum," he said. "I come here to offer you my aid in whatever you have to do to defeat the Demons as some recompense for my actions against you so many years ago."

"And why should I believe that?" asked Caelum.

"*None* of us believe that," Axis said.

Azhure opened her mouth to speak, but was forestalled by Zared.

"I believe Drago deserves the chance," he said. "Axis, have you or Caelum even thought of the fact that Drago is the *only* one among us who has had any firsthand experience of these Demons? Dammit, why kill that knowledge and potential help?"

"I think Zared speaks some sense," DareWing FullHeart said, finally braving his say. "Faraday, you ask a great deal of everyone here. I do not think," his mouth quirked and he gestured about the gathering, "that many here are ready to place their trust in Drago. Most of us have troublesome doubts. But most of us are prepared to trust you. Of *everyone* within this clearing, you are the one who deserves our full trust."

Axis' mouth hardened, and he turned his face away.

"If you say you will stand responsible for Drago's actions," DareWing finished, "and that he deserves the chance to finally help instead of hinder, then I will trust you and I will give Drago that chance."

"And I," StarDrifter said quietly, looking Faraday directly in the eye. Then he dropped his gaze to Drago. "Don't fail her."

Be his trust, the Survivor had said, be his trust. Suddenly Faraday knew what he had meant.

Axis started to say something, stopped himself, then stared at the ground for several moments, battling his fury.

Finally he raised his eyes. "Where is the Scepter?" he said flatly. "If Drago hands the Scepter to Caelum, then I will give him his chance."

"I do not know the Scepter's will, nor do I know its location," Faraday said. "I'm sorry."

"Sorry?" Axis stared at her. "Sorry! A trifling word to use as excuse for defending a traitor and a murderer!"

"No! Wait!" Drago struggled to his feet, the front of his tunic horribly bloodstained, his face white. He leaned heavily on Zenith, and looked about.

Where was the staff? Surely *that* was the Scepter, transformed?

"Well?" said Axis.

"Wait . . ." Drago cast his eyes frantically about. He had it when he stepped into the clearing, he was sure . . . had it fallen from his hand when Axis attacked him? Where . . .

"You were ever the consummate play-actor," Axis said, hate and sarcasm infusing his voice and face.

Drago stopped his search to stare at his father. "I—"

"*I* have had enough of you and your lies!" Axis said, and turned back to Caelum.

He took a deep breath, and calmed himself. "We still have hope, Caelum. Adamon and the other gods have gone to Star Finger and await us there. If we go to the mountain we will have the advice and knowledge of the past six or seven thousand years that is stored there. There must be something secreted in the damned mountain that can help us! Besides, I cannot help but believe the Scepter will find its way to the StarSon in time. It is fated thus, and thus it must be."

Unnoticed, the donkeys twitched their ears slightly, and one of them dipped her head to the ground, as if trying to hide unwanted mirth.

Caelum nodded, comforted by the surety in his father's voice. "And now that the Demons are through and no longer blocking the Star Gate, there's every chance that we might be able to regain a part of the Star—"

"The Star Gate has been destroyed," Zenith said, wishing she did not have to say it. "We will never hear the Star Dance again."

To one side StarDrifter groaned and sank to one knee, head in hand.

Axis' face worked, and he shot Drago a look of such utter malevolence that his son had to turn his face aside, but Axis finally managed to speak relatively calmly.

"Then there is no point in lingering here. StarDrifter, I say to you, and to you, DareWing, and to you, Zared, that if you want to believe Faraday's assurances then I cannot stop you—but don't try to stop *my* efforts to help this land! Azhure and I will take Caelum back to Star Finger. Already, Adamon and the others who were once gods gather there.

"Zared, in Caelum's absence I need you to take command of the army. DareWing, through you Zared will command the Strike Force as well—support him."

DareWing nodded.

"And my task while you and Caelum are in Star Finger?" Zared said.

"Perhaps the worst task of all," Axis responded. "Deal with the devastation as best you can. Save as much and as many as best you can. Save a Tencendor for my son . . . for us all."

"I will do my best, StarMan."

"Do not call me that," Axis said dryly. "Now I am no more the StarMan than you."

He turned about, meaning to talk to Azhure, but his eye was caught once more by Drago, and his face darkened.

"Drago," Axis thrust a finger at him, "come within shouting distance of Star Finger and *no one* will be able to stop me killing you. *Do you understand?*"

Drago was standing still, patiently enduring Zenith's bandaging of his throat. "I, like you," he said, "will do whatever I have to in order to right the wrongs done to this land, Father. I wish you would believe me. *I will do anything I can.*"

"Neither I nor this land nor Caelum needs your aid," Axis said. "You are filth! I disowned you as a child, Drago, and there is nothing in this life that will ever make me accept you now. I do not love you, and I never will, and I swear before every Star that can still hear me that I wish you the death you deserve for your misdeeds. Damn you! You are nothing but worm-filled shit in my eyes!"

Drago flinched and his already white face went whiter.

Axis spun about on his heel. "Zared, may Azhure and I requisition a horse apiece? We must ride our way north as Spiredore is undoubtedly useless now that Star Dance is dead."

Zared nodded. "I will also send a unit of men with you. You will surely need some protection wandering north—gods know where the TimeKeepers are now."

"Good. Azhure, my love," Axis held out his hand to her. "Say your good-byes . . . to whoever deserves it. Caelum, fetch whatever you need to bring with you."

"Axis?"

Axis turned to look at Faraday.

"Axis, keep to shelter—whether beneath trees or inside houses—during the Demonic Hours. You will remain safe that way."

Axis continued to stare at her, then he spun about and

walked away. Faraday turned her attention back to Drago's
wound.

The gathering slowly dissipated as people drifted off, to
prepare for departure or to sink back before fires and mull
over the scene they'd just witnessed.

Sicarius melted back into the shadows, rejoining the pack
of Alaunt.

Faraday pushed Drago back to the ground and helped
Zenith more securely bind his neck.

"The staff!" Drago said. "It was *here!* I know it! Where—"

"Hush," Faraday said, and laid gentle fingers on his lips.
"Hush now, please."

"I have to help," Drago said. "I *must!*"

"I know," Faraday whispered. "I know."

She and Zenith tucked the loose end of the bandage in,
then Zenith smiled, patted Drago on the shoulder, and rose
and walked off to talk with StarDrifter.

Faraday waited until she had gone, then laid an apologetic
hand on one of Drago's.

"StarDrifter was right," she said softly. "I should have
thought before walking you so blatantly forth into this glade."

"I deserved much of that, Faraday," he said, and sighed.
"No one knows better than me that I deserve both Caelum's
and my parents' distrust."

"Don't ever say—" Faraday began fiercely, when Azhure's
voice behind her stopped her.

"Zenith?" she said.

Azhure very pointedly did not look at Drago.

Faraday felt for her. Torn between son and husband,
watching the world that she'd fought for so hard die about
her. Losing immortality. Losing enchantment.

Wondering why Sicarius had attacked her husband, rather
than Drago.

"She went that way," Faraday inclined her head, "with
StarDrifter."

Azhure nodded, risked one glance at Drago, then walked off.

Azhure found Zenith standing close with StarDrifter by a
group of tethered horses. They were talking quietly, sharing
information about their movements since they had parted on
the Island of Mist and Memory.

As Zenith looked up at her approach, Azhure asked bluntly, "Zenith—or Niah?"

"Zenith," her daughter replied softly. "*Zenith* reborn, not Niah."

Azhure hesitated, then nodded. She stood indecisively, as if wondering whether to touch Zenith or not. "Will you tell me what happened?"

"I know what your mother meant to you," Zenith said, "and I know what sacrifice she made for you. We have all treasured and revered her memory. But . . . but the soul that tried to seize mine had changed. She was warped by her dreadful death. All pity had been seared from her. Mother, I was *never* Niah, and I could not agree to let her kill me so she could live again."

Azhure's eyes were bright with tears, and she put a trembling hand to her mouth. "How?"

Zenith glanced at StarDrifter, both of them remembering that dreadful night that Zenith had forced the Niah-soul into the girl-child she carried, and had expelled the child from her body, killing her.

But how could Zenith tell Azhure that? Her mother loved Niah deeply, and treasured her memory, and it would only wound Azhure to be told the manner of Niah's second death.

"Something of the Niah who had so sacrificed herself for you remained, Mother. When she realized the extent of my distress she acquiesced, and let me be. She said . . . she said that she had already lived her life, and was content that I should be allowed to live mine."

Azhure stared at her, then burst into tears. Zenith leaned forward and gathered Azhure to her, rocking her gently as if she were truly the mother, and not the daughter.

For his part, StarDrifter just stared at Zenith, realizing for the first time how deeply he felt for her. And how differently he felt for her.

As Caelum inspected his horse's gear, Askam stepped quietly up beside him.

"Yes?" Caelum said.

"Was it wise of Axis to leave *Zared* in full control of the army, StarSon?" Askam said, and dropped his voice still further. "Remember that he has crowned himself King of Achar. Do you so agree with his actions that you watch as your father virtually presents him with the entire territory of Tencendor? Gods, man! He's even got control of the Strike Force!"

Caelum thought carefully before he answered, but when he did his voice was very firm. "Axis made the right choice," he said. "Zared can command more loyalty than you. Do you not remember what happened when you tried to command his army the morning after the battle?"

Askam recoiled. "I have lost my sister to him, now must I also lose land *and* troops? Where is the justice in this, Caelum? *Where?*"

"The problems between you and Zared must wait until the TimeKeepers lie broken at our feet, Askam."

"And the fact that he apparently stands with Drago against you and your father? Does that not concern you?"

Caelum paused, unable to answer immediately. "Zared, like so many of us, simply does not know what to do. And like DareWing, perhaps, he wants as many choices as possible left open to him."

He sighed. "My friend, giving Zared control of the army is no reflection on you. He is simply the best man to do it."

No, Askam thought, no reflection at all. I am simply "not best." I understand, Caelum StarSon. I understand very, very well.

"I understand, StarSon," he said, and then he drifted away into the gathering darkness.

Zared organized the unit of men, then went to check that Axis had suitable horses for Azhure and himself.

"Is there such need to rush off so soon?" Zared said quietly to his brother.

Axis looked at him. "I cannot stay, Zared. Not with Drago here. You must surely understand that." He paused.

"Zared, I cannot explain this, but somehow I *know* the answer to those Demons lies in Star Finger. I cannot wait to get there. And to get Caelum there."

Axis stopped and glanced to where Faraday and Drago sat, then moved a step closer to his brother and placed a hand on his shoulder. "I cannot trust Drago. I *cannot!*"

"I can understand, Axis."

"And yet you support him?"

Zared hesitated. "I trust Faraday when she says that Drago has pledged himself to Caelum. Axis, I do *not* believe he murdered RiverStar. Caelum treated him badly, the trial was a farce, for the gods' sakes!"

"And yet the vision WolfStar conjured showed that Drago murdered—"

"And have *you* ever trusted WolfStar?"

Axis was silent, and Zared let him think for a moment before he continued. "I am prepared to give Drago a chance, Axis. I think that he deserves that one chance."

Axis' face tightened, but when he spoke his voice was calm. "Then will you promise me one thing?"

Zared raised his eyebrows.

"Promise me that you will kill him the moment you suspect he works, not for Tencendor and Caelum, but for those Demons. Promise me!"

Zared slowly nodded. "I will not allow him to betray this land, Axis."

"To betray this land any further than he has!" Axis said bitterly, but he accepted Zared's words, and, after a moment's thought, gripped his younger brother's hand. "I do not envy you your task," he said.

"Nor I yours," Zared said quietly. They stared at each other, then Zared turned and walked away.

Caelum finished checking his horse, disquieted by Askam's visit, then went to say good-bye to Zared and DareWing. Zared would look after Tencendor—what was left of it—as well as anyone could.

Drago watched him, then pushed Faraday's gentle hands away. "Faraday, I must speak with him."

"Wait! Drago, your neck—"

"Faraday, a few steps won't hurt me, and I *need* to talk with Caelum. Neither of us should leave it like this."

Faraday dropped her hands. "Then stay well clear of your father."

Drago nodded, his expression bleak, and walked slowly away.

Caelum conversed briefly with Zared and DareWing, and then began to walk back to where he could see his parents with the unit of twenty men that Zared had given them. Axis and Azhure, the Alaunt milling about them, were obviously impatient.

Caelum sighed. On the one hand, he hated to leave Tencendor like this. He felt as though he were abandoning his responsibilities. On the other hand, Star Finger represented such a haven of safety that he could hardly wait to get there. Well might Faraday say that Drago was now the most trustworthy soul this side of death, but Caelum could not believe it. Not when each night the nightmare still thundered through his sleep, and the lance still pierced his heart.

Suddenly Drago stepped out from behind a tree and stood directly in Caelum's path.

Caelum stopped dead, his heart thumping. Drago was pale, and the blood-stained bandage about his neck hardly improved his appearance, but Caelum thought he looked strong enough for mischief. He quickly checked the surrounding trees—no one was close, although he could see his parents start in concern; Axis had taken a step forward.

"Get out of my way," Caelum said.

"Caelum, please, I do not come to hurt you—"

"Why should I believe that?"

Drago held out a hand. "Caelum, the only reason I came back through the Star Gate was to right the wrong I did you so many years ago. Brother, I pledge myself to your cause. Please, believe me."

His only answer was a hostile stare from his brother.

Drago's hand, still extended, wavered slightly. "I can understand why you hate and fear—"

"You understand *nothing* if you can say you have pledged yourself to my cause, and you ask me to trust you. Why should I believe that?"

"Caelum—"

"How dare I ever trust *you?*"

Drago dropped his hand. "Because when I came back through the Star Gate all enchantments fell from my eyes, Caelum."

Caelum's eyes widened, appalled at what he'd heard. He stared at Drago. "And still you say, 'I come only to aid you'?" he whispered.

Drago nodded slowly, his eyes never leaving those of his brother. "I swore to aid you and to aid Tencendor, and so I will do."

"You lie," Caelum said, "if all enchantments fell from your eyes as you came back through the Star Gate, then you *must* lie! You are here to destroy me. No more, no less."

Then he stepped past his brother and walked into the shadows where waited his parents.

As they mounted and rode into the forest, Sicarius stood a moment, looking first at the retreating riders, then at Drago standing watching them.

He whined, hesitated, then finally bounded after Axis, Azhure and Caelum.

The pack of Alaunt followed his lead.

High in a nearby tree, the feathered lizard inspected one of its twinkling talons, then slowly scratched at its cheek, thinking. After a moment it glanced down to the two white donkeys and the blue cart they were still harnessed to.

In its tray lay the staff.

6

The Rosewood Staff

"Drago?" Faraday placed a hand on his arm. "Do not blame Caelum too much."

"I do not blame him at all."

"Then do not blame yourself too much, either. Come, let us walk back to Leagh and Zared's fire. We need to eat, and I think I can see Leagh dabbling in some pot or the other. And I sincerely hope she spent *some* of her princesshood attending lessons in the kitchens," she added, almost in an undertone.

Despite the emotion of the past hour, Drago's sense of humor had not completely deserted him, and Faraday's words made him grin. For someone who had lived on a diet of grass, grass and yet more grass for the past forty-odd years, Faraday should be the last person to criticize anyone's culinary imagination.

They walked slowly toward the campsite. Leagh was still obviously disturbed at the scene between Drago and his father, but she composed herself and then smiled and held out her hands as Drago and Faraday approached.

"Drago, come and sit down. There is a pot of stew here. Not much, but it will warm you, at least."

Drago thanked Leagh as she passed him a bowl and then, as he sat, asked her to fetch Zared, DareWing, StarDrifter and Zenith. "And any other who commands within this force, Leagh. I need to talk, and they have done the honor of trusting me."

Leagh nodded, and walked off.

"Are you sure you want to do this?" Faraday said.

"Yes. They—all of you—deserve an explanation of what I did. And . . ."

"Yes?"

"You should never doubt Leagh's talents, Faraday. This stew is right flavorsome given the restrictions of her kitchen."

The others arrived and grouped quietly about, taking places as they could about the fire. Zenith was one of the first to arrive, StarDrifter close behind. He sat down close beside Zenith, closer than need be. Zenith tensed slightly, then relaxed and smiled as StarDrifter murmured something to her. Zared sat with Leagh across the fire from Drago. DareWing and his two most senior Crest-Leaders were to his right. Herme sat between Leagh and Faraday, but Theod and Askam preferred to remain standing just behind the seated circle, several of their lieutenants still further behind them.

Everyone studied Drago curiously. StarDrifter and Zared had known Drago previously, and, as Zenith had, they well noted the changes his experiences had wrought. A certain weariness from his struggle through the Star Gate and some pain from his wound remained, but his face was otherwise determined. The resentment and bitterness that had so characterized the old Drago had gone, and the lines they'd left in his face were now humorous and bold, and added character, rather than emphasizing his previous dampening blanket of futility. His skin was still pale, but the tincture of his violet eyes and copper hair gave him vitality and the appearance of endless energy; his wounding seemed to have brought no lasting damage to body or spirit. His was the lean, thoughtful face of a man in the midst of contemplative midlife, but there was something else . . . something in his eyes, or perhaps in the way he held his head, that hinted at far, far more.

It was a face that not only projected a profound and reassuring calmness, but also invited a further exploration of the man it represented.

For her part, Leagh thought his face and his overall demeanor extraordinarily sensual, and that surprised her, for she had never thought of Drago in that manner previously. Casting her eyes about those grouped around the fire, then back to Drago, Leagh thought he looked like a prince who had just woken from a very long enchanted sleep, and who yet did not know the talents or weaknesses of the court that surrounded him.

Neither did they know him.

There was wariness about this circle, and a little suspicion, but the general sense was of an overwhelming curiosity.

"When I went beyond the Star Gate," Drago began with no preamble, "I thought I had found all the love and all the meaning I had been searching for all my life. The Questors, as the five Demons called themselves, and the children and StarLaughter seemed so like me. All of us had been betrayed; all of us had seen our heritages stolen from us. It seemed so right to be with them. It seemed so right to aid each of them to regain their heritage as I needed to regain mine."

He smiled, but it was sad, and faded almost as soon as it had appeared. "They said they would give me back my Icarii power. Oh, Stars! To regain my power! To be like Caelum, and Zenith! To be an Enchanter again."

Everyone was quiet, watching.

"But the longer I spent with them," Drago continued, "the more I came to realize that their hatred and bitterness and their need for revenge had twisted them. Darkened them. StarLaughter, and the children—they were once so powerful, and so enchanted. Now . . ."

Drago paused, and his hands trembled. He clasped them together. "Their thirst for revenge at all cost had made them nauseating. Worse, I realized that I was very much like them, and I could not bear that thought. I grew to despise myself."

"Drago," StarDrifter said. "Do not so hate yourself. Few possess the courage to acknowledge their own shortcomings. It would have been easy for you to drift away among the Stars, regretting what you'd done but making no effort to right your wrongs. You had the courage to come back, and face the fruit of your sin."

"I had almost no choice, Grandfather," Drago said. "The Demons propelled me through the Star Gate. I could not have said no had I wished to."

"Nevertheless," StarDrifter said, "having come through the Star Gate you could have run for Coroleas, or made across the Widowmaker Sea. But you came here, to face those who have most cause to hate you."

Gods, Askam thought, his face carefully hidden in shadow, Drago has everyone convinced he is the hero of the moment, doesn't he? But what if, StarDrifter, you feathered idiot, Drago still aids the Demons? What if Axis is right, and Faraday is wrong?

Drago shrugged aside StarDrifter's words. "In actual fact, I first planned to die, for I did not particularly want to come back. But then," he raised his face and smiled at Faraday, "the Sentinels spoke to me—"

"The Sentinels!" Faraday's green eyes widened. "They are alive? You saw them? Did they come back?"

Drago smiled at her excitement. "Yes, they live, but no and no to your other two questions, Faraday. I did not 'see' them, for they are spirit only, and they did not wish to come back through the Star Gate, preferring to spend their eternity drifting among the stars. They love you, Faraday, but they did not want to come back."

"Are they still arguing?"

Drago laughed, and most about the fire smiled at the sound. "Yes, they still argue. I think the stars must ring with the music of their debates."

"So, they helped you to survive," StarDrifter said.

"Yes, but only after they persuaded me to aid Caelum and Tencendor as best I can." Drago sighed. "Not that Caelum will accept my help."

"Drago, do not blame him for that," Zared said.

"I do not. Instead I reproach myself for creating such a fear within him."

"And now?" DareWing asked. This sitting about and listening to confessions was all very well, but there were over thirty thousand men and Icarii standing about, waiting for direction.

For the first time an expression of uncertainty crossed Drago's face. "I want to help," he said, "but—"

Faraday put a hand on his shoulder, interrupting him. "There are many things that I have come to know over the past few months," she said, "and, regrettably, few that I can tell you for the moment. In time, it will become Drago's story to tell, and I ask only that you wait."

"Faraday—" Zared began, as eager as DareWing to make a start to *something*.

"Hush. Listen to me. At the moment none of us know much, but that can be remedied. First, may I ask what you all know, and understand?"

"Demons, through the Star Gate," Herme put in. "They

have ravaged this land." Briefly, he gave details of what hours were safe to venture forth, and what not.

"And we are thankful, Lady Faraday," Theod said, smiling and inclining his head at her, "that before the Demons broke through you spread the word that safety could be found indoors during those hours the Demons ravaged. Without the warning, most of Tencendor would be lost."

"As it is," Zared said, "our scouts at the edge of the forest report seeing crazed people wandering the plains, sometimes alone, sometimes in groups."

"And there are also herds of livestock," DareWing added. "Animals that are caught in the gray miasma of the Demonic horror seem to behave . . . most peculiarly. As if they, too, have gone mad."

Faraday's eyes narrowed thoughtfully. She had not thought about the animals. "Do you know why the Demons have come to ravage?" she asked, pushing the conversation forward. They could think about the animals later.

"To find what lies at the foot of the Sacred Lakes," Leagh said, "in order to resurrect one of their number, the worst of all. Qeteb, the Midday Demon."

Faraday nodded. "The answer to all our woes must lie at the foot of the Sacred Lakes. All I know is that Drago and I must go to the Cauldron Lake, as soon as we can. What is there needs to speak with Drago."

Everyone, including Drago, started to speak at once, but Faraday hushed them.

"I will take Drago there, and once we get back . . . well . . . once we get back I hope that we will have some answer to our current dilemma."

"Cauldron Lake?" Zared said. "But that is far south. It will take you days to get—"

"Seven or eight days to get there and back," Faraday said.

"What?" Zared exploded. "Wait! A *week?* Gods, Faraday! Tencendor lies ravaged and you say, 'Sit here and smile and wait *a week*.'"

"Zared," Leagh said, glancing at Faraday. "What can we do *but* wait? Where can we go? We cannot move beyond the shelter of this forest for more than a few hours at a time, and that is no time to get an army anywhere. We must wait.

Drago—what *will* you be able to tell us when you get back?"

"Leagh, I don't know. I am sorry."

Zared sighed, accepting. Leagh was right. They needed some answers. "Well, at least take two of our best horses. You might as well move as fast as you can."

Faraday laughed. "I thank you, Zared, but no. My two donkeys can carry us, and they know the way well enough." Faraday sat awake late into the night, watching as Tencendor's army slept curled up in blankets or wings in an unmoving ocean spreading into the unseeable distance.

Drago lay close to her, and she reached out, hesitated, then touched his cheek briefly.

He did not stir.

She sighed, and turned her gaze to the forest canopy, needing to sleep, but needing more to think. She was appalled by the scene earlier, and the face of hatred Axis had chosen to show Drago.

All Axis could see in Drago was the malevolent infant, using every power he had to try to put Caelum away so that he, DragonStar, could assume the name and privileges of Star-Son. Faraday could hardly blame Axis and Azhure, and certainly not Caelum, for their distrust of Drago—but it was going to make things difficult. Very difficult.

At that thought Faraday almost smiled. Here she was fretting at the fact that Drago's parents did not welcome the prodigal son with open arms and tears of joy, when beyond the trees ravaged such misery that SunSoar quarrels paled into insignificance.

But to counter the misery there was Drago. And somewhere, secreted within his craft, there was Noah. Between them, those two must somehow prove the saving of Tencendor.

Faraday let her thoughts drift for a while, content to listen to the sounds of the sleeping camp. Somewhere a horse moved, and snorted, and a soldier spoke quietly to it. The sound of the man soothing the horse made Faraday think, for no particular reason, of the stunning moment when Sicarius had leaped to the aid of Drago. *Drago?* Faraday knew how devoted those hounds, and especially Sicarius, had always been to Azhure, but she also remembered that for thousands of years they had run with the Sentinel, Jack, and she wondered if their origins lay not in Icarii magic, but deep below the Sacred Lakes.

Perhaps no wonder, then, that Sicarius had leaped to Drago's defense.

There was a slight movement at her side, breaking Faraday's thoughts.

She looked down. Drago had rolled a little closer, and now lay with his head propped up on a hand.

"Faraday—what did I come through the Star Gate as? You transformed me somehow, back to this form . . . *but what did I come through the Star Gate as?*"

"You came through as a sack of skin wrapped about some bones."

A sack, he thought . . . an empty sack, just waiting to be filled.

"And the rosewood staff was with me?"

"Yes. You insisted on searching for it before you would let me drag you from the Chamber."

Drago frowned slightly. "I can remember almost nothing of the Star Gate Chamber, or the first few hours afterward. Everything, until I woke refreshed in the cart, is blurred and indistinct."

Faraday remained silent, content to let Drago think.

"You evaded Axis' questions about the Scepter very nicely," he said finally. "You *know* the staff is the Scepter."

"Probably."

"I wanted to give it to Caelum. Damn it, Faraday, I stole it. It belongs to him, and he needs it back."

She tilted her head very slightly so he could not read her eyes, and again remained silent.

"When Axis taxed me about the Scepter I looked for the staff, intending to hand it to Caelum. But it had disappeared. Later, hours after Caelum and our parents had gone, I chanced upon it. Faraday, do you know where it was?"

She turned her face back to him again. "No."

"It was in the blue cart."

"It has its own purpose, Drago. And, undoubtedly, it did not want to be handed back to Caelum."

He sighed and rolled onto his back, staring at the forest

canopy far above. "Like all beautiful things," he said, and glanced at Faraday, "I do not understand it."

She bit down a grin, but he saw it anyway, and smiled himself.

"Why do you help me, Faraday? Why were you there in the Star Gate Chamber, waiting for me?"

"Someone needed to believe in you. I found that no hard task."

"You evade very well."

"It comes naturally to me."

Drago smiled again. He did not know why Faraday was with him, or how long she would stay, but he hoped it would be a while yet. It was a vastly new and immensely warm feeling to have such a beautiful woman walk by his side and say softly at night, "I believe in you."

Drago's grin subsided and he silently chastised himself for romanticizing Faraday's motives. It was obvious she knew some secret of Cauldron Lake, and it was that knowledge, or that secret, that kept her by his side. Like himself, she wanted only to aid the land, in any way she could, and at the moment she apparently felt the best way was to continue at his side.

He felt her fingers at his neck, gently feeling the bandage, and he looked at her. Gods, she was beautiful.

"Does the wound hurt?" she asked, trying to divert his attention.

"A little."

She drew back. "It should heal without giving you too much trouble. At least your father has enough experience with a blade to give you a clean cut and not some jagged hole."

"Then I am grateful for the small mercies of parental experience and skill," he said, "for, frankly, I thought he had me dead on the sliding edge of that blade." He paused, his own fingers briefly probing the bandage. "Faraday . . . at some point after you dragged me from the collapsing chamber I asked you who I was."

He frowned. "Why did I ask that?"

"I have no idea," she lied. "But do you remember that you answered your own question?"

He nodded very slowly. "And yet I do not understand my answer, nor the impulse that made me mouth it.

"*The Enemy, I am the Enemy*. What does that mean?"

"Go to sleep," Faraday murmured, and turned away and lay down herself, and although Drago stared at her blanketed back for a very long time, she said no more.

Drago dreamed he was once again in the kitchens of Sigholt. The cooks and scullery maids had all gone to bed for the night, and even though the fires were dampened down, the great ranges still glowed comfortingly.

He smiled, feeling the contentment of one at home and at peace.

He stood before one of the great scarred wooden kitchen tables. It was covered with pots and urns and plates, all filled with cooking ingredients.

But something was missing, and Drago frowned slightly, trying to place it.

Ah, of course. Of what use were a thousand ingredients without a mixing bowl? He walked to the pantry and lifted his favorite bowl down from the shelf, but when he returned to the laden table, he found that the bowl had turned into a hessian sack, and that the plates and bowls on the table no longer contained food, but the hopes and lives and beauty of Tencendor itself.

"I need to cook," he murmured, and then the kitchen faded, and Drago slipped deeper into his sleep.

Night reigned. Terror stalked the land. To the south of the Silent Woman Woods seven black shapes, a cloud hovering above them, thundered across the final hundred paces of the plain, and then vanished into the forest west of the Ancient Barrows.

Zared woke early, just as Drago and Faraday were rising and shaking out their blankets.

"Are you *sure* you won't take two of my fastest horses?" he asked, standing up and buttoning on his tunic.

"No," Faraday said. "The donkeys will do us well enough."

"However," Drago said, and his face relaxed into such deep amusement that Zared stilled in absolute amazement at the beauty of it, "there is one thing I would that you give me. I had a sack, and have lost it. Can you find me a small hessian sack? I swear I do feel lost without it at my belt."

And he grinned at Zared's and Faraday's bemused faces.

Far, far away he stood on the blasted plain, wondering where his master was. Last night he'd dreamed he'd heard his voice, dreamed he felt him on his back. Was there a use for him, after all? No, no one wanted him. He was too old and senile for any use. His battle days were behind him. His legs trembled, and he shuddered, and the demonic dawn broke over his back.

7

The Emperor's Horses

They sat, arms about each other, under the relative privacy of a weeping horstelm tree. Outside the barrier of leaves moved Banes and Clan Leaders, whispering, consulting, fearing.

Isfrael, Mage-King of the Avar, lifted a hand and caressed Shra's cheek. She was still handsome in her late fifties, and even if the bloom of youth had left her cheeks, Isfrael continued to love her dearly. She was the senior Bane among the Avar—had been since she was a child—but she was beloved to him for so many other reasons: she was his closest friend, his only lover, his ally, his helper, and he valued her above anything else in this forest, even more than the Earth Mother or her Tree.

When Isfrael's father, Axis, had given his son into the Avar's care when Isfrael was only fourteen, it had been Shra who had inducted him into the clannish Avar way of life, and into the deep mysteries of the Avarinheim and Minstrelsea forests and the awesome power of the Earth Tree and the Sacred Groves. She had made him what he was, and he owed her far more than love for that.

"Can you feel them?" she whispered.

"Yes."

He trembled, and she felt the shift of air against her face as he bared his teeth in a silent snarl. "*Demons* now think to walk this forest!"

She leaned in against him, pressing her face against the warmth of his bare chest. "Can we—"

"Stop them?" Isfrael was silent, thinking. He pulled Shra even closer against him, stroking her back and shoulder.

"Who else?" he whispered.

"WingRidge said that—"

"WingRidge said many things. But what has the StarSon done to help? Nothing . . . *nothing*. The Avar have ever had to fend for themselves."

"Can we stop them?"

"We must try. Before they get too strong."

Shra laughed softly, humorlessly. "They are strong enough *now!* Did they not break through the wards of the Star Gate? Isfrael—those wards were the strongest enchantment possible! Made of gods, as well as of the trees, earth and stars!"

"The Demons used Drago's power to break those wards."

They sat unspeaking a while, thinking of the implications of Isfrael's words.

Then Isfrael trembled again, and Shra leaned back. His face was twisted into a mask of rage—and something else.

Nausea.

"Their touch within the trees *desecrates* the entire land!" Isfrael said. "I cannot stand by and let them stride the paths unchallenged. And see, *see*."

His hand waved in the air before them, and both saw what ran the forest paths.

"See what abomination they have called forth," Isfrael whispered. "I *must* act."

The seven beasts snorted and bellowed, hating the shade that dappled their backs underneath the trees. They ran as fast as they dared. Their escort had not entered the forest with them, and they were fearful without the comforting presence of the Hawkchilds. So they ran, and as they ran the trees hissed and spat, trying to drive these abominations from the paths of Minstrelsea.

But something more powerful—and more fearsome—than the trees pulled the beasts forward.

Mot lifted his head, and laughed. "They come!" he cried, and the Demons rose as one from the rubble where they had been waiting.

StarLaughter scrambled to her feet, her lifeless child clutched tight in her arms.

"What comes?" she said. They'd been waiting here for days, and although the Demons had waited calmly, Star-Laughter had been almost beside herself with impatience. Her child awaited his destiny—and all they could do was sit amid the ruined Barrows. This was all they had come through the Star Gate for? She lifted her head. Something did come, for she could hear the distant pounding of many feet.

There was a movement beside her, and Sheol rested a hand on StarLaughter's shoulder.

"Watch," she said, and as she spoke something burst from the forest before them.

StarLaughter's eyes widened as the creatures approached and slowed into a thumping walk. She laughed. "How beautiful!" she cried.

"Indeed," whispered Sheol.

Waiting at the foot of the pile of rubble were seven massive horses—except they were not horses at all, for although they had the heads and bodies of horses, their great legs ended not in hooves, but in paws.

StarLaughter thought she knew what they were. When she'd been alive—before her hated husband, WolfStar, had thought to murder her—she'd heard Corolean legends of a great emperor who had conquered much of the known world.

This emperor had a prized stallion, as black as night, which had been born with paws instead of hooves.

The stallion had been as fast as the wind, according to legend, because his paws lent him catlike grace and swiftness, and he was as savage as any wild beast, striking out with his claws in battle, and dealing death to any who dared attack his rider. No wonder the emperor had managed to conquer so much with such a mount beneath him.

And here *seven* waited. Tencendor would quail before them.

Seven, one for each of the Demons, one for her—and one, eventually, for her son.

"DragonStar," she whispered, cuddling her child close, and started down the slope.

They rode northwest through the forest through the night, heading for Cauldron Lake. The Demons leading, Star-Laughter, her child safe in a sling at her bosom, behind them. They rode, but it was not a pleasant ride.

The horses were swift and comfortable to sit, but they were unnerved by the forest.

StarLaughter did not blame them, for she hated the forest herself—no wonder the Demons wanted to leave it as quickly as they did. To each side, trees hissed, their branches crackling ominously above, the ground shifting about the base of their trunks as if roots strove for the surface.

Barzula laughed, but there was a note of strain in his laughter. "See the trees," he said. "They think they can stop us, but all they can do is rattle their twigs in fury."

None of the others replied. Mot, Sheol and Raspu were tense, watchful, while beside Barzula, Rox rode as if in a waking dream. This was night, his time, and terror drove all before it. Rox had his head tilted slightly back, his eyes and mouth open. A faint wisp of gray sickness slithered from a nostril and into the night. He fed, growing more powerful with every soul he tainted.

If the trees unnerved the Demons and StarLaughter alike, then even worse than the trees were the beings that slunk in the shadows. Scores, perhaps hundreds, of strange creatures crept, parallel with the path, through the forest. StarLaughter caught only the barest glimpses of them—but they were creatures such as she had never seen before: badgers with horns and crests of feathers, birds with gems for eyes, great cats splotched with emerald and orange.

StarLaughter did not like them at all. She tightened her hold about her son, and called softly to Raspu who was immediately in front of her: "My friend, can these hurt us?"

Raspu hesitated, then twisted slightly on his mount so he could reply. "Once your son strides in all his glory, my dear, this forest will wither and die, and all that inhabit it will run screaming before him."

StarLaughter smiled. "Good." She started to say something more, but there was a movement a little further down the path before them, and then a great roar tore into the night.

"Get you gone from these paths! Your tread fouls the very soil!"

The horses abruptly halted. They hissed and milled about agitatedly. StarLaughter peered ahead—and laughed.

Before them stood the strangest man she had ever seen. He wore only a wrap—a wrap that seemed woven of twigs and leaves, for Stars' sakes!—about his hips, and was otherwise barefooted and chested. His hair was a wild tangle of faded blond curls, and two horns arched up from his hairline.

True, he had the feel of power about him, but StarLaughter did not think it was any match for what her companions wielded.

To one side and slightly behind the man stood a slender woman, dark haired and serene-faced, wearing a robe with leaping deer about its hemline. Her hand rested on the man's shoulder.

StarLaughter's lip curled. A Bane. How pitiful.

"Leave this place!" the betwigged man cried, and took a belligerent step forward.

"And who are you to so demand?" Sheol said pleasantly, but StarLaughter could hear the power that underlay her voice, and she smiled. This man was dead. The only question was who would strike the match.

"I am Isfrael, Mage-King of the Avar," the man replied.

"And the woman?" Sheol asked. It was polite, perhaps, to

find out the names of those about to die, but StarLaughter had always thought such niceties well beyond Sheol. Mayhap she was but toying with her prey.

"I am Shra," the slender woman said. "Senior Bane among the Avar."

"The Avar were ever troublesome," StarLaughter said. "Grim-faced and petulant-browed. Perhaps it is time they were finally put away."

Surprisingly, Isfrael smiled. "You do not like this place, do you? Why is that?"

Sheol shifted on her horse, and shot a look at Raspu, but when she spoke, her voice was even and calm. "It is a place that has no meaning, Mage-King. I do *not* like it."

"You do not like it, Demon, because you cannot touch it."

Sheol literally hissed, then she swiveled about on her horse. *"Rox!"*

The Demon of Terror slowly focused his eyes on the two before him, then his face twisted, and he cried out. "I cannot! The trees protect them!"

Isfrael smiled, and took another step forward. He raised a hand, and in it StarLaughter saw that he clutched a twig.

"You ravage freely across the plains, Demons, but know that eventually the very land will rise up against you."

"When we are whole, we will tear **this** land apart, rock by rock, tree by tree!" Sheol said.

Isfrael's grin widened . . . and **then** he threw the twig at Sheol.

Sheol *knew* what that twig was. It was not simply a twig, but the entire shadowy power of the trees that hurtled toward her.

She screamed in stark terror, reflexively raising both arms before her face, and then her scream turned into a roar and the twig disintegrated the instant before it hit her.

"Filth!" she screamed, and she grabbed the mane of her horse and dug her heels cruelly into its flanks.

The horse leaped forward, bellowing, its teeth bared, its neck arching as if to strike.

As if from nowhere, another twig appeared in Isfrael's hand, and this he brandished before him. "Shra! Stand firm!" he cried. "I rely on you now as never before!"

The horse lunged, snapping at the twig, but it did not seize it.

"Filth!" Sheol screamed again, and now Barzula and Mot also drove their creatures forward.

Unnoticed, the seventh, and riderless, horse, slunk back a few steps until it merged with the night.

"Shra!" Isfrael murmured. As mighty as he was, he still needed her power to sustain him. The three black beasts roiled before him, snapping and snarling, swiping their claws through the air.

Yet still they held back, so that their teeth and claws came within a finger span of Isfrael, but did not actually touch him.

"The very land will rise up against you!" Isfrael shouted one more time, and at his shout the trees themselves screamed.

Shra staggered, almost unable to control the power that Isfrael was using. She could feel it rope through her, feel it burn up through the soles of her feet where they touched the forest floor, flood through her body, and then flow into Isfrael through her hand on his shoulder.

All the Demons were screaming now, unstinting in their efforts to drive their mounts forward over this man before he could bring the full power of the trees to bear upon them. The air before Isfrael was filled with the yellowed teeth of the horses and the fury of their talons—but he was holding, and with luck he might even manage to drive the Demons back.

The seventh horse abruptly materialized out of the darkness behind Shra. Utterly silent, it surged forward, reared up on its hind legs, and then brought all its weight and fury to bear in one horrific slashing movement of its forepaws.

Neither Shra nor Isfrael had realized it was there. All their concentration was on the Demons before them, on driving them out, on. . . . Shra's eyes widened in complete shock, and she staggered backward, breaking the contact between her and Isfrael. Claws raked into her flesh from her neck to her buttocks, ripping the flesh apart to expose her spine.

"Isfrael!" she cried, and collapsed on the ground.

At the loss of contact Isfrael spun about—to see the massive beast tear her apart. Blood splattered across his face and chest.

"Shra!" he screamed.

Behind him the horses lunged, but as they did so Isfrael dropped to his knees by Shra's side under the flailing paws of the black horse, and tried to scoop her into his arms.

The other horses, the screaming Demons on their backs, milled above the two, biting and slashing.

StarLaughter, who had kept her own steed back, sat and smiled. The scene reminded her of the kill at the end of the hunt. She could see nothing save the plunging bodies of the horses, the Demons—now laughing and screaming hysterically—on their backs. Or almost nothing, except for the scattering drops of blood that flew through the air.

"A Mage-King," she murmured to herself. "How utterly, indescribably useless."

And then something swept past her.

She spun about, gasping. It was so fast that she did not get a good look at the creature—all she had was an impression of white. Of white, and of horns.

Something horned.

An owl fluttered down from the forest canopy and nipped at StarLaughter's hair.

She screamed, crouching over her baby.

Something else slithered out from between the trees—a snake, but a snake with small wings just behind its head. It sank its teeth into her horse's back paw, and the creature panicked and bolted, careening into the bloody melee before it.

StarLaughter, clinging desperately to the horse's mane, and trying to protect her baby, only had momentary impressions of the nightmare her horse had plunged her into.

The Demons were now silent, fighting an enemy that she could not immediately see.

Horses' heads, rearing back, eyes rolling white with terror.

A bloodied mess on the ground, and the horses' paws and lower legs thick with ropy blood and flesh.

The Mage-King—still alive—slowly rising, his face terrible with vengeance.

All StarLaughter wanted to do now was escape, any way she could. She fought to free her hand from her horse's mane, but it was tangled tight. Her wings beat futilely, trying to lift her from the horse's back, but she couldn't free herself, she couldn't free herself, she couldn't—

Suddenly a white form rose, almost as if from the very earth beneath her horse.

StarLaughter screamed in utter terror. A huge white stag reared before her, and then it plunged down, sinking its teeth into her horse's neck.

Both beasts writhed, both trying to gain the advantage. The stag's horns razored through the air, inches from StarLaughter's face, inches from her precious child—and still her hand was trapped in her horse's forever-damned mane!

She screamed again, thinking herself finally dead, when Sheol, Barzula and Rox simultaneously drove their horses onto the stag. It let her horse go, and suddenly StarLaughter was free, her horse bolting down the forest paths, the Demons' horses pounding behind her.

In the forest to the west, Drago's eyes flew open, and he fought for control as panic and terror flooded through him. In some part of him he could feel the Demons, feel their fingers reaching into him, feel them draining him. He could barely control the impulse to rise and flee through the forest, flee from something *horrid* that nibbled at him, that sunk sharp teeth into his heels, that lunged for his soft belly with razored horns—

He rose on his elbows, his eyes jerking from side to side. Faraday slept serenely by his side, and the ranks of soldiers that rippled out from Zared's campfire likewise lay calmly, lost in sleep.

Finally Drago managed to control his sense of panic. He looked to the east, troubled, and after a long, long time drifted back to sleep.

They rode for an hour, and then, as their mounts finally slaked their terror, pulled to a halt in a glade.

"When Qeteb walks again we will *raze* this forest to the bedrock!" Sheol screamed, turning her horse so she could see back the way they'd come, as if she might still see Isfrael standing there.

"Every one of the creatures that hide here shall become our fodder," Rox said, with more calm but equal venom.

StarLaughter looked between them, shaken to the very core of her being. She'd thought the Demons completely invulnerable, she couldn't believe that . . .

Sheol turned to stare flatly at her. "It is this forest. It is too *shady*," she said. "But we will grow stronger the more we feed. And one day, one day . . ."

StarLaughter nodded. "How far are we from Cauldron Lake?"

The Demons relaxed, and smiled. "Not far," Mot said. "We will be there in a day or so. And after Cauldron Lake, we will be stronger."

He looked at the flaccid child in StarLaughter's arms. "More whole."

There was a movement overhead, and all jerked their heads skyward, expecting further attack.

All relaxed almost instantly.

Black shapes drifted down through the forest canopy. The Hawkchilds.

"Sweet children," Sheol whispered as they landed, and dismounted from her horse so that she could scratch the nearest under the chin.

As a whole they tilted their heads the more easily to feel her fingers, whispering softly.

"I think," Raspu said, "that it is time we put our friends to good use."

The other Demons nodded.

"I admit to a dislike at being so ambushed," Sheol said. She dropped her hand, and when she spoke again her tone had the ring of command about it, even though she spoke softly.

"Scout, my sweet children. Find for us those who think to stop us. Where are the magicians of this world? Where is this StarSon who thinks to rule from the Throne of Stars? And where the armies who think to trample us underfoot?"

Behind her the other Demons laughed, but Sheol continued without paying them any heed.

"Find for us and, finding, set those who run to our song against them. Do you understand?"

"Yes, yes, yes, yes," came back the whispered answer. "Yes, yes, yes, yes."

"Then fly."

And they flew.

Isfrael stood staring down the forest path for almost two hours. About him Minstrelsea's fey creatures milled, touching him briefly, gently, grieving with him.

Eventually, Isfrael sank to one knee beside what was left of Shra. He stared a long moment, then he dropped his face into one hand and sobbed. He had loved Shra as he'd never loved another. She'd been the warmth of his youth, and the strength of his manhood. She had shown him the paths to the Sacred Groves, and she had inducted him into the laughter of love.

She had been his lover, his only companion, his only friend.

Isfrael bent down and wiped the fingers of his right hand through her torn flesh. Then he raised it and ran three fingers down his face, leaving trails of glistening blood running down each cheek and down the center of his nose.

"By the very Mother Earth herself," he said, looking again down the path where the Demons had disappeared, "this land *will* rise up against you."

And then he rose, and walked down the path.

Toward Cauldron Lake.

Toward the man WingRidge had told him would aid Tencendor.

But Isfrael had changed. The debacle of the Demons' passage through the Star Gate into Tencendor had suddenly become very, very personal. Now Isfrael had his own agenda, and the StarSon could be damned to a bloody mess if he thought to get in its way.

8

Toward Cauldron Lake

There was a disturbance last night," Drago said quietly to Faraday as he watched Zared rummaging through some gear for a sack. "In the forest."

She looked sharply at him. "Yes," she said. "To the southeast." She twisted her thick chestnut hair into a plait. "How did you know?"

Drago hesitated, trying to put emotion into words. "I could *feel* it, somewhere within me. Terror and savage pleasure both. It was the Demons . . . but what happened I do not know."

The feeling had disturbed Drago more than he revealed. It was almost as if . . . almost as if he had a bond with the Demons.

"Death," Faraday said. "Death happened. But who or how I do not know. Only that the Demons were involved."

She grimaced. The Demons were involved in every terror that struck Tencendor now. She watched Drago carefully as he walked a few steps away, pretending an interest in a saddle thrown carelessly against a tree trunk. He'd lapsed into his introspectiveness again, but Faraday was not surprised or perturbed by it. He needed to accept, and to explore, and for that he needed time and quiet.

There was a step behind her. Zared. In his hand he held a small hessian sack.

"Is this what you needed, Drago?" he asked. Zared was hesitant. There was something puzzling him about Drago, but he could not quite fix the puzzle yet in his mind, and that irritated him.

Drago took the sack from Zared, shaking it out. It was of rough weave, tattered about the edges, and with a small cloth tie threaded through its opening.

He smiled again. "It is perfect, Zared."

He turned to Faraday. "Faraday, may I ask a favor of you?"

She frowned, still bemused by the request for the sack. "What?"

For an answer, Drago leaned down swiftly and took a sharp knife that was resting by the loaf of bread Leagh had just put out for their breakfast.

"A lock of your hair," he said, and without waiting for an answer, reached out and cut a short length of Faraday's hair that curled about her forehead.

She jumped, surprised but not scared. "Drago, why—?"

He grinned impishly, and dropped it into the sack. "I like to cook," he said, and then laughed at all the surprised faces about him.

"Drago?" Zenith said. She and StarDrifter had just walked up. "What kind of answer is that? Look at us!" She gestured about to the circle of bewildered people. "Explain!"

"No," he said, still grinning. "Sometimes an explanation would only confuse the matter. StarDrifter?"

StarDrifter shared a quizzical look with Faraday. "Yes?"

"Will you trust me enough to give me your ring?"

StarDrifter looked down at the diamond-encrusted ring on his finger. It was his Enchanter's ring, although not the original, for that he'd given to Rivkah many, many years ago. He twisted it slightly. It was useless without the Star Dance, but still . . .

He looked up. "Yes," he said, "yes, I will trust you enough. Here," and he slid the ring off his finger and, as Drago opened the mouth of the sack, threw it in.

There was a brief glint as it fell into the darkness, and then the depths of the sack—and the lock of Faraday's hair— absorbed it.

"Would you like *me* to contribute anything?" Zared asked, half-expecting Drago to lunge at his person with the knife to snip off whatever took his fancy.

"No," Drago said. "I apologize for this mystery, but one day . . . one day I hope to explain what I do. There is one more thing I need, though. Leagh, will you take this knife," he handed it back to her, "cut me a slice of that bread, and place it in the sack?"

She half-frowned, half-smiled, and did as he asked.

"I thank you," Drago said quietly, and impulsively leaned forward to kiss her cheek. "And I am more glad than you know to see you and Zared together as husband and wife. Now, Faraday, perhaps we can eat before we go?"

They all sat, utterly intrigued by the scene, and accepted the bread, cheese and tea that Leagh and Zenith handed out.

Faraday chewed thoughtfully, watching Drago eat from under the lids of her eyes. He was growing into his heritage, and his destiny, by the hour.

It pleased her, and yet frightened her. Drago could save Tencendor—but not if the TimeKeepers came to understand who he was. No doubt the Demons were moving toward Cauldron Lake, and what would happen if they met her and Drago?

They had believed Drago dead—what would they think, what would they *understand,* if they saw him in the flesh? But what did it matter what they knew or understood? No doubt the Demons would do their best to kill them anyway.

"Be careful," Zared said, and Faraday jerked out of her thoughts, and nodded.

"Can we take some of this bread with us, Leagh? I do not know if we will find much on our way."

"Take what you like," Leagh said, and shared a glance with Zared. "Faraday, what are you doing? None of us understand what—"

Drago leaned forward and touched his fingers briefly to her lips. "Wait," he said.

Zared, watching, suddenly realized what it was that had been fretting at his mind. Since Axis, Azhure and Caelum had left, command had passed to Drago.

And everyone had accepted it.

None of us wait on what Caelum or Axis might do, Zared thought, but only on Drago. We have all turned to him, even though very few of us realize it yet. We wait for Drago's word.

"I wish you luck," Zared said, and stepped forward to grip Drago's hand and arm in both his hands.

"Are you *sure* we shouldn't have accepted Zared's offer of the horses?" Drago asked, squirming about on the donkey's ridged back. The forest had completely closed in about them, absorbing even the sounds of the donkeys' hooves, and it seemed that Zared's camp was more like a week behind them rather than two or three hours.

Faraday smiled a little to herself. "Uncomfortable, Drago?"

Drago sighed, and patted the donkey's neck. "I can understand why you like these beasts, Faraday, but for Stars' sakes! Surely they'd be better left to run free through the forest?"

"They are safe," Faraday said without thinking, and then wondered why she'd said it. "Safe," she repeated, half to herself.

Drago turned his head slightly so that he could watch her. A shaft of sunlight filtered through the forest canopy, and touched her hair so that deep red glints shimmered through the chestnut.

Drago's breath caught in his throat.

She lifted and turned her head to face him fully. "My beauty has never helped me, Drago. Never."

"And yet you are not bitter?"

She shrugged a little. "I have spent many years consumed by bitterness, Drago—and you of all people should know that bitterness does not help, either."

Drago let that pass. "Faraday, who do you take me to meet?"

"A . . . man, I suppose . . . a man called Noah. Noah exists within the Repositories at the foot of the Sacred Lakes, and he asked me to bring you to him."

She explained to Drago how, when he'd unleashed the power of the Rainbow Scepter in the Chamber of the Star Gate, the light from the Scepter had enveloped the Faraday-doe and wrapped her in vision.

Faraday laughed, a trifle harshly. "And you do not know how I had come to loathe visions, Drago. As a young, naive and stupid girl I first laid hand on the trees of the Silent Woman Woods, and they imparted to me a frightful vision that propelled me into my dreadful service to the Prophecy of the Destroyer. And to WolfStar, that damned Prophet!"

Drago almost asked what had happened to WolfStar, but thought better of it. "But this vision in the Chamber of the Star Gate . . . ?"

"Was better." Faraday smiled, remembering. "I was in a room—such a strange room, filled with twinkling lights and knobs, and with windows that commanded such a wondrous view of the stars—and a man rose from a deep-backed chair to greet me. He said his name was Noah, and that the room was within one of the Repositories at the foot of the Lakes, and he asked four things of me."

"And they were?"

"He asked me to be your friend."

"Ah." Drago's mouth twisted cynically. No wonder she walked by his side. She had promised to do so, and the world and every star in the heavens knew Faraday kept to her promises, even though they might be the death of her.

"Drago, why must you find it so hard to believe that people can like you, even love you?"

"Because for forty years I was told over and over that I was totally unlikable."

"And yet Zenith liked you, loved you, and believed in you."

Drago let that hang in the air between them awhile before he answered. "Zenith is special."

Faraday smiled softly. "I think that one day you will find that all of Tencendor, and all of its people and creatures are also special, Drago."

"Hmm. Well, what else did this Noah ask of you?"

"He asked me to be your trust."

Drago nodded, knowing that over the past day many had decided to trust him only through their trust of Faraday. "And?"

"Third, he asked me to bring him to you—and that is what I do now."

"Fourth?"

"Fourth, he asked me to find that which was lost."

"Am I among the lost, Faraday?"

"Oh yes," she said. "Most definitely."

Just as Faraday finished speaking, Drago's donkey snorted and tossed her head in alarm.

Something had seized her from behind.

Above the plains of Tare a black cloud wheeled and whispered. The old speckled blue eagle, now watching from a vantage point under the roof of one of the watchtowers on the walls of the city of Tare, shifted, ruffled its feathers, then opened his beak for a brief, low cry.

It did not like the cloud. During those hours of the day when the eagle had learned it was safe to venture out, it had flown as close as it dared to the cloud.

And that was not very close, for that cloud was dangerous, very dangerous.

It was composed of hundreds of . . . bird-things. The eagle did not understand them. They had the scent of the Icarii bird-people about them, but that scent was somehow tarnished and warped. They also carried the scent of hunting hawks, a scent the eagle was familiar with, for he had spent many a cold winter's night huddled safe within a nobleman's hawk stable murmuring love songs to unresponsive lady-hawks.

But as they were not quite Icarii, then they were also not quite hawks.

They behaved as a flock with one mind—yet that mind was not theirs, for the eagle sensed that the mind that controlled them was far distant.

These bird-things spent many hours of the day hunting and eating. They hunted anything that moved, horses, cattle . . . people. When they had spotted a target, the bird-things swooped, and tore it to pieces. Once they had fed—and they left nothing uneaten, not even a speck of blood—they rose again as one, and recommenced their whispering patrol of the skies.

There was a brief movement on the streets below, and the eagle glanced down, distracted. A group of three or four people, scurrying from one house to another, baskets of food under their arms. The people of this land had been almost as quick as the eagle to realize that certain hours of the day were . . . bad . . . to venture forth. Now they, like the eagle, spent the bad hours huddled inside, or under whatever overhang provided shelter.

Many—thousands—had not been so wise. In his forays over Tencendor, the eagle had seen bands of maniacal men and women, and groups of children, roving the land. Some had been ravaged by despair, some by terror, others by disease; still others by internal tempest so severe some extremities looked as though they had self-destructed.

And still others wandered, so hungry that they consumed everything in their path. For several hours one day the eagle had roosted under a chimney stack, watching in absolute horror as an aged man had literally eaten his way across a stony field. He had crawled on his hands and knees, and everything he touched that could be picked up he stuffed into his mouth and swallowed.

Stones, brambles, thorns, dried cattle dung—the man had even bitten off four of his own fingers in his quest to assuage his hunger.

He had died, eventually, by the low stone wall that had bounded the field. His internal organs had finally exploded with the weight of the rocks he carried within him. He'd died stuffing scraps of his bowel and liver into his mouth.

Sickened, the eagle had watched it all, and wondered if, eventually, he also would be caught outside when the badness billowed abroad.

Now he sat safe under the watchtower roof. The black cloud swooped low over a band of pigs that roamed savage and crazed to the west of Tare—yesterday, that band of pigs had caught and devoured several people trying to scrabble among the fields for some scraps to eat—and then rose into the sky again, and flew eastward.

The eagle shuddered as their whispering sounded directly above him, and then slowly relaxed as they continued to fly westward.

Drago lurched forward as the donkey bucked and kicked, and tried to grab at her brushlike mane.

But it was no good, and with a grunt of surprise, he slid to the ground.

He rolled to his feet immediately, grabbing his staff to use as a weapon—and then froze in utter astonishment.

Faraday already had her hands to her mouth, stifling her laughter.

The donkey bucked and kicked in a small circle, trying to dislodge what appeared to be a blue-feathered lizard that clutched at her tail trying with narrow-eyed determination to climb onto the donkey's back.

Drago slowly rose to his feet, laid both staff and sack on the ground, and then cautiously approached the aggrieved donkey, holding out one hand and murmuring soothing words.

The donkey gave one final buck—the lizard still gripping her tail—and halted, trembling, allowing Drago to rub her cheek and neck.

The lizard gave a hiss of triumph, and then, with almost lightning speed, scrabbled up the donkey's tail and onto her back.

Drago looked at it, looked at Faraday—who had quietened herself—and then ran his hand down the donkey's neck and across her withers toward the lizard. He hesitated, then gently touched the lizard's emerald and scarlet feathers just behind its head.

They were as soft as silk.

The lizard's crest rose up and down as Drago scratched.

"What is it?" he asked, raising his eyes to Faraday.

"It is one of the fey creatures of Minstrelsea," Faraday said. She explained how, when she'd planted the last tree for the forest, the borders between the forest and the Sacred Grove had opened, and Minstrelsea had been flooded with the strange creatures of the Groves. "I think it likes you."

Drago grinned and ran his hand down the lizard's blue back. "It's beautiful," he said, watching the shafts of light glint from its talons. "Entrancing . . ."

The lizard twisted a little, and grabbed at his hand with its mouth—and then began to wash the back of Drago's hand with its bright pink tongue.

The donkey, grown bored, sighed and shifted her weight from one hind leg to another.

The lizard slipped, and Drago instinctively caught it up into his arms.

"What am I supposed to do with it?" he asked helplessly.

"I think it wants to come with us," Faraday said. "And as to what you are supposed to do with it . . . well, I think it expects you to love it." For the rest of that day, and all the next, they traveled further south through the Woods. The lizard traveled with Drago, curled up in front of him on the donkey, the crystal talons of its fore-claws gripping the donkey's mane for purchase.

The donkey put up with it with some bad grace, her floppy

ears laid back along her skull, and she snapped whenever the lizard slipped. But at night she did not seem to mind when the lizard curled up beside her for warmth.

On the morning of the third day they neared Cauldron Lake, descending through thickening trees, and Faraday indicated they should dismount and walk the final fifteen or twenty paces to the edge of the trees.

The lizard, silent and watchful, crawled a pace behind them, careful of its footing on the slope.

"There," Faraday murmured as they stopped within the gloom of the line of trees. "Cauldron Lake."

Drago's breath caught in his throat. As with so many of the wonders of Tencendor, he'd heard tales of this Lake, but had never seen it previously.

It lay in an almost perfectly circular depression, the entire forest sloping down toward it on all sides. To their left, perhaps some two hundred paces about the Lake's edge, stood a circular Keep, built of pale yellow stone. Its door and all its windows were bolted tight.

But it was the water of the Lake that caught Drago's attention. It shone a soft, gentle gold in the early-morning sun.

Without warning, a vicious hand clenched in his stomach, and Drago gagged.

Faraday grabbed his arm and dragged him behind a tree.

"Look," she mouthed, and pointed across the Lake.

On the far shore a blackness had coalesced, and spread like a stain. It took Drago a few minutes to realize that it consisted of seven black and vaguely horse-like creatures.

And the Demons and StarLaughter.

9

Cauldron Lake

Curse them!" Faraday cried softly. "Gods! I'd hoped we could get here before them!"

"Should we—"

"No," Faraday said. "If we try to get to Noah now they will see us."

Drago sank down to the ground. He felt physically ill this close to the Demons, and he wondered again at the bond that existed between them.

"Will Noah survive them?" he asked.

"He'll have to," Faraday replied.

She sat down next to Drago and regarded him with concerned eyes. "Are you all right?"

He nodded, briefly closing his eyes, then he managed a small smile for her. "I am sick with frustration, no more. All I want to do is to see this friend of yours, and find out what it is I must do to help this land. Yet here the Demons have arrived before us, and so we must sit, and wait, and hope there is still a Noah to speak to once they have done."

She touched his arm briefly, but did not reply.

The Demons had not enjoyed a particularly pleasant ride through the Silent Woman Woods. Their encounter with Isfrael and Shra had unnerved them and, even though they grew progressively stronger each hour that they hunted, the trees had made their way difficult.

Tangled roots had snapped at them from the soft, treacherous soil.

Branches had dipped and swayed and snapped.

Leaves had flowed through the air, burrowing beneath robes and into corners of eyes.

And *things* had hissed and wailed at them from behind trees.

StarLaughter had been terrified, not only by the malevolence of the Woods themselves, but by the fact that the Demons seemed unnerved by them as well. Surely they were too powerful for such as this?

But maybe they needed the power of Qeteb before they could rise to their full potential.

And that power was not so very far away, surely. Soon Qeteb would be reborn, and her son would rise to *his* full potential.

And sometime, WolfStar, StarLaughter thought, hugging her child to her and casting her eyes about the shadowy spaces of the Woods, sometime we will catch up with *you!*

StarLaughter lowered her eyes, and looked about. They sat their mounts at the very edge of the Cauldron Lake, the five Demons staring silently at the strange, golden waters.

"Well?" StarLaughter asked.

There was a silence, and StarLaughter wondered if she ought to speak again, louder this time, but Rox finally answered her.

"Tens of thousands of years we have traveled," he said in a voice not much above a whisper. "Eons. And here . . . so close . . ."

Sheol raised her brilliant sapphire eyes and stared at StarLaughter. "We must proceed carefully, for the Enemy will have laid traps."

"But surely they are so old they will have lost their potency?" StarLaughter said. Why were the Demons always rattling on about traps?

Mot shook his head, then slid off his horse. Bones poked helter-skelter through his pallid skin, but his face had a satisfied plumpness about it. Mot had fed well at dawn.

He squatted down by the Lake's edge, and ran a hand through the water. It glowed, and filtered between his fingers, but it did not run as a liquid would, rather . . . as a mist.

"Ssss," the Demon said, and jerked his wrist so that the remaining globules of mist scattered over the surface of the Lake. They were absorbed instantly. "The magic lives, more potent than ever!"

"But not too potent for us, my friend," said Sheol, joining him. "We will go down at dusk, I think, for that will give us the power of Raspu and then Rox. An entire night to ravage through this craft and find what we need."

"Nevertheless," Barzula said slowly, casting his eyes about the Lake. "I feel the Enemy powerfully here. We must be careful."

"We did not come this entire way to waste our chance on thoughtless rush," Sheol said shortly.

She sat down on the damp earth and crossed her legs. "StarLaughter, my dear, come join me, and let me cuddle your child."

Across the Lake, Faraday and Drago likewise sat, hidden in shadows.

Drago's eyes hardly blinked, so intent was he on watching the Demons.

"Why do they wait?" Faraday asked.

"They wait for *their* time," Drago said. "It is only just noon. They will wait for the sun to set."

"And then?"

"And then they will leap."

It grew dark earlier within the trees than elsewhere, but the Demons waited until the entire land was wrapped in dusk before they began.

First they stood in a perfect line on the shore, about a hand span back from the water's edge.

Raspu, whose hour was at hand, stood in the center of the line, his head tilted back slightly, his eyes closed, the veins in his neck taut and throbbing.

A gray haze enveloped his head, and tendrils lazily lifted off and floated into the night air.

"What is happening?" Faraday whispered.

"He is feeding," Drago said. "As that gray mist spreads, so does pestilence sweep the land; gathering to itself all those who are not within some kind of shelter."

"Why did they wait until now?"

"Now they have the longest time span in which to work—from dusk to dawn. Once Raspu's time is done, then Rox will spread his terror over the land for the entire night. See, even now Rox prepares himself."

Faraday grimaced. Rox was trembling—so violently she could see it even from this distance—and his mouth was working; every so often his lips would tighten into a silent snarl, showing slippery, yellowed teeth.

Something about him, not his actual appearance, but something else, reminded Faraday vividly of the Skraelings and she shuddered.

Now all the Demons were trembling violently, almost convulsing. Behind them StarLaughter paced back and forth. Her child, as always, was tight in her arms.

One of the Demons—Drago could not tell which—screamed, and StarLaughter cried out and jerked to a halt.

Behind her, the dark horses milled and tossed their heads, pawing at the ground, although whether in fear or ecstasy, Drago could not tell.

The Lake began to boil—to *seethe*.

"What is happening?" Faraday whispered, one of her hands clutching Drago's arm in tight fingers.

"They are channeling the power Raspu and Rox have gathered into the water."

"But they are—"

"Destroying it. Yes, I know. Faraday, I . . . I don't think this Lake will ever be quite the same once the Demons have worked their will with it."

Faraday remembered what she and Zenith had seen when they'd walked the shadowlands: Grail Lake burned so completely away that the waters had disappeared to reveal the Maze beneath. A Maze that had grown to envelop Carlon. A Maze that had held such horror Faraday could hardly bear to remember it.

She lowered her head and closed her eyes. This was a beloved Lake, and she could not bear to see it die.

The next instant her head jerked up and her eyes opened as a sharp crack sounded behind her. She twisted about, and gasped. The trees were writhing and moaning, their bark splintering, yellowish cracks appearing in trunks and branches alike.

"Drago!"

"I can do *nothing*, Faraday. What do you want me to do? *What?* Whatever I am supposed to be, or supposed to do, lies at the foot of this Lake—at the moment I can do *nothing!*"

Faraday linked her arm through his, and leaned against him. "I'm sorry, Drago. I . . . this Lake is special to me. It is hard watching it die."

"They are all special," Drago said, and somewhere in a corner of his mind came the unbidden thought, *And they will all die.*

No!

The scene before them had turned into a nightmare. The water was boiling, great bubbles breaking the surface to send gouts of golden mist spurting into the night air. Soon the trees nearest the water's edge were laced with tendrils of gold.

The Demons were forcing the Lake to empty out its life over the Silent Woman Woods.

Beyond the seething water the Demons still stood in a line, but they were rocking and twisting violently, and screaming and shrieking unintelligibly. StarLaughter was crouched at one end of the line, by Sheol's feet, staring at the water.

She was laughing.

Suddenly the entire Lake exploded.

Drago threw himself over Faraday, rolling her as far behind the nearest tree as he could get her. He felt something crawl over his back, and almost screamed before he realized it was the feathered lizard. It scrambled under one of his arms and thrust its head under the neckline of his tunic, its feet scrabbling, trying to drive itself completely inside.

"Cursed—" Drago began, catching at the lizard with one hand, trying to prevent it getting any further, when a frightful silence fell as suddenly over the Lake and forest as the explosion had erupted only moments before.

Drago slowly raised his head, Faraday beside him.

The lizard took the opportunity to scramble completely inside Drago's tunic.

But even the frantic tickling of its feet could not tear Drago's eyes from the sight before him.

The golden waters had vanished. Now the slope of the forest floor continued down, down, down . . .

Down into another forest, one not of wood and leaves, but of crystal and gold.

The Demons and StarLaughter had disappeared.

10

The Crystal Forest

StarLaughter stood and stared. She could hardly believe the beauty of the crystal forest. She lifted one hand and stroked the trunk of the tree nearest her. It was cool and solid, but somehow vibrant.

"Exquisite," she said.

The Demons were grouped two or three trees beyond her. StarLaughter could see their dark and distorted forms through the transparent trunks.

"Dangerous," Barzula said. He had his arms wrapped about himself, and his golden eyes flickered uncertainly at the trees.

StarLaughter walked up to them, slipping a little on the glassy footing, and noting that the golden leaves of the trees—and how smooth and silky they felt!—were exactly the same shade as Barzula's eyes.

"Dangerous?" she said. "How so?"

Mot rounded on her, baring sharp teeth, but he pulled himself up at the look of surprise on StarLaughter's face.

"A trap," he said, and waved his hand about. A thousand hands reflected back at him from a myriad of trunks and branches. "This is a trap designed by the Enemy."

StarLaughter frowned, and tightened her hold on her son. "You must not let it harm him."

"Fear not, Queen of Heaven." Sheol slipped an arm about StarLaughter's shoulders and gave her a brief hug. "No harm shall come to your son. Now . . ."

Her tone suddenly brisk, Sheol turned to Rox. "How do we proceed? Which way?"

Rox shrugged. "Down. Everything slopes down. The Enemy's craft is *down*. What we need is *down*."

"Then why do we still stand here?" StarLaughter asked, raising one eyebrow. She shifted her son to a more comfortable position, and took a step forward. "Can't you use your power to scry out the . . . the place?"

Rox looked at the others. "Shall I? It is my time—my power grows each minute as terror feeds off this pitiful land."

"We need to move," Raspu agreed. "If we stand about and wait the trap will only snap shut."

But will it snap shut the instant we move? Sheol shared her thought with her companion Demons, but not with Star-Laughter.

Rox looked her in the eye. *There is only one way to find out.*

Sheol nodded. "We must risk it. Let loose your terror, Rox. Shatter these trees, and find the hiding place for us."

Rox smiled. He shifted so that he stood with his feet wide apart, and tipped back his head. His grin widened, became more feral, then he spread his arms out wide, his fingers trembling slightly . . . and screamed.

Terror raged through the trees. Every nightmare possible, every fear imaginable, every horror that was ever conceived, flooded rampant through the crystal forest.

Far away, hidden at the edge of the crystal trees at the point where it joined the waterways, WolfStar cried out and sagged to the floor. His breath cramped in his chest, his eyes bulged, and his limbs trembled.

His hands convulsed, and tightened about the tiny, cold corpse he carried.

"No!" he whispered, and then gagged.

In yet a different part of the crystal forest, the Survivor leaned against a tree, and grinned. His brown eyes danced with merriment.

"Predictable," he whispered. "But foolish. Very, very foolish."

Terror raged through the crystal forest. It bounced and jangled through the trees—and then it reflected, reflected back toward its source a thousand times stronger than it had been born.

Straight back to the Demons and StarLaughter.

It hit them with unimaginable force.

Every one of them, StarLaughter included, fell to the crystal floor, bruising flesh and jarring joints, their mouths opening for screams that never came because of the sheer weight of the terror that consumed them.

The baby slid out of StarLaughter's arms, rolling downhill until he slammed against a tree and lay still.

Completely still, his eyes wide open and blank, unaffected by the terror that assailed those who cared for him.

As quickly as the terror had hit the group, it dissipated. Rox had withdrawn his power in the extremity of his own fright, and once the source was shut off, so the terror dimmed until there were only faint shadows left to chase each other through the forest.

Mot was the first of the Demons to recover. He struggled to his feet, his pallid flesh quivering.

"I had always wondered how the Enemy had trapped Qeteb," he said hoarsely. "Now I know. They must have used his own power against him. They must have *reflected* it back at him!"

Sheol bared her teeth, arched her neck, and then howled, letting the sound echo through the forest a full minute before she shut her mouth with a snap.

"Then, knowing, we are the stronger," she said. "*No one* can ever use that trap against us again. Come, rise, and we shall set off on foot to find our stolen treasure."

StarLaughter came out of her fugue with a start, and suddenly realized that her child was missing. She cried out, then spotted him some paces away. She scrambled over on her hands and knees, ripping the hem of her robe where it caught under one knee, and gathered him into her arms, crooning softly.

"Was he hurt?" Raspu asked.

StarLaughter shook her head. "He is well, *see* how well!"

The five Demons were now gathered about her in a circle. They stared down at the unmoving infant, then lifted their eyes and stared at each other.

And smiled.

*   *   *

The Survivor ran one hand back through his silvered hair.

Then he straightened his black leather jacket with a tug at its hem.

"Good," he said. "Good girl." He patted the tree affectionately. "That scared them! Now, we may as well let them have what they want, and let them leave. No use holding them up any more than we have already."

The Survivor smiled slowly to himself. "But that *was* fun to watch."

Then he tensed, his eyes on a far distant form moving stealthily from tree to tree. He caught a brief glimpse of golden wings, and coppery hair.

WolfStar!

Noah swore. He hoped the Enchanter wasn't going to make a nuisance of himself.

He stilled, watching the distant form carefully. Noah suddenly realized that WolfStar had outlived his usefulness by many, many years.

"Something should have been done about you a long time ago," he murmured.

Then suddenly Noah's face blanched, and his right hand clutched at his chest, and he forgot all about WolfStar as the craft wreaked their deadly havoc within him.

In the end, it wasn't the Demons that Noah had to fear at all.

Sheol stood talking quietly to Rox, making sure he hadn't been harmed too greatly by the sudden reflection of his power, then turned and gestured to StarLaughter and the other Demons.

"Come. Let us waste no more time here than we must."

She turned and walked deeper into the forest, her feet slipping and sliding on the treacherous floor.

After an instant's hesitation, the others followed her.

They found the going difficult and nerve-wracking. Feet constantly slid out from underneath them, and their hips and knees were continually jarred and bruised by sudden heart-lurching tumbles.

StarLaughter, her arms so tightly wrapped about her unliving son that they sunk into his flesh, had to spread her wings in order to maintain even the semblance of balance.

But even that worked against her, because the feathers invariably got caught in low-slung branches. Sharp crystal twigs dug into her feathers until blood speckled the path behind her, and she was constantly being spun about as a wing was securely lodged between branches.

StarLaughter gritted her teeth against the pain, and struggled forward. *Damn all the Stars into eternal darkness that she no longer had her power!*

And why didn't she? Hadn't the Demons promised that her power would be returned to her when she came back through the Star Gate?

Raspu caught her thought and paused, leaning a hand against a tree trunk to maintain his balance.

The ground was now sloping alarmingly, and yet the slopes below showed more tangled crystal branches and golden leaves for as far as the eye could see.

As StarLaughter drew level, Raspu slipped an arm about her waist and drew her tight and hard against him.

StarLaughter, her breath momentarily jerked from her body, looked into his eyes in fright—and then relaxed, feeling the power and warmth of his body against hers.

"Be still, Queen of Heaven," Raspu whispered, his breath warm against her cheek, his arm still warmer about her waist. "Power *shall* be yours, but you must wait a little longer for it. Once our own power has been strengthened by this Lake, then we will have some to share with you. A different power than what you once commanded, but still power."

"Of course," StarLaughter said, accepting. "The Star Dance is no more, is it?"

"No," Raspu whispered, and leaned down to softly brush her lips with his. "No more."

The Demons struggled lower and lower. No more tricks leaped out at them, but their tempers grew progressively shorter as they went deeper, until they lashed out as they stumbled, their arms and hands striking twigs and leaves from branches, leaving a scattering of crushed crystal and trampled leaves in their path.

"Where?" snapped Sheol.

"Where?" snarled Rox.

"What is wrong?" StarLaughter whispered, now walking close to Raspu.

"It *must* be here somewhere!" he said, then jerked to a halt. "Wait!"

"What?" Sheol asked, turning to look at him.

Raspu stilled, sending his awareness slinking out between the trees. There was something . . . something . . .

"Something is out there!" Mot said.

"What we are looking for?" StarLaughter asked, her eyes bright.

Raspu shook his head slowly.

"Something . . . else. Something . . . watches."

Noah stilled in his efforts to get back to his craft. Pain still arced through his chest and arm, but it wasn't as fierce as it had been previously.

Or maybe he was simply getting used to it.

He raised his head slightly and peered about. Could the Demons see him? Sense him somehow? He tried very hard not to even breathe. No doubt the pain they would visit on him should they catch him would be even worse than this he currently endured.

Noah remembered the horror that had been wreaked on his own world, the frightfulness of the campaign to trap Qeteb, and he shivered.

"Drago," he mouthed soundlessly, and looked up through the crystal-clogged slopes rising above him. *Drago!*

And agony such as he could not have even imagined knifed through his body.

"If feels almost like the Enemy," Sheol said, a deep frown twisting her face. "I remember how they felt, how they tasted. And this tastes so familiar."

Rox shook his head. "It could not be. They were mortal, they could not still live."

"But still," Raspu said, and looked about. "Still . . . there is *something* out there."

"But it is not a danger," Mot said briskly. "Come."

And he set off again.

The other Demons looked at each other, shrugged, and followed him, Raspu holding StarLaughter's hand.

But still they kept their awareness sensing out about them.

They found what they where looking for eventually, when they were so tired and impatient that they were at the point of sinking their teeth into each other.

It sat before them, bubbling quietly.

"Warmth!" Sheol whispered, and sank to her bruised knees.

StarLaughter stood, staring, unable to believe that after so long, the first of the jewels of the Grail stood before them.

A large, spreading pool of blood in the very pit of the crystal forest, gently steaming and bubbling.

"*Yes!*" Raspu screamed . . . and then lunged at StarLaughter.

She pulled back instinctively, her arms tight about her son, but Raspu was far too quick and far too strong for her, and he yanked the baby from her arms.

"Yes!" he cried again, and tossed the baby toward the pool of blood.

The child arced through the air—and then fell, hitting the pool with a sickening heavy-wet splash.

Blood splattered out in a great circle where he had hit the pool, covering both the Demons and the nearest crystal trees.

StarLaughter cried out in horror, her hands to her face. Her child had gone! Disappeared!

"Wait," Raspu said, his voice now calm. "Wait."

Every one of the Demons was now still, tense.

Waiting.

Suddenly there was an agitation within the pool of blood, as if it were being stirred by an unseen hand, and then something floated to the surface.

A child.

But an infant no longer. A toddler of perhaps three or four. A boy, his hair thickened and clotted by the blood in which he floated, his eyes closed under gelatinous clumps of the stuff, his pale skin made rosy by the blood running off him.

"DragonStar!" StarLaughter cried, and waded into the pool.

She sank to her thighs almost immediately, but she struggled on, the blood rising up through her pale blue gown and soaking her breasts and wings. She lunged for the boy, missed, lunged again, and grabbed him by the hair, pulling him to her.

"DragonStar," she whispered this time, and drew the boy to her, offering him her slimy, crimson breast.

The nipple plopped out of his unresponsive mouth, but there was a difference in him—and the difference was not only his size.

StarLaughter looked up to the Demons anxiously standing at the edge of the pool.

"He is warm," she said, tears slipping down her cheeks. "He is *warm!*"

WolfStar watched from his hiding place twenty paces distant. He lay flat along the forest floor, his head raised only enough so that he could see through the transparent roots before him.

This was his first sight of the Demons—and of his wife, StarLaughter.

He was shocked that after four thousand years she could still rouse emotions in him. There she stood, so dark and beautiful, her coagulating robe clinging to the body he still remembered, could still feel.

And in her arms, their son.

DragonStar.

No, he thought, trying to drive down his feelings for StarLaughter—

—remember the nights they had shared? Remember the love and the laughter?

And remember also that she plotted to take your place on the throne, and conspired with our unborn son to that purpose.

—no, not DragonStar. Qeteb. Born and yet unborn.

StarLaughter was willing to let a Demon inhabit the body of their son.

WolfStar's lips drew back in a silent snarl. No wonder he

loathed her. She had deserved her death, and he wished she'd been made to suffer more than she had.

Perhaps he could still arrange it.

The Demons grouped about StarLaughter, drenched in clotted blood and now standing out of the pool. As their hands patted at the boy, and their faces bent to kiss him, WolfStar slithered carefully forward, one hand dragging the tiny corpse behind him.

There. Again! Raspu thought, sharing it only with the other Demons.

Who?
What?
Where?
WOLFSTAR!

Yes, Raspu nodded to the others. WolfStar.

StarLaughter, unaware of what was going on about her, crooned and laughed at her child, one hand trying to wipe the clots of blood from his body.

What should we do? What is he doing?

They considered, their jewellike eyes sharp.

Watch, Sheol thought, and the others silently agreed. Watch—and learn what it was that WolfStar did here.

Raspu laid a hand on StarLaughter's arm and pulled her gently back up the slope.

"It is time to leave, Queen of Heaven," he said. "Time to move to the next site."

"Yes." StarLaughter had a great smile of happiness on her face. "Yes."

As they moved off, Barzula lagged behind, concealing himself with power and keeping his senses focused on the blood pool.

Thus he was aware when WolfStar furtively ran forward to the pool, now considerably smaller in circumference than previously, and threw in his own still corpse.

A tiny girl bubbled back to the surface, as still as the male-child had been, but just as warm.

Barzula frowned, only barely repressing the urge to confront WolfStar—how dare he use the pool!—when he stopped himself, and smiled.

They could use this. Indeed they could.

And so he hurried after the other Demons, formulating his plan as he ran.

Drago pulled Faraday back down to the ground when the Demons emerged, sheltering her with his body.

Both drew in shocked breaths at the appalling sight of the bloodied StarLaughter carrying a toddler.

"Look!" Faraday whispered. "Look!"

Drago nodded, his face composed but thoughtful. "Their first goal is achieved. Qeteb now warms."

"And they? The Demons?"

"Will be stronger now. More confident. They have braved and won the first of the obstacles. They will know they can win through the others, as well."

StarLaughter sat, the child in her lap, completely absorbed in him. Her eyes shone soft and happy.

A few paces away the Demons stood huddled, talking urgently.

"WolfStar?"

"He had an *infant* that he threw in?"

Barzula nodded. "The corpse of a girl-child. I do not know what she means or is to him that he so dares."

"And she . . . ?"

"She was . . . warmed."

"How dare he?" Rox seethed. "How dare he—"

"Wait," Barzula said, and laid a hand on Rox's arm. "We can use this."

"Use? How?"

And Barzula spoke.

After a few minutes all the Demons nodded, their eyes glowing with satisfaction.

"And StarLaughter?" Sheol asked.

"She will not like it at first," Barzula said, "for she aches for revenge. But she will accept, and then she will approve. Think how much sweeter the revenge will be!"

Sheol gurgled with merriment, startling StarLaughter into looking up.

All the Demons were laughing, and clapping their hands. They must be pleased for her son, she thought, and smiled at them.

Sheol quietened as she watched StarLaughter. She turned to her companions. "It it time?" she asked. "Should we?"

They considered the possibilities, finally nodding.

"A little," Raspu said. "Not too much."

"Just enough," Sheol agreed. "Enough so she can be useful—"

"—but not a threat," Mot said.

StarLaughter, her head once more bent to her son, looked up as she heard the TimeKeepers approaching. Their faces were gentle, their jewel-bright eyes loving.

"When you originally came to us," Sheol began softly, "we promised you power for your help."

Her eyes shifted to the boy-child in StarLaughter's lap. "Now we are on the final path, our goal is in sight, and we have come to fulfill our promise. Stand."

StarLaughter obeyed, her eyes hungry. Rox stepped forward, and took her shoulder in his hands. "Beautiful woman," he whispered, and kissed her full on the mouth.

Power flooded through StarLaughter. Her mouth gobbled at his, desperate for more of the sweet stuff, but Rox pulled away, laughing.

Barzula stepped forth, and offered StarLaughter his mouth. She clung to him, drinking in as much power as he was willing to give her, and then almost fell when he pushed her back.

StarLaughter regained her balance, and clung to each of the other Demons in turn as they let her feed from their mouths.

As Sheol, the last, pushed her away, StarLaughter tried to understand the power that now flooded her. It was not Icarii power, and not tied to the now-silent Star Dance, but something far different—and far, far more exhilarating.

"I thank you," she whispered. "Now I shall be a true mother to my son."

The Demons smiled.

* * *

Faraday swallowed her revulsion as the Demons gathered StarLaughter to them. Once they had done, they mounted their dark horses, moving back through the Silent Woman Woods.

"Drago," she said, "it is time we went. Noah told me that we could find a way down through the Keep—"

"No." Drago laid a hand on her shoulder and pushed her gently back down. "You stay here. I want to do this by myself. Please."

"But how will you—"

Faraday never finished. With a low cry the feathered lizard stuck its head out of the neckline of Drago's tunic, looked about, then scrambled forth.

Drago almost fell over with the strength of its exertions, and grabbed at the nearest tree for support.

The lizard scuttled for the border between the Woods and the crystal forest, and then jumped between the first two of the crystal trees, its feet scrabbling on the slippery surface.

Drago looked at the lizard, looked at Faraday, then shrugged helplessly. "It looks like I will have some company after all."

"Be careful," Faraday said.

Drago stood looking down at her, very still. Her face was upturned to him, her eyes bright with concern.

Hesitantly Drago reached out a hand, then stopped it before his fingers touched her face.

"Wait for me," he said, then turned and walked between the first trees of the crystal forest, one hand now on his sack, the other hefting his staff.

11

GhostTree Camp

Fleat was an old, old woman. She had seen more than seventy Beltides, she had seen her daughter and her husband's second wife, Pease, torn to pieces by Skraelings, and she had seen this man who sat before her now drive the Destroyer and his minions from Tencendor.

She had thought to be able to die in peace, but that was not to be. Now another force invaded, far more vile than anything the Destroyer had thrown at them, and this man before her was utterly helpless.

Her eldest son, Helm, was now the leader of the Ghost-Tree Clan. Grindle had died twelve Beltides ago, and since then Helm had done his father proud. Now Helm was watching his wife, Jemma—eight months pregnant with a child that would surely be born into darkness—serve Axis and Azhure with malfari bread and the flat-backed fish she'd caught earlier in the day.

Both accepted the food, bowing their heads in thanks, but refrained from eating until Jemma had served Caelum, a little further about the fire, and sat down herself.

The twenty men and horses were camped fifteen paces about a bend in the path. Helm had not felt comfortable with them so close, and had wondered how Minstrelsea could tolerate their weapons.

Maybe, Fleat thought, the forest thought the weapons a lesser evil than the one that currently slithered through her southern skirts. Well, and wasn't that the case? Even weapons were palatable when compared to the TimeKeeper Demons.

Helm lifted his fish, slicing it open with a thumbnail, and laid layers of fish on his malfari bread.

"Where are you going?" he asked.

Azhure fingered her bread, unable to bear the thought of

eating it, but knowing that not only did she need the strength, Jemma would be gravely insulted if she left it.

So she broke off a piece, looked at Fleat, remembering how the GhostTree Clan had once taken her in when no one else seemed to want her, and responded to Helm's question.

"We travel north," she said. "To Star Finger. The Maze Gate," Azhure briefly explained what it was, "has told us that Caelum is the one to defeat Qeteb."

She put the piece of bread into her mouth and discovered to her astonishment that she was ravenously hungry. She began to chew enthusiastically.

"How," Fleat asked, her voice still strong despite her age, "if the Star Dance is gone?"

"We will find a way," Axis said. He looked about the circle of faces, lingering on Caelum's. "You must all believe that. We *will* find a way."

Some of the tension among the Avar of the GhostTree Clan dissipated. Axis had always found a way previously, and he would again this time.

Helm swallowed his mouthful of bread and fish. "There has been word from the southern borders of the forest, StarMan."

"Yes?"

"Shra is dead. Slaughtered by the TimeKeepers."

Azhure cried out, her hands to her face. She locked eyes with Axis, who was as horrified as she. Both of them remembered the day they had first met, that scene in the cellar of the worship Hall of Smyrton. Raum, half dead; Shra—a tiny child then—almost completely dead. Touched beyond words, Axis had gathered Shra into his arms and had instinctively sung the Song of Recreation over her. Then, he'd been BattleAxe of the Seneschal, committed to fighting against the "Forbidden," and had no idea he was of Forbidden blood and an Enchanter himself.

Shra was—had been—very special to both of them.

"How?" Axis said.

"Isfrael and Shra confronted the Demons, for they could not bear it that they so boldly walked the paths of Minstrelsea. They threw all the power they could command at them, and it was not enough."

Axis and Azhure shared another glance, then one with

Caelum. If Isfrael could not touch the Demons . . . then it *would* all be left up to Caelum.

"The Demons tore Shra apart," Helm finished.

"And Isfrael?" Azhure asked. A tear trailed down her cheek.

"He lived. The Stag intervened, and saved him."

Azhure nodded. The White Stag. The most magical beast in Minstrelsea. The creature that had once been Raum.

"Drago killed Shra as surely as if he had plunged a knife into her heart himself," Axis said savagely, and Azhure laid a hand on his arm. She had little love for Drago, and none for the harm he'd done her family and Tencendor, but she wished Axis could move beyond his all-consuming enmity for their second son. What good would that do them now? She glanced at Caelum.

"Where is Isfrael now?" Caelum asked. Even if Isfrael had failed in his own attempt against the Demons, he would be a valuable—and powerful—ally later.

"I am not sure," Helm said, "although forest whispers have him moving westward through the trees. Perhaps to the Cauldron Lake."

"Surely he wouldn't think to attack the Demons there!" Azhure said. Isfrael was not of her blood, but she had raised him until he was fourteen, and loved him as much as she did Caelum.

"Mother, be calm," Caelum said. "Isfrael is no fool, and I am sure he has a purpose to his movements. Trust him."

Later, they lay curled in each other's arms, not talking, listening to the other's breath and heartbeat, and to the sounds of the Avar camp settling about them.

After a while Azhure lifted her hand and ran it softly down Axis' cheek, letting her fingers brush against his short-cropped blond beard and then down his neck to his chest. How she loved this man! She leaned down and kissed his neck, and then his chest.

"Think you to make love here and now?" Axis asked.

She grinned in the dark. "I was remembering Beltide."

He smiled also, his hand stroking her back. "A long time ago, my love."

"Perhaps we ought to re-create a little of its magic now. It might comfort us."

Axis' smile died. "There is no magic to re-create, Azhure."

She lifted her head to study his face. "We will persevere, Axis."

He was quiet a long time, his eyes distant. When he spoke, his voice was so quiet that, even as close as she was, Azhure had to lean yet closer to catch his words.

"If I had known that day in that rank cellar," he said, "that Shra's life would have been so needlessly wasted then I may never have—"

"Hush." Azhure laid her fingers across his mouth. "Shra's life was not needlessly wasted. She lived to a full age, and even if the manner of her death was . . ."

"Vile." Axis' voice now had a hard and dangerous edge to it.

"Even if the manner of her death was dreadful, then do not deny her life because of it."

Axis was silent again for a few minutes, thinking.

Azhure thought she knew the trail of his mind, for his body had tensed. "Axis, nothing *we* did was useless."

"Wasn't it?" Axis' voice was very bitter. "Wasn't it? Was all the death, all the pain, all the suffering that I dragged so many men, that I dragged *Tencendor,* through, 'worth it?' "

"Yes!" Azhure said. "Yes!"

"Damn you!" Axis said, angry not with her, but with the pain that had now been visited on Tencendor. *"Damn you, Azhure!* Between us we bred the son that is solely responsible for—"

"And between us we have bred the son who will be solely responsible for Tencendor's salvation!" Azhure said.

"*If* we can find a way to give him the power to do so." And the confidence, Axis thought, but did not voice it.

His despair and anger was deepened by the knowledge that, once, Azhure would have caught that thought with her own power.

No more.

"We will!" Azhure said. "Axis, with something so deep inside me that I cannot tell what it be. I *know* that Star Finger holds the key to Qeteb's defeat! *I know it!*"

"And if it doesn't?"

Azhure raised herself on one elbow and looked her husband full in the face. "If it doesn't, then our task will be to witness Tencendor through its dying. And if that is fated to be our task, then let us do it gracefully."

"Stars, Azhure . . ." Axis said brokenly, and she leaned down and stopped his words with a kiss. He resisted an instant, then his arms tightened and he pulled her close to him.

Even after forty years, even in the midst of this disaster, his desire for her had not slackened.

Five paces away, hidden under the gloom of a purple-berry bush, Sicarius lay with his head on his forepaws, watching them. The hound's loyalty and love had been with Azhure for so very long that he now found it difficult to contemplate leaving her.

But he knew he would have to.

He had other loyalties, and other loves, far older than those he gave Azhure.

There was a movement behind him. His mate, a bitch called FortHeart. She nuzzled at his shoulder, and Sicarius shifted a little to give her room.

She too studied Axis and Azhure, then as one the pair shifted their heads to look south.

Caelum lay for a long time, listening to the sounds of the night forest, listening to the faint whispers of his parents, thinking.

He was glad that they were finally moving, finally doing something. He hoped his parents' faith that Star Finger held the key was justified . . . for if it wasn't, then there was no hope at all.

No, no, he couldn't think that way. He had to keep hope alive . . . somehow. Star Finger *did* hold the key, and it would give him what he needed to free the land from the horror that enveloped it.

And then no one, not even the ever-cursed Drago, could whisper behind his back that he didn't have the strength or courage or resourcefulness of his father. No one could ever say that he didn't deserve to sit the Throne of Stars in his own right.

Drago. Caelum felt a coldness seep over him as he thought of his younger brother.

When I came back through the Star Gate all enchantments fell from my eyes.

Curse him! Curse him! Curse him! If Drago's eyes were clear, then Caelum had no doubt that his brother was currently planning to scatter Caelum's blood over all of Tencendor.

How could it be otherwise?

All this pretense of contrition was a foil for Drago's deadly revenge and never-ending ambition.

"Stars help me," Caelum whispered, "if Star Finger holds nothing but useless hope." He dreamed.

He dreamed he was hunting through the forest. A great summer hunt, the entire court with him. His parents, laughing on their horses. His brother, Isfrael, and his sisters, even RiverStar. It was a glorious day, and they rode on the wind and on their power, and all the cares of the world and of Tencendor seemed very, very far away.

But then the dream shifted. They still hunted, but Caelum could no longer see his parents or his brother and sisters. The hounds ran, but he could no longer see them either. The forest gathered about him, threatening now.

And now even his horse had disappeared. He was running through the forest on foot, his breath tight in his chest, fear pounding through his veins.

Behind him something coursed. Hounds, but not hounds. They whispered his name. Oh, Stars! There were hundreds of them! And they hunted him.

They whispered his name. *StarSon! StarSon!*

Caelum sobbed in fear. *What was this forest?* It was nothing that he had ever seen in Tencendor. He cut himself on twigs and shrubs, fell, and scrambled panicked to his feet.

Something behind him . . . something . . . something deadly. Running.

He heard feet pounding closer, he heard horns, and glad cries. They had cornered him.

Caelum fell to the forest floor and cowered as deeply into the dirt and leaf litter as he could.

But he couldn't resist one glimpse—even knowing what he would see.

DragonStar was there, wielding his sword, riding his great black horse. But now he was different.

He still wore his enveloping armor—but it was black no longer. Now it ran with blood, great clots that slithered down from helmet, over shoulders, hanging dripping from arms and legs.

Heat radiated out from him.

DragonStar's voice whispered through his head. *And so shall you run with blood, Caelum.*

Caelum opened his mouth to scream, then halted, transfixed. Behind DragonStar's horse stood a woman.

Dark-haired. Beautiful.

And on her face a predatory smile of unbelievable malignancy.

"Zenith?" Caelum whispered, and then said no more, for DragonStar's sword sliced down through his chest, twisting and slicing, and, as promised, thick, clotted blood swamped Caelum's throat and mouth, and flowed out over his chin and chest to drown the land.

12

The Hawkchilds

Find for us and, finding, set those who run to our song against them.

So Sheol had commanded, and so the Hawkchilds had done. In truth, they already knew much of what the Demons needed to know. Since their return through the Star Gate the Hawkchilds had flown virtually the length and breadth of their ancient homeland, watching, seeing, noting.

Where the armies that think to trample us underfoot?

There, in the north of the Silent Woman Woods. Many of them. Tens of thousands. Crouched about small campfires, waiting for who knew what.

Where the magicians of this world?

Those that are left crouch within the forests. That so *few* were left made the Hawkchilds whisper their glee to the darkened skies.

They were those of the earth and the trees, and while they retained some powers now, the Hawkchilds knew they would eventually lose it. When Qeteb walked again beneath the heat of the midday sun. When the trees were blackened stumps smoldering under his fury.

These magicians, these Avar, were impotent now and would shortly be completely useless. The best they'd had, Israel and the Bane Shra, had thrown themselves against the Demons, and had lost.

And so the Hawkchilds paid them no heed. They would pose little, if any, danger. They soared through the dawning sky, whispering joyful melodies. There was no magic left in this land that could touch the Demons.

None.

Where this StarSon who thinks to rule the Throne of Stars?

Harder. He was here, somewhere, in the forests, but the Hawkchilds could not spot him.

Their joy faltered, and they hissed.

Where this StarSon? His name is Caelum. Caelum SunSoar.

As one mind they soared and dipped, thinking. Eventually, as mutual decision was reached, twenty-seven of the Hawkchilds veered away from the main flock and flew east. Over Minstrelsea. Hunting. Tracking.

The main body flew westward, seeking to carry out Sheol's command. *Find for us and, finding, set those who run to our song against them.*

Easy.

They whispered their joy, and then broke apart, the Hawkchilds scattering over the entire land.

In the very southwestern corner of the Skarabost plains, an old white horse stood in the rosy light of the dawn, hunger raging unnoticed about him.

He slept, dreaming of glory days past.

Sheltering on the ground under the shade provided by his belly, the ancient speckled blue eagle sat fluffing out his feathers in utter indignation that he'd been driven to find such shelter from the Demonic Hour.

But this was all there was, and somehow the eagle felt a kinship with this senile old nag.

Overhead there was a rustling, and a whispering.

The eagle started, terrified, knowing that what hunted was worse than the most crazed Gryphon.

But the Hawkchilds swept over, not minding the horse or the bird he sheltered. As if they had not seen either of them.

Little did either horse or eagle know it, but apart from the fey creatures of Minstrelsea, they were among the very few sane creatures left alive in the plains of Tencendor.

Five times during the day and night, the Demons sent forth the gray miasma, carrying their horror throughout Tencendor. The peoples of the land came to know that if they stayed indoors during those times and tightly shuttered doors and windows, then they could not be touched.

It was a dismal existence, but it *was* an existence.

Tencendor's fauna were not so fortunate.

Apart from the creatures of the forests, or those livestock who were continuously sheltered within barns or even homes, most of the creatures of Tencendor had been touched at one time or another over the past few days by the Demons.

Touched, and changed. Birds, badgers, cattle, pigs, snakes and frogs. All changed.

All now running to the song of the Demons.

The Hawkchilds hunted them down. Most of the creatures were roaming uselessly through grain land or the plains. And over the next few days all were visited by one or two of the Hawkchilds.

Whispering instructions.

An army in the northern Silent Woman Woods.

Destroy.

A myriad thousand people sheltering in Carlon.

Destroy.

Scores of hamlets and isolated farmhouses, still sheltering those who refuse to heed the sweet song of madness.

Destroy!

And when you roam, you will find the two-legs who, like you, have been touched. Absorb them into your flocks and herds. Use them.

The brown and cream badger led forth his slaughterhouse band at the behest of the Hawkchilds. He was tired of the years spent huddled in his burrow hiding from the horsed hunters after his fur.

Now was his time.

The Hawkchilds flew west and found a further friend huddled in a pool of weak sunshine outside the walls of Carlon.

A patchy-bald gray rat, sick of a lifetime of torture at the hands of the small male two-legs who ran the streets of the city.

In the city, tens of thousands of people crowded inside tenements, hiding from the Demons.

The Hawkchilds whispered in the rat's mind, and it turned its head back to the walls rising above it and bared its yellowed teeth in what passed for a grin.

Now was its time.

13

The Waiting Stars

Drago hesitated at the edge of the crystal forest, and then stepped onto its slippery floor.

He paused and, as StarLaughter had done, rested a hand on the trunk of the nearest tree.

It was warm, and solid, and somehow comforting.

Drago dropped his hand and straightened, his eyes surveying the forest before him. He took a deep breath, then stepped forward, following the flash of blue feathers between the trees below him.

Like the Demons, he walked for hours, marveling that the forest extended so far. Always the feathered lizard scrabbled, and sometimes slid, two or three trees in front of him, leading him downward.

In time the creature stood before a blackened crust that lay on the forest floor in a small glade. Drago stopped, and looked about him. He could feel the faint resonance of Demons in this place. What had they done here? He looked down at the crust. The feathered lizard was snuffling about its edges, reaching out one claw to scrape hesitantly at the stuff. His talons came away encrusted in flaky red filth, and the lizard backed off, hissing.

"What is it, my friend?" Drago said, squatting by the lizard and stroking its feathers. "What is this . . ."

He dropped his hand to the crusty stuff, and made a sound of disgust as his fingers touched it. Dried blood! Drago screwed up his face and stood, rubbing his fingers free of the crumbling flakes.

His fingers stilled, and he bent down again, scraped up a handful of the blood and dropped it into his sack.

His other hand momentarily tightened about the rosewood staff, and without thinking, Drago lifted the staff forward and scraped away a part of the blood.

He fell motionless, and looked awhile, and the lizard raised its eyes and studied Drago curiously.

"I think," Drago said tonelessly, "that we have reached our destination."

Underneath the dried blood was a trapdoor.

Grimacing, Drago bent down and swept away as much of the blood as he could. Then he lifted the door, revealing a well of steps circling down into darkness.

Much as, had Drago but known it, steps had once led from each of the Ancient Barrows into the Chamber of the Star Gate.

"Well," Drago began, speaking to the lizard, but he got no further, for the lizard had leaped into the stairwell and was already slithering and sliding his way down.

Drago smiled, and stepped after him.

He did not walk very far down the narrow, twisting staircase before it opened into a corridor that stretched some fifty paces, ending in a circular door. The lizard was snuffling about its hinges.

Drago stepped onto the smooth, gray metallic floor of the

corridor, and paused to study it. The floor was slightly leveled out, but only about the width of an arm, otherwise the passageway was completely circular, rising to a point about half an arm's length above his head. The roof of the corridor was lit by gently glowing circles, each a pace apart down its entire length. The walls were cool to the touch, but vibrated very gently.

As if they were alive.

A line of inscriptions ran at shoulder height down the walls. Drago stared at them, then lifted his staff and compared the inscriptions set there with those on the wall. They were the same, the strange black circles with feathered handles rising from their backs, running in a dancing, weaving line.

"These ancients," Drago said to the lizard, "had a strange script indeed."

Then he walked down to the door and inspected it.

There was no handle, although one side had hinges. Obviously it opened. But how?

Drago pushed, but with no success. He frowned, his fingers tapping gently against the door. On the wall by the door was a recessed rectangular section, filled with nine slightly raised knobs of the same cool, gray material as door and corridor.

Drago stared at them, then slowly raised his hand and rested his fingers on the raised knobs.

Instantly his mind flooded with an extraordinary vision.

Two old men, one short and squat, the other tall and thin, had marched down this very corridor once.

Drago's frown deepened. Who? One of the men turned and spoke to his companion, and Drago recognized the voice instantly. They were the Sentinels, Ogden and Veremund, and this was the doorway by which they had accessed the Repository.

He watched as the vision unwound itself.

The Sentinels walked to the spot where he now stood, and the tall one, Veremund, lifted his hand and placed it as Drago now had his placed.

Then he had hummed a fragment of melody, and his fingers had danced accordingly.

The memory faded, although the short melody lingered; it was a part of the same tune the Sentinels had taught him before he'd been dragged back through the Star Gate.

Drago stood, almost as if in a trance, replaying the vision over and over. Then, in a flash of inspiration, Drago realized that Veremund had transferred the melody into a pattern, and had then transferred the pattern onto the raised knobs.

Drago ran the tune through his head, translating it from melody to pattern almost without thought. He transferred the pattern onto the rows of knobs with his fingers.

Instantly the door swung inward with a soft hiss.

The lizard gave a soft cry and scampered through.

But Drago stood still, his head bowed, thinking. Something very, very important had just happened, and he struggled to understand it. He . . . he . . .

"Damn it!" Drago whispered. *"What did I just do?"*

He had used the pattern of melody to accomplish a purpose. Is that not what Icarii Enchanters did?

And yet there was no Star Dance, no power, no magic. No enchantment left.

Drago shuddered, and the grip of his left hand tightened about his staff. He had not only opened a door, he had also just been taught something.

Ah! Frustrated, feeling that the answer danced just beyond the reaches of his mind, Drago put the problem to one side and stepped through the door.

It swung shut behind him.

Drago paid it no heed. Before him stretched yet another corridor, similar to the last with the pattern of feathered circles on the walls, but curving into a left-hand bend some twenty paces ahead.

Beyond the bend the corridor branched into two. Drago took the left-hand fork without hesitation and then, when it again branched, took the right-hand fork. It led into a flight of steep steps leading to a higher level, and Drago grinned as he imagined how the two Sentinels would have grumbled about climbing them. Somehow, their presence was still very much here.

There was a large rectangular room at the top of the steps. The walls were literally smothered with the feather-backed circles. Metallic racks stood in three ranks, almost empty, save for half a dozen glass jars.

They were empty.

Drago looked about. There were three doors, rectangular now, in the far wall, each of them open. Which one?

From the door on the far right came the faint hum of vast power, but Drago understood he should not take that one.

He walked through the middle doorway instead. Before him stretched yet another corridor, but very short, and ending in yet another doorway through which . . . through which Drago thought he could see stars.

Stars?

Hesitant now, Drago walked down the corridor to the door, took a deep breath, and stepped through.

He stood in a strange room. The walls, ceiling, benches and even parts of the floor were covered with metal plates, and these plates were studded with knobs and bright jewellike lights. Before him were the high backs of several chairs, facing enormous windows that looked out upon the universe.

One of the chairs before him swiveled, revealing a silver-haired man in its depths. He wore a uniform made of a leathery black material; gold braid hung at his shoulders and encircled the cuffs of his sleeves, and in his first glance Drago saw a black, peaked cap, gold braid about its brim, sitting on the bench behind him.

But it was the man's face underneath his silvery hair which riveted Drago's attention.

It was lined with care . . . and more. Agonizing pain had scored a network of deep lines into the man's skin. His right hand clenched spasmodically in the tunic over his chest, and he breathed erratically, great deep breaths that tore through his throat.

A slight movement distracted Drago's attention momentarily. The blue-feathered lizard sat to one side under an empty chair, his black eyes unblinking on the man in the chair.

"Drago," said the man, and Drago looked back to him.

"You are Faraday's Noah," he said, and then stepped forward to touch Noah's shoulder. "What is wrong?"

Noah's mouth twisted. "I am suffering the ill effects of redundancy," he said. "No, no, that is wrong. I am simply being recycled."

"I don't understand," Drago said. He touched Noah's

shoulder again, leaving his hand resting there this time. "What can I do to help?"

Noah lifted his own hand to pat Drago's. "First of all, you can sit down. Then you can listen and accept."

"I meant," Drago said softly, "what can I do to aid *you?*"

"Me?" Noah raised tortured brown eyes and looked into Drago's violet gaze. "You can do nothing to help me. I am dying. After all this time, I am finally, finally dying."

Then he grunted with pain, doubling over in the chair.

Drago dropped his staff and grabbed him, wanting to help, but not knowing what to do. In the end he just knelt by the chair and held Noah, trying to give some measure of comfort.

Noah managed to straighten. His face was slick with sweat.

"We have all been waiting too long," he whispered harshly, "for me to die before I tell you what you must know."

"All?" Drago said.

Noah lifted a trembling hand and pointed to the window filled with the tens of thousands of stars beyond.

"All of us," he repeated. "The Stars."

14

In the Chamber of the Enemy

Noah looked at one of the empty chairs, as if considering asking Drago to sit in it, then gave a tired sigh and took Drago's hand in his. He glanced at the newly healed scar on Drago's neck, but said nothing.

Drago settled on the floor, moving the staff to one side as the lizard crept over and curled up against his legs.

"Tell me," Drago said, and Noah nodded, raised his head, and searched the panels under the window.

"Will you press the copper knob on the panel?" Noah asked, and Drago leaned over, hesitated, then firmly pressed a glowing knob.

Instantly the view from the forward window changed. The stars disappeared, and Drago found himself looking out on a world filled with mountains and valleys, plains and oceans.

He frowned. "I have not seen this place before."

"Nay. This is not Tencendor, although it is much like it. It is my world. My home."

Drago looked at Noah. Beneath his pain, the man's face was lined with memory and regret.

"And its name?" he said.

Noah's hand clenched a little more deeply into the black leather of his tunic. "Not important. For all I know it no longer exists. It has been hundreds of thousands of years since I have seen it."

The view altered. There were the same mountains and valleys, plains and oceans, but all had changed.

Now they were a wasteland of pain and despair, of tempest, pestilence and starvation. Maddened people and animals roamed, tearing at their own bodies and at the bodies of any who ventured near them. Their eyes were blank save for their madness, and ropes of saliva hung from their mouths. All the people were naked, their bodies emaciated and covered with boils and streaks of rot. They lived, but in a hell that Drago could barely comprehend.

"The same world," Noah rasped into the silence, "after the TimeKeeper Demons had come to ravage. Drago, listen to this, my story."

The view in the window shifted again, back to the stars.

"We do not know from where they came. We simply woke one morning to find half our world gone mad with hunger, and the pain continued through the day, and then into the night."

Drago remembered how the TimeKeepers had leaped from world to world. No doubt they'd found some other poor soul to drain in order to enter Noah's world.

"Hunger, then such tempest as we'd never before endured, and then midday—oh God! *Midday!*" Noah shuddered violently, struggled to control himself, then continued, his voice hoarse with the remembered horror.

"Midday is too terrible to even speak about—thank every god you pray to, Drago, that Tencendor has not yet been subjected to Qeteb's malice!"

Yet. The word echoed about the spaces between them.

Drago studied Noah's face. The man seemed in more pain than when Drago had first entered. "But you found a way to trap him."

"It took us forty years, Drago."

"Forty years?"

"Can you imagine," he whispered, "what those forty years were like?"

"How did your people survive?"

"In caves and tunnels and basements, mostly. Drago, your first lesson, and one Faraday already understands, is that the Demons, even Qeteb, cannot touch any who rest under shade. They cannot work their evil in shade. For some reason, the mere fact of shade protects the mind and soul from their touch."

There was more, but Noah was in too much pain to be bothered explaining it to Drago. The man would discover it soon enough, in any case.

"Ah, thus the forest keeps myself, Zared and his army," Drago slid a glance toward the feathered lizard, "and all the fey creatures safe."

"Until the Demons gain enough power to strip the leaves, yes."

"And Qeteb? How did you manage to capture him?"

"With mirrors. We trapped him inside a chamber that was completely mirrored. He could not escape, and any power he used was turned back against him."

"Mirrors? How could they—"

Noah grunted, and his face paled even more than it was already. He took several deep breaths, and then spoke rapidly, as if he knew he had not much longer.

"Mirrors . . . we mirrored him back to himself, we mirrored his *hate* back to himself. But . . ." Noah suppressed a groan, and momentarily closed his eyes, "unfortunately you will not have the same success now. The TimeKeepers are somewhat wary of mirrors and reflections."

"And so you—"

"And so we—or those who had the skill among us, for not all among us commanded the strength—dismembered him. They took his breath and warmth and movement and soul and separated them."

"His body?"

Noah shrugged. "It was useless. I think we burned it, although I am not sure."

And thus the need for a new body to house Qeteb, thought Drago.

"No one initially knew what to do with these life components," Noah continued. His voice and breath were easier now, as if his pain had leveled out. "In themselves they were still horrendously dangerous. We tried to destroy them, but found we could not. The other TimeKeepers were doing their best to steal them back from us—and they were powerful. Too powerful for us to hold out against for very long."

"So you decided to flee through the universe with them."

"Yes. It was the best we could do. I volunteered to lead the fleet of craft—"

"Craft?"

Noah looked up at the chamber. "We sit in the command chamber of the command craft. The craft are, ah, like ships that sail the seas, but these sail the universe."

Drago nodded hesitantly, struggling to come to grips with the concept.

"We set sail with four craft, one for each of Qeteb's life components, for we dared not store them in the same place. It was a mission that all of us—"

"Us?"

Noah's mouth thinned at the constant interruption—could the man not see he was in pain? "We had twelve crew members in each of the craft. Well, anyway, it was a mission that we all doubted we could return from."

"You *knew* you would never go home again. Noah . . . who did you leave behind?"

Tears slid down Noah's cheeks. "A daughter—my wife was dead. Her name is . . . was . . . Katie. It was . . . it was hard, but I went knowing she would live in a better world for my flight."

Drago placed a hand on Noah's knee. "I am sorry, Noah."

"I know you are. Thank you. Well, we fled through the universe. For many thousands of years."

Drago frowned, noting Noah's deteriorating state. "You are immortal? How else could you survive a journey of so long?"

Noah gave a harsh bark of laughter. "Immortal? Nay, obviously not! Our craft were equipped with . . . sleeping chambers, I guess you can call them, and in these we spent most of our time. The craft were set with self-guidance systems, and we generally slept, trusting in them to do their best."

Noah paused. "As a race, we had traveled parts of the universe before, but never so far or for so long as our fleet did. We did not realize what such lengthy travel through the stars would do to our craft."

Noah paused, remembering, and this time Drago did not bother him with a question.

"Our craft were woken by the music of the stars," Noah eventually continued. "And from that music they learned."

"Learned?"

Noah did not speak for some minutes, and when he finally did, his voice was soft with wonder. "Drago, your Icarii race speak of the Star Dance, the music that the stars make as they dance through the universe. While we slept, the music of the Star Dance infiltrated the craft, changing them, creating an awareness that was not there previously.

"They changed, and were filled with a purpose of their own. They changed," he repeated, as if still trying to understand it himself.

"Periodically we woke from our sleep to make sure the craft were operating normally. On one memorable occasion," Noah actually managed a smile, as he remembered the shock of his crew, "we woke to find that the craft would no longer obey our instructions. We found ourselves passengers, as much cargo as Qcteb's life parts.

"The craft altered course, heading for a different part of the universe than that which we intended to go."

Noah paused, his face emptying of all expression. "Gradually, I became 'aware' of the craft, and of the music that filtered through the stars. No one else among us did. I was the only one graced."

"You were the only one picked."

Noah's mouth twitched. "Aye, Drago, you are right. I was the only one picked. I learned that the craft headed for a world—this world. I was appalled. Infect another world with what we carried? And with the other TimeKeepers?

"We knew," he added, "that the five remaining TimeKeepers would follow us as best they could, hunting down Qeteb's life parts. It was one of the reasons we fled through the universe, knowing that in doing so we would rid our own world of all the TimeKeepers."

"And so you brought them to this world."

Noah turned his head and stared out the windows. Faint starlight illuminated the scores of lines about his forehead and reflected the pain in his eyes.

"The *craft* brought them to this world," he said softly, still not looking at Drago. "Not I. Not my race."

"You thought only to flee, not thinking of the eventual consequences."

Noah turned his eyes back to Drago. "Do not condemn us, Drago. Not *you*."

Now Drago dropped his eyes. "Then why did the *craft* bring them here?"

"It has taken me a long time to come to the understanding, Drago. Let me speak, and do not interrupt me. What you hear will be hard."

Noah swiveled his chair back to the windows. "Behold what will happen to your world when the TimeKeepers reconstitute Qeteb."

When, not if? But the view in the window shifted before Drago had a chance to ask the question.

As Drago had seen the Demons ravaging Noah's home world, now he saw them ravage Tencendor. Wasteland. Insanity. Deserts. People with no hope, nowhere to go. All beauty, love, hope and enchantment destroyed.

Drifting ashes where once had been forest.

Bones littering dust-swept streets where once had been cities.

Maddened animals ravening at will.

Horror.

Hopelessness.

"Tell me how to stop this!" Drago said.

The lizard stirred from its doze, lifted its head, stared at the image in the window, and then at Drago. Then it momentarily locked eyes with Noah.

Drago was too appalled by the vision of a devastated Tencendor to notice.

"I asked you to remain quiet," Noah said, a note of command ringing through the pain in his voice. "What you will hear *will* be hard, and you must hear it all before you speak again."

Drago jerked his head, apparently in acceptance. His violet eyes were very dark, and very hard.

Noah looked at him, and then waved a hand. The image of the devastated Tencendor was once more replaced with the tens of thousands of stars.

Drago relaxed very slightly.

"The craft brought Qeteb's life parts to Tencendor," Noah said, "because, drifting through the universe, they had come to the understanding that here, and here *only*, could Qeteb and his fellow demons finally be destroyed."

Noah sighed. "Drago, you must allow the TimeKeepers to reconstitute Qeteb. Allow them to destroy Tencendor."

"No!"

Noah did not chastise Drago for the outburst. He had the right.

"It is the *only* way to defeat him, Drago. *Listen* to me. We tried to destroy his life parts, and could not. But a whole Qeteb *can* be destroyed. This land is steeped in magic, although you—as so many of your brethren—are completely blind to it. Once Qeteb walks again, then, yes, Tencendor will become a true wasteland. The Demons will completely destroy it. Nothing will be left."

Nothing save the existence it will gain through death, thought Noah, but he knew he did not have the time to explain that to Drago. It was a knowledge better learned than told. "Nothing but its inherent magic," Noah said. "And nothing but you."

"Me? I came back through the Star Gate to *aid* Tencendor, Noah! To aid Tencendor and Caelum. Yet now you ask that I allow it to be destroyed." Drago gave a bitter laugh. "Yet what else could be expected of Drago the treacherous, Drago the malevolent? No wonder all hate me."

"Few truly hate you, Drago, although most are puzzled by you."

"How will allowing Qeteb to rise again help? How can allowing Tencendor to be devastated—"

"Qeteb *must* be defeated this time, Drago. He must be dealt to death."

Drago's face was tight and tense, a muscle flickering uncertainly in his lower jaw. "How?"

"Listen," Noah said, and he spoke for a very long time, his voice soft and desperate, his words tumbling over each other, and this time Drago did not interrupt at all.

When he finished Drago sat motionless, his own face almost as ashen as Noah's, his eyes despairing. "No."

"Yes. You have always known it."

"No."

"You knew it as an infant, it was *instinctive* knowledge! You acted badly, but you cannot be blamed for what you believed."

"No!"

"You know it now. Why else that sack that hangs from your belt?"

Drago fingered it. "I . . . I just thought it . . ."

"Yes," Noah said softly, and finally sat back down. "You just 'thought.' Instinctively you knew it was necessary. Drago, from your parents you have inherited the magic of the stars and of this land. From . . . elsewhere . . . you have inherited the magic of this craft. You have been *born* and you have been *made* exclusively for this task. Qeteb will be defeated only by a combination of these craft—which are now entirely star music—and Tencendor's enchantment."

Drago shook his head slowly, trying desperately to deny what Noah had told him. "I cannot do this to Caelum again. I *cannot*."

"You must."

"I have already destroyed his life!" Drago cried. He scrambled to his feet and stared at Noah huddled in his chair. "Now you would have me feed him to the Lord of Darkness all over again?"

Drago took a deep breath. "*He* is the StarSon, Noah, and I will not again deprive him of that right!"

"I think you will find he may insist," Noah said somewhat dryly.

"No," Drago said in a very quiet and almost threatening tone. "Caelum *is* the StarSon. Caelum will meet Qeteb, and I will do everything in my power to aid him in that quest. I will *not* betray him again."

"You have very much to accept," Noah said quietly. "Very much."

"I—"

"But if you want to do your best to aid Caelum and Tencendor, then do this. Go north, north to Gorkenfort. Seek your mother."

"Azhure?"

"Nay," Noah said, and smiled with such love that he unsettled Drago. "Your true mother. Your ancestral mother. Listen to her if you will not listen to me."

And ignore her if you dare.

Drago stared at him, then slowly sank down to the floor before the dying man.

"How can I let Tencendor be destroyed?" he asked again, his voice breaking. "I came back through the Star Gate to *save* it, and yet you tell me to stand witness to its destruction! Would you have me *deepen* my sin against the land?"

Noah reached out a hand and gently cupped Drago's chin. "You are a Pilgrim," he said, "and all pilgrims must first learn their own soul, and the power of their own soul, before they can save anyone else. If you take but one piece of advice from me, Prince of Flowers—"

Prince of Flowers?

"—then take this. Go north, and listen to your mother."

Drago was silent a long time. The lizard crawled into his lap, and Drago sat stroking it absently, his eyes unfocused.

When he finally spoke, his voice was heavy with acceptance. "I will go north to Gorkenfort. What else can I do?"

"The craft are not insensitive to the devastation that will occur. Somewhere within the waterways, I know not where for I have not been granted the knowledge, lies a sanctuary. A place of shelter. The craft would not let the peoples of this land suffer ultimate extinction. Do you understand?"

Drago nodded. "If the craft have that much compassion," he asked, "then why do they let you die?"

"So that another may be reborn," Noah said, but speaking with the voice of the craft.

So that another may be reborn? he thought, and then his eyes filled with tears as he understood what the craft were doing. They were using his life to create another, and the beauty of that other was enough for Noah to accept his death with gladness.

"Drago," he said, "I have not much time. Will you tell Faraday something for me?"

"What?"

"Ask Faraday to find that which I lost. She will know. Now go, Drago. Go. I would die alone, as I have spent an eternity alone."

Drago slowly stood, picking up his staff. "Good-bye, Noah."

"Good-bye, Prince of Flowers."

He sat in his chair in the empty chamber, staring at the screen full of stars, and let their love and comfort infuse him. He could feel the life ebbing from him, but it no longer hurt, and it no longer distressed him.

"Katie," he said. "Be strong."

His chest heaved, and again, then fell still.

In the dank basement, surrounded by dark and the stale air of a thousand years past, a light glowed faintly, and then flared into sudden brilliance.

When it faded, the thin voice of a desperate child filled the darkness.

"Mama? Mama? Where are you? I'm lost! Mama? *Mama!*"

The sacrifice had begun.

15

Hidden Conversations

Drago hesitated outside the doorway to Noah's chamber, then turned back.

The doorway had closed behind him, and there was no longer a panel of knobs by which to gain access.

"How can I do this to Caelum?"

But no one in this barren corridor, least of all the lizard, was going to answer him, so Drago took a deep breath and walked slowly back to the rectangular chamber.

Here he again hesitated. He'd meant to retrace his steps to the crystal forest, and from there to rejoin Faraday, but on impulse he took one of the other open doorways.

And found himself in the waterways.

Drago stopped dead. Before him a tunnel disappeared into the distance, a deep channel running down its center. He walked to the white-stoned edge of the waterway and looked down. The river that ran there was deep emerald. In its depths shone the stars.

The stars are everywhere, thought Drago. *Somewhere, surely, still lingers the Star Dance. But where? In these waterways? In the craft of the Enemy? Or will this puzzling "mother" awaiting in Gorkenfort tell me?*

"We must find it," he said aloud to the lizard, "if Caelum is to defeat the—"

"Did you listen to nothing Noah told you?" a soft voice said, and Drago spun about.

Walking along the banks of the waterway were Wing-Ridge CurlClaw, Captain of the Lake Guard, and the unmistakable red plumage of SpikeFeather TrueSong behind him.

Where had they come from?

"What are you doing here?" Drago said, taking a step back. WingRidge stopped a pace away, SpikeFeather just behind. Both birdmen studied Drago carefully, and both glanced curiously at the blue lizard under his arm.

"You know why we are here," WingRidge said softly. His face was a mixture of awe, determination, and sheer unadulterated relief. He lifted a hand and placed it on Drago's chest.

"You are here as I am here," Drago said, a hard edge to his voice. "We must do all we can to aid the StarSon."

WingRidge's mouth curled. "And what do you mean by that, Drago?"

Drago stared at him. "Caelum needs our help."

WingRidge inclined his head. "Caelum will need aid, assuredly."

Drago looked at WingRidge, then at SpikeFeather standing obviously confused behind the Captain of the Lake Guard's shoulder, then turned to look back the way he'd come.

"Noah told me . . . he told me . . ."

"I do hope you had the grace to listen, and the courage to accept," WingRidge said, and now his voice was hard, and his eyes flinty.

Drago looked back at him. "Why are you here, WingRidge?"

"I am here to aid the StarSon."

"Then why are you *here?*"

WingRidge remained silent, his eyes unblinking as they regarded Drago.

A muscle flickered in Drago's cheek. "I came back through the Star Gate to aid Tencendor."

"Good," WingRidge said quietly.

"In whatever way I can."

"Even better."

"I did *not* come back to disinherit my brother!"

"There is no question of that."

"Then we understand each other?"

WingRidge startled the others by bursting into laughter. "Yes, Drago, I think that we do. Now, in what direction did Noah set your wandering feet?"

"I must go north. To Gorkenfort."

For the first time WingRidge looked mildly disconcerted, but with a languid shrug of his shoulders said, "North is good. You will meet with Caelum in the north, eventually."

"Noah . . . Noah told me that Tencendor must die. We must allow Qeteb's resurrection."

"Surely we can stop the Demons before—" SpikeFeather began, his face horrified, but WingRidge turned about and placed a hand on the birdman's shoulder.

"Trust," he said. "Please. Did you not see this in the Maze Gate?"

SpikeFeather nodded unhappily.

"The Maze Gate?" Drago asked.

"Under Grail Lake lies a Maze," WingRidge said. "Each of the craft have grown into different forms over the millennia. Here, the crystal forest cradled Qeteb's warmth. The Maze cradles Qeteb's soul. At the entrance to the Maze lies a Gate, and it is the script about the Maze Gate that the craft used to speak to . . . well, to whomever, over the eons. The Maze Gate tells of many things. It, too, awaits the StarSon."

Drago ignored the last remark. "And this Maze Gate speaks of Tencendor's destruction?"

"It has been written," WingRidge said, "and thus it must be. Do not dread it too much, Drago. Does not the field need to lay fallow for it to flower full bright in the season that follows the night?"

The man speaks in nothing but riddles, Drago thought irritably, and then remembered that Noah had also mentioned flowers. Prince of Flowers. He stared at WingRidge, and the captain smiled at him, his eyes now soft.

Still pondering the consequences of turning Tencendor into an uninhabitable wasteland, SpikeFeather had completely missed the exchange. "And Qeteb is to be allowed a resurrection," he said. "How can this be?"

WingRidge did not look away from Drago as he answered. "How can the StarSon defeat a memory? A ghost? Only when Qeteb's scattered life parts unite in flesh and blood can they be destroyed. Eventually, the StarSon and Qeteb will face each other."

"And Caelum will defeat him," Drago said.

"The StarSon will defeat him," WingRidge said. "Will you agree to that, Drago? That the StarSon shall defeat Qeteb?"

SpikeFeather shifted, uncertain what to make of the conversation. He had the uncomfortable feeling that WingRidge and Drago were somehow weaving a hidden dialogue over and above their spoken words.

"I can agree to that," Drago said softly. "The StarSon shall defeat Qeteb."

"Then our purpose is as one," WingRidge said. "We both serve the StarSon and we both serve Tencendor."

He held out his hand, and after a brief hesitation Drago took it.

"That is an interesting staff you hold," WingRidge observed, not letting go of Drago's hand.

"You know what it is."

"Aye. I know what it is." WingRidge clasped his other hand over Drago's, holding it securely between both of his. "The Scepter. Never let it go."

"But—" SpikeFeather said, remembering the entwined symbols of StarSon and Scepter about the Maze Gate . . . and then suddenly the entire conversation between WingRidge and Drago fell into place.

"Ah," he breathed.

WingRidge laughed again and let Drago's hand go. "So you are to go north, my friend. Will Faraday go with you?"

"Yes."

"Good. And your new friend?" WingRidge indicated the lizard, now leaning over the edge of the waterway and splashing at shadows with one of his claws, light glimmering in shining shards from his talons under and over the water.

"His intentions are hidden from *me*," Drago said.

WingRidge cocked an eyebrow. "And you think *I* know? Not I. The beast is a mystery to me as well. What else?"

"You do not know?"

For the first time WingRidge looked uncomfortable. "If there is more, then, no, I do not know it."

"Remarkable," Drago said, but grinned to take the sting out of the remark. "Well, there is actually a little palatable news. Noah spoke of a Sanctuary somewhere within the waterways."

"A Sanctuary?" SpikeFeather queried, and WingRidge narrowed his eyes thoughtfully. Sanctuary. This *was* news!

But Drago took no notice of WingRidge's reaction.

"Gods!" he whispered, and shuddered. His eyes lifted upward, as if he could see through the tons of rock above them. "I can *feel* the Demons on the move. Every hour they are on the loose more souls are lost."

He dropped his gaze to the two birdmen before him. "I must go north, and I hardly know these waterways. Can I ask you to—"

"You know I serve no one but the StarSon," WingRidge said carefully.

Drago's face worked. "Then in the StarSon's name," he said, grating the words out, "will you hunt for Sanctuary while I go north?"

WingRidge grinned at Drago's discomfiture. "You had but to ask, Drago."

SpikeFeather hesitated, not wanting to be the one to break the tension, but finally the words burst out of him:

"Drago, these waterways spread not only under the complete landmass of Tencendor, but leagues out under the oceans, too. It might take a lifetime—*three* lifetimes!—to find this 'Sanctuary.'"

"Nevertheless," Drago said, "you possibly have a few months. No more. It will not take the TimeKeepers long to travel between Lakes, and before then we . . . someone . . . must manage the evacuation of Tencendor."

"A few months!" SpikeFeather muttered.

"I will help," WingRidge said to him. "The Lake Guard will help. Won't it be fun to keep company, SpikeFeather?" He threw an arm about SpikeFeather's shoulders. "You and I. Brothers in quest."

SpikeFeather glared at the Captain. He'd never seen WingRidge full of such high humor before. WingRidge kept his arm about SpikeFeather, but again addressed Drago.

"And once you have achieved your north and Gorkenfort, Drago? What then?"

"I . . . I don't know."

"Then I am sure your feet will find the right path," WingRidge said softly. "Drago, there is something you must know. WolfStar haunts these waterways. With him he carries the corpse of a girl-child. I do not know why."

Drago frowned, not sure what to make of this. What was WolfStar up to?

"Be careful," he said. "If WolfStar has a hidden purpose, then he can hardly be trusted."

WingRidge grimaced. "You hardly need tell me that, Drago. But don't worry, my friend and I shall find this Sanctuary. Won't we, SpikeFeather?"

SpikeFeather nodded, his mind full of the problems that conducting a search of the entire waterways would entail. He'd spent at least fifteen years wandering the tunnels and had never had a whiff of this secret place—and Orr had never mentioned it. Had the Ferryman even heard of its existence, let alone known its location?

"Come," WingRidge said, and took a step back along the tunnel. "We have a long—"

"Wait!" Drago cried, and touched the Captain's chest as he turned back to face him. "What's that?"

"This?" WingRidge looked down at the maze. "It represents the Maze, my friend. It represents my bond to the StarSon."

Drago stared at him, then he deftly picked out a golden thread from the embroidery and dropped it into his sack.

Then he gave a smile, almost apologetic, turned and walked away.

The lizard scampered after him.

16

Destruction Accepted

Drago retraced his steps through the craft and the crystal forest. When he finally entered the green shade of the live trees he stopped, hesitated, then turned and plucked one of the golden leaves from one of the crystal trees, and slipped that into his sack as well.

He was not sure why he did so, as he was not sure why he'd plucked the thread from WingRidge's emblem nor collected some of the dried blood, in each case yielding only to a sudden urge.

"I am glad *you* do not ask questions!" Drago said to the

lizard crouched beside him. It opened its mouth in a parody of a grin, and then bounded forward. Drago smiled to himself as he walked the final few paces into the Silent Woman Woods.

Faraday emerged from behind one of the trees, her face relaxing in relief.

"Drago!" She halted a pace away from him, her eyes searching his.

"Well?" she asked softly.

He stared at her, wondering what she knew. Did *she* also think . . . ?

"You cannot hide from who you are," Faraday said, watching the denial in Drago's face, "nor from your heritage."

She started to say more, but Drago cut her off.

"We have to go north. To Gorkenfort—"

Sudden emotion flared in Faraday's eyes, but Drago did not see it.

"—where," his mouth thinned, "I must meet with my mother. My 'ancestral mother.' Do you know what this means?"

Emotion relaxed to puzzlement in Faraday's eyes, but she did not question him. She shook her head. "What else?"

"And you are to find that which Noah lost," Drago continued. "He said you would know what he meant."

"Katie's Enchanted Songbook," she said. "It will, I believe, be a help against Qeteb."

At the name of the Midday Demon, Drago stared into the trees at Faraday's back.

He took a deep breath. "Faraday, Noah told me Tencendor must die and Qeteb must walk. How can I let this be? Gods, *how can I let this?*"

Faraday stared at him, almost unable to believe what he'd said, then she collected herself and gave him a brief hug. *But all she could think of was the land dying, the trees toppling, the lakes disintegrating, the dust drifting . . . drifting . . .*

She turned her head aside, not wanting him to see the tears in her eyes.

"It must be," Drago repeated in a soft voice. He was still staring into the forest, almost unaware of Faraday, and certainly completely unaware of her own distress. "Whatever it takes, I will let nothing, *nothing,* stand in my way. I came back through the Star Gate to help Caelum and to save this land, and *damn me to the pits of the AfterLife if I cannot repair the horror I helped sow."*

Faraday jerked her gaze back to his face, disturbed by his determination without quite knowing why. Drago would let nothing stand in the way of his quest. Tencendor would always come first in his affections and loyalties.

The land would always come first.

Faraday had known another man like that, and had been hurt beyond compare by him.

She turned away and walked back to the donkeys.

They took four days to move back to Zared's camp. They could have moved faster, but both wanted to put off the moment when they would have to share their grim news with Zared. Both Drago and Faraday, each driven to chronic loneliness by either circumstance or choice, also needed the time to forge the bonds of a friendship that would prove comforting, but not taxing or dangerous or potentially painful.

Both found themselves very much aware of the other, and aware of the other's reaction. For one that was a welcome surprise, for the other a frightening and unacceptable risk.

"Can you tell me what happened with Gorgrael?" Faraday asked one day as the thin Snow-month sun filtered down through the forest canopy and she caught Drago watching her from the corner of an eye. The lizard rode with her that day, curled up behind her back, snuggled between Faraday's warmth and that of the donkey.

Drago nodded. His passage back through the Star Gate had shattered all the enchantments that had crippled his memories. "I came to awareness early." His voice was very quiet. "I was growing in Azhure's womb, RiverStar wrapped tightly about me. Maybe the third or fourth month of life. I knew even then that I had . . . that I had a task. I believed I should be Axis' heir. I *knew* it!"

He turned to stare at Faraday. "I cannot know how. But I knew it. I was so stupid. I imagined a life full of greatness and pride, of reverence and of muscle-throbbing power. I thought of thrones and courts and the masses of Tencendor spread at my feet."

Drago's eyes slipped back to the path before them. "I understood the power of both my parents. I reveled in it. And I thought to be twice as powerful as them because in me was combined the power of both.

"And then . . . then I became aware of Caelum. Gods, Faraday, you cannot know the resentment that swept me! *Another* son? Born *before* me? A son that my mother rocked to her breast, only thin layers of flesh between us. A son that my father tossed high in the air and proclaimed StarSon.

"I thought that title should have been mine."

To that Faraday said nothing. But now? she wondered. Now?

Drago glanced at Faraday, his mouth crooked. "Of course, I set about my ambitions all the wrong way. I wanted to escape from that womb and set things to rights so badly. The moment I knew I could survive beyond it I beat my way out, dragging RiverStar with me."

"You almost killed Azhure."

"I know that now. Then, I did not care. She was useless. She had done her task in breeding me."

"And so you conspired with Gorgrael?"

Drago was silent awhile before he replied, and when he did his voice was distant. "Yes. So then I conspired with Gorgrael. With his help, I hoped to be rid not only of Caelum, but also of my parents. One or both of them would surely die in Caelum's rescue."

"You underestimated Azhure."

"Yes. I surely did." Drago sighed. "Gorgrael's mind was so easily manipulated. My success with him blinded me to the fact that my parents might have greater power."

"You were very stupid."

Drago stared at her, but let the remark lie. "Then I almost ruined Caelum. Now I will do my best to help him."

"Of course you must," Faraday said, and Drago glanced at her, trying to interpret her remark.

But her face was in shadow, and he could not read her expression.

As soon as Drago looked away, Faraday spoke again. "If circumstance shows you a path that is distasteful, Drago, but one that will result in a freed Tencendor, will you take it?"

He took a long time to reply. "Stop trying to convince me that—"

"Will you?"

"There is only one person who can persuade me to—"

"Then Caelum will do that," Faraday said.

Drago's face closed over. "I can hardly imagine that ever being the case. He rightly loathes me."

"Will you do whatever you have to in order to aid Caelum and Tencendor?"

"Yes!"

"Then that is enough," Faraday said. "No one can ever ask more of you."

Drago sat on his donkey and wondered if he had just been outwitted. She was as smooth-tongued as WingRidge. He suddenly grinned, dissipating the tension between them. "You retain the sharp skills of a Queen immersed in court intrigue, Faraday."

She laughed softly. "Naturally. One never knows when they will come in handy."

"We worry," said a soldier by the name of Gerlien.

"I know," Zared answered, rubbing the bridge of his nose between forefinger and thumb. He'd hardly slept the past few nights. "But—"

"Sire? We do not know if our wives and children are safe or wander the plains demented. We must find out."

To one side, Askam lounged against a tree and watched. Zared had command. So be it. He could deal with this nasty mess, then.

"We must wait for Drago and Faraday to—"

"How much longer must we wait?" Another man stepped forward from the group facing Zared.

"What do you propose?" Zared snapped. "That we just march out into the plains? How long do you think we would last before one of the Demons' miasma found us? There is no shelter out there, and at least two weeks between us and Carlon!"

"Zared, hush one moment." Leagh stepped to her husband, and took his arm, although she kept her eyes on the knot of men before them.

"Gerlien, Meanthrin, my husband speaks the truth. Do not blame him that at least he knows where his wife is."

She smiled to take any sense of chastisement out of her words.

The soldiers relaxed a little, impressed with the fact that Leagh knew their names. But then, she'd been tireless this past week, moving among the campfires of the army each night, spending a few minutes and words at each. And although Zared had done the same, Leagh had always managed to raise a few more, and far more genuine, smiles.

"I ask you to wait," Zared said. He smiled lopsidedly. "None of us can know where, or how, to move until Drago and Faraday return."

"And yet," Askam's voice cut in from the side, "some people might think you should be out there, saving as much of Tencendor as you can, Zared. After all, is that not what Axis asked you to do?"

"And I will do so," Zared said, keeping his tone even, "when I know how it is that I may keep most of these men alive."

"You would put your trust in someone as treacherous as Drago?" Askam asked. "Or as unknown as Faraday?"

"Faraday is hardly 'unknown,' Askam," Leagh said, her voice sharp. If her husband necessarily had to guard her tongue in front of Askam, then she did not. "She died for—"

"Ah," Askam said dismissively, turning away as if to walk into the forest. "And yet here she walks again. Not quite 'dead,' is she? What did she promise to the Demons to get her life back? The green fields of Tencendor? The jeweled corridors of the Minaret Peaks? And I hardly need start on Drago—that man has never had anything but deadly intentions for Tencendor, or for anyone who steps in his path."

"No one can blame you for being scared, Askam," said a voice to the side, "but you should learn to look beyond past grievances. Don't fight that which may well save your life."

"Faraday!" Zared strode forward and helped her from her donkey, relieved beyond measure that she was back. He looked over to Drago. The man was different. Sadder, almost.

"Drago?"

"Soon, Zared, but—"

A lizard scrambled from the donkey's back and scrambled up the nearest tree. Everyone's eyes widened in surprise.

"—a meal first would surely be appreciated."

Sitting about the fire with Zared and his immediate command, Drago told them what he could.

There was little to say but the worst, and no way to say it but in the worst way possible.

Drago studied his hands, and when he looked up his face was neutral. "Qeteb must be allowed to live," he said.

The listeners erupted with exclamations, and Drago held up his hand for silence.

"There is worse."

"And why am I not surprised?" Askam muttered under his breath, but none heard.

He shot a glance at Faraday. Askam wasn't fooled by her. She sat close by Drago's side, her lovely face demure, her eyes downcast, but Askam wondered if she wasn't casting some spell to enchant all into Drago's web.

"Tencendor will be devastated by the Demons," Drago said softly. "Especially with Qeteb at their head. The land will be destroyed. It must be."

"Why say this?" Zared cried. "You think this is going to *help?*"

"Zared . . . everyone . . . please listen to what I say before judging either the speaker or the message."

Drago paused and thought carefully before continuing. The journey through the Silent Woman Woods with Faraday had given him time to think and to reason things out, and what he'd come to understand needed to be said carefully, and yet plainly.

"You all know the tensions of the past, tensions that have been present within Tencendor for over a thousand years. Not even Axis' battle against Gorgrael managed to truly unite the three peoples of Tencendor. Sin, bias, bigotry, dissent and distrust still walk the land. Tencendor must be ravaged clean to . . . wait! . . . let me finish! All the bigotry and distrust must be burned clean before the peoples of Tencendor can find the heart and the courage to truly unite against the Demons.

"The field must be left fallow for it to flower full bright in the season that follows the night."

Zared dropped his gaze. He could not trust himself to speak.

If Zared thought it best not to immediately vent his anger, then StarDrifter had no hesitation in speaking his mind.

"But to allow Tencendor to become a wasteland." His face was tight and ashen, his pale blue eyes furious. "Allow Qeteb to arise? How can—"

"I am sorry, StarDrifter. But Qeteb must be allowed to live before he can be killed. Nothing 'unalive' can be made dead."

"And how is this killing to eventuate?" StarDrifter asked, no less angry.

"With the magic of this land combined with the magic of the Enemy's craft," Drago replied.

"There is no magic of the land remaining," StarDrifter said, making an emphatic gesture with his hand. "None."

"No." Faraday turned from watching Zared to look at StarDrifter. "You are wrong. This land reeks with enchantment. We must learn how to use it."

"And the magic of the craft?" Zenith asked. She hated what Drago said, but she also believed they had no option but to trust him.

"We must learn to use that as well," Drago said. "Faraday is to seek—"

"For the gods' sakes!" Askam shifted irritably. "No doubt you are going to blind our senses and woo our favor by speaking of some glittering and glorious quest. Bah! You speak of nothing but dreams. *Caelum* will help us, and he will do right by us. *He* will not allow this Qeteb to raise from whatever crypt he is stored in. *He* will not allow—"

"Askam," Drago said, fixing the man with his eyes. Both his stare and his voice were steady, and very compelling. "You speak nothing but truth when you say that Caelum will help us and do right by us. I am here to serve this land above all else, and I am here to right what wrongs I have done, to both land and Caelum. But Qeteb *must* be allowed to rise, for there is no other way he can be destroyed. No one can fight a memory, not even Caelum."

"Ha!" Askam said, but his tone was unsteady, and his eyes wavered from Drago's.

Zared studied Drago. There was something troubling the man, some doubt that ate away at his soul. *What* doubt? Damn him. What was he hiding? *Was it worth the destruction of Tencendor?*

Leagh laid a hand on his arm, and Zared lowered his head, fighting to contain his anger and frustration.

"Caelum can't defeat Qeteb without the Scepter, Drago," DareWing said. "All who have seen the Maze Gate agree with that. I do not mean to cast doubts on your words, but—"

"DareWing, there is no offense taken." Drago paused. "I will return the Scepter to Caelum. I stole it, and I must return it. Faraday and I will go north to do just that."

Faraday gave him a sharp look, and then turned her face away.

"I have heard enough," Zared said in a low voice, then raised his head and stared at Drago. "I have heard *enough*. I am charged with the care of the peoples of this land, and yet you sit there and say, 'Let them die.' You are nothing but—"

"You will listen to what I have to say," Drago shouted, visibly shocking most in the circle.

He stared at Zared, then moved his eyes to each and every one who sat about the fire. "I am a SunSoar. I am the son of Axis SunSoar and of the Enchantress Azhure. I am a Prince of the House of Stars, and of this moment I am claiming my birthright. Among all of us here, *I* have the highest birthright, *I* have the best claim to authority, and *I* know what must be done! In the absence of the StarSon you will, you *must,* heed my wishes and do as I ask."

Drago paused, his entire face set hard, then he leaned forward, stabbing with a stiff finger to give his words more emphasis. "Now you will shut up and you will *all* damn well *listen* to what I have to say."

Utter silence. Shock not only at being spoken to in this manner, but because the words and tone came from a man that most had been used to seeing only as a skulking, sullen backdrop to any scene.

It was still hard, StarDrifter thought, to think of Drago as a SunSoar Prince. He glanced about the circle. Faraday was as watchful as he. They locked eyes for an instant, and StarDrifter was the first to shift his away. Zared's face was unreadable, but StarDrifter thought he knew the man well enough to know that unreadability in itself did not bode ill for Drago. He looked at DareWing. The birdman was tense, and looking at Drago with such ambiguous speculation that StarDrifter thought it could mean either murder or unquestioning loyalty. Askam was clearly hostile. Theod and Herme looked entirely out of their depth; they would follow Zared's lead.

StarDrifter looked briefly at the birdwoman by his side. Zenith caught his look, and gave a half-smile. She trusted Drago implicitly. Leagh? She was worried, upset by the confrontation between her husband and Drago, and uncertain whom to believe.

"Yes," Drago said. "Tencendor will be destroyed, but if everyone within this circle works hard, then its peoples will be saved. Deep below us in the waterways is a Sanctuary, a place to which every person and creature that remains untainted can be evacuated. This land is going to be torn apart in the struggle against Qeteb, but its peoples can be saved, and eventually, once Qeteb is dead, the land can be resurrected."

Again, silence. Then Askam leaned back and laughed. It was a harsh and sarcastic sound.

"I can hardly believe *you* have the gall to sit here and say that," he said. "You. *You?* I haven't heard anything so ridiculous in—"

He got no further. There was a blur of movement from the trees and suddenly Askam was flat on the ground, the blue-feathered lizard on his chest and hissing in his face.

Drago ignored both Askam and lizard. He looked Zared directly in the eye. "Zared, you are King of Achar. If I tell you how to save your people, will you listen?"

He did not wait for an answer. Instead, Drago swung his fierce stare to StarDrifter. "StarDrifter, you are a Prince of the SunSoar House, and uncle to the Talon. If I tell you of a way to save the Icarii race, will you listen?"

Again, Drago did not wait for an answer. He dropped his eyes for an instant, then raised his face and stared into the gloom of the trees.

"Isfracl! You are Mage-King of the Avar. If I tell you how to save your people from destruction, will you listen?"

Everyone else started, and turned to look in the same direction as Drago.

There was a stillness among the trees . . . and then Isfrael stepped forth. He looked wilder and more dangerous than any could remember seeing him. His lips were curled in a half-snarl, his arms tense beside him, his hands clenched.

There was blood streaked across his naked torso, and three trails of blood ran down his face.

"No one tells *me* how to save the Avar!" he snarled.

Isfrael paused, and then closed the distance between himself and Drago. He leaned down, and thrust a bloodied hand in Drago's face.

Everyone except Drago automatically leaned back a fraction in shock.

"See Shra's blood," Isfrael said, his voice almost a growl. "See what the Demons have done to her."

Drago stared at the hand, then back to Isfrael's face. "If I tell you how to save the Avar, *will* you listen to me?"

"If you live to see the Demons die," Isfrael said, "then you have my loyalty."

He held Drago's eyes an instant longer, then turned and stared at Faraday.

She returned his stare, trying to reconcile her memory of a lovable baby and child with this wild man. All she wanted to do was rise and embrace him, but she was kept still by the unexpected—and horrific—antagonism on his face.

"Where were *you* when Shra died?" Isfrael hissed.

Shra dead? Faraday did not know what to say. Did he blame *her?* Could she have done something? But she hadn't known. Was there a way in which she—

"I do thank you for your loyalty," Drago said, and Isfrael snapped his gaze back to him.

The Mage-King gave a stiff nod and moved away a pace or two.

Faraday dropped her eyes, shocked by the encounter and by Isfrael's hostility. There was something more than anger at Shra's death feeding that hostility, but Faraday could not even begin to think what it might be.

"If you can tell me how to save the Icarii from the inevitable destruction ahead, then I am also yours to command," StarDrifter said quietly. Gods, *someone* had to say something!

Drago looked at Zared.

"And I," Zared said, although his willingness to accept Drago's command clearly had not eased his frustration. "Tell me how to save my people."

Askam, who had finally managed to push the lizard to one side, leaped to his feet. "Fools!" he cried. He started to say something else, but was so angry that he couldn't get any more words out. He stared, then stumbled away, the lizard nipping at his heels.

"I'll speak with him," Leagh murmured, then rose and hurried after her brother.

"Drago," Zared said, "where may we find this Sanctuary?"

"It is somewhere in the waterways—" Drago began.

"Forgive me," Zared said, "but I do not like this 'somewhere.' *Where?*"

"WingRidge, as indeed the entire Lake Guard and Spike-Feather TrueSong, are already engaged in the hunt for Sanctuary. Trust, Zared. That is all you can do."

The Lake Guard are aiding Drago? StarDrifter's heart began to thump as if it had shifted position into his very mouth. *WingRidge and the Lake Guard are working for Drago?* Oh merciful Stars above, StarDrifter thought. *Oh Stars! Now I understand!*

It was as well that no one addressed StarDrifter at that moment, for he thought himself incapable of speech. He almost moved a hand to his eyes, then realized they were shaking so much it was impossible.

Across the fire from StarDrifter, Zared was fighting his own doubts. He wanted to be able to trust Drago, but he had the responsibility for hundreds of thousands of people. And what had Drago given him? Just vague mention of a Sanctuary that even Drago admitted he couldn't find. Damn you, Zared thought, staring at Drago. You *demand* trust of us, and yet you cannot tell us where it is that—

Something jerked within Zared's body, and he had to fight to keep his face expressionless. For an instant . . . for an instant he'd been overpowered with the sweet fragrance of a field of lilies, and the bizarre, but utter, conviction that this was what Drago would lead Tencendor into. Both scent and conviction were so compelling they literally took his breath away.

Zared regained his equilibrium within a few heartbeats, and the scent faded. He could have sworn that somehow Drago had cast an enchantment over him, save that Drago was himself looking at Zared with a clearly puzzled expression.

"Zared," Drago said, watching the man carefully. "I need you to go back to Carlon, taking this army with you. Gather together as many of your people as you can, and ready them for the word I will send when WingRidge finds Sanctuary. Isfrael, will you allow the Acharites in the eastern parts of Tencendor access to the shelter of the forests?"

"As long as they bring their own food with them," Isfrael said, but Drago nodded. It was enough.

"StarDrifter, I need you and Zenith to go to the Minaret Peaks. Tell FreeFall what I have told you, and wait for word on Sanctuary."

StarDrifter's mouth quirked. "The Icarii will not take kindly to news of another exile," he said. "But we will do as you say. *Anything* you say, Drago."

StarDrifter stared at his grandson, his eyes intense, and Drago looked away quickly, not liking the knowledge he saw there. He began to say something else, but Zared forestalled him.

"I do have one small problem," he said.

Drago raised an eyebrow.

"How do I get myself and my thirty thousand back to Carlon? Isfrael and StarDrifter shall have the forests to protect them, but you seem to calmly assume I can just wander back across the Plains of Tare with my army and all their cursed horses as if we are out for a seventh-day picnic. There is no *shelter!*"

"Shade will protect you," Drago said evenly. "All you must ensure is that your army can access shade during the Demonic Hours—"

"There is no shade between these damned Woods and Carlon!"

"Carry it with you."

"Carry it with me? *Carry it with me?* Shall I uproot these trees, then, and carry *them* with me?"

"A cloth against the sun or moon is all you require, Zared. Perhaps stretched over poles. The most basic of tents, enough to shelter you and your horses."

"A tent? How am I supposed to get enough material—"

"I can give you what you need to move your army," Isfrael said.

Zared's eyes widened. "Do you have a thousand bolts of cloth secreted somewhere?"

"You will be surprised by what I and mine have secreted within these trees."

Zared almost pressed Isfrael, then realized there was no point. "I thank you," he said, then looked back to Drago.

"I have spoken as I did through anger," he said. "Anger and frustration. Drago, Prince of the House of the Stars, I will give you everything I can and then more, but only if you *can* provide my people this Sanctuary. If I watch them shrivel and die because you are wrong, if I watch this land desecrated into nothingness because you are wrong, then know now that I will curse you for all eternity."

"If I am wrong, then I will deserve to be so cursed," Drago said, "and I will embrace it for all eternity. But for now, you will do as I say."

Zared stared at him, remembering again the all consuming scent of lilies, and he nodded.

As the meeting broke up, Drago moved to speak with StarDrifter and Zenith.

"Zenith," he said low, "I need to know what happened in your battle with Niah. How exactly *did* you expel her?"

Zenith exchanged a glance with StarDrifter, then told Drago of how Faraday had found her in the shadowlands. Moving back toward the Island of Mist and Memory, where lay Niah, Zenith had eventually forced the Niah-soul into the baby girl that the shared body carried.

"And then?" Drago asked.

Zenith took a deep breath, her eyes stricken with the memory. "Then I forced the child from my body, and killed her."

"And *then?*" Drago said.

"WolfStar took the corpse," StarDrifter said, sliding a protective arm about Zenith. "Drago, why push Zenith on this? It is over and done with."

Drago rubbed his eyes. "No," he said quietly. "It is only just beginning. WolfStar is in the waterways. He is moving between the craft—with the baby's corpse."

"But why?" Zenith said.

"I think he seeks to reconstitute her in the same way that the TimeKeepers look to—"

"No!" Zenith cried.

"And the Demons?" StarDrifter asked. "How is it possible that WolfStar can—"

Drago looked him directly in the eye. "I think the Demons are allowing him to do it. I do not know the 'why' of it, but I most certainly do not like it."

17

The Donkeys' Tantrum

Leagh walked slowly among the trees, smiling at the groups of soldiers she passed. Sometimes she found it difficult to believe over thirty thousand were sheltered in these Woods. Separated by the trees into small groups, the entire army seemed to merge into the gloom.

She stopped by one lieutenant. "Jaspar, has the Prince Askam passed this way?"

"Through there, my lady." Jaspar, one of Askam's command, was not quite sure what to call Leagh. Princess or Queen? What did his allegiance dictate? And who did he owe his allegiance *to*? Askam . . . or Zared?

Leagh almost walked off in the direction Jaspar indicated, then paused. "Jaspar, the *Prince* Drago—" why was it that no one had thought to accord him *his* proper title, either? "—has just said something that I think is very pertinent. Tencendor can no longer let petty rivalries and bigotries continue to tear it asunder. If nothing else, Jaspar, give Zared your loyalty because Caelum has asked it of you."

Jaspar nodded unhappily, and Leagh sighed, and turned away.

She found Askam standing among the horse lines, stroking the neck of his bay stallion.

"Askam?" Leagh walked up and smiled, giving the horse a pat herself. "I think the horses appreciate the gentle rest they find among these trees."

He didn't answer her, refusing to even meet her eyes.

"Askam . . ." Leagh's voice almost broke, and she had to clear her throat. "Askam, we are tied by blood so close that *nothing* should come between us. Please—"

He turned to stare at her. "Zared has come between us, sister. You *gave* him the West when you decided to run away with him and marry him against all wishes. *You*, only you, denuded me of my heritage."

Leagh dropped her eyes, burying her fingers in the glossy coat of the horse in an effort to find strength. "I apologize with every beat of my heart for that deception. But Askam . . ." She raised her eyes, and now they were bright with tears. "Askam, it was what our *people* wanted, too. Can't you understand that? Carlon rang with joy when Zared rode in—"

"He must have paid them to—"

"Oh, damn you to everlasting torment in the Bogle Marshes, Askam! No one can *pay* for unfeigned joy! It is freely given, not purchased! I struggled for weeks myself, not knowing what to do, thinking that I had betrayed you for love of Zared—"

"You had!"

"—but what he did was not through blind ambition, Askam, but for the people of the Acharite—"

"*You* are blind, Leagh, to so argue. Gods! The man took you because through you he could gain control of the West. Of Achar. And now? Now he has virtual control of *Tencendor* while Caelum meditates in Star Finger!"

Askam was shouting now, his hazel eyes furious, his cheeks flushed. "No! What am I saying? That eternal traitor Drago has control of Tencendor. Leagh, *I cannot believe what I witnessed there!* Everyone from erstwhile Enchanters to the be-twigged Isfrael himself rolled over to let him scratch their bellies. What are they going to do next? Learn to crouch before him and beg for morsels from his plate? What about *Caelum* for the gods' sakes? *He* is the one to whom they owe their ultimate loyalty."

Leagh tried one last time. "If there is one thing I have learned over the past months, Askam, it is that people will willingly tear out their hearts for a man who will *do* rather than *expect*."

"I expected loyalty," Askam said flatly, "and I received nothing but treachery. Even from my sister, who I should have been able to trust more than anyone else. But you? You prostituted yourself for a crown."

Leagh flinched. She tried to think of something to say, then finally turned her back and walked away.

Askam watched her disappear among the trees, then stood by his horse thinking for a long time. Eventually he retraced his steps until he found Jaspar, and the sergeant-at-arms now standing with him.

"My friends," he said, "I need to have a word with you. It seems we find ourselves among a nest of traitors. If you care for your wife and children, waiting, vulnerable in Carlon, then you will listen well to what I have to say."

Drago and Faraday did not linger. They told Zared they needed to move north as soon as they could.

"Deal with whatever you find as best you can, Zared," Drago said.

"And this Sanctuary?"

"I will send word as soon as I can."

"Do not delay it, Drago."

"Be prepared, Zared."

Zared sighed. "Do you need supplies?"

Drago nodded. "I would appreciate it. Who knows what we will be able to scavenge from the plains?"

"Why not stay within the forest for a while?"

"We need to move fast, Zared."

As do you. The words hung between them, and Zared stared at Drago a moment before moving off.

Drago smoothed his hair with both hands, wishing he had the time and opportunity to bathe and shave. Gods! How many days since he'd been able to shave? He ran a hand over the stubble on his chin, and grimaced. Enchanted forests were all very well, but Drago truly thought he would gladly bargain one of Faraday's donkeys for an hour in a marbled and steamy bathroom.

As if in direct response to his thought, there was an indignant bray to one side, and Drago turned to look.

Faraday had gone to harness the donkeys to the blue cart—but with obvious lack of success.

Leather harness lay strewn about the clearing, and the cart itself had somehow lost a wheel and was leaning drunkenly to one side. As Drago watched, it creaked, trembled, and then fell apart completely.

Faraday jumped back, tripped over one of the harness collars lying on the ground, and fell over.

Drago walked over and helped her to her feet. "What's going on?"

"I . . . I don't know!" Faraday raised both hands, then let them fall helplessly to her sides again.

The donkeys had retreated several paces, and were now staring at both Drago and Faraday with patent stubbornness.

For his part, Drago studied Faraday. Over the past two weeks since he'd returned through the Star Gate, he'd never seen her anything but calm and sure of herself. Now her cheeks were flushed, her hair in disarray, and her eyes bright—with tears, Drago realized with a start.

"Faraday?" She jumped as a soft hand fell on her shoulder. Zenith.

As Drago had done, Zenith stared about her, unable to believe what she was seeing. The donkeys adored Faraday. They had comforted her during the time Faraday had planted out Minstrelsea, and Zenith herself had seen their devotion to the woman on their trip from Ysbadd to the Ancient Barrows.

Zenith looked at Drago, registering his own shock.

"The cart just fell apart," Faraday said. "It just fell apart!"

"Shush," Drago said, and took one of her hands between his. "Both cart and donkeys doubtless have their reasons."

Faraday made a helpless gesture with her other hand, and a tear ran down her cheek.

Drago looked impotently at Zenith.

"And the donkeys *kicked* at me," Faraday whispered.

Zenith glanced at her brother, then wrapped an arm about Faraday. "Hush, Faraday. Drago is right. They have their reasons."

"But to *kick!*"

Drago dropped Faraday's hand, not knowing what to do. He watched Zenith rock the woman to and fro, crooning to her, and then heard a step behind him and turned, grateful for the interruption.

Zared, his face puzzled, an eyebrow raised. "Do you want horses, Drago?"

Drago started to nod, then stopped himself. "No," he said, and wondered why he said that. Why refuse horses? "We will walk. It is what the donkeys want us to do."

The donkeys relaxed, their ears flopping, and each shifted their weight onto one of their hind legs, resting the other.

The feathered lizard suddenly appeared, investigating the wreckage of the cart. It rippled sinuously between the spokes of one of the wheels, and then disappeared under the tray.

"We will walk," Drago repeated softly, watching the donkeys.

Faraday walked slowly into the grove. It hardly deserved the name, for it was only some three paces across the four or five deep, but it was beautiful nonetheless, with heavy-scented scarlet brambry bushes and clumps of spiked blue and pink rheannies filling the spaces between the trees.

Isfrael was standing in the shadows at the far end of the grove.

"It has been so long," Faraday said softly. She felt like weeping. Seeing him standing here within the forest made her remember vividly the betrayal in which he'd been conceived—those glorious eight days with Axis when she'd thought to become his wife, while he'd thought of his mistress, Azhure—and the pain and misery of crawling on her hands and knees across half of Tencendor, her belly heavy with her baby, replanting the forests.

The agony of his birth in the Sacred Groves. The far deeper agony of saying good-bye to the infant to fulfill her destiny in dying for the Prophecy.

Azhure and Axis had raised him. Not Faraday.

Faraday had been left to wander the forest paths as a doe, hating her confinement there, and knowing that she slipped from everyone's minds, including her son's. It was difficult to reconcile the knowledge that she'd been relegated to legend, with the need to live . . . *live!* . . . and hold her son for just one day in her arms.

Spending brief hours with him in Niah's Grove when Isfrael had been a child had not been enough, for either of them.

"Mother," he said, and took a step forward into a shaft of sunlight.

She drew her breath in. In his own strange way he did remind her of Axis, although his wildness was all Avar. His hair was the same faded blond, the musculature of his chest and arms . . . his hands. He had Axis' hands.

Faraday stared at them, remembering how Axis had touched her, and betrayed her with that touch.

"Why did you leave the forests to walk with Drago?" Isfrael asked.

Faraday walked forward a few steps until she was within a pace of her son. "You know why."

He nodded. "WingRidge told me who he was. But why did you leave the forests?"

Faraday thought about telling Isfrael of how the Scepter had pulled her to Drago, and thence to the Ancient Barrows. She thought of telling Isfrael how Drago had saved her with the Rainbow Scepter, when Axis had refused to use it to save her from Gorgrael. She thought of telling him about Noah, and her promises to him.

But none of this did she say.

"Because I think I can help," she said eventually, speaking such a colorless truth it was almost a lie. She dropped her eyes to her hands clasped in front of her.

"So you would walk with Drago," Isfrael said, folding his arms across his chest, "but you would not walk to my cradle when I was an infant and croon me to sleep?"

"Isfrael, I have hardly had a choice in what—"

"I wish," Isfrael said, and his voice was wistful, almost tender, through its bitterness, "I wish that just once during my childhood you had been there to rock me to sleep. I wish you had cared that much."

"I have *loved* you with all my being—"

"No. No, you cared more for those donkeys than you have for me. No wonder Axis preferred Azhure's love to yours."

He paused, and his lip curled slightly. "You have no place in my life, Faraday. As you deserted me as an infant, as you deserted Shra to her death, so now I abandon you."

And he turned and walked into the trees.

Faraday stood and stared at the spot where he had disappeared, absolutely stricken.

It was not my fault, she wanted to cry, but . . . but was it her fault? *Could* she have aided Shra? No, no, there was nothing she could have done.

But the other accusation hurt more, because Faraday felt so guilty about it.

Should she have stayed within the Sacred Grove with her son and let Azhure die in her place? If she had, things would not be much different now, would they? Gorgrael would be here to face the TimeKeepers and Qeteb instead of Axis, and Gorgrael would be as powerless as Axis was.

But the most important factor, Drago, *would* still be here, because Drago had allied himself with Gorgrael and would have survived the Destroyer's push into Tencendor.

"What *did* I accomplish by serving out the Prophecy's wishes," Faraday whispered into the empty shaft of sunlight. "Not much at all, really, save for the abandonment of my son. No wonder he curses me."

She stood for a while longer, the tears coursing freely down her face, and then she walked back the way she had come.

Drago was waiting for her, two packs leaning against his legs.

"Did you say good-bye?" he asked.

Faraday bent down and picked up one of the packs, slipping her arms through the straps and settling it on her back.

"I said good-bye to him forty years ago," she said, "and that was the only good-bye he cares to remember."

Drago studied her face, almost reaching out to her, then he thought better of it and shouldered his own pack. He picked up his staff, made sure his sack was securely attached to his belt, and whistled for the lizard.

It scrambled out of Askam's sleeping roll where it had chewed several large holes for the sake of self-amusement, and ran toward them.

"North," Drago said.

18

Shade

After Drago and Faraday had left, Zared went in search of Isfrael. The Mage-King had melded with the shadows when the meeting had broken up, but now Zared needed to know how the man could possibly help him acquire enough shade to move an army westward.

"Shade!" Zared muttered, striding down one of the forest paths. "*Shade!* What next? Must I carry my own river with me in case we meet up with a band of renegade Skraelings?"

His mouth quirked at the thought. One of Axis' main foes during his battle with Gorgrael had been the Destroyer's army of Skraeling wraiths. They had been fearless of everything but water, and Zared was sure that Axis had managed to clog most of the rivers of Tencendor with the Skraelings' misty bodies at some point or the other.

"Zared."

Zared turned. Herme was jogging down the path after him.

"Gods," the older man panted. "I am glad finally to have caught up with you. Where are you going? I need something to occupy me. This inaction is killing me."

"Something to occupy you, Earl Herme?"

Zared whipped about. Isfrael—in his irritating, fey way—had appeared on the path before him. Behind him were six or seven Avar women.

"You need shade, Zared?" Isfrael waved at the women behind him. "I bring it."

Numerous possibilities and images jumbled through Zared's mind at the thought of just how these women might provide shade . . . and none of them were repeatable.

"Ah . . ." he said.

Isfrael grinned, stunning Zared even more. He'd never previously seen the Mage-King *grin,* but even now, there was something slightly malevolent about the expression.

"We need some twenty to thirty of your men," one of the women said, and Zared's mind was now so choked with unspeakable thoughts he could only stare at her. She was young and comely, with a clear creamy complexion and dark, wavy hair cascading down her back. She was dressed in a smoky-pink hip-length tunic with a pattern of clam shells embroidered about its hem, and brown leggings and boots.

"Layon," Isfrael said, "of the ClamBeach Clan."

Layon? Zared opened his mouth to say something, *anything,* and then was startled by Leagh's voice speaking behind him.

"ClamBeach Clan?" she said, and walked to stand close by Zared's side. "Do you live along the Widowmaker coast?"

Facing both Zared and Leagh, Layon inclined the upper half of her body and placed the heels of her hands on her forehead. "Yes, Queen Leagh."

"Then you have traveled far to help us," Leagh said, and smiled, stepping forward to take Layon's hands. "Will you introduce me to your companions?"

Zared stepped back and managed to reorder his thoughts as Layon introduced Leagh to the other women. He turned to Isfrael, and was silenced by the look of cynical amusement on the Mage-King's face.

"No doubt," Isfrael said, "you wonder *exactly* what these Clan wives need with your men?"

Zared nodded, and then turned slightly to speak with Herme. "Um, Herme, perhaps you can fetch thirty men to aid these women."

"Make sure they are strong, Earl," Isfrael said as the Earl turned to go. "Their constitutions will be sorely tested by—"

"Oh for the gods' sakes, Isfrael," Zared snapped. "What *are* you going to do with them? I need shade, not innuendo."

"'Twas not me who first thought the innuendo," Isfrael said softly, and then spoke normally. "The forest is replete in materials that can be woven to form mats. These women can show your men how."

Zared stared at him, then smiled himself. "Now I *have* heard of everything, Isfrael. Do you think to give my army weaving classes?"

It was exactly what Isfrael proposed. For the rest of that day, and all through the next, teams of men hunted through the forest for what the Avar women called the goat tree. It was a variety of beech, but with a peculiar stringy bark that the tree continuously shed. Once a tree had been located, men spent an hour or two pulling as much of the fine, fibrous bark from the tree as they could, sweating and grunting as they climbed into the heights to reach the finest bark.

"As long as the men do not pull the under-bark free from the trunk of the tree, it will not be harmed," Layon explained to a curious Leagh who trailed after the woman from work site to work site.

"What do you normally use the bark for?" she asked.

Layon paused to give a soldier carrying a massive bundle of the bark across his shoulders directions back to the main camp, and then turned back to Leagh. "It is useful for weaving into a rough fiber. We use it, as you shall, to provide summer shelters, although it does not provide much protection against the rain. Once sufficiently prepared and cured, it dries out to become very easy to work and then to carry as a woven cloth."

"Do we have that long?"

Layon shook her head. "Not unless you want to waste two weeks or more waiting for the fiber to dry out completely. It is workable now, and will dry out further on your trek west. Each man will be able to carry enough on his horse to provide them both with shade, and yet not have it prove too heavy a burden."

They walked in silence for a while as they moved back toward the campsite. Leagh, as so many "Plains-Dwellers" before her, was overawed by the forest, especially by the sense of light and space and music within it.

"I do not envy you your trek," Layon eventually said softly. She did not look at Leagh.

"I fear it," Leagh admitted, equally as softly. "Not only the march west, but what we will find on the plains, and in Carlon itself. I, as Zared and every man with us who has a family and loved ones left behind, worry each moment we are awake about their fate. And at night our dreams . . .''

Layon looked about her, lifting her eyes to study the forest canopy so far overhead.

"The forest remains a haven," she said. "But for how long? The Demons grow stronger each day . . . and even when relatively weak they still managed the murder of Shra."

Leagh's eyes filled with tears at the grief in Layon's voice. "We will prevail—"

Layon turned to her, anger in her face and voice. "We will *what?* Prevail? And at what expense? This Drago tells us that we must watch Tencendor be turned into a complete wasteland. What does that mean? The destruction of the forest?" Layon waved a hand about her. "That this should *burn?* I cannot believe that!"

"We must all endure—" Leagh began.

But Layon now let the Avar's well-tended harvest of bitterness swell to the surface and would not let Leagh finish. "You Acharites know nothing of endurance," she said. "Nothing."

After that there was not much to be said. They walked in silence back to the camp, and then separated, Layon to one of the groups of Acharite men under the instruction of an Avar weaver, Leagh back to her husband.

Zared was standing in their personal camp, a bridle hanging from his hands. His face was set in a frown as his fingers struggled with a particularly stiff buckle, and he cursed and dropped the bridle as his fingers slipped one more time.

"You are too impatient," Leagh said, and bent to retrieve the bridle. "Look, work it gently, so, and . . . lo! The strap slips through easily."

Zared grinned wryly, and then noticed Leagh's face. "What's wrong?"

She hesitated, then threw the bridle down on top of a pile of tack and stepped into the protective circle of his arms. "I am afraid."

"So am I," he said. "Leagh?"

"Yes?"

"I want you to stay within the forest. Who knows what we will encounter—"

"No."

"Leagh—"

"*No!*" She raised her face to his. "Twice no, Zared. First a no because I refuse to let my husband ride off without me—and you know what will happen if you do that."

Zared grimaced, remembering how he'd left Leagh in charge of Carlon, only to have her ride off to Caelum's camp.

"And a no because, as *you* taught me, I have a duty to my people. I am not only Leagh. I am Queen Leagh, and I, as you, have a people to put before my personal desires and wants."

Zared grinned down into her face, unable to be cross with her. "I shall remind you of that next time you start to whisper your personal desires and wants into my ear late at night."

She returned his smile, then leaned in close against him, resting her cheek against his chest.

"But, for my sake," he whispered into her hair, "keep safe. Keep safe."

"And you," she said. "And you."

They stood and held each other, both silent.

Once the fibrous bark of the goat tree had been stripped, separated and then combed—a process that took the best part of a week—then every man was given the task of weaving his own shelter.

Some took to the work better than others. Many among the army were sons of craftsmen, or were craftsmen themselves, and they quickly sat down to the job, whistling as the fine fibers spun through their fingers.

Others needed persuasion . . . and much instruction. The Avar women, now numbering almost fifty, moved among the army, bending over shoulders, laughing and scolding, and correcting fumbling fingers. Zared, Herme and Theod sat in a circle, with Leagh hovering on the outer ring, amused that the highest nobility of Achar could use man-welded weapons to destroy with ease, and yet could not use the fingers they'd been born with to create.

"I wish I had a court painter with me now!" she said, among her laughter, "so he could record this scene for posterity."

All three men looked up from the knotted and uneven weave in their laps and scowled at her, but their eyes danced with merriment also.

"One day," Zared said, "I am going to see how well you wield a sword."

"Oh, my dear," she said, and winked at him. "Not half as well as you do, I am sure."

"Wait," he murmured so that none about him could hear. "Wait."

19

The SunSoar Curse

During the midafternoon of their third day out of the Silent Woman Woods, Zenith and StarDrifter stopped to exchange news for malfari bread and honeyed malayam fruit with a band of Avar, then flew until the dusk penetrated the forest canopy and flight was no longer enjoyable, let alone safe.

"How far do you think we have come?" Zenith asked StarDrifter as they cleared a space beneath a whalebone tree and sat down.

He glanced about him, wincing as a twig stabbed into his back, and readjusting his position slightly to accommodate it. Then he pointed to a shrub huddling close to the small stream that ran eastward.

"See that kianet shrub? They only grow near the Bogle Marsh. So we have not done badly for three days' journey."

Zenith nodded, and handed StarDrifter his share of the honeyed malayam on a thick slice of malfari. A fair distance indeed, but if they'd been able to fly direct to the Minaret Peaks they would only have another day's travel, if that.

Forced to keep to the sheltering forests, they were swinging in a great arc to the east. Tomorrow, perhaps, they could swing back west.

"I have a hankering to spend tomorrow night in Arcen," StarDrifter said as he broke away some of the fruit and ate it.

Zenith glanced at him sharply. "Why? We can overfly it and continue straight on. There's no point—"

"Zenith, what difference will a half day make?" StarDrifter said around his mouthful. "That's all we'd lose, and I confess myself tired of these beds of pine needles and sharp-elbowed twigs."

Zenith grinned and tore herself off a slice of malfari. Aha! StarDrifter was missing his comforts! It seemed an age since they'd been on the Island of Mist and Memory. StarDrifter had gone with Axis to the Ancient Barrows to try and strengthen the Star Gate—a useless exercise, as it turned out—and Zenith had traveled north with Faraday in the blue cart drawn by the donkeys.

"It has been a rare long time since I've had you to myself," StarDrifter said, and Zenith smiled softly again, and replied without looking at him.

"Have you recovered your Enchanter powers then, StarDrifter, to read my mind so?"

StarDrifter did not reply immediately. He stared down at his fruit and bread, turning a crust over and over in one hand.

"And I find," he said, very hesitatingly, but encouraged by her response, "that I do so very much enjoy this time spent alone with you."

He looked up. Now Zenith was staring at the food in her hands. Again StarDrifter hesitated, but he was not a man for leaving unsaid that which needed to be shared.

"I also find," he finally said, "that I resent every moment that I must share you with someone else. Dear gods, Zenith, I adore Faraday, but she trailed so happily—and so damnably consistently!—about after us on the Isle of Mist and Memory that I could have thrown her over the cliff face!"

StarDrifter stopped, wondering if he had said too much. But, curse it, it needed to be said! And so, having come this far, StarDrifter leaped over the cliff himself.

"It is the SunSoar curse that our blood calls out so boldly

for each other," he said. "But I find it no burden, and no curse, to love you as I do."

There, it was said.

"StarDrifter—"

"Let me say one more thing," he said, in gentler tones. "I know WolfStar hurt you, and that the introduction to love you suffered at his hands has likely scarred you for life. But—"

"Now is not the time to be talking of this," Zenith said. Her voice was very brittle.

StarDrifter raised an eyebrow. "Now, in this gentle companionship under the trees, is not the time to be speaking of 'this?' "

She looked at him steadily. "The TimeKeeper Demons are tearing this land apart. Surely there are more important things we should be—"

"Don't evade me, Zenith."

Zenith's eyes filled with sudden tears, and she jerked her gaze away from StarDrifter's face.

"Zenith . . ." StarDrifter reached over, took the now damp and useless food from Zenith's hands, put it to one side, and clasped her hands very gently in his own. "Please, talk to me."

She took a deep breath. StarDrifter had been courageous enough to speak of the bond that both knew had been developing between them, and she knew she should be as well. "RiverStar . . . RiverStar always chided me for not taking a lover. She said it was not the SunSoar way."

StarDrifter grinned mischievously, his eyes twinkling with undemanding humor. "She was right."

Zenith allowed herself to be reassured by his grin, and half-smiled herself. "I always told her I wanted to wait for the right man, she always said it was Mother's Acharite primness showing through."

Maybe RiverStar was right, StarDrifter thought. And maybe it was just that Azhure, like Zenith, had preferred to wait until she found the man she loved.

"I wish," Zenith's smile faded, "I wish that I *had* succumbed to the blandishments of some Icarii Strike Leader, or Enchanter, during those wild Beltide nights that I spent watching from beneath the safety of the trees. I wish that I *had,* because then I would not have been left with WolfStar as my only memory of love!"

"Shush," StarDrifter said, disturbed by the emotion in Zenith's voice.

Zenith took another deep breath, calming herself. "But . . . but I waited, because I felt that somewhere was the one man that I could love more than any other."

StarDrifter's heart was racing. Why would she have said that, unless . . . unless . . . "And have you found him yet?"

Zenith stared at StarDrifter, wishing he had not forced this conversation, and yet relieved beyond words that he had. Had she found the man she could love beyond any other? Yes, she had, and she'd known it for a very, very long time. Why else had she been so frantic to know if he'd survived the Demons' push through the Star Gate?

"Yes," she whispered.

Strange, StarDrifter thought, strange that I do not feel overwhelming triumph at this moment. Ever before when a woman has looked into my eyes and whispered "yes," all I have felt was triumph. Now? Relief. Sheer relief.

He leaned forward to kiss her.

Zenith jerked her head away, her eyes round and fearful, and StarDrifter pulled back as if he'd been burned.

"Why let WolfStar ruin your life? Love does *not* have to be what he showed you. Zenith, do you *want* WolfStar to color your perception of love for the rest of your life?"

"No," she whispered, and StarDrifter nodded slightly.

"Good." He leaned forward, very, very slowly, giving her every chance to move away if she wanted, and then, having hesitated as long as he was capable, he kissed her.

Zenith tensed as his lips touched hers, but he was so gentle, and so tender, that she forced herself to relax and to accept his kiss. Feeling her muscles lose their rigidity, StarDrifter drew back slightly, his eyes searching Zenith's face, then he drew her close and kissed her again, this time with more passion, and more insistence.

The kiss of a lover.

Zenith's initial reaction was absolute immobility. She'd admitted that she loved him, but Zenith still found this sudden metamorphosis of grandfather into lover a profoundly unsettling experience. She was shocked by the warmth and taste of his mouth, a potent mixture of sweetness and maleness, and she was shocked by his insistence.

It reminded her far too much of—

"No!" she said, and pushed him away.

StarDrifter stared at her, remembering himself. Remembering the feel of Azhure in his arms, and the delight of her mouth, when he'd kissed her in the training chamber of Star Finger so many years ago.

She'd pushed him away, too, and he'd acquiesced.

And lost her to Axis.

What would have happened then if he'd insisted?

StarDrifter's face closed over and he turned away from Zenith. Rape. That's what would have happened. And whatever else StarDrifter was, and might be capable of, he could not now insist with Zenith. He could not be a WolfStar.

"I'm sorry!" Zenith was crying, feeling the burden of guilt and uselessness. What kind of woman was she? She owed StarDrifter more than this. "I'm sorry! It was just that . . . just that . . ."

"Hush," StarDrifter said, and gathered her into his arms as he would have gathered a child. "Hush. We have time, and I think we have love between us, and I think that we will eventually manage."

Zenith clung to him, grateful that the lover had transformed (for the moment) back into the protective grandfather. Did she love him? Yes, she did, but nevertheless . . .

"Just give me time," she whispered, leaning her head against his chest and letting herself be comforted by the beating of his heart. "I just need time."

Above her head StarDrifter's mouth twisted wryly. He was heartily sick of being the understanding grandfather.

20

Sicarius

Axis sat his horse—a fine roan stallion—and wished he had wings with which to fly. Perhaps he should have taken up StarDrifter's long ago offer to coax his latent wing buds into growth. Too late now.

He tried not to think of the enchantments he had once commanded that could have seen him travel the breadth of Tencendor in an instant.

Over the past week they had pushed both horses and men hard, northward through the Minstrelsea forest, skirting Arcen, and then straight through the tree-sheltered passes of the Minaret Peaks in the dead of night. Both Axis and Azhure would have liked to stop to talk with FreeFall, but time was more important for the moment, and they could always send him a message from Star Finger if they needed.

Besides, no doubt FreeFall had his own problems in this Demonic-controlled world.

Now they rode through the northern Minstrelsea a few hours distant of the southern extremities of the Fortress Ranges. Good time. Excellent time. But . . .

"We're moving too slow," Axis said, turning to look at Azhure and Caelum sitting their horses to his left. Behind them were the twenty men of the accompanying unit, while the Alaunt ranged to the sides and the front, snuffling among trees.

Axis shifted impatiently, his face clearly showing his frustration. "Damn it! These Demons grow in strength from one day to the next—I can *feel* the horror seep from the plains in among these trees!—and yet we *still* march northward . . . and we're barely halfway!"

Azhure shared a look with Caelum. They were all worried. It would take them weeks to get to Star Finger, and Adamon would be growing anxious.

"Could we cut time by traveling through the Wild Dog Plains?" Caelum said.

"A day or two at the most," Azhure answered, "but a day or two is not worth risking being caught in the open by the Demons."

"We could ride hard for the Urqhart Hills—there is shelter there—and then cut directly north into the Icescarp Alps."

Axis shook his head. "There is no way we could do any of those legs in the open in the five or six hours that we'd have free during the afternoon."

He sighed, and looked behind him at the silent escort, as if one of them might have an inspiration.

They were impassive, waiting orders, and Axis shook his head imperceptibly and looked back at Azhure. Her face was expressionless, and her eyes dead ahead—but they were unfocused.

Axis frowned. "Azhure?"

She hardly heard him. She was thinking. Remembering. Remembering a time many years ago when she had just been Azhure, daughter of Hagen the Plow-Keeper. She'd fled her home to first live with the Avar, and then the Icarii. She'd come down to the Earth Tree Grove to celebrate Beltide with the Icarii and Avar, and had been seduced by Axis. Thinking to remove herself from his life—what could she contribute save his ruination?—Azhure had then traveled south into Sigholt with Rivkah and the two Sentinels, Ogden and Veremund.

Through the Avarinheim, through the Fortress Ranges, and then down the WildDog Plains until Arne and his escort had found them and delivered them to Sigholt.

Through the Fortress Ranges. But not over . . . *under.*

Ogden and Veremund had led her and Rivkah into a tunnel that had wound beneath the Fortress Ranges. It had cut many days from their travel.

That particular tunnel would not be much use to them, but . . . but Veremund had said . . . "This tunnel exists . . . and others like it in various parts of Tencendor," she murmured.

"Azhure?"

She blinked, and looked at Axis.

"Azhure?" Axis' voice was impatient.

"I think I know a way," she said, and explained what she'd remembered.

Axis sat on his drowsing horse and thought about it. Azhure had told him about this tunnel many years ago, but neither she nor he had had an opportunity to think about it, much less explore for others since.

He locked eyes with Caelum. His son was clearly excited, looking between him and Azhure.

Axis looked back at Azhure. "Do you think there is a chance?"

She was almost as excited as Caelum. Her dark blue eyes shone, and she tossed her head, shaking out her black hair. "We can but try."

"How?" Axis said. "Where *are* these tunnels?"

Azhure chewed her lip. "The Alaunt," she finally said.

Silence. All three shifted their eyes to the pale shapes still nosing about the trees. Since they'd left the camp in the Silent Woman Woods, the Alaunt had caused no trouble, but none could forget Sicarius' astounding attack on Axis.

"Do it," Axis said. He waved back to the captain of the escort. "We camp here for the time being."

Azhure dismounted slowly, and whistled Sicarius to her.

He came instantly, loping along in easy strides, his golden eyes steady on her.

Azhure had to repress a shudder. There was something unknowably different about him. She didn't know if it was just a result of the sudden cessation of her powers—even when she'd thought herself just Azhure, daughter of Hagen, she'd been able to subconsciously access them—or whether it was because the hounds themselves had changed in some subtle way.

Whatever, she had a problem, because Azhure had always used her powers to communicate with the hounds.

How could she do so now?

The hound sat before her, and Azhure slowly dropped to her knees. She lifted both hands, taking Sicarius' head gently between them.

"Sicarius," she said, and stopped, a little unnerved by his dark gold eyes. Traces of silver flecked in their depths, and

Azhure could no longer read them, and could no longer understand his mind, nor his heart.

She heard Axis step up behind her, and out of the corner of her eye saw Caelum still on his horse, but leaning over the pommel of his saddle and watching intently.

Azhure wet her lips, wondering what words she could use, and tried again.

"Sicarius, I need you to seek."

Something shifted in the hound's eyes.

"An entrance to a tunnel leading north. *Seek!*"

Damn it! Azhure kept her face as impassive as the hound's, but she wanted to curse to the very stars themselves. This was so . . . so *cumbersome!*

Sicarius stared at her, his gaze unwavering.

Azhure fought to keep both her hands and her voice steady. "Seek, Sicarius."

He whined, and shifted. Not anxious . . . Azhure had the distinct impression he was bored and just wanted to get back to his investigation of the forest.

In desperation, Azhure closed her eyes and formed a mental image of Star Finger.

Massif . . . blue . . . mantled with ice . . . reaching for stars.

The hound shifted again.

Behind him, his mate FortHeart walked up and sat down, curious.

Azhure fought to repress her frustration, and tried yet again.

Massif . . . blue . . . mantled with ice . . . reaching for stars. Need to get there. FAST! Seek a way . . . seek . . . seek . . .

Now FortHeart whined, and Sicarius' ears flickered. She had picked up a faint flicker of what Azhure was trying to tell Sicarius, and now in her own peculiar way, and with power that was born of the craft, not of the Stars, FortHeart shared her understanding with Sicarius. He trembled, then yelped and wrenched his head out of Azhure's hands.

Within an instant both he and FortHeart had disappeared among the trees.

As had all the other Alaunt. There was not a pale shape to be seen anywhere, only silence from the spot where they'd disappeared. When the Alaunt hunted, they did so silently and with deadly accuracy.

At least, that's what Azhure hoped they were doing now.

"Mother?" Caelum dismounted and squatted by her side, taking her hand. "You look exhausted. Are you all right?"

Azhure smiled for him. "Yes." She glanced at Axis. "That was . . . hard."

"Do you think they understood?" Axis asked.

She shrugged, then laughed with genuine humor. "Who knows? Either they will seek out what we need or they will return with a rabbit for our dinner."

Axis grinned as well, and helped Azhure to her feet. "Well, at least they'll prove themselves useful one way or the other."

"Axis," Azhure said, as she dusted her tunic and leggings down, "where did the power of the Alaunt derive from?"

"From the Stars, surely," Axis said.

"I think not," Azhure said, even more slowly now. "I think not. They ran with Jack for thousands of years. Before that . . ."

"Before that they came from WolfStar, didn't they?" Caelum said.

"Yes," Azhure said. "But where did *he* find them?" She looked Caelum in the eye. "What if they are the creation of the Maze Gate as much as the Prophecy was? And if so . . . *do they retain their power?*"

"Stars!" Caelum breathed. "Do you mean they might have the same power as the Scepter?"

"Who knows," she said, and then took Axis and Caelum by the hand. "But if they *do* . . ."

"If they do," Axis said, "then we have a chance. A good chance."

"And one that Drago does not control," Caelum said, and grinned.

"But can we trust the Alaunt?" Axis murmured, and turned to stare southward.

The Alaunt ran.

At least for a while.

Sicarius commanded them to a halt by the banks of a small stream, and the other fourteen hounds obeyed instantly, sitting down in a perfect circle about their leader.

The forest waited.

Sicarius moved about the circle, seeking each of his companions' thoughts, needing a decision.

Do we find her this dark space?

Do we follow her to the blue massif?

Do we aid her? Do we aid her?

Do we have any choice?

For the moment they were purposeless. They had a while yet to wait before they could leap into the fray. A while yet before the man opened the gate into the garden.

It has been so long in coming.

But yet is nearly here.

We help them, Sicarius thought, *until the hunter is ready and we course again.*

Azhure had once hunted with the Wolven Bow, and had once directed the Alaunt to the hunt, but there was a greater hunt, and a dearer master, and it was only for this hunt and for this master that the Alaunt had been bred. Their puppyhood had been spent fawning at the feet of Noah, not Wolf-Star or Jack.

His companions silently agreed.

Is there time to hunt before we scent out this dark space? FortHeart asked.

Sicarius turned on his haunches and nipped her on her shoulder.

We do not hunt in this forest. Not yet. There is a bloodier prey awaiting us than rabbits and mice and deer.

FortHeart yelped and leaped to one side, but did not retaliate.

They loped off, traveling pathways that had not been explored in years, and some that had never been trodden by mortal feet previously. They sought . . . and they found.

They knew these secret pathways better than any of the Sentinels had ever done. They were of the land, and part of the land.

Far above circled almost thirty black shapes. Their wings were stretched tight in the thermals, the scrawny clawed hands at their tips opening and closing with frustration that they could not yet hunt.

Their bright black eyes, as sharp as the birds they'd been named after, watched the prey scurry far below the forest canopy.

"Hounds?" whispered one, watching their flickering shapes move through the shadows.

"Magician hounds!" whispered another, and the entire small flock of the Hawkchilds wheeled and dipped, agitated almost beyond measure.

Magicians! Had not their masters set them to hunt out the magicians remaining of this world?

"Magicians?" whispered one. "Magicians? They are no magicians that I have ever known."

Its words tumbled fast over its tongue, warped in their speaking.

"Dogs!" cried another.

"Hounds!" cried yet another.

"They run for that man and woman and their son."

"StarSon?"

"StarSon?"

StarSon?

"What name is he called by?"

"Caelum!"

As one they hissed and fluttered. "That is the name!"

And then, in a single, smooth and totally coordinated movement, they all flipped onto their backs and floated in the thermals, their eyes staring blankly upward toward the sun, their minds communing.

The TimeKeepers traveled the central Skarabost Plains. Their black horses strode forth on untiring legs, their paws eating into the grass and killing the distance that still needed to be traveled to the Lake of Life.

Sigholt lay before them.

Sigholt!

StarLaughter sat her horse with ease. She had never been happier in her . . . well, in *any* of her lives or existences. She had power again, and she reveled in its soothing caress. In her arms she rocked the toddler boy, rejoicing in his warmth. Next—breath. StarLaughter could hardly wait to hear him draw breath for the first time, and she longed to be woken in the midnight hours by his squalling.

And then to feel him squirming in her arms.

But he would be too large then, wouldn't he? By the time they got to Fernbrake Lake and he gained movement, DragonStar would be a youth.

"My baby!" she whispered, and smiled. By that time she would no longer be able to hold him to her breast, but by then, the loss would be no loss at all.

She kicked her horse into greater efforts, and fixed her eyes on the Demons ahead.

About StarLaughter fluttered her torn, blue robe, rusted into great stiff patches by dried blood, and behind her streamed her dark hair and white wings.

The Queen of Heaven she might be, yet StarLaughter looked more demonic than any of her companions.

"Sssss." Raspu held up his hand, bringing the group to a halt. "Listen."

The Demons crooked their heads slightly to the east, and StarLaughter looked that way, too. She knew what was happening—the flock of twenty-seven Hawkchilds that was scavenging the forests looking for the StarSon were communing with the TimeKeepers— but she could not hear them herself.

"What is it?" she asked. "What do they say? Have they found him?"

"Shush!" Barzula said, his eyes intense, but his voice was not unkind, and StarLaughter tried to stifle her impatience.

Slowly Sheol smiled, and then the other Demons followed suit. Smiled, and then howled with laughter.

"What is it?" StarLaughter cried.

Sheol turned her head to the birdwoman. "They have located the StarSon," she said, "and he walks into a dark trap."

She lifted her face into the sun. "Trap!" she screamed.

21

Why? Why? Why?

Faraday was terribly wounded by the donkeys' rejection. Never previously had they snapped so at her, or kicked. Why, if they had wanted some different path from hers, had they let her know it in such a mean-spirited manner?

She traveled silently, and Drago let her be, walking by her side, only speaking in low tones when they needed to camp and erect their tent, or to warn her of a particularly deep chasm in the desiccated earth that intersected their path.

They'd been appalled by the sight that had greeted them on the northern border of the Silent Woman Woods.

The Demons' influence had laid waste to the land. Vegetation had either disappeared completely, or had bleached out to gray stalks running with red rust. Cracks angled crazily across the dried plains, and balls of vegetation and dust rolled with a horrible languidness toward distant horizons. Sometimes they dropped out of sight into the unknown depths of dark chasms that split the earth.

Small creatures—lizards, grasshoppers, beetles—scurried in and out of the cracks in the earth. Most had terrible suppurating wounds, most behaved . . . oddly.

It had only taken Faraday and Drago a few minutes to understand why the creatures were so wounded: they attacked each other without provocation, mindless, soulless attacks that gained them only a brief mouthful of flesh that they sometimes swallowed, sometimes spat out.

They tried to attack Faraday and Drago as well, but the blue-feathered lizard hissed at them violently, and the creatures eventually kept their distance.

The journey through the Plains of Arcness was hardly enjoyable. This was a cold, bleak desert, scorched of life and laughter, and running with madness.

"And this is only what the Demons can accomplish in two weeks," Faraday murmured, heartbroken by the sight. "What can they do in six months, or with Qeteb at their side?"

She glanced at Drago, but his face was as bleak as the landscape, his thoughts obviously no better, and she was glad he did not answer her.

The feathered lizard ranged ahead of them as they walked north. It scared away what life there was, sniffed out cracks—and poked its talons down particularly interesting ones—and curled up as if to sleep when it got so far ahead it had to wait for its companions to catch up.

Sometimes they could see his blue clump of feathers far ahead, a bright, incongruous splotch of color in a drained landscape.

They walked northward in as direct a line as they could go, heading for the hills of Rhaetia and then the Nordra. Drago hoped they could find a boat to carry them further northward faster than their current rate of travel.

At odd moments of the day Drago felt a sickness sweep through him, a knowledge of where the Demons were and, to some extent, of what they did. The link that had been forged between them was both help and hindrance. Drago knew it was invaluable to know where the Demons were. On the other hand the link was so sickening (and reminiscent of the horrific pain he'd endured during the leaps, a memory of hooks dragged from his heels up through his body), and the knowledge of the speed and joyousness of the Demons' travel so disconcerting, that Drago often wished he could remain unaware of their presence, and their progress.

He was glad they did not yet know of his survival, and wondered what they would make of it when they did find out . . . and what they might do.

Sometimes he looked skyward, expecting any moment to see the great dark sweep of the cloud of Hawkchilds. But the Demons obviously had them occupied elsewhere, and Drago felt some measure of sympathy for whichever poor soul they'd decided to torment.

He pushed Faraday northward as fast as he could, although their progress was slowed by the necessity to shelter within their tent during the Demonic Hours. They became adept at traveling until the last possible moment when they would whip the tent from Drago's pack and erect it almost in the blink of an eye, dropping their packs outside and snatching the lizard to safety as they scrambled inside.

There they would sit, often talking, but just as often snatching some sleep as the gray miasma settled its heavy infection over the land.

Some few days after they had left the Silent Woman Woods, Faraday began to dream.

At first the dreams were formless, just a feeling of dread and helplessness, but after the third one Faraday began to distinguish the lost voice of a child.

A small girl, helpless, vulnerable, lost, desperate.

Mama? Mama? Where are you? Why won't you come? Mama?

The child's lost voice tore into Faraday's sense of frustrated motherhood. She struggled to reach out to the girl, but she was too far away to reach.

Too far away.

North.

Drago became aware of the dreams one night when he woke to feel Faraday tossing beside him. He lay a moment, staring at her face, then laid a hand on her shoulder and shook her gently.

Faraday jerked away, her eyes wide and desperate.

She stared about the tent, as if trying to remember where she was, then she turned to Drago and grabbed his hands. "Did you hear her?"

"Who?"

"The girl, the little girl." Faraday sat up. "I can still hear her! Drago, can't you hear her?"

He shook his head slowly, his eyes concerned. At his back the feathered lizard raised his own head and stared at Faraday.

"Lost," Faraday whispered. "Somewhere north . . ."

Drago stroked her thick hair back from her forehead, worried for her, and wondering if her dream was Demon-inspired. *Had* they scried him out?

As he smoothed her hair back, Faraday's eyes gradually lost some of their wildness, and she calmed down a little.

"It was a dream," Drago said softly. "Nothing else. A dream."

Faraday was not ready to be soothed completely. "Must we go to Gorkenfort first?"

"Where else?"

Faraday suddenly realized she was more aware of Drago's hand stroking her hair than she was concerned about the lost girl, and she jerked her head back, angry that he should have distracted her away from her purpose and frightened by her reaction to him. No. No! No more love. Drago let his hand drop without comment.

"We need to reach her," Faraday said. "She's lost."

"Who?"

"I don't know . . ."

"Perhaps after Gorkenfort—"

"No! We should go now. I don't want to go to Gorkenfort."

"Faraday . . ."

But she turned her face away, and after a moment Drago sighed and settled back into his blanket. "We can go nowhere now, Faraday, and Gorkenfort is north anyway. It was a dream. A dream, nothing more."

But the dreams continued, and they drove their own angling cracks into Drago and Faraday's relationship. As they turned westward toward the Nordra, Drago noticed that Faraday kept glancing true north, and she became quieter and quieter the more they moved northwest.

"Star Finger," she said one morning as they broke camp. "She's in Star Finger."

Drago stood and watched her. She was bustling about the tent, folding it as quickly as she could, lifting an impatient hand to jerk stray tendrils of hair out of her eyes and face.

"Faraday," he said, but she did not look at him, and Drago was forced to walk over and take her by the arm. "Faraday."

She straightened and stared at him. "Do you not hear her?" she whispered. "She tears into my mind every time I close my eyes. Drago, she's so lost . . . so lost!"

Drago looked into her eyes, then drew her against him, trying to give her what comfort he could with his presence. She was stiff and unyielding, and Drago was not sure whether it was because she was impatient to reach the girl, or because she disliked him holding her.

Drago suddenly found himself hoping very much that it was because Faraday wanted to reach the girl.

"We will go to Star Finger after Gorkenfort," he said quietly. "To see Caelum, and to find this girl of yours."

She pulled away from him.

"It may be too late then," she said tonelessly, and stuffed the tent into Drago's pack.

Two nights later, sleeping in their tent pitched in the western foothills of the Rhaetian hills, the girl also reached out to Drago.

She was tiny, frail, helpless. Winds of demonic intent buffeted her, pushing her closer and closer to the razor edge of an infinite cliff, and she wailed and cried, *Help me! Help me! Mama? Mama?*

Even caught as he was in his dream, Drago felt tears slide down his cheek, and he understood Faraday's desperation to reach the girl. Indeed, he could feel Faraday within the dream. She was somewhere in the darkness that surrounded the girl, and Drago could feel her reaching out, reaching out, but never quite reaching the child.

He opened his mouth to call out to the girl that they would reach her soon, very soon, be calm, hold on, we're almost there . . . when suddenly he felt another presence within the dream.

Something dark and loathsome, something heavy and cruel, and something much, much closer to the girl than either he or Faraday.

He turned his attention back to the girl. She was silent now, terrified, her eyes jerking about the darkness, trying to see what it was that approached. She was crouched protectively about something, but Drago could not quite make it out. The child's eyes jerked to her left, focusing on something moving toward her.

Drago looked, and cried out. A gigantic figure loomed out of the blackness, a man several hand spans taller than any man Drago had ever seen before, and encased entirely in black armor.

In his mailed hand he held a gleaming, wicked knife.

A kitchen knife.

The girl hiccupped in terror, and almost choked on a sob that wrenched up from deep within her.

Drago could hear Faraday screaming, but he could not see her, and he could not free himself from the dream, nor could he move to aid her.

The black-armored man stepped to the girl's side—

Run, run, run! Drago screamed at her, but she was so stricken with terror she could not move.

—and seized the girl's glossy brown curls in his left hand, jerking her head back to expose the slim whiteness of her throat.

Then the knife slashed through the air, and all Drago could see and taste and feel was the thick redness of life pouring forth from the girl's throat, and—

He jerked awake, sitting upright and staring about wildly. Beside him Faraday was screaming in her sleep, throwing herself from side to side, her hands reaching up and groping uselessly into the air above her.

Drago heaved in a great breath, orienting himself out of the dream, and turned to Faraday. He lifted a hand, intending to wake her from the nightmare, when her eyes flew open. She stared at Drago, and then, before he could stop her, she leaped to her feet, dived through the tent flap, and ran outside.

Into the terror of the night.

"No!" Drago screamed and, without any thought, ran after her.

He felt the cold fingers of the Demonic terror intrude into his mind as soon as he left the safety of the tent. Faraday was a pale shape struggling on the ground several paces away, the wind whipping her hair about, her hands groping at the ground about her.

She was screaming uncontrollably.

Drago knew that madness was only an instant away, and he knew it had already claimed Faraday, but all he could think of was that he had to reach her, that somehow he needed to be with her before he lost his own mind completely.

The cold fingers dug deeper and more agonizingly into his

mind, and Drago screamed and threw himself on Faraday's struggling body.

In her fright and horror she instinctively hit him, and Drago caught at her hands, rolling himself atop her and pinning her hands down to the ground.

"Faraday!" he yelled above the storm of madness about them. "Faraday, it is only me! Drago! Please, be still, please . . . please . . ."

She ceased to struggle and stared at his face a hand span above hers, and suddenly Drago realized that he stared into the eyes of a woman who was terrified beyond measure . . .

. . . but sane.

"Faraday?" he whispered. "Faraday?"

The cold fingers of terror continued to probe at his mind, but Drago slowly realized that although they probed and probed—and stung horribly in that probing—they could not enter.

His mind was still his.

As was Faraday's.

"Why?" she whispered. "Why are we safe?"

He laughed softly, not caring that the fingers still pushed and prodded at his mind, but reveling in his—and her—strange immunity.

The Demons could not touch them.

"I don't know," he whispered back. "And I do not particularly care why."

At that moment, staring into each other's eyes, both forgot the girl and her terrified cries for help, as they forgot the winds of terror howling about them and the thick tendrils of gray miasma that clung to their clothes and hair.

Very, very slowly Drago lowered his head and kissed Faraday.

She closed her eyes, accepting his kiss, and then from nowhere came the memory of Drago swearing that nothing, *nothing,* was to get in the way of his determination to save the land, and from that memory her mind leaped back forty years to the moment when Axis stood before her in Gorgrael's chamber and lifted not a finger to save her so that he, too, might save Tencendor.

She twisted her head away.

"No!"

Drago did not protest. He lifted himself from her and stood, holding a hand to help her rise.

Reluctantly she accepted his aid.

"Why?" she repeated. "Why aren't we mad?"

Drago stared about him. The night landscape seemed to be in the grips of a fatal insanity.

The air itself was alive, twisting and writhing and roping under the Demon Rox's influence. A small rabbit, caught outside its burrow, was winding and contorting in a dance of madness, chewing at its own paws and dribbling thick saliva down the matted fur of its chest. Somewhere a dog howled and screamed, and then gurgled into quietness.

And yet here he and Faraday stood, their minds aching from the insistent probing of the Demon, and yet safe.

Why?

Why?

Slowly Drago turned his face to the east.

Far away Rox turned and stared across the western Skarabost Plains. There was something wrong. Something . . . different.

He sent his senses reeling out across the land.

There! A man and a woman, standing close together in the night, their minds invulnerable.

The man was staring at him, as if he could somehow see him so far to the east.

Who? Who?

Why? Why? Why?

Slowly Rox turned his eyes back to his east. There the StarSon was, walking into the dark trap, so who was this to the west? Who? Who?

Why?

He sent a message screaming through the night to the Hawkchilds: *It seems we have a stray magician or two to the west. Find them. Find out why they can resist us. And then kill them.*

22

Arrival at the Minaret Peaks

*T*hey arrived in Arcen by late afternoon the next day. The mayor greeted them enthusiastically, begging for news, hope, anything . . .

"I am sorry," StarDrifter said. "We know little, but what we do we would be happy to share. Perhaps over dinner . . . ?"

The mayor apologized, embarrassed at his lack of civility, and bustled StarDrifter and Zenith into his townhouse. His servants laid out a good meal, and the mayor and his wife were pleasant and entertaining conversationalists, but StarDrifter and Zenith spent the time far more aware of each other than of the mayor.

"You must be tired!" the mayor eventually declared, as his guests lapsed once more into silence. He clapped his hands. "Let my servants show you to your rooms."

They had separate but adjoining rooms, and Zenith was not surprised to hear the gentle knock at her door after an hour.

"Come in," she called softly.

"I missed you," StarDrifter said as he closed the door behind him. "Even the feather bed is not enough compensation for the lack of your company."

Zenith smiled awkwardly. This was so strange, so uncomfortable. She felt as if he thought she should just invite him straight into her bed, she knew that was what he wanted, and maybe she *should* do that, but—

"I just came to say good night, Zenith," StarDrifter said, watching the play of emotions over her face.

She nodded, relaxed, then smiled. "Good night, StarDrifter."

Then, suddenly bold, she walked up to him, put her hands on his chest—his skin was so warm!—and kissed his mouth softly. She leaned back slightly, but she did not step back, and she did not take her hands from his chest.

Feeling certain that the time for hesitancy was past, StarDrifter slid his hands into her hair, pulled her close, and kissed her again. She tensed slightly, but did not pull back, and so StarDrifter held her tight against his body, and let both hands and mouth grow bolder.

More than anything else Zenith wanted to be able to accept StarDrifter as a lover—it was why she'd been bold enough to kiss him—but now she fought to keep still as unwelcome images tumbled through her mind. StarDrifter gently chiding her when she was a child, and holding on to her chubby arms as she learned to walk. WolfStar's harsh kisses, the scrape of teeth and rasp of tongue against her neck. StarDrifter rescuing her from the cliff face, and telling her he'd always be there to catch her. WolfStar's repulsive rape, feeling him force himself inside her body—

She pulled back.

"I won't hurt you," StarDrifter said. "I won't."

"I know," she whispered, feeling even more the failure. "I *know* you won't . . . but . . ."

"But?"

"But it just doesn't feel right," she said.

StarDrifter reached out a hand and stroked her cheek. "I can wait," he said, planted an undemanding kiss on her forehead, and walked from the room.

Zenith stared at the door, then turned and looked at the bed.

A tear slowly ran down one cheek.

Two days later, Zenith and StarDrifter arrived at the colonnades and spires of the Icarii city nestled in the forests and ridges of the Minaret Peaks.

What they found shocked them.

To avoid the deadly miasma of the Demons, they'd had to approach via the forest paths rather than drop down from the sky—the infinitely more preferable way for any Icarii to approach the city. They initially assumed that the sense of gloom they experienced as they approached was due to their restricted flight underneath the trees. But the instant they'd alighted before the entrance to the Talon's palace they had to reassess their initial assumption.

"Why is it so dark?" Zenith said, drawing her wings in close against her back and hugging her arms about her.

StarDrifter hesitated before answering.

"I should have expected this," he murmured, and Zenith looked at him.

"Expected what? Why?"

In answer StarDrifter took her by the elbow and led her under the great pink stone archway. A long corridor stretched before them, and Zenith frowned. In previous visits she remembered this corridor as glowing with soft light, and pleasantly warm.

Now rank torches sputtered fitfully down its length, and chill air swept out to envelop them.

The corridor was empty of all life. Where the guards? Where the always hovering servants ready to provide a welcome for unexpected guests?

StarDrifter stood and stared, and felt an inexpressible sadness sweep over him. He knew what was wrong, but because he hadn't thought through the full implications of the Demons' effects on the daily lives of the Icarii, he'd not been prepared for this sight.

"StarDrifter?" Zenith said, and he turned and half-smiled reassuringly at her. She was unsure, and nervous, and StarDrifter's heart went out to her. He ran his hand softly along her arm and gently disengaged one of her hands from her tightly crossed arms and cradled it in his own.

"There has always been so much we took for granted," he said. "So much."

He sighed and looked back down the corridor. "Why no light? No warmth? Because for thousands of years the Icarii have relied on their Enchanters to weave light and warmth from the Star Dance."

"Oh," Zenith said, and then shivered. "This place feels like a tomb."

"It might well become one," StarDrifter said. "Come, let us find a friendly face."

As they walked through the outer corridors and halls, StarDrifter contemplated the potential ruin of Icarii life with sadness and, he was surprised to realize, more than a little cynicism. For too long, perhaps, no Icarii had ever soiled his or her hands with agricultural pursuits, for had they not always had Enchanters who could coax the most delicious of foods into existence with merely a breath of Song? No Icarii had ever chopped wood, nor lugged it about the corridors of Talon Spike or their Minaret Peaks, nor had they spent their mornings choking as they cleaned out their ash-filled hearths; always there had been enchantment to provide them with clean glowing braziers. No Icarii had ever scorched his or her hand on a hot pot, or a wayward candle, or cursed the hours spent peeling vegetables in a cold kitchen. Their lives had been spent in pleasurable pursuits, whether physical sports and games, challenging intellectual conundrums or the ever-appealing pursuit of love.

Now enchantment had disappeared from their lives, and the Icarii were obviously finding it hard to cope with the most simple demands of daily life.

As they walked down the cold corridor, StarDrifter's thoughts drifted from the Icarii's ever-appealing pursuit of love to his own problems with Zenith. He glanced at her walking quiet at his side. Since Arcen, StarDrifter had been careful not to scare Zenith by pushing her on the issue of their relationship. He hadn't realized how badly Zenith had been scarred by WolfStar's rape, but now that he *did* know, StarDrifter was determined to give Zenith the time and space she needed. She loved him, she'd admitted that, and there was no Axis lurking in the wings to steal *this* woman from him, and so, somewhat uncharacteristically, StarDrifter was prepared to bide his time.

His thoughts meandered, wondering what it would be like when Zenith finally did come to his bed . . .

"Watch where you're going!" a hoarse, unknown voice cried.

Zenith gave a sharp cry of surprise and wrenched StarDrifter to one side.

StarDrifter blinked, concentrated on the moment rather than the wishful, and then his eyes widened in surprise.

He and Zenith had rounded a bend in the corridor to meet a group of four Avar and a male and female Icarii, all six now staring angrily at StarDrifter. There was an overturned basket and a dozen pieces of halo fruit scattered over the floor, and

StarDrifter realized the group had been in the midst of an acrimonious argument over the possession of the crop of fruit the Icarii pair had obviously plucked from the Minstrelsea forest.

It was extraordinary, StarDrifter thought, that the Avar had pursued the Icarii inside the city. He opened his mouth to say something, but the Avars' attention had swung back to the fruit and the guilty Icarii.

One of the Avar jabbed his fist angrily in the direction of the Icarii male.

"The forest is *ours* to forage, birdman! What gives you the right to—".

"My starving children give me the right!" the birdman yelled, his bright yellow feathers standing up along the length of his neck and across his shoulders. "The forest is not yours exclusively."

StarDrifter and Zenith shared a shocked look, and StarDrifter decided he ought to do something. He stepped forward and held out his hands placatingly.

"My friends, what is wrong? Surely," he turned slightly to the birdman, "there is no need to expend such anger over a simple basket of halo fruit?"

"That fruit," the birdman said in a voice still vibrating with emotion, "means survival for my wife and children."

He paused and looked at StarDrifter carefully. "You are StarDrifter SunSoar, are you not?"

StarDrifter nodded. "And this is Axis and Azhure's daughter, Zenith SunSoar."

The Icarii birdman's lip curled slightly. "And as always, the SunSoar clan looks remarkably well-fed. Does your family have stocks of food, SunSoar, that might feed *my* family?"

The Avar had stepped back slightly, looking carefully between the two groups of Icarii. Nevertheless, the largest Avar male, probably the Clan leader, had not stepped so far from the fruit that he could not seize it if the opportunity presented itself.

"I am sorry, we have no food ourselves," Zenith said. "Forgive me, I do not know you and your wife's—"

The birdman belatedly found some manners. "My name is

GristleCrest SweptNest," he said, with only the barest inclination of his head. "And this my wife, PalmStar."

GristleCrest very slightly stressed the "Star" of his wife's name, conveying just the faintest touch of disrespect. StarDrifter shivered involuntarily. If Enchanters had lost their powers, had they then lost all value and respect in the eyes of ordinary Icarii?

Zenith nodded at the two Icarii, and then politely inquired after the Avar.

"Jokam, of the StillPond Clan," the man said. "My wife, my brother, and my nephew."

He did not extend Zenith the courtesy of their names.

GristleCrest took a deep breath, his neck and shoulders corded with tension. "StarDrifter, Zenith, do you retain your enchantment?"

For an instant hope flared in PalmStar's eyes, but it faded as StarDrifter and Zenith shook their heads.

"No," StarDrifter said. "We have lost the Star Dance, as have all Enchanters."

"Then you can well imagine life in the Minaret Peaks without enchantment, SunSoar," GristleCrest said. "No light, no heat, no food."

"We have seen the darkness, and felt the chill," Zenith said. "But we had not thought that you might be—"

"Starving," PalmStar said. Her voice was flat. "And worse. Scores of Icarii have died trying to fly through the corridors and shafts we have no torches for. My own sister, an *Enchanter* for the Stars' sakes!, died yesterday evening—she slammed into a rock face when flying to find food for her children."

She turned her face away, unable to look at StarDrifter or Zenith. "Other Icarii lie crippled, their wings broken through accident. Others yet lie unable to move because of the cold, or because they have not eaten enough to find the strength to move."

StarDrifter briefly closed his eyes. All this sadness and misery and death within only weeks of the Demons' arrival. Would there be an Icarii race *left* in a year? In six months?

"Even our gods have deserted us," GristleCrest said, very quietly now, his eyes fixed on StarDrifter. "Where are they,

SunSoar? Where your son? Where Azhure? Where the Star-Son? How long before all the Gods survey is a pile of bones? Even the Acharites could not bring us to our knees so effectively."

"We have news," StarDrifter said, "but should share it first with the Talon—"

"Ah," GristleCrest spat, "and no doubt you SunSoars will decide to save only each other!"

"That is not fair!" Zenith said. "We will do all we can—"

But GristleCrest and PalmStar were gone, snatching a few pieces of fruit as they went.

The Avar silently gathered the rest into the basket, stared equally as silently at StarDrifter and Zenith, and then walked away.

Within heartbeats they were lost to the gloom of the corridor.

A few minutes later StarDrifter and Zenith met the Master Secretary of the palace, StarFever HighCrest, wandering down a side hallway. His well-remembered saffron brightness was undiminished, but his skin was pale and his eyes overbright.

At least he, they were relieved to see, offered them more respect than GristleCrest had.

"StarDrifter! Zenith! Welcome." StarFever bowed deeply, spreading his wings out behind him.

StarDrifter returned StarFever's bow, noting that the Master Secretary of the Palace's face was haggard and lined (the effects of hunger and frustration, *or was his age showing?*).

"We greet you well," he said, Zenith murmuring the same words at his side. "StarFever, things do not seem well here."

To StarDrifter's horror, StarFever's eyes glimmered with tears. "Have you brought hope with you, StarDrifter?"

"As much as I am able," StarDrifter said, his voice soft with pity. "Please, Zenith and I need to see Talon FreeFall."

StarFever nodded, then raised the lamp he held at his side and led them down a hall. StarDrifter thought nothing epitomized the depths the Icarii had sunk to more than that lamp. It spluttered fitfully on a thin diet of animal fats and the oil of the limapeg tree; it smelled frightful and threw an utterly inadequate light about them—several times StarDrifter stumbled across a step he had not realized approached, and Zenith likewise had trouble with her footing.

Who had ever seen an Icarii *stumble* before?

As they progressed deeper within the palace complex, what brightness the lamp did cast revealed an increasing number of gaunt-faced Icarii. All they passed were huddled in their wings (none dared fly the spacious corridors) and some even in fur capes; the fitful lamplight revealed thin fingers of ice running down stone walls. Whatever beauty the inner chambers of the Peaks had once possessed had been lost with the Star Dance, or was hidden in the gloom.

There was no music save careful scuffling movement and the occasional exclamation and thump as someone fell down a step that had surprised their feet, and it was to that accompaniment that StarFever led them into the Talon's audience chamber.

There was more light in this chamber, for the roof soared into one of the massive spires that characterized the Minaret Peaks, and welcome sunlight filtered down from the skylight far above. The chamber, decorated with swirls of gold and silver on its walls and ceiling, was empty of everything save a round table and chairs directly beneath the spire, a glowing brazier to one side (a dusty pile of coal beside it), and FreeFall and his wife EvenSong, standing close together by the heat. They turned as StarFever led StarDrifter and Zenith into the room.

"Uncle! Zenith!" FreeFall strode across the room and enveloped StarDrifter in a huge hug, turning to embrace Zenith as EvenSong wrapped her arms about her father.

Behind them, StarFever quietly exited the Chamber, closing the door as he went.

"I swear," FreeFall said, as he stepped back from Zenith and studied StarDrifter, "that you look better than I do."

StarDrifter tried to smile, but was unable to. Both FreeFall and EvenSong looked careworn and tired beyond measure. As with StarFever, their skin was abnormally pale and their eyes overly bright, and StarDrifter realized the toll that maintaining a constant facade of strength had exacted on his daughter and nephew. He thanked every Star in existence that Rivkah had died before she could see the fate that had enveloped her daughter. At least, he thought, she died thinking that EvenSong would live out a long life in joy and comfort.

"Things have not been good here," he observed.

FreeFall grimaced. "As good as they are on the unprotected plains, no doubt. We might not be subject to this disgusting miasma I am told issues forth during the Demonic Hours, but the loss of enchantment, and all that means to us, has been devastating."

"We have tried our best to cope, Father," EvenSong said. "We have tried so *hard,* but trying to find the food to feed over a hundred thousand Icarii, and the means to warm them and light their way, has been . . . taxing."

Zenith shot her a sympathetic glance. EvenSong was a resourceful and emotionally strong birdwoman. Seeing her face wreathed in so much helplessness bespoke the difficulties of life in this dying complex.

"But at least you two look well," FreeFall said. His voice tightened. "What news? We are as starved for news—and hope—as we are for bread and warmth."

"Zenith and I are weary," StarDrifter said, "for we have come many leagues to see you. May we sit?"

"Oh!" EvenSong cried, distraught at her rudeness. "Please. And we shall find some refreshments for you—"

"Just something to drink, EvenSong," Zenith said. "We do not need food."

"You need it as much as EvenSong or I," FreeFall said dryly, "and as much as the smallest child among us. We can manage a cup of warm ale at the least."

He rang a small chime, then escorted StarDrifter and Zenith to the table.

"So," FreeFall said. "Talk."

And so they talked, their hands gratefully wrapped about the warmth of the ale cups the servant brought them. First Zenith, telling FreeFall of her adventures with Drago, and then her struggle for life with the Niah-soul that battled to claim her.

EvenSong and FreeFall listened silently, their eyes wide, their hands clasped together on the table before them.

Then StarDrifter spoke of Faraday's reappearance—

Both FreeFall's and EvenSong's mouths dropped open at that point. Her return could mean only hope, surely?

—and her help in saving Zenith, and then leading her toward the Star Gate.

"Oh, Stars, FreeFall," StarDrifter said, his voice hoarse with emotion as he remembered the hopelessness and horror of the chamber of the Star Gate. "Axis and Azhure, as well, the other Star Gods, WolfStar and all the Enchanters the Icarii nation could summon—"

"*And* Isfrael and his Banes," Zenith put in.

"—and then with all the strength of the Mother and trees behind us . . . and yet we could do nothing. Nothing."

"And now," FreeFall said, leaning forward and staring at StarDrifter, "what is to be done about the Demons? Am I to be Talon of nothing but a disintegrating people? Are we to watch Tencendor destruct before our eyes?"

StarDrifter exchanged a glance with Zenith—how could he say blandly that, yes, that *is* what Drago wanted them to do?

"There is more we must tell you," Zenith said softly, and she began to speak of Drago, and how he had come back through the Star Gate to help, not hinder. She spoke of her own belief in him, of the man who'd had his own incredible potential strangled in retaliation for his infant crime, and yet who nevertheless had shown her humor and compassion. She spoke of what he'd said when he'd returned from Cauldron Lake, and hoped she'd been as persuasive as Drago had been.

As FreeFall and EvenSong both opened their mouths to speak their objections, Zenith hastened on, speaking of Faraday's similar belief in Drago, and of Drago's peculiar connection with the craft that lay at the foot of the Sacred Lakes.

"Caelum—" FreeFall began, but Zenith did not allow him to continue.

"Caelum is firstborn of Axis and Azhure, and he has been named the StarSon, true, but I believe more in Drago."

Zenith looked steadily at FreeFall and then EvenSong. "Caelum has gone with our parents to Star Finger, and the other Star Gods try and determine a method by which these Demons can be beaten back. I wish them success, but my heart . . ." She lay her hand on her breast, ". . . my heart tells me that Drago will be the one who will return to us and say, 'I have found a way.' "

FreeFall exchanged a dubious look with EvenSong. "I find it hard to transfer my hopes to Drago. *Drago?* Did he not murder his sister, RiverStar? And I have heard it was he who led the Demons toward the—"

"I, as many, believe Drago innocent of RiverStar's murder," StarDrifter said. "And if he aided the Demons, then he was driven to it by a lifetime of wrongful accusations and resentments. Now his life is dedicated to righting whatever part he had in the wrong that has happened. I *believe* him, FreeFall. You have not seen Drago recently, nor spoken to him. He has my trust, as well as Zenith's, and Zared, who has been given control of both ground and air forces of Tencendor, has given his support. And Isfrael listens to him, and accepts what he says."

That did cause FreeFall to raise an eyebrow. "I thought Isfrael listened to nothing but the thoughts roaring about his own head."

"Why," EvenSong said, getting back to the kernel of the matter, "should we trust a man who says we must watch the destruction of Tencendor? That is equal to saying, 'Die, and be glad of it!' Damn you, Father. Your wits must be addled to listen to such nonsense!"

"There is more, EvenSong," StarDrifter said, "and the 'more' encompasses hope."

He told them of Sanctuary, and the shelter that all would find there.

"And while we shelter in Sanctuary, then by whatever means Caelum and Drago and Axis and Azhure and every one of the Star Gods and scholars in Star Finger can devise, the Demons shall be destroyed without the risk of destroying every innocent soul in Tencendor as well."

"Yet the land must be destroyed?" FreeFall said. "I cannot imagine why—"

"Sometimes," Zenith put in, "destruction precedes new life. Think of the joy of spring after the death of winter, and imagine with what zest Tencendor will manage its own regeneration."

"Still . . ." EvenSong said.

"Would you sit here and freeze to death?" StarDrifter said.

"Our people will be eating each other within the month! Already Icarii are dying needlessly. Will you refuse Sanctuary out of stubborn-headedness?"

"I will personally carry every Icarii into Sanctuary myself if it will save a single life," FreeFall said. "So, when do we leave? How far to the Sanctuary?"

"Well . . ." StarDrifter glanced at Zenith. "It has yet to be found—"

"Ha!" EvenSong said. "So you proffer hope, and then snatch it away."

"—but SpikeFeather and WingRidge and the entire Lake Guard are searching for it. Believe, EvenSong. Please."

EvenSong stared into her father's eyes, then shrugged and dropped her own gaze.

"Wait," she said softly. "Very well."

She straightened on her stool and reached for the chime. "I shall have servants prepare you apartments. No doubt you are tired after your long journey north."

Zenith lay awake for long hours that night, staring into the cold blackness of her chamber. There was a candle on the table by her bed, but she preferred not to light it.

Better the darkness, where she could think without distraction. Better the darkness, where no one could read her thoughts.

StarDrifter. Gods! What could she do?

She trusted him, she loved him, and she even found him sexually appealing (was there a woman alive who did not?) but the thought of actually bedding with him made her stomach heave with repulsion. Over the past three days they had kissed several times, and every time they laid mouth on mouth Zenith had thought she was finally learning to conquer that repulsion. But then his hands would become more demanding, his body harder, and Zenith would panic.

Her hands clenched into the bedclothes, and she stared into the oblivion above her. StarDrifter was being so patient, so kind, so tender—so loving and protective, dammit! He was sure, as she'd been sure, that time and patience would cure the damage WolfStar had wrought.

But in these past wakeful hours Zenith had come to realize that her hesitation about being intimate with StarDrifter had nothing at all to do with WolfStar. True, WolfStar had raped and humiliated her, but that in itself formed no barrier to Zenith's sleeping with StarDrifter. StarDrifter was everything WolfStar was not: kind, patient, gentle. Zenith was well aware that StarDrifter's loving would be a very, very different thing to WolfStar's rape.

But that was not the issue. While she and StarDrifter had been talking with FreeFall and EvenSong, Zenith had finally realized just why she felt so uncomfortable about forming an intimate relationship with StarDrifter.

StarDrifter was her grandfather, and her perception of him as her grandfather was the greatest barrier to being able to perceive, and accept, him as a lover. Zenith had realized, as she'd sat about the table with her family this afternoon, that if she and StarDrifter had been lovers, and that if EvenSong and FreeFall had realized it, then she would have been consumed with self-disgust and crippled with humiliation. Sleeping with her *grandfather?*

No matter that FreeFall and EvenSong would not have felt that way, nor even been able to understand it. They were first cousins, and had indulged in sexual love since childhood. Sexual relations between Icarii grandparents and grandchildren were not forbidden, nor even unknown. Gods! EvenSong and FreeFall probably would have welcomed the news that StarDrifter was bedding Zenith! Zenith and StarDrifter could provide the heir to the throne of Talon that EvenSong and FreeFall were unable to.

At that thought, Zenith's stomach literally did heave, and she rolled onto her side and curled up into a tight ball. Pregnant with StarDrifter's child?

No!

Then Zenith was consumed with self-loathing that she should feel so repulsed by the idea of sleeping with StarDrifter, or bearing his child.

There was no one to stop them, and no one to blame them, if they did become lovers. *There was nothing to stop Zenith loving StarDrifter except her own prudery!*

How could she be so ungrateful?

It was StarDrifter who had believed in her enough to beg
Faraday to find her when to all others it seemed as if Niah had
conquered her completely. It was StarDrifter who had stood
guard the long nights when she and Faraday walked through
the shadow-lands, StarDrifter who had no thought of his own
safety when he attacked WolfStar in order to protect her in
those first vulnerable minutes when she reclaimed her body.

StarDrifter. Always StarDrifter had been there for her. And
surely now he deserved some reward? Something back?

She loved him, so why couldn't she give him what he
wanted and had every right to expect?

Because she was ashamed. Disgusted by the idea of taking
a grandfather as a lover.

Zenith put her hands to her face and wept.

23

The Arcness Plains

It took time to get thirty thousand odd men and horses to
move anywhere save in a forced march or a blind panic,
and Zared did not want to do it either way. Ten days after
Layon had first appeared with her companions to show the
men how to weave their shade cloth from the bark of the goat
tree, the army was ready to move.

"North out of the Silent Woman Woods," Zared muttered
as he sat his horse, studying the pathway as it wound its way
through the trees, "and then west, west, west to Carlon, to see
how much of its pink and gold beauty remains."

Leagh sat her fine-boned chestnut mare beside him, glad
beyond measure to be moving, but fearing the journey ahead.
She wished she still had Zenith here for company. She smiled
to herself. How could she lack for company in this twenty-
thousand strong army? *And* the man she loved more than any
other person beside her day and night?

But it would be better, she thought, if she could have the
empathy of a sister-companion.

For an instant her hand touched her belly, but she moved it back to the rein immediately. Best not to think about that. Not now.

Zared turned his horse and studied the ranks of men stretching into the distance behind him. Every horseman had a large roll of the goat tree cloth strapped to the cantle of his saddle. Pack horses further back carried poles gleaned from dead wood and what the trees of the forest had been prepared to give them. There were far fewer poles than men, but each pole could take the corners of four cloths, and there would be enough to set up shelter.

Among his entire command, only the members of the Strike Force were not burdened with any cloth. It was too weighty for them to carry, but there was enough shade for them to shelter with the ground units when they needed to.

What they would have to do, Zared thought, was practice raising poles and cloth as quickly as possible. He decided that for the first few days they would have to stop well before one of the Demons was due to spread his or her horror to give them enough time to erect their safety.

He raised his eyebrows at Theod and, just behind him, his captain of the guard, Gustus. Both men nodded. The Strike Force was already lining the forest path, ready to take to the skies.

Zared swung his horse back to the empty path and raised his hand, about to signal the march . . .

. . . and stopped, his hand suspended midair, amazed.

Standing on the path before him were the two white donkeys, gazing placidly at him, their long white ears flopping every which way over their narrow, bony skulls.

After the donkeys had kicked their way clear of the traces when Faraday had tried to harness them to the cart, they had disappeared into the forest. All presumed they'd wanted to resume their meandering.

The donkeys blinked, snorted, then turned and trotted up the path. One paused just long enough to send an inquiring glance Zared's way.

He shrugged, and waved his hand. "Forward!" he whispered, then collected himself. "Forward!"

The army slowly snaked its way north through the Silent

Woman Woods, led by two white donkeys, covered from the air by the Strike Force, and watched by an invisible Isfrael crouched among the branches of an everheart tree.

They reached the edge of the woods by midmorning.

Beyond the trees, tempest reigned in the swirling gray miasma of Barzula's hour.

There was no storm as such—no roiling winds nor gusting hail—but merely the overwhelming impression of a tempest waiting, waiting with gleaming teeth, to plunge into the mind and sanity of everyone foolish enough to dare the open spaces.

Tendrils of the gray haze drifted through the air, clinging to everything it could find.

"Gods," Leagh whispered by Zared's side. "It's sickening! How will we manage to survive that?"

"It is not too late to turn back now," Zared said. "If you wish you can stay here."

He shifted his eyes to all within hearing distance. "I would not begrudge anyone a fear that would not let them leave these Woods."

Men stared back at him, but all stayed their ground.

Leagh shook her head slightly. I will stay with you, her eyes said.

Zared nodded to himself, satisfied, and turned his face back to the exposed landscape. He hoped to every god in existence that Drago knew what he was saying when he swore shade would protect them from this.

Once the miasma had dissipated, Zared waved his column forward. The Strike Force wheeling overhead, they rode silently out from the Woods into a desolate landscape.

The two white donkeys trotted some ten paces in front of the army, their ears flopping with irritating cheerfulness. But Zared, Leagh, and every man and Icarii within the force, was sickened by the sight that met their eyes, just as Faraday and Drago had been. The lush Arcness Plains had been ravaged into a desiccated landscape, swept with the cold winds of Snow-month and left hopeless with the touch of the Demons.

Bones lay scattered everywhere across the cracked earth.

"We will be lucky indeed to find water in this desert," Herme said, pulling his horse up beside Zared's.

Zared nodded. "Pass the word back. We drink enough to sustain us. No more."

A movement to his left caught his eye. Something crawled out of a crack, scuttled several paces, and dropped into another crack.

Zared narrowed his eyes, peering as hard as he could, but he could not make it out.

"Another one!" Leagh cried, pointing to a movement directly in front of them.

It stayed aboveground long enough to be recognized . . . partly. This one was a lizard of the variety that could normally be found hunting grasshoppers through the grasslands. But was it hunting grasshoppers now?

Zared quietly sent back the order to stand ready. They'd barely been out of the Woods a half hour—was it going to be like this the entire way to Carlon? Riding heart in mouth, expecting attack by lizards and mice and sundry other insects and rodents?

Suddenly Leagh cried out. Her horse shied violently to one side, crashing into Zared's mount, and almost throwing Zared to the ground.

He steadied himself, and grabbed at Leagh, making sure she was all right.

She nodded, her face tight, and they both looked down on the ground.

There were two lizards there, each half out of a crack in the earth, each tugging at what remained of a baby's head.

Leagh gagged, and turned away.

"Ride on!" Zared ordered, his eyes hard, and the column wheeled to the left to avoid the lizards.

Ahead, the donkeys started forward from where they'd been waiting patiently.

Zared held his horse back for a moment, then spurred it forward, crushing both lizards and the infant's head beneath its hooves.

They rode through the late morning, past noon, and into the early afternoon. Zared pushed his men and horses as fast as he could, and yet not so fast they would be forced to consume too much water.

The landscape did not change. The plains were stripped of grass back to the red, drifting earth. Cracks zigzagged as far as the horizon.

"And this is the depths of winter!" Leagh said to Zared. "Imagine what it will be like next summer."

Zared did not answer for a moment, and when he did speak, he kept his eyes straight ahead. "If we have not won out against these Demons by next summer, then I doubt we shall be here to endure its horror."

Pray Drago finds this Sanctuary, Leagh thought. Pray all the gods of creation he finds it *soon*. Yet even that thought did not comfort her. Unless this promised Sanctuary sat smack in the center of Tencendor, then it would be nigh impossible to manage to evacuate all of the nation's peoples into its safety.

And how *does* one evacuate a nation? Leagh wondered. How, if we must travel through this kind of wasteland?

An hour after noon, the two donkeys abruptly halted, swung about, and stared at Zared.

He reined in his horse, returned the donkeys' stare briefly, then called a halt.

"Midafternoon draws nigh," he said, and spoke to Herme. "Quick! The shelters!"

Herme turned without answering, and spoke urgently to the lieutenants and captains behind him.

The army had practiced this maneuver a score of times while in the Silent Woman Woods, but out here, so vulnerable, nervousness and haste made for thickened fingers. The Strike Force dropped out of the sky, helping where they could, but even their normally implacable temperaments were disturbed, and their agile fingers awkward.

Zared sat his horse, watching the sky, the horizon, *anything,* for some sign that Sheol's time approached. The scouts had previously announced that the gray miasma swept over the land in the blink of an eye . . . was there *no* warning? What if his sense of time was out and they all died in madness while still erecting their pavilions?

The donkeys slowly walked back toward the army.

"Zared, *move!*" Leagh said behind him, and jolted out of

his thoughts, Zared swung his horse about, casting his gaze over the army behind him.

The column of men and horses had rearranged itself into a vastly different formation of seventy-five squares. Each square comprised several hundred men and horses, and each man had unrolled his shade cloth and attached it to those of his neighbors with poles that were shared about.

Seventy-five squares of shade.

What happened if a storm hit, as was likely at this time of the year? What if the Demons saw these tempting squares, and blew a tempest down upon them?

"Gods help you, Drago," Zared muttered, "if this isn't enough!"

He swung down from his horse, unrolled his own length of shade, and helped Leagh attach it into the square they were assigned to.

He glanced anxiously about. "Herme? Theod? Gustus?"

Each man reported in. The squares were up. Everyone was under.

"Then we wait," Zared said. "And watch."

The donkeys shouldered their way under the square that sheltered Zared's company, and stood to one side of Leagh, their heads turned out into the landscape.

Despair descended upon the land. It rippled out in gray concentric circles from Sheol's location in the northern Skarabost Plains, breaking against the western borders of the Avarinheim and Minstrelsea forests, but flowing smoothly south and west.

In the southern Skarabost Plains it flowed over the dreaming, ancient white horse.

Despair surged further south. The gray tide broke and screamed and wailed over the walls of Tare and Carlon, snatching at the few dozen people who had not been fast enough inside.

It sailed straight over the shade that sheltered Zared's army, leaving them untouched.

But hardly unaffected.

Every member of that force watched the gray twilight areas beyond their shelter. They could somehow *feel* the despair of that gray contagion, even though it did not seep beneath their shade. It felt as if a thousand eyes waited within the haze outside. Waited for a single toe to creep unnoticed over the dividing line between madness and sanity. It felt as if ten thousand bony fingers creaked and flexed out there, waiting for that mistake, that single instant it would take those fingers to *grab*.

Leagh watched for ten minutes, and then could bear no more. She turned and buried her face in Zared's shoulder, feeling his arms wrap about her.

"I do not know if I have the strength," she whispered.

"You must have the strength," he replied. "You have no choice."

The donkeys crowded closer to the pair, and their warmth and apparently unruffable cheerfulness gave both Zared and Leagh strength.

Within the hour, despair passed and the wasteland was once more safe to traverse.

But Zared did not break camp. There were perhaps some three hours before dusk and the onset of the ravages of pestilence, but Zared did not think the effort of breaking camp, riding for one hour, and then setting up camp again was worth the effort.

"We stay here until dawn has passed," he said. "Everyone has three hours to stretch their legs, eat, forage for fodder, whatever, but half an hour before dusk, I want all back in here."

At dusk the world changed. Pestilence reigned, and a low and utterly horrible whirring and droning came from within the miasma, as if great clouds of insects flew within its gray clouds. As the hour deepened, the surface of the earth itself developed great boils that eventually burst to reveal writhing masses of grubs and worms.

When full night descended, terror replaced pestilence. Men swore they could hear teeth gnashing in the darkness beyond the sheltered areas, or the whispers of nightmares too terrible to be contemplated. Terror writhed amid the untamed landscape of the night, and it waited—as had pestilence and despair—for that single error that would let it feed.

Few managed any sleep, and the horses jostled nervously the entire time, forcing men to their heads to try and keep them calm.

A league beyond the boundaries of the camp, coalesced a terror more terrible than any could imagine.

For days the Hawkchilds that flew over the central plains had been driving southeastward an army many thousands strong. It had been instructed by the Hawkchilds, and given its purpose by them, but it was led by an immense brown and cream badger intent on its own hunt after a lifetime of being hunted.

All that it saw in its mind and smelt with its nose was the heady brightness and aroma of blood.

It wanted to feed.

As did every creature that lurched, scampered, hopped and flew behind it.

There were hundreds of once-white sheep, their wool now stained with madness and the blood of those who had proved themselves a nuisance.

There were twice that number of dairy cows, their udders straining with accumulated pestilence, their minds fixed on destroying those who had abused them in their former life. For the past week they'd been sharpening their horns on every stone they came across.

There was a mass of pigs, *thousands* of them, grown strange tusks in hairy snouts, their eyes almost enclosed by thickened, puffy eyelids, grunting with every step they took. They too wanted revenge against those who'd bred them exclusively for the table.

Among the sheep and cattle and pigs scuttled sundry dogs and cats, many of them far longer-limbed than they'd been several weeks previously, their sides gaunt-ribbed, their mouths open in permanent snarls, rabid saliva flickering from their jaws to dot the paths they took. There were rats and hamsters, mules and oxen, and a thousand maddened chickens, geese and turkeys.

And among all these beasts who had formerly been enslaved, ran those creatures who had once commanded them. Naked, febrile men, women and children, sometimes running upright, sometimes scuttling on all fours, snapping at any creature that came within reach.

All lost to the Demons.

All wanting blood, and revenge for whatever slight their madness had magnified in their mind.

They adored this wasteland, and they would do anything— *anything*—to protect it.

They attacked at dawn when hunger ruled the land.

Zared and his army had no knowledge of their approach. The air was dark about them, and they were muddle-witted from an almost sleepless night. They were still broken up into their seventy-five squares, a formation hardly conducive to effective defense.

The donkeys gave the first warning. They had been curled up beside Zared and Leagh's sleeping roll when they jerked awake, their eyes wide, and scrambled to their feet.

If that alone was not enough to startle those about them into wide-eyed apprehension, it was the low, rumbling growl that issued forth from one of the donkeys' throats.

Zared followed the donkey's stare into the lightening gloom, and then drew his sword with a sharp rattle.

"Ware!" he shouted, and the shout was taken up a hundred times until it echoed about the camp.

Ware! Ware! Ware!

Then the maddened army was upon them.

That those they wished to kill currently rested under shade did not worry them in the slightest. Shade or sun, they could still attack, and attack they did against an army that had never, *never*, trained for defense against scuttling cats, or vicious-eyed hamsters, or sharp-toothed sheep, or the sheer weight of a charging cow or ox. Or the sight of a scrawny, naked woman who had twisted her hands into claws and who threw herself into the fray with no thought for the swords that were pointed at her belly.

Horses—and men—panicked.

Zared found himself, and those who sheltered with him, almost overwhelmed by the first wave of attack. A pig knocked him to his knees, and he only just managed to run his sword through its left eye and into its brain before its teeth would have sliced into his throat.

He looked up. "Leagh!"

She had shrunk back among the horses—now rearing and plunging. A howling, naked boy of about ten was darting under the plunging hooves, trying to reach her. He held a great rock in one hand.

"Leagh!"

Zared tried to rise and go to her aid, but a cat sprang and wrapped its legs and claws about his head. Blinded, Zared jabbed the hilt of his sword into the cat's body, over and over, until he felt its grip loosening.

Something massive and foul-breathed loomed to one side, and Zared ducked, flinging the body of the cat as far away as he could.

He tried to turn to meet the new threat, but something bit into the calf of a leg, and he grunted in pain, momentarily distracted.

The huge creature—an ox!—lunged, its forelegs stiff and murderous, but in the instant before it crushed Zared, something white flashed in from the side, and suddenly the ox had no head, and half its left side was gone as well.

It toppled to the ground.

Zared blinked, clearing his own blood from his eyes, then blinked again.

What? He had the hazy impression of something white, more massive even than the ox, moving swiftly through the mayhem.

There was an inhuman shriek, and he vaguely saw the boy who was attacking Leagh fall under the onslaught of the white beast. And there was another white creature, leaping the distance between his shelter and the one adjoining.

Was it a Demonic beast as well, that it could run between shelters?

One . . . roared? Zared blinked again. There. Yes! It roared, and swiped with a huge paw, and suddenly animals were scattering everywhere, fleeing back into the wilderness from whence they had come.

Zared concentrated, but he could not clearly see what it was that had come to their aid. The two white forms—they were so immense!—were leaping from shelter to shelter, and setting to flight any crazed animal that fell within their field of vision.

"Leagh?" Zared scrambled to his feet. "Leagh?"

"Here. Safe." She emerged from behind one of the horses, now strangely calm, and looked at Zared.

"What was that?"

He shook his head. "I don't know." He made sure that Leagh was, indeed, unharmed, then moved among his men within the shelter. Some carried deep wounds, several were dead, but most had survived the encounter relatively physically intact. Their frightened eyes, however, made Zared wonder how well their souls had survived.

"Gustus?" Zared called to the next shelter and, gradually, as men shouted between shelters, he managed to get an idea of how badly his force had been hit.

High overhead, a swarm of Hawkchilds hissed and whispered in frustration. What had gone wrong? There had been an enchantment worked below—but what kind? *How?* They were far from any forest. Was not the Star Dance dead? Was it the stray magician or two that had aided the army below? They screamed, then veered north to commune with the Demons.

Also to the north, the brown and cream badger snapped and snarled his own force back into some form of order. They'd had their chance, and wasted it. But the badger had learned. He'd wait, and grow, and next time . . . next time . . .

Zared let the surgeon suture the wounds on his forehead— that cat had truly been murderous—and talked to Herme, Theod and Leagh through the man's twisting fingers.

"What happened?" he asked.

Theod and Herme looked at each other.

"We were attacked—" Herme began.

"By *what?*" Zared snapped.

Leagh looked at Theod and Herme, and placed her hands on her husband's shoulders, smiling her thanks to the surgeon as he packed his bag and left.

"They know no more than we do," she said gently. "We were attacked by crazed animals."

"They moved as one force," Zared said. "Under direction."

"Yes," Herme said. "We knew that numbers of demented creatures wandered the plains, but we did not know of this organized force."

"And the people among them," Leagh shuddered. "I swear that I recognized one or two of those faces."

"They were more animal than the creatures they ran with," Theod said softly. "Is this what awaits all of us?"

"Unless Drago finds this Sanctuary," Zared said, and stood up. He gazed slowly about, and eventually looked back at his wife and two closest friends.

"What was it that saved us?" he said, his tone almost a whisper.

"I don't know," said Herme, shifting from foot to foot. "But . . . but in the one brief glimpse of it as one lunged past me, I could have sworn . . . I could have sworn that it was an enormous bear."

"Whatever," Zared said, "we can afford to linger here no longer. Roll up the shade cloth, stow the poles, bury the dead, and put the wounded on horses or litters as need be. We must keep on moving."

Herme glanced at Theod, then addressed Zared.

"Sire, there is a problem."

"What?"

"When Theod and I collected the names of those dead and wounded, we discovered . . ."

"You discovered *what?*"

"We discovered that Askam, and some four hundred men, horses and weapons had gone."

24

The Dark Trap

Sicarius returned within five hours.

Axis, who'd been sitting talking with the captain of the escort, slowly rose to his feet as he saw the hound enter the glade and sit down.

"Azhure," Axis called softly, and she turned from grooming her horse.

"Sicarius?" she said, and the dog whined and shifted.

"There are no other hounds," Azhure said, breaking into a large smile. "They must be waiting at . . . well, at whatever they have found."

Both Axis and Caelum stared at the hound, wondering to what he would lead them.

"Do we wait the night . . . or follow Sicarius?" Azhure asked.

Axis hesitated, then made up his mind.

"Mount up!" he called, and men leaped to tightening girths and untying reins.

Sicarius led them northward, then veered east. The land slowly rose toward the southern foothills of the Fortress Ranges. No one in the group, not even any of the men among the escort, had ever explored the southern Fortress Ranges. They were rocky, barren hills, lofty and difficult to pass. Apart from the tunnel Azhure had once traveled with the two Sentinels and Rivkah, Axis knew of only one way through—the Valley, once known as the Forbidden Valley, directly north of the site of the now destroyed Smyrton.

"I sincerely hope there *is* another way through—or under—these Ranges," Axis muttered, "for I do not wish to be out on their open slopes during those hours when the Demons rage."

Azhure shot him an anxious look, but it was Caelum who responded. "Should we just ride for the Valley, Father, and continue our journey through the Avarinheim?"

"Let's see what this hound has found for us first," Axis said, and spurred his horse after Sicarius' form in the distance.

The hound led them to a square hole in a cliff face.

Axis reined in his horse. "A mine?" he asked, looking back at Azhure and Caelum.

"I have heard of no mines in this area," Caelum said, frowning. "Several years ago I commissioned a survey team to see if we could cut a road through to the bay that opens into the Widowmaker Sea just south of here. It would have been useful to open that bay up as a port. But . . ."

"But?"

"The survey team reported back that beneath the surface soil, about an arm's length down, was solid rock. It would be more than difficult to cut a road through here, especially as we would have to cut into some of the hills themselves to avoid disturbing Minstrelsea. So we gave it up as a bad idea.

"The team surveyed this entire southern line of the Ranges. No mines. And from what they'd reported to me, I cannot see how there *could* be any mines."

Sicarius was sitting in the entranceway to the mine, watching them.

"Someone could have mined down a natural fissure in the bedrock," Azhure said softly, her eyes on Sicarius rather than the dark opening of the mine. The pack must be waiting inside somewhere, for they were nowhere to be seen.

"The point is, Mother," Caelum said, "there *was* no mine opening here three years ago. And look!" His hand waved at the entrance. "Those beams are ancient, and the track that leads inside has been worn down over countless generations."

"So what do you suggest?" Axis asked, looking steadily at his son.

Caelum shrugged. "We go inside. See where it leads."

"It's a trap," Azhure said. "I can feel it."

"As can I," Axis murmured. His right hand rested on the hilt of his sword. One half of him was wary about riding into a black hole that stunk of entrapment, the other half of him yearned for a brutal fight so that he could ease some of his frustration at the events of past weeks with the swing and thrust of his sword. "I can *smell* it!"

Caelum looked between his parents, remembering Kastaleon. Then his stupidity had seen four and a half thousand men die. Here? Not four and a half thousand lives, but the hopes and dreams of a nation would be lost if they went inside and failed to meet whatever challenge awaited them.

"We could always swing northwest again," he said, "but we have already lost a day, and will lose at least one more in recovering our ground. The hounds have led us here to this . . . possibility. We would be mad to ignore it."

Caelum's eyes slid toward Sicarius. Would he also be mad to ignore the fact that the Alaunt were not quite as "reliable" as they had once been?

"And if it is a trap?" Axis said.

"We have to risk it," Caelum responded. "We *need* to get to Star Finger as fast as we can. But we also need to get there safely. We go in, but we post a guard of three men at this entrance with a fire. On our way through we post men at regular intervals—until we are down to five men—who will watch for the signal from the entrance that something attacks from our rear."

"So our retreat will be secured," Azhure said. "But what if the trap lies already set deep within the tunnel?"

Caelum grinned, a peculiarly charming and boyish gesture. "Then we deal with it as best we can, Mother. Life is full of risks."

Axis smiled also. Caelum had suggested what he would have done. "Good," he said, and waved to the captain. "Station three men here—and tell them to keep sharp watch!"

The tunnel air was damp and peculiarly thick. Each rider held both reins and a burning brand in one hand, leaving one free to fight with. Small, sharp-edged stones littered the steeply sloping path, forcing the horses to a sliding walk.

Stars help us, Axis thought, if we have to retreat hurriedly.

On the other hand, the rock-littered floor would hinder any enemy as well. Save for anything winged, for within thirty paces of entering the tunnel the roof had lifted into cavernous proportions. The tunnel might only be some four paces wide, but it was at least twenty high.

Axis shivered.

At every turn in the tunnel he motioned a guard to pull in his horse and wait. He did not envy them their solitary vigil.

Before them Sicarius wove sinuously through the darkness, certain of his movements.

The three guards left at the mouth of the tunnel built themselves a bright fire and stood about it, nervously stamping their feet and clapping their hands as if cold, even though the air was mild.

"I'm glad *I* am not down that hole," one muttered, and his companions nodded their agreement.

"Wish I was back with King Zared," a second said.

"What?" the third remarked with forced jocularly. "Do you feel safer in a crowd, then?"

"I just feel safer with *Zared.*"

To that there was nothing to say, and the three lapsed into silence.

An hour passed.

"What was that?" one of them hissed suddenly. He spun about to his left, but there was nothing but the gently shifting trees. He turned again, but here was nothing but the steep cliff face. He turned yet again.

Nothing but the black hole.

"I don't *like* it," he muttered.

"No one ever asked you to *like* your orders, Brandon," one of the others said, "but only to —"

"There! Again!"

Brandon whipped about with his back to the tunnel. He pointed with a hand into the trees before them. "There! I am sure of it!"

His hand trembled slightly.

The other two exchanged glances, and hefted their swords.

All three stared into the forested gloom.

A shadow moved, and they jumped.

"Best signal the first man inside," Brandon said, and bent down to the fire, but before he could grasp a torch something stepped out of the forest.

Brandon, as did his two companions, froze in horror.

They were used to the Icarii—but nothing like this. Even the tales of the Gryphon that their fathers told paled into insignificant bedtime stories compared to this abomination.

It walked at the height of a small man, but there the resemblance ended. Its head was almost that of a bird, except that its forehead was manlike, and its lower beak was not a beak at all, but a full, pouting lip. Its beaked mouth was open, and the men saw that it had no teeth, only hard-ridged bone where once had been gums. It had wings held out behind it—but at their tips clenched and unclenched small hands . . . a child's hands, and that recognition made the horror even worse.

It walked forward on a bird's legs, tufted with black feathers down to the midjoint, and then scaled to end in a four-toed claw that alternatively flexed and splayed delicately as the creature walked.

It was entirely feathered in dull black.

"Hello," it whispered, tilting its head to one side curiously. Abruptly, its head tilted the other way, as if the creature tried to view its prey from all angles, assessing the possibilities.

Completely frozen, none of the men moved or spoke.

"Hello," it said again.

It had now walked to within several paces of the men, and Brandon finally found the courage to heft his sword before him.

"Who are you?" he challenged. "One of the Demons?"

The creature laughed, a peculiar dry whispery sound that sent chills of fear through the men. "Nay. I am a child, come to look for its home."

It took a step closer.

"And for he who condemned me. Do you know of him? WolfStar?"

Suddenly whispers surrounded the men. They rippled in from all sides—seemingly coming from within the rock itself.

The creature spread its wings, and lunged.

Reflexively, Brandon thrust his sword forward—but it had hardly moved before he found his wrist grasped from behind.

A black-feathered wing had wrapped about him, and the small hand at its tip had caught at his sword arm with frightening strength.

There was one at his back!

Brandon twisted his head, registering that both his companions were now gripped by two of the creatures, but before he could do or say anything else, a beak sliced down into his neck.

"Blood," whispered the creature in front, and sank its own beak into Brandon's belly.

It withdrew, holding a lump of something wet and red in its beak. "This is what it feels like to die a murdered death, man," it said, the words gurgling out past the lump of flesh. "Pity us, that we have had to wait so long for a revenge."

Then, pitiless, the Hawkchild ripped the man apart.

The flock fed quickly, before, as one, they turned to the dark entrance. They lifted into the air and swept inside.

None of the sentries stationed along the way ever saw or heard them approach. The black-feathered Hawkchilds were absorbed by the darkness of the tunnel, and by the time they swooped down into the circle of light cast by the brand each sentry carried, it was far, far too late.

Axis, Azhure and Caelum were left with five of their escort when the tunnel abruptly leveled out—and changed.

It changed into the same kind of tunnel that Azhure remembered from her previous experience. The floor was coated with a hard, shiny black substance, and as soon as Axis' horse placed its first hoof on it, a light blinked on overhead. Another lit up some five paces ahead.

Sicarius trotted ahead, lights blinking on as he went. After some forty paces the lights revealed the rest of the pack of Alaunt, sitting patiently in a group, waiting for Sicarius and those he led.

"No trap," Axis said, his shoulder slumping in relief.

Azhure nodded. "The way will be easy from here on, if hard sleeping at night."

She looked about. "I wonder how long we will have to travel this roadway?"

"As long as it takes us to get to Star Finger, I hope," Caelum said. "Come, let us ride. This surface will allow us a good pace before we stop to rest."

Axis murmured to the captain, and then signaled to the rear rider to go back and fetch the rest of the unit. It would take them a while to catch up, but catch up they would.

The rider died after the second turn he took.

They'd ridden for perhaps half an hour when Axis began to feel cold.

"Azhure?" he said, turning his horse slightly so he could look at her. "Do you—"

He stopped, appalled. Past Azhure and Caelum, past the remaining four men of their escort, at the very farthest reaches of the portion of the tunnel that still remained lighted, Axis saw a cloud of darkness billowing toward them.

"Stars!" he whispered. "What is that?"

Sicarius heard the horses stop, and turned to look over his shoulder.

The coldness of pure horror passed through him.

Everything that was in him screamed at him to defend those he was with, everything within him screamed to *Attack! Attack! Attack!*

And yet he could not. He could not.

The StarSon needed his pack intact for the hunt, and Sicarius could not risk them in a fray now.

With a half-yelp, half-howl of sheer frustration and anger, Sicarius led the Alaunt in a flat run down the tunnel, as far away from the black cloud as they could get.

Leaving his charges to defend themselves as best they could.

25

Askam

Askam had been able to come to terms with nothing since Caelum's astounding decision to accept the traitor Zared into his force in order to meet whatever threatened from beyond the Star Gate. In a matter of weeks, Askam had seen his entire inheritance—Carlon and the lands of the West—disappear through Zared's treachery, his sister's disloyalty, and Caelum's incomprehensible decision not to hang Zared the instant he'd got his hands on him.

Had his father, Belial, fought for nothing? he wondered. What would Belial have thought, knowing that all he'd achieved had been lost within a generation?

Well, Askam had learned one immensely valuable lesson from all he'd witnessed—and lost—and that was that bold action more often won the day (and the land and the inheritance) than did complaining about the actions of traitors.

Action provided what justice this world harbored, and possession was more potent than right.

And so, even while he fumbled one-handed with the *cursed* piece of weaving under the trees of the Silent Woman Woods, Askam decided on a course of action that would regain him the possession of that which was his.

Damn it! Zared was using every opportunity, even this invasion by the TimeKeepers, to consolidate his hold on the West. And no doubt Zared was working hand in hand with Drago who, in his own fashion, was simply the pawn of the Demons.

"Well," Askam had said, his eyes sliding over his empty coat sleeve, "as Zared does, so will I take every opportunity offered me."

Among the combined forces there were still men confused about the issue of leadership. How was it that one day Zared could be the hunted, and the next the commander? Askam played to those confusions, and added in the spice of uncertainty about what was happening to families back home.

"Zared intends to course out into the Arcness Plains to win himself yet more territory," Askam whispered around carefully selected campfires at night. "He wants to conquer *all* of the old lands of Achar! But wait . . . maybe that is not his plan. Zared listens to the vile Drago, and we all know that Drago walks in the company of Demons!"

Askam would lean forward to drive home his point, his eyes glittering with passion.

"Tencendor is doomed if we blindly follow Zared. What about your wives and children back in Carlon? Who will protect them from the horrors that now sweep Tencendor? Caelum has gone north to study at Star Finger, Zared has his personal ambitions to cater for, but I . . . *I* . . . sit here and worry for you, and for your families."

His words fell on fertile worries. What *did* happen to their families in Carlon?

"But what can you do to help us?" Jaspar asked. About him some fourteen men sat listening intently.

"I can *act*," Askam said, remembering Leagh's words: *People will willingly tear out their hearts for a man who will do* rather than *expect*.

Jaspar looked at Askam for a long moment, then turned and conversed with his companions in low tones.

Satisfied, Askam rose from that campfire and left them to their decision. He knew what it would be.

By the time Zared led the horsed soldiers and Strike Force out of the Silent Woman Woods, Askam had almost four hundred men who would follow him. They wanted to go home, they wanted to be able to look after their families, and they were not particularly thrilled with the notion of chasing about Tencendor in the employment of the Demonic-inspired Drago or the land-hungry Zared.

Askam's lies had worked their evil well.

He chose the first night they were camped, making sure that all the men who were his were under the same squares of cloth. Askam had noted how cleverly the shade cloths worked, and in the dead of night, when they had the space of many hours before first light, he managed to persuade his men to silently uplift the poles that supported the shade overhead and, keeping the cloths in position, move very slowly and carefully to the northeast.

"We will get above Zared's forces," he whispered to Jaspar to spread among the men. "Wait for him to move on, and then we can make a run for Carlon."

Trying to move while keeping the shade cloths steady overhead was no easy task. Three hundred of the men carried the poles, the others led the horses. The nighttime terror spread all about them, but it did not infiltrate under the shade.

Askam had smiled in satisfaction. He was acting, he was being *bold,* and it would win him the day yet.

After several hours' movement they heard the sounds of a distant battle.

"See!" Askam cried. "You did well to come with me! Zared and his men die, while we are safe."

The men nodded, reassured, and they kept moving northeast until well after daybreak.

Then Askam had them roll up the shade cloth and remount their horses.

"We ride!" he cried, "west then southwest for Carlon!"

They rode for the rest of the day, keeping a sharp watch for any signs that they were about to encounter Zared's force. But Askam had led them several leagues to the north, and if—*if,* for all had heard the sounds of the terrible battle—Zared still commanded anything resembling a force, then it would be moving to the south of them. Having only four hundred men, Askam found it considerably easier to dismount and maneuver the shade cloth into position than did Zared and his massive force, so Askam rode the periods between dawn and midmorning, midmorning and midafternoon, and then between mid-afternoon and dusk. Thus Askam covered far more territory than Zared, but he was also angling slightly more south than he realized.

They rode until they were an hour away from dusk, and Askam started to look for a likely spot to camp in this arid, cold wasteland, although it all looked uniformly inhospitable.

Jaspar, riding at his right, lifted slightly out of the saddle and tried to shade his eyes from the setting sun they rode into.

"My Prince? There is a depression ahead. A small valley perhaps."

A small valley? Here? Well, who knew what the winds had blown out. Or maybe it housed one of the small streams that fed the Nordra.

Askam peered into the sun. It was about a half-hour's ride away. "Good. We will camp there. At least it will provide us with some shelter."

They spurred their horses faster, wanting to reach the campsite as fast as possible.

As they neared, Askam waved his men back to a trot, and then a halt as they stood at the rim of the valley.

Valley was too grand a word for this depression. About twenty paces deep and ten wide, it stretched for about a league north-south.

Askam shrugged. It was shelter.

He waved the men forward, and they turned their horses onto the faint path that led down the eastern slope of the depression. The floor was sandy, and gave way alarmingly in places, but it would suffice for the night, and they could not afford to ride any further.

"Set up camp," Askam ordered.

As dusk settled about them, pestilence raged. Then terror swept in at pestilence's heels, and the men huddled underneath their shade cloth, trying to catch what sleep they could.

The horses shifted, nervous.

Askam jumped out of his doze as a horse snorted and half-reared. Damn! Would they never grow used to the Demonic Hours? Their mounts would be worn out before they got halfway to Carlon.

Askam cursed, and rolled over, drifting back to sleep.

The sentries posted at the borders of the square of shade remained alert, but their eyes tended to be averted from the landscape outside, for there terror and horror raged, and they feared that even by looking on it, it might yet infect them.

Thus they did not see it when great lumps and forms arose out of the sandy soil about them.

The badger had been busy. After his failed attempt at Zared's force, he'd decided to lay a trap . . . a trap into which Askam had inadvertently blundered. Among his force the badger had set the burrowing animals to work, digging out great traps under the sandy floor of the depression. There he had secreted the most violent and crazed of all his command.

Attack at night, and silently, and maybe they would escape whatever enchantment had defeated them previously.

The badger realized this smaller force was not the one he'd wanted to trap, but he also saw its possibilities, and as night moved in he'd changed his mind about his method of attack—and the results he wanted to see.

A score of scrawny and scratched men and women crawled closer to the square of shade. Among them writhed a dozen small children, as well as three infants barely able to crawl. Almost a thousand poultry, eight hundred rabbits and hamsters, and six-score cats crept with the mad humans.

All wanted to taste blood. But all had very strict instructions not to kill. Just to drag.

Behind this first wave of attack came the pigs and cows and sheep, ready to charge in once the first wave had created its terror.

The sentries, alert, still kept their eyes averted from the terror of the night, and thus it was that the first they knew of the attack was when hands and paws and claws and beaks reached out from the darkness of the night and snatched their ankles.

The men cried out, waking their companions, but their cries cut off suddenly.

They had been dragged out from the shade and into the terror of the night. For a heartbeat they thought they were safe, and then terror such as they had never imagined forced its way down their throats and between the spaces of eye and eyelid, and tunneled its way into their bodies. The men's minds did not snap immediately. The terror let them *feel* it, *feel* how it enjoyed feeding on the spaces within their bodies, before it finally let its full force explode through their minds. The men screamed and writhed, voiding themselves on the sand, some snapping the delicate bones of fingers and wrists as they scrabbled for an escape, any escape.

But there was no escape. The terror finished its work, and when it *was* done, the men stood, shaking almost uncontrollably.

Their minds were gone. They had been consumed, and now these men turned their swords and eyes back to the squares of cloth, their loyalty now belonging to the badger, not Askam.

Askam, as everyone else, had leaped to his feet, appalled by the screaming. "What . . . what happened?"

Suddenly there was a frightful wail outside, and a wall of appalling creatures rushed the square. Some were cut down the instant they met the swords of the men, but most were not, and they dragged and clawed and chased men out from under the protection of the shade.

"Gods!" screamed Jaspar as an ox seized his collar in his teeth and pulled him toward the night. "*Askam! They mean to drag us outside.*"

Askam could no longer reply. He was already outside, lying on his back, staring at the stars overhead.

Completely mad.

Within a space of only minutes, the entire force of four hundred men lay twitching under the stars, their minds a ghastly thick soup of madness, pain, and gleeful whispering voices.

The brown and cream badger trotted triumphantly among the victims. He had lost a few of his command, yes, but they had now been replaced by four hundred men and horses, all relatively intact and capable of obeying his every command.

There was a whisper of feathers overhead, and the hiss of satisfaction. At last! The beginnings of a true army for their masters. Soon the entire landmass of Tencendor would ring to the booted footsteps of an army swaying to the battle songs of madness.

26

The Hall of the Stars

Sicarius!" Azhure cried, unable to believe the Alaunt were running. *"Sicarius!"*

But none of the hounds paid her any heed. Within moments they had disappeared from sight.

She looked at Axis, her eyes stricken.

"We will manage without them," he said, and squeezed her arm briefly.

She nodded, and turned her eyes back to the cloud that was slowly advancing toward them.

"There must be somewhere to hide—" Caelum began, turning his horse about in tight, anxious circles, but his father interrupted.

"Hide. Where? This tunnel is bare of any secret spaces. Captain. Arrange your men behind me. Azhure, take Caelum, and ride as fast as you can. Get him out, at least."

She nodded, silencing Caelum's protests with a curt wave of her hand.

"Be careful," she whispered to Axis. "Come back to me."

He grinned for her, although the effort cost him dearly. "I have not battled through all these years to lose you now," he said, and kneed his horse close to hers so he could lean over and kiss her hard on the mouth. "Now, get our son to safety."

Azhure turned for one last look at the cloud, her face tightening in horror. There were no bodies distinguishable in the cloud, but here and there she could see the brightness of eyes gleaming, and in one or two places she thought she saw hands reaching out . . . grasping . . .

"Ride!" Axis shouted, and whacked the rump of her horse with the flat of his hand.

It leaped forward, desperate itself to escape what advanced behind them, and Axis waved Caelum after Azhure. "Damn it, Caelum—follow your mother. You can do nothing here!"

Caelum held his horse back long enough to give his father one hard stare, trying to imprint Axis' face in his memory for all time, then he spurred his horse after Azhure.

Axis swung his horse to meet the threat. "Hold fast, man!" he told the captain and the other three men, and they tried to quell the growing agitation of their mounts, as well as the horror in their own bellies, as the cloud seethed down the tunnel toward them.

He risked a glance over his shoulder to make sure Azhure and Caelum had managed to escape—and froze.

Both were only some twenty paces away, and moving no further.

The tunnel floor had disappeared.

As had the walls, and the roof.

Even as he watched, Azhure's horse screamed and reared, tossing her. Frightened into total panic, it leaped into the darkness in front of it—and vanished.

Caelum bent down and hauled Azhure up behind him, kicking his horse to guide it back to his father and the four escorts.

"It is no use," he said. "The tunnel has gone."

Axis swung his eyes forward again, expecting to see the black cloud filled with its eyes and hands ready to pounce.

Instead, it had completely disappeared. As with the tunnel behind his back, twenty paces ahead of him the floor and walls of the tunnel had vanished.

Replaced with darkness . . . and stars.

"What is happening?" one of the men whispered.

Axis shook his head slowly. "I do not know. I do not know."

The Demons and StarLaughter stopped their horses, and arranged themselves in a row, facing east.

All of the Demons stared with unblinking eyes, and Star-Laughter alternated between watching them, and staring east herself. She could feel the power bubbling within her, and she sent it coursing east, trying to see what the Demons did.

She closed her eyes, allowing the power to rope free, and when she opened them again, she did not see with her eyes, nor did she see the flat of the Skarabost Plains.

She saw through the eyes of the Hawkchilds in the tunnel under the Fortress Ranges, and she saw the group of riders, their faces a mixture of confusion and panic. Dimly, Star-Laughter heard the thump of a great paw next to her horse.

Queen of Heaven, Sheol whispered into her mind. *Do you see?*

Yes.

They are trapped. Sheol's mind voice was filled with irrepressible glee.

Yes!

Watch, Sheol commanded, *and follow our lead.*

"Gods save us!" one of the men-at-arms screamed, staring at the floor beneath his horse.

Like the floor and walls elsewhere, it was slowly fading.

The man tried to wheel his horse about, but he lost control and the horse panicked. It reared and plunged and then . . . both man and horse vanished. They had fallen through into the darkness beneath.

"Stand fast!" Axis yelled. "And dismount! These horses will be no use."

Everyone did as he commanded, grateful to be off the increasingly panicked horses, yet well aware of the risks of trying to meet whatever danger threatened them on foot.

Axis felt Azhure by his side, and he looked at her.

She was calm, and in complete control. "We will do the best we can," she said.

"Yes," Axis answered, and looked to his son. "Caelum?"

Caelum was as calm as Azhure, and he managed to give his father a confident nod.

"What I need to know," the captain ground out, "is what we face and how to deal with it! I—"

His voice abruptly cut off, and Axis turned to look at him. He was struggling to find his footing. Beneath him the floor had disappeared.

Strangely, the captain managed to stay upright, and he lifted an ashen face to stare at Axis.

"It's all gone," he said unnecessarily. *"There's nothing under my feet!"*

Within a moment all six found that the tunnel had entirely disappeared, taking the remaining horses with it. They were standing in blackness, surrounded by blackness—except for the bright stars where once had been the black cloud.

"Look," Caelum said softly. "The stars . . ."

Once stationary, now the stars were flowing toward them, the sense of danger growing so palpable that Axis thought he could reach out a hand and snatch at it.

"Stand fast," he said, although he had no idea how—*if!*—they could meet the danger . . . or what the danger even was.

Stars swirled about them and Axis, as Azhure and Caelum were reminded of their experiences inside the Temple of the Stars. Then the stars had streamed and danced by them within the great cobalt beacon that had speared up from Temple Mount. Here they were locked, trapped within a blackness. Here the stars were malevolent, not benign.

"It is as though we are in a hall," Caelum said softly, turning slowly to look about him. "A hall of stars."

"A hall of stars," Azhure repeated. "Is there any . . . can you feel the Star Dance?"

"I feel *something*," Axis said, his senses desperately seeking the Star Dance.

But there was nothing.

Nothing but danger seeping all about them.

Axis' frustration exploded. "Damn you!" he called into the starry void. "What are you? *Where* are you?"

"Look!" one of the men cried, pointing.

They all turned to follow his hand. From one of the constellations spinning about them a dark, cloaked and hooded figure had emerged. It was hard to say exactly how they could *see* it, but it was there. They could sense it, taste it.

Fear it.

"And there!" cried the captain.

Again they looked, and again they saw *(sensed)* another dark hooded figure moving toward them from a galaxy overhead.

"And there," murmured Azhure. "And there."

"How many?" Axis asked after a few minutes. They were surrounded by a circle of cloaked and hooded figures, slowly gliding toward them from among the stars.

"Twenty-seven," Caelum answered. He slowly drew his

sword from its scabbard, hearing the scrape of steel about him as the others did the same.

The circle tightened until the figures were no more than five paces away, and standing so close each to the other that passage through them would be impossible.

"My name is Axis SunSoar StarMan," Axis called. "Who are you?"

One of the figures took a step forward, and they spun in its direction. A faint light glowed about its head, and they saw the pale shape of hands lift to pull down the hood, revealing the face.

Azhure gasped, and she heard the swift intake of breaths about her.

It was a young birdwoman, fine gold hair curling about her forehead, deep violet eyes filled with sadness.

"She is so beautiful!" Azhure whispered.

"Aye," Axis said. "And deadly."

"You are Axis SunSoar StarMan?" the birdwoman said. Her voice was strange, as if harsh from disuse. Whispery. All had to strain to hear her.

"Yes," Axis said. "And you?"

She half-turned her face, the starlight catching a tear that ran down her cheek.

"My name is StarGrace SunSoar," she said. "Murdered StarGrace. Betrayed StarGrace."

She turned her face back toward them, and they saw her eyes glittered dangerously. "*Lost* StarGrace!" she hissed.

"Oh Stars!" Azhure said, and grasped Axis' arm. "Star-Grace was the niece of WolfStar, daughter of CloudBurst. She was one of those he—"

"Murdered," StarGrace said. "Who are you, woman?"

Azhure tilted her chin but before she could answer, Axis spoke.

"Who stands with me does not matter, StarGrace. Why do you trap us here? Let us go!" Whatever else, Axis did not want to reveal that among them stood Caelum StarSon.

"You do not *know* the meaning of trapped!" StarGrace cried, and flung an arm behind her, indicating the starry universe. "*Here* is where we drifted a thousand wasted lifetimes. Here is where—"

"You betrayed this land of Tencendor to the Demons," Axis said.

StarGrace cocked her head to one side, as if curious. "You are a fool, Axis SunSoar StarMan, and most physically deformed. You bear no wings. What has this come to, that a man who dares to bear the title of StarMan wears no wings? I can see that the SunSoar house has become ill-bred over the millennia. Corrupted."

Go, Sheol whispered in StarLaughter's mind. *Go, and have your fun. But do not—*

I understand, Sheol, and StarLaughter handed her child to the Demon to mind.

"It is more than time, then," said a new voice, "that the true heir return and put things to rights."

Axis snapped his head about so fast that his neck cricked in protest.

From somewhere beyond the circle a woman stepped forth. She wore no cloak, and no disguise, but was garbed instead in a robe that—Axis almost gagged—appeared to be made of blood. It trickled down over her breasts and belly, congealing over her hips at the juncture of her legs, then running in thick, ropy strands down to her ankles.

Axis instinctively knew who she was. "StarLaughter."

She inclined her beautiful head, a lock of her dark hair dragging through the bloody shoulders of her robe, and laughed. "Indeed, Axis SunSoar. Now, will you introduce me to the others standing here?"

She stopped just past StarGrace. "Do it!"

"No!" Axis said. "There is no need to—"

StarLaughter's face contorted in fury. She jerked her right hand, and the captain and the two remaining men-at-arms disappeared.

"They are *pointless*," she said, swinging her eyes between Axis, Azhure and Caelum. "And eminently dispensable. Just as your swords are."

And they too vanished, leaving only empty fists where once had been steel.

"Will you not introduce me to your wife and son, Axis?" StarLaughter said.

Axis silently cursed the fact that he had named himself in the first instance. Perhaps if he'd kept a still tongue, this woman would not have known that—

"Oh, I have *always* known!" she hissed, and swung to face Azhure.

"Bitch!" she screamed, the veins on her forehead and in her neck throbbing into knotted fury. *"You are the fruit of my husband's betrayal!"*

Azhure reeled back, one hand half-raised before her. "I am not responsible for WolfStar's faults—"

"You are his flesh and blood! *You* carried his blood into power, not *my* son."

StarLaughter abruptly stopped, still staring at Azhure, her face contorted in fury, her hands clenched at her sides.

"Where is she?" she growled.

"Who?" Azhure shot Axis a stricken look, and he moved closer to her side.

"The bitch WolfStar lay with. Your mother."

Azhure managed to keep her composure. "She is dead. She died when I was six. Burned to death by—"

"Then why is it that I can *feel* her?" StarLaughter said, her voice quieter now, but her gaze no less intense. "Why?"

Her nostrils flared, almost as if she could scent her rival. "She is here," she said. "Somewhere. Niah. Even if I have to hunt her beyond the gates of death, Azhure, be sure that I will do it!"

Now Azhure was visibly shaken, not only at StarLaughter's venom, but at her knowledge of Niah's name. "How did you—"

StarLaughter shook her head of hair, and smiled. "How did I know Niah's name? How do I know anything?"

She paused, and shifted her eyes to stare directly at Caelum. "Drago told me. Drago told me *everything*."

The tip of her tongue flicked out between her teeth and ran over her top lip.

"He was extraordinary in bed, Caelum. The SunSoar blood, I suppose."

She smiled and took a step toward Caelum. "I would *beg* him to take me. I would *grovel* on the floor before him. Do you know what I mean, Caelum?"

He paled. "Drago is a traitor," he managed.

"As are you!" StarLaughter erupted into a frightful fury. *"You claim the Throne of Stars when it should be my son who claims that right!"*

StarLaughter took another step forward until she was so close to Caelum she could thrust her face in his. "And do you know what, StarSon?"

She spoke the title as a curse.

"He will come to get you. He will *kill* you." She smiled. "And nothing you can do will stop that now. Look at you, you pitiful lump of mortal flesh. You dare to name yourself heir and ruler of Tencendor. Ha! You were bred beyond the bonds of marriage. *The legitimate heir, my son, will come to kill you!"*

The entire circle of robed watchers broke into agitated whispering.

"He will revel in your pain and blood," StarLaughter continued, triumph and laughter replacing the fury in her voice.

"See." The circle of Hawkchilds broke into howls of laughter, and they parted so that there was an unrestricted view of the part of the universe to which StarLaughter pointed. "See!"

Axis grabbed at Azhure and Caelum, pulling them into a tight group. Stars! What could they do! Even though he had no power himself, Axis could feel the power that vibrated from StarLaughter, as from each and every one of the robed children about them.

It must have taken unimaginable strength and skill to create this hall of stars. Had StarLaughter and the children done that, or had it been the TimeKeepers?

Of what use were swords against such enchantments as this?

"Look!" Azhure whispered, but both Caelum and Axis were staring anyway.

Caelum shuddered, then wrenched himself out of his father's grasp. "No!"

"Caelum—" Axis began.

"No!"

"Yes!" StarLaughter whispered. "Here comes DragonStar to drink your blood, fool boy!"

Wheeling out of a galaxy of swirling stars came a figure as black as the others that had circled the three. Save this one rode a horse, and brandished something in his hand that caught and reflected the starlight.

Caelum screamed, a thin wail of utter terror, and turned to flee.

But the circle of children—now hawks—crowded in about him, wrapping him in their wings, pecking at his face, his eyes.

Axis jumped to help, grabbing at legs and claws and wings, trying to free his son.

Azhure would have tried to help as well, except at the very moment that Axis leaped, Azhure felt cruel hands grab her arms and hold her back.

"No," StarLaughter whispered in her ear. "Why not let them both die together? They will only stand in the way of the true heir, DragonStar."

Azhure struggled, baring her teeth in a desperate attempt to bite her way free, but StarLaughter countered every move Azhure made with power and mirth.

"Damn you!" Azhure cried.

"Nay," StarLaughter said. "*You* are the one who is damned. Can you not feel it?"

Caelum was completely enveloped in feathered wings and bodies. Struggling to battle his way in, Axis still managed to wonder in one corner of his mind how the children had transformed themselves. They were as dangerous and powerful as StarLaughter and the Demons. He managed to get a good grasp of one wing, and used his entire strength to tear it back.

Something screamed, and a body fell away from the writhing black pile that contained Caelum.

Axis grabbed at another wing, but this time a horrific head rose up and pecked violently at his face so that he was forced to stumble back, his arms covering his bleeding forehead and cheeks.

"Axis!" he heard Azhure scream. *"Look!"*

Axis raised his head, wiping blood out of his left eye—and felt his heart falter, and then thud violently.

Thundering toward them was a massive black horse. Atop him was a man clad in enveloping black armor, and wielding a sword in his right hand such as Axis had never seen before.

The rider swept it through the air in great hissing arcs.

Caelum.

The word blasted through his head, and Axis saw Azhure clutch at her own skull and cry out.

Caelum!

The horse and rider drew nearer, and Axis, even though he could see no floor where he stood, could nevertheless *feel* the vibrations of the beast's approach.

The rider now stood in his stirrups, slowly waving the sword above his head, and Axis heard a scream of triumph tear through his mind.

He screamed himself, battling the gut instinct to fling himself out of the way, and instead leaped for Caelum, still struggling with the bird-children.

As Axis leaped, they all rose in the air, leaving Caelum writhing on the floor, covered in a thin layer of blood from a myriad of scratches.

At first Axis thought it was because of his own precipitous leap, but at the moment he gathered his son into his arms, he felt the horse's hooves slam down next to his head.

Instinctively he rolled closer to Caelum, gathering him into his arms—

Caelum . . .

"No," Axis gasped. "Don't listen to him! Don't look at—"

Look at my face, Caelum.

And Caelum had to. He had to. He had to see the face of the being that was about to kill him.

He twisted about in Axis' arms, and looked up.

The rider slowly lifted the visor of his helmet.

"Drago!" Caelum screamed, and then the rider's sword arm was flashing down, and Caelum felt the tip of the sword slice into his chest, slice *deep* into his chest, and he choked on the blood and pieces of sliced tissue that filled his lungs.

The rider leaned down from the horse, leaned down his entire weight, and twisted the blade.

"*No!*" Axis screamed, reaching around Caelum to grasp the blade in his bare hands. "*No!*"

"Yes," whispered StarLaughter.

Yes! whispered the voice of the rider through their minds, and he twisted the blade again, and now Axis screamed, but still he held on to the blade, even though he could feel it slicing his fingers away, trying, trying, trying to wrench it out of his son's chest.

"A foretaste of the hunt," StarLaughter said conversationally, and then she, the children, and the black rider disappeared.

The instant she felt the restraining arms vanish, Azhure fell down on top of her husband and son. The blade was still embedded in Caelum's chest, and Axis still had his hands wrapped about it.

Stricken, Azhure looked into Caelum's face.

"Drago!" he said, through a mouthful of clotting blood, and died.

Azhure blinked, and her son lay dead before her.

She blinked again, and her husband writhed screaming as he clutched his ruined hands to his chest.

She blinked once more, and she found herself kneeling on the hard black surface of the tunnel, staring at her husband and Caelum lying before her.

Perfectly whole.

The sword, the blood, the horror, all had disappeared.

StarLaughter took a deep breath, and opened her eyes back to awareness of the horse beneath her and the cold winds of the Skarabost Plains whipping past her.

She turned her head slightly to look at the Demons.

They were all watching her with expressions of half-ecstasy, half-wild amusement.

"He is weak," StarLaughter said, "and filled with hopelessness. If the StarSon can let a vision impale him, then think what will happen when the real thing hunts him through the Maze!"

There was silence as the Demons and StarLaughter smiled at the thought.

It would be a good hunt.

"Those were the three," said Mot, "who, if there had been any power remaining, could have wielded it."

Barzula smirked. "The Mage-King of the Avar was useless."

"*Everyone* is useless!" cried Rox.

"Tencendor is ours," Raspu said.

"Forever and ever and through all time," Sheol said, and looked reverently at the child in her lap.

They had, for the moment, forgotten about the two worrying magicians to the west.

27

Drago's Ancient Relics

Did you not live in southern Skarabost, Faraday?" Drago asked one night, idly stroking the lizard as it cuddled against his thigh.

They were crouched in their cramped tent on the shores of the Nordra as it sliced through the Western Ranges and the Rhaetian Hills. Drago had spent the best part of the day looking for a boat, but had found none. In the morning they would continue their northward journey to Gorkenfort on foot, crossing the Nordra when they found a ford or a boat. Faraday had remained silent when Drago had mentioned Gorkenfort; he knew all too well of her need to go directly north to Star Finger, and she knew it would be of no use to tell him yet again.

They sat shoulder by shoulder, with space not even for a fire. The terror raged outside, and while they knew it could not touch them, the confinement of the tent was still preferable to sitting outside by a fire with the Demons nibbling at their minds . . . *Why? Why? Why?* During the day they continued to travel through the Demonic Hours, ignoring the cold fingers of the gray miasma as best they could, but at night they rested, both physically and spiritually, within the warm comfort of the tent's interior.

Faraday took a long time to answer, and Drago was surprised that she finally did.

"Yes," she said. "On an estate called Ilfracombe. But it is far to the east of where we will travel."

Her voice had a decided edge to it, but Drago ignored it. He also dreamed of the girl, but he found his need to get to Gorkenfort greater, and he hoped that the answers he would find there would also help solve the riddle of the girl.

"Do you still have family there?"

"Why these questions?" she said, and raised her face. "Will whether or not any of my family survive or be damned save or damn Tencendor in its turn?"

Drago was horrified to see the brightness of tears in her eyes. "Faraday . . . we will get to the girl soon enough."

She was silent a long time, wiping the tears away with the back of a hand. It was not only the fretting for the girl that made her irritable, but her growing feeling for this man now so close to her.

Faraday didn't like that . . . she didn't like it at all.

"It is not just the girl," she whispered. "There is another wound which will not close."

This, at least, she would tell him.

Drago was silent, willing to let her tell him at her own pace.

"Before we left the Silent Woman Woods I said good-bye to Isfrael," she said, her voice stronger.

Drago remembered how curt Faraday had been when she'd mentioned her talk with Isfrael as they'd left the Silent Woman Woods.

"I know," he said gently.

Tears threatened again. "I loved that child so much!" Faraday said, and she spread her hands across her belly, as if she could still feel him growing inside of her. "And I loved Axis so *much*. I did so much for both of them. And yet both of them have preferred to cut me from their lives.

"Isfrael said . . ." Her voice broke. "Isfrael said that he wished that just once I'd been there to rock him to sleep as a child."

Furious with both Axis and Isfrael for hurting Faraday so much, for *continuing* to hurt her, Drago wrapped his arms about Faraday and hugged her close.

"Shhh, Faraday," he whispered into her hair, gently rocking her. "Shush now."

Very slowly and very hesitantly, as if she regretted every movement, he felt Faraday slide her arms about him.

"I shouldn't have abandoned him," she whispered. "I shouldn't have abandoned him."

"Shush now, Faraday," he said again. "Shush."

They sat in silence, and gradually Drago rocked Faraday to sleep as if she were a child.

Drago dreamed.

But this night it was not the girl who intruded into his subconscious.

He dreamed he stood outside a great abandoned fortress of ice-covered black stone. Winds and snow buffeted the fortress, and he had to fight to maintain his feet. The great gates hung open on rusted hinges, and Drago struggled inside.

The courtyard was bare of anything but snow and ice drifts. Drago looked about, shielding his eyes as best he could from the gusts of ice-needled wind.

Twenty paces away was the door into the Keep, and Drago slipped and slithered his way across the courtyard, hoping the door was not bolted.

It opened with a painful squeal as he leaned against it, and Drago stumbled inside, grateful to be out of the wind. But it was no warmer inside. Ice crept down stone walls and cascaded in a frozen waterfall down the stairs.

They were impassable.

Drago walked slowly into the great hall, then stopped. Here a fire roared in the fireplace. A table was set before it, and on that table lay a dead seal, its blank eyes staring in Drago's direction.

There was a rustle of movement in a shadowed space at the rear of the hall, and Drago swung his gaze in that direction.

A woman emerged from the shadows. She was tall and willowy, dressed in a pale gray robe that clung to her form. Iron-gray hair, streaked with silver, cascaded down her back. On the ring finger of her left hand she wore a circle of stars.

She had very deep blue eyes, and a red mouth, curved in a welcoming smile.

"North," she whispered, and yet the whisper reached Drago easily. "Come north to *Gorkenfort,* Drago. Listen not to Faraday's pleadings. I have more need of you than the weeping girl."

Her smile widened momentarily, and then she moved gracefully to stand behind the table, her back to the fire.

She continued to stare at Drago, and then suddenly, horrifically, she snarled, revealing sharp fangs, and she bent to sink them into the spine of the seal.

Bones crackled, and blood spattered about the table.

She lifted her head. Her mouth and chin were red.

"Come north," she said. "I need to talk to you."

His mother. His ancestral mother . . .

Drago nodded, understanding even though he could put no words to his understanding, and turned and left the dream.

Terror buffeted the tiny tent, and when dawn broke, hunger tried to poke its skeletal fingers through the openings.

But the two inside did not notice, nor fear.

They slept.

Drago let Faraday sleep until it was full daylight.

"It's late!" she cried, springing into instant awareness. She pushed her hair back from her face and hastily twisted it into a long plait down her back.

"We have not lost long," Drago said, watching with amused eyes as Faraday leaped to her feet and stuffed their few possessions into their packs.

"We can eat as we walk," she said, handing Drago a dried apple and a piece of cheese. "Get moving! I cannot dismantle this tent while you still sit there!"

Drago did as he was told. He unlaced the top of the tent from his staff, which doubled as a pole, and helped Faraday fold it.

Then he checked that his pack was properly loaded, swung it onto his back, made certain his sack was securely hung at his belt and picked up his staff. "Ready?"

"At this rate, it will be full summer by the time we reach Gorkenfort," Faraday grumbled, swinging into step beside Drago. *And we will never reach Star Finger in time.*

Drago heard both spoken and unspoken words, but he did not answer. He stared at the landscape about them. It was still windswept, but here, at the edge of river and the Rhaetian hills, there was more vegetation and dozens of deep burrows where, Drago thought, might huddle those creatures not yet driven insane by the Demons' touch.

Every so often, as if to confirm his hopes, he spotted the glint of dark eyes watching him from deep within the shadowed burrows. Sometimes the lizard would investigate the burrows, and he always seemed to emerge grinning.

Drago and Faraday had seen evidence of the maddened creatures that roamed the plains, but they had not been attacked, nor had they seen the creatures in groups of any more than four or five.

The lizard emerged from a burrow to Drago's left, and trotted over to him.

Drago leaned down and scratched his head, smiling.

"How will we cross the Nordra?" Faraday asked.

He turned back to her, watching the northerly wind whip fine strands of chestnut hair about her face and press the material of her dress close to her body.

"Until we find a boat, or a ford, we shall have to travel north along this bank. I . . ."

His voice trailed off.

"Yes?" Faraday said.

"I dreamed last night of she who we go to meet at Gorkenfort."

Faraday arched an eyebrow, but did not speak, and Drago thought she had never looked so beautiful.

"Urbeth," he said. "Urbeth waits impatiently for us at Gorkenfort."

"*She* is your ancestral mother?"

Drago gave a little shrug. "I understand it as much as you."

Faraday dropped her eyes. Urbeth awaited them? She lifted her eyes again and stared directly north toward Star Finger. Then she sighed and bent down to lift her pack.

"We had better walk," she said, "for there is a long way to go, and many directions to be taken."

The lizard heaved a great sigh and got to his feet.

* * *

They walked through that day, stopping only to eat a brief meal at midday. Their food was getting low, but Drago hoped they'd meet with some Aldeni communities, or find their abandoned homes, which might have stocks of food.

Faraday privately wondered about Drago's optimism on that score. With the devastation that had struck at land and lives alike, people were likely to be wary of strangers, and even more wary of sharing what little food they had left.

They camped that evening still on the east bank of the river. Drago was clearly impatient at the delay in finding a way to cross the Nordra, for the river was now angling back to the east. They spent the evening in silence, each lost in their own thoughts, and when it came time to sleep they slept wrapped tight in their individual blankets, and tight in their individual dreams.

"Why do you continue to deny your birthright?" Faraday said unexpectedly over the dried apple they shared for breakfast.

Drago took his time in answering. "I am not ready to deny Caelum *his* birthright," he said.

"You are a fool." Faraday stood up. "Especially since you say that you will let nothing stop you from aiding the land. What if . . ."

She stopped folding her blanket and fixed him with her eye. "What if you can best serve Tencendor as StarSon and *not* Caelum's lackey?"

Drago drew in a sharp, angry breath. "I am *not* StarSon. That was but a childish dream. I will not stand in Caelum's way again!"

"It is your denial that is childish!" Faraday snapped, and turned her back to him.

They walked in silence that morning.

An hour before midday Drago halted, his hand shading his eyes. "There's something ahead," he said.

Faraday strained to see, but could see nothing. "What? Is it dangerous?"

Drago chewed his lip in frustration. "I can't see it properly. It's too far away. A pale smudge . . . but it doesn't fit into the landscape. It's not natural."

Faraday glanced at the lizard ranging some fifteen paces ahead of them. It showed no fear, or sign of any consternation.

"Then we must walk," she said, and shifted her backpack into a more comfortable position. "We cannot let a smudge deter us."

Drago could not help a grin at her words, but Faraday, who had walked ahead, did not see it. Within a few minutes she could see the smudge as well, and both she and Drago quickened their stride, trying to get close enough to see.

When they did make it out, they both slowed slightly in amazement. It was a white horse, sway-backed with age, standing as still as death.

"Is it crazed?" Faraday asked.

"It must be," Drago said. "We're too far from any shelter for the horse to be anything other."

Faraday checked their surroundings. "Perhaps we should give it a wide berth."

"Another few paces," Drago said. "We can see better from there, and we'll still be a safe distance away."

They halted within twenty paces of the horse. It gave no indication that it was aware of their presence, standing with its head drooping almost to the ground, apparently fast asleep.

"We'd best give him a wide berth," Faraday said again.

Drago did not answer immediately, standing staring at the horse.

"No," he finally said slowly. "No. I want to have a closer look at him."

There was something about that horse . . . something . . .

Faraday looked at him oddly. "Are you certain it's safe?"

"No." Drago gave a sudden grin. "If he tries to bite, will you save me?"

She shot him a hard glare, and his grin widened slightly.

"If the horse refuses to wake, then perhaps we can throw him into the Nordra, and use him to float us across."

Faraday's mouth jerked, but she managed to keep her face

straight, and waved Drago forward. "Off you go then, if you're so curious. But I would have thought one old horse was surely much the same as the next."

Drago walked forward, and after an instant's hesitation, Faraday followed him.

The lizard ranged ahead of Drago, dropping to its belly and slithering toward the horse, almost like a snake.

The horse stood with his head drooping so close to the ground his nose almost touched the soil. He did not seem aware of the two people or the lizard. The lizard slowed as it neared, then carefully planted its clawed feet on the ground and walked very carefully about the horse.

"Stop here," Drago said, his hand catching at Faraday's arm, his eyes still fixed on the horse.

"Be careful," she said.

Drago eased the pack from his back and put it on the ground, then cautiously approached the horse. How, if the horse was *not* one of the Demons' minions, had it managed to survive without shelter? And why, if the horse *was* crazed, did it not attack? Was this a trap?

Were the Demons aware that he was still alive, and that he could resist their incursions?

Doubts raced through Drago's mind, and though he was wary, *something* about the horse bothered him, *something* about the horse tugged at his mind, at his memories.

Something told him this horse was no foe.

"Quiet now, old boy," he said softly as he got to within a pace of the beast. "Quiet now."

The horse did not move, perhaps wondering in some deep recess of his mind how he *could* get any quieter.

"Quiet now," Drago repeated, reassuring himself far more than the horse, and reached out a cautious hand to the beast's neck.

He patted it lightly.

The horse did not stir.

Bolder now, Drago stepped close to him and ran his hand down his neck in bold, reassuring strokes.

"What a fine old boy," he said, his tone warm but gentle. "What a handsome old fellow. What are you doing here? Lost? No one to care for you?"

The stallion *must* have been a handsome beast in his prime, Drago thought. He was at least eighteen hands high, and with good bones, although his flesh hung limply enough from them now. His chest was deep and, even ancient as he was, the horse's legs were clean and straight.

The horse sighed, and Drago tensed and then relaxed as the horse made no further movement. Beneath him, the lizard was engaged in careful exploration, sniffing about the horse's fetlocks and hooves. It moved behind the horse, and sniffed at the yellowed tail that hung almost to the ground.

"No," Drago said, and fixed the lizard in the eye.

The lizard blinked, its crest rising rapidly three or four times, then it walked stiff-legged to the other side of the horse and pretended a great interest in a small stone.

Drago smiled, and turned his head slightly so he could speak to Faraday.

"Come closer. I do not think there is any danger."

"Are you sure?" But Faraday slipped her pack off and walked closer.

"I think this horse is so ancient," Drago said, "that his mind has wandered. He's as senile as a wine-soaked octogenarian."

Faraday had to think a moment before she understood. "Ah. The Demons' influence has just slid off his mind like sunshine off a mirror."

"Yes. I had wondered if he somehow shared our strange immunity . . . but maybe it *is* just his senility that has protected him." Drago had moved down the horse's side, running his hand down his ridged back, and then down his flank. "But there's something about this horse . . . something . . ."

His hand drifted lower down the horse's near hind leg, and Drago squatted to inspect it more closely.

"I am sure that I've seen this . . . *Oh Stars! Faraday!*"

Stunned by what she thought was utter panic in Drago's voice, Faraday grabbed him by the shoulders and pulled him back.

Drago toppled over in the dirt, but his eyes remained on the horse's hind leg . . . on the faint scar that ran down the horse's hock.

His father, Axis, shouting at the stable boy who had so

startled the stallion that he'd kicked down his stable door cutting his near hind badly.

Axis, holding the stallion's bridle to keep him still as the surgeon stitched the leg.

Long nights when the lamps had burned in the stable block as watch was kept on the fevered stallion.

The day, the final horrible day, when Axis had realized the horse's leg would be too weak for him to ever be ridden again.

Drago sat up and squatted back at the horse's leg, his fingers exploring the scar. "Faraday, I know this horse!"

Axis, tears running down his face, turning the stallion loose in the Urqhart Hills so he could live out the rest of his life in freedom.

The horse woke from his dream, opened his eyes, turned his head, and stared at Drago.

This was the boy who had fed him apples . . .

This was the boy who had spent so many nights asleep in his manger, escaping some horror within Sigholt's gray walls.

This was the boy who for months after the horse had been released into the hills, would come to seek him out to bring him apples, and make sure he was not too lonely.

Drago stood and faced the horse, now gazing at him with deep black intelligent eyes. This was no senile nag. This was . . . "Belaguez," Drago said in wonderment.

"Belaguez?" Faraday said. "But it *can't* be! Axis rode him when he was BattleAxe—"

"He must be fifty years old," Drago said, now rubbing Belaguez's ears. The old horse sighed in contentment, and butted Drago's chest with his head.

"No horse lives that old," Faraday said, her forehead creased in a frown as if cross that the horse had dared to contravene holy law.

Drago shot her an amused look. "And no woman lives, and dies, and wanders forests as a deer, and then lives again . . . does she?"

Faraday managed a small smile. "Perhaps some of Axis' enchantment seeped into the horse. What happened to him?"

"He was crippled in a stable accident," Drago said, indicating the scar, "when I was about eight. Axis decided he could no longer be ridden, so he turned him loose in the Urqhart Hills."

"He must have been wandering all these years," Faraday said, and now she, too, was stroking Belaguez's nose.

"We must take him with us," Drago said softly. "At the very least he'll be strong enough to help us ford the river."

At that announcement, the lizard—who had crept back behind the horse's haunches—launched itself into Belaguez's tail, and began to haul itself upward, claw over claw.

Belaguez snorted, and tossed his head, but otherwise made no objection as the lizard happily attained the summit of the horse's haunches and sat, surveying the view.

Faraday's eyes drifted between Drago and Belaguez. She finally crossed her arms and squared her shoulders.

"Well," she said, "as long as you're comfortable traveling with an ancient relic from your father's reign . . ."

Drago took his time in responding, and when he did, his eyes were merry with mischief. "Oh, I'm getting quite used to traveling with ancient relics from my father's reign."

28

Sunken Castles

Find this Sanctuary," Drago had told WingRidge and SpikeFeather, and so they had done their best.

But Sanctuary, whatever that might be, was proving difficult to locate.

WingRidge had set the entire Lake Guard to the task, six hundred birdmen and -women, haunting the waterways in small punts or walking the banks with smoking torches held aloft.

"I know *nothing*," SpikeFeather kept telling WingRidge, "of any place beneath here that might harbor so many hundreds of thousands of people."

"Then why," WingRidge invariably shot back to his companion, "did you spend so damned many years down here with the Ferryman, if not to learn these secrets?"

"I do not think even the Ferryman knew," SpikeFeather finally said stiffly one day as they stood in a cavern in the waterways halfway between the Lake of Life and Fernbrake Lake. "Apparently Orr was not privy to this secret, nor were any of his Charonite predecessors."

"He who seeks only finds what he wants to find," WingRidge said obscurely, and then placed his hands on his hips and looked about the cavern. There were several other members of the Lake Guard standing to one side, their ivory uniforms gleaming softly in the lamplight, the golden knots in the center of their chests sending bright sparks of light about the cavern.

"We have wandered these passages for weeks," WingRidge said, now studying the blank rock walls as if he might find inspiration there. "And nothing. In the meantime the Demons have retrieved what they needed from Cauldron Lake and must now be drawing close to the Lake of Life."

"There must be a clue *somewhere!*" SpikeFeather said. "Does the Maze Gate say anything?"

WingRidge shook his head, still studying the rock. He, as with most members of the Lake Guard at various times, had gone back to the Maze Gate under Grail Lake to study more carefully its inscriptions—but nothing. There were only the symbols depicting the rise of Qeteb and StarSon, the devastation of Tencendor, and the beginning of a final battle between Qeteb and the Crusader.

There had been a new symbol depicted among the script devoted to destruction, a lily, but WingRidge did not think the lilies related anything of Sanctuary.

The Maze Gate was mute when it came to sanctuaries.

"Then do you suppose Drago misheard?" SpikeFeather asked.

WingRidge finally turned back to the birdman. "No. He heard correctly enough, and we have been set to the task, and we are failing, dammit!"

"Captain?" One of the Lake Guardsmen had stepped forth.

"Yes, GapFeather?"

"Captain, there must be a clue somewhere. Something that stares us in the eye, and yet we remain blind."

"I thank you for that observation, GapFeather," WingRidge said, "but unless the blindfold has been suddenly removed from your eyes, I fail to see how this—"

"Captain, pardon my interruption, but here in these waterways we *are* blind. We can explore only a small portion of the whole. What we need to be able to do is see the whole."

"What do you mean?"

GapFeather glanced quickly at his companions for support. "We need to see a map of the waterways. That may well give us an indication of where to look. Even what to look for."

WingRidge nodded. "A good point. SpikeFeather?"

"What?"

"A *map*, SpikeFeather! Do you know of a map of the—"

SpikeFeather threw up his hands in disgust. "No. Gods, WingRidge, don't you think I would have thought of that first? I have never seen a map of the waterways. Orr never spoke of one, and—"

"Sigholt," WingRidge said quietly, his eyes still on Spike-Feather.

"Sigholt?"

"Sigholt. Sigholt is ancient, it is in itself almost a part of the waterways, as it is so closely tied to the Lake. And . . ."

"And?"

"And it has at its heart a map room."

SpikeFeather was still not convinced. "But I've never seen a map of the waterways there. And Axis, and then Caelum, who both used the room, have never mentioned one to me—and I'm sure they would have."

WingRidge stood silently, his fingers thumping gently against his hips, his wings held tense against his back.

"That room has ten thousand maps in it," he said softly. "There are even vaults under the floor with maps stuffed into cabinets. I would swear that no one has ever, *ever*, investigated them all."

Sigholt felt empty and spiritless without a member of the SunSoar family in residence. There were still many people who lived there, and thousands more in Lakesview a little further about the Lake, but the silvery-gray stones of the Keep seemed duller, as if in mourning.

All present were nervous, and WingRidge and Spike-

Feather had no doubts why. The Demons were on their way, and would be only days distant.

"Can we not do something to help the people here?" SpikeFeather said as they crossed the bridge into Sigholt's courtyard. "Once the Demons arrive . . ."

"Lakesview perhaps," WingRidge said, impatient to get to the map room.

"Too close," SpikeFeather said. They had entered the Keep and were now climbing the steps of the great staircase three at a time. He wished there was more overhead space so they could fly. "Perhaps the Urqhart Hills—"

"And perhaps Sanctuary, if we find a clue here," WingRidge said, flinging open the door of the map room.

They both came to a halt just inside, looking at the room as if for the first time. Completely circular, the room had windows opening on to all aspects of the Lake and its environs. Between the windows were deep map cases filled with maps both rolled up and laid flat. There was a brazier to one side, filled with wood, but currently unlit, and the very center of the room was occupied by a table and several chairs.

It looked purposeless without either Axis or Caelum here, pacing back and forth worrying out a problem.

"You said there were vaults?" SpikeFeather said quietly.

"Yes." WingRidge led the way into the room and then turned to speak quietly to the half dozen men and women of the Lake Guard who had accompanied them, setting them to searching through the map cases about the walls.

Once they were at work, WingRidge motioned Spike-Feather to the western window. Outside, the Lake ruffled gently, hedged about with its blue mists, but WingRidge ignored the view and squatted down by the floor.

"Few people know about the vaults," he said. He slid his finger into a cunningly hidden ring and lifted a trapdoor.

"How do you know about them?" SpikeFeather asked, craning his neck to look into the square of darkness.

"I found them," WingRidge said, and looked up, grinning. "At least Caelum and I did. I was about twenty, and Caelum ten. Axis and Azhure often set me to be Caelum's companion, to keep an eye on him. One day we were working at strengthening our hearts by running up and down the grand staircase, counting each step as we did, when Caelum realized that there were more steps between the floor the map room is on and the one below it than between any other level in Spiredore—and yet the chambers on each floor are no higher. We realized there must be a space below the floor of the map room. So, while Axis and Azhure were still out riding the hills, we investigated the floor of this room. I was the lucky one to find the hidden catch."

WingRidge's grin widened. "Caelum was disgusted that I'd found it and not he. Whatever, we set to investigating." He took a lamp that one of his Guard's handed him, and stepped down onto a narrow wooden ladder. "We thought to find treasures and secrets, but only found yet more maps."

He stepped swiftly down the ladder, his voice now muffled. "Who knows? Perhaps there *are* secrets and treasures down here yet."

SpikeFeather also took the lamp proffered him, and climbed down after WingRidge. He found himself in a room the same size as the map room above, but without any of the windows, and with a low ceiling only a hand span above his head.

Chests, bookcases and crates crammed floor and wall spaces, and there was barely room enough to move between them.

"Where are we going to start?" SpikeFeather whispered.

"You take that side, I this one," WingRidge said, and bent down to the box he'd just opened.

Sighing, SpikeFeather set to his task.

They searched for hours. All through that day, through the night, and into the next morning. As soon as the search of the map room itself had proved useless, the members of the Lake Guard went below to help WingRidge and SpikeFeather.

The space became awash with curses, bruised wings, and ancient dust as elbows jostled and feet tripped over upended cases and piles of discarded maps.

There were maps of the road systems of Tencendor, maps of the ancient castles that had once dotted the countryside, maps of cattle trails, starling nesting sites and the pattern of gem mines in Ichtar. There were maps of population densities in a Tencendor of two thousand years ago, maps showing the location of lace factories; and maps of the shadows the stars threw over the land during full moon. There were even maps of the gloam mines in far away Escator.

But no maps of the waterways, and no maps with thick, black arrows helpfully pointing to "Sanctuary."

Finally, toward noon, they crawled out of the space into the map room, brushing dust off their clothes and wings and out of their hair.

SpikeFeather sneezed and, tired out, sank down into one of the chairs at the table. He pushed a pile of maps to one side to make room for his elbow and leaned his head in his hand.

"Nothing," he said, his voice emotionless.

WingRidge took the chair next to him. "Perhaps we will think of something after we have slept," he said.

"Perhaps," SpikeFeather replied.

For a while both birdmen sat in silence, too tired to speak, too tired to contemplate the implications of their failure. The members of the Lake Guard who had helped them had either left, or had sunk down to sit against walls, their eyes closed, their skin ashen with exhaustion.

SpikeFeather finally stirred. "At the very least we should think about what to do to protect the people here against the Demons."

WingRidge grimaced. "Yes. I suppose you're right. I'll set the guard to shifting them into the Urqhart Hills . . . perhaps the mines will shelter them until the Demons have gone."

"How are you going to tell Drago you couldn't find Sanctuary?"

WingRidge laughed humorlessly. "What do you mean, how am *I* going to tell Drago?"

He sighed and sat up straight, shuffling maps haphazardly across the table. There were several that they'd brought up from the vaults to study.

"Look at this ancient network of castles around Tencendor," he said idly. "It is a shame most of these are no longer here. They might have proved useful."

SpikeFeather rested his eyes on the map. He was too tired to think. Maybe WingRidge was right. Maybe they *would* think of something after they'd slept a few hours.

Then his whole body jerked. "WingRidge!"

"What?"

SpikeFeather's eyes were fixed on the map of the ancient castle systems in front of them. "Gods, WingRidge—why didn't we see that!"

"What?"

About the room, birdmen and -women were stirring from their lethargy, their eyes brightening.

"Look!" SpikeFeather jabbed his finger at Fernbrake Lake. "What do you see?"

WingRidge shrugged. "There's a castle on its edges. Gone now. Like three dozen more such castles that have disappeared from the ancient landscape."

"No, no! It's not a 'castle' . . . it's a Keep."

WingRidge raised his eyes and stared into SpikeFeather's face. "What are you trying to say?"

SpikeFeather made a gesture of irritation. "Every one of the other three Lakes have Keeps associated with them. Highly magical Keeps."

"Yes . . ."

"But not Fernbrake Lake. Why not?"

WingRidge shrugged again. "I don't know. Maybe there was no need—"

"Yes, there *was* a need. *Every one of the Lakes is supposed to have a Keep!* But Fernbrake's has gone."

"So where is it?"

SpikeFeather hesitated, trying to think it through, trying to find out what was wrong with his idea. But there was nothing. It was perfect.

"It's sunk," he said.

WingRidge stared at him, then quickly glanced at the others present before he looked back at SpikeFeather. *"Sunk?"*

SpikeFeather nodded. "Sunk." His finger tapped the map. "The waterways under Fernbrake Lake hold the Sanctuary, my friend, and the lost castle is the key. Perhaps even *is* Sanctuary. Now all we have to do is find it."

WingRidge leaned forward and laid his hand gently on SpikeFeather's arm. "Are you *sure* your weariness has not addled your wits, my friend?"

29

The Mountain Trails

Still in shock, Azhure helped Caelum and Axis to rise. She was trembling badly, and as she gripped both men's hands, she realized they were, too.

Azhure opened her mouth to ask if they were all right, but thought better of it. She contented herself with patting Caelum's chest as if to reassure herself it was still whole, and took Axis' hands and kissed his palms.

Then she looked around. Azhure's first impression that all the blood had gone was wrong. They were surrounded by it. The bodies of their horses, and of the captain and the men of the escort, were strewn about the floor of the tunnel, splintered bones poking through ragged flesh.

Their swords lay to one side, blades gleaming spotlessly.

She raised her eyes and looked at Axis, and he stepped forward and took her hand.

"Come," he said. "We will walk the remainder of the way."

They picked up their swords and walked forward in silence. Azhure battled back tears. Never had she been as helpless in her entire life as she had been in the past hour. Her son and husband apparently torn to pieces before her eyes, their escort slaughtered, laughed at by beings that but a few months ago would have barely dared to threaten her shadow.

Even Azhure the Plow-keeper's daughter would have done more against them than she had, she berated herself. But no, Azhure the once-god could not even find the words to fling in their defense.

For his part, Axis was thinking much the same. Could he not have done more? Gods! Even a junior Ax-Wielder could have helped more than he'd managed!

They approached a gentle curve in the tunnel. Once around it, the three saw that the tunnel apparently stretched into infinity.

There was no sign of the Alaunt.

"I sincerely hope this *does* lead to Star Finger," Axis muttered, then straightened his shoulders and looked at Caelum, marching silent and tight-faced by his side.

"Caelum, that black rider . . . is he the one who has hunted you through your dreams?"

"Yes. The dreams started soon after Drago fled from Sigholt with the Rainbow Scepter. They have rarely left me since."

"*Cursed* be the day I conceived my second son!"

Azhure frowned, remembering what StarLaughter had said. "Axis . . . are you sure that rider is Drago—"

"He has *always* hunted me!" Caelum cried, halting and swinging to face his mother. "Who else?"

Azhure glanced at Axis—his face was as stubbornly set as Caelum's—and then took Caelum's hands in hers.

"Caelum, might it not be StarLaughter's son, *her* Dragon-Star, that hunts you through your dreams?"

All she received by way of reply was a hostile stare.

Azhure took a deep breath and tried again. "Caelum, Axis. StarLaughter was angry that Caelum is heir to the Throne of the Stars and all that it implies. She said that her son should be the heir. *She* had the legitimate son. That black rider, that DragonStar, rode out of the stars, as her son would—"

"No," Caelum said, pulling his hands from Azhure's. "Did you not see his face? That was the face of *Drago*, not some long-dead unborn child!"

Again Azhure glanced at Axis, but she could see she wouldn't get any help from him.

"Caelum," she said, "both would look very similar. Drago takes after WolfStar in coloring and features, and naturally StarLaughter's son would, too. After all, they are virtually brothers—"

Caelum shifted impatiently, angrily. "*Drago* is my enemy, Mother, perhaps more so than any of these Demons. It is the dagger from behind that always strikes home first. And did you not hear StarLaughter? Drago has passed across to her every secret of our family, as he has undoubtedly passed across the Scepter. The Demons *must* have it, and I think they will use it to destroy us completely—"

"Caelum," Axis said. "Enough. We need to talk about this

in calmer surroundings than this gray tunnel. Star Finger is all we have left, and I would prefer that we expend our energies on walking there instead of arguing among ourselves."

Star Finger is all we have left? Caelum wondered. But Star Finger stores only Icarii knowledge and magic, and Icarii knowledge and magic has as much hope of defeating these Demons as a feather does of surviving a tempest. Is it time to give up? Is it time to say, "enough"? Surely we have done what we can. What more can one do against the treachery of a brother?

They walked in silence, time out of mind, the overhead lights clicking softly on as they approached, then turning themselves out some minutes after they'd passed.

They walked in an isolated island of light and time and desperate bravado.

They eventually walked about a long sloping curve of the tunnel to come face to face with the pack of Alaunt sitting facing them.

Every one of the hounds, Sicarius included, had shame-faced expressions.

Azhure stared at them. Could she blame them for fleeing before the dark cloud of murdered children?

She sighed, rested her hand briefly on top of Sicarius' head, then walked past. Axis and Caelum followed her, and the hounds fell into step behind the three.

They emerged, eventually, in the Avarinheim forest beneath the first of the Icescarp Alps.

"Stars!" Axis said, as they stood in the dawn air, looking at the trees and the rising cliffs. "How did we come so far, so fast?"

Azhure shrugged. "The tunnels still contain some enchantment, perhaps."

Caelum paid no heed to his parents, instead inspecting the faint path that led through the last of the trees to the rising cliffs. On the several occasions he'd been to Star Finger, Caelum had always used the Song of Movement to transport himself, but now he and his parents would be forced to use the treacherous cliff paths that Rivkah had once traversed.

"We should get moving," he said. "The paths will only be traversable during daylight hours."

He stepped forward, but Azhure grabbed at his arm, looking anxiously between her son and Axis.

"And the Demons?" she said. "And the hours when they roam? How will we protect ourselves once we are past the safety of the trees?"

"There are caves along the trails, Azhure. You must remember those, surely."

She stared at Axis, recalling their own journey so many years ago down the mountain trails in order to join the Avar for Beltide. At night they had sheltered within the many caves that ate into the mountainsides, singing and telling stories, and falling deeper and deeper in love.

She nodded slowly. "They will be all the protection we'll have."

Caelum scanned the skies. "We must watch for those children, too."

Axis shifted irritably. They were frighteningly vulnerable. Their escort, equipment, horses and food had all gone. They had their swords, true, but swords would not be very useful against any attack that plummeted from the sky, nor would they feed them at night. The mountain trails were notoriously barren of food.

Axis looked about them, wondering if any of the Avar were close, but the forest was silent and still, and they could not waste the time to search a Clan out.

"Caelum's right," Axis said. "We should get moving, and deal with any threat as it arises. Azhure, send the hounds ranging ahead. If nothing else, they should spring any trap before it closes about us."

She nodded, and ordered the Alaunt down the path before them. Azhure half-expected them to disobey, but they sprang to their feet and loped out of sight down the path the instant she'd finished speaking.

Caelum watched them go. "I do not trust them," he said.

Azhure opened her mouth to defend them, then thought better of it. "It is hard to know who or what to trust now," she eventually said.

Caelum hugged her. "I trust you, and Father," he said, and lifted his eyes and smiled at Axis.

For some reason, whether it was the open air or Caelum's smile, Axis felt more optimistic and light-hearted than he had in days.

"Come," he said. "The mountains await."

The path wound through a final hundred paces of forest before it rose steeply into a curve about the skirts of the first mountain.

All three of them were puffing within minutes.

"How long did it take Rivkah to climb these paths?" Caelum asked after an hour or so of climbing.

Axis tried to remember what his mother had told him of her experiences. "Many, many days," he said. "A week or more."

"A week!" Caelum said, and looked at his mother ruefully. "Or more."

"Perhaps the Alaunt can forage for rabbits, or small birds," Azhure said. "Damn! I wish I had my bow with me."

"We can set traps, Azhure," Axis said, and then conversation lapsed as they fought for breath.

The climb was almost impossibly steep, and the footing treacherous. The trail wound up, up, up through black-rocked ravines and gorges, following the paths carved out by mountain streams and waterfalls. They remained almost entirely in the shade of the cliffs, for the mountains were high and steep and the gorges narrow. The sun also rarely penetrated the mist from streams and waterfalls.

Far above, black specks circled, sharing their vision with the Demons and StarLaughter who were approaching the Nordra as it ran below the Urqhart Hills.

May we attack? the Hawkchilds asked.

The Demons considered. *You may have your fun*, they finally decided, *but do not tip them from the mountain trails, for we need them for the final hunt.*

The Hawkchilds circled lower.

Caelum and his parents rested at midmorning and then midafternoon under the shelter of overhangs and tumbled rocks.

They felt the corruption of tempest and despair sweep up through the gorges to break against the mountain ridges, but were heartened by the relative weakness of the Demons' influence within the Alps.

"Maybe it is the rarefied air," Caelum said, fighting his urge to pant.

"Or perhaps merely the distance," Azhure said.

"Or maybe," Axis said slowly, turning to look at his wife and son, "they do not like the mountains. Who knows? But if their influence is weaker here, then what will it be like at Star Finger?"

As despair died after the midafternoon, they struggled from under their sheltering overhang and prepared to climb for another few hours until they came to a suitable cave where they could shelter for the night.

They had been on the trail barely an hour when the Hawkchilds decided to play with them.

The Hawkchilds had descended deep into the gorge behind the three, so they could launch an attack from behind. The first Axis, Azhure and Caelum knew of it was when they'd swung about at a horrible whooshing noise from behind, only to realize that nine or ten Hawkchilds were rushing up the trail toward them, running on clawed feet, their wings outstretched for balance, hands grasping, beaks whispering.

The Alaunt, further up the trail than Axis, Azhure and Caelum, turned and snarled, then cringed, apparently unsure of what to do against the threat. Azhure shot them a look that was both sympathetic and damning, then joined her husband and son in drawing her sword, prepared to kill as many of the creatures as she could before she was killed in her turn.

But the Hawkchilds did not come close enough for the sword thrust. When they were five or six paces away from the group, they rose up on wings, and passed overhead barely a sword's length above the three.

There was a rush of a foul wind, and a whisper on the air. *DragonStar comes, Caelum. Do you hear the thunder of horses' hooves on the path behind you? Do you feel his heat?*

Caelum cried out, swinging wildly around to look down the path, and Axis had to grab his arm to prevent him falling over the edge of the cliff.

"They only taunt you," Axis hissed. "No one comes!"

Wrong, StarMan, the Hawkchilds whispered as another cloud of them spun over their heads. *He comes. Can you not hear him, Caelum?*

"I will kill him," Caelum shouted.

They howled with merriment, and a cloud some twenty strong blocked out the sun.

Relinquish the Throne of the Stars and he may allow you your life!

"Ignore them," Azhure said softly, placing a hand on Caelum's arm. "They seek only to distract you."

Caelum hesitated, then nodded.

"They do not attack," Axis said. "They fear you."

Caelum's back straightened. "Yes. I——"

The Hawkchilds howled with laughter. *Fear you? Nay, we merely keep you warm so that the true heir can baptize his accession in blood!*

"Walk," Azhure said, and turned back to the trail rising before them. "Walk, and ignore them."

They did their best, but the Hawkchilds hovered close for the remainder of the afternoon, alternately creeping along the path behind them, or swooping low overhead, whispering, whispering, whispering.

The Alaunt crept just in front of their two-legged companions, their tails between their legs, their bellies close to the ground, as useless as sheep before a cavalry charge.

When finally Azhure spotted the gloomy entrance to a small cave off the main trail, all of them, two-legged and four, stumbled inside as quickly as they could, grateful for the shelter and quiet the cave provided.

"Damn it!" Caelum said as he sank down, resting his back against the rough rock wall of the cave. "Why *don't* they attack? Why not try to kill me?"

"They fear you——" Azhure began, but Caelum shook his head.

"No," he said quietly into the darkness. "They merely toy with me."

He was being blooded for the hunt.

30

Home Safe

Askam's mind was a tangle of black feathers, razored talons and the bright, bright eyes of the brown and cream badger.

He had no thoughts of his own. He listened only to the rustle of feather and the commands of the badger, and was content in the febrile embrace of madness.

He sat his horse— its mind equally as feathered and mad— before his four hundred mounted men, all insane and under the control of the badger.

They waited.

Zared pulled his horse up as Herme waved the column to a halt. "Askam?" he said softly.

Herme reined in beside him. "No other. And his four hundred."

Zared didn't know what to think. In the days since Askam had disappeared they'd continued their push for Carlon, now only a day or two away. Zared had not wasted effort trying to track Askam down. He'd believed that Askam had finally succumbed to resentment and had fled to fulfill his own purpose, which no doubt included some plan to wrest control of the West back from Zared.

Well, let him try. Zared had no time to deal with Askam's desertion and what it might mean for his own security on the throne of Achar. Gods! Did Achar still exist? Or Tencendor? So, Zared had let Askam go with barely more than a shrug of his shoulders. Leagh had been upset by Askam's disappearance, but had not insisted that Zared mount a search for him. Her brother was old enough to know his own mind.

Now Gustus and Theod joined Zared, Leagh not far behind them.

"Askam!" she said, and would have urged her horse forward, save that Zared snatched at her reins.

"No. Wait," he said. "I do not like this. What if—"

"No!" Leagh cried. "He knew how to protect himself."

"Askam may be a fool personified when it comes to running the West," Herme said, "but he would not risk himself, or the men with him, to the ravages of the Demons."

Zared stared before him. Some fifteen paces ahead, Askam sat his horse in front of the neatly ranked four hundred men and horses, the only movement the lifting of manes and tails in the frigid northerly wind.

"I will ride ahead," Herme said, and Zared nodded.

"Be careful."

Askam made no move, and his face remained set into its carefully neutral expression as Herme rode forward.

As the Earl reined to a stop before him, Askam inclined his head in greeting. "No doubt you wonder what I have been doing," he said.

"No doubt," Herme said, his tenseness communicating itself to his horse, which shifted and fidgeted nervously.

"The attack of the crazed beasts—and worse—came as a shock," Askam said. "I understood how vulnerable our—Zared's—force was to them. I decided that I might assist in some small way by breaking off with a smaller force and scouting the way ahead—springing any trap that might exist."

"So you absconded in the middle of the *night?*" Herme asked, and in response to the touch of his legs his horse backed away several steps.

Askam grinned as if embarrassed. "Foolish, I know, but I also knew that so long as we kept the shade above our heads we would be safe. Herme, *have* you been attacked in the days since we've been gone?"

"No," Herme said.

"Well, then," Askam said. "I may be guilty of absconding, but mayhap I have done some good!"

Herme stared at him, trying to see beyond Askam's bland eyes. "So you and your four hundred safely dealt with what almost brought Zared's thirty thousand to their knees?"

"A smaller force is more maneuverable," Askam said, "and I must add that we met only much smaller groups of the crazed creatures. But, as I said, mayhap even that did Zared some good. Look, Herme, are you going to sit there screwing your face into lines and studying me all day? Midafternoon approaches. I and the hundreds behind me are hungry—we forgot to make off with any of the supply mules—and, for the gods' sakes, do we *look* as if the Demons have us under their sway?"

Herme gave in to the irritation in Askam's voice. Whatever else Askam might be lying about—and frankly, Herme thought this tale of trying to spring any traps to make Zared's life easier was a fabrication to hide Askam's own ambitions—he surely did not look crazed.

"Then join up with the main force," Herme said, "and answer for your foolishness to Zared himself."

He wheeled his horse about, and cantered back to his King.

Zared sighed and rubbed his tired eyes. Gods, but he would appreciate being back under the shelter of his palace in Carlon and not have to stop three times a day to shelter under these shade cloths.

"Did you happen to come across any hamlets or farmhouses in your, ah, sweep ahead, Askam?" he said, raising his eyes again. He sat with Leagh and his subcommanders under the shade cloths, Askam sitting cross-legged before him, waiting out Sheol's midafternoon despair.

Askam shrugged slightly. "A home or two, the peasants sheltered inside. They stared at us as we passed, their faces pressed to glass and their fingers locked into the catches of shutters."

Zared shook his head. "I hope Carlon has managed to fare better than what we've seen so far. Ah! What kind of life is this, hiding from the hour of the day itself."

"And what will happen when they have eaten their way through their winter stocks?" Leagh said softly. "Few will be able to forage for food, or hunt for meat—and what food does still linger about on four hooves must truly be contaminated beyond belief by the Demons."

There was silence for a while as all contemplated Leagh's words. Askam, apparently still chastened by Zared's earlier sharp-tongued words on his desertion, dropped his eyes and studied his fingers.

"Dare we eat madness?" Theod eventually said.

"Enough of these thoughts," Zared said, his voice stronger. "By noon tomorrow we will be in Carlon. Enough shelter to give us time to consolidate, and perhaps plan a means to strike back."

"How?" Askam said. He raised his head, and all who looked at him put the peculiar blankness of his eyes down to hopelessness.

Zared hesitated before he found a reply. "There *must* be a way. And if we can't find it, then we must trust Drago to find it for us."

Askam's entire body jerked, and the others looked at him curiously. *Drago!* The name thundered through his mind, rippling out first to the badger, and then to the minds of the Hawkchilds hovering far, far overhead.

Drago. Drago? He lives?

And from there . . .

The great black horses responded instantly to the command of their riders, and slowed to a halt, flexing their claws into the earth to anchor themselves against whatever might strike.

"Drago lives," Rox said, gazing first at his fellow Demons, and then to StarLaughter, cradling her son. They had all shared the Hawkchilds' thoughts.

"But I thought you killed him," StarLaughter said. "What can this mean?"

Sheol furrowed her forehead, angered that Drago *had* managed to survive the final leap through the Star Gate. But how? They had used all of his enchantment and power and life to accomplish that final leap, she was certain of it. How?

"What enchantment was used to save him?" she asked softly. "What is it that we don't know?"

"There was something we felt in the chamber of the Star Gate," Barzula said, and they fell quiet remembering the slight, but odd power they'd felt floating about the chamber as they'd come through.

Directional power, Sheol had said of it then . . . but what if it was more than that?

"It was enough to re-create Drago," Sheol said. Her voice was expressionless.

"The magicians you saw to the west?" Barzula asked Rox.

"The man was too . . . too vague for me to pick out his features. The woman I did not know."

"I do not like this!" Raspu cried. "How did he survive? *How?*"

"For Stars' sakes!" StarLaughter said. "Drago is worse than useless. He had no power left . . . *nothing.* His Icarii potential was burned completely away. If he *did* survive, then I imagine he is crawling about the landscape seeking some crevice in which to grovel. *Drago?* We have all seen how pathetic and useless he is. Why worry about him?"

"Perhaps you are right," Sheol said. "He is a nothing. An inconsequent."

She smiled at StarLaughter, and as she smiled she shared private thoughts with her Demon companions.

Nevertheless, we shall set the Hawkchilds to him. He knows us, and even that knowledge could be dangerous. I would feel better with him dead.

Aye. Kill him.

Yes. Kill him soon.

Moreover, why should StarLaughter speak on his behalf? Did they exchange more than fluids in that bed they shared? Allegiances, perhaps?

Shall we kill her?

Not yet. Not yet.

The Demons sat their horses and smiled at StarLaughter, and she smiled back, and hugged her child to her breast. All was well.

Leagh pressed closer to Zared, listening to the night roil outside their shelter. But it did not terrify her, for here she lay safe in her husband's arms, and if Tencendor lay ravaged, then surely it would only be a matter of time before Zared, or Drago, or even Caelum and his parents, found the solution to the TimeKeepers.

"You must be happy that Askam is back," Zared murmured into her hair.

"Relieved," she whispered. "I had thought . . ."

Zared did not answer with words, but tightened his arms about her, wishing his love was enough to keep her safe. He knew what she'd thought, for he had thought the same. But whatever motives had driven Askam out into the night, he was safe back now, and if that made Leagh happy then Zared supposed he should be happy for her sake.

But he could not quite rid himself of his own self-serving wish that Askam had died out there in the terror-swept Plains of Tare.

"Tomorrow you will be home," he murmured, then tilted her face to kiss her. He had his own reasons for wanting the privacy of their own bedchamber again.

In the shadows the two indistinct white shapes of the donkeys shifted. They were disturbed and uncertain, and they were not quite sure why. They did not trust the blandness of Askam's eyes, nor the similar blandness in the eyes of the men and horses he'd led back to Zared's camp.

"Carlon!" a joyful voice rang out from the ranks behind him, and Zared grinned, as relieved and as happy as his command.

"Carlon," he said, and let his eyes roam over the rising pink walls before them.

Then he quickly checked the sun. Noon. They had two hours to ford the Nordra at the crossing north of Grail Lake and get inside. Not long enough. Perhaps a third of his force—and, of course, the Strike Force who could happily wing the distance—could get inside the city gates by midafternoon.

Zared sighed, and turned about to issue orders to Gustus and his other captains. Most would camp on the eastern banks of the Nordra, but perhaps ten or eleven thousand could safely make the dash for the city before despair closed in.

"Leagh," Zared said as Gustus spurred his horse away, "do you mind?"

"No," she smiled, and reached out for his hand. "We will wait for the afternoon. A few hours will do us no harm."

Several ranks behind them, Askam smiled.

Zared sent the Strike Force ahead, then gave the order for seven thousand, including those still wounded, to make the push across the ford and then into Carlon. As the remainder of his force busied themselves erecting the shade cloths for what they hoped would be the last time, Zared stood on the banks of the river, Leagh beside him.

"It looks so beautiful," she said, and leaned against her husband.

Zared nodded. "See? People wave from the walls."

Perhaps several score of the Carlonese had lined the walls, waving banners and faint smudges of hands. They were too far away for their voices and cheers to reach Zared's and Leagh's ears, but they could hear them in their hearts.

As the first of the men from Zared's force crossed the river and spurred toward the city, the gates swung open.

"Safe," Zared said again. "I have brought you home safe."

The midafternoon hour seemed to drag forever. All who yet waited on the eastern banks of the Nordra shifted impatiently; horses loaded with gear were ready to be urged across the river and into Carlon the moment despair had evaporated.

From a small gap in the pink walls a patchy-bald rat stared across the distance to the waiting army.

More two-legs. Well, all the more to sate his hunger. The patchy-bald rat couldn't wait for the badger to get here. Couldn't *wait* for the feast to begin.

A thin drool of saliva ran out from between its yellowed fangs and trickled down to its claws. In the blink of an eye, the rat scampered down a drain set into the walls.

Down to the sewers under the city.

Zared hoped the three hours between midafternoon and dusk would be enough to get everyone safe within the walls. He did not fancy spending another night in the open when shelter sat so close.

A few paces away from Zared and Leagh, the white donkeys dozed, their heads nodding with the weight of their thoughts.

The instant it was safe, men leaped to the poles and shade cloths, pulling them down haphazardly and parceling them up into rough bundles.

There would be no need to use them that night.

Zared mounted his horse. "Gustus, will you watch Leagh? I need to be—"

"I will watch her," Askam broke in. "You need Gustus with you, and I will be sure to bring Leagh safely home."

Zared hesitated, but Leagh smiled and took her brother's arm. "I will be safe enough with Askam, Zared."

Zared looked from one to the other, and then nodded. He *did* need Gustus at something other than nursemaid duty, and watching Leagh would keep Askam out of mischief.

"Then watch her as if your soul depended on it," Zared said, and Askam inclined his head.

"As if my soul depended on it," he agreed, then took Leagh's hand and led her toward her horse.

For the next two hours Zared's full attention was given to the mechanics and logistics of getting tens of thousands of men and horses and mules across the ford and then into Carlon without clogging river, road or streets.

Rank after rank of men urged horses and supply mules into the muddied waters, and then up the far bank and onto the road for Carlon. The muscles of man and beast alike, still frozen from the icy waters of the river, shuddered with the effort of pulling body weight and supply bundles up the western bank and then through the increasingly trampled road surface. Dust rose in a cloud along the road to Carlon, men and beasts obscured by the murkiness thrown up by the host of hastening hooves and feet.

"Leagh?" Zared shouted as he saw Askam leading a column of men and horses down into the Nordra.

She waved as Askam nodded. A faint cry reached Zared's ears, but he could not distinguish words, and within the instant both Leagh's and Askam's horses had plunged into the Nordra. Zared felt sick, remembering the near tragedy of the Azle crossing, but the Nordra was shallower and less angry than that river had been, and Leagh's mare retained her footing easily.

"She will be safe," Herme murmured at Zared's side, and Zared nodded unhappily.

"I will not relax until she, as all my command, rests safely under Carlon's eaves," he said, and checked the horizon. Already the sun was sinking low into the clouds of dust—now even Carlon was obscured—and they had perhaps an hour left before they must all be safely sheltered.

Herme noticed the direction of Zared's eyes, and he checked the remaining units on their side of the Nordra.

"Perhaps eight hundred men left," he said. "Sire, you must think about leaving yourself."

"Not until the last of the men is on his way," Zared replied, then he grinned. "Look! The donkeys guard our rear."

Indeed, it seemed as if that was what the donkeys did. They had positioned themselves at the very rear of the final column, but facing eastward, as if they feared an attack from the rear.

Zared's grin faded. "What are they?" he whispered.

"Our friends," Herme responded quietly, "and that is all we need to know."

Within twenty minutes the last column had braved the ford, and Zared, Herme and Gustus—Theod having gone on earlier—pushed their horses into the water.

Behind them, the two donkeys plunged in as well.

Within a heartbeat Zared felt the icy water creep up to his thighs, and felt his horse falter as the current caught. But it found its footing surely enough, and pushed forward, and within minutes Zared felt the water cascade away from their bodies as the horse leaned into the slope of the western bank.

"Home!" Zared shouted joyfully, and dug his heels into his horse's flanks. It needed no encouragement.

The final few hundred men, Zared, Herme, Gustus and the two donkeys at their rear, galloped for the city, racing to reach its gates before the sun sank below the horizon.

"Home!" Zared screamed, and the cry was taken up about and before him.

"*Home! Home! Home!*" men screamed, and then the shadow of the walls embraced them, and Zared heard the gates groan and then thunder closed behind the donkeys.

"Home safe," he cried, and waved at the cheering crowd overjoyed to have him home. "Home safe."

* * *

"Theod!" Zared clapped the man on the shoulder, still suffused with the joy of bringing virtually his entire command safe into Carlon's shelter and not noticing the man's frown. "Theod. Did Leagh go straight to the palace?"

"Zared," Theod stumbled. "I thought she and Askam were riding with you."

A coldness such as he'd never known before crept through Zared's entire existence. "*Where is Leagh?*"

"I thought she was with you!" Theod repeated in a whisper, his face white.

Zared stared at him a moment longer, then spun for the gates. "Leagh!"

"No!" Theod screamed, and grabbed at Zared's arm. "Night falls. See?"

Zared paid him no heed.

"*Leagh,*" he screamed, and it took five men to drag him away from the exposed air of the street and into a nearby shop as twilight fell over the city.

"*Leagh!*"

"Why, why, why?" she cried, twisting in the one-armed grip of a brother she no longer knew.

As they had ridden for the city, and under cover of the dust haze, Askam had seized the reins of her horse and, surrounded by the men he'd led back from the wilderness, had kicked their horses into the shelterless fields north of Carlon.

Now they milled about as dusk swept in from the east, the safety of the city a useless half-league to the south.

"Why?" she cried, too confused to be scared. Yet.

Askam let his madness reveal itself in his smile, and though it was his voice that answered, he spoke with the words of the brown and cream badger.

"Welcome to the new Tencendor, my dear. I am sure you will be a useful addition to our company."

Leagh opened her mouth to say something, but just then the corruption of dusk swept over them, and a thin whimper was all that issued from her mouth.

Pestilence raged, bubbling through the minds and souls of all those exposed.

For one horrible brief moment of sanity, Leagh understood her fate, and understood that she had been betrayed by her brother.

One hand clutched uselessly at the air, and she opened her mouth for one final, despairing shriek.

But no sound came forth. Madness ravaged her mind and tore her soul to pieces, and Leagh stared blindly into insanity.

Then, quietly, she began to babble, her fingers itching madly at her belly.

31

The Fun of the Blooding

For several days Caelum and his parents climbed ever higher into the Ice-scarp Alps. The climb was hard, the cold wretched, and the lack of food debilitating—what game may have once existed on the sides of the mountains had apparently disappeared—yet all these discomforts paled into insignificance when compared to the constant sweeping shadow of the Hawkchilds far above them.

The three tried to ignore them as they climbed, but it was hard to drive the shadow and the intermittent whispering and hissing laughter from their minds.

They spent each night huddled in frigid caves or under drafty overhangs, clinging close to each other and the hounds for warmth.

On the fourth night, they had found a slightly more substantial cave. It had been formed from a fault in the rock, and stretched some twelve paces back into the cliff face, and was at least five paces wide and five high. There was room enough for all to curl up at the rear of the cave, a mass of arms and legs and furred bodies, out of the draft that eddied in from the narrow mouth.

No one had spent much time on conversation after they'd stumbled in and checked the cave for any dangers that might be lurking there. Axis had just nodded tiredly once he was certain the cave was as safe a shelter as they'd find that night, and had then sunk down to the dirt, pushing aside some of the cave rubble to make himself a reasonably flat space in which to sleep. Azhure and Caelum lay down on either side of him, and then the hounds snuffled and scratched and turned about in ever-tighter circles, finally dropping down as close to the three as they could.

It was as much comfort and warmth as any could expect.

Once settled, no one spoke. All were too hungry and cold and tired to be able to conjure anything vaguely cheerful in the way of words, and there was no use speaking the pessimism that gripped all their minds.

Outside the darkness deepened, and the cave lost all form in the gathering night.

Axis wondered where the Hawkchilds spent the nights. Did they cling to the rock face outside the cave entrance, like gigantic bats protecting their nest? Or did they spend the entire night spiraling ever higher in the joy of their masters' expanding destruction? Waiting for the morning, and for the pale faces and forms of their prey to peek out from the cave, and emerge to creep ever higher into the mountains?

When would they attack? Axis did not think it would be very long, for he, Azhure and Caelum were growing weaker, and soon would not be able to defend themselves from an irate millipede, let alone the Hawkchilds' spiteful wrath. He sighed, irritated with himself. None of them could afford to even contemplate defeat. And yet, did he have the strength to go on fighting? How much *would* Tencendor demand of him?

Azhure leaned in tight under Axis' arm, wishing she could give him more comfort. She remembered how he'd once provided them with magical fires to warm them the last time they'd traversed these mountain paths. She lifted her head slightly, and glanced into Axis' eyes, and wondered if he, too, remembered.

Stars! How she wished she could enjoy her power again, if only so she could revel in the intimacy of sharing Axis' every thought.

Azhure dropped her gaze and clung as tightly to her husband as she could. Behind her Sicarius and his mate, Fort-Heart, pressed their warm backs against hers. Azhure briefly scratched Sicarius' head, then relaxed, and slipped into a dreamless sleep. A few minutes later Axis, too, slipped into sleep.

Caelum, already deep in sleep on Axis' other side, was not so fortunate. Again and again that night DragonStar hunted him through forest and plain. But in the fifth visitation, the dream hunt took on a different aspect.

Caelum found himself running through a maze, trapped by walls that rose three paces above his head and stopped his headlong flight again and again with their frightful blank dead ends. Behind him echoed the sounds of the hunt. Again and again Caelum found himself having to retrace his steps, certain each time that he would retreat directly into the jaws of the hunt, trying to find an escape from the twisting, confusing paths.

Every time, just as he was sure he'd found a straight run, it would curve into yet another cul-de-sac. And every time he ran into the blank, mocking wall, he thought he heard the faint sounds of laughter behind him.

The sound of the hunt closed. Caelum could feel, if not yet see, DragonStar urging his great black horse forward, could feel it as his brother raised his arm and steadied the sword.

Could hear his breath come quick with excitement and the lust of the hunt, could *feel* its fevered warmth at his back.

Caelum's entire body tightened as he dreamed, and Axis murmured in his own sleep, as yet not disturbed enough to wake.

One of the hounds whimpered, and curled into a tighter ball.

Suddenly Caelum stopped, leaning heavily on a wall with one hand, his breath heaving in and out of his throat. What was he doing? Why was he running? DragonStar would eventually find him, whatever Caelum did to try and evade him, and it was surely better to turn and face him with what courage he had left than continue to waste his energy on flight.

For the first time, for the very first time since this horror had started months ago, all fear left Caelum.

Its sudden absence left him feeling exhilarated. Why hadn't he done this before? Embraced his fate, instead of running from it?

He straightened, and his breathing steadied. He dropped his hand from the wall, and turned to face the way he'd come.

The sound of the hunt pounded closer. Now that his own breathing was calmer, Caelum heard the labored breath of the closing horses.

He felt the pavement tremble under his feet.

Caelum carried no weapon—either the dream or fate would not allow it—and so he just stood, the tension of months of uselessness draining from his muscles, and waited.

A quiet joy filled him.

There was a howl from the way he'd just come, and then the dark shadow of the Hawkchilds as they swept low overhead.

Trapped! He's trapped!

And just standing, resigned, the weak fool!

"Resigned?"

The voice filtered about the turn of the Maze before Caelum.

"Resigned?"

And for the first time Caelum heard a measure of uncertainty in the voice. It was a dream of many firsts, he decided, and smiled.

And then a third time—

"Resigned?"

A long shadow moved on the pavement before him. Again it moved, and then again, and then DragonStar rode his horrid beast about the corner . . . at an extremely careful and controlled walk.

Whatever the black beast had once started out as, it no longer resembled a horse. It had four stout legs, with four rippling talon-tipped paws to tread on. Its body was twice as long as a horse's, and had only a waggling stump where its tail had once been. The head of the horse was gone, replaced with a gigantic eel's head at the end of a lithe, snaking neck.

Caelum stared at it, wondering that it engendered no fear in him.

Then he raised his eyes—and sorrow enveloped him.

DragonStar sat the beast, his black armor absorbing all light. His visor was raised, and Caelum saw that his brother's thin, lined face was remarkably sensuous when it was enlivened with power.

DragonStar was smiling.

He raised his right arm, and in his hand Caelum saw that he held a great sword of light, its hilt guard a mass of writhing serpents that twisted about hilt and DragonStar's wrist alike.

"Fool," DragonStar hissed. "Why don't you run?"

And Caelum said to him what he needed most to hear himself. "I forgive you."

DragonStar screamed, and dug his heels into his beast's flanks. It cried with the warbling voice of a bird, and lunged forward.

The sword arced through the air.

Caelum did not move, nor even flinch. "I forgive you," he repeated.

"*I do not need forgiveness!*" DragonStar screamed, and the sword whistled down through the air and sliced deep into Caelum's chest.

Yet even as he felt his lungs and then mouth fill with blood, even as the face of his tormentor filled his eyes, Caelum finally came to an understanding. That face beneath the helmet was like, but unlike, his brother.

This DragonStar was not his brother.

"Forgive *me*," he mouthed, and then his world disintegrated into clouds of pain and black feathers and sharp blades and claws and beaks that tore into his flesh and drove spikes of agony deep into his mind.

Despite his resolve, he felt himself begin to thrash about on the point of the sword.

Maybe he *did* want to live, after all.

He twisted, and opened his mouth to shout, but found it filled with feathers and a taste so foul he gagged.

Agony continued to slice through his body. If anything, it had gotten worse. Far worse.

Caelum opened his eyes, and found he had woken into a nightmare as bad as his dream. The entire world was a mass of black feathers, mad whispering, and claws that scratched and beaks that bit deep into flesh.

The Hawkchilds had attacked.

The cave was literally packed with them. So completely

did they fill the space between floor and rock ceiling that it seemed they'd driven out all the air.

Caelum gasped for breath, trying to beat the three Hawkchilds that clung to him back far enough to allow him to draw his sword.

To one side he could hear the sounds of his parents similarly fighting for their lives, and the howls and snapping jaws of the Alaunt.

But however Caelum struggled, the Hawkchilds only clung closer. One of them drove his beak deep into Caelum's shoulder, tearing away a strip of flesh, and Caelum screamed, only to have another thrust the clawed hand at the tip of its wing into his mouth, the claws tickling and scratching deep into his throat.

Caelum's scream was cut off, and he gagged, his entire body shuddering with the effort. Again he gagged, so badly one part of his mind wondered if he would vomit his entire gut up through his mouth, and then again, and again.

The claws tickled deeper, and then more struck at his face, his eyes, and something vile sank into his belly. Caelum's consciousness grayed, his mind unable to cope with the horror of the attack and the pain and weight of the Hawkchilds.

They began to sing.

It was a lullaby, something that Caelum—even in his extremity—remembered Azhure singing to him as a child, but a frightful parody of the lullaby.

Here were no sweet, comforting verses, but words that jested at the futility of life, words that spoke longingly of the embrace of pain and disease, words that wished upon the listener a life marked with the rewards of disappointment and the joys of despair.

And while the lullaby embraced him and drifted through his mind, the Hawkchilds sank their beaks and claws deeper and deeper into Caelum's body, tearing at belly and throat and neck. Far away Caelum thought he heard Azhure scream, and wondered what they could possibly be doing to her to cause such horror to suffuse her voice.

And then he drifted deeper toward unconsciousness, *pushed* himself toward it, because it would be the only escape from this—

Suddenly, the pressure eased. He felt one Hawkchild lift away, and another fall away, tearing its claws out of his throat as it did so.

Caelum finally managed to retch, spitting filth and his own blood from his mouth.

The taste brought him back to full consciousness. He slammed one of his elbows into the remaining Hawkchild that clung to him, simultaneously grasping his sword and swinging it in an arc.

There was a screech, and the sound of a body scrabbling about on the floor.

For an instant black wings thrashed in his face, and then the Hawkchild had scrambled free.

"Father?"

"Caelum!" Axis' voice was breathless, and somewhat distant, but it was strong.

Caelum blinked his eyes, adjusting them to the darkness, and finally began to discern shapes.

Pale hounds were leaping and snapping into the air, and both his parents were fighting to the rear of the cave, their backs to the wall.

He took a step toward them, when, stunningly, a hand fell on his shoulder.

"You are wounded," someone said behind him, and the hand thrust him against the side wall of the cave. "Stand back. We will help your parents."

Several people leaped past him, seizing wings and legs and literally hurling Hawkchilds away from Azhure and Axis. Swords flashed, and Caelum thought he saw two of the new arrivals lunge forward with deadly pikes.

"Adamon," he said, abruptly realizing who had spoken to him. Then he slid to his knees, his injuries finally draining him of strength. It was Adamon, and six or seven companions, some of them winged. Relieved he didn't have to fight either dream or reality anymore, Caelum finally let the grayness claim him.

He awoke to the feel of something dabbing at the wounds on his belly.

It hurt.

"Be still," a soft voice said. "The Hawkchilds have scored your flesh deeply."

Caelum blinked, and then focused on the face bending over him. Xanon, Adamon's wife.

She lifted her head slightly and smiled at him, then turned back to her cleansing of his belly wounds.

"What . . . how . . . ?" He could hardly force the words past his damaged throat.

Then his father appeared at his side, bending down to him.

"Adamon and Xanon came to our aid," Axis said, laying a hand on Caelum's shoulder. "With Pors and Silton and four Icarii from Star Finger."

"We were worried." Now Adamon's face appeared over Xanon's shoulder. "You were taking so long to join us at Star Finger that we thought to come down the trails in the hope of meeting you."

"Thank the Stars you did," Axis said softly.

"Mother?" Caelum asked.

"Scratched, but not as deeply as you," Axis answered. "She's with the hounds. One or two of them sustained some deep wounds."

Caelum relaxed a little. "And the Hawkchilds?"

"Gone," Xanon said. She sat back on her heels, and reached for a rough bandage she'd torn from a robe. "Wounded, but not dead. They have flown into the distant night. For the moment."

"Well, at least we know they, too, can bleed," Axis said, and then looked at Adamon. "We have no time to waste."

Adamon nodded. "I know." Then his eyes brightened, and he leaned forward and rested his hand on Axis' shoulder, his excitement flowing down through Axis' body and arm into Caelum.

"We have found something!" he said.

32

A Seal Hunt . . . of Sorts

He strode down through the palace corridors, ignoring the glances of those he passed, down to the courtyard, across to the stables and to the bracket of two loose boxes that held his stallion and the placidly munching donkeys.

All Zared could think of was how he'd lost Isabeau.

If only he'd been more careful. Not let her ride to the hunt while pregnant. Restricted her to the palace and gentle walks about the garden.

If only . . . if only he'd been able to keep her from death.

And now he'd lost Leagh, too. If only he'd kept Leagh with him.

If only he'd not trusted his wife to her Demon-rotted brother!

And now, was Leagh also . . . ? No! He could not think of it.

"I *will* rescue her," he said to his stallion as he threw a saddle across its back. "How far can Askam have run?"

"Don't be such a fool, Zared!" Herme cried, running into the stable. His face was red and sweating. He had dashed all the way from the audience chamber of the palace where a guard had told him of Zared's stern-faced march through the corridors and down to the stables.

Thank all gods in creation he'd got here soon enough. He began to say something else, checked himself, then continued in a moderate voice that was nevertheless tight with frustration.

"Sire, I entreat you to listen to reason. There is no shelter beyond Carlon's walls, and dusk fell many hours ago. Leagh . . . Leagh would have succumbed—"

"No!" Zared jerked the girth of his saddle tight and reached for the bridle hanging on a hook nearby. "Askam and his men had shade cloth with them. They could have . . . they *must* have . . ."

Theod entered the stable, his own face flushed, and looked mildly surprised that the older Herme had managed to get there first.

"Zared," he said, somewhat breathlessly, "you know as well as we that Askam and his command must have been infected by the Demons. They would not use the shade cloth. My friend, Leagh is . . . is . . ."

He could not continue, and turned away, his hand over his eyes.

Zared stared at Theod, then shifted his eyes to Herme. "I *will* rescue her," he repeated. "Damn it, I cannot let her lie out there."

"For the gods' sakes, listen to reason!" Herme roared, startling the other two men. "You owe responsibility to your people before you do to your wife. Have you forgotten already who you are? You are a *King,* Zared, and married to your people as much as you are married to the woman who is your wife."

Zared stared at him flatly, almost hating Herme for his words, and hating his own mind for dredging up the memory of using almost the exact words to Leagh when he was trying to persuade her to marry him despite her doubts.

Herme swung an arm dramatically toward the stable door leading to the courtyard and the streets beyond. "Your people need you to help *them,* Zared. The very last thing they need of you is to waste your own life trying to rescue a woman who is already surely as mad as her brother."

"How dare you say those words to me!" Zared screamed, and would have lunged forward had not Theod seized his shoulders and held him back.

"How dare you say to me she is mad," Zared said again, this time in a whisper. "How dare you say to me she is lost."

Again Theod's and Herme's eyes met, and they were almost as despairing as Zared's were.

"We can do nothing," Herme murmured. "Nothing."

Very gently he eased the bridle from Zared's trembling hands.

"Nothing," he whispered again, and then gathered Zared into his arms. "I am so very, very sorry, my friend."

Zared stood stiffly for a moment, and then he broke down, sobbing.

Herme stood there and held him as he wept, Theod standing close to one side, a hand on Zared's shoulder.

Theod raised his eyes and looked at Herme, and neither man was surprised to see that the other had tears sliding down his cheeks. For his part, Herme knew that Theod was thinking of his own wife and two young sons far to the north. Gwendylyr was of an age with Leagh.

In the adjoining loose box the donkeys had stopped their munching and were staring at the three men. One of them shifted her gaze slightly, and the single lamp hanging on a post glinted in her eyes. For one instant the donkey's eyes reflected the carnage of dead seals atop the ice pack.

The donkeys stayed still long after the men had gone.

Then one turned to the other and spoke with the mind voice.

It has been a very long time since we have hunted, sister.

That is so.

And meanwhile the man-Zared laments for the woman-Leagh.

That is so.

We have been quiescent too long. Shall we hunt the seal tonight, sister?

Aye!

The streets of Carlon were still, deserted. Nothing moved, save the gray terror that hung down in thick veils from the sky and the two white donkeys who moved silently between the tenement buildings.

The terror did not touch them . . . it did not even notice them.

The donkeys plodded forward, their heads nodding with every step, their ears drooping amiably.

Their tongues hungered for the wetness of blood.

Eventually, the donkeys drew close to the postern gate. It was bolted shut, and heavy beams were propped against the door as further protection against invasion.

One of the donkeys stepped forward and nudged one of the beams gently with her nose. It fell soundlessly to the ground, and the two other beams toppled with it.

The other donkey nudged the bolt, and it slid soundlessly into its carriage.

The gate opened and the donkeys walked through. It swung shut behind them and the bolt slid home.

The donkeys ambled forth placidly into the night.

Askam had not moved his party since the previous evening. The badger was coming from the east, and would not ford the Nordra until the next morning.

And so Askam sat and waited. His maniacal command sat with him, forming concentric circles that rippled out in the night, at their edges hemmed in by their horses standing legs akimbo, heads down, drool roping from slack jaws to the ground.

In the center of the circles lay Leagh, her eyes wide, staring at something no one else could see. Her limbs moved slowly and purposelessly, her hands alternatively scrabbling at the dirt she lay in and picking at invisible scabs on her belly.

She was completely naked.

None among this mad company cared, or were even aroused by the sight.

Their minds communed with that of the brown and cream badger, dreaming of the day when all in this land lay under the sway of the Demons.

The hours passed.

Dawn filtered from the eastern sky, and Mot's hunger ravaged the land. Some of the men who sat with Askam absently carried handfuls of dirt to their mouths, chewing happily on the dry, crumbly earth, their teeth cracking and shattering on the rocks within the soil. They swallowed this breakfast without apparent effort. Again and again they lifted their hands to their mouths, stuffing their bodies with so much earth they eventually groaned and fell over, writhing silently as their stomachs and then guts burst with the pressure of the rocks and soil.

Eventually blood trickled from their mouths and they lay still, although their bellies continued to swell with the fluids and gases created by the internal destruction. Some one or two, their internal buildup so extreme, looked like ghastly parodies of women who had died in the extremities of childbirth.

Askam paid the swelling corpses no heed. The badger was only a few hours away, and soon Askam would be reanimated with its purpose.

Everyone save Leagh, who still writhed under the weight of her own internal agonies, sat completely still. Likewise, the horses stood motionless on their skewed legs.

Waiting.

Something else found them before the badger did.

The donkeys had trotted through the night, unerringly headed straight for the spot where Askam and his demented force waited. As they drew to within a quarter of a league of their quarry the donkeys broke into a canter, and their heads snaked forth before them.

The donkeys' bony spines padded out and their flanks thickened. Their hooves grew larger and flattened into plate-sized paws, wicked talons curving outward in the anticipation of dealing death. Their heads, snaking ever lower to the ground, broadened and shrunk back toward shoulders that had attained the bulkiness of bears.

Icebears.

One of them opened her massive jaws and snarled, and her sister replied with a full-throated roar.

Far, far to the north, Urbeth raised her head from where it lay on her paws before the fire. If she had been any less drowsy, she would have smiled, but as it was, she only listened, then let her head drop back to her paws and sleep. She dreamed of the time, fifteen thousand years earlier, when she had walked the Underworld on two legs, and with the man who had once been her husband.

Noah.

Then, Urbeth's mouth had spent a great deal of its time curved in laughter and hardly any of her nights in sleep at all.

The icebears burst through the outer ranks of horses and men with the full fury of a winter storm on the Icebear Coast.

Men and horses scattered, bowled aside by a combination of the bears' weight and the force of their huge paws.

Those not directly affected by the bears' intrusion leaped to their feet, hands reaching for swords or stones, their faces contorted with howls of hate.

Who was this, come to destroy their contemplation?

Askam himself jumped up, jerking about to see what it was that caused such a commotion.

Even in his preoccupied madness, his face slackened in momentary disbelief before he grabbed his sword.

Askam ordered the compliant Leagh to her feet, and simultaneously holding her against him and wielding the sword, Askam placed the sword against her throat.

She did not protest, nor move away.

One of the bears stopped several paces away, her head moving slowly from side to side, deep growls rumbling through her throat.

The fur of her neck and chest was stained bright red, but Askam was way beyond fear. His sword tightened against Leagh's throat so that a trickle of blood crept down to circle one breast. Still she did not move, nor give any sign that she knew a great icebear stood before her.

"Go away," Askam said to the icebear, "or she dies."

The icebear sat down with a thud, and tilted her head to one side. "I can eat her dead or alive," she said, "as I can you."

"Why do you not listen to the badger?" Askam asked, the first hint of puzzlement infusing his voice.

The icebear grinned. "Oh, but it *is* the badger who has sent me."

"It is?" Askam asked hopefully. His arm slackened slightly and the sword point drooped.

"The badger of death," the icebear said, and laughed.

Askam frowned, and his arm twitched as if he meant to lift the sword, but in the heartbeat before he did so, the other sister slunk silently up behind him and seized his head in her jaws.

Askam screamed—the sound horribly muffled—and dropped the sword as he desperately grabbed at the slavering mouth that encased his head.

It was useless.

With three quick movements the icebear savaged Askam's head from his shoulders, and then dropped his corpse.

She bent down and snuffled Leagh lying unperturbed on the ground.

"I like this not," she said to her sister.

"Nevertheless," said the other icebear, ambling over, "she will make a lily yet."

And then she grinned, and looked about at the slaughter that surrounded them. "The hunt was a good one, sister. Shall we feed before we go back?"

The badger stood and surveyed the scene of carnage.

What had happened?

He snorted and nuzzled the remains of a soldier. There was not much left.

What to do now?

He raised his head and gazed southward. He could just make out the rising walls and spires of Carlon—the stone maze where the two-legs hid.

Many two-legs . . . more two-legs than his mind could grasp. All hiding from his masters' hunger.

He looked back over his shoulder. Several thousand creatures of all varieties stood waiting his instructions.

His eyes swiveled forward again, and the Demons spoke in his mind.

Carlon! Carlon!

The brown and cream badger grunted, and started forward. Behind him his force followed in blind, obedient madness.

At noon that day a shout from one of the guards brought Zared rushing from palace to gates.

Outside stood the two white donkeys, Leagh's still form draped across one of them.

In the ensuing rush no one had time to even *think* about how it was that the two donkeys had not only escaped Carlon in the middle of the night, but now stood here in the noon chill with Leagh. Zared broke several fingernails in his desperate attempts to get the bolts drawn back from the gates, and had hauled Leagh from the donkey's back with no other thought than to get her inside.

No questions asked.

No thanks given.

No one even remembered the donkeys who stood watching with great sad, dark eyes as the gates slammed and bolted shut again in their faces. They sighed, and wished Zared luck with what was left of his wife.

After a moment they turned and trotted north, their duty done.

Theod stood with Zared, surrounded by Herme, Gustus and several other captains and anxious servants, staring at the closed door to the bedchamber.

Nothing had been said as Zared carried Leagh back to their rooms—save for a shout for the palace physician—and there were few words to be said now.

And so they waited in silence, all eyes on the closed bedchamber door. Zared had wanted to go inside with the physician, and the five soldiers he'd needed for safety, but both Herme and Theod had held him back.

Now they stood, and watched, and waited.

The door opened, and the physician emerged. His face was gray, and marked as if scratched. His eyes searched for Zared, then he walked over and dropped to one knee before his King.

"Sire," he said, his voice hoarse, "there is nothing I can do—"

"How dare you tell me that!" Zared yelled. "There must be *something* you can do."

Silence, and the physician turned his eyes away from the agony in Zared's face.

Zared fell to his knees before the physician. "Good sir, I apologize. I . . . I . . ." The physician looked at Zared, his eyes compassionate. He reached out and took Zared's hand between both his own.

"Sire, I have done all I know how, but there is nothing I can do for her as there has been nothing I have been able to do for the scores of people who have been caught outside during . . . well, caught outside."

He paused, and when he resumed his voice was a whisper. "Sire . . . sire . . . did you know that the Queen is some three months gone with child?"

33

Of Sundry Travelers

Winter had firmed its grip on the northern plains of Tencendor. Above the Azle, frost carpeted the ground until midmorning, and the clouds that billowed over the distant Icescarp Alps were heavy with snow.

The plains were empty, save for the old white horse that plodded unceasingly northward, two figures blanketed against the cold on his back.

Drago and Faraday had traveled faster than they had a right to, but Drago was not surprised. The Scepter had done this to him previously, pulling him south through the Minstrelsea forest toward the Star Gate at close to three times normal speed. Now he wondered if the staff did a similar thing, pulling them north, north toward whatever awaited them at Gorkenfort. Drago hoped he would learn some of its secrets in Gorkenfort. He spent many an hour in the evening, seeking refuge from Faraday's silence, in contemplation of the strange notations that wound about the ancient rosewood. Wondering.

Neither Drago nor Faraday could deny that Belaguez aided their journey as well. An ancient relic Belaguez might be, but he could still remember the commands of a rider, and he could still place one hoof in front of the other.

Once Drago had decided to bring the horse with himself and Faraday, he'd simply vaulted onto the stallion's swayback, leaned down to give Faraday a helping hand up, adjusted the packs behind them (on which the lizard happily curled), and gently tapped his heels against Belaguez's sides.

The horse had heaved a great sigh, but had obediently started forward, although Drago was never able to persuade him to anything more strenuous than a slow, shuffling trot. But Belaguez could keep that up for hours at a time—even through the Demonic Hours. Drago and Faraday had wondered at his seeming inability to be affected by the Demons, so like their own strange immunity, and they wondered if his mind was so senile the Demon's ravages and many-fingered mental cruelties made no difference to him.

Or was it whatever aided *them?*

So, together with the influence of the Scepter, and the senile mental murkiness of the old horse, Drago and Faraday traveled ever further north toward Gorkenfort.

Faraday spent most of the long days on Belaguez's sharp-ridged spine huddled against Drago's back. She'd given up trying to persuade Drago from Gorkenfort. The knowledge that it was Urbeth they were going to meet calmed her somewhat. Maybe Urbeth knew who the girl was, and might say how they might help her.

But deep within her Faraday knew exactly who the girl was. She was that which was lost. If not the Enchanted Songbook, then something very, very close to it, and Faraday had to find her, find her as soon as she could. The girl was too young to be left so lost. She needed to be loved and hugged and sung to sleep, and most of all she needed to be protected, and told that no harm would ever come to her again.

At night the urge to go to the mountain was almost unbearable. Faraday could now hear the child cry on every breath of wind, and when she lay down her head to pretend sleep, Faraday could feel the child's low sobs vibrating through the very earth itself.

She sounded so lost. So alone. Whatever power Noah and the craft had infused her with, it combined with Faraday's frustrated maternal instincts to make the urge to get to Star Finger almost overwhelming.

Faraday could not drive away the image of the dark-armored knight leaning down driving the blade into the child's throat, and the remembrance of the dark spurt of blood into the night made her feel sick at odd moments of the day.

But the child was not the only problem that ate at Faraday's serenity. She had promised Noah she would be Drago's friend and his trust, and she had promised she would go north with him. None of this she had minded, for she had thought Drago an enigma she would enjoy learning to know better.

She had not thought to fall in love with him. Like him, yes. Love him? *No*, and thrice no again.

Faraday had endured enough of love, and of love's betrayals. She would not let herself love Drago. *She would not do it!*

But it was hard when his eyes crinkled at her with such humor, and when his warmth enveloped her in the tent at night. It was hard when Drago left no doubt hanging between them how he felt about her, and it was hard remembering the feel of his weight on her body and the taste of his mouth on hers when they lay under the stars and the Demons' terror.

But Faraday was determined. Both would eventually live happier lives if she was strong and kept him away. They *would* live better lives. They would . . . they would . . .

So day by day Belaguez plodded indefatigably north across featureless landscape—and through the wind and snow-swept bones of those who had died during the infected hours.

The riders on his back rarely spoke.

One day, a black speck in the sky spotted them, and reported their presence to the Demons.

No man or woman in either the Strike Force or the regular ground force could account for it beyond attributing it to sheer courage and strength of will, as refugees from the desolate and raped landscape of western Tencendor found their way to Carlon. Sometimes they would scamper or creep to one of the bolted gates in ones and twos, sometimes in groups of a score or more. Many of them fell victim to the increasing number of crazed animals the badger had grouped about the walls and approaches to Carlon, but many made it through.

As yet, the number of animals was not great enough to stop all passage to and from Carlon.

Theod, for Zared took little interest in life beyond his palace these days, ordered that the guards and gate-keepers should let in the refugees once every two hours—the last opening to be just before the commencement of one of the Demonic Hours. The gates could not be left open constantly because of the creatures that now attacked whenever they saw an opening, and two hours meant there was enough of a buildup of desperate people outside to make the opening worthwhile.

Once the gray haze had settled over the landscape and roofs of the town the gates were opened for no one, no matter how desperately—or cunningly—they pleaded and bargained.

Theod spent much time with them, finding out where they'd come from, and how they'd managed to escape demonic infection during their journey. To Theod's surprise— and hope—the refugees not only came from the relatively close provinces of Avondale and Romsdale, but from the much more distant southern and western parts of Ichtar; many even from Zared's erstwhile capital of Severin.

"How did you know how to keep safe from the gray fingers of the Demons?" he asked, and always the response came the same, and always with flat voice and apathetic eyes.

"We watched how our neighbors died or were captured by madness, and we observed. We learned. Fast."

Then there would be a pause, and a spark would appear in the refugee's eyes. He or she would ask whether Caelum was about to rescue them, or if the Star Gods prepared to do battle with the Demons, or if there was any hope, please, my lord, *any* hope at all?

And Theod would smile and pat their shoulders, and direct them to shelter and food, and he would not answer any more of their questions.

After two weeks of talking to new arrivals, Theod made his way to the palace.

Unlike the streets and tenements of Carlon, which were necessarily becoming crowded from the constant arrival of refugees, the palace halls and corridors largely echoed only with the footfalls of ghosts. There was the palace secretary, and a few servants, and DareWing slouched dark-browed in a shadowed corner, and a few nervous men-at-arms manning the doors, or Strike Force members outlined in windows.

And there was Herme.

Herme kept an almost constant vigil outside the room where Zared sat with Leagh. Or with what she had become.

Theod paused as he neared Herme, then resolutely strode close. "Herme? Has Zared come forth this day?"

"Nay." Herme heaved a great sigh. "And not likely to. He spends all day in there. All day! I cannot understand how he can bear it."

Theod looked at the door. For an instant uncertainty crossed his face, then it disappeared as fast as it had come. Theod was rapidly growing out of his youthful exuberance and its accompanying hesitancy. He had also lost much of his joy for life, but Theod supposed that was to be expected under the present circumstances.

"We need to talk, he and you and I," Theod said. "Get him."

Herme stared at Theod in surprise. Despite the difference in ages the two had always been close friends, and Theod had always treated Herme with the deference due his age and experience, even if Theod technically outranked the Earl.

Previously, Herme had never seen this hard edge to Theod.

"Get him!" Theod barked, and then turned on his heel and walked to a meeting chamber several doors down the corridor.

Herme stared, hesitated, then wiped his hand over his eyes. He suddenly felt very, very tired. Then he leaned his weight against the door and opened it a hand span.

"Zared. Theod has urgent business."

"It can wait." Zared's voice sounded hollow, and underneath it Herme could hear a savage hissing, and then the sound of a globule of phlegm hitting a wall.

He swallowed, and then wished he hadn't. "My Lord King, I think you need to speak to Theod. Please."

Gods! Was he going to be reduced to begging?

But Zared came forth after a long moment, his feet shuffling, and closed the door behind him.

Herme was glad he hadn't had to witness what the closed door hid.

"Where is he?" Zared asked. His voice sounded even hollower in the spaces of the corridor, and his face was sunken and gray.

Herme indicated with his hand, and the two slowly walked down the corridor and into the meeting room.

"Well?" Zared asked, sitting slowly down in a chair by a table. Herme sat to one side of him, while Theod chose to stand at the end of the table. DareWing stood by a window, his arms folded, his face lost in shadow.

"Sire," Theod said, putting to one side his concern for Zared's appearance. It could wait. "Sire, as you know many thousands of refugees have entered Carlon over the past two weeks, and—"

"Really?" Zared's face showed a faint glimmer of interest.

Theod gaped at him . . . hadn't Zared taken note of *any-thing*? Had he concerned himself with nothing but Leagh's plight, when many thousands of Leaghs wandered the hills of Tencendor, wailing and howling?

He glanced at Herme, who shrugged slightly, and continued. "Sire, many of these refugees are from the extreme north, Ichtar and Aldeni."

Zared sat forward. "Go on."

"They learned to cope with the ravages of the Demons, and learned how best to travel, *and* they learned how to repel the increasing swarms of crazed beasts that hunt the sanc."

"Yes, yes, but what is so urgent?"

"Sire, several of the groups who have arrived in the past few days have mentioned as many as twenty thousand refugees sheltering in the mines of the Murkle Mountains."

Zared nodded, as if considering the information as trivial as the latest score from the games of hoopball the street boys played. "Yes. That would be a good place to hide, wouldn't it?"

Theod bent his head, and fought with his temper. Eventually he raised it again, and leaned forward over the table on his hands. When he spoke, he carefully enunciated every word.

"Sire, these people need to be brought to the safety of Carlon. Someone needs to lead an expeditionary force north to bring them to Carlon. Sire, has not Drago promised us this Sanctuary? Would it not be best for all concerned if we had as many people sheltering in Carlon when word arrives of its location?

"At the very least, these people cannot remain out there much longer. Food, as hope, is in short supply, and the swarms of the maddened grow daily—you only have to look over the walls to see that."

Zared blinked. He had not looked over the walls for a very long time. "Do you want to lead this force, Theod?"

"Sire," Theod's voice was very quiet now. "Sire, my wife and two sons might be among them."

Zared's eyes deepened with emotion. For the first time, the import of what Theod was saying sank in. What despair and horror did those twenty thousand live through?

And Theod's *wife?* Oh gods, why hadn't he *thought?*

"*I* should be the one to—" Zared began, but Herme interrupted him.

"No, sire. You should *not* be the one to go. Carlon—Tencendor—needs you here, and we can ill afford you to lead this force north for the many, many weeks it will keep you away."

Zared bowed his head, sighed, and gave a slight nod. Then he raised his face. "Very well. How many men will you need, Theod?"

"Will you spare me the Strike Force, sire?"

Before Zared could answer, DareWing stepped forth from the shadows. "I will assist the Duke, sire. The Strike Force can do more than twenty thousand ground troops can."

Zared's mouth twisted. "I see the decision has been taken away from me, Theod. Very well, you may go. Take two thousand men with you to complement the Strike Force."

"By the time we get to the northern plains of Avonsdale with as many of the thousands that we can find," Theod said, "we will need vastly more than the Strike Force and two thousand men to protect them. Will you ride to meet us and bring a force of some few thousands?"

"Ah . . . sire?"

They looked about, surprised. Jannymire Goldman, Master of the Guilds of Carlon, was standing in the door.

"Sire? Sir Duke?" Goldman walked into the room, ignoring the looks of mild surprise on the faces before him. "Sir Duke? I believe I may be able to aid you."

"I have no room for a trading coterie, Goldman," Theod said.

Goldman bit down his temper. Over the past weeks he'd seen his beloved country reduced to tatters, his people in disarray and, worse, the extensive network of contacts he held across Tencendor virtually useless. But not yet dead.

"Nevertheless, my lord," Goldman said, "I assume you will have need of rapid transport?"

Theod stopped. "Transport?"

"How *do* you propose to reach those stranded in the north, sir Duke?"

Theod glanced at DareWing, then back to Goldman. "How would *you* propose to reach them, Goldman?"

"Sir Duke, there are two score merchant ships waiting in the ports of Nordmuth, Ysbadd and Pirates Town."

Unnoticed, Zared lowered his face into a hand. Why hadn't he thought of those ships!

"You would want to sail up the Nordra?" Theod said. "That would be cumbersome at best. That many ships could not hope to navigate the Nordra safely at once, so it would take several relays of ships, and each relay would require some two weeks for the return trip. The men from the first two relays who had been disembarked in eastern Aldeni would be vulnerable to attack while they waited for the rest of the force to catch up. And after all of this, you could still only set us down ten days' ride away from the Murkle Mountains. It would be quicker to walk north to the Mountains."

"Not the Nordra. The Andeis Sea. Straight to the Murkle Mountains."

Zared looked up, wondering if hope *did* still exist.

DareWing drew in a sharp breath. "How long to get a force to the Murkle Mountains from Nordmuth?" the Strike Leader asked.

"Six days."

Theod stared at Goldman, thinking it would take him at least three weeks, if not four, to *ride* that far north.

"When can those ships be ready to sail?" he asked.

"We've had them ready for weeks, sir Duke," Goldman said. "I owed it to the Acharites to have some form of escape at hand."

Zared winced. "If you find the twenty thousand," he said, "you could sail many of them straight south for Coroleas. Carlon certainly cannot hold that many, and I profess myself rather sick of waiting for Drago's Sanctuary to emerge from the gray sorceries that hang about us. Goldman, how many could your fleet hold?"

"Twenty thousand, sire."

Everyone in the room relaxed. The Andeis would be horribly treacherous this time of year, and normally would never be considered, but better the threat of a sea storm than the maddening dangers of the plains of Tencendor.

Zared rose. "Good, Master Goldman. Again Achar owes you its thanks. Theod, I wish you every last remaining speck of luck in this land of ours."

Theod nodded, took Zared's hand, then turned for the door.

"Theod." Zared's soft voice halted him. "Theod, I hope you find Gwendylyr and your two boys safe and well."

Theod nodded again, and then he, DareWing and Goldman were gone, and Zared sank down into his chair.

WolfStar sat in pitch blackness in an ancient conduit deep within the waterways. His fingers idly stroked the warm skin of the girl child in his lap, his wings drooped behind him, his eyes stared unfocused into the dark.

His thoughts consumed him.

Where were the Demons now? Well on their way to the Lake of Life, no doubt, but not close enough for WolfStar's liking. He'd arrived at this site close to the chambers beneath the Lake many days ago—and now he must needs wait, wait, wait for the Demons to take their own sweet time traversing the plains above.

More than anything WolfStar itched to throw the girl into the next power trap and infuse her body with breath and another spurt of growth, but he couldn't find the ancient site without the Demons to show the way.

And so now here he must linger. And hope that he could escape the Demons' attention at the Lake of Life as easily as he had at Cauldron Lake.

WolfStar's fingers continued to stroke the warmth of the child. Back and forth, back and forth, but driven by impatience now, rather than love.

In WolfStar's constantly shifting, plotting mind, Niah had become a tool rather than an object of love or even of desire.

His eyes sharpened, and he grinned into the darkness.

34

Poor, Useless Fool

Drago was drowsing, lulled by the rhythmic swaying of Belaguez's gait, when the shadow swept over his face. His eyes jerked open instantly, and he drew his breath sharply in horror.

His slid a hand down to where Faraday's hands were clasped loosely about his waist.

She was heavy against his back, fully asleep, and unaware of the danger.

"Faraday!" he whispered fiercely.

She stirred.

"Faraday . . ."

"Mmm?"

"Whatever happens next, *take my lead*. Do you hear me? *Take my lead!*"

"But—"

"Where's the lizard?"

"Against my back. Why?"

"Make sure your cloak is covering him, and pray to the gods he doesn't move!"

"But—"

Faraday broke off as she saw what was circling down from the sky. "Oh, dear gods!" she whispered.

Drago's hand tightened briefly about hers. "Just follow my lead, Faraday, please."

There was no time to say more. Belaguez sighed and halted, stopped by the dozen or so Hawkchilds now crouched in a semicircle across the snow-swept path.

Belaguez's head drooped, his eyes closed, and he was asleep within a heartbeat.

The central Hawkchild, a small, black-eyed boy, took several hops forward and spoke with whispery accusation. "You were dead. We ate of your flesh. Why do you now walk, Drago?"

Drago gave a high-pitched giggle, as if nervous—which, in truth, was a reaction he did not have to feign. "I don't know . . . I felt the . . . Questors . . . tear me apart, use me for the leap . . . and then I woke up in the Star Gate Chamber."

The Hawkchild tilted his head to one side, and regarded Drago silently. Drago suddenly realized that everything it saw and heard was being relayed directly back to the Demons.

"You were a sack of bones," it said, and its head tilted back the other way.

Drago arranged his face into a sullen expression. "They said they would give me back my Icarii power, and they didn't."

The semicircle of Hawkchilds edged closer, whispering, their heads tilting as one, first to this side, and then to that.

Several of them were flexing their hands at the tips of their wings.

"Who is that with you?" one asked.

"This?" Drago shrugged disinterestedly. "A woman. She keeps me warm at night. I have not thought to ask her name." He sighed. "She is not StarLaughter, but at least she is not dead."

"You wander unsheltered through the barren plains, Drago. How is it that you keep your minds?"

"I have no idea how I have kept *my* mind. As for her, well, she lost hers a hundred leagues to the south. I mean, *look* at her!"

The Hawkchilds peered closely at Faraday's face.

It was slack-jawed and vacant. A thin drool of saliva hung from lower lip to chin. Her eyes were closed. Not even Faraday could have hidden either the fear or the intelligence in them.

One of the Hawkchilds stepped closer and lifted one of its wings. The fingers of the hand at its tip ran down Faraday's face. One of the hardest things Faraday had ever had to do in her life, as hard as keeping her sanity while wrapped in Gorgrael's talons, was to keep her face slack and relaxed at that moment.

"Do you want her?" Drago asked. "She's useful enough at night, but a bother to feed and keep moderately clean."

The Hawkchild lifted its wing and stroked Faraday's face again. Its head tilted curiously to one side, and a pink tongue glistened momentarily in its beak.

"You can have her if you want," Drago said, "although I'd have the bother of finding another one."

The Hawkchild switched its gaze to him, and it suddenly snarled. "You should be dead."

"Don't kill me!" Drago gibbered. "Don't kill me!"

The Hawkchild drew back its wings, and its head began a long, low sweeping movement . . . back and forth . . . back and forth . . . as if seeking the best spot to attack first.

The others drew closer until Belaguez—still contentedly asleep—was completely ringed by rustling, whispering black-feathered Hawkchilds.

"Take her!" Drago screamed, and grabbed Faraday's arm as if he meant to hurl her from the horse. "Take her, but not *me*." The Hawkchilds drew closer.

"Take her! Take her! Please, please don't kill me!"

"The poor, useless fool," StarLaughter said. "Perhaps we should kill him and have done with it. Although . . ."

"Although?" Sheol said, arching an eyebrow at her.

"It might be fun to play with him a little," StarLaughter said, and grinned. "*And* her."

"I don't know that we should—" Rox began, and then every one of the Demons swiveled southwest and snarled.

"The magicians!" Barzula cried. "I can feel them."

StarLaughter watched her companions, puzzled . . . and then they thought to share with her what they saw and felt. Far away, somewhere just south of the Western Ranges, stood two white-clad figures staring northeast toward the Demons.

Power radiated off them in concentric ripples.

"Destroy them!" Sheol cried, and she was not meaning Faraday and Drago.

Drago didn't know what else he could do. He'd hoped to fool the Hawkchilds, and the Demons, into just letting himself and Faraday go (what else could he do?) with his act, but it wasn't working.

The Hawkchilds were drawing their net about the horse, their beaks snapping, their hands reaching, and then, just as Drago thought he'd have to try and defend them both with his staff . . . they leaped into the air, circled once, then sped south.

As they disappeared, he relaxed. "Faraday?"

"What did you mean," she hissed, "by asking, 'Do you want her'? What would you have done if they'd said, 'Why, yes, thank you'?"

"Faraday," he said, "I honestly have no idea."

When the Hawkchilds, by dint of effort, and a good deal of power lent them by the Demons, arrived at the spot where the magicians had spied their way northeast, all they found was a herd of deranged cattle with two white donkeys running in their midst.

Hissing with disappointment, the Hawkchilds veered east, and then further south, trying to find the elusive magicians.

They, as the Demons, had totally forgotten about poor, useless Drago and his equally useless woman.

35

Andeis Voyagers

The voyage north through the Andeis Sea was frightful beyond anything Theod had ever experienced. True, as a youth he'd sailed the Azle River and the upper reaches of Murkle Bay during the summer calm, but that now seemed an experience of another world, and could hardly equip him for this monstrous voyage.

The Andeis Sea was treacherous in the best of seasons, and in the late winter was . . . beyond the furthest reaches of any nurse's nightmarish midnight tale.

The forty merchantmen sailed north in two fleets of twenty vessels each, separated by more than a half-day's sailing. Theod, his two thousand, their horses, and the Strike Force sailed in the leading fleet, and spent the time rolling about the three-quarters empty holds of the ships, hanging on to whatever they could, cursing every god, fish and lord of the wind that they could remember.

The merchantmen were built to hold as much cargo as they could, not provide smooth sailing for landlubber tastes. They were great heavy vessels with bellies built rounder than the most gravid whale, and with little in their holds to stabilize them they rolled from side to side like drunken parrots. Their motion was worsened by the fact they were sailing due north, and the crews had to tack across the prevailing northerly and norwesterly winds.

"It will be kinder sailing south," Goldman said, clinging to the side of his bunk but actually looking reasonably at ease. He had spent much of his youth sailing these waters as an apprentice whaler, until he'd decided his true skills lay in the courteous but deadly cut-and-thrust of trading diplomacy. "The wind will be directly behind us then."

Theod grunted, and eyed the bucket just beyond the end of his bunk. It was sliding about the floor, to and fro, to and fro, and its grating across the floorboards made Theod think of the horrible moaning that gripped Gwendylyr during childbirth.

His stomach cramped and then roiled violently, and Theod did not begrudge his wife a single moan. He lunged for the bucket and retched into it, his fair hair hanging in damp strings over his face.

Gods!

He sat for a few minutes until he thought his stomach had finally emptied itself of everything he'd eaten over the past six weeks, then pushed it away and struggled back to his bunk, wiping his mouth.

"I wish I could get some fresh air," he muttered.

Goldman glanced up at the prism set into the deck above them. "Nay, sir Duke. 'Tis still dark night. Terror clings to every mast and railing, and slides down the sails, seeking entrance belowdecks."

Theod lay down on his bunk and closed his eyes, pretending he might be able to sleep. He had hoped—they had *all* hoped—that the Demons' influence might not extend over the sea, but although the gray hazes seemed slightly diluted, they were still powerful enough to drag any caught in them deep into the bowels of madness. Everyone had to spend the Demonic Hours trapped below deck. Theod had worried that the ships might strike rocks, or whales, or whatever sea monsters lurked beneath the rolling gray waves, but the master of the ship, Hervitius, had said the ships' helms were roped and locked onto course, and there wasn't much the ships could strike in this weather.

"All monsters will have dived deep," Hervitius had soothed the previous afternoon, "for they dislike the slap of the rolling waves as much as we."

If the sea monsters couldn't stand it, thought Theod, wishing sleep would come steal him away from this horror, then how can we cope with it?

"Sir Duke?"

Theod repressed a sigh and opened his eyes.

DareWing had entered, and was standing as easily on the rolling deck as if he stood in the sunlit audience chamber of a Queen's palace.

"Gods, DareWing," Theod whispered. "How do you manage?"

DareWing raised a black eyebrow in feigned surprise, although in truth he was rather enjoying the predicament of the majority of Acharites. Once the Icarii had contemptuously referred to them as Groundwalkers. Now DareWing wondered, although not unkindly, if they should resurrect that as Waveretchers.

"This?" DareWing said, and looked about the cabin as if it were indeed a pleasant audience chamber in some pastel, scented palace. "'Tis nothing compared to the turbulence of a summer thunder thermal."

Theod tried to glare at the Strike Leader, but managed only a slight frown.

Holding his breath against the demands of his stomach to retch yet again, he rolled slowly over and sat up.

"What is it?"

"Dawn lights the eastern horizon. Another hour, and we can emerge from this wooden coffin."

"Good." Theod managed to stand up, clinging white-knuckled to the bunk support. "Does Hervitius have any idea where we are?"

DareWing nodded, and generously placed a hand under Theod's elbow. "The first light reveals the coastline, some two leagues to the east. Peaks . . . mountains."

Theod's face brightened. "The Murkle Mountains?"

"Aye," DareWing said. "We should be in the Bay by this afternoon."

"The gods be praised!" Goldman said, standing up himself. He slapped his belly. "Has breakfast been laid on?"

DareWing looked disgusted. "Sailor food, Goldman. Fried whale blubber. In oil. With cold salted herring."

Theod groaned, bent over, and surrendered to the howling of his stomach.

By noon the ships had tacked into the relative calm of Murkle Bay. The waters were clearer now than they had been for generations. With the destruction along the lower reaches of the Azle during the battle between Timozel's and Axis' forces, the tanneries that had once poured their thick pollutants into the bay had disappeared, and neither Theod nor Zared had wanted to rebuild them. During summer, Murkle Bay had become something of a summer retreat for many of the wealthier Tencendorians, and several small houses had been built along its shores.

The mountains themselves rose tall, grim and silent about half a league inland from the gritty beach. Theod had never been able to understand the attraction Murkle Bay had for the rich and idle, but supposed a summer weekend spent here constituted the closest many of them would ever come to adventure.

Well, now he supposed that a good many of them were lining the mines of the mountains, embroiled in an adventure they would never have willingly paid for in a thousand lifetimes.

"The beaches are deserted," DareWing muttered by Theod's side, his eyesight far keener than that of the Acharite.

Theod nodded, keeping his own eyes slitted against the cold, salty wind. "*If* they had scouts posted, and *if* they had spotted us, then it is doubtful that any would actually want to leave the safety of the mines."

He squinted at the leaden sky, searching out the brightness of the sun behind its layered grayness. "We have but an hour to go before mid—"

The ship suddenly keeled over to starboard, and Theod slipped and would have fallen had not DareWing, half in the air, grabbed him.

"What's wrong?" Theod said, echoing a half dozen shouts behind him from crew and soldiers alike.

The ship lurched again, and this time it felt as if it were being bodily lifted out of the waves. Theod clung to the deck railing, and peered over the side. They *were* being lifted out of the waters! He could see exposed barnacles on timbers normally hidden, and below them . . . below them . . . something glistening gray and purple.

Something scaly.

"DareWing," Theod shouted, "get the Strike Force into the air!"

DareWing was already airborne and shouting orders himself.

Theod, struggling on the damp decks, managed to look back to the other ships.

At least a third of them were in a similar predicament to his vessel, rolling alarmingly on the backs of . . . of *some* kind of sea creatures, and raised at least the height of a man, perhaps two, out of the waters.

On all of the ships men scurried, seizing weapons, some tying themselves to railings and masts, while members of the Strike Force rose into the air, fitting arrows to their bows.

Theod looked back along the deck of his own vessel. "Hervitius," he yelled at the master, clinging grimly to the useless helm.

Hervitius shook his head. *I don't know what it is!*

Theod looked about. "Goldman!"

The Master of the Guilds, for once pale-faced, struggled along the deck toward him.

"No one knows what they are, Theod," he gasped, forgetting all formalities amid his fear. "I can't tell if—"

The ship lurched again, and threatened to founder completely. Theod glanced over the side—sweet gods, they had been raised more than the height of a house above the waters!—and then lunged for a pike from a rack attached to the forward mast.

He seized it, started back for the railing, slipped as the ship lurched again, then managed to scramble across the deck and lean over the side.

He steadied himself, took a deep breath, and then stabbed the pike down with all his force. It speared into the scaly surface of the creature with a wet thud, leaving only a third of its length protruding.

For a breath, nothing, then . . .

. . . then the entire ship rocketed for the sky. A frightful wail rent the air, and Theod screamed with it as a head from nightmare shot above the level of the deck. It looked like that of a horse, save there were no ears, it was covered in bright purple scales, and was the size of an entire horse itself.

Purple lips peeled back from rows of squat thick teeth that looked like anvils, and then the head shot downward, seized a piece of railing between its teeth, *and ate it.*

Someone grabbed Theod's arm, and as the sea monster's head darted downward again, felt himself being pulled backward.

The sea monster's head slammed into the deck where Theod had been standing, and emerged with a mouthful of splintered planks. It chewed, swallowed, then seized the edges of the jagged deck again and shook its head. Several nails pierced its bulbous tongue, but this did not appear to overly concern the creature.

The entire deck began to rise, screaming as wood splintered and nails gave way. The sea monster shook its head, trying to worry the wood free, and Goldman dragged Theod back to the shelter of the cabin, where Hervitius and several of the crew were huddled.

Another head appeared over the side of the ship, and then another, and then a fourth.

"Dear lords of Tencendor," Hervitius whispered, "it is but the one creature. Look!"

The beast had now risen sufficiently from the waters to

show that its serpentine body had four heads snaking from it at various intervals.

"A Sea Worm!" Goldman cried. "But they're only . . ."

Only legend, he'd been about to say, but this was, apparently, a time when legends were to be resurrected. Perhaps by whatever demonic influence had penetrated the sea's depths.

Theod grabbed on to the door frame as the ship rolled over so far it lay on its side. He stared into the sky and prayed for a miracle, or at least the Strike Force.

Even before he'd managed to form the thought, an arrow flew through the air and skewered an eye on one of the four heads. The head shook, weeping pale green blood from its shattered eye. It wailed agonizingly through a mouthful of half-chewed timbers.

The other three heads let go the ship and snapped at the creatures hovering above, but the Icarii kept well out of the way, and continued to rain down arrows.

Two of the other heads had their eyes punctured, and the Sea Worm decided it had suffered enough. All four heads reared back, viciously smashed once more into the deck, then slithered over the side of the shattered railings.

The ship lurched, shuddered, and then fell, slamming into the water in a plume of spray.

It landed, not on its keel, but on its starboard side, and water rushed over the deck and inundated the cabin.

"Jump overbo—" Hervitius started to scream, but the rush of water stopped his words, and hurled him against a far wall . . .

. . . hard against a row of spikes meant to hang wet-weather gear on. The initial rush of water receded, and Theod blinked, and rubbed his eyes clear. Hervitius was pinned high against the wall, blood trailing from his mouth, and a vaguely surprised look in his staring, dead eyes.

The ship shuddered once more, then rolled over with a quiet sigh.

Far below in the hold, horses and men screamed.

"Get off this ship," Theod ordered. "Now!"

Then he knew no more save chaos, and the feel of water flooding into his lungs, the touch of icy hands already drowned, and the cold silence of the deep sea.

Above, far above, a small flock of Hawkchilds whispered and wondered.

"How . . . interesting," Rox remarked, blinking as he came out of his semi-trance.

The other Demons, and StarLaughter, did likewise. They were standing in a tiny hut in a small village in the northern Skarabost Plains. The remains of their meal, a middle-aged woman and her teenage daughter, were a blood-soaked and splintered muddle before them. They had been talking about these troublesome and unknown magicians to the south when the Hawkchilds had sent their vision.

"Why would the Acharites be sending a fleet to the north-western coastline?" Sheol asked StarLaughter.

She shrugged. "How could I know? I don't—"

"Then think!" Mot hissed. "This is an act we should inquire into."

"There is *nothing* in those mountains save mines and caves," StarLaughter said. "Pitiful enough in my time, and I cannot imagine they'd be more beauteous or plentiful now."

"Mines," Rox said slowly. "Caves . . ."

Sheol looked about her companions and smiled. "A fleet . . . sailing to a place where there are mines and caves . . . what *else* can they be doing but effecting a rescue? An evacuation?"

"But where to?" StarLaughter asked.

"Away from us," Raspu snarled. "Away from our *hunger*."

Simultaneously all the Demons bared their teeth, and then equally simultaneously jerked their heads toward the west.

Search! they commanded the Hawkchilds in the area. *Watch! Tell!*

36

Gorkenfort

By early Hungry-month Drago and Faraday were in the extreme northern plains of Ichtar, now moving directly north along the ancient road toward Gorkenfort and then Ravensbund. The Hawkchilds had troubled them no more, although both spent much of the day anxiously scanning the heavy skies for their sweeping shadows.

Drago had pushed Belaguez as fast as the ancient horse would go. He knew he wouldn't survive another interview with the feathered horrors.

During the day Faraday's obsession with finding the lost child faded in a flood of gloomy memories. She had come this way once before, a long, long time ago. Then she'd been, if not exactly naive, then too innocent. Too determined to play her role in a Prophecy that demanded only her death. She had ridden with Timozel and Yr, escorted by Lieutenant Gautier, toward Borneheld.

Borneheld.

Faraday's arms tightened instinctively about Drago, and he turned his head slightly, feeling the warmth of her body against him keenly.

"Faraday?" he asked softly.

"Memories, Drago."

"Ah." Drago was not unaware that Gorkenfort was an unwelcome destination for Faraday, for more reasons than that she would have preferred to have gone straight to Star Finger. "Was there *no* happiness for you in Gorkenfort?"

As Drago had, so did Faraday hesitate. "I don't think I had much happiness anywhere, Drago."

To that, Drago had nothing to say.

They saw no person, and no animal, on the final few leagues of road leading to Gorkenfort. The cold, bleak wind had swept the land completely bare; the sense of hopelessness in the air was palpable. During Magariz's time as Prince of the North, Gorkenfort and town had been reestablished as a major juncture of Ichtarian and Ravensbund trade, but now both had apparently been abandoned again. Drago wondered where the people had gone. There was too much horror to the south, and he suspected they may have fled yet further north through the Gorken Pass into Ravensbund itself.

Perhaps the Ravensbund Necklet, the series of curious sinkholes stretching from the foot of the Icescarp Alps to the western coast, might be harboring more than the Ravensbund. Drago hoped so. He did not think he could bear it if the entire population of northern Tencendor had been lost.

Belaguez plodded on, his nose pointed ever north, his mind lost in the mists of age.

Gorkenfort was indeed deserted, as was the town that spread out beneath its walls.

As they drew close to the town in the late afternoon, Drago tugged at Belaguez's mane, pulling the horse to a halt.

Both Drago and Faraday stared ahead. Several months of winter snow had collected in frozen drifts about the walls of the town; one particularly large mound had propped open the gates.

Behind the town rose the black walls of the fort, and behind that, leagues distant, but still so massive they blocked out much of the sky, the sheer cliffs of the Icescarp Alps surged toward the stars. The peaks were lost in mist and cloud, and thicker clouds billowed beyond the alps and streamed through the mountain passes toward Gorkentown and fort.

A gust of icy wind hit them, and Belaguez momentarily struggled with his footing.

Faraday shivered, and clung as close to Drago's back as she could with the feathered lizard curled between them.

"There's a storm coming," Drago murmured over his shoulder. "But we can find shelter enough in the fort, and build a fire to see us through the night."

"'Tis not the cold that makes me shiver so," Faraday said.

Drago twisted so he could see her face. Her green eyes appeared abnormally bright in her face, and her lower lip was an angry scarlet where she had caught it between her teeth. Tendrils of her bright hair fluttered in the wind, making her seem even more lost and uncertain.

"Borneheld still lives for you, doesn't he?" he said.

Faraday blinked, and a tear ran down her left cheek. "I didn't realize how much I loathed him until I saw this place again."

"You don't have to go in—"

"What?" Anger had replaced the sadness in her voice. "Do you expect me to wait out here for you? No, you say we must go inside, so inside we will go. Both of us!"

She slammed her heels into Belaguez's flanks, and the horse obediently plodded forward.

"Faraday—"

"Don't say anything," she hissed. *Just don't say it.*

Drago held her eyes a moment longer, then he turned back and looked into what awaited them.

Gorkentown was not only deserted, it appeared as if it had been destroyed in some siege. As if by memory, Belaguez took them through the gates, then along the main thoroughfare that wound between gaunt-windowed and gape-doored tenement buildings toward the town square, and then up to the gates of the fort itself.

Not only were the buildings in sad disorder, goods lay in disarray as if piled by inhabitants preparing to evacuate and then fleeing in terror without them. A few walls had half-tumbled down, and the tiles of several roofs were scattered, as if they'd been caught in a spiteful whirlwind.

Although, outside the walls, snow had lain in only occasional drifts, here it lay stacked shoulder high against walls, icicles hung an arm's length down from eaves and abandoned doorframes, and a thick layer of ice glittered in the late afternoon sun from the spires of the town and the towers of the fort.

Winter had claimed Gorkentown far earlier than it had anything else.

"Something is wrong," Drago said, leaning to one side to scoop a handful of snow from a door ledge into his sack. "Why is everything destroyed? Magariz rebuilt this town as a major trading point with the Ravensbundmen."

"We have ridden into memory, I think," Faraday said. "For this is how Gorkentown appeared when it had been attacked by Gorgrael's Skraelings. And thus . . . thus I rode into the town to meet Borneheld."

"Borneheld is dead," Drago said roughly. He wondered if she surrounded herself deliberately with the ghosts of dead husbands and dream-children to protect herself from him.

"For you, perhaps."

Drago wished he hadn't brought Faraday here, and wondered what he could do to bridge the distance between them.

He tried to push Faraday from his mind—hard when she clung so close to his back—and studied the town. Should it be *this* sunk in ice? Was it the effects of the Demons? Or the power of Faraday's memory?

Or she who awaited them in the fort?

He remembered the gray-haired woman, sinking her teeth into the spine of the seal, and he shivered himself.

"We have no choice," Faraday said. "Either of us. Come, let us urge this ancient horse forward a trifle faster. Night approaches, and I'd prefer to be in the shelter of the Keep when it falls."

The gates to Gorkenfort stood as open as had the gates to the town. Belaguez halted of his own accord as he approached them, and he lifted his head and whinnied, as if caught in memory himself.

"Your father fought all along this street," Faraday said, indicating the curved road that ran between a row of tenements and the fort walls. "It was their final line of defense against the Skraelings after a night spent retreating toward the fort. Borneheld . . ."

She lifted her head and stared at the walls rising high above them. "Borneheld had ordered that the gates not be opened to admit him. He wanted him dead."

"But . . ."

"Margariz ordered them open," Faraday said. "And I sank my hands into your father's body and healed him. I loved him so desperately. I could not see him die."

Drago tensed, then booted Belaguez forward.

As the town, so the fort. The inner courtyard was deserted, piles of goods left adrift as if everything had been abandoned in a hurry so terrifying that precious belongings were dropped forgotten as people fled in a thousand differing directions.

Hinges moaned in the wind, and a squall of four or five ravens launched themselves screaming into the twilight air high above.

A door banged, and Faraday jumped and cried out.

Drago swung a leg over Belaguez's wither and dropped to the ground, slipping slightly in the ice. He turned and held out his arms for Faraday.

"Come—we need to seek shelter. I can smell a storm on this wind."

She stared at him, as if lost in some appalling memory.

"I am *not* Borneheld," Drago said. "*Come on*. Can you not hear the wind? We have little time."

Faraday blinked, then leaned down to Drago. He seized her waist and lifted her down from the horse, slapping Belaguez's rump so that he ambled—apparently totally unconcerned about the nearing tempest—into an open stable door.

The feathered lizard gave a high-pitched cry and slithered over Belaguez's hindquarters, scampering over the snow- and ice-covered paving stones to follow Drago as he carried Faraday inside the door to the Keep.

The lizard scrambled in behind them, and Drago let Faraday slide to her feet, and slammed the door closed.

Then he turned and looked about him.

They were in an entrance chamber, bare save for its ancient, rotted tapestries and banners.

Nothing but cold, damp, dark stone walls and the fungus-encrusted wall-hangings. Not a lamp or a candle, and certainly no gilt-edged explanation.

"Through here," Faraday said, stepping over to a closed door. "The Great Hall."

Surely, Drago thought, *surely* whatever he needed to find would be in here. But the Hall was as bare as the entrance chamber, except for a table and chairs scattered around the massive fireplace at the far end.

The Hall was freezing, far worse than outside, and Drago pulled his cloak tighter about him, trying to repress his shivering.

Faraday stood and looked at the far fireplace.

There Borneheld had stood and stared at her with his frightful, open lust as she'd entered, stunning in an emerald and ivory silk gown that had bared her breasts more than concealed them . . .

The same gown that Gorgrael, with equal lust, had forced her to wear so he too could—

"No!" she cried and spun about.

Here, in this Hall, Axis had stared at her, believing she'd betrayed him with his brother, and so precipitating, perhaps, his own betrayal of her.

"No!" she cried again. *"No!"*

Appalled, Drago caught her to him. She struggled blindly, sobbing, and Drago dragged her from the Hall, realizing the horror of her memories, even if he was unable to participate in them.

In the antechamber Faraday calmed, although she still shook, and tears continued to course down her face.

"There must be a room upstairs where we can light a fire and warm ourselves," he said. "Faraday, can you—"

"I can walk," she said, and hastily wiped the tears from her cheeks.

"I shouldn't have brought you here," Drago said, but took her arm and led her yet deeper into the Keep.

Up the stone stairwell he found a bedchamber with enough wood stacked into the grate to sustain a hot fire for the night. Leaving Faraday standing by the bed, the lizard playing with the laces of her boots, Drago squatted down and lit the fire.

Finally he rose once the flames took hold and caught sight of Faraday, completely still, looking at him with her great eyes. Gods, she was so lovely!

"You should wear silks rather than that peasant gown, Faraday."

"I have had enough of the lies and betrayals silks bring."

"Why so cold to me, Faraday? What have I done?"

She turned her face away.

"Is it Axis, is that why you refuse to love me?"

She looked back at him, her eyes even more stricken than before. Why had he spoken those words?

"Why should I love *you*, Drago?"

He winced, and she immediately regretted her words. She

fought to find something else to say, and then said the first thing that came to her mind.

"Did you know that this was the chamber of my marriage night, Drago? That this was where Borneheld took my virginity?"

"Are you determined to throw every past lover in my face, Faraday?"

"I am determined *never* to be betrayed again, never to be hurt again," she countered.

Drago strode across the room, angry with her. Damn it, why did she deny what he *knew* existed between them?

He took her shoulders in hands suddenly surprisingly gentle. "I would not betray you, Faraday."

"And yet you betray this land by refusing to accept what Noah told you, by refusing to accept what *I* know, and what WingRidge and all his damned Lake Guard knows, and what Isfrael and StarDrifter and Zenith know!"

Drago shifted his eyes so he did not have to bear the angry scrutiny in her own.

"*You* are the StarSon, Drago. *You!*"

Still he did not speak, and Faraday, her frustration at his obstinacy almost unbearable, tore at the throat laces of the gown. She pulled the bodice apart, exposing the swell of her breasts.

"If you accept your heritage, Drago, if you accept your role as StarSon, then you may bed me. Tonight. Here. Now. But tell me that *you* are the StarSon."

"And what shall I tell Caelum?" Drago said softly, once more looking her in the eye. "That I again betrayed him? And this time for a night with our father's lover?"

The color drained from Faraday's face and she wrenched away from him, jerking the bodice closed over her breasts.

"What lies between us," Drago snapped, "needs no blackmail to force a consummation!"

He turned and strode over to the door. "I'll get some food from our packs," he said, then slammed the door behind him.

Faraday lowered her head into her hands, and her shoulders shuddered.

"Never, never say you love me," she whispered into the lonely night, "for that I could not bear."

* * *

She trod the snowdrifts with the firmness of one who regarded the winter as a lover.

About her Gorkentown lay windswept and frosty, and she raised her great head and sniffed the thickening wind, half-expecting to find the scent of prey upon it.

But there was nothing, and so she rumbled a great sigh, and padded further into the town. Puffs of snow lifted into the air with every step she took.

She did not like it. It was too close, the streets too narrow, and she yearned for the vastness of the ice packs to the north.

But it was time, more than time, that she came south to see to her miscreant children. There were lessons to be learned, and no one left but she to teach them.

Of course, Noah could have been a trifle more forthcoming, but that was a man for you, and it was no wonder that Drago, as all her children, was mildly confused.

She halted, raising her head to stare at the rising bulk of Gorkenfort with dark eyes suddenly sharp with knowledge. So. One side of her razor-toothed red mouth lifted as if in a smile—or perhaps a feral grin—then she dropped her head and resumed her slow padding toward the fort.

One of her ears was so badly tattered it was virtually nonexistent, as if it had been lost in some ancient ursine dispute.

She wished she could sink her teeth into the back of a seal, but they lay many days' journey to the north, and she'd have to wait a little longer before she could look forward to that pleasure again.

The fire had died down to glowing coals, but the chamber was warm. Faraday lay curled up in her cloak before the fire, having refused to lie once more in the bed she'd shared with Borneheld.

Now Drago lay there, snug under the heavy quilt, yet cold in its lonely spaces.

The fire cracked and popped, and both sank deeper into their dreams.

Then a massive, frightful roar echoed about the chamber, disintegrating both peace and dream.

Something grabbed and clawed at the foot of the bed, and Drago jerked awake, momentarily too disorientated to do anything save clutch uselessly at the covers sliding toward the floor.

He shouted at Faraday, but she was already awake and crouching against the back wall, staring at something between the door and the bed.

Drago wrenched his eyes away from her and to the foot of the bed.

A dark shape loomed over the mattress. It roared again, and then a flame flickered among the coals, and Drago and Faraday saw that a great icebear stood with its forepaws on the foot of the bed, shaking its head to and fro, and growling around the feathered lizard it held between its teeth.

37

The Lesson of the Sparrow

Faraday blinked, and she saw a great icebear savaging the feathered lizard.

She blinked again, and she saw a gray-haired woman, clothed in ice, impossibly lifting a bull seal in her bare ivory arms and sinking great white fangs into his spine. Blood ran down the seal's fur, and pooled in the quilt tangled about Drago's feet.

"It's all right," Drago said to Faraday, and she blinked one more time, and the visionary woman vanished.

The icebear spat the lizard out with a disgusted growl. The lizard squealed, landed in Drago's lap and immediately scrabbled for a hiding place among the disarranged quilt.

Blue feathers drifted about in the air.

"It *bit* me," the icebear said, her tone disgusted at the temerity of the lizard, and then she tipped her head and looked at Drago, her black eyes gleaming with interest.

"You are Drago," she said. "You were but a babe when Azhure talked of you to me."

"And you are Urbeth."

Urbeth, the mysterious icebear of the northern ice-packs, worshiped by the Ravensbundmen and feared by every seal, seagull and fish in existence.

"Quite so," Urbeth said, then sat down on the floor, her hind legs splayed, one of her forepaws absently combing out the yellowed fur of her belly.

Drago slid out of the bed and pulled on his clothes. "Why did Noah send me north to see you?"

Urbeth ignored him. She had turned her head to regard Faraday curiously. "So, I finally meet Faraday. When Axis and Azhure gossiped with me on the Icebear Coast so many years ago, images of you suffused both their thoughts.

"And then, of course, Gorgrael had you brought north into his ice fortress. I came too late to that place to meet you." But Urbeth remembered how she'd met Axis, on one knee in the freezing snow and wind, his head bowed with grief. And, looking into Faraday's eyes, the bear knew she was remembering, too.

"We all had our different purposes then," Faraday said, and threw her blanket aside, pulling her dress straight.

"Why do you need to speak to me?" Drago said.

Urbeth sighed. "Have you no patience? I have walked many leagues and have blistered my paws to meet you. The least you could do is share with me what gossip you have before badgering me with bald questions."

"No doubt you have heard of the Demons, Urbeth?" Faraday said, stirring the embers into life again.

Urbeth snarled, causing both Drago and Faraday to stare at her.

"Curse Noah, to hide in this land cargo to tempt such Demons through the Star Gate!"

"If you know of Noah," Drago said quietly, "then what gossip *can* we tell you?"

"Everything," said the bear. "Well may I know a name or two, but those damned Ravensbund are too reticent to share every piece of gossip from the south. When did the Demons come through? How? And how lies Tencendor?"

Drago exchanged a glance with Faraday, then sank down on a stool by the fire.

"There is much to tell," he said, as Faraday sat across the hearth from him.

"Then tell," said Urbeth.

Drago and Faraday shared turns to talk through the night of what they knew. Urbeth stretched out by the fire, her eyes half-closed, occasionally rolling on to her back with her four paws dangling in the air to toast her belly.

Every time either Drago or Faraday paused, Urbeth would widen one of her eyes and press them to continue. And yet, Drago had the oddest feeling that little of this was new to the bear.

Finally, as Drago brought their tale to the gates of Gorkenfort itself, he asked again, "Why did Noah ask me to come north to Gorkenfort to meet you? What did he mean, our 'ancestral' mother?"

Urbeth lay on her back staring at the ceiling for a while before she answered.

"Noah wanted me to remind you of something," she said.

"What?" Drago asked.

"A story," Urbeth said. "A lesson."

Drago exchanged a puzzled glance with Faraday. "A story?"

Urbeth rolled over onto her side, and pushed herself into a sitting position with her forepaws. "The Story of the Sparrow," she said. "Do you know it?"

Drago half-laughed. "But that's—"

"*Necessary!*" Urbeth said, and a growl rumbled from her chest. "Tell it!"

Drago looked again at Faraday, whose eyes were bright with curiosity, then acceded to Urbeth's request—or demand.

"This story has only been found relatively recently," he said. "It was discovered among the ancient books that my father and StarDrifter found in Spiredore when they freed it from the Brothers of the Seneschal."

He paused, clearly disquieted about something. "No Enchanters pay it much heed. I mean . . ."

Drago stopped, and Urbeth grinned and scratched her stomach. "I can well imagine why they would want to disregard it, boy. But please . . ."

"It is only a myth," he said. "Unverifiable. A children's tale only. StarDrifter told it to me to amuse me one evening."

"So now amuse *us* with it," Faraday said.

Drago sighed and capitulated.

"Well," he said, shifting about in his chair, "there has always been some mystery about the origins of the four races of Tencendor. The Avar's origins remain shrouded in the secret mysteries of the Sacred Groves, and they have never shared that mystery with any outsiders, even the Icarii. So," he shrugged, "of the Avar I cannot tell.

"The Story of the Sparrow, however, tells a little of the ancient Enchantress, of the origins of the Icarii race, of their father, of how they found their wings, and of the SunSoar affection each for the other."

Again Drago paused, but this time it was only for reflection. The firelight played over his face, lending it both warmth and mystery, and Faraday's own expression stilled as she watched him. Here, now, where the shadows of the fire hid her face and Drago concentrated on something else, it was safe to let herself love him a little.

But only a little . . . enough to pull back before it hurt.

"Listen to the Story of the Sparrow," he said, and leaned forward, his voice taking on the hypnotic quality of a court troubadour and the rhythmic beauty of a SunSoar:

As you must both know, the Icarii, as the Charonites and the Acharites, were all born of the ancient Enchantress. She had three sons, fathered by the gods only knew, and of those three sons she favored only the younger two. To them she whispered some of her myriad of secrets, while the eldest she cast from her door and turned her back on his pleas. This eldest wandered desolate into the land, which he eventually destroyed to assuage his grief at his mother's rejection, while his younger brothers stayed many more years learning at the Enchantress' knee.

"You have a duty," she told her middle son, "to wander and watch." He nodded, and thought he understood.

"You have a duty," she told her youngest son, "to dance your delight to the stars." And he too nodded, thinking he understood.

Her two younger sons made their way into the world. The middle brother was reflective, and haunted shadows, thinking there to catch a glimpse of the unknowable. Eventually, his eyes turned downward to the chasms that led into the earth, and there he made his way.

The youngest brother was wide of smile and bright of curiosity. He clutched in his hand his mother's ring, that which would give birth to all of the Enchanters' rings, and it impelled him to cast his eye to the high places, and to there he climbed.

All three brothers took to themselves many wives from among the humanoid races that populated the land, and these wives bore them many children. These children took to themselves husbands and wives, and they likewise bred many children. Within a thousand years the plains and the chasms and the mountains rang with the voices of the brother races. Mankind, the Acharites, who followed their cattle through dusty plain trails and built themselves houses of brick. The Charonites, who explored the misty waterways beneath the trails and took the houses others had left behind. And the Icarii, beloved of the gods, who climbed the crags and cried out to the stars and built themselves houses of music and mystery.

Then, the Icarii did not have wings.

The story of how the Icarii found their wings is rightly the love story of EverHeart and CrimsonStar. CrimsonStar was an Enchanter unparalleled in the as yet young history of the Icarii, but his love for the stars and for the Star Dance paled into insignificance beside the love he bore his wife, Ever-Heart. CrimsonStar and EverHeart lived in the lower ranges of the Icescarp Alps. Then, long, long before the Wars of the Ax, the Icarii populated most of the mountain ranges of Tencendor, the majority living in the Minaret Peaks. But CrimsonStar and EverHeart were newly married and preferred to enjoy the relative isolation of the Icescarp Alps. Talon Spike was only just being opened up and hollowed out, and the few dozen Icarii within their immediate vicinity were, truth to tell, a few dozen too many for CrimsonStar and EverHeart.

They did what they could to keep themselves distant, climbing frightening precipices to achieve privacy to indulge their frequent cravings for love, clinging to razorbacked crags to evade curious eyes and to allow the winds of thrill and danger to deepen their passion.

They were in love and they were young, and so they were indulged by their elders. Time enough, in fifty years or so, for them to descend from the heights of newly married explorations.

But fifty years they did not have. Eight years after they were married, when they had barely recovered from the breathless passion of their initial consummation, EverHeart fell. She fell from a peak so high even the winds were frightened to assail it. She fell so far she was swallowed by the clouds that broiled about the knees of the mountain.

She fell so fast even CrimsonStar's scream could not follow her.

It took him three days to find her, and when he did, he thought he had found a corpse. She lay broken, unmoving, her spilt blood frozen in crazy patterns across the rocks that cradled her. CrimsonStar's tears felt as if they, too, were freezing into solid grief as they trailed down his cheeks. He touched his wife, but she did not move, and her flesh had the solidity of rock.

Frozen.

He wailed, then screamed, then wrenched his wife from her resting place, tearing her skin where it had frozen to the surface of the rocks. He cuddled her close, trying to warm her, then realized through his grief that, somewhere deep within EverHeart, her courageous heart, her ever heart, still thudded. Slowly, achingly slowly, but still it thudded.

He carried her back to their home, and there he cared for her, bringing to her side all the Healers of the Icarii people, and even calling to her side Banes from the distant forests. They restored her warmth, and the color to her cheeks. They restored the brightness of her eye, and even the gloss of her golden hair. They restored the flex to her arms and the suppleness to her long white fingers.

But they could not restore movement or usefulness to her shattered legs, and they could not restore the laughter to her face. EverHeart was condemned to lie useless in her bed, her lower body anchoring her to immobility, its flesh a drain on the resources of her upper body and, more importantly, on her spirit.

At CrimsonStar's request, the Icarii Healers and the Avar Banes left. They farewelled the pair as best they could, certain that EverHeart would not survive the year, and even more certain CrimsonStar would not survive his wife's inevitable death.

For seven months CrimsonStar held EverHeart's hand, and sang to her, and soothed her as best he could. He fed her and washed her and ministered to her needs. He lived only to see her smile, and to hear her tell him she was content.

But EverHeart could do neither of these things without lying, and this she would not do.

One night, late into the darkness, EverHeart asked CrimsonStar to kill her. It was a brutal request, but EverHeart was too tired of life to phrase it more politely.

"I cannot," CrimsonStar said, and turned his head aside.

"Then build me wings to fly," EverHeart said, bitterness twisting her voice, "that I may escape these useless legs and this prison bed."

CrimsonStar looked at her. "My lovely, I cannot . . ."

"Then kill me."

CrimsonStar crept away, not wishing EverHeart to see the depth of his distress. Knowing she knew it anyway.

He climbed to the crag from which EverHeart had fallen so many months before. He had no intention of throwing himself from the peak, but some instinct told him that he might find comfort at the same point where he and she had lost so much of their lives. He sat down in a sheltered crevice, and watched the stars filter their way across the night sky.

Tears ran down his face. EverHeart had given him an impossible request . . . and if he didn't help her die now, then what agony of wasting would she go through over the next few months until she died of unaided causes?

"You should not weep so at this altitude," a soft voice said, "for your tears will freeze to your face and leave your cheeks marred with black ice."

CrimsonStar jerked his head up.

A sparrow hopped into the crevice, its feathers ruffled out against the cold.

CrimsonStar was so stunned he could not speak.

"I have been disappointed in you, my son," the sparrow continued, and hopped onto CrimsonStar's knee to better look the Icarii man in the eye.

"Disappointed?" CrimsonStar managed, but he straightened his shoulders and brushed the tears from his eyes. Who was this sparrow to so chastise him?

"I am your father, CrimsonStar."

"No . . . no . . . my father is FellowStar . . . alive and well . . ."

The sparrow tipped his head to one side, his eyes angry yet sadly tolerant of his wayward child. "Do you not understand, CrimsonStar? I am the father of the Icarii race."

CrimsonStar could do nothing but stare at the sparrow.

"I lay with the Enchantress, and she waxed great with our child. Her third and last son for her life . . . and my fourth son that spring. It was a good spring for me that year."

"I . . . I did not know . . ."

"Few knew who the Enchantress took to her bed, child. The fathers of her elder sons are unknown to me. And I . . . I should not have told you of my role in your generation, save that I could not bear your sadness and that of EverHeart's. Still," the sparrow sighed, "I had no choice, for you have proved such a disappointment, and all fathers reserve their right to chastise and redirect their children."

CrimsonStar slowly shook his head from side to side, almost unable to comprehend that this sparrow (*a sparrow!*) was the father of the proud Icarii race.

"Listen to me, CrimsonStar. I shall tell you of a great joy and then I shall curse you, because you must pay for the privilege of hearing my advice—"

"No . . . I have been cursed enough."

"You have no choice, my son. Now . . . watch."

And the sparrow fluttered his wings, and rose a hand span above CrimsonStar's knee before settling gently down again.

"Why have you no wings, CrimsonStar?"

"Wings . . ."

"Wings, CrimsonStar. You are my son, and yet you refuse to wear your heritage."

"I . . ."

"Do you not sing the Flight Song to your children as they lay nesting in their shells?"

"Flight Song . . . ?"

The sparrow spat in disgust. "Listen . . ." And he trilled a simple song, paused, then trilled it again. "Repeat it."

His surprise giving way to a small tingle of excitement, CrimsonStar repeated the tune, stumbling over one or two of the phrases, but correcting himself instantly.

The sparrow laughed. "You are my son, CrimsonStar. Now go home and lay beside EverHeart and sing her the Song. Run your hands down her back, rub, probe, encourage, and soon she shall have movement again. Soon she will soar free from her prison bed and let the sky ring with her laughter. Teach her the Song, and let her minister to you as well. And when she swells with your child, then place your hands on her belly and sing to the child what I have taught you. It is my gift to my children, CrimsonStar."

"Thank—"

"Do not thank me, CrimsonStar. Not until after the pain has faded, for you are both late in age to spread your wings. Besides, for the knowledge I have imparted and the gift I have given I must curse you."

CrimsonStar waited, sure the curse would match the gift.

"Oh, it will, it will, CrimsonStar. Listen to me now. You and EverHeart will be the first among the Icarii to spread your wings and fly into the heavens. But for this there is a price. I name your family SunSoar, a regal name, for your feathered backs must bear the burden of the sins of the Icarii. Wait . . . there is more. As you and EverHeart can consider no other love save that you bear for the other, so no SunSoar will love beyond the SunSoar blood. Never will you and yours find happiness save in each other's arms. Do you understand?"

CrimsonStar nodded soberly, considering the implications.

"Then go down to your wife, CrimsonStar. And then to your people . . . and tell them the heavens wait."

The fire had died down, and Drago's face was lost in shadow.

"StarDrifter told me that," he repeated, "and he also told

me that somehow the story must have been corrupted by the Seneschal, for how could the proud Icarii be born of a *sparrow*?"

Faraday managed a small smile. Poor StarDrifter. No doubt he preferred to think that the Icarii race was fathered by one of the stars themselves, falling down the ladder of the Star Dance to impregnate the Enchantress.

"It is no myth, but truth," said Urbeth quietly, her eyes fixed on some distant point in the roof beams. "For I am she who lay with the sparrow, and I am she who mothered the three races."

As Drago and Faraday stared at her, Faraday motionless with shock and Drago silent with understanding, Urbeth—the Enchantress—rolled over on her belly and bared her teeth at them.

"Noah sent you to me to learn, Drago, and there is a lesson in what you have just related. Shall we speak of it?"

38

The Sunken Keep

Zenith sat at the table and tried not to listen to the conversation. StarDrifter and EvenSong were chatting happily about their long-gone life in Talon Spike. All Zenith could think of was that EvenSong was her aunt . . . and how could she sleep with her aunt's father? Zenith suppressed a grimace. She was becoming obsessed with guilt, and yet all she and StarDrifter had ever done was share a kiss or two!

Zenith looked at the table, trying to find something else to think about. The table held the most splendid platter-ware—the richest crimson-gilded Corolean manufacture—but it sat horribly bare. That noon they'd lunched on dried biscuits and a single apple apiece.

The only thing they had in abundance was wine. The cellars of the palace had always been well-stocked, and whether it was the accessibility or the peace of mind it gave Zenith did not know, but over the past few weeks she had begun to avail herself of it a little too freely.

She had not been able to resolve anything regarding StarDrifter. He remained warm, loving and patient. She wanted desperately to please him, to thank him for his belief in her, and had come to the conclusion that if she was unable to bring herself to sleep with him, it was nothing but her fault. There was no *reason* to feel such repulsion . . . was there?

Perhaps RiverStar had been right to taunt her. Maybe she should have taken lovers well before this. Maybe she was nothing but a prim bitch with a hall as cold as any in this complex. Why was she such a *prude?*

She crumpled a napkin in one hand, and felt like screaming. All Zenith wanted to do was escape . . . escape from this chill-chambered prison, and from her own confusion and guilt. In the next instant, escape was handed her.

StarFever bustled in the door, and behind him came WingRidge CurlClaw, Captain of the Lake Guard, with SpikeFeather TrueSong at his side.

StarDrifter gaped at them an instant before he remembered that Drago had sent them off to find Sanctuary. He stood and took a step in their direction. "Have you . . . ?"

"Well," WingRidge said, one eyebrow raised in amusement, "SpikeFeather *thinks* he knows where it is."

"But we need your help," SpikeFeather said.

Both birdmen remembered their manners as they caught sight of FreeFall, and they bowed low, sweeping their wings behind them.

"StarDrifter has spoken of this Sanctuary," FreeFall said as he rose and walked slowly over to WingRidge. "He has also said that you trust implicitly in Drago. Is this correct?"

"Talon FreeFall," WingRidge said, holding the birdman's eyes. "If I say that I believe in Drago, then what I mean is that the Lake Guard believes Drago . . . and trusts Drago."

FreeFall stilled, his back very straight. He knew as well as any other that the Lake Guard dedicated their lives in service to StarSon. "And so now you aid Drago," he asked. "You do as he asks?"

"I can do nothing else," WingRidge said. "The Guard can do nothing else."

FreeFall rocked slightly on his feet as the implications of what WingRidge said sank in.

The Lake Guard acknowledged Drago as StarSon.

He looked at EvenSong, their love and many years of closeness allowing them to know what the other was thinking, even if they had never had the benefit of enchantments with which to share thoughts.

FreeFall breathed deeply, trying to accept it, but finding it hard. Why had no one told him before now?

"The Icarii starve in this cold-halled hell," he said to WingRidge, and walked back to his place at the table. For the moment he did not want to think about accepting Drago as StarSon. "And the Avar can hardly feed themselves, let alone us. Every day we are inundated with more refugees from the plains to the west. StarDrifter could tell me little about this Sanctuary . . . can you add to that meagerness?"

FreeFall sat and indicated two stools, and the two birdmen took them, tucking their wings neatly against their backs. Briefly SpikeFeather spoke about what they knew of Sanctuary. It was not much.

"Drago knew nothing of it himself," SpikeFeather said, "save that it exists and that it is within the Underworld. He tasked WingRidge and myself with the burden of looking for it."

"And of course," WingRidge said, managing to combine both sarcasm and affection into his tone, "despite all Spike-Feather's knowledge gained from the Ferryman, he could not cast a gleam of light upon this mysterious Sanctuary."

"Nevertheless," SpikeFeather said firmly, throwing the captain of the Lake Guard an irritated glance, "I now know where it *must* be."

He told his four listeners of his and WingRidge's hunt through the ancient maps of Sigholt.

"And you found evidence of Sanctuary?" Zenith said. For the first time in weeks she felt a surge of optimism . . . and sheer relief in being given something else to think of other than her problematical relationship with StarDrifter.

"Not quite," WingRidge said, his eyes firmly on Spike-Feather.

"What we found," SpikeFeather continued, "was an ancient map of Tencendor that showed the Sacred Lakes and their accompanying Keeps. All four Lakes, and all *four* Keeps."

"But . . ." EvenSong said and shared a glance with her husband, father and Zenith.

"Quite," SpikeFeather said with evident satisfaction. "Now there are only three Lakes with Keeps, or Towers. Where is Fernbrake Lake's Keep? It was there on the ancient map, but now? Gone."

He grinned and waved his hands about as if his discovery had magically solved Tencendor's every last problem.

"My friend does tend to be slightly overenthusiastic on what can only be sheer supposition," WingRidge said.

"But surely he has a point, otherwise you would not be here with him," Zenith said.

"Zenith is right," StarDrifter said slowly. "Tell me, have you searched for this lost Keep in the waterways?"

SpikeFeather nodded. "Of course—but we found nothing. Besides . . . would not the Charonites have found something before now if it were in easy view?"

WingRidge thought about observing that the Charonites had managed to miss the Maze Gate, as well as any evidence of Noah's occasional ramblings through the waterways between the craft, but decided not to spoil SpikeFeather's moment of excitement.

"There is much in the Underworld that lay hidden in deep enchantment even from Charonite eyes," SpikeFeather went on. "I think that the entrance to Sanctuary must be in the Overworld somewhere—for the peoples of Tencendor to have easy access to it—and leads down to a completely hidden region of the waterways. I think the door to Sanctuary must be Fernbrake's Keep—what else *can* it be—and we must only find it, and then—"

"And then I suppose every one of Tencendor's problems will be instantly at an end," FreeFall said, with more than a hint of sarcasm in his voice.

"At the least," StarDrifter said, "you may find shelter and food for the Icarii, FreeFall, and room enough also for the Acharites and Avar, should the forests ever fail."

"You are right, StarDrifter." FreeFall looked at Spike-

Feather. "I apologize for my tone, SpikeFeather. What needs to be done?"

"Well," WingRidge said, "we need to search the shoreline of Fernbrake Lake for evidence of the Keep, and we must do it fast. I need willing legs and eyes to help in that. At the moment the majority of the Lake Guard are busy aiding the population of Sigholt and Lakesview into hiding within the Urqhart Hills, for surely the TimeKeepers will be there any day now. Then the Demons will turn for Fernbrake, aided by the gods know what increase in their power. We need to get as many people into Sanctuary before then—and *all* must be secreted before the TimeKeepers manage to resurrect Qeteb completely."

"Surely Caelum will have acted by then," FreeFall said, but he was not the only one who heard the doubt in his voice.

WingRidge fixed him with his stare. "We must needs act fast," he repeated. "Who will aid me?"

In the end, WingRidge and SpikeFeather led only a small party of some eight Icarii, including StarDrifter, and Zenith, who'd flatly refused to be left behind in the gloomy chambers of the Icarii palace, toward Fernbrake Lake. They had not food to spare for a larger group.

SpikeFeather thought ten should be enough. The Lake and its surrounds were not so extensive that they couldn't search the entire area, and besides, he knew where the Keep had once stood.

StarDrifter, although cheered by SpikeFeather's enthusiasm, nonetheless wondered if it was misplaced. It *was* only sheer hope, after all, that saw SpikeFeather put his entire trust in this single idea, and if he was wrong, then would they have time enough to canvas other possibilities? And if Spike-Feather was right, and they found the entrance to Sanctuary—what if it was guarded by wards and enchantments? None of them had the ability left to work them. StarDrifter remembered the enchantment in the carved rock-face that covered the entrance of the stairwell leading down to the waterways at the junction of the River Nordra and the Icescarp Alps. Then StarDrifter had entranced Rivkah and

Azhure with his power to open the stairwell—but he could not do that now. So what if—

"Peace, StarDrifter," WingRidge said by his side, a smile on his face. "Your shoulders alone cannot carry the weight of Tencendor."

StarDrifter grinned, liking the birdman, although they'd hardly passed more than a half-hour in conversation previously, and put his effort back into the path ahead.

They had climbed out of the Minaret complex about half a league below the crest of the ranges. Minstrelsea rose above them, for Faraday had planted it not only up to the rim of the crater that housed the Lake, but right down into the crater as well.

"I will be glad," StarDrifter said, his breath now short as the pathway steepened, "when we can finally take to the sky again without fear of the Demons striking us down. Gods! To be virtually deprived of flight as well as of power!"

They reached the rim of the crater by late morning, and stood a while to catch their breath and look down. It was a beautiful sight.

The center of the crater was filled with a vast circular emerald lake, surrounded not only by trees, but by thick ferns that in places rose higher than a man's head. Birds chirruped and cavorted among the fronds, safe within the shadows and the nearby magic of the Lake.

"I hope," muttered a young birdman by the name of Jest-Wing BlueBack, "that SpikeFeather does not expect us to crawl *all* through that bracken!"

"I sincerely hope I won't have to ask it of you," Spike-Feather said, then waved the party down the path.

The air was milder within the crater, but whether because of the sheltering height of its walls, or the influence of the magical water itself, StarDrifter did not know. Whichever, the extra warmth was welcome and invigorating. For the first time in many days he felt the muscles of his wings and shoulders relax, and he shook out his silvery white feathers and walked down the gravel path with confident strides.

For her part, Zenith looked about in wonder, distracted for once from her own thoughts. She had never previously been to Fernbrake Lake. Although magical and sacred, the Lake was more important to the Avar than the Icarii, and figured in none of the Icarii's religious rituals. Zenith had heard her mother speak of the Lake, and Faraday had mentioned it once or twice (hadn't something happened to Faraday in these waters?) but nothing prepared her for the sheer beauty of the Lake.

The water was a deep emerald in hue, yet nevertheless it remained beautifully translucent. Pausing at the edge of the waters, Zenith stared into depths that appeared to go on forever. Down to the very mysteries of the unknown, she thought, and then jumped, for she thought she saw the reflection of a stag in the water.

Zenith straightened and looked behind her, but there was nothing, and she shrugged slightly and hurried to catch up with the others.

"Here!" SpikeFeather proclaimed as they reached a semicircular grassy area between a stand of trees and the water. The clearing extended some sixty paces, in an almost perfect crescent about the edge of the Lake. "The Keep stood here."

"The grass is smooth and flat," StarDrifter said. "There is no rubble, or evidence of foundations."

"It *was* here," SpikeFeather insisted, "but it must have collapsed into the earth hundreds, if not thousands, of years ago. Naturally, the grass will have grown smooth over it. Now . . ." and he proceeded to instruct his companions in the manner of search they should undertake.

Zenith glanced at StarDrifter, then dropped her eyes as he sent her a small smile to share his amusement at Spike-Feather's bustle.

WingRidge noticed StarDrifter's expression and smiled wryly himself. "Is this what I have spent my entire life training for?" he murmured. "Crawling about on my hands and knees in a grassy clearing looking for pebbles?"

"Well," StarDrifter said, "at least you shall have the joy of watching two of the vaunted SunSoars doing the same."

WingRidge burst into laughter, and SpikeFeather shot him an irritated glance.

Zenith grinned despite herself, then sank to her knees. If it was here, then they would find it.

In the end, it took less than an hour. JestWing, disinclined to crawl about on his hands and knees, had taken a sturdy branch he'd found lying under its parent tree, and searched the grassy flat by poking the jagged end of the branch down through the soil. For almost an hour, he sank the branch again and again into the soft earth, encountering no other obstacles than the roots of the grass carpet.

This time, as he probed into the earth, the branch slid only a hand span in before it hit stone.

The force jarred JestWing's arm, and he frowned. He lifted the branch out of the earth and stepped forward a pace, sliding it down again.

It slid only a hand span before it stopped.

Another pace, and then five or six more, with the same result, and JestWing knew he'd found an extensive flat stone surface just under the grass.

He opened his mouth, meaning to shout his discovery to the others, but as he turned about, JestWing saw all were standing silently, watching him.

"Sanctuary," Zenith whispered. By late afternoon they had cleared the grass and soil away from the flat stone surface. Situated halfway between the edges of water and trees, it formed a massive circle some twenty-five paces across. The large cream flagstones were laid out in the form of a twisting maze.

"WingRidge?" SpikeFeather said, raising his eyebrows at the captain of the Lake Guard. Like everyone else, he was tired and dirty, soil smudging his face and dappling the skin of his hands and arms.

WingRidge did not raise his eyes from the circular maze. "I do not know it," he said, the fingers of one hand absently tracing the golden knot on his tunic. "Knots—mazes—may take a thousand varied forms, and this one is very different to the Maze beyond the Gate. I cannot understand it."

If WingRidge expected SpikeFeather to be disappointed, he was wrong. The red-plumed birdman simply shrugged, and asked everyone to stand outside the circle.

"It will be simple enough to decipher," SpikeFeather said, and walked slowly over the maze.

"Ah!" he exclaimed after only a few minutes. "Here is where it begins!"

He began to follow a pathway over the maze, his body swaying with the natural rhythm of the Icarii.

"What is he doing?" Zenith said, finally moving to stand next to StarDrifter.

He did not answer, and Zenith looked at him. StarDrifter was frowning, staring at SpikeFeather, but Zenith thought she could see just the faintest glimmer of excitement in the pale blue of his eyes and the skin stretched tight over his cheekbones.

"StarDrifter?"

"I don't believe it!" he whispered. "I can't believe we have all been so *stupid*."

Then he strode into the circle, grabbing a startled Spike-Feather by the elbow.

"Out," StarDrifter said. "Let me, SpikeFeather. Please, *let me do this*."

SpikeFeather almost objected, then stopped himself. StarDrifter had once been a powerful Enchanter, second only to Axis and his family in strength. He would do this far better than SpikeFeather could. So he nodded, and left the circle, joining Zenith and the other Icarii grouped about her.

StarDrifter moved to the spot where SpikeFeather had originally said the pathway began, and stood completely still, his golden head bowed, his luminescent white wings spread across the stone behind him.

Zenith frowned herself, and laid a soft hand on Spike-Feather's arm. "What is happening?"

SpikeFeather caught WingRidge's eyes, then glanced briefly at the other Icarii standing about, as puzzled as Zenith.

"I found the entrance to the Maze Gate by executing a dance," SpikeFeather explained. "The pattern of the Maze here describes the pattern of a dance, a dance that will open the doorway into Sanctuary."

Zenith jerked her head back to StarDrifter. A dance? A pattern?

An enchantment?

Now StarDrifter commenced the dance. He used his entire body, wings, arms, legs and torso all twisting and dipping in exquisite deliberateness that described the movements of the dance.

Zenith stared at him, everything else forgotten. All she could think of was how stunningly beautiful StarDrifter was. She saw the strength and beauty in the line and swell of muscle over his naked arms and torso, the indefinable air of mystery that clung to the chiseled bone structure of his face and saved it from arrogance, the pale, fine skin, the golden hair, and the sheer loveliness of his long-fingered hands, now sweeping slowly through the air.

Stars! Why couldn't she allow herself to enjoy him as a lover?

For the first time, Zenith realized that that was what she wanted above all else. She *wanted* StarDrifter as a lover, but she did not know how to *accept* him as a lover. He came with too many complex confusions and emotions.

Why couldn't he be my cousin, or even uncle? *Anything* would be better than grandfather. Anything.

Tears filled Zenith's eyes, and she felt SpikeFeather place a hand on her shoulder. She glanced at him, and he nodded and gave her a small smile, and even though Zenith knew he couldn't possibly know her dilemma, she let herself be comforted nevertheless.

StarDrifter moved ever more deliberately into his dance. He proceeded slowly, and with precision, but with such supple fluidity no part of his body was ever still. Feet, hands, wings all followed the movement prescribed in the stone patterns before him.

Now he increased the tempo of his dance slightly, and Zenith realized he was repeating the pattern.

And then . . . then StarDrifter began to sing.

As an Enchanter, when he'd had the use of the Star Dance, StarDrifter had been renowned for the power and beauty of his voice. Now, even though he no longer had the use of the Star Dance, his voice was still beautiful and utterly compelling.

Zenith felt the tears slide down her cheeks, feeling the waste of her life to this point. She had sat in her chamber in Sigholt, and done what? Nothing, save use her power to frivolous ends. Meanwhile, StarDrifter, who had enjoyed only a fraction of the power of Axis' brood, had studied the beauty and mystery of the very air about him.

The SunSoars had squabbled and plotted and torn their

lives to shreds. StarDrifter had learned to understand the rhythms of life itself, and had *enjoyed* life.

Had any of his grandchildren?

StarDrifter twirled and dipped, his voice soaring into the gathering dusk, his arms fully extended, his wings catching the final rays of the sun to send slivers of silvery light scattering about the clearing.

Zenith put a hand to her mouth, unable to stop herself from crying. She cried for the waste the SunSoars had made of their lives, she cried for the beauty that StarDrifter was forcing her to witness, and she cried for herself that she could not allow herself to love the man she had been born for.

Now StarDrifter twirled, so fast she could hardly distinguish individual movements. She sensed the warmth as someone halted behind her.

"All my life I have heard stories of StarDrifter," WingRidge whispered, one of his hands now on her other shoulder. "I had heard of his self-absorption and selfishness. Of his quests and lusts for women. Of his pettinesses. But no one ever told me . . . no one ever told me that he was a Master."

At that precise moment StarDrifter's song and his dance soared to a climax, and he came to a halt, flinging his arms and wings out.

Somewhere a bell tolled, its rich melodious tones reverberating about the clearing. Individual stones started to move, sliding silently to one side.

StarDrifter rose into the air on his wings, twisting higher and higher in an ecstasy of joy, then dropped down to alight before Zenith, SpikeFeather and WingRidge.

"Don't you understand?" he cried, and, seizing Zenith by the shoulders, he pulled her from WingRidge's and Spike-Feather's grasp.

She did not object.

"Don't you *understand?*"

"StarDrifter?"

"Zenith, you are lovelier than the very stars themselves, but must I shake you to move your thoughts into coherence? My darling girl, *don't you understand what I just did?*"

She stared into his eyes, too consumed by emotion to speak.

"I just used the same enchantment to open the door into Sanctuary as I used to open the rock door before the Nordra door to the Underworld. *Don't you understand?*"

Now StarDrifter looked over Zenith's shoulder to all the Icarii standing behind her.

"I did not use music at all, but—"

"But *dance!*" SpikeFeather cried.

"Yes," StarDrifter said, quieter now. He dropped his eyes back to Zenith's face, and she felt his hands tighten on her shoulders.

"Music and dance are but patterns, Zenith. Icarii Enchanters once wove the pattern of music to channel the power of the Star Dance. I just used the pattern of dance."

"But . . . how did you use the power of the Star Dance?" Zenith said. "It has been cut off."

"I . . . I don't know. Perhaps—"

"You did not touch the power of the Star Dance," WingRidge said, "but the power of the craft themselves." The power of the Star Dance that had infused the craft during their millennia in space. Then he grinned. "And I do not think it would have required the power of an Enchanter to open the Sanctuary door. SpikeFeather would have been as successful."

He laughed. "And had a beetle crawled about in the right pattern then the door would have opened for it, as well."

But *no one,* thought Zenith, could have used that power or executed that dance with the grace and beauty of StarDrifter. Still excited, StarDrifter slid his arm around her shoulders, and Zenith did not object.

The patchy-bald rat scrabbled its way through the darkness, embracing the foul scents and dampnesses of the sewer.

This was home, and it was where he would eventually launch his revenge on the two-legs who had harried him and his kind all their lives. He paused, and listened. Ten thousand claws scrabbled behind him, and this was only one sewer. Many other sewers, ten times a thousand sewers, were filled with the sweet sounds of scrabbling, gnawing revenge.

And hunger.

It was not only revenge that drove the patchy-bald rat. His masters wanted those who sheltered in the tenements above . . . but they'd promised him his fun, first.

There, another voice probing his mind. The badger, checking on the rat's progress. The rat quivered in delight at the thought of the slaughter ahead. As he burrowed and tunneled and probed underground, so the badger and his ever-growing crowd of beasts and demented two-legs thronged and probed the sheer walls of Carlon.

The city was surrounded by increasing numbers of Demon-controlled animals. While the guards might lean from the walls and worry about the deranged cattle and sheep and pigs that humped and bumped against the stone, and shudder at the foulness of their human cousins shifting among the beasts, they did not think for a moment of what might be crawling under their feet.

39

The Mother of Races

"The *Enchantress*?" Faraday said. "But . . . but I thought . . ."

Urbeth waved a paw lazily in the air, admiring the way red shards of firelight glinted from her talons.

"You thought what?" she asked.

"I . . . I thought . . ."

"All who know of you," Drago said, "believed you long dead. Or just a myth, or legend."

Urbeth laughed softly, but her humor was edged with cynicism, and neither Drago nor Faraday smiled with her.

"And of that you would know much, would you not?" Urbeth said, addressing Faraday rather than Drago. "For were you not virtually forgotten in but forty years? I have had some fifteen thousand years of forgetfulness, of being consigned to legend."

She almost spat the last word.

Faraday bowed her head in understanding. "And yet I have

managed to escape my entrapment in the flesh of a doe," she said, shooting Drago a glance, "while here you still linger in the flesh of a—"

"Bear!" Urbeth cried. "A *bear*. But you don't understand." She waved a languid paw over her form. "I enjoy this form, and I wear it by choice. Now . . ."

Urbeth slapped her paw on the floor in a businesslike manner. "Noah sent you north to talk with me, yes, and thus we must talk. First, I would tell you a little of myself, and of my purpose in life, and perhaps that will allow you to realize the significance of the Story of the Sparrow."

The feathered lizard peeked from under the bedcovers, then slowly crawled out as the bear continued to speak.

"My name *is* Urbeth, and has always been, although legend has assigned to me the title of Enchantress. Bah! It is a glib title, given how it has been bandied about these past years.

"I was born to loving parents into a world heavy with magic."

"Wait," Drago said, then apologized for his interruption. "I thought that magic only came with—"

"With the Icarii. And their Star Dance." Urbeth grinned. "Learn the first lesson, Drago. This *land* itself is invested with magic—you should know where it comes from—and it does not need the tinkling accompaniment of the Star Dance to work its wonders.

"Well, to continue. I was entranced by the magic, and captivated by it. It used me to its will, and from my body issued forth three sons, three sons who founded the Icarii, Charonite and Acharite races.

"The sparrow founded the Icarii race, and perhaps it is more than enough time that they should learn his humility."

"And the Charonites?" Drago asked.

Urbeth glanced at the lizard, which had now crept down to the very foot of the bed, his eyes bright upon her.

"Who fathered the Charonites has no bearing on this tale," Urbeth said, and shifted uncomfortably.

"But he was of undoubted magic," Faraday said, "for he fathered a race of magicians."

"Quite so," Urbeth said. "I chose my lovers well. All of them planted enchanted seed."

There was a silence.

"All?" Drago asked softly. "But the Acharites have no magic at—"

Urbeth snarled. "Are you not listening?"

"Urbeth, who fathered the Acharite race?" Faraday asked. Her voice trembled slightly.

Urbeth took her time in answering. When she finally did, her voice was heavy with memory, and perhaps even love. "He was the best lover of all. I would have kept him more company, save that he lived in a place I could not share."

"Noah," Drago said suddenly. "*Noah* fathered the Acharite race."

Urbeth nodded. "He did."

"And the Acharites are *magical?*"

In answer, Urbeth looked to Faraday. "Faraday. You carry only Acharite blood. Tell me, *are* the Acharites magical?"

Faraday opened her mouth to answer in the negative, but then she slowly closed it again, remembering. Besides herself, there *had* been others with certain skills, hadn't there?

"Goodwife Renkin," she said. "She was infused with magic, but I thought it a product of her association with the Mother."

"Mostly, yes, but Goodwife Renkin came from a long line of Goodwives who were able to somehow tap into a tiny portion of their ability," Urbeth said. "Women who muttered spells over their newborn children, and their husbands' corn-blistered feet. Women who knew the right paths to keep the sheep from harm. But there is more, Faraday, and you know it."

Faraday stared at her. "Noah gave me power—"

"No!" Urbeth snapped. "He gave you nothing. He merely awoke your latent powers." Her voice softened. "He is, after all, and in a manner of speaking, your father."

She turned back to Drago. "The TimeKeepers destroyed all the Icarii power that your mother had buried, boy, you know that . . . but what of your Acharite blood?"

Drago did not answer her, but merely stared.

"I can see that I shall have to explain more, and tell some of my own tale," Urbeth said, and settled herself more comfortably. "Throw another log on that fire, Drago. It is not often I get the chance to toast my belly so efficiently.

"Ah, that's better. Now, as you related in the Story of the Sparrow—ah! he had a wit rarely found!—I bore three sons. The eldest, who eventually founded the Acharite race, I cast from my door, and turned my back on all his pleas for love."

"You favored the younger two," Faraday said, trying to think it through. "The founders of the Icarii and Charonite races. Magical races. And yet you said that the eldest son had as much magic . . ."

"As much *potential* magic," Urbeth replied. "I cast him from my door and from my heart because he denied his heritage. He found the very word 'enchantment' distasteful, let alone the concept and the power itself that lay in his breast."

She shot Drago a significant glance, and Drago averted his eyes.

"The Acharites have ever been distrustful of magic," Faraday said. "Thus the Seneschal were able to attain such a tight grip on their souls."

"Aye," Urbeth said. "My eldest son was a *fool*. He had so much! And yet yet denied it. He buried it deep, and refused to allow its presence. When I realized that he would never accept his heritage, I grew angry, and cast him from my heart and my house before I gave in to the overwhelming temptation to eat him."

Urbeth paused, and bared her teeth in a silent snarl, as if she could see her eldest son standing before her now—a tempting meal.

"The pain must have been the greater," Faraday said very softly, "for that the son was fathered by he whom you loved most. To lose a child made in such great love . . ."

Drago shot an unreadable look at her. Did she think of Axis *all* day? And long for him *all* night?

Urbeth chose not to comment on Faraday's words. "So my son wandered onto the plains," she said, "and interbred with the humanoid peoples he found there. From his loins sprang the Acharites, a breed hatefully resistant to all forms of magic, a breed given to murdering all wielders of magic they encountered, and yet a breed who carried the seed of profound magic within their breasts."

"And what does this magic consist of?" Drago asked. "How may the Acharites use it?"

"Ah," Urbeth said. "Thereby lies a problem. Both you and Faraday have managed to touch the magic within, and with investigation and acceptance, you will learn how to use it, and to what uses it may be put."

"Thus our ability to withstand the ravages of the Demons," Faraday said.

She turned to Drago, her eyes bright with excitement. "All the Acharites will be able to—"

"No!" Urbeth barked, and Faraday turned back to her.

"No," the Enchantress repeated more softly. "*Hear me out.* My eldest—I can no longer bear to utter his name!—rejected his heritage so completely that the ability to use it has now virtually been lost to all Acharites. There is only one way that a person of Acharite blood can touch his or her enchantment. A process they must experience that can shock their power to the fore. Faraday? Drago? What experience did you both share, what shattering process, that enabled both of you to touch your power?"

They sat in silence for some moments, and when Drago spoke, his voice was peculiarly flat.

"We have both died," he said, "and been reborn. Re-created."

"Yes," Urbeth said. "The only way you can use the heritage your ancestor chose to deny for you is to die—and then somehow manage a re-creation."

Again, silence.

"But the Goodwives . . ." Faraday said.

"They touched what can only be called a ten thousandth of their heritage," Urbeth said. "And Goodwife Renkin was so powerful *only* because the Mother chose her as a conduit."

"As I," Faraday said, nodding slowly. "The power I had as Faraday Tree Friend was the Mother's power."

"Yes," Urbeth said. "And now both of you enjoy power, your *own* power, via death and then rebirth."

Drago thought of Noah, and thought of the power of the craft. "Over the hundreds of thousands of years the craft have lain in the ground," he said in a voice so low the others could barely hear him, "they have infused their power into the land. Noah infused that same power into the child he and you made. Thus the Acharites—*potentially*—wield the power of the craft and the land itself."

"Aye," Urbeth said quietly. "You understand."

"What about the Scepter?" Drago said in a slightly louder voice. He glanced toward the staff leaning against the wall by the bed.

"The Scepter," she continued, "was a way by which the Acharite power could be used by those who denied their heritage. Axis wielded some of that power when he destroyed Gorgrael—and part of the reason he was able to do that was because he combined Acharite power with Icarii and Avar power—but he was able to do so only because of the Scepter."

"Thus the symbols of StarSon and Scepter intertwine," Faraday said. "The power of the Scepter, the power of the land, has been infused into the StarSon. *Not* via the Scepter, but via death."

"Aye," Urbeth said, pleased with the woman. Then she shifted her sharp black eyes to Drago.

"You remind me of my eldest son," she said. As Urbeth continued to speak her tone rose until she was almost shouting. "Denying your heritage. Fool! Don't you realize that *you* must be the one to meet Qeteb? Only *you* have the power to do so?"

"But Caelum must meet Qeteb . . ." Drago said. No! He could not seize Caelum's heritage again. He couldn't.

Urbeth looked at him pityingly. "Drago, you know the answer to that. Caelum relies exclusively on Icarii power, and to defeat the TimeKeeper Demons you need—"

"You need Acharite power!" Faraday shouted, jumping up and startling both Urbeth and Drago. "Because Noah is one of the Enemy who originally trapped Qeteb, and because Noah fathered the Acharites, and thus we bear his blood—and power. *And thus the Acharite race is the Enemy!*"

She whipped back to Drago, taking his face between her hands, and he caught his breath at the beauty in her excited face.

"Drago! That's what you said after you'd come back through the Star Gate. You said you were the Enemy. And you literally *are!* You," she thumped his chest with her hand, then hit her own chest, and turned back to Urbeth, "and I, as all Acharites who eventually manage to worm their way through death and accept their heritage, *am the Enemy!*"

"And thus you all have the ability to turn against the Demons," Urbeth said. "Although you, Drago, as StarSon, are the one who must face the final confrontation. But, yes, the Acharites all carry within them the seed of the power that initially trapped Qeteb."

"StarSon," Drago said tonelessly.

Faraday knelt before him and again took his face between gentle hands. "Ah, Drago," she said. "Surely you must understand. *You* were born StarSon. The Maze Gate named the Crusader as the StarSon at *your* birth, not Caelum's. As an infant, you *knew* instinctively that you were the StarSon. And Azhure, caught in fate, did the one thing to ensure your inheritance . . . she stripped you of your Icarii blood and made your Acharite blood dominant. Don't you see? Don't you understand? The StarSon is the Enemy reborn, and you are the StarSon. You have always, always been."

Urbeth watched silently as Drago hung his head. Faraday leaned closer, cradling his face against her shoulder.

"Stop denying it, please," she whispered. "Stop denying your heritage, stop trying to foist the title of StarSon on Caelum. What good will that do anyone? Don't you want to save this land?"

"How can I do this to him again?" Drago said, and leaned back a little so he could look Faraday in the eye. "How can I deny Caelum his—"

"It is not his heritage, you *stupid* man," Faraday hissed. "It is *yours*. And if you don't have the courage to take it in both hands, then . . . then . . . oh!"

She let go his face and got to her feet, standing to stare into the fire for a heartbeat, then swiveling to face Drago again.

"Stop playing the remorseful penitent. It doesn't suit you. You swore to me that you would do your utmost to save this land . . . will you now do it?"

"It is not only that I feel I am betraying Caelum all over again," Drago said. "That is bad enough. But Noah also said . . . he also said that Caelum . . ."

"Caelum was born first for a very good reason," Urbeth put in, "and all of us here in this room know what it is."

There was silence. Drago stared at Urbeth, and then dropped his head again.

Faraday stared between the two of them, her thoughts racing, and then suddenly realized what they were talking about. Caelum . . . Caelum was born as a decoy, a false StarSon. While Drago wandered the land, learning the secrets of both the land and his soul, the Demons concentrated on Caelum. *No wonder Drago felt so guilty.*

And guilt at her own treatment of the man abruptly infused her. She sank to her knees in front of him, and took one of his hands between both of hers.

"I think you will find," Urbeth said very gently, "that Caelum is a fine man and a worthy brother. This will not be as difficult as you think."

"I want to go north to Star Finger from here to see him," Drago said.

"Yes," Urbeth said. "That would be good. And I think that he will be more than ready to speak with you. A peace needs to be made between you. Caelum needs to come to terms with his own nightmares."

"The girl?" Faraday said, abruptly reminded of her when Urbeth mentioned nightmares. "Do you know who she—"

"Hush!" Urbeth cried. "Does no one relish the adventure anymore? Does no one revel in the delight of finding out for *themselves* anymore? It is not the quest, but the *questing* that is important."

She heaved a great, theatrical sigh and waved a paw languidly in the air. "Go to Star Finger. Speak with Caelum. Find that which is lost."

"And when I *do* find her, she need never fear again!" Faraday said in a low but vehement tone.

Urbeth stared at her, concerned, then shared that concern in a glance to Drago.

"You cannot be the protective mother to every lost child," Urbeth said, and touched the hem of Faraday's gown with one of her paws. "Sometimes, that which is lost . . . returns to loss."

"What do you mean?" Faraday asked, her tone sharp.

Urbeth shrugged. "I speak in the riddles of the ice-pack, girl. I cannot help it."

"And from Star Finger?" Drago asked. "Where from there? What do I *do*, Urbeth? I am wandering the land and watching it sicken about me. Each hour the Demons stretch their gray miasma across Tencendor more creatures fall under their influence and lose their souls! What do I do? How do I confront—"

"Hush!" Urbeth cried again. "What *did* happen to all the adventurers of history? Ah!"

She took a deep breath and calmed herself. "Journeying in itself is learning, Drago. Go where you feel driven."

"Go where I feel driven," Drago muttered. "All fine and good!"

"You *do* remind me of my eldest," Urbeth said, "for you are certainly as annoying." She sighed. "From Star Finger take your staff to Sigholt. Learn the heritage of the Enemy that lives in you. And once you have learned that, learn to trust *instinct*. One more thing, seeing as I have fallen in the habit of spilling secrets, Drago . . . I have spoken of how the Acharite magic is released only through death. Use that knowledge to create your allies and the magic that will destroy Qeteb. Destruction through death, resurrection into magic."

Drago nodded, thinking he understood, and they sat for a long while without speaking. In that silence Drago finally came to an acceptance of Caelum's fate . . . the fate Drago had to send him to.

I was ever the treacherous brother, Drago thought, but the thought was tinged only with sadness, not with resentment.

Eventually, when the fire had burned down to hot coals, Urbeth spoke. "I would that you leave the stallion here in Gorkenfort."

Drago, dozing in the warmth and comfort of the chamber, jerked his head up. "Why?"

"I have need of company, and for the moment you will have no need of him."

Drago shrugged. "Very well."

Urbeth's words made Faraday ponder on the lonely life the Enchantress must have led. "It must have been very sad for you," she said, "to lose all your children to the world. Three sons, and they all left home eventually."

Urbeth smiled, her eyes dreamy. "Yes, it *was* sad to lose my sons, but I had my daughters to keep me company."

Faraday and Drago sat up in interest.

"Daughters?" Drago said.

"Yes. Two daughters. They traveled with you for many, many months. Do you know them?"

"Oh gods!" Faraday breathed, and looked at Drago and laughed.

The Crimson Chamber of the ancient Icarii palace in Carlon was one of the fairest rooms the palace contained, but now it reeked with the stink of madness—and worse.

The beautiful crimson dome reigned over a chamber that was entirely bare, save for the stake driven into the very center of the floor, and the single wooden chair placed next to the locked and barred door.

On that chair sat Zared, King of the Acharites. His gray eyes were absent of all expression, save hopelessness. His face was ashen, his hair uncombed, his cheeks and chin stubbled with days-old beard.

He stared, and as he stared, he was caught yet again in the recurring guilt he had about his first wife, Isabeau.

He should never have let her ride to the hunt. He should never have given her the horse that killed her. He should never have let her *near* a horse, for the gods' sakes, when she was five months gone with their child.

Now she was dead, crushed beneath the horse that failed a single stone fence.

Their child, never given the chance of life, was dead.

As was the woman before him, and the child she carried.

Both dead, or as good as.

From the stake in the heart of the chamber snaked a chain that almost—but not quite—extended as far as the surrounding circular walls.

At the end of that chain was bolted a woman. Naked. Smeared with filth, for she would allow none near to clean her.

And savage. She snarled and spat at Zared, her eyes clouded with insanity and demonic rage. Her fingernails had been torn free in her desperate attempt to claw across the floor to reach him.

Blood smeared the tiles and her pale skin.

Zared's eyes flitted down to the faint swelling of her belly. Her body lived, but Leagh was dead to him.

As was the child.

Zared's eyes filled with tears. It was his fault. He should never have let her ride with Askam. He should *never* have trusted Askam!

Leagh—or what had once been her—snarled and jerked at the chain that had been bolted to her left ankle. She spat, trying every way her mad mind knew to reach him . . . to hurt him.

Her only purpose in life now was to destroy the man who sat weeping on the chair just out of her reach.

"I love you," he said.

40

Murkle Mines

*T*he Sea Worms had decimated the twenty-strong fleet. Most of the ships had been attacked and crippled or sunk in the initial attack, and in the cold late afternoon air, as the survivors huddled on the gritty beach, the Worms attacked the remaining floating vessels from the safety of the bay's depths. In one moment a ship floated peacefully, the next it would rock violently as teeth sunk into its keel, ripping away timbers and exposing the belly of the ship to the invading icy waters.

Theod, as all those who survived the sinking of their ships, had swum to shore with only bare minutes to spare before the onset of the midafternoon despair. They'd frantically dug themselves holes in the loose shale of the beach with limbs shaking with cold and exhaustion and fear, burying themselves even as the gray corruption rolled over the mountains.

Many had not covered themselves in time, and they and the horses which had managed to escape the holds of the sinking ships, had succumbed to the madness.

Now the horses floated in the water, useless hulks of skin, flesh and bone. Maddened, they had forgotten to swim, and had died drowning in despair.

The men, either those in the water or those who'd found the beach, but not the safety of shelter, had scuttled away into the first gullies of the Murkle Mountains, although not before a few had stabbed down into the mounds of shale with their swords.

More men dead.

The Strike Force had escaped with no casualties at all—if you did not consider the wounding of their spirits as they watched, horrified, the fate of their wingless companions. The Icarii could do little, for they could not bear the weight of a man to safety of either shore or shadowed gullies, and in the end they were reduced to sheltering in the caves of the first line of mountains, watching and listening as horses and men went mad.

As despair passed, and the afternoon once again became relatively safe, DareWing FullHeart sent a farflight scout back to the fleet of ships still at sea.

"Tell them to turn for the safety of ports in the south," he ordered, "for it would be death to venture into Murkle Bay."

Now Theod, with DareWing, Goldman, the Strike Force and what remained of the two thousand men—some nine hundred—sat on the beach watching the Sea Worms eating the remaining planks floating in the sea.

"Enough!" Theod said, and rose wearily to his feet. "DareWing, send a Wing into the mountains to make contact, if they can, with those who shelter in the mines. Keep the rest of the Strike Force in the air for . . . for whatever protection you can give us."

"And us?" Goldman asked, gesturing to the white-faced, sodden soldiers standing about in listless ranks.

"Us? Why, we walk into the mountains," Theod said. "I do not fancy spending this night breathing shale."

And without waiting for an answer, Theod turned his back to the sea and walked toward the first of the gullies leading into the mountains as the Strike Force rose into the air about him.

No one wanted to think about what kind of journey home

awaited them. A league out to sea, the farflight scout winged his way toward the distant masts.

Relieved that he would reach them in time, the scout increased his efforts, but then slowed, horrified. The mast of the leading ship was keeling over, and before the scout's appalled eyes, hit the water with a great splash.

The ship rolled over, showing a massive hole in its side.

The farflight scout descended, desperate to try and help the men struggling in the water.

As he skimmed the waves, not thinking about the danger, a huge purple head reared out of the sea and snatched him from the air, disappearing beneath the waves again.

The water roiled, and then resumed its heavy rolling motion, the only reminder of the farflight scout's foolhardy bravery being a few white feathers scattered across the flowing waves.

Another ship, and then another, and then yet another rolled over and sank, and by the time Raspu settled his pestilence over the gray sea there was only the odd sailor left clinging to a plank to seize for his own.

Tencendor, as its people, was on its own.

Theod trudged up the gully. His outer clothes were drying off, but his underclothes clung damply to his skin, and the leather of his boots was soaked through, chafing at his frozen feet.

He'd lost the ships, dammit, but he had some nine hundred men, and the Strike Force, and that would have to be enough. Get the people to the Western Ranges . . . they could travel east-southeast through the lower reaches of the Murkles and then into the Western Ranges, sheltering through the unlivable hours under overhangs and in caves and the shadows of cliffs. It would have to be enough.

From the Western Ranges, DareWing could send farflight scouts to Zared, and Zared could meet them with enough of a force to get them safely to Carlon.

"We could stay in the mines," Goldman said quietly as he strode beside Theod. He could see the younger man's face, the determination in his mind, and he knew what he must be thinking.

"For how long?" Theod's voice was hard, and he did not look at Goldman. "For how *long?* We must trust in a man whom no one has ever trusted before, and trust him to find us this unknowable called Sanctuary." Theod abruptly halted and faced Goldman. "And no doubt if all the unknowables resolve in our favor, do you know what will happen? This Sanctuary will be found in a delightful little glade in the furthest corner of the Avarinheim, and what hope, *what bloody hope,* would we have of getting to it?"

Goldman said nothing, just returned Theod's look with all the sympathy he could manage.

"Besides . . ." Theod turned his eyes to the nearest cliffs of the Murkles. "I do not want to spend what is left of my life lurking in the depths of these abominations."

His voice softened almost to a whisper. "Look at them. They are so bare, so lifeless. No vegetation. Not even a lizard left to crawl over them. Just gray peaks and shale-covered slopes. No beauty. Nothing. Are my people in there, Goldman? Gods be damned, that all the hope and beauty of Aldeni should have come to this!"

Goldman did not follow Theod's eyes, but merely looked at the Duke. He wondered if the man knew how much of his grandfather shone out of him at this moment. Not his looks, for, luckily, Theod took after his maternal side in litheness and blond coloring, but in the sheer humanity shining from his face. Roland had been a man who had suffered with every one of his people when Gorgrael's ice and loathsome minions had crawled over his province, and the man had died before he could see it restored to its former beauty. Goldman hoped that Theod would live to see Aldeni released from its current horror.

What was he saying? Goldman twisted his face and stepped forward again. He hoped *he* would live long enough to see the entire nation restored to its sanity.

He heard Theod fall into step behind him, but just as he was about to turn and say something to him, a shadow swept overhead, and a voice hailed them from above.

"My Lord Duke. See!" a hovering scout cried.

Goldman lifted his head, Theod beside him, but it was the younger man who spotted the waving hand first.

"There," Theod said, pointing, and Goldman nodded. A man, no, two or three men, climbing down the shale face above them.

Aldenians.

"I have found three," Theod said, "now there are but nineteen thousand and some hundreds to go."

And he pushed past Goldman and climbed upward.

The mines were dense with darkness. There *was* torchlight, the men who met them explained, but fuel was so precious they did not want to light them until it became absolutely necessary.

"The way here is smooth, and the downhill slope relatively slight," the man's voice said out of the darkness before Theod. "Keep your hand on the wall, and you will not fall."

Theod heard DareWing and another Icarii mutter some paces behind him. The Icarii must loathe this enclosed space, Theod thought, but he wasted little pity on them. They were alive, and they were in shelter for the night's terror, and no one could ask for more than that.

"How long have you been down here?" Theod asked.

"Weeks, is all I know," the man replied. "Time loses all meaning in this darkness."

He paused, and when he resumed his voice was harsh. "We are crowded like rats into these mines. Everyone gets a space the width of their arms outstretched. Everyone eats, shits and sleeps in the same patch of darkness. We never see the sun, and we grow tired indeed of the same stale voices about us. Many among us have gone mad, even without the touch of the gray haze."

"I have heard," Theod said softly, "that there are twenty thousand within these mines."

"Twenty thousand?" The man laughed unpleasantly. "Was that before or after the darkness began to eat at us?"

Theod shuddered, and remembered the tales his father had told him of these mines. Hadn't his grandfather been trapped down here once, trapped by Gorgrael's sorcery even as he was now trapped by that of the TimeKeepers?

And hadn't Ho'Demi, the old Chief of the Ravensbund-men, found something lost down here?

Lost souls, was it?

Theod's hand slipped on the damp wall, and he stumbled into the man before him.

"Mind!" the man called angrily, and Theod mumbled an apology.

They descended in silence now. No one was willing to speak, or to ask the guides in front any more questions. Who wanted answers? The sooner out of here the better, and in the mind of every one of those men who had stepped into the mines for the first time, the same thought tumbled over and over again.

What is worse? The madness of the Demons, or *this?*

They descended perhaps an hour, perhaps ten—time was unknowable in this darkness. When the way became rocky and uneven, and the guides in front announced they'd reached the first of the chasms—

Chasms?

—they lit a score of brands, and passed them down the long line.

Theod blinked in the sudden radiance of the fitful, smoky torch, and slowly regained his bearings. They were in a spacious enough tunnel, Theod could not reach the roof even if he jumped, but when he looked ahead, he saw that the floor was rent with a chasm some three or four paces wide, with a narrow beam stretching across it.

"It drops to the bowels of the earth," one of the guides said, and smiled sourly as he saw the pale, shocked faces of those behind him. "I know, see, because my son dropped down one of these, and we heard his scream for an eternity before the darkness ate it."

Theod caught the man's eyes, and he looked away at the pain he saw there.

"We walk across," the guide continued, "and if you fall, then where you land there will be no one but ghosts to cradle your soul into the AfterLife."

"Why isn't the beam broader?" Theod asked. "Why not have two side by side? This is not safe—"

"You're bloody lucky you don't have just a rope to balance

on," the man said. "We need wood for fuel, and we don't waste it on luxuries like wide avenues for the likes of noble visitors!"

Theod's face hardened, but he made no reply. Instead he turned slightly to Goldman behind him.

"Will you manage?" he murmured.

"Aye," Goldman said. "If I could balance Askam's demands for taxes, then I can manage this."

He smiled—a considerable effort—at the concern in Theod's eyes. "I *will* be all right," he said.

"I'll watch him." DareWing stepped up behind Goldman. "There are two Icarii for every Acharite. All will pass safely."

Theod nodded his thanks, and stepped forward to cross over the first of many beams.

The chasms—there were fourteen in all—claimed no one, for the Icarii did their task well. After an infinite time of trudging downward, ever downward, when Theod thought his legs would drop off from his hips and his buttocks turn into liquid, they reached a gigantic cavern in the mountain.

Here, had they but known it, Gorgrael's army of Skraelings had once hidden until the Chitter Chatters had driven them forth, but now it was home to the twenty thousand who'd managed to escape from Aldeni.

A few torches sputtered erratically, and the stench of unwashed bodies and barely covered latrine trenches was appalling, but Theod strode forward, and stood on a great rock that loomed above the floor of the cavern.

"I have come to take you to Carlon!" he called, and a sea of pale faces lifted and turned in his direction amid a swelling murmur. *Carlon?* It was but a word from a dream, surely?

"Carlon," Theod called again, hearing the disbelief, and not blaming them for it. "Carlon!"

And then there was a cry, a woman's voice, and then a figure pushing her way through the crowd.

Thin, but with black hair neatly braided about her ears and her face free of smudges, Gwendylyr, Duchess of Aldeni, threw herself into the arms of her husband.

41

An Angry Foam of Stars

Far to the north, the old horse stood in the courtyard of Gorkenfort, sinking deeper into dream as the snow eddied fitfully about him.

Nothing moved, save the flurries of snow.

Drago and Faraday, the feathered lizard balancing on Drago's pack and grabbing playfully at the top of his staff, were well north of the fort, climbing into the Icescarp Alps.

Belaguez had not even missed them, nor noticed the man's gentle pat on his shoulder, nor the woman's soft kiss on his nose as they left him.

Left him to Urbeth.

The snow gusted strongly now, and it piled in drifts about the horse's fetlocks, and in a strange, shifting mound on his rump.

He dreamed on.

A shape moved within the snow.

Urbeth.

She growled, but the horse's only response was a thin twitching of the skin on his near shoulder. Urbeth's growl barely penetrated his dreaming.

She snarled, vicious, a hunter scenting prey, but still the horse did not wake.

There was a billowing of snow as a sudden gust of wind scraped it from the ground, and out of this cloud of snow and ice sprang Urbeth.

First her gaping, scarlet snarling mouth, then the glint of her talons, and then her massive body sliding after. Straight for the horse.

He did not notice.

Urbeth landed on his back, digging her talons into his flanks and potbelly, and sinking her teeth around his windpipe in the predator's death clutch.

Belaguez screamed awake. His whole body spasmed, then convulsed in a great buck, trying to throw the bear off. *I am a Skraeling, come to eat you,* she whispered into his mind, and suddenly she *was* a wraith in Belaguez's understanding, and he bucked and struggled, his breath wheezing horribly through his tortured throat.

Blood ran in rivulets down his body and stained the snow.

An IceWorm, come to eat you!

And Belaguez could *see* the frightful horse-head of the worm plunging for his body, could see it vomiting its Skraelings until he was covered in the writhing wraiths.

Danger! Danger!

Something surged within the old horse, some vague memory of strength, and a sudden spurt of his old intelligence and cunning. He gave a huge buck and then, instead of landing on stiff, splayed legs, allowed himself to collapse, rolling over in the snow.

Urbeth lost her grip, and she was thrown several paces.

In one smooth movement, strange in such an ancient horse, Belaguez gained his feet and, instead of running, attacked. His head snaked down toward Urbeth, still lying on the ground, and she seized his nose in her jaws.

Blood sprayed about them, and Belaguez shook his head, trying to dislodge her.

He was angry now, very angry, and fear seemed a thing of the past.

Urbeth suddenly let go, and although Belaguez slipped, he re-found his balance almost instantly. He reared, bringing his stiff forelegs down on Urbeth.

She rolled out of the way barely in time, and scrambled to her feet. She reached out a huge paw and raked it down Belaguez's exposed shoulder, and the horse screamed in fury.

Again he turned and attacked, and now the bear was laughing, and doing enough only to tease the stallion and to keep just out of his reach.

Belaguez! Belaguez! Do you want to run, Belaguez?

The stallion stopped and stared at the bear, his ears flickering uncertainly. He was streaked with blood, but under that blood his flesh seemed firmer, his neck more muscled, his belly tauter than it had been previously.

Do you want to fight, Belaguez?

The stallion reared and screamed, his fore-hooves plunging through the air. Urbeth reached out with a lazy paw and again swiped it through the air, but this time it did not come near the horse. Instead, a spray of tiny stars fanned out from her paw and caught themselves in the stallion's plunging mane and tail.

He halted, surprised, then lowered his head and shook it, snorting.

"Run, Belaguez," Urbeth whispered, and the magnificent white and silver stallion pranced about uncertainly, not knowing what to make of the stars that blazed out from his forehead and neck and streamed from his haunches.

Suddenly he reared and screamed again. The dream was gone, forgotten, and Belaguez was alive and young and angry, and he needed something to vent that anger on.

Run, Belaguez! South! South! South!

And Belaguez plunged one more time, shaking his head at Urbeth, and then he was through the Keep's gate and skidding through the deserted streets of Gorkentown.

He exploded through the town's gates into the snow-covered wastes beyond, a shifting apparition of white and silver.

South! South! South!

South! Nothing stood in his way. A league south of Gorkenfort a Demon-controlled bull plunged at him, but Belaguez sailed into a mighty leap that carried him well over the bull and five paces the other side. His nostrils flared red and he screamed again, but he did not stop to challenge the bull. He ran south, ever south, sometimes so indistinct against the snow he seemed only a streaming, glittering whirlwind.

The terror of the night could not touch him, and the hunger of the dawn shaken off without thought.

Risen from death, and filled with the magic of the land his bones had lain on for twenty years, Belaguez ran south, an angry foam of stars.

42

The Lake of Life

They sat their black beasts and stared into the waters of the
Lake of Life. The trip through the blue mists surrounding
Sigholt had not been difficult; the mists had hindered, but not
overly, and the Demons had laughed at the inefficiencies of
the bridge's magic.

"She is such an inconsequential thing," Sheol had observed
as they had ridden to the shores of the Lake, "but irritating. And
after we finish here, then I think we might . . . remove . . . her."

And yet even as she boasted of the bridge's destruction,
Sheol, as all the Demons, felt the first stir of danger emanat-
ing from the Keep. Something was wrong there. Something
dangerous. Something . . . something to be wary of.

Did the Enemy somehow—impossibly—wait in its shadows?

"This Lake is still water," StarLaughter said, not realizing
the concerns shared by the Demons. Her child was clasped,
as ever, protectively to her breast. "How do we enter the
Repository?"

"With ease," Barzula said. "The waters will not hinder us.
And after we have collected what we need from here, we will
have to go *down* no more."

"What do you mean?" StarLaughter asked.

"You will see," Rox replied, irritatingly obtuse. He looked at
the child in StarLaughter's arms, and his gaze softened slightly.

"Your boy," he said, placing a very slight—and somewhat
sarcastic—emphasis on the *your,* "will be too large to carry
once breath has infused his body. You will have to relinquish
him to his mount."

StarLaughter glanced at the spare black mount, and her
face suffused with a deep unreadable emotion.

"Soon," she whispered. "Soon! After so many years."

The Demons turned back to a contemplation of the Lake's surroundings. Directly across from them was a substantial town.

Deserted. A few doors swung in the wind, and a shutter slammed shut so violently the Demons heard the sound from across the Lake.

"They have fled," Raspu observed.

The others shrugged. "It will do them little good," Sheol replied. "We shall feed from them eventually."

From the town their eyes drifted over the similarly deserted barracks of the Lake Guard and, as the barracks held no interest for them, continued around the curve of the Lake to the great silvery stone Keep of Sigholt itself.

"Magic," Sheol said in a soft voice. "StarLaughter? Tell me what you know of this place."

StarLaughter adjusted her child a little more comfortably. "Sigholt is a place of great magic, although few know where it originates, nor even how to use it. When I lived in this land as wife to WolfStar, it was used part as a residence for the Talon and his family, and part as a staging post on the long flight from the Minaret Peaks to our summer palace in Talon Spike. The bridge guards Sigholt, and demands of all who enter if they are true, or not."

"True to what?" Rox asked.

StarLaughter shrugged. "I do not know. And when I lived, and entered Sigholt, the bridge always let me past."

Barzula stared at her, then burst into loud laughter. "But you are hardly 'true,' StarLaughter! Not to this land, nor to anything *in* this land!"

StarLaughter kept her eyes on the Keep. "I was then," she said softly.

"The question must be," Rox said, ignoring both Barzula's mirth and StarLaughter's reply, "is the Keep *still* magic? If so, why? Where does the magic emanate from? The Star Dance is dead, and surely this Keep has little connection to the great forests far to the east."

"And which we will shortly deal with, anyway," Sheol said, almost automatically. "But if the Keep is still enchanted, then *how*?"

She paused, then turned slightly so she could see all her

companion Demons. "It makes me uncomfortable for I would know why." Her voice changed, became harder. "As I would know how Drago survived the Star Gate."

The TimeKeepers had come to repent of their tardiness in disposing of Drago. They'd been distracted by those magicians, still not found, and by the time they'd thought to look for Drago, he'd disappeared.

There was silence as all contemplated Drago.

"When we find him," StarLaughter eventually said, "may *I* kill him?"

"Why is it you claim all the joy in revenge and killing?" Barzula asked, a petulant lilt in his voice. "First you want WolfStar, now Drago."

She shrugged slightly. "They both thought to use me."

"When we find Drago again," Sheol said, "he is *mine!* He thought to trick me of his death once . . . he will not do it again."

StarLaughter thought about protesting her right to Drago, then let it drop. Sheol seemed particularly strident over this issue, and besides, her revenge on WolfStar would be sweet enough by itself.

"As you wish," StarLaughter said, and Sheol smiled at her. *Always as I wish, you irritating birdwoman.*

"Now," Sheol said, and turned to Raspu, "will you work *your* magic on this Lake?"

Raspu bared his teeth, and hissed. He dropped the reins of his horse, and flexed his fingers into claws.

Watching, StarLaughter was struck by how skeletal they seemed.

With jerky movements, almost as if he was consumed by a desire so great his muscles had gone into involuntary spasm, Raspu threw a leg over his mount's wither, slid to the ground, and tore the clothing from his body.

He stood, naked and trembling, staring at the water.

StarLaughter suppressed a grimace. Raspu's body was so emaciated his bones almost protruded through his skin, and boils and pitted scars of long dried-out pustules littered his body from the base of his neck to the backs of his knees. As the Demon began to jerk and tremble, she ran her eyes down his body, noting every sore, the knotted, swollen joints of his limbs, and the withered, browned genitals shrunken up against his pubic bone.

StarLaughter had once considered Raspu a potential lover, but the sight of his naked body dissuaded her completely. Even Drago, as boring as he had been, at least had a body worth caressing.

If Raspu was aware of StarLaughter's caustic scrutiny, he gave no indication of it. His attention was completely on the waters of the Lake of Life before him. He stepped toward it, rocking violently on his feet as his muscles continued to spasm. His arms and hands jerked in a violent dance by his side, seeming completely beyond his control, and his mouth had dropped open to allow his swollen, reddened tongue to loll down almost as far as the bony bulge of his chin.

As a foot touched the waters, Raspu jerked even more violently, and tipped back his head, screaming and wailing. Star-Laughter's eyes widened, and she glanced at the other Demons. They watched with beatific expressions on their faces, as if it were the greatest wonder they had ever beheld.

StarLaughter looked back at Raspu. The Demon had walked into the Lake far enough that the waters lapped at his thighs. He still jerked and spasmed, so uncontrollably Star-Laughter wondered how he kept upright, and a thin shriek now came from his mouth. Dribble streamed down to connect chin to chest. StarLaughter's mouth twisted in repulsion . . .

And the waters of the Lake began to churn.

She stared. It was as if Raspu had infected the waters with some foul pestilence. The water bubbled, not as if it had been heated to a boil, but as if its surface was erupting in great pustules, sending spurts of fetid steam into the warm air.

"Look," Sheol said, and she pointed to a spot some twenty paces before Raspu.

Here the water had formed into a gigantic pustule some five paces across that, having burst, had then solidified as its effluence drained from it. In the center, a scarred and pockmarked walkway sloped downward.

"Bring your child, Queen of Heaven," Sheol said, and she dismounted from her horse and walked past Raspu, still standing jerking and keening, and waded through the water toward the horrific opening.

* * *

StarLaughter found the journey downward somewhat loathsome. It reinforced her growing belief that she must really find some more suitable companions. Perhaps when her son was fully grown . . .

She followed Sheol toward the opening, and was followed in turn by Mot, Barzula and Rox. As Rox passed Raspu, the Demon of Pestilence abruptly halted both jerking and wailing, and fell into quiet step behind Rox.

The walkway sloped down at a gentle gradient, but StarLaughter found the going difficult.

The entire surface was slicked with something thick and fetid, and StarLaughter did not want to dwell on what it might be.

"Sheol?" StarLaughter called to the Questor several paces before her. As she spoke, StarLaughter had to fight to repress a gag caused by a sudden mouthful of the putrid air. It smelled (tasted) as if a herd of diseased cattle had chosen to die in this place . . . several weeks previously.

"Yes, Queen of Heaven?"

"Will . . ." StarLaughter fought her stomach again, and barely managed to suppress her nausea. Now they had descended well below the level of the water, they were surrounded by close, suppurating walls of sickly pink. It was almost as if they walked through a tunnel of corrupted flesh. "Will the Enemy attempt to trap us here as they did at Cauldron Lake?"

"Undoubtedly, StarLaughter. But I do not think they will have much success at—".

Something lunged out of the floor of the walkway and sunk sharp teeth into Sheol's ankle. She shrieked, and stumbled back into StarLaughter and her son.

A bright blue fish clung to her flesh.

Sheol lifted her foot and tried to shake the fish free, but it clung tenaciously.

"StarLaughter!" she shrieked, fury more evident in her voice than fear.

But encumbered as she was by her heavy son, StarLaughter could do nothing. She shook her head, stumbling out apologies, her eyes fixed on the rivulets of blood running from Sheol's ankle, and eventually Mot was forced to push past her and lean down to Sheol's aid.

But as his hands wrapped themselves about the fish, ten more wriggled out of the suppurating floor of the walkway, and snatched at Mot's hands.

He lurched back, shouting, but several managed to sink their teeth into his hands, and he waved them about, hitting Star-Laughter in the face with both his and the fishes' loathsome flesh.

Something dropped down from the close ceiling above them, and snagged in StarLaughter's hair. She screamed, her arms at first loosening, then tightening about her son just before he dropped from her grasp. He was too heavy for her to hold in only one arm, so she could do nothing as she felt . . . *something* . . . chew among her hair, trying to find her scalp.

Raspu grabbed at the thing for her, and flung it far down the walkway. It was an eel, as bright blue as the fish that yet clung to both Sheol and Mot.

He grabbed at the fish clinging to Mot, tore them off—causing Mot to shriek in pain as he did so—and flung them likewise. Then he bent to the remaining fish still chewing grimly on Sheol's ankle.

"There!" he said, as that, too, went slithering down the walkway. As they watched, all the fish and the eel wriggled back into the floor and disappeared. "I don't think that we will be—"

He halted, transfixed with horror. Slithering up the tunnel of rotting flesh toward them was a massive fish-creature, its girth almost filling the entire tunnel. Its mouth yawned open, revealing row after row of razored triangular teeth, disappearing into a dark red gullet that eventually shaded into black in its considerable depth.

It roared, and every one of the Demons shrieked and clambered backward.

Only StarLaughter remained still and silent, staring at the creature as if transfixed with horror.

Something grabbed at her, and she jumped.

It was Sheol, who had overcome her own fear to fetch StarLaughter.

No, not StarLaughter, but the child. Sheol tried to jerk it

out of StarLaughter's arms, but StarLaughter's grip tightened automatically.

"No!" she cried, suddenly finding her voice.

"Give him to me!" Sheol screamed, tugging with all her might. "Die if you want, fool, but *give him* to *me!*"

The huge fish-creature was now only fifteen paces away, slithering closer with every lurch of its body.

"Give him to me!"

"No!" StarLaughter cried desperately, and the two females rocked back and forth, arms and hands locked tight about the child, pulling him to and fro.

The child paid no attention, its blank eyes fixed unsighted on a spot in the ceiling above.

"I am his *mother!*" StarLaughter shouted and gave a final, desperate heave.

She was far, far too successful.

Sheol's grip suddenly gave way, and StarLaughter fell backward, completely losing her footing. She fell straight into the yawning chasm of the fish-creature's mouth.

All StarLaughter saw was Sheol's horrified eyes, and the other Demons rushing up behind her, and then she felt the clamminess of the creature's tongue, and felt the first rows of teeth slice open the skin of her back and buttocks.

Agony swept through her body, and StarLaughter screamed once, and then again, and then a third time.

The creature's jaws snapped closed about her.

There was blackness, and more pain, and then a period of unknowingness, and when StarLaughter opened her eyes again she saw the Demons standing over her, Sheol cradling the child in her arms.

StarLaughter scrambled to her feet, wiping her hands free of slime on her gown, where new and more putrid stains had added themselves to the rust brown blood that already streaked the once fine, pale-blue gown.

"Give him to me," she cried, and snatched the child from Sheol's arms.

Sheol shrugged. "You tripped and fell," she said, "and *I* saved the child."

StarLaughter glanced behind her. The fish-creature had disappeared. "Where is it?"

"The Enemy's attack was a delusion only," Raspu said. His naked body was streaked with filth. "Hardly worthy even of the term 'trap.' What remains of their power fades fast, and I doubt we shall be overly troubled by them again."

StarLaughter stared at him. His words were bravado only, and StarLaughter had the horrible feeling the Enemy—or whatever remained of them—was toying with them only.

"Shall we go?" Sheol said, raising an eyebrow at Star-Laughter. "Your son's breath awaits."

They descended in silence, StarLaughter now at the back of the line, her arms possessively tight about her son. Her misadventure had made her realize the Demons cared only for her child, but who would he care for, when he spoke and smiled? His mother? Or the Demons?

Far, far behind her, WolfStar slipped and slithered his way down the walkway, his own child's corpse tight under one arm.

Nothing bothered him on his journey down.

The Demons found what they wanted an hour later. The walkway descended into a massive vaulted chamber, bare save for a pedestal of golden stone in the center.

On this pedestal sat a great black bird. It had a thick body, but an overly long and completely bald neck, topped by a tiny head with a long, sharp beak.

It stood unmoving on thick, yellow, scaled legs and claws.

The Demons filed into the chamber, and Sheol waved Star-Laughter forward.

"Place the child on the pedestal before the bird."

"But what if he hurts him? What if—"

"Place the child on the pedestal!" Sheol took one threatening step toward StarLaughter, her shoulders hunching as she flung her arms outward, the shadow she cast on the wall behind her making her seem like a great predatory bird herself.

StarLaughter's face tightened, but she did as Sheol commanded, turning to walk slowly toward the golden pedestal. The bird's head turned slightly to watch her.

StarLaughter halted a pace away. The bird was far larger than it had originally seemed, almost twice the size of an eagle, and the beak was wickedly sharp.

"Place the child on the pedestal," Sheol whispered.

Slowly, very slowly, her eyes not leaving those of the bird, StarLaughter took one more step forward, then lifted her beloved child onto the cold stone before the bird's claws.

The child shivered, as if discomforted by the chill against its newly warmed flesh.

"Now rejoin us," Sheol commanded.

StarLaughter hesitated, terrified at what the bird might do to her son, but then she turned and walked back toward the Demons.

She only got halfway when she heard a frightful shriek behind her. StarLaughter whipped about. The bird's head was now a blur as it plunged its beak again and again into the child's chest.

StarLaughter cried out, and would have rushed to her son's aid, but tight arms closed about her.

"Watch only!" Barzula hissed in her ear.

StarLaughter struggled and wailed. The baby, too, shrieked again and again, the level of his screams rising each time the bird stabbed its beak down.

Blood spattered across the entire chamber, spattering Star-Laughter's face and hair, and slivers of flesh slipped down the golden sides of the pedestal.

"No!" StarLaughter howled, struggling vainly against Barzula's grip. *"No!"*

"Wait!" Barzula whispered, and StarLaughter felt his arms tighten yet more until she had no breath to cry out.

The bird continued to hack at the child's body, and the child continued to scream. Impossible amounts of blood flowed from his body, and ribs glinted through the ruined flesh of his chest.

Suddenly the bird stopped, tilted its head curiously as it stared into the ruined flesh before it, then stabbed its beak down a final time.

But this time it did not withdraw. It kept its beak buried deep within the child's body, and it took a great breath through its tiny nostrils, and then exhaled through its beak.

The boy quietened.

The bird withdrew its beak, and took one careful step away from the child to the very back edge of the pedestal. There it stayed, its eyes still fixed on the child.

The child's chest expanded in a huge breath, and in an instant so quick StarLaughter's eyes could not follow it the ravaged flesh healed itself before her eyes, and the boy's limbs and body lengthened and thickened.

A youth of some twelve years now lay on the pedestal, his legs and arms drooping over its sides. His chest rose in regular movement, but his eyes—now a clear, deep violet—still stared blankly above him.

Barzula's arms loosened, and StarLaughter walked slowly toward the pedestal.

The bird watched her, but did not move.

StarLaughter halted and ran one hand softly down her son's body, marveling at the beauty of his sturdy figure and the well-defined muscles of his arms and legs. His head, once only covered with a fine down, was now thick with rich copper curls and as StarLaughter slid him off the pedestal, she saw he had golden adolescent wings emerging from his back.

"My boy," she whispered. "DragonStar."

"If you like," Sheol murmured unheard behind her.

They waited, all of them, in a corner of the chamber hidden by shadows and the power of the Demons.

The boy stood obediently, his eyes blank, his body unresponsive to StarLaughter's murmurings and caressing hands.

"Be silent," Barzula hissed at her. "He comes!"

StarLaughter fell silent, lifting her eyes from her son.

WolfStar entered the chamber on feet silent with caution. His eyes slid about the walls, but he saw nothing, and he visibly relaxed.

StarLaughter stared, so shocked she did not know what to think. She moved slightly, and felt a Demon's hand clutch at her arm. *Be silent, StarLaughter!* It was the combined voice of the Demons in her mind.

But that is WolfStar!

Aye.

But—

Watch, StarLaughter, and once he has gone, we will tell you something very, very amusing.

WolfStar was completely unaware that anyone else re-

mained in the chamber. StarLaughter watched him, her mind
in turmoil. She had waited so long for this moment. Gods, but
she wished the Demons would allow her to rush forth and
claw his eyes out! Her chest constricted in loathing, remembering how he had gladly wasted her life, and that of their
son's, in his quest for all-consuming power.

Her fingers grazed slightly against the warm flesh of her
son's chest, marveling at its rise and fall, and then her attention was consumed by WolfStar. In his arms he carried the
still form of a toddling girl. As StarLaughter had done, now
he stepped forth and placed the child on the pedestal.

The instant he had moved back, the bird took one pace forward, and tore into the girl's chest as he had into the boy's.

StarLaughter turned eyes wide with anger toward the
Demons.

*We understand, StarLaughter. But be still and silent, and
do not fret too much. There is good reason to allow WolfStar
this moment.*

StarLaughter looked back to her husband . . . and she almost sneered. His face wore an expression of open ambition
as he stared at the girl.

Who was this girl? It could be no one else save Niah, the
woman he had betrayed StarLaughter with. Who else would
he bother to go to this trouble for?

Me he murdered, StarLaughter thought, and this girl he
resurrects.

Hate consumed her, and were it not for the power of the
Demons that held her back, StarLaughter would have rushed
forward to tear the child into such pieces that WolfStar would
never have been able to contemplate a resurrection, let alone
accomplish it.

Be still, StarLaughter.

Now the bird had finished, and he stepped back to the edge
of the pedestal again.

As had the boy, so now did the girl transform. Limbs and
body lengthened into the form of a twelve-year-old girl. Her
skin was pale and fine, her hair as black as the bird and falling
to the very floor, her limbs long and shapely, and her breasts
just beginning to emerge from their childish entrapment.

Will you wait until she speaks and moves before you slake

your lust on her, WolfStar? StarLaughter thought. Or will you
take her now, and enjoy her silence?

But WolfStar was apparently in no rush to slake his lust,
for he stepped forward and took the girl's arm in a perfunc-
tory manner. He gave an impatient tug. Then, when she did
not move, he picked her up and slung her over a shoulder before exiting the chamber.

"What have you done!" StarLaughter cried. "That was Wolf-
Star. And no doubt that child was the woman he craves so
much. Why let him—"

"We, too, were angered when first we realized WolfStar
trailed us with his own child that he wishes to return to life,"
Sheol said. "But we quickly lost our anger when we realized
how we could turn this situation to our advantage, *and* gain
you your revenge at the same time."

"How?"

"StarLaughter." Mot now stepped forward and took both
StarLaughter's hands in his. "Would you have your son rule
this vast land without a bride at his side?"

StarLaughter's eyes widened as she grasped what the Demon's meant to do. "But she will be as powerful as—"

Sheol grinned, her teeth glinting behind red lips. "Not if
we stop him after Fernbrake, beloved Queen of Heaven.
Then your son will have a bride any husband would covet.
Beautiful, willing . . . and completely soulless. And Wolf-
Star? Sweet StarLaughter, why not let your *son* have the
eventual revenge on WolfStar? After all, while he murdered
both of you, it has been your son who has been deprived of
all chance at life. Imagine what *he* can do to the father who
denied him the chance to draw a single breath."

StarLaughter stared expressionlessly at Sheol, then in a
sudden, horrific movement, she bared her teeth in a gesture
half-smile, half-snarl.

43

The Bridges of Tencendor

StarDrifter hurriedly dropped his arm from Zenith's shoulders, realizing that he may well have gone too far. Stars! How long did she need before she would accept him?

Zenith turned away slightly, lowering her eyes so that StarDrifter would not see the guilt she was certain shone forth.

"Well?" SpikeFeather cried. "Shall we go down?"

"Yes," StarDrifter said, a little too quickly. "Let us go and see this Sanctuary of Drago's."

The stairwell curved down in a spiral, as did most of the entrances to the Underworld, but the steps down were wide and the gradient gentle. They wished they could have used their wings to float down, but the internal space that the stairs encircled was too tight for the Icarii wingspan. And so not only do I lose the sound of the Star Dance, StarDrifter thought, but I also lose the use of my proudest possession, my wings. But the thought did not cause him too much distress, for he was still tingling with the excitement of his discovery.

What if he could map all the Songs he knew into dance? Could he then regain the same power as he'd once enjoyed? But he did not know how to map music into movement.

StarDrifter had succeeded in the enchantment necessary to open the door to Sanctuary only because the pattern of the stone maze had shown him the steps to take.

But if I think, StarDrifter reasoned, if I think it through, surely I will learn the secret. Thus encouraged, he stepped lightly down into whatever mystery awaited them below.

Behind him trod Zenith. Her eyes and thoughts were not on the mysteries below, or even on StarDrifter's discovery, but on the play of the tendons and sinews of his back, and the smooth transition they made from flesh to wing. Then her eyes traveled further and were trapped by the hidden play of the muscles of his buttocks and thighs beneath the skintight fabric of his golden breeches.

Why *can't* I put my pruderies to one side? she thought. Are my inhibitions destroying me?

The walk was long, hours long, and legs ached and tempers frayed well before it was over. Darkness, and terror, had fallen in the world above, but here in the sheltered entrance stairwell of Sanctuary the shadows were dissipated by the subtle radiance that emanated from the pink walls. Even if legs ached, then terror did not find them, for from deep below rose the hope of Sanctuary.

StarDrifter's eyes occasionally wandered to the walls. They reminded him of the walls on the stairwell leading from the Nordra down to the waterways. Patterns of women and children engaged in joyous dance had been traced into the walls, and sometimes StarDrifter lifted his hand and let his fingers trail over the tracings, wondering at the dance they performed, and wondering at its use.

Behind, Zenith's eyes were trapped by his lean-fingered hand drifting so lightly across the carvings.

Finally, when by WingRidge's calculation it had reached midnight in the world above, they came to the end of the stairwell. The Icarii sighed and jested in relief, bending to rub calves and stretching their hands upward to ease cramped muscles.

They stood in a circular domed chamber. Some fifteen paces directly across from the foot of the stairs were two massive, arched doors.

WingRidge and SpikeFeather walked closer to inspect them.

As with the Maze Gate, while the doors were of plain wood, the stone surrounds had been carved into the symbols of the Enemy.

"What does it say?" StarDrifter asked, walking up.

"Again and again it mentions StarSon," WingRidge said, pointing to the recurring symbols of the sun-surmounted star. "But basically the script states that behind these doors lies Sanctuary, a haven for all the races of Tencendor. It is a welcoming message, and full of hope."

The others had wandered up.

"Will you open it?" JestWing asked. All he could think of

were the Icarii huddled miserably in the Minaret Peaks, hungry and cold and with nothing but their despair to comfort them. Stars! Fernbrake was so close that the majority of them could be safe in Sanctuary within a week.

"I don't see why not," WingRidge said slowly, his hands still moving gracefully over the symbols. "There is no caution or bar against entry, as there is on the Maze Gate. SpikeFeather? Do you concur?"

"I am not as practiced as you at reading this language, WingRidge," he said, and took a deep breath, "but nothing ventured, nothing gained."

"Or lost," someone muttered at the back, but no one took offense at the remark.

WingRidge dropped his hand from the stone and looked back at his companions. "Shall I?"

"Yes!" StarDrifter said. "Yes!"

WingRidge stepped before the double doors and took firm grip on the brass handles. The muscles in his arms and shoulders visibly tensed, then his wrists turned, and his whole body leaned forward.

The doors swung silently and gracefully open.

As soon as WingRidge felt them move, he let go the handles and stood back. For a very long time they stood there, silent, stunned by the beauty and wonder of Sanctuary.

All of them had wet eyes or tears sliding gently down cheeks.

Zenith stood open-mouthed, and StarDrifter's wings had sagged in astonishment.

"I . . . I had no idea." SpikeFeather stumbled over the words. "None. Whoever thought . . . the Charonites never knew . . . oh, *Stars*."

Beyond the gates arched a graceful bridge constructed of what appeared to be silver. It managed to convey both the strength of fire-tempered steel and the grace and beauty of an orbed spider's tracery web. It covered a chasm whose depths were lost in billowing white clouds.

Beyond the bridge, a road wound across a grassy plain that was liberally sprinkled with flowers and spreading shrubs. Above soared the dome of a deep blue sky, a sun shining incongruously over this UnderWorld landscape. The road extended perhaps half a league and it led toward a blue and white mountain range with jagged peaks surpassing even those of the Icescarp Alps. The mountains formed an impenetrable wall . . . save for the mouth of a valley that absorbed the end of the road. Even though it was distant, the Icarii could see that the valley was beauteous beyond any they had ever seen before.

StarDrifter walked slowly forward. He passed through the doors, and then set foot on the bridge.

He did not take his eyes off the distant valley.

"Are you true?" the bridge asked with the cadence of a songstress.

"Yes," StarDrifter said. "I am true," and took another step forward until his full weight rested on the bridge.

"You are not *he* who is true," the bridge cried, and without further ado, vanished.

StarDrifter plummeted into the chasm in a flash of white and gold.

"Ah," said WingRidge, his voice heavy with the sagacious wisdom of hindsight.

The TimeKeeper Demons sat their black horses through the midnight hour and stared at the bridge stretching into Sigholt.

They were powerful, more powerful than they had been in many, many tens of thousands of years. They had fed well of the souls of Tencendor, and they had increased their power further with each Lake they visited. They still had some distance to go before they attained their full powers—two lakes' distance—but now they were more dangerous, and hungrier, than Tencendor had yet seen them. Or felt them.

They hated the Keep rising silvery gray before them. They hated it because of its inherent beauty and gracefulness, but mostly they hated it because it did not fear them.

In fact, the Keep of Sigholt chose to ignore them.

Slightly to one side, StarLaughter watched the Demons rather than the bridge. She did not totally understand their antipathy toward the Keep. It was irritating, yes, and the bridge was more than annoying, but why worry about one stone Keep when further power and glory awaited them to the south?

Her son was more important.

She turned her lovely head slightly to run her eyes over her boy. Surely no fairer youth than he had ever existed. It was all she could do not to lean across the distance that separated them—for now the boy's size required him to ride his own black mount—and run her hand over his soft, *warm* skin. *Feel* his chest rise and fall with every breath.

He was only movement and soul away from wholeness, and when that happened StarLaughter thought she would not be able to bear the strength of her happiness, nor her love for her boy.

So why did the Demons waste time here, staring at the Keep, when they should be hasting south toward Fernbrake?

"Something waits within that stone," Sheol said.

"But the Keep is deserted," StarLaughter said. "All have run for the hills."

She swiveled a little in her saddle so she could see the first of the Urqhart Hills guarding the entrance to the Hold-Hard Pass.

"Fools!" she cried. "Do you not know your masters when you see them? Will you not come and do them honor?"

The TimeKeepers ignored her, and, for the moment, her boy. Their mission was to give him life, but they must also guard against the Enemy's traps that might yet defeat their hopes.

And they sensed *something* in this Keep.

Something powerful, something dangerous, something wrapped in deep, deep enchantment.

Something that might make a mockery of the Hunt.

"I do not know what it is," Mot whispered in a voice papery-harsh with frustration.

"StarLaughter," Sheol said, finally wrenching her eyes from the Keep to the birdwoman. "You said that the bridge guards the Keep."

"Yes. The blue mists we passed through are in part her creation."

Sheol glanced at her companions, and shared thoughts they did not allow StarLaughter to hear.

"I will go," Rox said. "It is my time, and perhaps terror will disconcert the bridge."

The other Demons finally, grudgingly, nodded.

"Take care," Raspu said. "And seek out that which the silvery stone hides."

Rox nudged his horse-beast forward, and it placed a firm black paw on the bridge.

"Are you true?" the bridge asked.

"Yes," Rox answered. "I am true."

"Then cross, Demon," the bridge said, "and I shall test the strength of your words."

Rox was halfway across when the bridge spoke again.

"Rox, Demon of Terror," she said, "I have a message for you."

"Yes?" Rox looked over his shoulder and smiled at the other Demons. He could feel the bridge's magic all about him, and it was as they'd originally thought—an inconsequential thing. Rox knew he could best it himself, and with the combined power of his companions, they would easily tear this bridge apart stone by stone.

"A message," the bridge repeated. "And yet it will not be my voice that imparts it."

And the air before Rox shimmered, and a red-haired young man dressed in very ordinary breeches and a white linen shirt stood there. His entire body was relaxed, almost lazy. Both hands rested on his hips, his weight on one leg.

"Hello, Rox," he said. "Remember me?"

Rox took one huge breath, held it . . . and then screamed, as did every one of the Demons behind him.

The man laughed. "Will you step into my parlor, Rox?"

StarLaughter, acting on the pure fear generated by the Demons—for she could not possibly see what was so fearful about this man—leaned over from her mount, grabbed the reins of her son's horse, and then urged both horses into a flat run toward the HoldHard Pass.

The red-haired man vanished as quickly as he had appeared, but the moment he disappeared from view, the bridge began to alter.

Sinewy black legs, eight of them, branched out from her sides. The portion of the bridge that rested at Sigholt's foot reared into the air, and became a black rounded head with a hundred eyes and a gaping mouth.

The end of the bridge closest to the Demons—although they had quickly retreated to follow StarLaughter—swelled into the black abdomen of . . . of a massive, frightful black arachnid.

Eight legs closed about Rox and his horse with an audible snap. The rounded head darted in and out of its legs, and each time it reappeared, it was covered with the sweet wetness of torn flesh. Then, with a huge splash, the spider and her catch dropped into the moat surrounding Sigholt.

The waters foamed and roiled for several heartbeats, and then gentled into stillness.

The bridge glimmered into substance over the moat again.

There was no one else about, but the bridge spoke anyway. "Are you true?" she asked the night air, and then broke into pealing laughter. "Are you true?"

And Sigholt smiled, and wrapped itself ever closer about the treasure it harbored.

All around Tencendor men and women, beasts of the air and plain alike, shivered and wondered at the sudden beauty of the night.

Terror had vanished.

44

Aftermath

What do you mean, you thought Drago would have to be the first to cross?" StarDrifter demanded.

With barely a ruffled feather, but with considerable angst, he'd risen from the chasm and alighted before WingRidge.

Zenith breathed a gentle sigh of relief. For a moment . . .

WingRidge had the grace to look discomforted. "Undoubtedly, approach to Sanctuary is intimately linked to the presence of the . . . of Drago."

StarDrifter blinked, biting down another angry outburst.

"StarDrifter," WingRidge continued. "I *am* sorry. I just didn't connect the script around the door with the enchantments needed to cross the bridge."

Deciding to accept the apology with the merest of nods, StarDrifter turned slightly to stare across the chasm into Sanctuary. The valley was utterly extraordinary, and looked as if it stretched, in all its loveliness, into eternity. *We could fit the populations of fifteen worlds into that enchanted place,* he thought, *and there would still be room for all to dance the Hey-de-Gie with ease.*

"Couldn't we just fly across?" Zenith asked.

StarDrifter shook his head. "The other side of the chasm is warded tightly with enchantment. I tried to fly across to the other side when—" his eyes flitted momentarily to WingRidge, "—the bridge vanished, but could not penetrate the thick veil of sorcery that hangs to protect the other side."

"Thus must we fetch Drago," WingRidge said. "We can do no more here, and no more for those above who need to cross that bridge."

"Where is he?" one of the other Icarii asked.

"North," WingRidge said. "Come." He laid a hand on SpikeFeather's shoulder. "I need your knowledge of the waterways, my friend, to reach Drago."

SpikeFeather looked helplessly between StarDrifter and WingRidge. "I know the way, WingRidge, but *you* know how long it took us to get from Sigholt to the Minaret Peaks using the waterways. Days, at least, for I have not the enchantment to use the waterways as once did the Ferryman. Meanwhile, no doubt the Demons progress from Lake to Lake, breath quickens Qeteb's body . . . and Sanctuary remains denied to the peoples of Tencendor."

"We must do the best we can—" WingRidge began, but was interrupted by StarDrifter.

"Wait. Zenith, will you return to the Minaret Peaks with JestWing and his companions?"

"Yes, but—"

"Get them organized for an evacuation as quickly as you can. Within days," StarDrifter took a deep breath, "I hope we will have Drago here to open Sanctuary."

"And you?" Zenith asked.

"I will go with WingRidge and SpikeFeather."

She nodded, both relieved and disappointed that they would be parted for a while.

*   *   *

"What happened?" StarLaughter shouted. She had pulled her and her son's horses to a halt half a league into the shelter of the HoldHard Pass, waiting for the Demons to catch up.

Now four of them had, their horses still rolling reddened eyes in fear, their sides still heaving with panic.

The Demons were not in a much calmer state.

"Where's Rox?" StarLaughter screamed, both terrified and furious.

Sheol turned on StarLaughter and snarled, a vicious animalistic sound that sent StarLaughter reeling back in her saddle.

"Think to question *us*, girl?"

"Then tell me why Rox no longer rides with you, and why terror no longer patrols the night!"

"Rox," Mot ground out, "is gone."

StarLaughter shot a look at her son, as if somehow she thought he might have been destroyed by that revelation, but the boy sat his horse, motionless and devoid of expression.

StarLaughter turned back to the Demons. All four wore expressions of rage mixed with pure, unadulterated fright.

"I do not know who that red-haired man was . . ." she said with a certain caution.

"He was the Enemy—" Raspu began, his pockmarked skin even more ashen than normal.

"I thought all the Enemy were dead," StarLaughter said.

"As so they are!" Sheol snapped. "The bridge was, and has always been, a trap. The man was a vision only, a remembrance, meant to . . ."

She drifted off, but StarLaughter heard the unspoken phrase lingering in the air.

Meant to terrify us.

And more, StarLaughter thought, for has not that vision, that trap, killed Rox?

"He was one of the Enemy who had succeeded in trapping Qeteb," Mot said. "His name is unimportant, but it was his skill and knowledge that was the force behind snatching life from Qeteb. He died may eons ago, but his memory was encased in the trap."

"Rox?" StarLaughter said.

"Gone," Sheol said shortly.

StarLaughter glanced again at her son. "What does that mean for—"

"In the end, nothing," Sheol said. She had managed to calm herself now, although a thin drool of saliva still ran slowly down her chin. "Qeteb's resurrection may be accomplished without Rox."

"And your power?" StarLaughter continued, unable to conceal her concern. "What about that?"

Again she glanced at her son. "What about *his?*"

"Your *son's* power will be unaffected," Sheol said, her lip curling in a renewed snarl. "Never fear. As for us . . . we shall have to be more vigilant, but we will succeed, nevertheless."

She looked skyward into the blue mists that still enveloped them.

"When we emerge from this vaporous horror, we shall set the Hawkchilds to ravage and tear and punish this land for Rox's death. If his terror cannot haunt the night, then our winged friends can. We may still feed."

It took StarDrifter, WingRidge and SpikeFeather almost half a day to reach the waterways, and when they did, WingRidge and SpikeFeather stood back to watch StarDrifter. Perhaps he had connected pattern to dance, and thus to power, but the Ferryman had never used obvious enchantment to work his way through the waterways. Even if he had, and StarDrifter knew the enchantment, how could he know how to transfer the music, or words, into movement and dance?

But StarDrifter did not dance, nor sing, nor even wave his hands about and plead.

Instead, he merely climbed gracefully into the flat-bottomed boat that awaited them, and sat down on the bare plank in its stern, arranging his wings carefully behind him.

"Well?" StarDrifter inquired. "What are you waiting for?"

WingRidge and SpikeFeather glanced at each other and climbed in.

"How—" SpikeFeather began.

"It has become obvious to me," StarDrifter said, "that

these waterways are intimately connected with the Sacred Lakes and with the craft those lakes nurture. Correct?"

The two birdmen slowly nodded.

"And," StarDrifter continued, "are not the craft intimately connected with Drago?"

"Yes," WingRidge said. His forehead was crinkled in a slight frown.

"Then," StarDrifter said, and laid a hand on the smooth wood of the side of the boat, "I ask only that this boat, and the waterway on which it rests, takes us to Drago."

Instantly, the boat glided forward.

45

The Twenty Thousand

Move twenty thousand on foot, through territory that would be hostile to say the least, and with the entire night and much of the day spent scurrying for shelter? Some might say it was an impossible task, and one only a fool would contemplate, but Theod had no choice. They would die in the mines within a month, whether from the lack of food and water, or disease, or from the dark itself. He had to get them out.

The only thing in his favor was that at least they would not have to move through the open plains. The grain fields of Aldeni or Avonsdale were no different and the odd apple tree would do little to shelter his twenty thousand.

But Theod had the Murkle Mountains, and then the Western Ranges, and once he got them to a spot directly north of Carlon, then he could sigh with relief and send a farflight scout to beg Zared to aid them back to Carlon.

And so he began.

First, Theod sent scouting parties ahead, heavily protected by Wings of the Strike Force, to pick likely shelter spots through the lower Murkles and into the Western Ranges. These scouting parties would leave clear signs for the coming exodus to follow.

The twenty thousand could not move as one group, so, from among his own soldiers, the Strike Force and those sheltering within the mines themselves, Theod picked ten men and women who could lead groups of some two thousand each. These groups would leave the mines at intervals of twelve hours, in the hour after dawn, or dusk (now that the night had suddenly become inexplicably safe), and travel through each hour that they could and resting when they were forced to shelter. Of the ships Theod never spoke. They could have guaranteed the survival of the greater portion of these helpless and innocent people. Now, the Duke was certain he was about to lead many of them to their deaths.

When the time finally came for the groups of two thousand to leave, one group every twelve hours, day by day, their passing was noted by the Hawkchilds, and the information passed on to the TimeKeepers.

And, via the TimeKeepers, the information was sent to their legions in Aldeni and Avonsdale and, in particular, the brown and cream badger and the patchy-bald rat. The rat, emerging from his burrowings deep under the walls of Carlon, thought he had a plan—and the friends in right places to carry it through.

The badger's piggy eyes gleamed, and he approved.

The Hawkchilds agreed to carry messages north.

The Demons laughed, as Theod led his twenty thousand forward.

The way was difficult and fraught with hardship, but as the days passed Theod dared believe they might manage it. He led the first group, including Master Goldman, Gwendylyr and his two five-year-old sons. When they moved, a Wing of the Strike Force drifted overhead, keeping watch. When they sheltered, the Icarii fluttered down to huddle with them. They marched, walked and scrambled through landscape that was not hostile, but fatiguing. They generally moved among rocky slopes where there were no paths, they had little in the way of food supplies, and the weather remained cold and bitter during the early spring. It would have been difficult with a well-trained and hardened army unit; with groups of two thousand men, women and children it was sometimes heartbreaking.

Everyone bore up as best they could, but children stumbled

and sprained ankles, or grew tired and fractious. The adults already carried packs of blankets or food, and for many hours when they moved some of them also had to carry children, often as old, and as large, as eight or nine.

Whenever they set out, almost immediately everyone in the group began to worry about finding shelter before the next wave of gray madness oozed over the peaks. It did not matter that the Icarii wings above could spot adequate shelter ahead, people only worried that they might not make it. Some mornings and afternoons several, maybe even a score, among the group did not make it. Perhaps they misjudged the time, perhaps their exhausted limbs just could not get them into shade before the Demons consumed their minds. Whenever Theod heard the scream of terror, and then the screech of madness coming from beyond the shade of shelter, he flinched and lost a little more of his youth.

Then he would tighten his arms about his sons, and hang his head and weep.

So they struggled.

The Icarii kept Theod in touch with the groups coming behind him. They progressed hour by hour, day by day, as did he, and, as he, they occasionally lost a soul to the Demons, although because Theod could give them details of forward shelter it was that little bit easier.

They moved, and they kept on moving, for they had no other option.

Days passed, and Theod eventually managed to swing his group eastward into the Western Ranges.

"DareWing," he asked the Strike Leader softly one evening as they sat about a cold and cheerless canyon deep in shade. "I will need to send word to Zared soon about what has happened, and what we do. When do you counsel to be the best time?"

DareWing rubbed his tired face and thought. "To give the farflight scouts the best chance of getting through, we should get close to the ranges directly north of Carlon before we send scouts."

"How long will it take them to fly south to Zared?"

"My fittest and strongest scouts would take perhaps a day, but that would be flying nonstop, and they can't do that.

Every few hours they will need to seek shelter. Two days, maybe three."

"But they *will* get through?"

DareWing's mouth twisted grimly. "If we send enough, then perhaps two or three will get through, yes."

"What is enough?"

DareWing looked Theod in the eye. "I cannot answer that question."

DareWing and Theod may have hoped they passed through the southern Murkle Mountains and into the Western Ranges unobserved, but their every move was noted. Not by the Hawkchilds for they would have been seen, but by snails and grub worms and rodents and birds, once loyal only to their hungers and the land that fed them. Now mind and soul belonged entirely to the Demons who fed off them and now, in their madness, friends and comrades of the patchy-bald rat.

Early one morning, when the stars still sprinkled the predawn twilight, DareWing peered outside the entrance of the cave in which they'd sheltered and nodded.

"I can start sending scouts tomorrow," he said to Theod, who sat with his arm about his still-sleeping wife.

"Are you sure?"

DareWing nodded. "With luck, Zared can be preparing to meet us within the week."

Theod allowed himself a small glimmer of hope. "Then perhaps we will save some of these people."

He looked down to Gwendylyr's dark head cradled against his chest. Born an aristocrat, she'd lived a life of ease until the past few months, and yet she'd not once complained nor asked for favors. On the trek through the mountains she'd spent most of her time helping the elderly and sick who found the forced march difficult at best, and almost impossible for the rest.

Theod stroked the crown of her head, smiling gently, then looked over to where their two sons lay entwined in each others' arms. Theod knew he would gladly give his own life if it meant that Gwendylyr and the two boys lived.

"DareWing," he said softly, turning back to his friend. "Where do you think we should—"

He never got any further.

Someone among the bodies crowded into this particular cave suddenly screeched, and instantly there was panic.

People lurched to their feet—including Gwendylyr and the two boys—still half-asleep, but still fully within their nightmares.

Someone else screamed, and then another, and Theod shouted for calm.

But way back in the cave people were shoving and grunting, trying to push forward, and a mass of people were now surging toward the cave's entrance.

"No!" Theod screamed. "Stay where you are! *What's gone wrong?"*

He was answered instantly, but not by word. One of his sons screamed, and beat at something crawling up his body.

It was a bat, and behind it a snake, and then crawling up his other leg were four or five wolf spiders.

Theod ignored the tiny claws sinking into his own flesh, and instead tried to help his sons. Gwendylyr was beside him, alternately beating at something that clung to her back and the creatures that threatened to overwhelm her sons.

"Get a scout out!" Theod yelled to DareWing.

"I can't, damn you! It's dawn outside."

And then both of them were pushed to ground, as was Gwendylyr, by a wave of panicked people—some of them so thick with crawling creatures their human forms were blurred—surging toward the entrance.

"No!" Theod screamed yet again, but his voice was muffled, and his body buffeted by feet and sliding rocks, and by far, far worse . . .

One of his sons screamed in pure terror, and to *his* terror, Theod realized the sound came from very, very close to the mouth of the cave.

No! he wanted to scream yet again, but he couldn't rise, he couldn't, the weight of people above him was so great, the panic so all-consuming, he could hardly breathe, he—

Gwendylyr somehow managed to find her feet, and she saw both of her sons carried forward by the crowd. She fought forward, desperate beyond words to reach them and drag them back, but instead was caught in a surge of human-

ity crawling with horror, and could only watch helpless as her
two beloved boys were carried out into the dawn—

—*where horror worse, far, far, worse than a sea of biting
bats and insects awaited them*—

—and then was carried forward herself to experience with
horrible intimacy the feel of the Demons' hunger carving
into her mind, her sanity, her soul.

Gwendylyr, Duchess of Aldeni, beloved wife of Theod and
mother of their equally beloved sons, was crawling around
like a beast of the forest, tearing the clothes from her body.
She writhed naked in the dirt, groveling, groveling, groveling
before the black boar that now stood over her; weeping,
screeching, offering him her breasts to suck, her body to
take. Her life gone . . . And Theod, now left standing just inside the mouth of the cave, two Icarii with him, could only
stand and watch and scream, and scream, and scream.

Everyone, save those two left with him, had been carried
out into the dawn. DareWing, Goldman, the Strike Force . . .
and his wife and sons.

As the dawn brightened into day, Theod turned, and sank
down to the ground, for he could bear no more.

One of the Icarii squatted down beside him, lifted a hand
as if to put it on his shoulder, and then dropped it helplessly.

"We will fly to Carlon," he said. "Get help."

Theod nodded listlessly, not bothering to answer, and the
Icarii stood, beckoned to his companion, and lifted into the
morning.

A league south, just as they were about to fly out over the
northern Aldeni plains, they were attacked and utterly overwhelmed by a massive flock of birds that blocked out what
little sun there was.

Neither of the Icarii lived.

Theod sat through the day.

Outside, one of his former companions would sometimes
appear, gibbering, maniacal, filthy.

Once, one of Theod's sons appeared and that he could not
bear, so he moved back to the rear of the cave. A scratching
caught his attention—*anything* would have caught his atten-

tion, so desperate was Theod not to hear the horror babbling outside the cave's entrance—and he looked down.

There was a crack within the tumble of rocks that formed the back wall of the cave. No, more than twenty cracks, and from each of them shone beady eyes and glistening fangs.

"Gods!" Theod whispered. "This entire cave is a trap."

And behind him were moving nine more groups of Aldeni, each of them following signs that marked this cave as a safe haven!

He stood up and spun about.

What could he do? Where . . . who . . .

There was another movement outside the cave entrance, and all the gibbering and babbling abruptly ceased. Theod narrowed his eyes and stared into the brightness of sudden sun.

A great white horse pranced there, rolling his eyes. Stars flared about his head and streamed from his tail, and he seemed a thing of dream, not reality. Without thinking, without having any idea of why he did such a stupid, foolhardy thing, Theod walked forward, walked into the sun, and scrambled onto the stallion's bare back.

And so began the wild ride.

46

The Secret in the Basement

From the cave where they had all fought off the Hawkchilds' attack, Adamon and his companions led Axis, Azhure and Caelum into Star Finger. It was a day and a half's walk away, and too painful a journey for Caelum to manage on his own two feet. Eventually, Pors and Silton carried him on a rough stretcher made of a cloak and two spears.

The cloud of Hawkchilds did not return. No one knew whether it was because of the escort the three now had, or the injuries the Hawkchilds had sustained.

"What has been found?" Axis had demanded of Adamon before they left the cave, but Adamon had shaken his head.

"Wait," he said. "Yes, I have found something and I understand your impatience, but wait until we are in Star Finger."

And with that, Axis and Azhure, as their son, had to be content until Adamon could lead them to Star Finger's secret.

On that journey to Star Finger Caelum slept, swayed by the movement of the stretcher . . . and dreamed.

He dreamed he wandered, not through the entrapment of a maze, but through the freedom of a magnificent field of flowers, redolent with the colors and scents of poppies and lilies and cornflowers.

Always the dream would be disturbed with the thunder of a horse's hooves, and the cry from somewhere of "Star-Son!" Caelum would turn about, thinking the call was for him, but, invariably, all he would see was a woman dressed in a simple white robe wandering knee-deep in color and fragrance through the field. Thick chestnut hair flowed down her back, and she held the hand of a small girl who skipped at her side.

In her free hand she carried a single white lily.

A man rode toward her on a white stallion, its crest and mane shrouded with a glorious mist of stars. He halted the stallion before the woman and the child, and accepted the lily that the woman held up toward him.

"StarSon," she said, and the man smiled and leaned down to kiss her. And Caelum, seeing the man's face, wept in understanding—and a great deal of relief.

Sometimes the dream differed and he wandered the field of flowers, seeing no woman, nor man, nor stallion. But he did see the child. She would appear before him, holding a posy of flowers in her hand.

They would stare at each other, then the girl would hold out the posy of flowers, except every time she did that the flowers would turn to blood that stained her hand and dripped over Caelum's feet.

"Do you understand the need of sacrifice, Caelum?" she would ask, and whenever she said that, Caelum wept anew, and then listened as the girl pulled him down among the bloody flowers and spoke of love and of sacrifice.

* * *

Star Finger, once Talon Spike, had thousands of years of history in Icarii culture. Before the Wars of the Ax, when the Acharites had driven both Icarii and Avar from the southern lands, the great mountain had been the Icarii's summer playground, a place to laugh and sing and plan the pursuit of love.

After those desperate wars that had exiled the Icarii from so much of Tencendor, the mountain had become a thousand-year prison until Axis StarMan had led the Icarii southward to west Tencendor from the Seneschal's control. Then most of the Icarii had flown southward to reclaim the spires and citadels of the Minaret Peaks, but many thousands had remained in Talon Spike with the previous Talon, RavenCrest SunSoar and his wife, BrightFeather. While SpikeFeather had been able to persuade the majority of the Icarii to flee the mountain before Gorgrael set his Gryphon to its inevitable attack, RavenCrest and BrightFeather and many of the Elders had elected to remain.

They had all died, torn to pieces by the ravening Gryphon. Then, expecting to find tens of thousands of Icarii secreted within the shafts and winding passages of the mountain, the Gryphon had sunk ever deeper into the mountain's enchanted defenses, seeking, seeking, seeking.

They had sunk to the very bowels of the mountain (although they did not find the entrance to the Underworld, which the Ferryman had hidden). They had almost sunk to the chambers that had been excavated many thousands of years earlier to hide the mountain's population from an attack such as this.

Of course, now they hid no Icarii.

But that which the chambers did hide, which was neither feathered nor strictly alive, was kept safe from the incursion of Gorgrael's creatures, although the sense that there was *something* there, something *tasty,* drove the Gryphon almost insane with rage.

And when the Gryphon finally crawled exhausted from the mountain, the object remained as safe—and as lonely—as it had been for countless thousands of generations.

* * *

Star Finger was as lacking in enchantment as were the Minaret Peaks, but the mountain also housed far less Icarii than did the southern city, and they had managed to remain relatively comfortable. The corridors were gloomy and cold, but the chambers that were needed could be lit adequately for those who required them.

From the entrance in the eastern wall of the mountain, Adamon and Xanon led Axis, Azhure and a Caelum now rested enough to walk into one of the apartment complexes close to the peak of Star Finger. Here natural light filtering through thickened glass lit the chambers and coal-fired braziers warmed the air.

Two healers waited, and led Caelum and Azhure to benches so the healers could inspect their wounds and stitch those that needed it. Azhure was clearly impatient, but Caelum appeared very calm, almost cheerful, and the others put it down to the relative safety of Star Finger.

Azhure grimaced at the bite of the stitching needle, but managed a smile for Axis. "I have not endured a wound since the Skraelings scored my ribs in Hsingard."

Axis tried to return her smile, but found himself unable to. He'd never been able to regard the sight of Azhure bleeding, whether in field or childbirth battle, with equanimity, and he could not now.

So he touched her cheek, knowing she understood his concern, and turned to the healer attending Caelum. Only two of the wounds needed any stitching, and all were clean and healthy; Xanon's attentions at the cave had saved both Caelum and Azhure any lasting harm.

A movement caught his eye. Sicarius, moving among his pack, which was now lying close-grouped against a far wall. He was licking the wounds of the several hounds who had also been wounded in the fight with the Hawkchilds. Among them was FortHeart, who had a severe wound running down the left side of her skull. It oozed yellow effluent, leaving the pale fur of her neck and shoulder stained and fetid, and she bit off a yelp as Sicarius tried to clean it for her.

As Axis watched, Sicarius raised his head and stared at him. His golden eyes were flat and hard, and the corner of one lip raised very, very slightly, exposing the gleam of a fang.

Help her.

Axis jumped, stunned at the distinct request—nay, not a request, more a command. It had not sounded as voice, nor in the same way as the mind voice which all Icarii Enchanters had once been able to employ, but more as sheer emotion seething across the space between them.

Help her!

"FeatherTouch," Axis said quietly to one of the healers assisting with Azhure, "will you and another see to the hounds?"

"Yes, StarMan."

Again Sicarius' lip curled, but after a moment he dropped his head, and continued cleaning FortHeart's wound until FeatherTouch arrived. Then, having satisfied himself that the other members of his pack would receive attention in due course, he sank down to the floor, his head on his forepaws, and watched Axis steadily.

Axis tore his gaze away—damn those hounds! If they hadn't aided in repelling the Hawkchilds then he may have tried to persuade Azhure to have them placed under close guard in cells. He no longer trusted them, and knew that they no longer trusted him.

"Azhure," he murmured, and leaned back to her side.

Sicarius watched the activities of the Icarii, gods and Sun-Soars. He no longer felt at home with them, no longer wanted to be with them, although he did not feel animosity toward them as such. More than ever before in his life he felt the roar of the bear in his veins, and all he wanted to do was run with his true master.

When? When? When?

A movement in the open doorway caught his eyes. Sicarius pricked his ears, and every muscle in his body tensed. Then he relaxed, his lips almost seeming to grin, and his tail wagged once in a barely discernible movement.

There. Another of his pack.

In a manner of speaking.

The blue-feathered lizard flared its emerald and scarlet crest, then scuttled back into the shadows.

Sicarius slid his eyes back to Caelum, who sat with his eyes closed as he patiently bore the ministrations of the healer. Sicarius could sense the change in the man, sense the understanding, and as far as the leader of the Alaunt was concerned, that made Caelum an honorary member of the pack.

Caelum opened his eyes and caught Sicarius' stare.

He nodded slightly, and Sicarius' tail gave a single thump.

"You *must* rest!" Adamon threw up his hands in frustration, but Axis and Azhure would have none of his patience.

"You cannot say to us, 'I have found something,' with such high excitement," Axis said, "and then expect us to sleep quietly and spend an hour or two at leisurely supper while Tencendor decays about us. Tell us!"

Adamon glanced at Caelum, who merely smiled and nodded his head.

He shrugged. "Xanon, will you fetch the others?"

She nodded and walked to the door. "Come," she called softly, and Pors, Silton, Narcis, Flulia, and Zest entered. They had previously greeted Axis, Azhure and their son, and now sat quietly on chairs scattered about the chamber.

Several of the hounds moved to make room for the gods, but most remained still and watchful. Even though their interest and hope lay elsewhere, they still held a respect for the Circle entire.

Two Elder Icarii also entered. Axis knew them well, for they were the senior scholars of the Star Finger complex, respected for their wisdom and learning. Their names had long lost any importance, and they were addressed only by their titles.

"Respected Preceptor," Axis said, and inclined his head. "Respected Historian."

Azhure and Caelum also murmured a greeting, and the Preceptor and Historian sat together on a couch close by the brazier. They were dressed in plain white robes, and their bodies were unadorned with any of the finery Icarii usually adored. Even their wing feathers seemed oddly dulled, as if the two scholars assiduously bleached away their luminescence upon rising each morning.

Adamon, the only one who remained standing, inclined his head at those gathered, and then spoke.

"I, as my companions," he glanced at the other Star Gods,

"returned to Star Finger in the hope that the accumulated knowledge of tens of thousands of years held in its libraries might contain an answer to our current lack of effectiveness against the TimeKeeper Demons.

"Caelum StarSon must be the one to meet them . . . but how? How? If *all* his power, as all our powers, have disappeared with the Star Dance? When at first we returned, we had no luck," Adamon continued. "Even with the aid of all the respected scholars in Star Finger, we could find no hint of a solution to the problem. And yet where else could lie the answer to Caelum's dire need?"

Adamon's voice was tight with the frustration and anger of his initial lack of success. He sighed, and visibly relaxed his muscles.

"Then the Respected Historian came to me, and said there was an inconsistency. Historian, will you speak."

"Star Finger, once Talon Spike, has been used by the Icarii since their conception by the great Enchantress fifteen thousand years ago," the Historian said. His voice was rich and melodious, and Axis knew how he could hold a class, as any audience, enthralled for many hours. "The mountain has been burrowed into and hollowed out for fifteen thousand years. It holds fifteen thousand years of memories—and fifteen thousand years of secrets. In the very roots of the mountains lie secret basements, basements thick with enchantment."

"Surely those basements were always to be meant as hiding places for the Icarii nation," Azhure said, "should they ever come under attack. That SpikeFeather chose to evacuate the mountain rather than hide the people there speaks of the fear that all then regarded the Gryphon—and Gorgrael."

"Yes, yes," the Historian said, "but these were unusual enchantments. Preceptor, my friend, will you speak?"

The Preceptor nodded. "My primary task here in Star Finger was to instruct those Enchanters who chose to spend their years in study and contemplation of the most arcane and secret of enchantments. When my colleague the Historian came to me and engaged me in conversations about the enchantments surrounding the basements, and after some days of investigation and study on these most forgotten of enchantments, I realized there was an unusual conundrum present."

Caelum shifted slightly, easing his sore muscles, and again caught Sicarius' eyes on him. *How long have you known, my friend?* Caelum thought. *Did you run about Sigholt and Star Finger with my mother all these years and know the lie we all lived?*

Sicarius' tail thumped once again.

"The current problem surrounding the enchantments guarding the basement are twofold. One, why are they there in the first instance? The wards guarding the basements from attack should be erected only *after* they are full with refugees. Second, given that they are there, they should not be working. The Star Dance is gone—how can they still be in place?"

"But some enchantments do remain," Azhure said. "The mists surrounding Sigholt, for example. The magic of the Maze Gate."

"Quite," the Preceptor said. "What enchantments remain are those which we may have connected with the music of the Star Dance, but they are enchantments that perhaps draw their power from somewhere else."

"The Lakes," Caelum said. "They draw their power from the Lakes, or from the craft that lie within the Lakes."

"Yes," the Historian said. "So we wondered if the fact that the enchantments have remained in place, and the fact they are in place in the first instance, means that they *already guard something within the basements!*"

"Something connected to the Lakes, and the craft, perhaps!" Adamon said, now walking about the room, his movements restrained but tight with excitement. "We had to see. We had to search. We had to *know!*"

"And?" Axis said quietly.

"And . . ." Adamon took a deep breath. "My friends, do you feel you could manage the long walk down to Star Finger's cellars?"

They descended for hour past hour, and Adamon made them rest at regular intervals, passing out food and liquid at each stop. A score of Icarii, bearing burning torches and light packs with the food, came down with the gods, Caelum and the two scholars.

Behind all trod the Alaunt. Axis had noticed them rise to follow the party, and again had thought about asking that the hounds should be detained, but had eventually remained silent.

At first, as they descended the stairs that curved about the main shafts, the way was pleasant, if somewhat dark and chill. But after two hours they reached less traveled shafts, and then moved into stairwells that had lain forgotten for generations of Icarii. The odd feather and tuft of fur, covered with dust, lay as reminders that the only living beings who *had* descended into the bowels of Talon Spike had been Gorgrael's Gryphon.

The stairwells stank, stank from disuse, damp and the foulness that still remained of the Gryphon. All had to watch their footing on edges that crumbled and surfaces that glistened with ice.

Several turns of the stairwell behind the main party trod the Alaunt, the feathered lizard openly traveling with them, albeit at the rear.

"No one had any idea, really, that these stairs existed," the Historian murmured as they descended. He, like everyone, kept one hand on the wall for support. "They had lain so long forgotten."

"We came down here once, last week," Adamon said, "and found what we . . . well, found what we did, and then decided to await your arrival before coming back."

"What's that noise?" Azhure said, raising her head.

"What we have come to see," Adamon said, and the next instant the stair leveled out onto undulating flagstones. "This way. Come." And he led them across the floor to a corridor.

As they walked down the corridor the noise became louder.

"Oh!" Azhure cried, and her eyes filled with tears. It was the sound of a child weeping, a girl-child, and Azhure was reminded of her own painful and lost childhood. "Let me past! I must—"

"No." Adamon caught Azhure's arm as she tried to push past him. "Please, Azhure, there is nothing you can do for her, and no point in rushing on this damp and slippery flooring."

They walked through the dark corridor—it felt as close as

a tomb! Azhure thought—for another fifty or sixty paces, and then suddenly they were in a large domed chamber.

Empty, save for the figure of a five- or six-year-old girl huddled against the far wall, her arms wrapped about a great leather-bound book, crying disconsolately.

"Oh!" Azhure cried, and finally managed to push past Adamon and rush toward the girl.

Instantly, the girl's sobs became screams of terror and, as Azhure neared her, the girl literally convulsed with the strength of her fear. There was a flash of light, and Azhure was thrown against a side wall.

"No one can approach her," Adamon said, as Axis hurried to Azhure and helped her to rise. She was uninjured, save for a bruise where her shoulder had hit the stone, and wheezing from being badly winded.

"All have been repulsed who tried to near her, or comfort her," Adamon continued.

"But look," he pointed to the book held tightly within the girl's arms. She was relatively still now, although she still cried, but her eyes remained terrified as she stared at the intruders. "Look at what you can see on the front cover."

Between the white flesh of the girl's forearms, three words could be seen gleaming in gold.

Enchanted Songbook.

"I think there lies the one way we can re-find the power of Star Dance," Adamon said. "She waits, we think, for the Star-Son. Caelum. Will you—"

Caelum had recognized the girl instantly as the child who had spoken to him in the field of flowers. He hesitated, knowing it would be useless for him to approach her, but everyone was looking at him, and so he started forward.

He hoped the girl would understand.

She had calmed even more now, and all watching thought, hoped, that Caelum might be able to approach her when no one else could.

The girl's sobs stopped, and her blue eyes widened.

When Caelum was no more than seven paces away, the girl rose to her feet.

"You came!" she cried out with glad voice, and Caelum smiled . . . and then he realized that her eyes were fixed on something—someone—behind him. Very slowly, knowing who he would see, Caelum turned about.

There, barely visible in the gloomy doorway leading to the corridor, stood Drago.

He smiled, his eyes only for the girl.

"Hello, Katie," he said.

47

StarSon

Axis whirled about, shocked and angry at Drago's intrusion. How had he entered? How had he *known?* Axis had had enough. He'd promised Drago the last time he'd seen him that if Drago set foot in Star Finger he would die, and Axis meant to carry the promise through.

The instant he moved in Drago's direction, Caelum's voice cracked across the chamber. *"Father!"*

Every eye in the chamber, save those of Drago and the girl, swiveled to Caelum.

"Father," Caelum repeated, "let Drago enter."

Axis stared at Caelum, shocked by the command in his son's voice, looked back to Drago, then reluctantly took a step back. He felt Azhure at his back, and felt her take one of his hands.

Drago had hardly noticed his father, and had hardly heard Caelum. He only had eyes for the girl, as she him. Drago walked slowly into the chamber, the only display of emotion the slight clenching and unclenching of his hand about the staff.

Azhure watched him carefully. He seemed different, but she could not define it. Physically, he looked much the same; the copper hair slicked back into a tail, the leanness, the thin face that looked perpetually tired because of the deep lines that ran from nose to mouth.

But his eyes were subtly different. Still violet, but deeper, more alive. Deeply compassionate, Azhure realized with a start, and with a depth of knowing that she'd never, never seen there previously.

Power? Maybe. But how? Something the Demons had invested him with? Azhure abandoned that thought the instant it crossed her mind. No. This came from within him, *deep* within him, and *was* somehow him.

"DragonStar," she mouthed silently—and completely involuntarily—as he drew level with her, and for the first time since he'd entered the chamber, Drago's eyes flickered away from the girl and toward his mother. In the space of a heartbeat, a look, an understanding passed between them and Azhure dropped her eyes, stricken.

In that instant she had been consumed with love. Unimaginable love for her had coursed from him, but she had also felt her own love overwhelm her. Her love for her secondborn son . . . a love she had denied both to herself and to him for forty, long, horrid years.

Drago looked back to the girl.

She had clambered to her feet, still clutching the book, a final hiccuping sob escaping her lips. She was a beautiful child, with glossy brunette hair and dark blue eyes, and with fragile translucent skin.

"Katie," Drago murmured, and walked toward the girl.

Caelum stepped back to let him pass, his gaze riveted on his brother. His eyes were very bright and full of emotion, and Axis, watching him carefully, wondered at that. He would have said it was fright, save that Caelum's face showed no hint of fear.

Unseen by any in the room, Faraday slipped through the door into the chamber. Behind her crowded the pale shapes of the Alaunt. She stopped just behind Xanon, who stood behind everyone else.

Drago squatted before the girl. "Katie," he said, and his smile widened into embracing warmth.

She gave one final sniff, wiped her nose with the back of her hand, and stared at him with unblinking eyes. Slowly she took the book in both hands, and extended it toward him.

"For you," she said.

"No!" Axis' voice rang across the chamber. "That is meant for—"

"Axis," Azhure took his arm firmly, drawing him back against her body. "Please, just watch."

He tensed, angry, but he closed his mouth. Azhure could feel every muscle in his body tighten, and she gripped his arm the harder.

Drago laid his staff on the floor and took the book from the girl's hands. Then, balancing the heavy book under one arm, he took her hand in his, and held it loosely.

"Katie," he said. "See who I have brought for you."

And he turned his head slightly.

Faraday stepped out from behind the crowd, kneeling down on the cold, damp stone, and held out her arms. She was weeping silently.

Katie drew a breath in shock, and then she was flying across the chamber, pushing past Caelum, and ran into Faraday's arms. Katie was crying again, but this time with sheer joy as she felt Faraday's arms lock tightly about her, and felt Faraday's face pressed into her hair, and smelt the fragrance of the woman as it enveloped her.

No one knew where to look, whether at the girl and Faraday, or back to Drago and Caelum.

Drago rose to his feet, the book held in his hands.

"Drago and I must speak," Caelum said. "Alone."

Everyone left. No one spoke, no one demurred, no one offered any hint of resistance. Even Axis simply turned, and left.

Faraday gathered the girl into her arms, shot Drago a look of warmth and gratitude, and followed them out.

The door closed behind her. "This is a bad place to meet," Drago said. "We should talk, you and I, in a place of sunshine, where we can feel the weight of the wind in our hair."

"Nevertheless," Caelum said, his tone neutral, "this is what we have come to, you and I, a cold and damp cellar in the bowels of a mountain. A dungeon in all but name."

Drago dropped his eyes to the book. "Caelum—"

"No. Let me speak."

And having said this, Caelum hesitated. He wandered about the chamber in silence, as if involved in a deep inspection of the walls. Occasionally he reached out and touched the stone, running his fingers through the trails of moisture.

Drago watched him silently, content to let Caelum take his time. They had been moving toward this moment for over forty years. Who could blame Caelum for now wanting to delay the words a few moments more? It would be extraordinarily hard for him, for he would have to deny everything he'd ever believed in.

"For many months," Caelum eventually said, his voice not much more than a confessional murmur, "I have been plagued by dreams. The hunt. Running terrified through the forest, the hunter on a great black horse behind me."

Drago remembered his own dreams, of hunting, hunting, hunting, and of the joy he'd felt in the hunt.

His eyes filled with tears.

"Every time, no matter what I did," Caelum continued, "the hunter cornered me, and every time he would lean down and plunge his sword or lance into my chest. Every time I woke with the taste of blood in my mouth and the feel of it bubbling unhindered through my lungs."

Caelum turned from the wall and faced Drago. His arms were now relaxed by his side, and his eyes were bright with courage. "And every time, just before he sank his dreadful weapon into my chest, the rider would lift his visor, and I would see his face.·

"It has always been your face."

"I—"

"No. I need to finish. I feared you as I have never feared another, Drago. I have spent my *life* fearing you. You ruined my childhood, you scarred my adulthood, and you invaded my dreams. You have lurked in every shadow about me, and your malevolence has stalked my happiness, my resolve, and my confidence."

"I—"

"No!" Caelum screamed. *"Let me finish!"*

He strode forward, and stabbed a finger into Drago's chest. Drago flinched slightly, but at the pain in Caelum's eyes, rather than at his stabbing finger.

"You *bastard!*" Caelum spat, "you stole my heritage, you stole *everything* from me." A slight pause. "You have denied me even my self-respect." He took a great breath, trying to control his emotions.

"And yet," Caelum said, his voice now little more than a whisper, "you had every right to do that, didn't you?"

He turned and walked a few steps away before he faced Drago again. "DragonStar was the name of that rider, and he wore your face, and the malevolence and repulsiveness of his existence was the mirror of my interpretation of you.

"Yet a few nights ago, trapped in the dream again, I realized a frightful truth. He *isn't* you, is he, Drago?"

"No," Drago said. "It is the body of StarLaughter's son. DragonStar . . . the body that Qeteb will use."

Caelum nodded. Again he breathed deeply. "Drago . . . DragonStar . . . how *we* have betrayed *you,* and in betraying you, how we have betrayed Tencendor.

"As I realized that the fiend who hunts me was not you and has never been you, I realized something else. It felt so *right,*" Caelum raised a hand as if in appeal, "that I *knew* it was truth.

"I learned, brother, that *I* should have been the second son. *You* should have been heir . . . should have been StarSon."

"No!" Drago said. "You have been the best of—"

Caelum interrupted him with a low, deprecating laugh, and walked away a few more steps. "It *is* I who would have made a wonderful second son, DragonStar. I have all the qualities for it. The loyalty, the desire—the *need*—to serve someone else, the constant questioning of self-worth, the constant feeling that I always had to prove myself, and that I had to prove my right to sit upon the Throne of the Stars. I have not done well as Star-Son, and that is only right, because I have never been StarSon."

He turned back to face Drago. "*You* have. You knew from the instant you grew to awareness in Azhure's womb that you were the legitimate StarSon, and 'tis no wonder you developed such anger and resentment. You were right to rail against Axis as an infant, and correct in demanding your true birthright."

"No! I was *not* right to do what I did," Drago said. "To ally myself with Gorgrael and plot your death . . . I should have spent my life serving you, not betraying you, and surely not resenting you."

Caelum waved a hand dismissively. "We walk in circles with our words, brother." He paused. "You say you were wrong to ally yourself with Gorgrael and to plot my death.

But am I any better?" They stared at each other, and then, neither yet ready to speak of the greatest tragedy of all, Caelum continued: "I should have been the second son, but instead I was born first. Drago, I understand *why* I was born first, and I accept that, and I will do what is needed."

He half-smiled. "If you want me to continue on with the pretense of StarSon, then I will do so. It will serve the same end. If you think I must face Qeteb as StarSon, then I understand that I must do so."

He stopped, and stared at Drago. "You are weeping," he whispered. "Why?"

"For the loss of both of our lives, Caelum, but mostly for you. For your courage. For your dignity."

Caelum shuddered with emotion. "You said . . . you said in the forest, when last we parted, that when you came back through the Star Gate all enchantments fell from your eyes."

Drago nodded.

"Then how is it, brother, that you can stand there and weep for *me?*" Caelum's voice broke, and he had to pause to regain control of it, and of himself. "How is it that you can stand there and weep for me, when you *know* how foul I am?"

"Caelum—"

"How can you weep for *me,* when I did RiverStar to death?"

There was utter silence and stillness in the chamber. Here, finally, surrounded by the cold damp stone, the weight of the mountain upon them and Tencendor disintegrating outside, they dared to speak and confront RiverStar's death.

And remember.

RiverStar turned, and hungered.

"I thought you would not come tonight."

"I could not help myself," Caelum said. "I needed you."

She was on him then, her body tight against his, her hands daring, arousing. "Take me," she whispered hoarsely. "I demand it."

He half-pushed her away. "You are in no position to demand anything."

Her lip curled, hate and lust rippling across her face in equal amounts. "And are you, brother? How would Tencen-

dor react, do you think, to know that their StarSon spent each night deep inside his sister's body?"

"You foul-mouthed—"

"Oh!" she laughed, pushing back against him. "I can be much fouler than that, Caelum. As well you know. Do you think Tencendor would be interested in knowing just how foul? Do you think Tencendor would like to know just what you do to my body, Caelum? How you use it? How you scream and pant and sweat with every thrust?"

Now she had lifted one leg and wrapped it about his hip, lifting herself up slightly, and rubbing herself against his groin.

"Do you think," she whispered, her own lust now threatening to overwhelm her, "that Tencendor would like to know how much of yourself you expend within your sister's body?"

"Bitch!" Caelum spat, and he shoved her against the table behind her, ignoring her sudden cry of pain—and excitement—as the edge dug into her back. He slammed her along its surface, one hand tangled in her hair, one hand fumbling with her clothes and then his, and then he grunted and buried himself within her.

She laughed, writhing around him. "Do you think, brother," she whispered, her words barely audible above both their panting, "that Tencendor would like to know just how pregnant you have made me?"

He stopped, appalled, still buried deep within her. "You lie."

She wriggled against him, rocking her hips, intent on her own satisfaction, even if he had abandoned his. "Considering the amount of SunSoar seed you have planted in me, brother, I would be amazed if I did not give birth to a battalion of your sons."

Her movements intensified, and as Caelum continued to stare at her, she suddenly shuddered, then jerked, and cried out with hoarse gratification.

"You lie . . ." Caelum said.

"You must marry me," she whispered, her face running with sweat. "Or else I shall run to our parents and say that you raped me."

Caelum jerked himself away from her, fumbling as he re-arranged his clothes.

"I shall tell our mother," she sneered, continuing to lie on the table with her legs spread-eagled, "amid my tears of mortification, that you forced my compliance with savage threats. That you ignored my screams of pain as you—"

"No!"

"Then marry me, Caelum!" She raised herself on one elbow. "Marry me! Imagine the power we would enjoy together! Imagine the power our son," she splayed the fingers of one hand across her belly, "will enjoy! Imagine—"

"No!" Caelum screamed, and sprang forward. As he moved, music sprang into life about them. Music and power, and suddenly there was the gleam of steel in Caelum's hand, and then it vanished as he buried the kitchen knife to its hilt in her belly.

RiverStar shrieked, and writhed in an obscene parody of how she had writhed against Caelum's body.

"No," Caelum said again, in a strangely flat voice, and he wrenched the knife out only to sink it into her belly again, and again, and again. And then he turned his attention to her foul breasts and then to her throat although RiverStar had ceased to cry out long before.

As Caelum lifted the knife for yet another blow, a hand grasped his shoulder and spun him about.

"Are you mad, brother?"

Drago, his expression a mixture of fear and horror and anger. Behind Caelum RiverStar's body slid from the table to the floor with a sickening thud.

Caelum used his power to pull himself free from Drago's grip, and he raised his knife as if to attack his brother.

Then it suddenly stilled.

"No," he murmured. "I have a better idea."

Again music leaped into life about them, and Drago sank to his knees beside his sister's body, the knife magically, horribly, disappearing from Caelum's hand and reappearing in his.

Enchantment flooded Drago's mind, enchantment so powerful—and intrusive—he gagged, then leaned over and retched.

A memory block. An enchantment so potent, and so different, that only a SunSoar with the secret knowledge of how to manipulate the ring and the Star Dance could have wielded it.

A mind block, and a block that warped and rearranged Drago's memory of his sister's death.

"And now," Caelum said, waving his hand so that all blood about the room and on his clothes disappeared, leaving the only murderous evidence clinging to Drago, "I must be off."

He vanished.

And within heartbeats Isfrael and FreeFall had rushed into the room, only to halt in disbelief, and stare at the treacherous, now murderous, Drago crouched over his sister's body.

"Because of that, I will do as I must," Caelum said very quietly. "If you want me to continue on in the pretense of StarSon, then I will. And I will rejoice in it."

Drago stared at his brother. Forty wasted years lay between them, forty years of lies and denial. And yet were they a waste? Unbidden Drago remembered what Axis had hissed over his cradle the first time he'd seen his new son.

I will not welcome you into the House of Stars until you have learned both humility and compassion.

Drago realized that if he had been born into the title of StarSon, with all the potential power that entailed, then he would have been just another WolfStar, raging out of control.

The life wasted was not his, but Caelum's.

"Caelum . . ." Drago started, and was unable to finish. He had to turn aside slightly.

"Drago," Caelum said. "We must move on. Neither of us, nor Tencendor, has time for regrets."

Drago nodded, composed himself, then looked down to the book. "You will need this."

"Will you teach me how to use it?"

"As much as I am able."

He stepped closer to Caelum, and opened the book. "See these strange patterns? They are the same as on my staff," he indicated with a hand. "They form a strange script, representing music rather than words. This book contains Songs, Caelum, and I believe they are the Songs that will aid in the destruction of Qeteb. I hope to all the Stars above that they are!"

"But the Star Dance is dead."

"Caelum, I only know that this book *will* help. Here, feel it!" Drago passed the book into Caelum's hands, and his brother's eyes widened with surprise. The book vibrated gently.

"Mayhap the Star Dance lives on in the book, Caelum. It was written by one of the ancient Enemy, one of those who traveled on the craft, and he had many, many thousands of years to absorb the Dance. The craft are powerful . . . and so is the book."

Caelum nodded. "DragonStar," he said, and this time his voice did choke with emotion. "You are my brother."

"And you are mine," Drago said. "I love you, Caelum. I always have . . . I just had a cruel way of showing it."

Caelum smiled slowly, then he put the book down and took his brother's shoulders in his hands.

"This has been too long in the doing. Far too long," he said, and he took a deep breath.

"Welcome, DragonStar StarSon, into the House of the Stars and into my heart. My name is Caelum SunSoar, and I am your brother who loves you dearly. Sing well, and fly high, and . . ." Caelum hesitated slightly, "may your heart and mind and soul soar with all the enchantment that is your inheritance and your glory."

Without hesitation, and for the first time in his life, Caelum leaned forward and embraced Drago. "Welcome home, brother," he whispered.

And for the first time in *his* life, Drago hugged his brother tight against him, and buried his face in his shoulder, and wept.

48

Companionship and Respect

Outside the domed chamber people grouped in uncomfortable uncertainty, staring at the closed door, and wondering at what was happening inside.

"Pray to the Stars Drago does not harm his brother," Axis murmured, pacing back and forth before the door. Every two or three steps he stopped, stared at the door, then jerked back into his restless pacing.

"Why did the girl respond to Drago, and not Caelum?" Adamon asked. "And why Faraday?"

He turned, and looked at the two who were absorbed only in each other.

Faraday sat on the stone floor, her arms wrapped about the child. The girl—Katie—hugged herself as close to Faraday's body as she could get, burying her head in the coarse weave of Faraday's dress, her fingers digging great ravines and ranges into the fabric of her skirts. About them were grouped the Alaunt hounds. In a circle, facing outward, keeping guard.

"Who is she?" Axis asked, finally taking his eyes from the closed door behind which Drago was probably murdering Caelum in a fit of brotherly ambition.

Faraday looked up, her eyes swimming with tears, but nevertheless defiant.

"She is the child I was never allowed to hold," Faraday said. "And I the mother she lost."

"Who *is* she?" Axis repeated, his voice slightly colder now. Why must Faraday always throw the past in his face?

"Her name is Katie," Faraday said, "but exactly who, or what she is, I cannot know. She is connected to the craft, and mayhap she has still to play her role in the saving of this land, and mayhap she has already played it. All I know is that she has lost love, and yet needs love, and that I can give love to her."

Watching, Azhure's face softened. The girl reminded her of her own pain at that age.

"Leave them be," she murmured to Axis, and he turned his face away, his eyes still hard.

Pors, standing closest to the corridor down which they'd walked, suddenly stiffened, and stared intently down its gloom.

"Someone comes," he said.

Everyone tensed, save Faraday and the child. Faraday looked up, and then smiled slowly, her face lovely in its happiness.

"It is your father, Axis. And others as trustworthy."

Axis glanced at her, then returned his gaze to the group of three figures he could just make out at the far end of the corridor. "StarDrifter?"

Stars! How long had it been since he'd thought of StarDrifter? Wasn't he still with Zared?

"He, too, serves the StarSon, as he sees fit," Faraday whispered into the child's hair, and no one heard her.

"Axis?" StarDrifter's voice called down the length of corridor still separating them. "Azhure? WingRidge and Spike-Feather are with me. We bring stupendous news!"

Axis relaxed at the familiar sound of StarDrifter's voice, and within a minute StarDrifter was among them, embracing Axis and Azhure, and greeting the others respectfully. Behind him WingRidge and SpikeFeather bowed deeply to gods and scholars alike.

StarDrifter saw Faraday and the child surrounded by the hounds, and his eyes widened, but before he could speak to or approach her, Azhure spoke.

"News?" she said. "What news?"

"Hope," StarDrifter said.

In truth, he was, as were his two companions, disconcerted to find this crowd awaiting them here. They had disembarked from the boat where it had stopped at an ancient landing, and climbed a stairwell into a corridor a level below this. Trusting in the power of the waterways, they had followed the corridor, climbed the stairwell to which it led, followed yet another corridor hoping to find Drago before they became hopelessly lost, and had then instead run into this crowd—and Faraday and the girl she clutched. What was going on?

"We have found the Sanctuary in which the peoples of Tencendor may find shelter," StarDrifter continued, "and—"

"The Sanctuary?" Xanon asked, her soft query echoed by the other gods.

"Ah," StarDrifter said, suddenly remembering that Axis and Azhure had left the Silent Woman Woods well before Drago had returned with news of the existence of Sanctuary. How much should he tell them? In StarDrifter's hesitation, WingRidge took the initiative.

"The craft have provided for the shelter of the people of this land," he said. "We . . ."

WingRidge hesitated, thinking twice about saying that they needed Drago to open the bridge. "We have left Zenith to organize the evacuation of the Minaret Peaks."

"Where is this Sanctuary?" Adamon asked. Why had he not known of this?

"In the waterways," SpikeFeather said, inclining his head respectfully as he spoke. "Beneath Fernbrake Lake."

"Meanwhile," StarDrifter said, "we have come north with the news that we must share." He had no qualms telling them what he'd discovered about the ability of dance to tap into the power of the Star Dance. Gods knew it was knowledge that should be shared as widely as possible. "Axis, Azhure, I have managed to use the power of the Star Dance!"

The room erupted in sound, and Adamon had to shout for quiet. During the tumult Faraday shared a look with StarDrifter, then she looked at the closed door to the domed chamber. StarDrifter understood. He nodded slightly.

"StarDrifter?" Adamon's voice was tight with anxiety. *"How?"*

StarDrifter told them of their discovery of the foundations of the long lost Keep of Fernbrake Lake, and of the maze formed by the pattern of the stones. "SpikeFeather was the one who truly discovered the secret," StarDrifter said, and placed a hand on the birdman's shoulder, "and it is to him that we must owe all gratitude in—"

"What did you discover?" Axis all but shouted.

"What is important is pattern," StarDrifter said. "Music and dance, as do symbols and numbers, form patterns. We should have realized it, for the waterways work in the same—"

"What?"

"Each Song we sang manipulated the power of the Star Dance," StarDrifter said. "Manipulated by forming a pattern . . . we sang the pattern. Dance does the same thing. We may no longer hear the music of the Star Dance, but it still exists, and it still can be touched."

"Pattern can use the Star Dance?" Axis whispered. *"Dance?"*

StarDrifter nodded slowly, his eyes intent on his son. "And it is a method that anyone with the ability to move can employ, not just Enchanters, who were the only ones with the power to hear the music of the Star Dance. But—"

"But . . ." Azhure said, stepping forward. There had to be a difficulty, she *knew* it.

"So now all we have to do to regain our power," StarDrifter said, his eyes compassionate, "is discover the intricate dance movement appropriate for every purpose as once we discovered the appropriate Songs for each purpose."

Stars! Axis felt his surge of hope drain away into blank nothingness. It had taken the Icarii thousands of years to discover the Songs they needed. True, Axis and every one of his Enchanter children had been able to learn new Songs with the simple twist of their rings, but every ring had dulled into glassy-eyed sterility since the Star Gate had collapsed. Even Azhure's Circle of Stars now glinted with the despair of clouded and cracked glass rather than the joy of the stars.

No one had thousands of years. If anything, they had but a month or two to discover a means by which Caelum could face Qeteb and his companion Demons.

"Axis," StarDrifter said into the silence. "Why are you here?"

"Adamon found something unusual. A book," Axis said, "guarded by that child." He nodded his head at the girl in Faraday's arms. "I do not know how, but maybe—"

"There is no maybe about it," said Caelum's voice from behind him. "Combined with what StarDrifter has said, and this book in my arms, we shall have the means to rid this land of the Demons for all time."

Everyone spun around. Caelum and Drago were walking through the doorway leading into the domed chamber.

Watching them, all stilled, even Faraday and the girl in her lap.

Even the Alaunt held their breath.

Caelum and Drago walked close, not touching, but sharing, if not the deep love of years' standing, then companionship and respect.

Axis stared, but could hardly accept what he saw. Caelum . . . and *Drago?* His mind instantly took him back to the first time he'd met Drago. He'd walked into the nursery room of their apartments in Sigholt, Caelum in his arms, and met a violent wall of hate and mistrust, bounded and reinforced with a murderous blind ambition.

Caelum had been hurt—and terrified. Axis had been moved by such a profound rage it had colored his perceptions of Drago ever after. He had envisaged many futures for his sons, but never, *never,* one that had them walking together in silent companionship and respect.

"I have lived a very long time to see this day," Azhure murmured by his side. "And I wish to the heights of the Stars themselves it had not needed the destruction of Tencendor to bring it about."

"StarDrifter has discovered the power of pattern—dance—and this book provides the patterns," Caelum said, and smiled, a glorious expression of hope and joy. "We are saved!"

And yet . . . yet there was something about Caelum's eyes. A faint brittleness, so hidden that it was all but invisible to any but those who had occasion to look for it. And seeing it, Faraday looked at Drago, who had now stepped to one side of Caelum.

He saw her gaze, and very slightly inclined his head.

He knows, she thought. Caelum knows. And accepts.

She turned her face aside, lest others see the sorrow there, and question her.

The mood in the chamber had now sharply divided. Axis and Azhure, as their Star God companions and the scholars, were jubilant, but StarDrifter, WingRidge and SpikeFeather, and Drago and Caelum, were far more reserved. Their faces smiled, and their voices spoke glad words, but their eyes were guarded and hid a knowledge that the others, ignorant, could not yet share.

How indescribably sad, Faraday thought. How Fate brings to its knees those who thought themselves invulnerable. Within this shadowed, damp antechamber, buried so deep in the earth, Drago and myself, StarDrifter, WingRidge and SpikeFeather, know the truth of the matter. As did Caelum, for in his eyes Faraday saw the clarity of knowledge and the certainty, and tragedy, of fate.

Yet none of the others realized and knowledge had to remain hidden from them. Faraday knew that the salvation of the land, and its peoples, depended on an ultimately murderous and foul deception.

Again.

Faraday buried her face in the hair of the child she held. May Axis and Azhure forgive me and all those who work to keep the knowledge from them.

"StarDrifter?" Axis asked. "Will you join us above in the examination of this book, and a celebration at the news you brought?"

StarDrifter hesitated, his eyes carefully averted from Caelum. Gods, how could Caelum do this? How could Caelum stand there and smile so? Has he finally found the courage and the nobility to do what he must?

"No," StarDrifter said eventually. "Zenith, FreeFall and Zared will need help in evacuating Tencendor. I, perhaps with Drago and Faraday," again his eyes locked with Drago's, "will return to Fernbrake Lake."

"Drago," Axis muttered. Let him go? Alive!

"Drago will bother me no more," Caelum said, and turned slightly to his brother. "Farewell, Drago."

He held out his hand.

Drago gripped it, and nodded, but was unable to speak. After a brief pause he disengaged his hand and helped Faraday and the girl to their feet.

"StarDrifter?" Drago said.

"This way." StarDrifter nodded back down the corridor. "We will travel via the waterways." He shifted his eyes slightly. "Good-bye, Caelum. May the Stars always shine a path for your footsteps."

He embraced his grandson briefly, then turned away.

Axis frowned. That sounded almost like a final benediction. What was StarDrifter thinking of?

Then Faraday paused before Caelum. She, like Drago, was incapable of words, for all she saw was the baby boy that Azhure and Axis loved so much. She leaned forward, hugged him, and kissed his cheek.

The girl reached out a hand, and briefly touched Caelum's. When he glanced down at her fingers, he saw she held a blood-filled poppy in her hand and when he raised his eyes to her face he saw the blood reflected in the tears in her eyes.

No one else noticed the exchange. WingRidge saluted Caelum, and nodded, and SpikeFeather bowed.

And then they were gone. Drago, Faraday and the girl followed StarDrifter down the corridor, WingRidge and Spike-Feather behind them.

Save for Caelum, those left behind pondered the solemnity and formality, even the finality, of those good-byes. And, in so wondering, left no room to ask themselves why StarDrifter, WingRidge and SpikeFeather should travel all this way for that one brief message.

There was a scuffle, and suddenly the Alaunt sprang to their paws and dashed down the corridor. Amid their feet was a brief flash of sapphire.

"What was that?" cried Xanon, but no one answered her as Azhure leaped forward.

"No!" she cried. "Sicarius! Come back!"

Axis caught her and held her back. "Let them go," he said. "Azhure, they have changed beyond our understanding. Either they know their own destiny, or they have gone mad. Either way it is best to let them go."

Azhure pulled briefly against his hands, then relaxed in grief-stricken acceptance. They might be mad, but they had accompanied her for decades, and they were a living reminder of who, and what, she had once been.

They walked in silence. When they got to the stairwell that led down to the waterways, Drago halted them and squatted in front of the little girl.

"For many weeks now your cries have rung through our dreams," Drago said. "Mine and Faraday's."

She regarded him solemnly, nibbling her bottom lip. Then she nodded.

"I had been crying a long time," she said.

"We all have," Drago responded. He hugged Katie and kissed her cheek, then handed her back to Faraday and turned for the stairwell.

The stairs ended in a wide circular cavern, walled and floored in smooth gray stone. In the center of the cavern flowed a waterway, entering through an arch on one wall, and exiting through an identical arch on the opposite wall. The waterway was narrow, only three paces wide, but like most others in the Underworld it was edged in white stone.

Moored to the side of the waterway, directly across from the stairs, was a flat-bottomed boat.

StarDrifter walked half the distance between waterway and stairs, then halted and addressed Drago. "Should you have given that book to—"

"Yes," Drago said sharply. "Caelum will need it."

"But—"

"He will return it," Drago said, his tone more even. "In time."

"And he accepted . . . ?" Faraday asked. The girl clung close by her, unwilling to let her go even for a moment.

Drago nodded.

"Then the Stars will dance in his honor evermore," WingRidge said, in a tone far more respectful than he had ever used to Caelum's face. Drago almost told them that Caelum had been the one to murder RiverStar—but why should he? It changed nothing, and he had a feeling that most in this group realized it, anyway.

"And do *you* finally accept?" WingRidge asked Drago. His face was very still, his eyes fathomless, as he stared at Drago.

A thousand answers raced through Drago's mind, ten thousand words, a myriad excuses, and yet none of them would do, would they?

"Yes," he said. And this moment was, indeed, the moment when he truly did accept the burden.

WingRidge took a deep breath, and his face tightened with emotion. Then abruptly he fell to one knee, bowed until his forehead touched the knee of his bent leg, and splayed his wings behind him in the traditional Icarii gesture of homage.

"StarSon DragonStar," he said. "My name is WingRidge CurlClaw, and I commend myself and my life to your service. I am one of the six hundred, and I am their leader. Thus I speak with their voice as my voice when I vow them and myself to your name, your word and the vision you embrace. Our lives are yours, our souls are yours . . . StarSon, this entire land is yours."

He slowly lowered his head until his forehead touched the ground before Drago's feet, then he raised himself back into his kneeling position, his head still bowed.

"WingRidge," Drago said, and placed a hand on WingRidge's bowed head. "I do thank you for your belief, and I do thank you for your patience. I gladly accept your service, and that of your command."

Drago looked up at the others in the chamber. "I do thank all of you."

StarDrifter took a step forward, gazing intently at his grandson. "Has Caelum welcomed you into the House of the Stars?"

Drago nodded.

"Then I welcome you into my heart, StarSon, and into the House of SunSoar. Will you accept my service?"

Drago smiled gently. "Oh, aye, Grandfather," and he leaned forward and embraced StarDrifter.

Then SpikeFeather stepped forward, thinking how appropriate it was that Drago should take the first vows of service in this chamber where, so many years ago, Orr had taken SpikeFeather's life into service.

"I am yours, StarSon," he said, and Drago nodded and embraced him as well.

"I know it, SpikeFeather."

Then, slowly, he looked at Faraday.

She opened her mouth, but did not know what to say. If she vowed him her service, her life, did that mean she promised to love him? She couldn't do that, she couldn't.

Drago saw her distress, and understood her hesitation. He

took one of her hands gently between his. "Faraday, I pledge to you *my* service. You have already done enough for this land."

Emotion threatened to overwhelm her. She stared at him through eyes swimming with tears. If he'd said anything else, or demanded a single promise from her, she would have felt justified in hating him . . . and justified in denying him. Now she had to stand here silent and gape at him. What he'd said was, firstly, as formally bonding as any marriage vow—a stronger bonding, in fact, given who and what he was—and secondly . . . secondly . . . didn't it mean that he put her *before* Tencendor?

No. No! It could not be! He had already vowed that he would let nothing stand in his way in order to save the land. That was his father in him all over again. No, no, she could not, would not, believe him . . . she *dare* not!

"No," she whispered, and pulled her hand from his. "I do not accept your service."

There was an audible gasp in the chamber, probably from either StarDrifter or WingRidge, for Drago's face had gone stark white and he was so obviously shocked he was incapable of speech.

Faraday stared at him, wondering what she had done.

One part of her screamed to take his hand back before it was too late, another part screamed at her that she should turn and run, run before it was too late, run before she admitted to herself that she was so deeply in love with him she would murder herself all over again if it meant he could live . . .

"As you wish," Drago whispered in a frightful, rasping tone, and turned on his heel and walked toward the boat.

As he moved away, StarDrifter and WingRidge stared at Faraday with such utter incomprehension on their faces, such tightly controlled anger, she thought she *would* have to turn and run. Then . . .

. . . then the little girl, forgotten, slipped her hand into Faraday's cold one, and buried her head in Faraday's skirts. Faraday closed her eyes and shuddered, and from somewhere deep inside her drew the strength to carry on and walk toward the boat as if she had but brushed away a piece of inconsequential fluff.

49

Sigholt's Gift

"You see," StarDrifter said hurriedly, trying to think of *something* to say to cover the dreadful awkwardness in the chamber. "I have discovered the secret of the waterways. They are connected to the craft, they link them, and thus they serve the crafts' will. Thus, as long as the travelers' wish corresponds to the craft's overall intention, the waterways will do exactly what you will."

"That's very interesting," Drago said, and at the sound of Drago's voice StarDrifter shut up.

"Why would the waterways send us three boats?" Faraday asked, looking at a distant point over StarDrifter's shoulder, and trying to sound normal. Curse Drago for putting her in this predicament!

There had been a boat moored to the side of the waterway when they'd arrived, but during the conversation on the landing two more boats, linked by ropes, had drifted out of the tunnel entrance.

StarDrifter turned, stared, and faced the group again. "Obviously there has been some kind of—"

"Silence!" WingRidge barked, his entire body tensing, and he laid one hand on the hilt of the knife he carried.

Everyone stilled.

There was a distant sound . . . rather like soft rain. A scuffling, but regular, and very persistent.

"Something is coming down the stairwell," SpikeFeather said, who was closest to the stairs.

WingRidge looked at Drago. "Would Caelum have—"

"No. Whatever this is has not been instigated by Caelum," Drago said. But our parents? he wondered. Axis would have little reason to hold his hand.

The regular scuffling resolved itself into the padding of many paws.

"It is the Alaunt," Faraday said, and without reason all the childhood tales she'd heard of the hounds—mythical manhunters, ferocious devourers, child abductors—came rushing back, and she clutched Katie tight to her. The child caught some of her fear, and whimpered.

One of the Alaunt appeared at the curve of the stairs. Sicarius. He paused, looking carefully between the members of the company, and then he sunk as low as he could, whined, and crawled down the final flight of steps on his belly.

Behind him, successive Alaunt did the same.

Sicarius reached the floor, paused, then wriggled his way toward Drago, his tail wagging gently behind him. His golden eyes remained steady and unblinking on Drago.

Drago returned his stare with equally unblinking eyes, and Faraday frowned as she looked at him. His eyes were deeper, far more powerful than she'd ever seen them.

Compelling.

He is discovering more of his true nature every day, she thought, just as I did when I traveled south to the Island of Mist and Memory. Drago had spent much of their journey from Gorkenfort in deep introspection, exploring, growing, learning to trust his instinct and to recognize the ancient power of Noah as it coursed through his veins. The speed at which Drago learned and grew was almost frightening, and Faraday repressed a shiver, already regretting her dismissal of his vow. Not so much that she'd refused it, but that she'd done so in such cruel manner.

She had been *right* to refuse it . . . hadn't she?

Faraday closed her eyes briefly, and drove into a deep, dark place the nagging thought that she'd done the wrong thing, and that it might, just might, be safe to allow herself to love him, and to accept his love.

Drago squatted down before Sicarius and laid the palm of his right hand on the hound's skull.

"Do you present me your service?" he asked.

As one the entire pack of Alaunt leaped to their feet and burst into cry, the sound of their clamor resounding about the rounded chamber.

For an instant, Drago caught Faraday's eyes. *They* are not afraid of me . . . why are *you?* She turned her head away.

Just as Faraday thought they were over their quota of shocks for the day, there was a further scuffling on the stairs, and around the corner and down the final flight scuttled the feathered lizard, grinning cheerfully. Faraday's mouth dropped open. It was at least twice the size it had last been.

To save anyone the embarrassment of finding something to say, the two new boats bumped gently against the side of the waterway and the hounds and lizard happily scrambled in.

"A *lizard?*" StarDrifter said slowly. "I think, Drago, that you must tell me what you and Faraday have been up to."

"No time." Drago stepped into the front boat. "We have a detour to take before we can approach Fernbrake Lake. SpikeFeather. Here, come sit with me. You did well to find Sanctuary," Drago looked up and forced a smile, "before StarDrifter found a new source of enchantment to magic it up out of thin air."

"Detour?" StarDrifter said. He sat down. "What detour?"

"Sigholt," Drago said, and held out his hand to Faraday to help her in. After a brief hesitation, she took it, then let go as she turned to lift the girl in.

"There is something there I must collect," Drago finished, and settled himself into the boat.

Just as StarDrifter began to ask what Drago needed to collect, Drago's mood altered so sharply those watching could see the change sweep over his face.

"The Demons are well on their way to Fernbrake," he said. "They are more powerful than before, and travel with the speed of wind. Once at Fernbrake they will do their best to close Sanctuary forever."

"Then why waste time detouring to Sigholt?" StarDrifter cried, half-rising. "We need to get to—"

"Patience, StarDrifter," Drago said. "Sigholt can aid us. Well?"

"Well . . . *what?*" StarDrifter said.

"If you have discovered the secrets of waterway traffic, Grandfather, then I suggest you demonstrate your knowledge to get us to Sigholt."

StarDrifter laid a hand on the smooth wood of the boat.

"Drago needs to go to Sigholt," he said.

The boat glided forward.

"Although the Stars alone know why," StarDrifter murmured, "when the peoples of Tencendor need Sanctuary more than Drago needs his trinkets."

Drago chose not to respond to that.

The boat, SpikeFeather observed, took them on the normal route to the Lake of Life, although previously SpikeFeather had always had to use his muscles to travel the distance. Now the boats slid silently and swiftly through the tunnels of the UnderWorld. The two that contained the dogs and the feathered lizard, which spent the journey jumping enthusiastically from boat to boat (and once splashing into the waterway from where Drago had to rescue it), followed obediently behind the one that StarDrifter commanded.

"These waterways connect the craft under the Sacred Lakes?" Drago asked WingRidge.

"Yes."

"And extend yet *further,*" SpikeFeather said. "Over the years, I have traveled through waterways that stretch under the entire breadth and length of Tencendor and the Ferryman, Orr, told me that they also extend for leagues under the surrounding oceans."

"And every last one of them forming patterns," Drago mused, his eyes fixed on some distant spot.

SpikeFeather hesitated. "I suppose so. Why?"

Now Drago hesitated. His eyes refocused on SpikeFeather. "Is it much further to the Lake of Life?"

SpikeFeather swallowed his resentment that Drago chose to ignore his question. "At this rate? No. An hour, perhaps."

"Good," Drago said, and leaned back against the side of the boat and said no more.

Within the hour the three boats glided onto the Lake of Life, and Drago sat up and looked about keenly.

"Lakesview is deserted," he said.

"The Lake Guard arranged its abandonment when we knew the Demons approached," WingRidge said.

"Where are the people now?"

"In the surrounding hills. We did not know where, or how, to take them further. Should I now start moving them to Fernbrake?"

Drago shook his head. "Not by normal means, no. It would

take too long. We have . . ." he frowned slightly, "we have only some three or four weeks before the Demons will complete their quest. Before Qeteb—"

The others in the boat seemed to draw in their breath as one at the dreadful name.

"—walks again. The peoples of Tencendor must use other means to approach Sanctuary than their legs, methinks."

"How?" StarDrifter asked. "Dammit, Drago, stop giving us ambiguities to pin our lives on."

"StarDrifter, I am sorry. Sigholt will give all who linger nearby a direct route into Sanctuary. Believe me."

And with that, StarDrifter had to be content.

The boats glided to a stop at the wooden pier that sat some fifteen paces north of the moat that surrounded Sigholt. Everyone, dogs and lizard included, were glad to get out of the craft. The waters of the Lake seemed somehow corrupted; thick and loathsome, they yielded reluctantly to the demands of the boats.

"It has been the touch of the Demons," Drago said, looking back over the waters as StarDrifter helped Faraday and Katie from the boat. "The waters no longer wish to live. Within weeks they will have evaporated completely away."

Faraday looked back, and shuddered. She wished she could have seen this place when it had been vibrant with life and magic, but her duties, whether as wife to Borneheld, or as Tree Friend, had always kept her well away from it. She turned and looked up at the silvery-gray Keep. Here was Axis and Azhure's home, she thought. Here they lived for decades in laughter and love while I trod the byways of the forests, looking for tender grass shoots and missing my son.

Here is where my son grew up to adolescence. Without me.

Surprised by her sudden spurt of bitterness, Faraday dropped her eyes and looked at Drago, only to see sadness and bitterness in his face as well.

Sigholt contained no good memories for him, either.

Or was he thinking of her rejection?

"Come," he said, and walked forward without looking at the others.

"Wait!" Faraday cried. She ran after Drago, caught at his arm and pulled him to a halt, and then looked at StarDrifter.

"Will you take Katie on with you, StarDrifter? We won't be long."

He nodded, picked up the girl, and then the three Icarii walked forward, leaving Drago and Faraday by the shores of the Lake. He was silent, looking at her.

"I cannot, Drago," she whispered. "You know that."

He let his eyes drift over the waters. "I love you, Faraday."

She flinched. "I did not ask for that."

He looked back at her. "No. You didn't, did you? I apologize for putting you in a difficult position. It must have been embarrassing for you."

Her jaw tightened. "We have a journey to make, you and I, and it will be difficult enough without your sarcasm to add to its trials."

His eyes narrowed, and she could not tell if he was angry or trying to repress merriment.

"I am a SunSoar, Faraday. I do not take rejection well."

Her lips twitched—he was laughing at her! And suddenly she burst into laughter.

"Are we friends, Drago?"

"Friends, Faraday." He held out his hand, and she took it with only the slightest hesitation. He pressed it gently, then let it go, and they walked after the others.

"And you know the other thing about us SunSoar males, Faraday?"

"No . . . what?"

"We never give up."

They walked directly to the bridge, the hounds sniffing curiously about, the feathered lizard investigating the undersides of several stones, as if he expected to find a meal awaiting him there.

Drago stopped before the bridge, and turned back to the others. "Wait for me here," he said, and before anyone could ask him any questions Drago had stepped onto the bridge.

"Well, *second* son," the bridge said. "You return at last. Is Zenith well?"

"Yes," Drago said. "Far better than when she last crossed you."

"Good." The bridge hesitated. "Drago, you have surprised me."

Drago's mouth quirked. "I have surprised many people, including myself."

"And will surprise more to come," the bridge said. "Sigholt waits for you."

Drago nodded, glancing at the Keep. "Bridge . . . you destroyed Rox."

"Yes," the bridge said happily.

Drago sighed. "I can understand your wish to do so," he said, "but nevertheless the Demons need to succeed in their quest to resurrect Qeteb."

The bridge was silent, sulking.

"I only took a *bite*," she eventually said.

"Nevertheless," Drago repeated.

"The Demons will manage well enough without him."

"I hope so." Then Drago gave a quirky grin. "I'm glad you finally managed to take a bite at *someone*."

The bridge considered whether or not to be offended at this remark—was he referring to the fact that he'd managed to dupe her when he was but an infant?—then decided to laugh softly.

"I have waited eons for a chance like that," she admitted.

"Did he taste good?"

"Delicious!"

Drago laughed with her. "Well, then, despite my reservations, I do thank you for making the night a safer place. Bridge . . . bridge, from the depths of my heart I do apologize for my trickery of you so long ago."

"And I have been waiting some forty years to hear *that*," she said softly. "Go now, DragonStar SunSoar, and collect another trifle of your heritage."

Drago resumed walking along the bridge's back. When he was about to step onto the graveled walkway before Sigholt's open gates, the bridge spoke again: "I am glad you came home, DragonStar."

Drago faltered a little in his stride, then recovered. "Thank you, bridge."

And then he was through the gates and into the inner courtyard of Sigholt.

Everything was still, silent. Hay bales, half-empty crates and tangled tack lay scattered about the cobbles, bespeaking the haste in which the Keep had been evacuated. Wisps of blue mist drifted about the courtyard, losing and then refinding themselves among the half-open doorways. Yet Drago understood that Sigholt felt in no way abandoned. She was just waiting, waiting for whatever millennium approached.

And waiting for him.

There was a slight movement to one side, and Drago looked.

Nothing.

No . . . there it was again. A deeper shadow moving behind an overturned barrel, and yet another shadow behind that one.

Drago's eyes narrowed, then he squatted down and snapped his fingers, his mouth moving toward a smile.

Three of the shadows leaped out toward him—and resolved themselves into cats. Nine more rushed out in a group behind the first three. Tabbies, blacks, tortoiseshells and indeterminate patches, stripes and splotches—and there a sudden flash of white. All the result of countless generations of unsupervised and noisy breeding beneath the stamping hooves of the stable horses.

Sigholt's cats, come to greet Drago. Four purred and bumped about him, half a dozen leaped onto his shoulders and clambered down his back, sinking in their claws in an ecstasy of greeting and love. Two more batted at and played with the laces of his boots.

Drago grinned, trying to rub all of them at least once, and detaching the gray tabby that had decided to cling joyously to his hair.

"Have you missed me, then?" he asked, and the cats doubled their attentions.

"I have a pack of great hounds waiting the other side of the bridge," he said, laughing now. "Shall I invite them in?"

The cats knew an empty threat when they heard one. They shook with the strength of their purrs, dribbled with the power of their love, and kneaded Drago's flesh with the intensity of their adoration.

And Drago adored them in return. He hadn't realized how much he'd missed them over the past months, and now memories of their friendship and comfort in his otherwise friend-less and comfortless childhood came flooding back.

The toddling boy left to scream in fear and rejection on the damp cobbles of the inner courtyard. The cats, bumping sym-pathetic noses against his face, and cuddling their warm bod-ies next to his.

Drago closed his eyes, and buried his face in one of the furry bodies.

"Well now," he said, when he thought it time to introduce a bit of decorum into proceedings. "It seems Sigholt has some-thing for me. Do you perchance know—"

Before he'd finished speaking, every one of the cats had jumped away from him to stand stiff and watchful a pace away. Then, as one, the cats turned about and marched to-ward the kitchen door, their tails held high in the air.

"Either they want to be fed, or they *do* know more of Sigholt than its rat holes," Drago murmured, and followed them into the kitchen.

He stopped, surprised. According to WingRidge, Sigholt had been deserted for many days, yet the kitchen ranges lin-ing the far wall glowed with the strength of well-stocked firepits, and the tables lay dust-free and with cooking imple-ments laid neatly out in ranks for the sleepy hands of the morning breakfast cook.

Several mixing bowls sat in the center of one table, and Drago walked slowly over, ignoring the cats who had settled down in a semicircle before the ranges.

Stars, but he loved this kitchen almost as much as he loved the cats. How many nights had he whiled away the sleepless, loveless hours creating the perfect crust, the tenderest sir-loin? Drago ran the fingers of one hand softly over the table as he passed by, imagining he could feel warmth and friend-ship radiating out to him from the well-scrubbed wood.

"Why?" he asked softly, raising his head and looking at the cats.

They purred, and slowly blinked their twelve-pair of eyes in immense self-satisfaction, but they did not answer.

Drago's fingers glanced against one of the white ceramic mixing bowls, and he picked it up idly, balancing its weight in the palm of his hand. He stared at it, almost entranced, and then, with no idea why he did it, he slipped it into the sack at his side.

It should have almost filled the sack. At the very least, its weight should have made the sack too heavy and unwieldy to hang from Drago's belt, but to his amazement as soon as it had slipped from his fingers into the dark, close womb of the sack the weight vanished. Even the *form* of the bowl vanished, and the sack hung as close and as comfortable as if he only had two or three marbles in it.

Drago stood still, one hand still poised over the sack. Over the past weeks, since he'd come through the Star Gate, he'd been adding odd bits and pieces to the sack without ever knowing why. A piece of moss from a tabletop tree growing on the edge of the Silent Woman Woods; a crumbling handful of desiccated clay from the ravaged Plains of Tare; a crust he'd found on the doorstep of a deserted hamlet in northern Aldeni; a river-washed pebble from the Nordra; several white hairs from Belaguez's tail. Many, many things. He'd added them only on impulse—or so he'd thought. Now he realized there was something else at work, for he'd added so much the sack should be bursting at its seams by now.

Magic? Enchantment?

Certainly. But *what* enchantment?

And why?

Drago abruptly realized the cats were purring so loud the kitchen was vibrating very slightly with the strength of their rumbles, and he looked over to them. Again, as one, the twelve motley cats got to their feet and stalked, tails waving in the air, toward the door that led to the interior rooms and spaces of the Keep.

Drago followed.

They led him through the lower service corridors, past storerooms, servants' quarters and unknown, unexplored chambers, up the stairs leading into the main living and reception areas of Sigholt, and finally into the Great Hall.

A pace inside the door, Drago stopped, and then walked forward hesitantly. The cats had walked over to a far wall and sat down under one of the huge tapestries that lined its stone.

Drago did not look at them. Instead, his eyes were fixed on the dais at the far end of the chamber. This hall held no pleasant memories.

Here, the SunSoar family had sat about the fire and laughed without him.

Here, great Councils had been held. Without him.

Here, receptions and galas and the magnificence of the SunSoar court had glittered, and all, all of it, every last single bloody bit, without him.

And here Caelum and WolfStar had twisted and manipulated to do away with him once and for all. Here he had been falsely accused and then convicted of RiverStar's murder.

Drago's feet slowed even further as he reached the center of the hall. Caelum's enchantment falsifying Drago's memory of his sister's death had been powerful beyond compare.

"What a waste," Drago said to the hall, listening to his words echo about its vastness. "What a waste of a wonderful man and an extraordinary power."

And even as he said it, Drago did not truly know if he referred to Caelum with those words . . . or to himself.

His staff, almost forgotten, scraped against the stone flagging, and Drago jerked out of his reverie as it twisted in his hand. He looked about for the cats, saw them sitting patiently against the far wall, sighed and walked over. He stopped three paces away from the tapestry under which they had placed themselves, and stared.

He knew it well. How many times had he stood where he was now and gazed into its magic for hours on end, hungering for the power it portrayed, and hungering for the woman it portrayed to turn her eyes, just slightly, and see him?

And seeing him, laugh, and reach out to embrace him.

The tapestry depicted Azhure at the height of her magical frenzy at Gorkenfort, slaughtering hundreds of thousands of Skraelings with her magical bow, the Alaunt streaming out of the wraiths' nests and boltholes amid the rubble, driving the screaming and gibbering Skraelings before them.

It was fully nighttime, the moon casting a silvery glow upon the ethereal scene. Gray blocks of masonry piled into massive heaps of meaningless rubble. Moonwildflowers, drifting down from an unseen sky. Alaunt hounds, all spectral-pale save for their gaping, slavering scarlet mouths and golden eyes. Azhure atop her red Corolean stallion Venator, her raven hair flying and her face alive with magic, the Wolven singing destruction in her hands, and the quiver of unending arrows, all fletched in the blue of her eyes, strapped tight to her back.

Gods! Drago could almost swear he could see her lean backward to seize an arrow and put it to the Wolven, and then hear it scream as it flew through the night to plunge into one of the silvery orbs of a Skraeling.

And yet now something was very, very different about this tapestry. It had lost its magic.

It was only Drago's memory that gave Azhure's face its aura of enchantment. As he blinked and focused sharply on the tapestry, he saw that now the threads had worn and her face was . . . well . . . a trifle threadbare.

The bodies and faces of the Alaunt, once so clearly depicted, were even more shabby, almost as if only a memory lingered, not their form. Now they were truly ghosts in this wall hanging. Loose ends of thread hung out in unsightly tatters, and Drago had to narrow his eyes and concentrate to make out the individual hounds. Even then, four or five of them had so lost their definition they had merged into one unsightly splotch, the backing canvas clearly showing through the worn embroidery.

Everything in the tapestry had faded and unraveled, just as the Star Dance had been all but lost.

Everything, save one thing.

The Wolven *glowed*. Its warm ivory wood with its golden tracery, its scarlet and blue tassels, its silvered bowstring, all gave a sense of reality, of *impatient* reality, within the fading insignificance of the rest of the tapestry.

Sigholt's gift. The Wolven.

As the Alaunt had come to Drago, so here sat the Wolven. Waiting.

Drago tried to remember when he had last seen Azhure use the Wolven. It had been many, many years, and Azhure had probably handed it over to Caelum with the Scepter when he'd ascended the Throne of the Stars. As Caelum had hidden the Scepter with enchantment, so he had hidden the

Wolven—in plain view of everyone, and yet more hidden than if he'd secreted it in the deepest dungeon.

Drago still stared unblinking at the Wolven. Here it sat— trapped by enchantment.

"So, Caelum," he said, very slowly and very softly, "what was the enchantment you used? What must I do to retrieve this bow?"

And Caelum did not answer. Drago knew he faced a test: release the Wolven, and retrieve yet another part of his lost Acharite magic. Drago felt that if he understood how to release the Wolven, he would break the thickest barrier to the full use of his ancient Acharite power . . . the Enemy's power.

Was Sigholt's gift the Wolven? Or the ability to make full use of his power?

Drago sank down to the floor, sitting cross-legged, chin in hand, his staff laid before him. Thinking.

The cats, satisfied, curled up into tight balls, but they still kept their eyes on Drago.

"I am no Enchanter," Drago said, thinking it out aloud, "for the Demons have used up all my Icarii ability. And even had they not, there is no music of the Star Dance to manipulate with Song. But the Star Dance still *exists,* even if I cannot hear it."

Drago trailed off into silence. Power was still there for the using . . . StarDrifter's opening of the door to Sanctuary was proof enough of that. It was the power of the land, which was the power of the craft which had drifted for millennia among the stars, absorbing the Star Dance.

And Noah had bred it into the Acharites.

StarDrifter had tapped into the power of the land by using dance as a form of pattern.

"The Star Dance—or its power," Drago said, speaking his thoughts out softly, "is contained in the land, a gift from the craft. And now this power rests in me . . ."

So how to access it?

Pattern. Pattern was the key. Song and music was nothing but pattern. Dance was pattern. Drago took a deep breath and slowly rose, using the staff to help lift himself. He stood indecisively, leaning on the staff as if it, perhaps, held the answer. Could he use dance to form the pattern,. the enchantment, needed to release the Wolven?

But what was the enchantment that Caelum had used in the first instance? Drago would have to know that if he was to—

He cursed, absolutely stunned, and stepped back a pace, dropping the staff at the same time. As he'd been wondering what enchantment Caelum had used, the staff had vibrated in his hand. It had not been an unpleasant sensation, but surprising in the extreme.

Now Drago bent down and retrieved the staff. It still vibrated, and with a growing sense of excitement Drago realized that the pattern of fletched circles that ran about the staff was moving.

Showing him . . . showing him a pattern. The pattern of the Song Caelum had originally used to hide the Wolven.

The staff was acting in the same way that Drago suspected Zenith, and probably Axis and Caelum, had used their rings. How many times had he seen Zenith glance at her ring before she sang a Song of Enchantment? Did their diamonds alter the same way these circles now altered?

Yes!

It was a pattern, and knowing what it was, Drago found the reading of it easy. Translate the distance, both width and height between the fletched circles (*notes!*) into music—easy enough—and then the music into the steps of a dance.

Done!

But there was a problem.

StarDrifter was an accomplished dancer—his Icarii grace would be enough to make him elegant even had he two broken legs and moth-eaten wings.

But Drago had lost his Icarii grace and elegance, and as he now stumbled about in front of the tapestry—even the cats raising their heads to watch and grin—he knew that his skill on the dance floor would see him dead the instant he tried to outwit even the least of the Demons, let alone Qeteb.

No, no, there had to be a different way, and Drago realized it would have something to do with his innate Acharite power.

He stopped fumbling about with his feet, and stood again

staring at the tapestry. Pattern ... music was pattern ... dance was pattern ... and for different reasons both those were denied him.

Unbidden a memory surfaced. Standing before the doorway that eventually led to Noah. The recessed rectangular section beside the door, filled with nine slightly raised knobs. His fingers dancing over the knobs, pressing each in turn. Forming a pattern.

Symbols.

The Maze Gate was surrounded with symbols!

Song, dance, movement all formed patterns. As did symbols.

Drago lifted his right hand, studying it. Idly, he flexed his fingers, and then, in some almost subconscious process he was barely aware of, he transferred the pattern of the dance into a series of numbers, and from there into a complicated symbol.

"Do as I ask," he said, his voice strangely powerful, and his fingers sketched the symbol with fluid grace before the tapestry.

Instantly the Wolven glowed, then formed into solid wood from the silken threads that had trapped it, and it clattered to the floor. A moment afterward the quiver full of arrows likewise dropped to the floor.

The cats were now sitting, and as one, always as one, they looked from Drago to Wolven and back to Drago again.

Their eyes were wide with wonder.

Drago's heart was hammering in his chest. "Show me," he whispered, "the enchantment for creating a juicy mutton pie."

The staff again vibrated in his hand, and Drago noted the pattern the notes formed, translated them into music, then into the movement of dance, and from there into numbers and symbol.

"Do as I ask," he said, sketching the symbol in the air, and a juicy mutton pie formed a pace in front of the watching semicircle of cats.

Drago laughed, then spun about in sheer exuberance.

He had power back!

And his Acharite blood was truly in full ascendancy.

He stilled and smiled gently at the cats. "Eat," he said, waving at the pie, and the cats set to.

50

Sanctuary

StarDrifter paced back and forth, back and forth. Where was Drago? He'd been gone hours.

"We *must* go look for him!" he said, coming to a halt before WingRidge.

WingRidge, annoyingly calm, shook his head.

"Wait," he said.

Faraday smiled. She was sitting to one side, Katie asleep in her lap. "Wait," she echoed, and StarDrifter bit down a tart reply and walked away a pace or two.

Wait! Ah, bah!

The Alaunt sat and lay about in no particular order, half-asleep, utterly unconcerned. Just behind them the lizard lay, lazily combing out his feathers with a talon.

SpikeFeather had wandered off to chat to the bridge who was now happily engaged in relating the tale of how Rox had been foolish enough to step on her back. She'd told StarDrifter the same tale, and WingRidge; then Faraday and the girl, and now StarDrifter felt like shouting at her to shut up, for who needed it told an eighth time?

But he bit back his tongue. If it made the bridge happy to repeat the story for the next thirty lifetimes, StarDrifter supposed she had a complete right to. No one else had managed a single scratch on the Demons' equanimity, let alone eat one whole.

One of the Alaunt lifted his head, and stared at the bridge. StarDrifter spun about as Faraday tensed and Katie awoke.

Drago was striding back across the bridge, smiling and greeting both the bridge and SpikeFeather. Over Drago's left shoulder was slung the Wolven bow and quiver, and behind him trotted a dozen mangy cats in single file, all with their tails held up in complete feline self-satisfaction and superiority. StarDrifter's face went slack in disbelief.

"They are only cats, StarDrifter," Drago said, his eyes dancing, as he stopped in front of his grandfather. "There is no need to look so surprised."

"*What is this?*" StarDrifter said. One hand fleetingly touched the Wolven, as if it might scorch him.

"Evidence of Sigholt's gift," Drago said, and turned to help Faraday to her feet.

"*Evidence* of Sigholt's gift?" Faraday asked, her eyes searching his. Something had happened.

"I will tell you and you, StarDrifter," Drago said, "but not here. It is more than time Sanctuary released her secrets. Come, step back to the bridge."

He clicked his fingers, and whistled to the Alaunt, and they rose obediently and stepped onto the bridge. The feathered lizard yawned, blinked slowly at Drago, then did the same.

Cats yowled and greeted both hounds and lizard with the deep affection usually reserved for the most generous and softhearted of kitchen hands, and wound about canine, reptilian and Icarii legs with equal friendliness.

"Drago's traveling menagerie," StarDrifter muttered. "Please do not tell me you are going to add these courtyard cats to our retinue, Drago!"

Drago looked between the cats and StarDrifter. "If they want to come, then who am I to stop them?" he asked, and then faced the end of the bridge that led into HoldHard Pass and raised his hand.

"Connect this place to Spiredore," he said to the bridge. "Do as I ask."

And as he spoke, his right hand wove through the air so fast, and with such fluidity, that StarDrifter could not follow it.

"What . . ." he began, and then the road beyond the bridge shimmered and altered, forming into a close tunnel of blue mist.

"Come," Drago said, and led them into Spiredore.

In two days Zenith had accomplished miracles, although she felt that her voice would soon give out from its constant use. She'd been forced to use everything from sweet charm to strident threat to get the Icarii in the Minaret Peaks ready to evacuate toward Fernbrake Lake. Even FreeFall's support and backing was not always enough to convince the Icarii that they should once again prepare for exile from their beloved southern lands, even though to a place more wondrous than their previous exile.

Isfrael had not helped.

He'd been with FreeFall and EvenSong when Zenith had returned from Fernbrake with the stunning news of Sanctuary's discovery, and the slightly less exciting news that no one could yet reach it.

"Ah," he'd said, as Zenith had told her news, "Drago's Sanctuary. Why am I not surprised to hear, that while it does exist, it can't be approached?"

Zenith had rounded on him, furious. "It will serve to save you and yours, as well as the Icarii and Acharite," she'd snapped.

"The Avar will move nowhere," Isfrael had retorted, his tone very quiet. "The trees protect us."

"For now," Zenith had said, and turned her back on him.

Dubious, frightened, their cold and hunger the only reason to even consider exile, let alone attempt it, the Icarii had at last listened to Zenith's and FreeFall's arguments and threats.

Now they stretched in long, murmuring lines that wound under the sheltering trees of Minstrelsea, rose up the slopes toward the crater that cradled Fernbrake Lake, and then spilled over the ridge and down to the edge of the Lake itself, the line stopping at the edge of the trees.

And so they stood, while Zenith, FreeFall, EvenSong and Isfrael waited in the domed chamber at the doors of Sanctuary.

"He *will* return soon," Zenith said. "StarDrifter was certain they could quickly locate Drago—"

"Even if he *did*," Isfrael said, his arms crossed over his bare chest, and his curls in angry disarray about his horns, "will Drago return with StarDrifter?

"And . . ." he lifted one hand to wave it languidly at the silvery trace-work of the bridge spanning the chasm into Sanctuary, "will he have any idea of how to convince this bridge to let the Icarii past?"

"You should have more faith in your brother," a woman's voice said behind them, and they turned to see Faraday walk down the stairs into the chamber. She was holding the hand of the small girl who walked with her.

Behind her came StarDrifter and Drago, then WingRidge, SpikeFeather and, Zenith was astounded to note, the Alaunt hounds, together with the feathered lizard (which she could see was now much larger) and a line of cats. Zenith stood, transfixed, and then she laughed in sheer exuberance and stepped forward to embrace Faraday fiercely.

"I have missed you," she whispered, and Faraday murmured something back before Zenith extracted herself, smiled at the girl, and then stepped into Drago's arms.

"What have you brought us," Zenith said as she leaned back. "The Alaunt. The Wolven! What? Have you divested Mother of *all* her trappings?"

"Both Alaunt and Wolven have their own minds and their own choices," Drago said, "and for the moment it appears that they have chosen to walk with me."

"Along with half the cats of Tencendor," StarDrifter muttered, but his eyes crinkled with amusement, and he smiled as Zenith stepped over to him. She hesitated, then leaned forward and gave him a stiff hug and peck on the cheek.

The brightness in StarDrifter's eyes faded, and Faraday frowned as she looked between the two of them.

"The Icarii wait above," FreeFall said, after he'd greeted Drago and his companions. "Drago? Will you . . . can you . . . ?"

Even with the accoutrements of power that Drago carried with him, FreeFall's doubt was evident in his voice. Drago nodded, but he did not speak. He stared across the bridge into Sanctuary, transfixed by its beauty. Would anyone ever want to leave?

Brushing past Isfrael, Drago walked slowly through the door, pausing for a moment as his eyes scanned the symbols carved about its frame, then approached the bridge.

It was sister to Sigholt's bridge, he realized. The silver-tracery web to match her sister's many-legged skills.

Drago put a foot on the bridge, and then the other.

"Are you true?" she asked.

"Yes," Drago replied. "I am true." He took another step, running his right hand lightly along one fragile handrail.

"But," the bridge said in a voice almost a whisper, "are you *he* who is true?"

"Yes, I am he who is true."

Silence, then the bridge spoke again. "Show me."

Drago's mind spoke the request, and the staff vibrated slightly in his hand, and almost as soon as his eyes traced the pattern appearing on the wood, so he lifted his right hand and translated the pattern into symbol.

"Yes," the bridge said. "You are he who is true. Welcome to my heart, DragonStar SunSoar . . . and welcome home after so long away."

"I thank you, bridge," Drago said. "May I lead my friends across your back?"

"With pleasure," she assented, "although I must question each and every one of them." Drago's mouth twisted wryly—Tencendor would take months to evacuate if she paused to ask everyone of their truth.

"Don't you think you could do it in groups, bridge? The need is somewhat . . . urgent."

She thought about it. "Well . . ."

"I would not ask were it not important."

"Oh, very well. Groups. No more than seventy-seven per group."

"Thank you, bridge," Drago said with considerable relief and then lifted his head.

"Will you come, Faraday?" he asked.

She hesitated a moment before stepping forward, staring at the man on the bridge holding out his hand to her, fighting down the emotions that outstretched hand ignited in her. Damn him! Then, finding some refuge in humor (would he never give up?), she led the girl forward.

"Are you true?" the bridge asked.

"Yes," Faraday said.

"You speak the truth, Faraday," the bridge responded. "Welcome to my heart."

Then the bridge spoke to the girl.

"Are you true?"

The girl replied without any hesitation. "I *am* truth."

"Yes," the bridge said. "You are truth. Do well, Katie."

Katie inclined her head, and she and Faraday joined Drago on the far bank.

"You 'are' truth?" Drago questioned the girl, and when Katie remained silent he looked at Faraday, but Faraday shrugged her shoulders.

"All will spin to a conclusion eventually," she said, and with that Drago supposed he had to be content.

Sanctuary was not quite what Drago expected.

He walked slowly across the grassy plains toward the entrance to the valley. A gentle warm breeze billowed the grass and the blue-and-white star-shaped flowers into spreading ripples before them. By Drago's side walked Faraday and Katie, and StarDrifter and Zenith. Isfrael walked behind StarDrifter. He and Faraday had nodded to each other, but had exchanged no words. Now his face was carefully set in a neutral expression, although his current distaste had little to do with his mother. Isfrael did not like the idea of being underground, even though the sky yawned apparently limitless above, and the verdant valley and snow-capped mountains stretched infinitely before him.

WingRidge and SpikeFeather had remained behind at the bridge and stairwell, supervising the evacuation of the Icarii nation into Sanctuary.

As successive groups of Icarii successfully negotiated both the silver tracery of the bridge and her questioning and took to flight, the leading group was overtaken by the birdmen and -women. By the time Drago approached the valley mouth, Sanctuary had already been well-peopled with Icarii.

"How strange," Faraday murmured as they walked between the twin towers of rock that guarded the entrance. "I could have sworn that there was at least a half-league to travel between bridge and valley, yet here we are as if we have but just walked fifty paces."

"The grass ripples with enchantment as well as flowers," StarDrifter said. "Oh, look! It is an orchard."

All, except Drago, exclaimed at the beauty of Sanctuary. Before them stretched a valley that appeared to be almost entirely taken up with an orchard of astounding beauty. Thousands of trees grew well-spaced along mown lawns, their branches so laden with fruit they almost touched the ground. They could see the glint of ponds and streams here and there, and tasseled linen hammocks swung between trees above scattered silken pillows and cushions below.

Katie broke free from Faraday and ran to the nearest tree, taking a piece of fruit from a low-slung branch and sinking her teeth into it.

"Beautiful!" she cried, juice running down her chin, and Faraday walked over to her, and wiped it away with a smile.

"This place seems well enough," Isfrael said, "if you like ordered orchards before the wild beauty of the forests." He had his arms crossed and his legs placed apart. He looked like a judge about to deliver an execution penalty.

"There are palaces further in!" a voice above them cried, and a youthful Icarii called MurmurWing dropped down before them. "Filled with dormitories and fountains and well-fattened storerooms!"

He looked at the faces before him and, disconcerted by Isfrael's stiff stance and Drago's carefully bland face, stumbled out a few more words, and equally awkwardly rose into the air and flew back into Sanctuary.

"Drago?" Faraday said. "What's wrong? You look like a goat has stuck his hoof down your throat."

Drago jerked out of his reverie, and made a bad attempt at a smile. "Wrong? Nothing's wrong. I'm . . . I'm sure that all will be comfortable here . . . if we can ever get them past the bridge in time to enjoy it! Come," he held out his hand for Zenith, "let's explore this magical land a little further."

And yet as they walked and investigated and exclaimed at every new delight, all Drago could think of was that Sanctuary looked nothing less than an extended version of all the orchards of all the worlds that the TimeKeeper Demons had dragged him through. Every time a shadow flitted among the trees, or an Icarii descended from above, Drago jumped, more than half-expecting it to be one of the Hawkchilds.

What should he make of this? What?

Sanctuary, surely—but a Sanctuary for *whom?*

A few hours later Drago, Faraday and Katie, Zenith, and StarDrifter, sat about a cheerful fire in a side gully of the main valley of Sanctuary. Isfrael had sat with them a while before returning to the forests of the Overworld with a somewhat theatrical shudder at the well-ordered orchards of Sanctuary. All day the Icarii, eyes wide in wonder, had been walking down the stairwell to the door and then across the chasm—stopping in groups to be examined by the bridge—before launching themselves into the inviting thermals of the approach to Sanctuary.

"This place will be both a blessing and a curse," StarDrifter remarked, his eyes on the dancing flames.

"Why?" Faraday asked.

StarDrifter turned his gaze lazily toward her. "Who will ever want to leave?" he said. "Who, trapped in this wondrous prison, will ever want freedom?"

His voice was indescribably sad, and its melancholy communicated to all of them. The Icarii, trapped again in an exile, but one that might trap them for eternity. Who would follow a StarMan to leave *this* place, however urgent his summons?

Drago shuddered, and wondered again at the similarity of Sanctuary to the orchards seen in his rush with the Demons across the universe.

"Skies exist to be torn apart," Katie said, "and towers to be torn down."

Every eye in the circle riveted itself on her. She smiled happily, revealing two rows of tiny, perfect teeth. She laughed, and her glossy brown curls bounced about with the strength of her merriment.

"Katie," Drago said. "Who are you? *What are you?*"

She quietened, and regarded him solemnly. "Pilgrim," she said, "do you not know me?"

Drago shook his head, and Katie dropped her face, and wiped a sudden tear from her eye.

"Then I am no one," she whispered, and buried her face in the folds of Faraday's gown. "I have no meaning."

Faraday rested a hand on her head, her eyes questioning, *pleading* with Drago, but he only shook his head again.

"I do not know," he repeated, and spread his hands helplessly.

Partly because the movement of Drago's hands had reminded StarDrifter of the strange gestures he'd seen Drago making, and partly to divert the mood of the group, he spoke up. "Drago, what is it you have been working with your hands?"

Relieved to be given something to think about other than the orchards of Sanctuary or his failure to comfort Katie, Drago leaned forward, his face enthusiastic. "Enchantment, StarDrifter! I have found a means to access the power of the Star Dance again."

StarDrifter's face stiffened. "But I was the one to realize the power of dance to touch—"

"Yes, yes, StarDrifter. I did not mean to slight your achievement, and I apologize if I have hurt your feelings . . . but dance has such limitations!"

"What do you mean?" StarDrifter was not quite ready to accept the apology.

Drago's face grew more serious, his tone more compelling. "Think. If an enchantment must be worked by dance . . . then how vulnerable is the dancer to whatever danger faces him or her. StarDrifter, yes, dance manages to harness the power of the Star Dance, but of what use is dance if the TimeKeepers swallow you whole in the midst of a slow waltz?"

"But Song must have been as awkward," Faraday said before StarDrifter could answer. "Surely Enchanters had to sing an entire Song before—"

"No," StarDrifter said, a little reluctantly. "In an Enchanter's early stages of training he or she would have had to sing the entire Song, yes, but eventually the actual working of the enchantment became so instinctive that all we needed to do was to run a few casual bars through our head, or even only a few notes. Axis could act in seconds.

"Drago, surely we will learn of a way to modify the time it takes to dance a pattern?"

"I *have* already learned it," Drago said, and he proceeded to tell them what he surmised about the connections between Star Dance, music, dance and symbol. "All form patterns in their own way. The waterways do this with physical underground canals, Icarii Enchanters used to do it with Song, all apparently can touch the Star Dance with dance—"

"And you formed patterns with your hands!" Zenith said. "Show us."

"Not so much patterns. More like symbols. Condensed patterns." Drago hesitated. "A little like StarDrifter said about Enchanters eventually learning to run only a few notes through their minds to effect an enchantment. I take a full Song, convert it to numbers, and then those numbers into a symbol."

"Numbers?" StarDrifter sounded lost.

"Numbers form pattern as much as music does, StarDrifter. It is a simple thing to convert a Song to its equivalent numerical form, and then that to its condensed symbol."

A simple thing? Faraday looked at StarDrifter's and Zenith's bemused faces, and almost laughed. She swung her gaze back to Drago. Was this how he would use his Acharite magic? And to effect the conversion so effortlessly! Drago had noted StarDrifter's and Zenith's expressions as quickly as Faraday.

"StarDrifter . . . sing me one of the simplest of Songs, and I will show you how to convert to symbol."

StarDrifter glanced at Zenith, then sang a brief lilting melody.

"It is a Song for making a fire flarc," Zenith said as StarDrifter finished.

"Good," Drago said. "Now, all you have to do is convert the tune to its numerical equivalent," and without apparent effort he ran off a series of numbers, "and then those numbers to their symbolic equivalent, which you must visualize," and he very slowly sketched a complicated symbol through the air.

Then, Drago drew it again, but with such speed, fluidity and grace that those watching could hardly follow his movements.

Instantly the fire flared.

There was a silence.

"I have absolutely no idea how you did that," StarDrifter said. "Zenith?"

She shook her head. "It is beyond me. Those numbers, and the conversion of numerical formula to symbolic representation. Ah! No, I cannot do it. Drago, why can't you just teach us the symbols we need to sketch?"

"I don't see why not," Drago said, and slowly sketched the symbol through the air. "But you must do it with speed, for the form falls apart given too long to linger unaided in midair."

Both StarDrifter and Zenith—and Faraday, who was overcome with curiosity—attempted to copy Drago's hand actions, but none could sketch the symbol with the accuracy, speed and fluidity of Drago.

Frustrated words were spoken by StarDrifter, who could not believe he could fail at anything magical, and by Drago, who thought the whole process so impossibly simple that only a dullard could fumble it.

"Drago," Faraday eventually said, gently. "Do you remember what Urbeth said to us?"

"Urbeth?" StarDrifter and Zenith said together.

Drago stared at her. What?

"We have come back through death," Faraday reminded him, "and thus can touch our—"

"That doesn't explain why you fumble as badly as StarDrifter."

StarDrifter glared at Drago, but did not speak.

"I think," Faraday said, with a gentleness even more profound than in her last statement, "that much of the ability you display, Drago, is purely and simply *you*. It is StarSon DragonStar who works those symbols with such ease."

Zenith suddenly understood what Faraday was saying, and she, too, looked at Drago and smiled with exquisite tenderness. She laid a hand on his arm. "Drago, welcome to your own unique ability. You are a mage beyond that which Tencendor has seen before."

"You *are* StarSon," StarDrifter said, all trace of frustration and resentment now gone from his voice.

Drago dropped his eyes and stared at his hands, now carefully folded in his lap. "StarSon . . . as a man it has taken me a long time to come to terms with what I once demanded as my right. As an infant I destroyed Caelum and all he could be. As a man my actions have wreaked destruction upon Tencendor. It has been hard to snatch Caelum's heritage away for a second time."

Drago glanced at the staff, which lay at his side, and then looked about the circle. "If we survive this time, I think the legends will decorate Caelum with the glory, not me."

StarDrifter and Faraday lowered their eyes, wondering if Drago was right. Well, and who would not deny Caelum some bardic glory for his dreadful role?

Drago shuddered, and looked at the sky as if it were transparent. "I feel the darkness of the Demons drawing closer and closer to the Lake above."

"We must contact Zared," Zenith said, "and work out how best to get the Acharites into this shelter."

Drago nodded, too absorbed in his own thoughts to notice that Faraday was sitting stiffly, her eyes lost in some distant memory.

"We also, somehow, need to persuade Isfrael that the Avar need the shelter of Sanctuary. The forests will—"

"The forests will die?" Faraday suddenly asked, her voice brittle.

"Faraday," Drago said gently, finally catching some of her mood. "The Demons hate the forests, and while they cannot do much about them now, once Qeteb is risen they will work to make sure every leaf is stripped from every tree. The Avar can shelter under their shade for now, but . . . Faraday, you *knew* this."

"Ah!" Zenith said, far too brightly, "here comes WingRidge, no doubt with news about the length of the lines of Icarii above."

Later, Drago wandered slowly up to Faraday, who was seated on the ground with Katie, combing out the child's hair.

He smiled and squatted down beside them, and thought to make some light conversation, but even as he opened his mouth he was forestalled by an angry shout.

"Drago!"

Drago cursed silently and stood up.

It was Isfrael, his face dark with hatred and loathing, and for one dreadful moment Drago thought it was directed at him for daring to sit so close to his mother.

But Isfrael had other concerns on his mind. "WolfStar has been spotted lurking among the trees surrounding Fernbrake Lake."

Faraday rose, and pushed Katie behind her skirts, as if WolfStar would this moment appear and snatch the child.

Drago saw StarDrifter and Zenith nearby. His sister had blanched whiter than StarDrifter's wing feathers and

StarDrifter was standing awkwardly, as if he did not know whether to comfort Zenith or not.

"Zenith," Drago said. "WolfStar shall not harm you again, I *swear* it. I will not allow him to cross the bridge. Do you believe me?"

He had taken her hands in his, and now gave them a slight shake. Zenith nodded miserably, and Drago turned to Faraday.

"Faraday, will you . . . ?"

Faraday put her arms about Zenith. "I will look after her."

Drago turned back to Isfrael. "Where?"

Isfrael opened his mouth, but was not given the chance to speak.

"I'm coming, too," StarDrifter said. His entire stance radiated aggressive anger.

Drago hesitated, then nodded. "Why not?" he said.

Isfrael's mouth twisted wryly as he looked at StarDrifter—the Mother only knew what WolfStar would do to StarDrifter!—then he turned and led the other two back toward the bridge, pushing through the Icarii still coming across.

"Come on," Faraday said gently, putting her arm about Zenith's waist. "We can move further back into Sanctuary, if you like."

Zenith let Faraday lead her down a path toward a group of farrah fruit trees encircling a small, still pond that reflected the myriad of dragonflies and butterflies that hovered and danced above its surface.

Katie walked silently to Zenith's other side and slipped a hand into the birdwoman's. Zenith, surprised, looked down and gave the girl a hesitant smile.

Katie smiled back, and squeezed Zenith's hand.

"She is a lovely girl," Zenith said.

"Yes," Faraday said. She looked at Katie, loving her, and loving what she had brought into Faraday's life.

The sweetness of a child curled up against her breast at night. The exultation in knowing that it was to her that Katie would run whenever she had a question or needed reassurance. The sheer, quiet joy of Katie's laughter and the delight of her kiss as she wrapped her arms about Faraday's neck.

Faraday felt more protective of Katie than she did of anything or anyone else, although she did not know if that was because she'd been denied the love of her son, or because there was something innately special and magical about Katie that cried out to something deep in Faraday's soul.

Faraday knew she would kill without hesitation anyone or anything that threatened Katie, and she gloried in that protective instinct.

"You adore her," Zenith said as they sank down under one of the farrah trees and watched Katie chase butterflies about the pond.

"You cannot know how much," Faraday said in a low tone, and, watching Faraday's face, Zenith realized the strength and determination of the woman's love and fierce protectiveness.

"Where did she come from?" Zenith asked, and Faraday told her of how Katie had cried disconsolately in her dreams night after night, "Until I cried myself." Then Faraday spoke of how she and Drago had discovered the girl wrapped around the Enchanted Songbook in Star Finger's basement, and how Katie had run to Faraday, when she had rejected Caelum.

Faraday smiled in delight. "Zenith, it was worth almost every hardship I have ever gone through to watch Axis' face at that moment. This lovely little girl had rejected Caelum . . . and chosen me."

Zenith stared at Faraday, taken aback by this revelation of her continuing bitterness toward Axis. Then she shook herself, and changed the subject slightly.

"And Drago? How do you feel about him?" Zenith could not help but wonder what had developed between the two. Some of the looks she'd caught her brother sending Faraday were . . . well . . . almost unbearably frustrated.

Faraday's voice tightened noticeably. "I am here to help him, Zenith, and I will do all that I can for him."

"That doesn't answer my question," Zenith said quietly.

"I will never allow myself to love a man again," Faraday said. "How can I? All men have ever done is abuse me, trick me, hide my fate in shadows, and then stand by to watch me die. All for a greater cause, of course."

"Self-pity does not become you, either," Zenith said, and

Faraday whipped her head about to look at her with flashing eyes.

"I did not sit here to hear your sanctimonious advice, Zenith!"

"Then if you cannot trust yourself to love again, why bother clinging to life," Zenith snapped back.

Faraday took a huge breath, fighting to control her temper. "Then why is it I see you and StarDrifter circling each other like two callow adolescents terrified of the consequences of even holding hands?"

She managed to shock Zenith into silence for a moment, then Zenith looked away, her face working, her eyes suddenly bright with tears.

"Zenith," Faraday said. "I am sorry. Please . . . what is wrong? I would have thought . . . that you and StarDrifter . . . it just seems so natural that you and he . . ."

"And yet it feels so wrong," Zenith said, brushing her tears away with the fingers of one hand.

Faraday remained silent, waiting.

"I have always loved and trusted StarDrifter deeply," Zenith said, her voice low. She stared past Faraday at the dragonflies dancing above the pond. "So many people only see him as the superficial Enchanter, concerned simply with matters of lust and bright power, but to me . . . well, he has always been there for me, always willing to fight for me. Always willing to risk his life for me."

"And he has always loved you."

"Yes. And now . . . when we left the Silent Woman Woods to travel north to the Minaret Peaks we both admitted that the nature of that love had changed."

"But . . ."

"StarDrifter has no difficulties in perceiving me as a lover—"

Faraday repressed a small, wry smile. StarDrifter would have no difficulties in perceiving anything vaguely female as a lover if the mood took him.

"—but," Zenith finished on a whisper, "I feel repelled by the thought of bedding with my grandfather."

Faraday did not reply immediately. On the one hand she could understand Zenith's misgivings, her repulsion at the thought of sleeping with her grandfather. She remembered her own grandfather, a kindly, white-mustached man, and Faraday knew she could not even conceive of bedding with him.

On the other hand, Faraday was more than a little surprised by Zenith's reaction. Faraday well knew the SunSoar attraction each to the other, and if she had a grandfather who looked like StarDrifter, and who exuded sexual magnetism with every step . . .

But here was Zenith, and she was miserable, and she needed understanding, not wide-eyed wonder that she hadn't leaped into StarDrifter's bed at the first hint of an invitation.

"I think I can understand how you feel," Faraday eventually said. "Have you talked to StarDrifter about it? Has he been impatient with you? Has he scared you?"

"StarDrifter has been so patient, so tender . . . but I have not told him how I feel. He would only be puzzled. How could he understand how any woman, even a granddaughter, could feel shamed by his touch?"

Faraday could not help a laugh. StarDrifter would find it difficult, if not impossible, to believe any woman could not find him sexually attractive. Azhure may have refused him, but she'd been physically drawn to him, and StarDrifter had known it. "You must talk to him, Zenith."

"I know, I know. But I feel so ashamed that I cannot do this for him. I owe it to him, surely, after all he has done and been for me."

Faraday looked at Zenith sharply. "Zenith . . . *do* you want the relationship to change? *Do* you want to become his lover?"

"Of course!" Zenith said, perhaps too quickly, and Faraday nodded to herself in understanding. "Of course I do! Ah! This is *my* fault! *Mine!* There is no reason why I should feel as I do. Don't I owe him at least this? Isn't he responsible for saving my life? Shouldn't I be grateful enough to—"

"*Stop!*" Faraday said, and grabbed at Zenith's hand. "Stop saying that!"

She took a deep breath and continued more calmly. "Zenith, I have never seen two people more right for each other than you and StarDrifter. But the conflict inside you is not wrong, or anything to feel guilty about. You have spent your life loving StarDrifter only as a grandfather, while StarDrifter," she risked a grin, "has spent his entire life regarding everything female as a potential lover. I swear his eyes likely even followed MorningStar speculatively on occasion."

Faraday was rewarded with a small smile from Zenith as the birdwoman pictured StarDrifter intent on his own mother's seduction.

"You cannot berate yourself as you do," Faraday continued. "And you cannot bed with StarDrifter out of gratefulness, or because you feel that you owe him something."

Faraday gave Zenith's hand a slight shake. "Zenith, when it feels comfortable and natural, then go to him. Not before."

Zenith's mouth twisted. "And *when* is it going to feel 'comfortable and natural?' "

Faraday lifted a hand and softly stroked Zenith's cheek. "It will happen 'whenever,' Zenith. No one can tell the 'when.' For now bask in his love, trust him—and trust him enough to tell him exactly how you feel—but do not let misplaced guilt drive you into something you feel hesitant about. You owe StarDrifter nothing, Zenith. Nothing."

"And how long will StarDrifter wait? Wouldn't it be better to—"

Faraday's hands now cupped Zenith's face. "StarDrifter will wait for you, Zenith. Never, never doubt that." She kissed Zenith's cheek. "And I think a period of celibacy will do the man good. It will strengthen his character," she added with a grin.

Zenith stared at Faraday, then sighed, her entire body relaxing.

"Thank you," she said.

51

A SunSoar Reunion ... of Sorts

WolfStar crouched in the shadows of the forests surrounding Fernbrake Lake. Beside him, docile and soulless, sat the Niah-girl, her vacant stare emptying her face of any of the beauty that should have been her right. Black wings, almost fully grown, sprouted from her back. Her breasts were immature, but already temptingly full, and her hips curved with promise, but neither fullness nor promise was enough to tempt WolfStar to a tasting. His eyes flitted her way, and he barely suppressed a grimace—after this Lake she'd be able to walk for herself and he wouldn't have to cart her half-dead, half-alive body over his shoulder across half of Tencendor.

Gods, but if he'd known Niah was going to be this much trouble he'd never have promised her rebirth in the first instance!

No, no, he mustn't think like that. As a mate Niah had proved a disappointing failure (and even as that thought crossed his mind WolfStar let himself wonder where Zenith was), but as a weapon she would prove awesomely useful.

What better to counter and then destroy the Demons, than with a creation of their own kind?

WolfStar meant to re-create Niah, using the same source of power that the Demons used to re-create Qeteb, so she could become a weapon even more potent than the lost Rainbow Scepter. Who cared if Drago had made off with that gaudy bit of glassware? WolfStar would present the reborn Niah to Caelum, and let the StarSon use her to destroy the Demons.

It was such a simple plan, and yet so potent, that WolfStar knew it could not fail. Let Axis and Azhure and sundry other useless Star Gods scurry about Star Finger trying to find some dusty secret Caelum could toss in the Demons' general direction. *He,* WolfStar, would be the one to give Caelum what he truly needed to stop the TimeKeepers.

WolfStar patted Niah's knee absently, and then frowned as his eye caught a movement across the Lake. What was happening? Icarii by the thousand-fold were slowly moving along the pathway leading down from the rim of the crater to the Lake.

There they were descending through what appeared to be a hole in the ground. What were they doing? Where were they going? Were they stealing the power *he* needed?

"No!" he cried, and rose to his feet, his golden wings held out tense behind him.

"WolfStar," a man said, and WolfStar growled and spun about.

"You!" he spat, utterly shocked. "Why are you not dead?"

Drago smiled wryly. "How many times have I been asked *that* question during my lifetime?" he said, and walked slowly forward from the trees that had concealed him.

Behind him came two other figures, but WolfStar paid them no heed for the moment. He shifted so he stood between Drago and Niah, narrowing his eyes as he studied his grandson. The man *looked* ordinary enough, with his lined face and sad eyes. But he had the Wolven and its quiver of arrows slung over his back, and that only reinforced WolfStar's belief that the man was a traitor and a trickster. He'd not only stolen the Scepter—now he'd somehow wrangled the Wolven from his mother. WolfStar knew better than to trust the benign image that Drago now projected.

Drago halted two paces from WolfStar.

"What mischief do you do?" WolfStar asked, standing straight and tall. Even without the Star Dance, WolfStar knew he could best this fool before him.

"I think I do none compared to what *you* do," Drago said, and nodded at the Niah-form sitting unperturbed behind WolfStar. "What mischief do you make now, WolfStar?"

WolfStar moved slightly so he was between Niah and Drago. "Do not touch her, boy."

Drago raised his eyes back to WolfStar. "You think to mirror Qeteb's rise in her, don't you? Have you been stealing power from under the Demons' noses, WolfStar?"

WolfStar remained silent, but his lips curled in a snarl. Drago thought to snatch *her* as well!

Drago felt a coldness swamp him. That *is* what WolfStar

was doing! Damn him! Did he not know with what horror he played? In the name of all stars in creation, what did he think would emerge from this process? A sweet, pliable Niah? No, a demon escaped from the firepits of the AfterLife, more like.

"And what treachery are *you* up to, Drago?" WolfStar countered as he saw understanding sweep the man's face.

"I aid Caelum as best I—"

WolfStar brayed with laughter, and Drago involuntarily stepped back a pace.

"*You?*" WolfStar chortled. "Aiding *Caelum*? I can only imagine how thrilled Caelum must be about that."

"I can hardly see that *you* are helping Caelum, WolfStar," someone else said, and StarDrifter stepped out from the shadows behind Drago.

A step behind StarDrifter came Isfrael.

"Well," WolfStar sneered, trying to hide his disquiet. Damn! Would they try to take Niah? "Look what we have here. The pretty but completely ineffectual StarDrifter and the twig-encrusted Lord of the Avar. Has Drago ensnared you into his treacheries as well?"

"You are hardly one to talk of treachery," Isfrael said. "Why is it *you* do not move to aid Caelum?"

"I have ever walked alone," WolfStar snarled.

"Cursed be the day you were ever conceived," StarDrifter cried, and took a step past Drago. All he could see was the piece of filth that had raped and then repeatedly abused Zenith. And now here he was with the frightful fruit of his rape, hoping to re-create Niah again. Would Zenith never be safe?

Drago caught StarDrifter's arm and pulled him back. "You can do nothing. Be still."

Furious, StarDrifter tried to jerk his arm out of Drago's grasp, but found he could not; the man had more strength than appearances suggested.

"He wanders *my* forests," Isfrael said behind Drago. "Give him to me."

WolfStar had had enough. These fools would ruin what small hope Tencendor had left if they tried to snatch Niah away from him! He took a step backward, half-bent to grab at the girl's arm to pick her up and run, then caught a movement of Drago's hand out of the corner of his eye.

WolfStar cried out in surprise and some pain, and dropped to the ground. His legs would not move, and his wings were useless!

"A temporary device only," Drago said, "until we can hold you more securely."

"No!" WolfStar shouted. "Let me go! Curse you, *let me go!*"

He turned frantic eyes toward Niah. *What would Drago do with her?* Damn him, *curse him,* to everlasting torment at the gnawing jaws of belly worms!

WolfStar moaned, trying to struggle, yet finding his body would not obey him. He should have taken more care, been more circumspect—and yet how could he have known that Drago would reemerge and ensnare him with whatever Demon-fed power he'd grown?

"Let me go," WolfStar said, almost whispering with hate this time.

Drago stared at the Enchanter. What could be done with WolfStar? Drago knew that had he been Axis the decision would have been an easy one: kill him.

But Drago was not his father, and he could not forget that although WolfStar had done massive harm in Tencendor, he had also done much that was right.

Including killing many Enchanter children, and his own wife? Driving them into the arms of Demons to be thrown back against the land? And what about Zenith? How much harm had WolfStar done her *soul?*

"Well?" StarDrifter hissed.

Drago glanced at him. His grandfather's face was furious, but Drago knew that StarDrifter was hardly the right person to entrust with WolfStar's confinement.

He sighed. "Will you keep him, Isfrael?"

Isfrael took a deep breath of triumph, and placed a hand on Drago's shoulder.

"I do not mean for you to kill him," Drago said softly. "Merely to hold him until we can decide what to do with him."

Isfrael's face flushed with anger. "I—"

"You do *not* have the right to kill him," Drago said, and held Isfrael's stare. "He must face justice for what he has done, whether to those he murdered, to Tencendor generally, or to Zenith."

Drago shot StarDrifter a sympathetic glance, and finally let his arm go. "But not yet. Wait until we have bested the Demons and Tencendor is ours again. Then shall we let Tencendor sit in judgment of him."

Isfrael hesitated, then jerked his head in assent.

"Can you hold him safely?" Drago asked.

"Yes," Isfrael said, and from the surrounding forest sprang eight swarthy, well-muscled Avar men with coils of ropes and stakes. Once four or five of them had seized and bound the furious Enchanter, Drago waved his hand, dissolving the enchantment that had held WolfStar. Isfrael surely had enough skill left to keep the Enchanter out of mischief.

As six of the Avar men carried WolfStar away, another picked Niah up and followed them.

"Isfrael?" Drago said as the Mage-King moved to follow his men. *"Do not let him escape!"*

Isfrael stared at Drago, and then he was gone.

"He should have killed," StarDrifter said. "It would have been safer."

"There has been too much killing," Drago said, then silently walked the way back to the entrance to Sanctuary.

Once there, Drago asked one of the Lake Guard guiding the Icarii down the stairwell to send word to Faraday to meet him at the bridge, then he turned back to watch the horizon, his face creased in thought.

"What is it?" StarDrifter asked quietly, concerned by the worry evident in Drago's face.

"The Demons are but four days away—and it will take more days than that to get all the Icarii into Sanctuary."

"Can we suspend the evacuation while the Demons are here?"

Drago shook his head. "I would prefer not to."

"We have little choice—" StarDrifter began, but Drago turned and smiled at him with such sweetness that StarDrifter was taken aback.

"Perhaps there is," Drago said. "See?" He pointed to the north. "The Demons will come through from that direction. Not only because it is the most direct path from the Lake of Life, but because there are no trees on that side of Fernbrake's crater. They will want to steer clear of the trees."

"And the Icarii are filing down into the crater from the south, and through the trees."

"Exactly. Perhaps I can arrange it so that the Demons will never see the Icarii, nor the entrance to Sanctuary. Wait here."

Drago walked to the nearest tree and laid his hand on her trunk.

"I beg your indulgence," he whispered, "and crave your understanding in what I now do."

He leaned upward and broke off a small branch and then broke that into several dozen smaller pieces.

"What are you doing?" StarDrifter asked.

"Come with me," Drago said, and led the way around the gentle curve of the Lake to the point where the path wound down out of the forested slope and arced toward the entrance to Sanctuary. There, oblivious of the curious stares of the Icarii walking along the path, Drago bent and placed one of the broken pieces of wood in the ground.

He straightened. "StarDrifter, will you aid me by placing a handful of water from the Lake about each of these twigs I plant?"

StarDrifter nodded, his eyes narrowed in thought. Stars! Surely Drago did not command the power to . . . ?

He did as his grandson asked, and for each twig that Drago placed in the ground about the curve of the path, StarDrifter carefully placed a handful of the emerald water in the depression that surrounded it.

When Drago reached the entrance to Sanctuary, he planted the final half dozen twigs before it, and waited patiently for StarDrifter to water them.

"You can't do it," StarDrifter said as he rose from the final twig.

Drago grinned. "Really? Faraday did, so why can't I? Stand back a pace, StarDrifter. I would not want you damaged."

Frowning, StarDrifter stepped back, watching Drago. The man had lowered his eyes, as if in concentration, and he hefted the staff slightly in his left hand, his fingers opening and then closing about it. StarDrifter thought he saw a very slight flicker go through the muscles of Drago's hand where it clenched about the wood, but he could not be sure.

The next moment Drago raised his face, and his left hand

drew a symbol so fast and so fluidly that StarDrifter could not follow it.

"Do as I ask," Drago said, his voice curiously flat, and an instant later StarDrifter—as every Icarii within fifty paces—cried out in surprise.

Where Drago had planted the twigs, now rose massive trees. Even taller and more dense than usual for the Minstrelsea, they unraveled in the space of two breaths, and when they were finally still, the spaces between them were so filled with jutting branches and overhanging foliage that no one could see through them.

It was not only branch and foliage that protected the Icarii from view, for between each tree also hung such threatening shadow that StarDrifter knew no one would be tempted to walk through to investigate.

The passage from Minstrelsea to Sanctuary was completely hidden.

"Ye gods!" StarDrifter murmured, and looked at Drago.

"Faraday?"

She turned from where she'd been waiting at the valley end of the silver-tracery bridge and looked at Drago walking across the bridge toward her. Maybe they had come to some kind of compromise regarding their relationship, and maybe Drago had accepted her decision with unusual good humor for a SunSoar—but he had also pointed out he *was* a SunSoar male, and Faraday was only too well aware what difficulties might lie ahead for her.

Beside her Katie looked on patiently, her hand, as always, clasped in Faraday's. Now Faraday tightened her grip slightly on the girl's fingers.

StarDrifter was a step behind Drago and, as they neared, Faraday switched her eyes to him. "StarDrifter, we should talk—" she began, but Drago interrupted her.

"No. You can talk to StarDrifter some other time. For now we have to go to Carlon."

"Why?"

"Faraday," Drago said, as gently as he could. "The Icarii are not the only ones who will need the comfort of Sanctuary, and whatever Acharites are left will have a hard journey from Carlon. We *will* need to aid them."

"Yes. Of course . . . I'm sorry. StarDrifter? Will you talk with Zenith?" Faraday asked.

StarDrifter nodded, but looked puzzled. "About what?"

"About how much you love her, and what you would do for that love."

StarDrifter nodded again, but frowned a little. He inclined his head at Drago, and then walked past Faraday toward Sanctuary. Drago watched him go, then gave a sharp whistle. Almost instantly the hounds, cats and the feathered lizard bounded out of the grass.

Drago grinned at them, rubbing heads and patting flanks as they crowded about him, and then he looked at Faraday. He unslung the Wolven from his shoulder, as also the quiver of arrows.

"Will you take these? I am overburdened enough."

"Me?" Faraday kept her hands at her side, refusing to take the Wolven and quiver. She wasn't quite sure why she hesitated, but wondered if even the act of accepting something from Drago's hands might be construed as acknowledging a bond between them.

"Faraday, please. They will not bite."

Slowly she reached out and took them, handling them as gingerly as if she thought they might explode in her hands. At Drago's urgings, she eventually slung the bow and quiver over her shoulder.

"Good," Drago said, and held out his hand.

Faraday tensed, thinking he meant her to take it, but in the next instant he'd sketched a symbol in the air, and the far end of the bridge from Sanctuary dissolved into a blue-misted tunnel that led to the interior of a many-staired and balconied tower.

Faraday relaxed slightly, then she and Katie followed Drago into Spiredore.

Perhaps it understood the urgency of the matter, for Spiredore did not take long to transfer them to its outer door that led to the edge of Grail Lake. Three turns of a spiral staircase and they were there, the hounds, cats and feathered lizard close behind.

Drago pushed open the door and stepped outside. Then he halted, transfixed with horror as Faraday, Katie and sundry animals bumped into him.

The far shores of Grail Lake were dense with hundreds of thousands of animals—horses, cattle, feral creatures, birds of every variety—and wild-eyed humans, all milling about the walls of Carlon.

Even from the far side of the Lake Drago and Faraday could hear them howling and mewling and screaming. One of the cats, crouched low at Drago's feet, growled at the cacophony of sound drifting over the Lake.

Faraday's face went ashen, and she put a hand to her mouth. Drago leaned around to gather Faraday and the girl tight against him. Appalled and grief-stricken by the sight before her, Faraday did not object.

Katie merely studied the scene expressionlessly.

It was midafternoon, and the gray miasma of despair was settled upon the hand. Drago and Faraday had grown so used to their immunity, as that of the hounds and, apparently the cats, that it completely escaped them that Katie seemed unaffected as well.

In her, the power and magic of the Star Dance surged more powerfully than it did in the vast unfettered spaces of the universe, simply because it was concentrated into a vastly smaller space.

Inside her tiny body, Katie had enough power to ravage the entire land into a blackened, smoking waste, should she put a mind to it.

Katie grinned.

52

Of What Can't Be Rescued

*T*heod rode as if in a dream. Time passed him by unnoticed, and landscape and sun and night melded into one unknowable blur.

All he was aware of was the feel of the stallion's silken coat and powerful muscles beneath him, and the cold fire of the stars that foamed about his hands where they gripped within the mane.

All Theod thought about was Gwendylyr and his sons. Gone. Had he failed them? Should he have done something different? *Was she still somehow alive?*

No. The existence she currently enjoyed could in no way be called "life," but while her heart still beat, there was hope, surely.

Surely.

Somewhere there had to be hope!

He had to ride south, meet Zared who must be on his way north with his army by now, and go back and get her . . . and save the other groups crawling slowly, innocently, toward that horrid cave and all the beady eyes awaiting in its depths.

But Theod never met Zared coming north.

"Where are you?" he screamed one day into the blur that swept by him, but no one answered, and the stallion's gait did not falter. They sped south through days that folded inexorably from sunlight to night to sunlight again.

"Norden? Norden? Sir? *Wake up!*"

Norden mumbled and opened his eyes, irritated that Greman had woken him before his watch was due to start. What in the world could—

"Wake up, sir!"

The panic in Greman's voice woke Norden as nothing else

could. The captain of the northern wall watch struggled to his feet, cursing the lingering lethargy and stiffness of sleep, and moved to where Greman stood by the parapets.

He was staring at something beyond the wall.

Now *that* Norden could understand. The tens of thousands of cursed creatures were wailing and moaning with even more virulence than usual, but their cacophony in itself was nothing to be remarked on.

Were they preparing to attack?

Norden leaned on the stone blocks of the parapet, trying to see what it was that had disturbed Greman.

"There, sir, directly north. Do you see?"

Greman narrowed his eyes against the cold wind, ignoring the mass of creatures seething at the base of the walls for the moment.

"I—" he began, then concentrated. There was something . . . something . . . pale . . .

Beside him, Greman visibly relaxed. "It's a horse and rider, sir!"

Norden grunted, not wanting to concede that Greman's younger eyes were clearer than his.

"Perhaps," he said. "And if it is, then who would be so stupid as to ride straight for this psychotic circus below us?"

He blinked, and this time he, too, could see that it was a horse and rider. A white horse, with a peculiarly brilliant mane and tail, and a rider.

"Gods, but look how fast they're coming!" Norden said, and before he could add any more, or even think about informing someone of this peculiar event, the animals below roared into full-voiced fury.

Both guards instinctively dropped below the level of the parapet.

"Gods!" Norden whispered again, and carefully peered over the stone ledge.

What he saw this time stunned him.

The animals—while not abandoning the walls—had nevertheless turned to meet whatever it was that ran toward them. They were screaming with such vigor that Norden could actually see one or two convulsing with the strength of their hate.

The horse and rider were now very close, within only

twenty or thirty paces of the outer ranks of the animals. Norden's throat went dry . . . they would be torn to pieces! But even as he thought that, the white horse had closed the distance between it and the animals, and plunged into the first ranks that leaped to meet it.

Norden thought the horse and rider would be overwhelmed instantly, but suddenly creatures screamed and smoke rose from either side of the horse.

Norden blinked, then decided he *was* seeing true.

Tiny stars were falling from the horse's mane, burning a path through the now-frantic animals. The stallion—*the Star Stallion*—cantered through the crowd as though it paraded along a processional boulevard, the man atop him swinging somewhat uselessly to either side with his sword.

The creatures had backed several paces away from the horse, still snarling and howling, but terrified of the horse's magic.

"Open the gates," Norden whispered, then recovered his voice and roared down the ladder. *"Open the gates!"*

As the guards leaned to the bolts, Norden scrambled to his feet and headed for the ladder, sliding to the ground in three heartbeats. Turning from the ladder, he heard the horse leap through the gates, and then the thunder as the guards slammed them shut against the first of the creatures leaping after the horse.

But Norden had no eye for anything save the wondrous Star Stallion and his rider.

A man—it was the Duke of Aldeni!—slid off the stallion's back, and the horse reared, screamed . . . and disappeared.

The Duke saw Norden standing gaping, and dropped a heavy hand on his shoulder.

"Get me to the King. *Now!*"

Norden stared at Theod's haggard face, then moved hastily to obey.

Earl Herme rose slowly, unbelievingly, from his chair outside Leagh's chamber as he saw Theod and an officer of the watch approach. "Theod? My friend . . . what do you here?"

"I come wondering why Zared did not bother to ride to my aid. Where is he? Where is the carrion-cursed—"

"We have had no word, Theod." Zared emerged from the door, closing it softly behind him. "Nothing. No farflight scouts. No ships. We thought . . ."

He stopped, staring appalled at Theod's face. *"What has happened?"*

"No one got through?" Theod whispered. "Not *one* of the farflight scouts got through? Oh, *gods*!"

He sat and drank, glass after glass of the best Romsdale gold, and neither Zared nor Herme stopped him.

They listened to his extraordinary tale, and shared doubts in silent glances over Theod's bowed head. If all others had perished, then how was it Theod had got through?

How had he made it south safely through unprotected territory . . . unshaded territory?

How had he come so swiftly?

How had he got through the cordon about Carlon's walls?

Was he mad with grief . . . or mad with Demonic delight? *Was he another Askam?*

Zared's hand slipped about the knife in his belt, and saw Herme's silent nod.

"Sire?"

Zared's head jerked about. He'd forgotten Norden's presence.

"Sire," Norden said. "I saw him, and this horse. I cannot vouch for the earlier part of his tale, but of this magical horse I can say he speaks truth. And over a dozen of the watch on the northern wall will say the same thing."

"And where is this magical horse now?" Herme said.

"Gone, sir Earl. He vanished before our eyes."

Zared glanced again at Herme, and saw that doubts remained. Had they *all* been infected?

His hand tightened about his knife.

"How can we get across?" Faraday said. "Look at the water!"

The waters of Grail Lake were simmering. Great bubbles slowly broke across the surface.

Faraday jerked, and pressed closer to Drago in horror. A

huge slimy tail rose lazily in the air above the water, then slammed down again.

The water was not boiling, it was full of . . . of . . .

"Eels," Drago said. "Grown to gigantic proportions under the Demons' careful nurturing."

The water roiled, and several heads appeared. Fully five paces long and two wide, the eels had yawning mouths filled with razored, yellowing fangs. One of them had the remains of a cloak caught between its teeth, and as Faraday watched a neatly severed human leg dropped from the folds of the cloth and splashed into the water.

All three eels instantly lunged back into the water, fighting over the delicacy.

"There's a boat tied to the pier," Drago said, apparently unconcerned by what he'd just witnessed. "And large enough for our variety of furred and feathered companions as well."

Faraday pulled away from him. "No!" She hugged Katie tight to her, and buried the girl's head protectively in the folds of her skirts. Katie twisted her head about slightly to gaze quietly at Drago.

"We will never get across alive!" Faraday said. "Do you want to kill this sweet child before she has a chance to live?"

Katie now twisted her face about so she could look at Faraday.

"Faraday—" Drago began.

"*No!*"

"Faraday," Drago's voice became firmer. "Trust me. We can get across."

Faraday stared at him, her eyes panicked. She could not believe that Drago was prepared to risk the life of Katie with such equanimity.

A movement to their right broke the standoff. It was the feathered lizard—now, Faraday observed, far larger than any of the hounds—climbing carefully into the boat. It settled itself at the prow and began to preen, totally ignoring the glistening hump of an eel that had surfaced four or five paces out into the Lake.

Sicarius, FortHeart as ever at his shoulder, leaped in after the lizard, and the next moment the boat rocked as the remaining Alaunt and the cats all leaped in at the same time.

The lizard raised its head, its emerald and scarlet crest flaring, and hissed irritably at them.

There were three spaces left clear on the benches.

"Trust me!" Drago said, and held out his hand.

Faraday stared at him, then at the boat packed with sundry animals, then back at Drago.

She swallowed.

Drago gave a small smile. "Faraday, the worst that can happen is a rapid annihilation, and the best is an exhilarating ride. Will you risk it?"

His hand waggled a bit.

Faraday lowered her eyes, and made as if to speak to Katie, but the girl pulled free from her and ran to the boat, climbing in.

"Katie!" Faraday cried.

"I think," Drago said, "that you have been outvoted. If you do not wish to risk the journey, I can always leave you here. No doubt Spiredore will keep you safe and warm."

Faraday's cheeks reddened, and she marched stiff-backed past Drago and climbed into the boat.

His smile gone, Drago unmoored the boat and pushed it out into the water as he jumped in. He settled down in the remaining space, placed the staff carefully under the bench, unshipped the oars, and rowed strongly for the opposite shoreline.

Instantly the water came to life about them.

An eel reared out of the water, its huge head blocking out the sun, and lunged down at one of the Alaunt.

But in the instant before it seized the hound in its fangs, its head fell off, glancing off the side of the boat into the water.

The boat swung wildly, not only from the blow struck by the falling eel's head, but also because a half-dozen other eels began fighting over the head and body of their fellow.

Gripping her seat tightly with one hand, and Katie as tightly with the other, Faraday stared wildly about, trying to see from what direction the next inevitable attack would come from.

"How . . . what happened?" she gasped.

"Watch," Drago said, and pointed behind her.

Faraday twisted about, desperately trying to keep her balance, and saw that the lizard was sitting alertly in the prow. Another eel reared just to her right, and Faraday flinched, but not before she saw a shaft of brilliant light sear through the eel's head, sending it tumbling back into the water.

Again an eel reared out of the water, and this time Faraday saw exactly what happened. The lizard raised one of its claws and arced it through the air in a great cutting motion. As it did so, its diamond talons flared with light, and the beam flashed through the space between lizard and eel cutting off the monster's head.

Faraday looked back to Drago, absolutely astounded. "I had no idea it could do that," she whispered.

"I told you to trust me," he said, and his face relaxed into a wide grin.

Even Faraday could not resist that smile. Her mouth twisted, twitched, and then her resistance crumbled and she smiled. Katie clapped her hands delightedly, and the lizard joined in the fun by slicing off two eels' heads with a single flashing arc of light.

It was the last they were troubled by the eels. Whether the other eels had learned from the fate of their companions, or they were too busy feasting on the remains of those others, the boat sailed serenely across to the other side of Grail Lake.

As they neared the section of the city walls that rose directly from the waters, Drago lifted the oars from the water and let the boat slow to a glide.

"Carlon is ringed thirty deep with the Demons' minions. We could fight our way through—I am sure the lizard would prove more than useful—but I would prefer to arrive in a slightly more anonymous manner. I remember stories of the night my father bested Borneheld in this place. Did he not enter through a postern gate somewhere close to the water's edge?"

"Yes." Faraday did not particularly want to remember those eight days spent in the lie of Axis' arms, but she could not avoid it. First Gorkenfort and memories of Borneheld, and now Carlon and the shade of Axis' betrayal. What was Drago doing, dragging her to every site in Tencendor bound to stir up unwanted and painful memories?

"Yes?" Drago prompted.

"Ah." Faraday shook herself out of her train of thought. "Yes, Axis told me about it, as did Rivkah and Yr. It should be . . ." she twisted about so she could see the approaching sheer wall, ". . . it should be just beyond that corner there, tucked into an alcove that lies deep under a rounded tower. Yes. There!"

Drago leaned back into the oars, and the boat swung close to the tower. Five paces away he shipped the oars securely, and clambered forward to the prow, pushing aside sundry hounds and cats as he did so. A chorus of indignant grunts and yowls followed his pathway.

Once at the prow, Drago leaned over the form of the lizard, who had curled up and was watching proceedings carefully with one of its light-absorbing black eyes, and caught the iron ring by the door, tying the boat up with swift, sure movements.

Then he seized the door ring, and pushed.

The door swung inward—

—and instantly Drago was knocked to his face, only avoiding falling in the water by the most strenuous of actions, by the mad rush of lizard, hounds and cats for the open doorway.

Drago hauled himself back into a safe position, and looked back to Faraday. Both she and Katie were bent almost double in silent paroxysms of laughter.

Drago grinned himself, shaking his head slightly, then he held out his hand and silently helped Faraday and Katie, both still giggling, into the door.

"If you disbelieve me," Theod spat. "Then kill me now! I have *nothing* left to live for!"

Zared again locked eyes with Herme, and then he sighed and placed both his hands atop the table. "I cannot believe you are anything else but my friend. I am sorry for doubting you."

Theod's face did not relax. "And so when do we ride north? Ride to save—"

"My friend," Zared said as gently as he could, "we will not be riding north. By this time there will be nothing *left* to save . . . and you know as well as I that we can't help those who have been—"

"Coward!" Theod shouted, and stumbled to his feet. "I will ride back myself if I—"

He stopped, and stared at the door.

Zared and Herme turned to see what had quieted Theod. They, too, stilled. Sitting in the doorway, its tail swishing softly to and fro behind it, was an enormous blue-feathered lizard which had a brilliantly colored plumed crest on its head.

Norden had somehow managed to escape beyond the doorway, and they could see him edging slowly back down the corridor. He stopped and turned, as if he had seen someone. But Zared's, Herme's and Theod's attention was now all on the lizard.

It hissed, and Theod took a step back from the table.

His chair crashed to the floor behind him.

Zared rose to his feet, his hand now finally drawing his dagger.

"What?" he asked hoarsely. "Have the creatures gained entrance?"

"Not yet," a voice said, and Drago stepped through the door and—rather carefully—around the lizard. "But it seems to me that the miasma of despair has truly worked its horror within this room."

He stopped and looked at the three men. "Tell me, why so sad?"

Drago and Faraday sat on two chairs before the fire, Katie at Faraday's feet, their various creatures curled up about the room, and grieved silently as first Zared and then Theod spoke of the disasters that had befallen them.

"Why do *you* weep?" Theod said to Drago as he finished his tale. "Have you not returned successfully from the dead?"

Drago hesitated in his reply, Theod's words making him pause for thought. "I grieve for all this land, Theod, and for you and Zared and Herme."

Theod's mouth twisted, and he turned his face aside.

Faraday rose from her chair and walked over to a far wall, ostensibly to inspect a wall hanging, in reality to sorrow for Leagh in semiprivacy. Leagh! She didn't deserve such a dreadful fate. But then, who did? Did Drago truly know what he was doing, allowing Tencendor to be so ruined, and its people to be so decimated?

Katie, still sitting by Faraday's chair, looked between Drago and Faraday, her beautiful eyes swimming with grief herself. No one grieved more for Tencendor and its peoples than did Katie.

Drago sighed. "Faraday and I bring good news. Sanctuary is open—"

"—for those still able to enjoy it," Theod put in.

"Surely that must be enough!" Faraday cried, turning back from the wall. "Those left *must* be saved. Theod, how many are left in the western ranges, do you think?"

He shrugged, almost uncaring in his cynicism and grief. "It has been over a week, more, since I left. Zared thinks all must now be . . . gone. I agree with him."

He paused. "I went north to rescue twenty thousand, and ended by leading all to their deaths. Every one of them. Gone."

"Including the Strike Force," Drago said, and looked into the fire.

Including the Strike Force. His eyes stared dreamily into the fire. The Strike Force, lost to the forces of madness.

"Where is this Sanctuary?" Zared asked, uncertain of Drago's reaction to this disastrous news. "And how do we reach it?" He eyed the girl curiously, but was not inclined to ask about her. One small girl amid the tragedy that currently engulfed them was a problem that could be left to later, more leisurely times.

Faraday glanced at Drago, still deep in thought, and answered, "Sanctuary lies under Fernbrake Lake."

"That would be death for anyone trying to reach it from Carlon!" Theod cried, and turned and slammed his fist into the mantelpiece. "Have you not seen how hemmed in we are? How we sit and wait for starvation to claim us."

"The trip to Sanctuary will take little more than two hours for most people," Drago said, and looked up.

Theod merely raised his eyebrows disbelievingly.

"Spiredore," Drago said softly.

"You can work Spiredore?" Zared said. "But I thought . . . Axis said—"

Drago shrugged. "He should have trusted in Spiredore more. At the least it would have saved him, Azhure and Caelum a difficult journey to Star Finger."

"How is Caelum?" Herme asked. "Have he and his parents found any solution to the Demons?"

"Caelum has the means to do what he must," Drago said. "And I do what I can to make the path easier for him."

Zared glanced at Faraday, who had dropped her eyes into her lap at Drago's statement, then looked back to Drago.

"When do we start the evacuation?" he asked.

"Leave it several days, if only because there are still tens of thousands of Icarii filing down into Sanctuary, and the arrival of Carlon's bulk would only create more chaos."

"So we just sit here until—?" Theod began.

"No." Drago rose from his chair and picked up his staff. "There are several things to be done. First . . . Leagh."

53

The Enchanted Songbook

For two days the combined wisdom of Star Finger pondered the riddle of the Enchanted Songbook. It was read, fingered, examined, held up to the light and gently tapped for hidden spaces, and although Axis and Azhure shook their heads, as did the other Star Gods, and the scholars admitted themselves perplexed, Caelum seemed unperturbed.

After two days, as his parents and Adamon uselessly thumbed through the book in Caelum's apartment, he retrieved the book from their fingers, opened it up, and explained.

"Drago showed me how—"

"*Drago?*" Axis asked.

Caelum hesitated a little before answering. "He learned well in his journey through the Star Gate."

Axis bit back a tart reply. Drago had learned only treacheries, more like—and what twisted advice had he now passed on to Caelum?

Caelum opened the book, and pointed to the strange scribblings that meandered up and down lines.

"Yes, yes," Adamon said, leaning over Axis' shoulder. "A script, to be sure, but we know of none like it, and it is not like that about the Maze Gate—"

"Drago told me that it is written in the language of the ancient Enemy," Caelum said, "but it does not represent words, it represents—"

"Music!" Azhure cried. "It is music."

Caelum grinned and nodded. "Yes. Songs . . . and once we decipher the music, and learn the Songs, we will know to what purpose that can be put."

Axis slowly raised his head from the open book before him, and smiled.

Dance.

It did not take them long to decipher the script into music. The tune was easy, for the odd black-fletched circles ran up and down a series of horizontal lines, and to merely follow their progress was to decipher the tune.

Tone was a little more difficult, until Azhure noted the strange symbols at the start of every tune, and wondered if it was they that set the tone. From there it was merely a process of finding the tone that suited each symbol, and to a race which had spent its existence surrounded by music, that was but child's play.

And once they'd deciphered each Song and committed them to memory—again, a trifling chore to those addicted to music—there was the problem of discovering the steps that suited each Song.

Again, not a difficult task to those who were more Icarii than human, although all were careful not to complete an entire dance lest they call some unknown and dreadful destruction down upon themselves.

Within but a few days, Caelum not only had the book, he had the Dances the book contained. Once again, hope drifted about the corridors of Star Finger.

"We must test this," Caelum said one morning, as the dawn miasma cleared to reveal a glorious clear day atop Star Finger.

"I agree," Axis said, and walked some way about the platform that encircled the huge central shaft which fed light and air into the mountain.

They were alone on the peak. Caelum and his father had made it a habit to stroll the heights each morning to watch the miasma disappear. It always vanished from the high places first, and as they emerged, they could see the gray, bleak haze sliding down the mountain and rippling over the plains, back toward its source.

"They must be close to Fernbrake Lake now," Axis murmured, watching the miasma contract to a point far in the south.

"Yes. Father, I must meet them at Grail Lake."

Axis nodded, opened his mouth to say something, and then involuntarily ducked as something dark swooped down from out of the sun.

Caelum suppressed a cry, remembering not only Gorgrael's plunge from the sky, but also the Gryphon that had attacked him and Azhure atop Spiredore.

It was a lone Hawkchild, and it contented itself with one swoop, not daring to attack on its own.

"No doubt reporting our movements to its masters," Caelum said, biting down nausea.

"What better time to test out the dances," Axis said. Stars! How he wished this was his battle to execute. "Think only of the Hawkchild, direct all your concentration to it, direct the *dance* to it . . . and see what happens."

Caelum squinted into the sun. The Hawkchild was circling high in the sky above him.

He lowered his eyes to his father, and gave a curt nod.

Axis stepped well back, giving Caelum full use of the space available.

Caelum stood for a while, his head down, thinking and focusing his concentration. Which one to attempt? Eventually he decided that any would be as good as the next, for he could not know what any of them would do until he tried it.

And so he picked one of the shorter dances, one with savage staccato foot and leg movements and angry, violent body rhythms. Savage anger was something Caelum felt like letting out—but he also knew the dance would work. It had to. It was *fated* to.

Wasn't he the StarSon? He suppressed a grim smile.

Caelum commenced the dance, and, apart from keeping the image of the circling Hawkchild at the forefront of his mind, he lost himself entirely in its rhythms.

As he moved further and further into the dance, Caelum felt himself begin to seethe with hate and violence, *radiate* it. He felt power infuse him—not quite in the same manner as it had when he'd sung Songs, but just as powerful—and he let the rage and hate ripple forth.

Standing in the alcove leading to the stairwell, Axis gasped, and started in shock.

Caelum's face had twisted into a mask of malevolence, and his fingers were twitching violently—not a requirement of the dance.

"Caelum?" he said, and tensed as if to take a step forward.

Caelum roared, and Axis flinched in deep shock. The sound had been frightful, and he found it difficult to believe that it had come from Caelum—he had literally *felt* the waves of hate rippling off his son.

What was happening?

"Caelum!" he yelled, and prepared to stop his son . . . *What was this dance transforming him into?*

Just as Axis made up his mind to dash Caelum to the ground and out of the dance, there was a terrible scream from overhead. Axis jerked his neck up, cricking his neck painfully.

A black shape plummeted from the sky—the Hawkchild— but as it fell closer, Axis could see that it had been twisted and mangled as if by a brutal, angry hand.

Axis looked back to Caelum. He was moving so fast he was almost a blur, his arms and legs and head all jerking violently to the demands of the hate-filled dance.

"Caelum!" Axis screamed . . . and then the Hawkchild hit the platform about two paces from Caelum.

It broke apart on impact, splattering blood and flesh about the entire mountaintop. Both Axis and Caelum were covered in it.

Caelum faltered to a halt, staring down at the remains of the Hawkchild with eyes clouded with rancor. He roared again— a frightful sound—and threw himself upon the ground, tearing into the bits lying about with his fingernails and teeth.

"Caelum!" Axis screamed yet once more, and threw himself atop his son, dragging Caelum's head back until he heard his neck creak. "Caelum, damn you! Wake out of this rage!"

For an instant Axis thought he'd lost his son completely, then Caelum's body relaxed and the hate faded from his face.

"Let me go," he wheezed.

Axis hesitated, then decided that he'd heard enough reason in Caelum's voice to risk freeing him. He stood up, slipping a little in the blood and flesh that surrounded them, and let Caelum's head go.

Caelum rose to his hands and knees, then retched so violently Axis had to kneel down and support him.

"Stars, Caelum," he whispered when his son had finally done. "What happened?"

Caelum slowly sat up and wiped his mouth. "I have never felt like that before. It must have been a dance of pure hatred, and in performing it, I *felt* every nuance of that hatred and rage. Gods, father! It almost tore me apart. If I'd had to continue any longer . . ."

He looked about him. "Well, at least we know it works."

Sheol tipped her head back and screamed and roared and yowled. Every one of the other Demons did the same, and their demon-horses screeched and bucked.

Gray miasmic haze issued forth from their mouths, enveloping the company in a mist of corruption.

StarLaughter, fighting to gain some semblance of control over her own mount as well that of her son's, looked on in a combination of bewilderment and panic that the Demons should have suddenly reacted like this.

"What's wrong?" she yelled as soon as both Demons and horse had regained something resembling composure.

"The StarSon!" Mot hissed, and the other demons howled at the word. *"The StarSon!"*

"What about him?" StarLaughter cried. What had gone wrong now?

"He has eaten one of our Hawkchilds!"

"But . . . but . . . I thought his power had gone!"

"Well, he has found some *more!*" Sheol screamed so violently that spittle sprayed over the entire company. "And it tastes of the Enemy."

"The Enemy?" StarLaughter said. "But—"

Mot snarled, twisting his entire face like melting clay with the movement. "But he will not trick Qeteb with the likes of that! Not again! No!"

Suddenly all the Demons were screaming in laughter rather than rage.

"No! No! No!" they cried. "Qeteb will turn it against *you* this time!"

They went into convulsions of laughter, although the sound was still thin and harsh. Then, as one, they stopped.

"We will *slaughter* him," Sheol said.

Caelum slowly rose to his feet.

"Father, will you pledge me one thing?"

"Surely. What is it?"

"If I die, give the Songbook to Drago."

"No! I would rather cast it from the —"

"Do this for me!" Caelum screamed and gripped his father by the shoulders, shaking him. "If you love me, then *pledge me this!*"

Shaken to the very core of his being, Axis nodded jerkily. "If you wish."

"Then pledge it."

Axis ran his tongue about his lips. "Very well. Caelum, on everything I hold dear, I pledge to you that should you die, I will give the Enchanted Songbook to Drago."

Caelum stared at him, searching for any deception in his father's eyes. Then he spun him about, and flung one arm out to indicate the continent spread out below Star Finger.

"Tencendor is your witness, Axis SunSoar. Fail your pledge, and you fail this entire land!"

54

The Cruelty of Love

StarDrifter had not returned into Sanctuary immediately after leaving Faraday, Drago and the girl on the silver-tracery bridge. True, he'd begun to walk that way, but the thought of talking to Zenith made him feel uncomfortable, and so StarDrifter found himself walking back over the bridge and up the stairwell to the Overworld.

There he'd reinspected the screen of trees that Drago had erected, marveling at the skill of the man.

"But then, he is *my* grandson," StarDrifter murmured, and grinned at his own self-satisfaction.

From there he talked a while with WingRidge, and then with FreeFall and EvenSong, who had finally made the trek from their palace in the peaks to Fernbrake below, and then StarDrifter had found himself at a loss for something to do with the evening drifting in. He still preferred not to talk with Zenith. Above all else, he feared what she might say to him.

Obviously, Zenith had talked with Faraday. *So what had Faraday counseled her?* StarDrifter tried to think what Faraday might have said, and came up with twelve different responses—none of them comfortable.

"I swear to all gods that have existed and who are yet to exist," StarDrifter whispered, "that if WolfStar has scarred her irreparably, then I will kill him with my bare hands."

Lost and unsure, and terrified that Zenith might reject him, StarDrifter finally forced her from his mind and wandered into the night.

Without thinking about where he was going, StarDrifter found himself rambling in the forest of Minstrelsea below the eastern ridge of Fernbrake crater. It was peaceful, the shadowed walks of the forest as calm and as beautiful as they'd always been.

StarDrifter wandered further and further into the forest,

not truly looking where he was going, lost in his worries about Zenith, wondering how he would cope if she did reject him. Anything, he thought over and over, I will do anything for you Zenith—just don't leave me, don't leave me . . .

"StarDrifter? What are you doing here?"

StarDrifter leaped backward and hit a grumpian tree. He tumbled into an undignified heap beside it.

Isfrael emerged out of what little moonlight there was and leaned down, offering him a hand. "StarDrifter?"

StarDrifter accepted Isfrael's hand and stood up, dusting himself down. He grinned ruefully. "I was wandering and thinking, Isfrael. Obviously a combination of activities unsuited to my level of skill."

To StarDrifter's utter amazement, Isfrael laughed. "I did not think you capable of self-mockery!" he finally said. "But why here? This part of the forest is not a usual haunt of the Icarii."

StarDrifter looked at his grandson suspiciously. What was he hiding? A bevy of female Avar Banes that their Mage-King was personally inducting into a higher level of mystery?

Isfrael noted the look. "WolfStar is being held in a glade a short distance from here, StarDrifter. Do you want to see?"

StarDrifter nodded, sober now, and Isfrael led him down a side path and to the edge of a small glade.

They stopped at the edge of the glade, for its internal spaces were totally immersed in a dome of emerald light, similar to the one that Isfrael and his Banes, together with the Star Gods and Icarii Enchanters, had worked to guard the Star Gate against the TimeKeeper Demons. Isfrael hoped this enchanted dome would prove stronger than the last. Seven Banes squatted on their haunches about the glade, concentrating on the magic needed to maintain the ward.

Behind the ward, WolfStar was seething. His words did not penetrate the dome, but his vengeful expression was message enough. He paced to and fro, occasionally lunging at the Banes seated outside as if he hoped to distract them from their work, and slamming fists and heels into the walls of the dome.

As StarDrifter watched, WolfStar rose on his wings, and tore at the apex of the dome with his fingernails and teeth, until dark streaks of the Enchanter's blood became clearly evident on the inside surface.

StarDrifter turned away, wishing Drago had allowed him to kill the Enchanter. "Where is she?" he asked quietly.

"This way." Isfrael led him through a screen of bushes to a much smaller space.

The girl-woman—Niah, if this soulless automat dared be called by any name—sat motionless, expressionless, dead save for the rise and fall of her pubescent breasts.

Her beautiful, angelic face was almost identical to Zenith's, bespeaking the close soul and blood bond between them, although it lacked any warmth or charm, or Zenith's deep compassion.

"I wish we could kill her!" StarDrifter said, with a savageness that astounded Isfrael as much as his grandfather's previous self-mockery had.

"We already tried," he said.

Now StarDrifter was the one to stare. "You tried to—"

"Watch."

At Isfrael's nod, an Avar man stepped forth from the shadows of the ring of trees, a long curved knife in his hand. Isfrael nodded again, and the man stepped over to the girl, and plunged the knife into her belly, twisting and turning it mercilessly.

StarDrifter forced himself to watch, although the sight sickened him. The girl sat there, no change in her expression, nor in the gentle rise and fall of her breasts.

The Avar man withdrew the knife, clotted with blood and pieces of the internal organs he'd sliced apart, but as the knife slid out, so the girl's belly skin mended as if there had never been any attack made on her person.

"I myself have tried," Isfrael said. "We have surrounded her with dead wood and burned her. We have crushed her beneath rocks. We have—"

"Stop!" StarDrifter said. He turned away, then forced himself to look back a last time. "What will you do with her, and with WolfStar?"

Isfrael took his time in replying. "I do not know," he said, and walked back into the shadows.

StarDrifter went back to Sanctuary. It was time he talked with Zenith. Once he had walked across the silver-tracery bridge, the long line of Icarii wending their way down to the bridge seemingly never-ending, he lifted into the blue sky of Sanctuary and flew toward the valley mouth.

StarDrifter rose high, very high, and the wind felt warm and powerful under his wings. The sky, as Sanctuary, was apparently limitless, but StarDrifter wondered what would happen if he gave in to his urge to flip over onto his back and relax and let the thermals carry him ever higher.

Would he circle into infinity? Or would he smash against some ward that, like the emerald dome about WolfStar, would prove his imprisonment?

Unsettled, he flew further, soaring above the valley mouth and the first of the endless orchards, paths, ponds and palaces.

Everything was so perfect, so beautiful, so . . . so cloying.

A prison, just like a dark, barred cell.

Did those below perceive it thus, or were they still lost in Sanctuary's beauty and comfort? Did he only see it because he'd crossed to and fro some dozen times on various businesses?

"Stars grant Drago success," StarDrifter whispered as he began to descend, "for I would not want to be incarcerated in this prison forever more."

He hunted for Zenith for over an hour before an Icarii woman told him where to find her.

She was comfortably settled in a pretty crystal-domed chamber on an upper level of one of the myriad of palaces, staring at herself in a mirror.

"Zenith," StarDrifter said softly, and walked over to her as she twisted about on a stool. She was wearing a blue and silver gown, and he thought she'd never looked so beautiful . . . nor so vulnerable.

Her eyes were wide, almost frightened, and StarDrifter instinctively dropped to his knees before her, trailing his wings across the floor behind him.

Zenith hesitated, then held out her hands for him to take. "We have to talk, you and I," she said.

"Zenith, WolfStar is bound. Safe. He will never trouble you again. Isfrael has him—"

"No. StarDrifter, the problem between you and I is not WolfStar, nor even what he did to me. Will you listen if I talk?"

StarDrifter nodded, feeling with an icy certainty that he was going to lose Zenith before he'd even had a chance to love her.

His face was rigid, unreadable, and Zenith had to briefly close her eyes and summon her courage before she could go on.

"Dear gods, I love you, StarDrifter," she whispered, and dropped her eyes to their clasped hands, "but I do not know how I can ever be your lover—"

"No!"

"*Listen to me!* Please . . . please, just listen to me."

And so Zenith talked, haltingly at first, and then with more resolve. She told him that WolfStar's rape was not that which lay between them—gods, how desperately she wanted some other, more loving memory to overlay that one!—but that she could not overcome her revulsion at having a grandfather touch her carnally.

Zenith stumbled at that point, still feeling guilt that she should couch StarDrifter's love in such a shameful construct, then hurried on before he could say anything.

"Whenever you kiss me, or touch me, I feel such revulsion—"

Stars! Why had she said it so badly! What had she *done*? Zenith opened her mouth but, not knowing how to snatch back what she'd just said, said nothing at all.

Silence. StarDrifter did not speak, even his hands lay unspeaking and unmoving in hers.

She raised her eyes and looked him in the face.

And all she saw there was panic. Not condemnation. Not frustration. Not rejection. Not even puzzlement.

Panic.

"Zenith . . . gods! I had no idea . . . I don't know what to say . . . What can I say . . ." The words tumbled awkwardly, and the depth of dread in StarDrifter's face increased. "Zenith, I want you for my wife—"

And until those words were out StarDrifter had no idea how *desperately* he wanted Zenith for his wife.

"—and there is no shame in that. Is there?"

Zenith was crying. "No, no, there's *no* shame in that save what I feel in here!" She wrenched her hands from his and buried her fingers in her hair, giving her head a shake. "Oh gods! Why did RiverStar get all the wantonness and I all the inhibitions? Why can't I—"

"Zenith!" StarDrifter leaned forward as if to wrap his arms about her, hesitated, then gave an incoherent cry of frustration and, jumping to his feet, stalked over to the window.

Outside the sham sun shone over the sham world of Sanctuary, and StarDrifter thought he would scream if he saw so much as one smiling face.

And then, gently, hesitantly, stunningly, he felt arms slide about him, and Zenith's damp face press against his back.

"Please don't blame me," she whispered. "I want so much to be able to love you as we *both* want."

StarDrifter's heart broke. He turned around in her arms and hugged her to him.

"Don't run away from me," he whispered into her hair. "Please. I will do anything—"

She raised her face and looked at him. "Will you wait for me?"

Wait for *what?* he wondered. Wait for instinctive revulsion to fade?

"One day," and now she was smiling a little through her tears, "your silly granddaughter will grow up and become a woman who will see you with a woman's eyes. Will you wait for that day?"

StarDrifter nodded, and Zenith turned her face away so she did not have to see the tears in his eyes.

55

An Enchantment Made Visible

"Leagh?" Zared asked. "Why Leagh? Do you need to view her yourself? Would you like a portrait done of her in her current curious animalistic form? Would you like to see—"

"That's enough, Zared!" Drago snapped. "You are *King* of the Acharites, damn you, and you have been given responsibility for *all* Tencendor, not just one woman. How dare you sit here and go into a guilt-ridden fugue while Theod desperately tries to save the last remaining vestiges of your realm outside this city. *He* has a right to verbally lash me . . . but not you."

Zared visibly flinched, but he sat up slightly straighter. "I ask again, Drago. *Why* do you need to see Leagh? She does not deserve to be inspected like a curious freak displayed on fair days."

"I ask to see her so that I might help Tencendor."

"That makes no sense, Drago," Theod said, his voice hard. "At least I agree with Zared on the issue of displaying Leagh like a freak."

Drago bent down, retrieved his staff from the floor, stroking one of the cats as he did so.

He stood up, adjusting the sack at his belt. "Zared, is it your opinion that Leagh's mind is completely possessed by the Demons?"

"Yes."

"So," Drago said slowly, and he glanced at Faraday as he spoke. "Would you say that Leagh, as her own person, character, entity and soul, is completely dead?"

"Oh!" Faraday whispered, utterly shocked as she realized what Drago was going to attempt. "By all the heavens, Drago. *Can you do it?*"

"Can you imagine, Faraday," Drago said, ignoring the others' angry confusion, "what resources Tencendor would have at its side if we could?"

He held Faraday's gaze, and then he smiled, sweetly and tenderly, utterly transforming his face.

"What are you going to do?" Zared yelled, stepping forward and seizing Drago by the upper arm.

"I am going to bring Leagh back," Drago said. "With *all* the heritage of her Acharite blood."

"You can bring her back?" Zared whispered hoarsely. He paid no attention to the second part of Drago's statement.

"Indeed he can," Katie said, rising from her spot on the floor. "If I aid him."

Drago looked at her, puzzled, but he did not say anything.

Zared looked wildly at Herme and Theod, neither of them knowing what to think or say, and then his grip on Drago's arm tightened yet further, and he pulled him toward the door. "Come!"

Theod and Herme began to move as well, but Drago shook his head. "Only Zared, Faraday, Katie and myself," he said.

A movement at the corner of Drago's eye caught his attention.

"And the lizard," he added hurriedly, and allowed Zared to drag him forth.

The walk was relatively short in distance and time, but thick with Zared's wild hope and Faraday's unspoken queries.

Herme's place before the door to Leagh's chamber had earlier been taken over by a palace guard, and Drago dismissed him. "Go down to the kitchens and ask the cooks to prepare a light but nutritious meal. The Queen will require it soon enough."

The guard looked hesitantly at Zared, but when his King said nothing, he nodded and set off down the corridor toward the main stairs.

Zared still had Drago by the arm, and now he fumbled with the doorknob with his free hand. His hand slipped, and he lost his grip, but he pushed aside Drago's attempts to help him.

"I can do it!" he said.

Standing slightly behind the two men, Faraday felt sick. She had a very good idea of what she would see within the chamber, and she did not want to see Leagh thus degraded. She wiped damp palms against the rough weave of her gown. Could Drago truly do what he intimated? Had he come this far, this quickly?

By her side, Katie looked up into Faraday's anxious face. She patted at the woman's skirts, drawing her attention, and smiled when Faraday looked down. Faraday took a deep breath, and nodded. If Katie was confident . . .

The door swung open, and revealed the horror inside.

Leagh herself was not immediately apparent, but her stench flew out the open door and struck the faces of those who would enter. Drago and Faraday had to quell sudden nausea, and the lizard spat. Then it scurried past the hesitant legs before it, and disappeared inside.

Its entrance was greeted by a wild shriek, and the sound of a body shuffling about the floor.

Drago and Faraday forced themselves inside.

"Stars in heaven," Faraday whispered, and turned aside momentarily.

Now free of Zared, who had entered and then crept to one side of the door, Drago stared at the sight before him.

What had once been Leagh roiled at the end of its chains, a bare two paces from him. Its face had convulsed out of any resemblance to the woman who had once borne it, and its body was covered with sores and boils, scores of self-inflicted wounds and several layers of flaked excreta.

Ribs and hip bones jutted at wild angles, while muscle and flesh had shrunk into deep valleys between them. Its hair was knotted and dark with grease, dirt and blood, its fingernails were torn and bleeding, and yellowed saliva hung down from its mouth. But all Faraday could stare at, all she could see, was the frightful sight of the distended belly.

She was with child!

"Zared," Drago said, remarkably evenly, "that door in the far wall . . . does it connect to another chamber?"

"What? Ah, yes. To the diamond chamber."

"Good. I want you to go and arrange for a bath, medicinal supplies and some well-watered wine to be placed in there."

"But—"

"And then I want you to go and wait with Theod and Herme."

"I will not leave her!"

In an instant Drago was on him, seizing both his shoulders. "Do as I say, Zared. For the gods' sakes, *do you want her to realize that you have seen her like this*?"

Zared stared. "I never thought . . . I didn't . . ."

"She might forgive the fact that Faraday and I have seen her," Drago said more quietly. "But she will never, *never*, forgive you the sight of her in this condition."

"Help her, Drago. Help her," he begged.

Drago nodded, and gently shoved Zared out the door. "Go. Do as I ask."

He shut the door, paused to listen to Zared's footsteps shuffle down the corridor, and turned back into the room.

"We begin," he said.

He stood silent for a few minutes, his head down, his left

hand gently opening and closing about the staff, ignoring the shriekings and slaverings of the creature lunging two paces away at the end of its chain.

Faraday watched him silently, understanding that Drago was communicating with the staff in his hand.

Katie? Faraday dropped her eyes, and placed a gentle hand on the girl's head. Katie tilted her eyes up briefly, and smiled, but quickly returned her gaze to the scene before her.

Faraday looked back to Drago. She understood that she was about to witness a miracle unparalleled. A miracle not only in Leagh's own rebirth, and her redemption from the many-fingered madnesses of the TimeKeeper Demons, but in the rebirth of true hope for Tencendor.

For the first time Faraday understood why Tencendor had to die. It was the only way it could be reborn into its true nature. Drago looked up, catching her eyes, and perhaps even understanding a little of what she was thinking. He smiled, a movement that only just touched the corners of his mouth and eyes, but which, nevertheless, was rich with warmth and love.

Warmth and love for everyone, Faraday realized, not just for her.

Faraday could not help smiling back. She realized she also smiled with love, but for the moment she could not stop it. He was so extraordinary, and what he was about to do was so extraordinary, Faraday could not help but respond to his warmth.

She blinked, and the room had disappeared and she stood in a field of flowers. Drago still stood some paces from her, but here he wore nothing but a simple white linen cloth about his hips.

He held out his hand to her in the traditional Icarii gesture of seduction, but it was not empty. He held a single white lily.

"You will be," he said, "the first among lilies."

And he smiled.

Faraday's heart was thudding in her chest, and she could not tear her eyes away from his. There was nothing in his face of his father's arrogant confidence . . . nothing but that incredible warmth and tenderness, nothing but the promise of safety, and of the love she'd always been denied.

Faraday took a step through the flowers, and then she—

Two paces away the frightful thing that had once been Leagh snapped and drooled and dribbled thick urine down its thighs, and Faraday snapped out of her vision.

She blinked, disoriented, her heart still thudding. Drago was no longer looking at her, but considering Leagh.

"We will need to restrain her far more than she is now," Drago said, studying the lengthy chain attached to the iron spike in the center of the room.

He snapped his fingers at the lizard, who was sitting to one side of the door, and spoke to Faraday.

"Faraday? Will you take hold of Katie, and stand just here?"

The lizard ambled over, and Drago positioned him just in front of Faraday and Katie.

They were grouped directly in front of Leagh.

"Take this," Drago held out the staff to Faraday, who took it hesitantly, "and taunt her with it. Tease her. Keep her distracted."

"I cannot taunt her!" Faraday said.

"You must," Drago said gently. "I need to be able to wrap that chain about the spike, dragging her into the center of the room, and to do that," he paused, "with any degree of safety, I will need *you,* with Katie and the lizard, to distract her. Can you do that? The lizard will keep you safe."

"I am not worried about my safety," Faraday said quietly, her eyes on Leagh.

"I know that," Drago said. "Come, taunt her with the staff, and stay but one pace before her. She will see nothing else."

Taking a deep breath and steeling her nerves, Faraday pushed Katie halfway behind her skirts, then leaned forward over the lizard and struck the Leagh-creature a glancing blow across the cheek.

The creature screamed, and snatched wildly at the staff, which Faraday only barely managed to pull away in time.

The lizard shrieked as well, its crest rising up and down rapidly, and the creature went completely berserk, tearing at its chains, and flinging itself full forward, as if trying to stretch the metal links.

Drago moved quietly and smoothly about the side of the room until he was directly behind the creature, then he moved forward, step by careful step, until he was by the spike.

The creature backed up a pace, preparing itself for another lunge at the three tormentors before it, and Drago seized the chain and wrapped it twice about the spike. The creature lunged forward, and found itself brought up a pace earlier than it had expected.

It made no difference to the ferocity or single-mindedness of its attack, for the lizard and Faraday and the girl had also crept closer a pace, and the staff once more struck a glancing blow on the creature, this time across its back, drawing blood from one of its open sores.

Again and again the creature lunged, and each time the chain slackened slightly as it moved and Drago would wrap the links yet further about the spike.

Soon the creature's buttocks and heels were a bare pace away from Drago and the spike, and Drago motioned Faraday to further her efforts at distracting the beast. Again Faraday struck a glancing blow to the creature, and again, and then once more.

But on the third stroke the creature managed to seize the staff in its claws, and Faraday cried out as she felt herself being pulled forward.

Suddenly there was a flash of light. The creature screamed, and Faraday felt its grip on the staff lessen. She hauled it back, and seized Katie, pulling her out of harm's way as well.

The lizard, retracting its talons, also shuffled back, hissing and growling at the creature, who kept its eyes on him, although it had been frightened away from further attempts to reach the horrible light-wielding lizard.

Drago used the moment to secure the chain with the thong from the neck of the sack, then also retreated to a safe distance and rejoined Faraday.

"Did she . . . ?"

Faraday shook her head. "She did not touch me."

"Good. Faraday, will you wait by the wall for the moment?"

"Yes." Faraday hesitated. "Drago . . ."

"Yes?"

Faraday stared at him, wanting to say everything, but unable to say anything.

"Nothing," she said, and took the girl's hand and walked over to stand by the wall.

Drago faced the creature, almost completely restrained by the now short chain. He placed his hand on the lizard's head, and it sat down beside him, alternately looking up at Drago and over to the creature.

"Faraday," Drago said very quietly without looking at her, "what time of day is it?"

Her eyes flickered toward the window. They had come across the Lake during Sheol's midafternoon time, and had then spent at least two hours walking up through the palace and talking with Zared, Theod and Herme. "It lacks but an hour to dusk."

"Good," Drago said. "We are free of the miasma, and the Demons will not know what now we do."

He bent slightly, and the lizard raised its head to him. "Watch carefully," Drago told him.

Then he straightened, and sketched a symbol in the air. It was not accomplished with his usual speed and fluidity, but it was fast nevertheless, and Faraday was sure that if Drago wanted the lizard to learn it, he must surely repeat it several times.

But apparently not.

The lizard watched with its great black eyes, absorbing the symbol into their depths, and then it raised a languid foreclaw into the air and redrew the symbol.

With light.

Faraday gasped, and the child laughed delightedly.

The creature howled, and cowered.

Lines of light hung in the air before the lizard. It had drawn a symbol variously composed of circles and three-dimensional pyramids, the lines of both circles and pyramids interconnecting in two score places.

The symbol of light was large, perhaps the height of a man and the same dimension in width and depth.

"It is an enchantment!" Faraday said.

"Yes," Drago replied, not taking his eyes from the symbol. "An enchantment made visible.

"And," he placed his staff on the floor, "an enchantment with walls."

Without apparent fear, or even overdue caution, Drago reached out with both hands and seized the enchantment. It quivered lightly as it felt his grasp, but floated gently toward him as he pulled his arms back.

"Faraday?" Drago said. "Will you take hold of its other side?"

Faraday walked slowly about Drago, and the lizard—which had dropped to the floor and had its head resting incuriously on its forelegs—and took hold of the enchantment directly across from Drago.

It felt warm to her touch, and quivered softly with vibrant life.

She laughed, and Drago grinned at her wonder. "Lift it a little higher," he said, and together they raised it until their hands held it above their heads.

"Now, take a step back," Drago said, and as Faraday did this, so did he, and to Faraday's amazement, the enchantment stretched.

"And another," Drago said, and so they stepped yet further back until, under Drago's direction, they had stretched the enchantment to twice its former size.

Through all this the enchantment held shape and dimension, and the lines of light did not seem to lose any of their thickness or vibrancy. The lizard blinked, pleased with itself. Katie had sunk to the floor, eyes wide with marvel.

The creature had not stopped shrieking the entire time.

Under Drago's murmured instructions, Faraday helped him shift the enchantment until they held it high above the creature's head.

It was quiet with horror now, and cowered as close to the floor as it could get.

"Let it go," Drago murmured, and Faraday did so.

The enchantment trembled, then slowly sank.

The creature went completely wild, more than it had yet done. It howled and squealed, and threw itself about so violently that Faraday was sure it would manage to break every bone in its body.

"Drago!" she cried.

"Wait," he said. "It will be all right soon."

And so it was, for within the space of two breaths the enchantment settled to the floor, pinning the creature inside its cage of light. The enchantment had now taken a circular three-dimensional form, and it rose in a series of spheres and pyramids above the creature.

The creature was now still and completely silent.

Faraday looked over the rising, pulsing lines of light toward Drago, her eyes wide with questions.

He chose not to answer them.

Instead, Drago slowly walked about the enchantment, as if considering it. As he walked, he reached inside his sack, and drew out the mixing bowl he'd taken from Sigholt's kitchens.

Faraday's eyes, if possible, grew even wider. How had he gotten that bowl inside that tiny sack?

Balancing the bowl in the crook of his left arm, Drago— still walking slowly about the enchantment—reached inside the sack again, and drew out what appeared to be tiny pinches of dust, which he sprinkled into the bowl.

Faraday stepped back as he approached her, giving him room to move freely, and just watched.

Again and again Drago's hand dipped into the sack, always drawing forth what appeared to be nothing but pinches of dust. He continued to walk about the circle of the enchantment, his eyes never leaving it, until he had completed his circuit. Then he stopped, and stared into the bowl. His face was puzzled, as if he'd forgotten the recipe.

"You need this," Katie said, standing up and walking over to the lizard. She squatted down beside him, and gently lifted one of his claws.

Then, with a swift, stunning movement, she plunged the tip of the claw into the pad of her forefinger.

Faraday cried out softly and started forward, but Drago waved her away. Faraday halted, undecided, looking between first Katie, and then Drago.

A fat, bright scarlet drop of blood glistened on the end of Katie's forefinger. Slowly, and with the utmost caution and concentration, Katie rose and stepped over to Drago.

Once there, she slowly raised her hand, careful not to spill the drop of blood prematurely, and then, once it hung over the bowl, let it roll down into the mixture with an audible sigh of relief.

Drago stared at her with a mixture of awe and sadness, finally understanding what—or who—she was.

"I thank you," he whispered, and bowed slightly.

"Nay," Katie said, "it is I who will one day thank you."

She put her finger into her mouth and sucked it, and the wisdom in her eyes faded back to that of childish curiosity.

Drago put the bowl on the floor, and retrieved his staff. Standing very straight, he dipped the end of the staff into the bowl and began to blend the mixture.

His face was intense, every movement deliberate and almost part of a carefully rehearsed dance.

Faraday blinked. Her senses were overwhelmed by the scent and sight of a vast plain of wildflowers, dancing in the wind even as they reached for the sun. Birds and butterflies dipped and swayed above the waving sea of blossom, and Faraday thought that in the distance she could hear the crashing waves of the ocean.

All she wanted to do was to run through the flowers, run until she was exhausted, and then collapse wondrous within their midst, letting the beauty envelop her . . .

She blinked again. The flowers had vanished, and the room was before her.

Both Katie and the lizard were staring at her, but Faraday did not see them.

All she saw was Drago . . . Drago now dipping the staff into the bowl, now withdrawing it glistening with a liquid Faraday could not identify, and tracing the end of the staff over the lines of the enchantment.

Everywhere the glistening tip of the staff traced, flowed color—every color of the rainbow, until the entire enchantment glimmered and shifted with a thousand shades and permutations of color. Overcome with its beauty, and the sheer beauty of Drago's enchantment—had StarDrifter or Axis *ever* created anything so wondrous?—Faraday's eyes glistened with tears.

Drago had finished with the enchantment. He raised the staff one more time, dipped it into the bowl, and then sharply struck the floor with its tip three times, and then twice more.

The enchantment collapsed inward. It fell over the crea-

ture, covering every pore of its skin, and then . . . then it
slowly sank in.

Faraday could understand it in no other terms. For an instant she'd thought the enchantment was evaporating, but then
she'd realized it was actually sinking through the pores of the
skin of—

Leagh twisted over, and gave a hoarse cry of horror. She
wrapped her arms about herself, and curled up to hide her
nakedness.

"Faraday!" Drago said, and Faraday swiftly knelt beside
Leagh, gathering the woman into her arms, and hiding her
face against her shoulder so that she should never see the
pitiful state in which she'd been living.

Drago strode over to the door that connected to the adjoining chamber, ordered out Zared and the two waiting women
who stood there, and grabbed a blanket from the bed.

He returned, and helped Faraday to wrap Leagh in the
blanket.

"Leave us," Faraday said quietly, her arms tight about
Leagh, and Drago nodded.

He retrieved the bowl, slipping it back into the sack where
it apparently disappeared without trace, picked up the staff,
took Katie by the hand, and prodded the lizard with the toe of
his boot.

The outer door swung closed behind them, and Faraday
lowered her face into Leagh's filthy hair and wept.

56

The Field of Flowers

Faraday sat there a very long time, holding the shivering
woman in her arms, and weeping.

Then she sniffed, wiped away her tears with the back of
her hand, and resolved to cry no more this day—this was a
day for joy, not grief.

It took some effort for Faraday to persuade Leagh to her

feet, and even then she was weak and hardly able to walk. Finally, as they stumbled toward the adjoining chamber, Leagh found her voice.

"Askam," she croaked.

"He betrayed you," Faraday said, "and brought you to this."

"Why?" Leagh whispered. "Why, why, why?"

Faraday did not know if she was asking why Askam had done this to her, or why she'd sunk to such a dreadful physical state. Having considered, and not known what to answer to either question, Faraday chose instead to remain silent, guiding Leagh toward a great tub of water that stood steaming before a leaping fire.

"Oh, ye gods!" Leagh wept as Faraday let the blanket fall to the floor, and she saw the full extent of her depravation in the light of the fire. "How . . . did I get to such a state . . . what . . . Faraday? Why are you here? Where is Zared? Why am I—"

"Hush," Faraday murmured. "One of the first things my mother taught me was that no one can fully understand any answers when the first thing they need is a bath, a meal, and then some rest."

"But—"

"Lift this foot. Good. Now the other one."

Leagh gasped as she sank down into the hot water, partly in shock, partly in pain, as the heat bit into her scratches and sores, and part in sheer wonderment at the comforting embrace of the water.

Faraday rinsed out a cloth, lathered it with soap, and washed Leagh down, wondering wryly if she was to be condemned—through *all* her lives—to repeating the actions of her first. Here she knelt by the tub washing a pregnant Leagh as she had once sat on Azhure's bed and washed her, feeling the malevolence that even then had emanated from the belly swollen with the infant Drago.

Now? Faraday's hand slid gently over Leagh's belly, feeling the life within. What had happened to it? Had *it* been reborn, redeemed, as Leagh had?

Or . . . ?

Leagh's hand closed over hers, pressing it against her belly.

"Tell me," she said, staring at Faraday.

Faraday hesitated, then felt for the baby with all the power she possessed, bending her head down so that the ends of her chestnut hair trailed through the bath water.

Suddenly Faraday snatched her hand away and rocked back on her heels, covering her face with her hands. And then, despite her resolve of only a few minutes before, she burst into tears.

"Faraday?" Leagh cried in panic.

But Faraday slowly lowered her hands, and Leagh saw that she was crying in joy.

"Did you know," Faraday said, "that you have a field of flowers growing within you?"

Deep in the hours after midnight Theod and Herme sat at the small table, a jug of rich ale between them. Several empty jugs lay on the floor.

"What's happening?" Theod asked a fortieth time. His voice was hoarse, halfway between anger and desperation.

What was happening?

What?

A footstep, and both men jerked their heads up.

Zared.

He looked between the two of them, then his gaze settled on Theod.

"My friend," he said in a voice very gentle. "I think this is something you should see."

Theod stood up, stumbled, knocked the chair over, then gained enough control of himself to walk in a reasonably steady fashion over to Zared. Zared took his arm, and turned him for the door.

"May I?" Herme stood also, and Zared looked over his shoulder.

"Yes. If I thought it possible, I would ask the entire city to see this wonder . . . but I think it is a feat that perchance they will see soon enough anyway."

Theod stood before Leagh's bed, staring, not believing, not *daring* to believe. His shoulders shook, as if he was about to sob, but he gained control of himself with visible effort and stared toward Drago, standing in semishadow by the fireplace.

"Is she . . . can she . . ."

It was Leagh, rather than Drago, who answered. "I is," she said, and smiled, holding out her hand for Theod. "And I am. Theod, will you not come sit beside me?"

She was wan, and patently exhausted, but it was Leagh who sat there propped against the cliff of snowy pillows, not some demented fiend, and although Theod allowed Zared to guide him to Leagh's side, and sit him down, and even though Leagh took his hand, still Theod could not allow himself to believe . . . to believe . . .

Drago stepped forward into the light, although the leaping fire still sent shadows chasing across his face.

"Leagh has returned from death, Theod. And what I did for her, I can in some measure do for all those who screech and wail and crawl through the dirt."

Theod opened his mouth, then his face crumpled, and he sobbed. Faraday sank down on the bed behind him, and wrapped her arms around his shoulders, leaning his head against hers.

"There will be further miracles," she whispered. "Never doubt that."

There was a silence then, save for the crackling of the fire.

Leagh looked about the room. At her husband, whose haggard face revealed the extent of his worry for her. At Faraday and Theod sitting so close beside her on the bed, Theod weeping out his grief with silent tears that wracked his body. At Earl Herme who stood pale-faced just inside the door, but with a gleam in his eyes that Leagh had never seen there previously.

The girl who had come in with Drago earlier, the strange waif called Katie, sat by the fire, her face downcast, alternately scratching and then smoothing the feathers of the lizard.

Then Leagh turned her face and looked at Drago.

He was staring directly at her, his face showing the marks of exhaustion, as if he had recently been through some trial. Nevertheless, his eyes were soft, and he smiled a little at her regard. His legs were slightly apart, and his hands were folded before him, and as she watched he moved one of them slightly, as if he were . . .

. . . *as if he were tossing a flower into a field of flowers!*

As Faraday had been overwhelmed by a vision of a field of flowers, so also had Leagh been visited by a vision which, though similar to Faraday's, was also different.

She had been in a dark, dark forest, the trees completely stripped of leaves so that only dead limbs reached out. There was no sun, only a thick gray fog. The ground was thigh-deep mud, and this mud simmered about her legs; hot, horrid, sucking her down.

She was in a land called hopelessness.

Then a voice had called out. It had called a name, although she did not know she had a name. She looked up, and there, leaning comfortably in the fork of a nearby tree, was a man. A wonderful, glorious man, with a strong face and copper hair, and such dark violet eyes that they seemed to absorb all the gray fog into them. He was dressed only in a white linen hip wrap, as if he were about to leap into a bathhouse pool, but at his hip swung a golden sword, with an oddly shaped hilt that she could not immediately discern.

A fairy sword, and yet she sensed that it was sharp and deadly, and somehow hungry.

A movement caught her eye, and she looked away from the sword.

In his hand he had held a large, pure white lily.

"This," he said, holding out the lily to her, "represents your life."

And she had cried, for the lily was so beautiful, its scent was so extraordinary, that she knew it could not possibly represent her life.

"Please take me home," she had whispered.

With a sweeping, graceful gesture, he'd thrown the lily out into the mud.

And suddenly there was no mud, and no fog, and no bare dead trees.

She was standing in a field of wildflowers, an infinite field under an infinite blue sky.

And she had felt his hand in hers. "Welcome home," he said.

So now Leagh looked at Drago, and her eyes filled with tears, and his smile deepened very, very slightly, and she knew that he, too, was remembering the field of flowers.

"You are a magician," she said quietly, and at her words, Faraday lifted her head and looked at Drago herself.

"And you?" Drago asked Leagh.

"I am different," she answered and realized that, indeed, she *was* different.

She had now taken her place within the infinite field of flowers.

In that moment, Leagh had her first, true understanding of what Drago would do to Tencendor, and she gasped, and looked away, shaken beyond belief.

"The night beyond the next we will go to the Western Ranges," Drago said into the very quiet room. "All of us in this room, save Herme who will stay to watch Carlon."

Leagh looked at Faraday, and then both women looked at Katie.

"We will go to sow flowers," the girl said, and laughed.

57

Gorken Pass

Axis, Azhure and Caelum left Star Finger immediately after Caelum had destroyed the Hawkchild—and very nearly himself.

"There is no point sitting here and practicing, or brooding," Caelum had said, unusually assertive and almost confident. "The TimeKeepers quest, and we but waste away here in this mound of rock and ice."

"Where?" Axis had said, accepting Caelum's leadership.

"Grail Lake," Caelum replied, and had picked up the Enchanted Songbook and walked from the chamber.

It felt strange . . . no, worse than "strange," that she should set out on such a dangerous and desperate mission with nothing more to fight with than an ordinary bow. She had asked Caelum if they could detour via Sigholt to collect the Wolven, but he had shaken his head and said that it would be useless in the battle before them. But it was not only the lack of the Wolven that made Azhure feel so naked. As she had lost the Wolven, so also had the Alaunt gone. Azhure kept looking over her shoulder, but they were never there.

Where were they? Where? They'd disappeared in the hour or so after Drago had gone.

Had they gone with him?

Azhure shook her head, struggling to reconcile within herself the years of ingrained distrust she had for Drago, and that instant of overwhelming love she'd felt from him and for him when he'd looked into her eyes in that dank basement.

Something was going on . . . something was changing— but what?

Who was Drago?

Azhure gnawed at the thought as she might worry at a troublesome tooth.

Had she *ever* hated him, even after he'd proved so foul as to ally himself with Gorgrael against Caelum? If she had hated him, and thought him completely beyond redemption, then surely she would have killed him atop Sigholt, rather than just reversing his blood order. Wouldn't she?

What had stopped her doing that? Hope, or maternal blindness?

Or, some other guiding hand?

Caelum had loathed Drago since their babyhood, and had feared him even more than he'd hated him. Yet now, Caelum and Drago seemed to have reconciled. Why? How?

Axis had told her of Caelum's insistence that should he die, then the Enchanted Songbook must go to Drago.

"DragonStar," Azhure whispered into the cold northerly

that whipped her words away over the mountains. "Could you still be there?"

Is that why the Alaunt had gone to him?

Then a thought so devastating hit Azhure that she stopped dead in her tracks, staring unseeing at Axis and Caelum striding away before her.

Like Caelum, Drago had also been conceived wrapped in the magic of Beltide night. The infant DragonStar, so powerful, so *amazingly* powerful, had always claimed to be StarSon. No one had believed him. No one, because they were always blinded by the fact Caelum had been born first. Because Caelum had been so loved.

The Maze Gate had named the Crusader as the StarSon a year after Caelum's birth. They had thought it was because it was then sure that Caelum was the Crusader, and it was then that Axis named him StarSon. *But was it, in fact, because DragonStar had just been born?*

"Stars, Caelum," she murmured, her eyes thick with tears. "Is that why you now work in tandem with Drago? Why you insist that the book go to Drago?"

Was it . . . was it because Caelum expected to die? What *was* the understanding between Caelum and Drago?

"Mother?" Caelum had walked back to her, and now stood with an expression of such complete love on his own face that Azhure almost broke down completely.

No! No! Not Caelum! No! Not him!

He lifted a hand and gently wiped a tear from her cheek. "Mother, whatever I do now, I do with such joy in my soul, and such love for you and my father, and this land which we all strive for, that you do not need to cry. Please."

Azhure lowered her head. When she finally raised it again, her eyes were bright with naked pain . . . and acceptance.

She looked past Caelum to where Axis waited impatiently for them. "Does . . . does he realize?"

"No."

"Dear Stars above, Caelum, *I* cannot tell him!"

Caelum stepped forward and enveloped Azhure in a tight hug. "Azhure," he muttered, "you and Axis have another son worth as much love as you expend on this one. Tell him that, if nothing else."

"Caelum?" Axis called. "Azhure? What is it?"

"How can I ever tell him that the son he loves so much is going to—"

Caelum stopped her mouth with a hand. "Axis will need to acknowledge Drago one day, Azhure, he *must!*"

"But—"

"I have welcomed him into the House of the Stars, but Axis and you must also do the same, and Axis must also acknowledge him as—"

"I know, I know."

She pulled out of Caelum's embrace. "No one will ever take your place in my heart," she said. "No one."

And she pushed past him and walked down the narrow trail toward Axis.

Late that afternoon, as dusk approached, they camped in one of the final gullies of the western Icescarp Alps. In the morning they would enter Gorken Pass.

"Gorken Pass," Axis said softly as they sat within a small cave, its mouth blocked by a fire. "At Gorken Pass I had thought to have freed Tencendor once and for all."

No one said anything to that, but they all remembered the strange battle that had been fought in the pass. The tens of thousands of Gorgrael's Ice Worms and Skraelings, the Gryphon lurking among the rocks, and all defeated by Azhure and the trees of the great forests to the east.

It had brought a pause, nothing else.

Axis sighed, and stirred the fire. "It will be a long journey south, Caelum. How can we reach Carlon in time?"

"If we merely walk south, then we never will," Caelum said. "So we will continue west toward Seal Bay. Surely there must still be a sealer or two waiting out the winter there. We can voyage south on the Andeis in one of their whalers. They are well equipped to withstand the fiercest storms."

Axis shared a glance with Azhure, and frowned slightly when she dropped her eyes from his.

"The sealers rarely linger on the coast at this time of year, Caelum," he said, looking back to his son. "They see out the winter on Straum Island and do not come back until late spring."

"Then we can light a beacon fire," Caelum said, unperturbed by his father's pessimism. "One or two will surely sail across the bay to sate their curiosity."

"Surely it would be best to turn south and seize what horses we can find running loose in Ichtar—"

"No," Caelum said. "We will go to Seal Bay."

And with that he rolled himself up in his blanket and said no more.

Axis looked again at Azhure. She was curiously silent, and avoided his eyes. He shifted around the fire toward her, and smoothed the glossy black hair away from the face he loved so much.

"What have I said to annoy you?"

She shook her head slightly. "Nothing."

Axis' mouth quirked. "You forget how well I know you. *Something* is bothering you . . . frightening you."

She finally lifted her dark blue eyes and regarded him directly. "And nothing is bothering you?"

He hesitated. "Azhure, I had never thought to utter this, but I fear I might be growing too old for adventure. I hope," his eyes flickered across the fire to where Caelum lay rolled up in shadow, "I hope my son can fully take his place as the hope of this land."

"I am sure our son will do so," Azhure said, and suddenly hope suffused her, leaving her wide-eyed. Was that all it took, she thought? Belief in him? *Was that all it took?*

"Azhure?" Axis murmured.

She smiled. "Nothing. For now. No more words. Not now."

He smiled, moving his arm to encircle her shoulders, and he lowered his face to hers. There were some things Axis did not think he would ever grow too old for.

In the morning, they stepped down into Gorken Pass and met what, perhaps, Caelum had all along suspected they might.

Urbeth sat in the snow, hind legs splayed before her for balance, leaning back on one forepaw and cleaning the tufts of fur between the black pads of the other.

Her black eyes flickered at them as they stopped at the

sight of her, then she waved them over. Behind her was a great barrel of what appeared to be fresh fish.

"It has been a long time, Axis, lost God of Song, and Azhure, lost Goddess of the Moon."

She dipped her head at Caelum, but did not speak to him.

"And a fair morning to you, Urbeth, strange bear of the north," Axis said, a hard edge to his voice. "Have the Time-Keeper Demons driven you out of your den in the ice-pack?"

"My cubs have all grown and now seek their own way in the world," Urbeth said. "I have nothing to interest me in the ice anymore."

Azhure glanced up the Gorken Pass. "How do the Ravensbund fare, Urbeth? Have you seen them?"

Urbeth heaved a melodramatic sigh and rolled her eyes. "When the Demons struck I had every expectation they would appear at the edge of the ice-pack once more," she said, referring to the time when Gorgrael's Skraelings had driven the Ravensbundmen onto the ice where Urbeth had been forced to protect them by changing them into trees. "But for once they found their own methods of dealing with the bad hours," she continued. "They hide in their holes, and chafe at the fact they can no longer ride the ice-pack in search of seal."

"Ah," Azhure said. "The holes." The Ravensbund chief, Ho'Demi, had once shown her and Axis the holes: gigantic subsidences in the earth that sheltered warm springs, game and shelter.

"What do you here, Urbeth?" Caelum finally asked.

"Well," Urbeth said slowly, and stood up, shaking herself so rigorously the other three had to stand back. "It came to my attention that your good self, as your parents, seemed to be intent on getting to Carlon. And yet, pitiful creatures that you be without your powers, I thought to myself, how do they expect to manage it?"

"What do *you* propose?" Axis snapped.

Azhure laid a hand on his arm, smiling apologetically at Urbeth.

Urbeth shrugged in her own ursine way, and did not seem perturbed. Indeed, she seemed mildly amused.

"Axis, Azhure, the time has come to say good-bye to your son."

"No!" Azhure sounded terrified, and Axis took her arm, surprised at her emotion, even though he, too, was angry with the bear.

"We will go south with him," he said.

Urbeth shook her head, and although she kept her voice pleasant, her eyes were hard.

"This Caelum needs to do on his own. Let him go."

Caelum turned to his parents. "She is right. I do need to do this on my own."

"Caelum—" Azhure said, her voice breaking, and held out a trembling hand.

Caelum ignored the hand and enveloped her in a huge hug. "Thank you," he whispered. "For everything. For my life, and for your love and belief in me."

She clung desperately to him, weeping inconsolably, and Caelum had to lean back and push her slightly away so he could look into her eyes.

"Let me go, Azhure," he whispered. "It is time."

Azhure didn't know what to do, what to say. What *could* she say? And how could she just let him go and turn away? How could she?

"Azhure," Urbeth said. "Let him go."

Azhure wrenched herself out of Caelum's hands and stumbled a few paces away.

Axis stared at her, distraught by her emotion but not understanding its full depth, then embraced Caelum himself. "Stars go with you," he whispered, then stood back.

Caelum reached out and touched his father's face one last time, wishing that he could have been the son Axis had wanted.

"Remember what you promised, Father."

Axis nodded. "But Drago will not need it."

Caelum let that go. He half-smiled, lifted his hand again as if he wanted to touch his father just one more time, then let it drop. Axis nodded at him, then took Azhure gently by the hand.

"Come, my love," he murmured. "Come home with me."

The last Caelum saw of his parents were their backs disappearing into the wind and snow.

"Well?" he asked of Urbeth, "what now?"

"Now? Why, we sit by the fire and wait."

Caelum narrowed his eyes. "What fire? Wait for what?"

"*This* fire," and suddenly there was a fire burning several paces distant. "And we wait for Drago. He will let us know when the time is right."

Caelum hesitated, then he shrugged and walked over to the fire. "I am sure we will have much to discuss while we wait," he said.

"That we will," Urbeth said. "That we will."

She paused. "Would you like a fish?"

58

The Deep Blue Cloak of Betrayal

Faraday left Leagh, put Katie to bed, and wandered the corridors of the palace. It was a strange night, and a strange walk, and Faraday found herself in the clutches of some strange sensation—not of the Demons' doing, but of Fate's. She wandered the corridors, plunging from the extreme of hope and love to the nadir of despair and bitterness as she felt Fate's cold hand close about her. She loved Drago, but felt trapped by that love, and felt she would be lost if she ever admitted her love to Drago, let alone gave herself to him.

And, oh Gods, how she wanted to give herself to him, to tell him she loved him! Yet, if she did that, she would die. Faraday understood that very completely now . . . she'd understood it the moment she'd walked into this long abandoned chamber.

Very many things had become clear to her as she'd wandered into this chamber.

It was empty, save for a great wardrobe that stood against a far wall. The wardrobe stared at her, screaming at her to come closer, and fling open its doors.

It had a gift for her.

Faraday stared, then helplessly drifted over and flung open the doors. The wardrobe contained a deep blue cloak and nothing else. The deep blue cloak she'd worn when she'd gone to Axis the day he'd killed Borneheld.

She trembled violently, and stood back, wrapping her arms about herself.

Every muscle of her body, every nerve ending, screamed at her to now slip off her clothes until she stood white naked, save for the mantle of her desire. And then? Then to lift the cloak from its hook and slip it about her shoulders, tying the tassels at her throat, and walk the corridors of this palace until she came to Drago's chamber.

And when she slipped silently inside the door, Faraday knew what she would find.

Drago, asleep in a chair before the fire.

Thus had she found Axis, and thus had she given her body and love to Axis.

Faraday bent over, screwing her eyes shut, trying to find the courage to resist the call of both body and cloak.

Something, *damned fate*, now needed her to give herself to Drago as she'd once given herself to Axis. And what then . . . what then? Would he betray her love and need as Axis had done?

In the past weeks she'd found herself being dragged to Gorkenfort, and now to Carlon, retracing the steps of her previous life. Would she continue to retrace her previous mistakes and naiveties until she stood held in the talons of some foul Demon in some misbegotten chamber, watching Drago intent on saving Tencendor and not her?

Was this what Noah has re-created her for? Was this her fate through life after life after damned, accursed life?

"No!" she cried and slammed shut the doors of the wardrobe. She would deny her love for Drago, deny her need for him, and thus save her life.

"No, no, no!" she whispered now, and tore herself away from the wardrobe. "Never! This land must find itself another way to save it than *my* blood!"

For doubtless this land would need blood to save it.

"And always *my* blood," she said. "Always mine. *Why?*"

She had to get out of this chamber. It was not the one she'd used when she'd gone from being Borneheld's wife to Axis' whore within the space of a few hours, nor even the same palace, but it was a prison nevertheless . . . and the blue cloak had managed to find its way here.

Faraday took a deep breath, tucked a few stray tendrils of hair behind her ears, and wiped the wetness from her eyes.

It was night, and Demon-free, and even though the wind blew cold, a walk on the parapets might clear her mind enough to resist all the temptations and siren calls of fate.

But even so, Faraday's feet slowed outside Drago's chamber, and she paused to stare at his door for long minutes before she could force herself past.

Gods, but she wanted him. She loved and adored him as she had never adored Axis. Drago had a gentleness that his father had never had, and a depth of compassion that exceeded anything his parents had. Did he get that from Rivkah? Faraday could not think where else.

"Ah! Stop these thoughts!" she chided herself, and forced her feet briskly toward the stairs leading to the parapets. "Find yourself a peasant with no destiny and be content!"

At that she had to smile. Her? Wrapped contentedly in some burly, work-odored peasant's arms in a straw and lice-filled bed? And then her sense of humor truly resurrected itself, and Faraday laughed aloud at her own thoughts. *That* was her mother Merlion in her!

She opened the door to the parapets and breathed in the air gratefully, still smiling at what Merlion would have made of her daughter's thoughts on men and love. Sometimes Faraday pondered at the absurdity that her mother had ever submitted to the whole sweaty, thrusting business of love . . . but she must have done . . . at least once . . . unless her father got her so drunk one night she slept through the entire distasteful procedure.

Faraday giggled, and clapped a hand to her mouth to stifle her mirth. What could Merlion have thought when her belly began to swell with child? That a roving dark incubus had impregnated her during some nightmare?

Faraday's giggles increased, and she walked over to the stone walls to stare at the sight of Carlon spread out below the palace. Gods! She had to stop this line of thought!

"Why so merry, Faraday?" a soft voice said behind her, and she spun about, sobering into bright anger.

"What are you doing here!" she snapped.

Drago stopped, surprised by her tone. Hadn't they come to some workable arrangement? "I heard you pass my chamber," he said, "and I thought that I would—"

"Would *what*? Thought that you would open the door and seize me and drag me to your bed? Is that what you—"

"Stop it!" Now he, too, was angry. "For the gods' sakes, Faraday! What is the matter with you? I only wanted to speak with you."

Her face tightened, and she turned back to the view. "I only want to be left alone."

"Faraday." Drago's voice had softened. "I would never force myself on you. You have *very* clearly stated you do not want me."

"SunSoar love forces itself everywhere," she said bitterly. "Your father would not take 'No' as a suitable response. How can you?"

Drago risked stepping closer to her. He put out a hand, thinking to touch her shoulder, then thought better of it. "What is wrong?"

She turned back to him, leaning against the parapet, her face tilted up to his. "Did you know that earlier I was remembering Axis?"

"Is that why you were laughing?"

"I was recalling the night that I came to him here. The night I went to his bed for the first time. Although," she paused, "one strictly cannot call the hearth rug a bed, can one?"

Drago's face tightened, but he did not speak.

"What do you think of that, Drago? Did you realize that the first time I lay with your father it was here in Carlon? Did you know that, in the very chamber you now occupy, I spent many *long* nights with your father?"

"Would you like to give me a thrust by thrust description?" he snapped. "Would that appease your need to hurt me? To push me away?"

Faraday averted her face, angry with herself, but more so with him. Why was he here? *Why?*

Drago suddenly reached out and grabbed her to him, pressing her against his body. "Damn you!" he whispered. "I have traveled through the very stars to return to you. Do I deserve this much hatred?"

She tensed, her hands on his chest. "You journeyed back through the stars in your desperate need to redeem yourself to

Tencendor, not for me. Is it not Tencendor you should be forcing to your bed?"

"Curse you, Faraday!" Drago cried, and let her go. "Why do you stay with me if you hate me this much?"

"Because I promised Noah I would be your friend," she said. "And that is the only reason."

Drago stared at her a long searching minute before he replied. "I do not believe you. How hard did you have to fight with yourself, Faraday, not to come to that well-remembered chamber again tonight?"

"And how much do you wonder," she countered, "whose name I would have had ringing through my mind as I let you love me? Whose shoulders I would feel under my hands? Whose mouth I wanted to feel on mine before all others?"

"All stars damn you," Drago said weakly. "Why won't you accept love when it is given you freely? I have no paramour hiding in Spiredore across the Lake. No lover awaiting me in some secret bed. I would be yours, and yours only."

"No." Faraday shook her head slowly back and forth, and her eyes glistened with tears. "You lie. You have a paramour and a lover and one you are destined to betray me for."

"Oh, for the gods—"

"If I let you love me, if I let *me* love you, then I would condemn myself to the same fate I suffered at Axis' hands."

"Who would I betray you for, Faraday?" he asked softly. "*Who*, dammit?"

She stared at him. "You would betray me for Tencendor."

And then she pushed roughly past him and was gone.

59

A Fate Deserved?

They had come directly south, moving through the north-western portion of the ranges where the forest had not stretched so they could conserve power rather than expend it fighting the trees.

The trees could wait. Their time for destruction had not yet come.

The four Demons who were left were close to the maximum power they could achieve without Qeteb to aid them. They had drunk deeply of the souls available in Tencendor, and had deepened their own abilities, but until Qeteb walked beside them, snarling with the laughter of life, they were necessarily contained.

As Rox's death had demonstrated.

If Qeteb had been there, the struggle would have ended somewhat differently.

As they rode, each of the Demons' eyes drifted to the boy riding beside StarLaughter. Her get would provide the flesh and blood for their reborn savior, but not the reborn son she craved. StarLaughter somehow believed—foolish birdwoman—that it was her son DragonStar who would be reborn with the power of Qeteb . . . but the Demons knew a little differently.

There was no DragonStar SunSoar, son of StarLaughter and WolfStar. There was only ever a scrap of flesh that was suitable to be preserved until the time was ripe for it to be suffused with the life parts so horribly stolen by the Enemy. What StarLaughter had given birth to in the extremity of her murderous plunge through the Star Gate had been a mangled, dead clump of bloody flesh. Nothing else.

StarLaughter had clung to that scrap as she drifted through the stars, her madness and desire for revenge giving it form and life where there had been none.

None . . . until she'd come to the attention of the Demons. Not only was StarLaughter, as all the children who cried out for revenge with her, a link to the land the Demons needed to get to, she'd had the lump of lifeless and malleable flesh the Demons needed.

A house for Qeteb.

And so they'd given it back some form for the poor woman to cuddle, and so she had clutched it to her breast for four thousand useless years.

StarLaughter was completely, utterly, mad, and the Demons were not quite sure what to do with her once Qeteb was risen and the need for such tools negated. The Hawkchilds could still be useful—but StarLaughter?

Qeteb could decide, the Demons mutually, and silently, agreed. If he wanted he could eat her, if he wanted he could fuck her. They truly didn't care.

Of Drago they thought occasionally, but they did not waste any worry on him. He should not have survived the leap through the Star Gate, but he had. They should have killed him when they had the chance, but he'd done nothing with his un-expected life—no doubt he was now secreted in some cave dribbling resentment—and could be disposed of later, like StarLaughter, as Qeteb saw fit.

As *everything* would eventually be disposed of as Qeteb worked out his purpose.

For her part, StarLaughter was just as content as the Demons were. She knew the Demons regarded her son from time to time as they rode, and she knew that sometimes their unreadable eyes were cast in her direction. But that only made StarLaughter happy. She did not trust them, and in time her son would dispose of them as he saw fit.

StarLaughter was very, very sure of that.

Now, she stopped.

"He is here, *close!*" she hissed.

They had halted their black creatures—no longer even vaguely resembling horses, but rather immense black worms with stumpy legs—a few hundred paces from the western rim of Fernbrake crater.

"What?" Sheol said vaguely. She, and the Demons, were concentrating on the still-hidden Lake. There was something there . . . not quite right.

"WolfStar!" StarLaughter said, and half-turned her creature so that it faced south. "So close!" StarLaughter clenched a fist and struck her own breast. "I feel him. *Here!*"

Sheol looked at her fellow Demons. WolfStar? And with him . . . *her?*

That other lump of flesh could be more useful than they'd originally planned now that Rox was no more.

"Where?" Sheol said, far more interested now.

StarLaughter pointed. "Through there."

Through the forest. The Demons vacillated.

"Not far," StarLaughter said. "But a few minutes walk."
She paused. "Might that be too much for you?"

"We can afford a few minutes," Sheol said evenly, although she longed to tear StarLaughter to shreds. "Will you
lead the way?"

They abandoned their creatures, leaving them to snout
through the dirt for insects, and walked down the path Star-
Laughter indicated. The trees closed in about them, and whispers and eyes followed their steps.

Sheol's lips, as those of her fellows, curled in a silent snarl,
and the trees retreated slightly.

StarLaughter slowed, and she raised a hand to caution the
Demons. Then she lowered it and pointed into a small glade
ahead. *Here.*

The Demons nodded, and crowded at her shoulder to see
for themselves.

An enchantment! Mot cried through their minds. *He has
been jailed beneath an enchantment!*

Before them WolfStar sat rigid, his back to them, beneath
a glowing emerald dome. Several guards, Avar men, were
spaced about the glade. They did not realize the presence
lurking just beyond the first shadows of the bushes.

Do you recognize the enchantment? Sheol asked in Star-
Laughter's mind.

It is of the trees and earth, StarLaughter replied. *Easily
broken by such as you.*

Sheol again resisted the urge to reach out and slice the birdwoman to shreds—by the darkness itself, she had almost outlived her usefulness!—and looked more carefully about the
clearing.

I cannot see her, she said.

Who? StarLaughter asked.

There was an instant's pause as all four Demons resisted
the overwhelming urge to flay her, then . . .

The girl-child he had with him, Sheol said.

Ah, StarLaughter thought, *the one he betrayed me for.
Well, no doubt I can wreak my revenge on her as well. Wolf-
Star must know where she is.*

The Demons silently agreed.

We will remove the enchantment, Mot said, *and those who guard him.*

First . . . the men. Sheol opened her mouth, and her teeth lengthened and curved.

Her eyes glittered, and then changed, becoming dark fluid that roiled about in their orbits.

Her skin paled to a desperate whiteness.

The three Avar men, standing about the emerald dome, lifted their heads and stared toward the shrubbery where Sheol stood.

Their eyes were stricken . . . despairing.

WolfStar slowly raised his head and stared at the man nearest him. His back stiffened, and he turned his head very, very slightly, but otherwise made no reaction.

The Avar men were not armed, loathing any kind of weapon, but Sheol nevertheless had her way with them. One dug his fingers into his eyes, wriggling them in as far as he could go until he dropped dead to the ground.

Even then his fingers continued to worm.

Another took a great stone from the ground and beat himself over the skull with it.

When he, too, dropped dead to the ground, his hand continued to lift the rock and smash it against his skull until the crackle of wet bone gave way to the dull thud of pounded meal.

The third merely tore a wrist-thick branch from a sturdy bush and impaled himself on it. His body heaved up and down on the blood-soaked stick in a parody of love long after he had ceased to breathe.

WolfStar's head moved very slightly, enough so he could see all three Avar men from the corner of his eyes, but he otherwise still did not move.

He certainly did not look behind him.

Now the enchantment. Barzula waved a hand toward the glade, and a wind of immense power, and yet curiously without movement, lifted the emerald dome from WolfStar and smashed it against two nearby trees until it lay in useless shards amid the exposed roots.

WolfStar finally rose. He fastidiously dusted himself down, rearranged the feathers of one wing, and pulled one boot more comfortably along the close fit of his calf. His nonchalant behavior concealed horrified thoughts. The Demons! *Here!* WolfStar cursed his stupidity. He had allowed himself to be captured by Drago and held until the Demons had arrived.

What would happen if Niah fell into the Demons' control? What would they do to her?

What would they do *with* her?

Giving his breeches a final dust down, WolfStar slowly turned around.

If StarLaughter had expected him to show fear, she was disappointed. Even without power, WolfStar looked every bit as haughty, and every bit as malignant, as the day he'd hurled StarLaughter through the Star Gate.

"I would imagine," he said to the bushes before him, "that after four thousand years, StarLaughter, you have thought of the perfect curse to assail me with. Why so silent?"

She stepped forth, and her appearance—the bloodied and rent gown, the wild eyes—finally caused WolfStar to raise an eyebrow. For her part, StarLaughter could do little but stare at him. For so long she had hungered for this moment, for so long she had—

"At least you have managed to come back through the Star Gate," WolfStar said, "even if you have taken your sweet time about it. Have you brought me power, then, as I requested?"

Hate rippled across StarLaughter's face, and her hands jerked into fists. "*I* have power, WolfStar, and you have none. How does that feel? How does it *feel*, Talon-of-naught, to know you have no more sorcery than the smallest of worms?"

"Whatever I have done," WolfStar said quietly, his eyes not leaving her face, "I will go to my grave knowing I did not destroy this beloved land in order to—"

"But you were prepared to *kill* innocent children, weren't you, to gain power!"

"You were hardly innocent, StarLaughter. You lusted for power as much as I."

"Our *son* was innocent, and yet you murdered him," StarLaughter whispered. "Two hundred and more you sent to the grave to garner yet more power for yourself. Never think to judge *me* for what you would have done yourself had you the chance!"

"Our son was corrupted with your blood from the moment

he was conceived. Stars only know if I was the father, or if any one of the dozens of birdmen you coupled with behind my back planted him in you."

StarLaughter shrieked with rage. "I lay with no one but you! And Stars only know my experience of love at your hands was enough to dissuade me from anyone else's bed!"

WolfStar tensed, and his eyes blazed. Had he ever loved this woman? No! How could he have done!

"Your frigid character mirrored itself in your performance in bed," he said. "I sighed with relief when you said you were pregnant. I would as soon lie with a corpse as with you."

It was too much; all StarLaughter could think of was that he'd murdered her, and then betrayed her with another. Her face contorted with loathing, she summoned every last skerrick of power the Demons had given her and threw it all at WolfStar.

He gasped, and collapsed to one knee, doubling about the crippling agony that had but a moment ago been his belly.

"And so *I* suffered," she hissed, "giving birth to your son in the lifeless wastes beyond the Star Gate!"

"Is that the best you can do?" he rasped, raising his face to her. "The best? I would have expected more from—"

She strode the distance between them to kick him under the throat, but in the instant before her foot struck home WolfStar seized it and pulled her down by his side. In one furious movement he straddled her back, burying one hand in her hair and pushing her face into the earth.

"In the *dirt*, StarLaughter," he said. "In the *dirt,* where you belong! I curse the day I ever took you as my wife. I curse the day I ever took you to my bed. I curse the day I—"

"For our part, WolfStar SunSoar," a voice thin with hunger said behind him, "we are truly grateful you did all the aforementioned. Your son has proved a boon to us."

WolfStar gave StarLaughter's head a sickening wrench, then he leaped to his feet and turned about in the same graceful movement.

He stared at the emaciated man standing before him, knowing instinctively who—and what—he was.

"Demon," he said, his voice flat, "get you gone from this land!"

"Never!" a woman's voice said merrily, and Sheol stepped

forth, Raspu just behind her. "It feeds us too well, songless Enchanter, for us to ever want to leave."

"It is not your land," WolfStar said, hiding the revulsion that filled him.

"All lands that feed us are ours," Sheol said, gliding forward and circling WolfStar so close he could feel the graze of her robe against his skin. "But more to the point, has not this land of yours harbored what was stolen from us so long ago? You, and every sentient being as well as half-conscious beast that walks or crawls this land, is as much accomplice to the harm that was done us as those who brought our brother here."

"Then take him . . . and go."

"Nay, good birdman." Sheol had stopped her inspection, and now stood close beside him, a hand lightly resting on his belly. WolfStar had to fight the shudder of revulsion that threatened to ripple through him.

"Nay," she repeated in a whisper. "We think we like this land. We have traveled homeless and rootless too long. *This*," she stamped her foot lightly, "will become our paradise. And you . . ." her hand rubbed slightly, and WolfStar turned his head away, his jaw tightening, "shall become our plaything."

"He dies!" StarLaughter shouted. "You promised me he would die!"

Sheol pressed the length of her body against WolfStar's, and what he could feel roiling beneath her robe finally made his body quiver with disgust.

"There are many ways of dying," Sheol whispered, and her hand suddenly shot down, her fingers tightening like talons about his genitals, "and many states of death."

WolfStar screamed, doubling over, and Sheol let go her grip as he tumbled to the ground.

"Where is the girl-child you have filled with our property?" she asked tonelessly.

"Find her yourself, bitch!" WolfStar gasped.

Sheol half-smiled and she turned her head to Raspu. "My brother," she said, her voice almost gurgling out of her throat, "it seems WolfStar needs some persuasion."

She stepped back, taking StarLaughter by the arm and pulling her away as well. "Watch," she said in the birdwoman's ear, "as your murderer gets a fraction of what he has dealt out."

WolfStar blinked away the tears of agony in his eyes, and looked toward Raspu.

The Demon stepped forward, stopped, then tore the robe from his body. It was a mass of compacted sores, running with whatever pestilence Raspu had chosen to wear that day.

"You berate StarLaughter for her coldness amid the act of love," Raspu said, his voice far worse than Sheol's as it bubbled up through his throat from pus-filled lungs, "and yet I do not think you can possibly know the *true* coldness of love. Get to your knees, WolfStar, and then bend over, your face in the dirt."

"No!"

Raspu roared with laughter. "Do as I say, birdman!"

Power girdled WolfStar, and suddenly he was lifted up, thrown to his knees, doubled over, and his face pressed so far into dirt he began to choke on it.

Then, worst of all, he felt the presence of Raspu behind him, felt the Demon drop to *his* knees behind him, felt glacial hands tearing his breeches to shreds, and then felt the icy coldness of pure pestilent desire worm and shove its frightful way into his body.

WolfStar convulsed with horror, trying to struggle free from the rape being visited on him, but Raspu's power was too strong. WolfStar screamed, and then screamed again, inhaling dirt deep into his lungs as what felt like blunt frozen steel impaled his body, plunging deeper and deeper, until it felt as if the contents of his entire abdomen had succumbed to the invasion and were being clubbed into pulp.

"Tell us where the girl-child is!" he heard Sheol's voice scream from somewhere very far away, but WolfStar did not answer, *could* not answer, and he did not know what was worse, the feel of Raspu's horror punching and pummeling its way through his body, or the sound of StarLaughter howling with merriment.

"How does it *feel,* beloved husband?" she shouted from somewhere very far above him. "Do you now understand why *I* did not writhe with enjoyment every time you penetrated me?"

Tell us where the girl-child is! Sheol's insistent voice screamed in his mind, but still WolfStar could not speak. His hands groped blindly before him, and his face scored through the earth again and again as Raspu pushed home his rape with frightful eagerness.

Then the Demon screamed himself, and jerked about like a marionette, and WolfStar felt pestilence bubble forth and *boil* through his body, searing through him until its caustic effluent bubbled up through his lungs and throat and he choked on the foulness, dribbling it through his clenched teeth and down his chin.

Where is the girl-child?

One of WolfStar's hands, seemingly of its own will, clawed through the dirt until it lifted and pointed, quivering as if in the final extremities of the shaking sickness, toward a group of bushes on the eastern side of the glade.

"Very good," said Raspu, standing and rerobing himself in an unsullied garment with a wave of his hand. "Shall we fetch her?"

StarLaughter stared at the immobile and expressionless girl and loathed her. This, *this,* is what WolfStar preferred to her?

"As WolfStar, so her," Raspu whispered in her ear.

StarLaughter looked at him. His cheeks were still flushed, and his breath trembled with expectation.

"But far, far worse," he said, and StarLaughter smiled.

She turned a little further, and there was WolfStar, crouched behind her, his face ghastly wan and still wracked with pain, his eyes deep with hate, his naked body bruised, bloody and still smeared with Raspu's attentions.

A thick leather collar had sunk deep into the flesh of his throat, and a golden chain ran from it to StarLaughter's hand. She had not realized revenge could ever feel this good, and she glowed with love for her companions.

Later, perhaps, Mot could assuage his hunger upon WolfStar, and then Barzula could plummet his tempest deep into her husband. StarLaughter smiled with pure coldness, and sent her thoughts and images spearing into WolfStar's mind.

He quivered, but whether with hate or fear she could not tell.

I hope it is fear, earth-creeper, she whispered into his mind, *for you shall have much to fear.* Her smile widened. *Again and again. Morning, noon and night.*

"And there is always your son, WolfStar!" Sheol cried merrily, clapping her hands. Her sapphire eyes glowed very bright. "Don't you think *he* lusts for revenge as well? When cognizance finally fills your son's eyes, WolfStar, what revenge do you think *he* might like to visit on your body?"

"My son no more," WolfStar rasped. "If ever he was."

StarLaughter's face tightened, and she jerked the chain tight.

WolfStar choked, and fell over, his hands tight about the collar.

StarLaughter smiled sweetly.

"The Lake," Sheol said. "We have what we need, and we have wasted enough time here."

"Hardly a waste," StarLaughter murmured, and jerked again at WolfStar's chain. "For I find that I have enjoyed myself mightily."

60

Of Salvation

W hat I did to Leagh," Drago said, "I can do for only a few more. There are potentially twenty thousand out there running wild through the Western Ranges. It would kill me to bring them all back."

"But—" Theod said, his face tight.

"Three more," Drago said, "can I bring back as I did Leagh. Only three."

"You said that—" Theod started to shout.

"The others I can save," Drago said, his own voice tenser now. He'd realized over the past two days what the effort to return Leagh back had caused him, and he knew he could never repeat that twenty thousand times. Not all at once.

And knowing that broke his heart.

"I can save them," he repeated, "but only by moving them on."

"Moving them on?" Zared asked carefully. He, Leagh,

Theod, Faraday, Katie and Herme stood in one of the smaller chambers of the palace, a fire burning brightly and the drapes half-drawn to keep the bitterness of early spring at bay.

"Through death—" Drago said, and before he could say any more Katie finished for him.

"Into the field of flowers," she said.

Faraday and Leagh had told all present what they'd seen during Drago's enchantment, but even so Theod was slow to nod his head in understanding.

"Which three?" he asked.

Drago looked at Leagh and Faraday, then back to Theod. "Gwendylyr will be the first."

Theod's face crumpled in relief. "And then my two sons."

"No."

"No?"

"Theod," Zared said quietly, but with clear warning. He stepped forward to a spot where he could intervene between the two men if need be.

"Then *who* else?" Theod spat.

Drago hesitated. Gwendylyr had been an easy decision to reach. With Faraday and Leagh, she would make the third in the triangle he'd need against the Demons. Drago's three witches.

"Jannymire Goldman," he said.

Zared's face reflected his surprise, as did Theod's and Herme's.

"Goldman?" Herme said. He had kept very quiet until this point, reluctant to speak of things among those he did not truly understand.

Drago nodded, but did not explain himself. He walked over to the fire, standing before it, his hands clasped gently behind his back.

"And who is the third?" Zared asked.

"If suitable," Drago said, speaking into the fire, "I will also bring back DareWing FullHeart."

"If suitable?" Theod asked, his hand jerking in a curt, impatient and utterly frustrated gesture. *"If suitable?* Pray, what do you mean by, 'if suitable?' "

Drago turned about, looking at Faraday to answer. She was a little disconcerted. Since their clash on the roof of the palace, Faraday had been unsure of Drago, or of her reac-

tions to him. They'd passed some small time in company
since then, but never alone, and they had maintained a rigor-
ous politeness that tore at Faraday's soul.

But what else could she do? Did she want to live, or did she
want to love?

Drago raised his eyebrows, waiting, and Faraday forced
her mind back to the issue at hand. If DareWing was suitable? What did he mean? Then she remembered what Urbeth
had told them, and she realized what he meant.

"We went to Gorkenfort," she said, "and—"

*"What in curses' names does Gorkenfort have to do with
this?"* Theod yelled.

"Listen," Zared cautioned. "And let her speak."

"And while we were there we met with Urbeth," Faraday
continued, finally looking away from Drago back to the others. "You know of her?"

All nodded. The story of Urbeth had been one of the more
puzzling of those to emerge from Axis' battle with Gorgrael.

"She talked to us of many things, among which she passed
across the secret of the Acharite bloodline."

Faraday's mouth twitched in secret amusement as she told
them, if not the truth of the father of the Acharite race, then
of their potential for enchantment, but only once they'd
passed through death.

Leagh gasped, and then a beautiful smile graced her face.
"No wonder I feel . . ." her voice trailed off. "No wonder I
feel as I do," she finished quietly, and Zared looked at her
wonderingly.

"So why DareWing?" Theod asked, and all could hear the
unspoken question in his voice: if Acharites are so useful,
why bring the Icarii DareWing back and not one of my sons?

"Theod," Faraday said, and stepped forward so she could
take his hands in hers. "For countless generations before the
Wars of the Ax, Icarii men took lovers from among Acharite
women, believing their human blood would add vitality to
the Icarii race. When these women bore children, the Icarii
carried the babes off to raise them as full-blood Icarii."

"Thus many Icarii carry Acharite heritage in their veins,"
Drago said, "although they may not realize it. If DareWing is
one of those, then he will be more than useful."

"But this Acharite blood must be thin indeed by now," Zared said.

"Even the hint of its memory will be enough," Drago replied.

"But my sons . . ." Theod said helplessly, and Faraday's heart almost broke. She understood why Drago had chosen as he had, but the knowing could not lessen Theod's grief. She could not look him in the eye, and dropped her face.

Katie pushed between Faraday and Theod, and took one of the man's hands.

"Sir Duke," she said in a clear piping voice, shaking his hand so that he would look down into her face. "Trust in Drago. Your sons will be well."

Theod's face twisted, and he turned it away. "My sons will die," he said, his voice thick with emotion, "and I will mourn them all the days of my life."

Katie's hands tightened. "You will be too busy laughing *with* them to mourn them," she said. "Wait."

"We will go once dusk has passed," Drago said, "and the night is clean and peaceful."

The afternoon was spent either resting or pacing, depending on the temperament of each who waited. Zared sat a long hour at Leagh's bedside, watching her rest, until he could stand it no longer and got to his feet and wandered about the room, straightening that which did not need to be straightened, and neatening the already neat.

He did not like it that Leagh should go with them, however magically easy the journey that Drago might procure for them. She was still emaciated and physically drained from her ordeal, and her fatigue was doubled by the fact that her body sent what little vitality it had to spare into the baby she harbored.

And Zared did not want her to face any risk. He had lost Isabeau through his lack of foresight—through lack of *good sense, dammit!*—and he'd all but lost Leagh the same way, and the gods must be crazy if they thought he might be prepared to risk Leagh again.

But he had little choice, did he? Drago was insistent that Leagh come with them.

Ah! The tension and worry was almost too much, and Zared determined to find Drago and insist that Leagh stay in

Carlon. What could she do? Faraday would be there for whatever magical assistance Drago might need.

Checking to make sure Leagh still slept peacefully, Zared slipped quietly from the room and went to find Drago.

He found him, eventually, on the parapets. It was late afternoon, the dusk only an hour away but still currently safe enough to step into the open.

Drago stood at the far northeastern parapet, resting his chin on his folded arms on the chest-high stone, staring out at the mass of animals that crowded against the walls. He had his copper hair neatly tied in a tail at the nape of his neck, and was wearing light-colored breeches, calf-high close-fitting leather boots and a white linen shirt. He had his staff with him, but the sack was nowhere to be seen. Zared thought Drago looked far more elegant than he'd seen him in a long time . . . and more like Axis than Zared felt either Drago or his father would care to admit.

"Some sword practice, nephew?" Zared asked as he walked quietly up behind Drago, and was rewarded as Drago jumped.

Zared grinned. "Your newfound enchantments have not deepened your hearing, then?"

Drago returned the grin. "I was lost in thought."

Then his grin faded, and he looked back at the creatures spreading like a bleak wave of sin beyond Carlon's walls. "If I had ever imagined this horror . . ." he said softly.

"Then what?" Zared joined him in studying the force that swelled against the walls. "What? You would never have gone through the Star Gate? Drago, Fate has us all twisted in its relentless talons. If WolfStar hadn't thrown those children through, if the Enemy hadn't crashed in this land in the first instance . . . well, what chance that we would be here at all?"

Drago's eyes twinkled. If the Enemy hadn't crashed here, what chance that we would be here? None! Not if Noah hadn't seduced Urbeth into his bed!

But he said nothing, and let Zared continue.

Zared swiveled from the view and leaned on the parapet with one elbow, studying Drago's now unreadable face. "Spend no time bemoaning the past, or the fates that brought us to this moment, but instead think of the Tencendor that awaits."

Drago raised one eyebrow slightly. "I did not realize you

were the philosopher, Zared. Tell me, what *is* this Tencendor that awaits?"

Zared breathed deeply. "A Tencendor free of *everything*, dammit, but its own destiny. No prophecies, no long-buried Enemies, no Demons hurtling through space to tear it apart. Give Tencendor back the right to control its own destiny, Drago, and I swear that you will take your rightful place at its helm."

"Never say that!" Drago straightened, his violet eyes snapping with anger. "Once I have helped right the wrong that I helped perpetuate then I do not want leadership of *anything* save my own life and destiny. *I* do not want to snatch at a crown, Zared!"

Zared looked at Drago carefully, ignoring the jibe. "And if not you, Drago, then *who?* Neither Axis not Azhure retain the right to lead the land and its peoples forward. And Caelum . . . well . . ." He paused. "Who? *Who?*"

A muscle twitched in Drago's jaw, then his face relaxed. "We are indeed confident of victory, Zared, if here we stand fighting over who wants the glory afterward."

Zared's own mouth twitched in a smile. "I thought we were fighting over who did *not* want it!"

Drago laughed softly, then looked back over the creatures which thronged the plains beyond Carlon. "I do not like this, my friend."

"They increase by the day. The guards used to try and count them once a day, but they gave that up a long time ago. Now they just estimate the depth of the swarm about Carlon's walls."

"And?"

"And in the past week it has more than doubled," Zared said softly. "I think every creature—and every lost Acharite—that has been infected has found its way to Carlon."

To the Grail, and the Grail Lord, Drago thought, but did not speak it. "Zared . . . when did Theod arrive back?"

"Theod? The same night you and Faraday—and your menagerie—arrived."

"But how?" Drago waved a hand to the swarms beating against the walls. "*How?* I gained the impression he'd come through alone . . ."

"He had. And Herme and myself had the same suspicions you perhaps entertain—"

Drago shook his head. "His mind is his own, even if it is overburdened with grief."

"Well . . . Theod told us a remarkable story that, had it not been corroborated by several of the guards, I would find it hard to credit. He said that after he'd lost Gwendylyr, as the others, in the Western Ranges, a fabulous white stallion with a mane and tail of angry stars had appeared before him."

Drago stared, then smiled thoughtfully as he realized who the horse must be.

Zared only thought the smile a sign of skepticism. "Drago, this is true . . . I *believe* Theod!"

"Go on, uncle. I am not questioning you."

"Well . . ." Zared repeated the tale Theod had told him. "When the horse approached the ranks of the creatures outside, stars fell from his mane, burning a path before and about himself. The creatures howled and clamored, but they could not approach the horse. And so this star stallion carried Theod to the gates."

"Star stallion," Drago repeated to himself. "How appropriate."

He lifted his voice. "And where is this stallion now?"

Zared shrugged his shoulders. "No one knows. He vanished the moment Theod dropped from his back."

"North." Drago stared in that direction, then looked back to the closer problem of the hordes snapping and howling outside the walls.

"Apart from the obvious dangers to those who venture beyond the gates," he said, "have the creatures posed any other threat?"

Zared took his time in answering, and when he finally answered his voice was tinged with deep disquiet. "Look at them."

He waved his hand out, and almost as if the swarm of creatures had heard him, they screeched and screamed and howled, stamping a million feet from the tiny to the massive on the cold-baked earth.

Zared flinched. "Look at them, *hear* them. There are oxen and calves, vetches and ermine, cats and rats, snakes and creeping lice. *Everything* that once inhabited this land, that walked, crawled and hopped, has found its way here. I dread the moment that some of them find even the tiniest crack in the city's defenses. Gods, Drago! When are you going to get us to this Sanctuary?" Suddenly all thought of leaving Leagh safe behind in Carlon fled Zared's mind. Safety in Carlon? It was an illusory thing. Those creatures outside were waiting for something, and Zared did not want to be here when that something arrived.

"When we come back from the Western Ranges," Drago said. "Believe me, that needs to be attended first."

Zared stared at Drago. "You need Gwendylyr and Leagh and Faraday—"

"And Goldman and DareWing, if useful. Yes. Without them few people here would have a chance to get through. There are what . . ."

"Over two hundred thousand."

"Over two hundred thousand to get across to Spiredore, and I do not think Carlon has the fleet to ferry them over the Lake . . . do you?"

There was a silence between them for a while.

"And then," Drago said softly, peering yet further into the distance, "there must be still more trapped in the forbidding wilds of Tencendor. What of those in Skarabost? And in your native Ichtar? And Nor, and Tarantaise?"

"You cannot surely hope to retrieve *everyone?*" Zared said.

"I must," Drago replied, and turned his eyes back to Zared. "I must! If I leave even one soul that I could have saved to feed the appetites of the Demons, how then can *I* be saved?"

Caelum leaned back against the wind and laughed. Urbeth's eyes gleamed.

"And then . . . then, oh two-legged one, the seal said to me—"

"No! No!" Caelum said. "I do not want to hear what the poor seal said to try and save its life. No doubt it didn't succeed."

Urbeth grinned. "You are right. I sank my teeth into its back halfway through its pleading. It was boring me."

Caelum wiped his eyes, still chuckling. He had never thought to be so amused by a story of a seal's death, but the way Urbeth told it . . .

They had sat here swapping tales for what seemed like months—or was it years? Caelum had no way of gauging the time. There was only snow and cold that somehow did not perturb him, and the leap and twist of flame and words.

He remembered some vague wish he'd had as an infant to spend months wandering the northern wastes and talking with Urbeth, but as he'd grown he'd never found the time or the energy.

Now he had the time. He and Urbeth had shared not only tales, but also knowledge. Urbeth had talked to him about the craft and the Survivor. He told her of his sins. She'd shared her own sorrow at what she'd not done, and her joy at what she'd thought not to do, but had anyway. He'd hardly believed it when, halfway through one of her soliloquies, he'd realized her true identity.

Stars! She'd seen the look in his eye, and had nodded briefly, but that was the only concession either she or he had made to her ancient role as Mother of Races.

Mostly, Caelum had simply rediscovered the joy in life—something he realized he'd lost a long, long time ago.

"Ah," said Urbeth, looking over Caelum's shoulder at something approaching from the south.

He twisted about, expecting to see Drago, but all he saw were what he first thought looked like two small white donkeys, then gradually materialized into two great icebears, almost as large as Urbeth herself.

"My daughters," Urbeth said. "I would wager they have a tale or two to add to the warmth of this fire."

61

The Bloodied Rose Wind

Well?" Zenith asked anxiously, staring at StarDrifter. There was peace between them, although as yet neither was at ease with that peace. Despite StarDrifter's unconditional love, and his immense patience in a situation where he'd never before had to be patient, Zenith still felt guilty. As for StarDrifter, he felt as if Zenith might flinch every time he so much as glanced at her.

"They are there," he said quietly. He looked beyond the screen of trees and across the Lake.

"Where? I cannot see them!"

StarDrifter hesitated, then pointed. "There. Between the holyoak and the whalebone tree. Do you see?"

She stared, then nodded.

"And you, Isfrael?"

Isfrael stood with them, his entire body rigid with fury. News had been brought to him but an hour previously of the corpses found in the glade where WolfStar had been kept. Isfrael did not know if the Enchanter had gone with the Demons willingly, or if he had been forced—more blood found on the ground suggested that more force had been required than persuasion—but Isfrael did not care about the niceties of the difference. WolfStar was now with the Demons, as was that half-dead but bewitched she-creature he had carried about with him, and that, as well as the deaths of three good men, was all that mattered.

"And does the sight make you reconsider Drago's plea that you evacuate your people into Sanctuary?" StarDrifter asked. StarDrifter could not understand Isfrael. The Mage-King accepted that Drago was the StarSon, yet stubbornly resisted any suggestion that he send the Avar into safety.

Isfrael did not reply, not even blinking as he stared at the dim dusk-cloaked forms on their black creatures in the distance.

"Your magic could not stop them, Isfrael." StarDrifter's voice had hardened. "They discarded it as if it were a wisp of a child's imagination. Would you condemn the Avar to death for the sake of your pride?"

"The forests—" Isfrael began.

"The forests will be burned to the ground when Qeteb rises," StarDrifter hissed. "I trust that you will enjoy watching as your people roast for your stupidity!"

Isfrael finally turned to his grandfather. "I *know* what is best for *my* people," he said. "Cease your useless interfering!"

StarDrifter's mouth hardened into a thin line. Curse Isfrael! He was as stubborn—and as blind—as a brain-damaged mule.

Beside them, Zenith's breath jerked in her throat. Both

StarDrifter and Isfrael stared at her, then turned to see where she looked.

"Oh dear sweet gods of creation," Zenith whispered. "It is WolfStar! *What have they done to him!*"

StarDrifter's eyes jerked momentarily to Zenith's face. What was that emotion in her voice? Horror? Or sympathy? Then he looked back to the scene before him.

The Demons advanced from treeline to water's edge with more than usual circumspection. There was something odd, something different, in this place, but they could not smell it or taste it or see it or hear it, and that made them very, very cautious.

Was there another trap of the Enemy's here? Another bridge to snatch at one of them?

Their jewel-bright eyes glowed, searching the landscape. The Demons studied the terrain carefully, slowly, but their eyes did not linger when they passed over the line of trees that Drago had created to screen the Icarii evacuation.

Slightly to one side of them, and closer to the hidden entrance to Sanctuary, StarLaughter stood with WolfStar still collared and chained to her hand. The Enchanter crouched, as motionless as StarLaughter's still occasionally cruel hand would allow, for every movement ripped agony through him. He knew he'd been cruelly injured by Raspu's rape; not only the rape itself, but whatever essence the Demon had spurted into his body felt like it was eating away at his entrails, and corroding his lungs.

Even breathing was torment.

WolfStar wondered if he would survive whatever Mot or Barzula chose to do to him, but he wondered more whether Tencendor would survive what the Demons did with Niah. Was there a chance he could yet get her away from them?

Just behind StarLaughter and WolfStar, completely motionless and vacant, stood the boy and girl. Both were naked, their pale, gleaming pubescent bodies empty vessels for whatever would fill them here, and StarLaughter, in either cruel jest or hopeful anticipation, had put them hand in hand.

"Your son and your lover," she said to WolfStar when she'd done it. "Will you allow your son the pleasure of your lover? Will you smile indulgently when you watch them couple?"

WolfStar had turned away, refusing to respond to her taunts.

Now Zenith dragged her eyes away from WolfStar's battered body to the girl beyond him. "Gods! It's Niah!" she cried. "Oh dear gods, it's Niah!"

Her hands were to her cheeks, her eyes huge. Everything about the scene before her filled her with horror. Whether the sight of the Demons, or the bloodied and fouled WolfStar, or the horrible, horrible sight of Niah resurrected when Zenith had been *sure* that she had disposed of her once and for all, Zenith could not cope with it all at once, and she turned away, leaning on a tree for support.

As it was with Zenith, so with StarDrifter and Isfrael, although they did not have the same depth of revulsion at the sight of Niah as she'd had.

"That must be WolfStar's son," Isfrael eventually said quietly, inclining his head toward the boy.

"Qeteb half-reborn," said StarDrifter, also taking pains to keep his voice low, although it was apparent the enchantment shielded them from the Demon's eyes and ears. He glanced behind him. The lines of the Icarii were thinning now. In the past few days most had managed to find their way down to Sanctuary, and it was only the few who'd had to come from outlying areas that were now scurrying down the stairwell as fast as they could go.

He turned back to watch the Demons.

"How do we go down?" StarLaughter asked. She was impatient to see her son gain a little more of Qeteb's life. The sooner he could wreak his own revenge on his father the better. *And* the merrier! StarLaughter spared a glance in WolfStar's direction. She hoped the Enchanter would survive to endure his full-grown son's hatred.

Sheol cut back on her temper. "We have told you *before* we do not go down again. From this point what we need comes *up*."

The Demons had grown in power feasting on the souls of the living creatures of Tencendor. They were nowhere near their full power, but they'd glutted enough to pull what they needed to them, rather than the other way around.

Movement. Movement lay below, waiting lustfully.

Sheol moved forward to the very edge of the Lake, the waters lapping her toes, then seized the neckline of her robe in her hands, and ripped the cloth apart.

She threw the discarded halves to one side, and stood naked before the Lake the Avar called the Mother.

StarLaughter stared amazed. Sheol had the form of a female dog. Only her head and arms were vaguely human.

Sheol dropped to all fours, her arms in the water to the elbows, her hind legs resting on the sand. Her body was thin and covered with a brindle pelt. A short tail stood erect, and between her hind legs hung pendulous dugs, as if she'd only recently nursed a litter of puppies.

StarLaughter's mouth curled in distaste. Couldn't Sheol have thought of a more appropriate form?

Sheol growled, and hung her head down. Saliva dripped from her jaws in a gray foam, reminiscent of the haze that issued forth from the Demons' mouths during their hours of feeding.

There was a rasping to one side, and StarLaughter tore her eyes away from Sheol.

Raspu. Panting, his eyes on Sheol's hindquarters, and StarLaughter's mouth curled even further in distaste. Surely not!

In the next instant Raspu had torn away his own clothing, revealing a body also shaped liked a dog's—a great muscled mastiff—but with the flexibility of a serpent, and then he was down on all fours by Sheol's side, quivering and whining and drooling.

Another movement, and Mot and Barzula had also torn away their clothes, revealing doglike forms, and were prancing about in the shallows of the water, tipping their heads back to howl at the new moon just risen above the trees.

Their heads lengthened and sharpened into serpent heads, their tongues forking in and out, tasting the air.

" 'Tis not me who should be collared and chained," WolfStar said behind StarLaughter, and she turned and pulled viciously at the chain until he cried out and wept with agony.

"They are more faithful than *you*," she spat. "And doglike yourself, with the morals of a snake, it is no wonder you appeal to their lusts!"

She pulled and twisted the chain again, and was rewarded with a howl of pain.

"Grovel, WolfStar!" she whispered. "*Grovel* before me and I may yet grant you a speedy death!"

Only StarDrifter and Isfrael were now left to watch from the trees, their horror increasing with every moment that passed. As Sheol had revealed her bitch-form, Zenith had stumbled away, her hand to her mouth. WingRidge, who had been watching the three of them from the entrance to the stairwell, came forward, put his arm about her, and guided her down to Sanctuary. As they'd gone down, he had passed a quiet word to one of the Lake Guard, ordering him to stop the trail of Icarii and Avar through the trees toward Fernbrake Lake for the time being . . . until the Demons had got what they wanted and had gone.

Only StarDrifter and Isfrael—and the unseen woman on the top of the eastern ridge—were left to witness the passing of Fernbrake Lake.

The four creatures howled and cavorted in the shallows of the Lake, pausing only briefly to urinate and defecate into the waters. StarLaughter watched fascinated, WolfStar appalled, although he treasured the time it drew the Demons' attentions from him. He sat carefully on the ground, bent protectively over the arm wrapped about his belly, leaning heavily on the other. Every so often he glanced at the boy—he could not think of this creature as his son, even though his coloring and features were so much like his—as also at Niah.

Niah! If WolfStar had not believed it would call unwanted attention to him, he would have bent his head and wept at his own stupidity.

Now the Demons had ceased their prancing and defecating and stood still in water deep enough to lap against their bellies.

One by one the Demons began to tremble. They stared into the Lake, their noses almost touching the water, completely rigid save for the curious quivering that wracked their bodies. The trembling increased by the moment until it seemed as though they were in the final moments of some massive, hysteric convulsion . . . and yet still they stared down into the depths of the Lake.

The water changed.

It happened so subtly, and yet so swiftly, that WolfStar was not sure at what point the Lake ceased being a liquid and turned, instead, to glass. Emerald glass that trapped the Demons' legs and, in Sheol's case, her pendulous udders.

Still the Demons convulsed, the bodies a blur as their muscles spasmed faster than should have been possible, and the convulsions quickly transferred themselves to the glass.

It cracked, and then the entire surface of the Lake shattered into millions of tiny pieces. A great wind arose from beyond the ridge of the crater, and swept down over the Lake's surface.

The glass pieces turned to dust, whipped up into a maelstrom against which WolfStar had to screw his eyes closed and hide his face under an arm. He wanted to reach out for Niah, to shelter her against this murderous whirlwind of millions of razor-edged glass pieces, but he was not able to fight its force, and could only concentrate all his strength on protecting his own body against its fury.

StarDrifter and Israel, protected by Drago's enchantment, watched silently. Tears streamed down their faces, and Isfrael reached out and leaned a hand on his grandfather's shoulder.

Who comforted who, neither knew, but both drew strength from the physical contact. A piercing scream rose on the shoulders of the wind, growing in intensity and density until it seemed as if it filled the entire world.

It was the Lake, dying, and weeping in its death.

On the ridge, the woman wailed with it, and sank to her knees, tearing at her hair with her hands.

Almost as suddenly as it had arrived, the whirling maelstrom vanished, and WolfStar blinked, cleared away the glass shards that had embedded themselves in his eyelashes and hair, and stared out at what had once been the Lake.

All traces of water and glass had gone, and the Demons—now back to their humanoid forms and attired again in innocent pastel robes—pointed and exclaimed excitedly.

What had once been a Lake was now a garden, but a garden such as WolfStar had never seen previously.

It was a garden snatched from the darkest pits of the After-Life, a wasteland, an abomination. The ground, gradually rising to a small hillock in what had once been the center of the Lake, was cracked and scarred, bare-baked earth with no grass, no life, and no hope of life. Trees stood bare-branched and blackened, as if consumed in some ancient conflagration that they'd never recovered from. Rambling roses hung from trees and rusted trellises, their leaves and blossoms only a distant memory, flowering instead with needled thorns that reached out like traps.

The center hillock was barren, save for a windstorm that spun around and around on its crest, thick with dust and the thick, thorny tendrils of a rosebush.

"Movement," Sheol said with immense satisfaction. "Come."

StarLaughter tugged at WolfStar's chain, but he'd been ready for her, and rose and stumbled forward before she cut off his breathing. Mot and Barzula seized the boy and girl, throwing them over their shoulders, and striding into the wasteland with no mind for the thorns that reached out to scratch and mar.

WolfStar could not be so disdainful. He cried out each time a thorn hooked into his flesh, sometimes becoming so entangled in thorns that StarLaughter—the thorns appeared to completely ignore her—had to tug with all her strength to pull him free. By the time they approached the hillock he was covered in bloody scratches, and his wings had suffered so badly they were almost completely defeathered.

"Movement!" Sheol cried again. "Quick, Barzula! The boy!"

Barzula stepped forth, strode up the hillock until he was just outside the confines of the whirling wind. Then, in an abrupt movement, he hurled the boy inside.

Instantly, blood and flesh whipped out of the whirlwind as the boy's body was torn apart by the thorns inside. A piece of the ghastly meat struck WolfStar in the face and he gagged, reminded forcibly of the moment Zenith had flung Niah's poor dead body at him.

No one else minded. The Demons and StarLaughter were leaning forward in their eagerness, their eyes bright, their breasts heaving with excitement.

"When?" StarLaughter cried.

"*Now!*" Mot screamed, dancing from foot to foot in an obscene jig, and as he screamed, so a man stepped forth from the bloodied rose wind.

WolfStar's mouth slowly dropped open.

What now stood on the hillock was a nightmarish parody of an Icarii male. He was over-tall, and his naked body was obscenely roped with thick muscles which bulged so thick at chest and arm and thigh that WolfStar could not see how the man could possibly walk. From his back sprouted fully developed golden wings—*too* fully developed, for they were half as large again as a normal Icarii male's, and feathers sprouted unevenly from flight muscles that bulged as thick as they did on the man's body. The hands that dangled at the end of each arm were like spades; the fingers were as long and as thick as every other appendage, but flexible nevertheless.

They would miss no crevice that could be exploited.

The man's face was curiously flattened, with a broad and thick nose and forehead under dense, dull copper curls, and light violet eyes that were narrow and cunning—almost piggy—rather than bright and clear.

WolfStar looked closely. They remained lifeless, for Qeteb still had to be animated with soul, but they were chilling for all that they lacked spirit. The mouth was wide, its lips thick, red and moist, a pink flicker of tongue appearing between large, crowded white teeth.

Sheol turned slightly so she could see WolfStar. "The girl," she whispered.

"No!" WolfStar cried. "No!"

"Why?" Sheol said. "Is this not what you wanted? Mot! The girl!"

Mot stepped forward, the girl slung over his shoulder, but instead of hurling her into the rose wind as Barzula had done the boy, he handed her to the Qeteb-man.

"Take her," he said, and the Qeteb-man held out his arms and took her weight from Mot.

"The wind," Sheol commanded, and the Qeteb-man turned, but not before WolfStar had seen him run his spade-hands over the girl's breasts and belly . . . exploring, his body instinctively reacting to the feel of the female flesh under his hands.

No! WolfStar screamed in his mind, but at that instant the Qeteb-man flung his Niah into the rose wind, and particles of flesh and blood again streamed out across the wasteland.

When Niah finally emerged, completed in body, if not in spirit, WolfStar had to turn his face aside.

She was flawless, beautiful. Her alabaster body was female physical perfection, and glossy black hair streamed down her back to her buttocks.

Her face was stunning in its loveliness, fragile and yet strong at the same moment.

WolfStar knew in that instant that he'd lost. The Demons would use Niah, and her potential power, to their own ends. WolfStar felt nauseous: sick with self-disgust, sick with horror at how his plan to save Tencendor would now likely condemn it.

What had he done?

"There are many kinds of death," Sheol again informed WolfStar, her voice almost kindly, "and you shall now experience another one. She is female," she said to the Qeteb-man. "Take her."

The Qeteb-man seized the woman, his all-encompassing hands groping and kneading her unresisting flesh as he pushed her to the ground. The Qeteb-man dropped his weight upon her, forcing her to his requirements without any thought to the damage he might thereby do to her body. Coldly, his vacant eyes fixed on some distant point, the Qeteb-man drove himself roughly inside the Niah-woman and began to grunt and thrust, and each grunt and thrust ate into WolfStar's soul, tore into his being, and he lowered his head and wept as Niah lay on her bed of thorns, her hips and breasts jerking and jiggling with every movement of the Demon's frantically plunging body.

There, in that desiccated rose garden, Qeteb took his bride as WolfStar raved, StarDrifter and Isfrael watched in morbid fascination, and the Goodwife Renkin, still atop the ridge, climbed to her feet, her face hard, and descended into the forest below.

62

A Song of Innocence

Deep in the earth beneath Carlon, a writhing, twisting mass of voles, rats, and sundry burrowing insects and rodents continued to scrape their way through the earth. Among them moved the patchy-bald rat, biting and nipping, driving them on, on, on, for the day was coming, the day when the Lord would rise, and preparations must be made and souls must be in place for that moment.

The Day of Resurrection.

Above, the night was deep and moonless.

Drago stood at the open doorway by which he had entered Carlon, his sack tied securely to his belt. Drago had begun to think of it as his weapons sack; his father may have once slung ax and sword from his belt, now his reviled youngest son slung a hessian bag.

The Wolven was slung over Drago's left shoulder, the quiver of arrows hung down his back. In his right hand Drago held his staff, and in the other he held Katie.

By his feet crouched the feathered lizard. Its growth had stopped, and it had now stabilized into a form slightly larger than a mastiff hound, but still retaining the shape of a lizard.

Behind Drago came Faraday, wrapped in a bright scarlet cloak that she had hunted all afternoon for in the wardrobes of the palace, and with two blankets under her arm; Leagh, equally wrapped in a thick and warm black cloak and also with a blanket; Zared, his worried eyes rarely leaving his wife; and finally, Theod clad in light chain mail under his cloak and with his sword already drawn in his hand.

He'd heard of the eels that had attacked Drago's boat on the way over from Spiredore. The gods alone knew what else the Demons might launch at them. Theod did not want anything stopping him from reaching Gwendylyr this night.

He concentrated all his thoughts on her, and pushed the

memory of their two sons to the dim recesses of his mind. They were gone, sacrificed to Drago's unexplained plans, and Theod would not allow himself to dwell on them anymore.

"Well?" an anxious voice asked from far back in the dark passageway.

"The boat is still here, Herme," Drago replied, and he stepped carefully down, wishing that if he'd retained only one thing from his Icarii heritage it could have been their exquisite grace and balance.

The feathered lizard leaped in, causing the boat to rock violently, and Drago planted his staff firmly down and leaned on it, silently cursing the lizard with every gutter and kitchen oath he'd ever known.

Once the boat had settled, he laid the staff in the belly of the boat, lifted Katie in and saw her safely seated, helped Faraday and then Leagh into the boat, and seated himself, leaving Zared and Theod to manage as best they could.

Herme appeared in the dark hole of the doorway. "Be careful," he said. "And return quickly."

"Keep safe," Drago said, then briefly smiled, nodded, and leaned his weight into the oars, sliding the boat silently out onto the waters of Grail Lake.

Faraday drew the cloak yet tighter about her and shivered. Animals of all shapes, sizes and breed lined the shoreline about the city's walls. Men and women, as naked and vile as Leagh had been, crept back and forth, snatching at themselves or at whoever came close. All the demented were relatively silent, whether because of the night or some unknown plan, Faraday did not know, but they shuffled and moved in undulating waves, constantly pushing against the walls.

Pray we get back in time, Drago thought. He'd felt the increase in the power of the Demons, and knew they'd been successful at Fernbrake Lake.

How long would it take them to get to Grail Lake? Over a week, but less than two.

Not long. Not long.

Drago pulled harder on the oars.

The gigantic eels humped their bodies out of the water as the boat moved across the Lake, but they did not attack. Perhaps they could see the feathered lizard sitting sentinel in the bow of the boat, or perhaps their attention was focused on something within the Lake, for they rarely lifted their heads to watch the boat's progress.

"There is something different about the Lake," Faraday said, and Leagh nodded.

"I feel it, too. There is a . . . a thickness . . . here which I do not understand."

Faraday trailed a hand through the water. "A thickness . . ." she repeated, and then wiped her hand on her cloak with an expression of distaste.

Drago watched both women, sitting directly opposite him, with careful eyes. Leagh, while cautious about the danger surrounding them and their mission this night, was nevertheless serene and calm. She had come through death and found nothing but peace.

Faraday, on the other hand, was as jumpy as a cat. Drago remembered how sure she'd seemed when first he'd come back through the Star Gate. Gradually that confidence had dissipated.

It was him, Drago knew that. They'd fallen unwanted into love, and he thought that neither of them would find much happiness in it. Faraday did not want love, it had betrayed her too much already. And he? For weeks Drago had thought all he wanted was Faraday and her love, but after their conversation on the parapets, he now knew that even if she *did* come to him, would it be to him that she came, or the resemblance in movement and expression to his father?

Would she ever get over her love for Axis? She said she had, but Drago did not believe her. It continued to cripple her life, and Axis, utterly unintentionally, had returned to cripple Drago's as well. How pleased Axis would be, Drago thought, if only he knew.

Drago watched Faraday's eyes skim over the water, and remembered the passion in those eyes as she'd spoken of Axis and the nights they'd spent in love.

Would she ever look thus when she spoke of him?

He grimaced, and dropped his face, and bent back to the oars.

They reached the far shore without incident, and the moment the boat scraped against the gravel bottom of the Lake, all knew what was different about it.

The level of the Lake had dropped considerably, possibly by about the height of a man. Now they had several paces of dry lake bed to walk across to reach what had once been the shoreline and the now-waterless pier by Spiredore.

"But," Faraday said, turning about on the exposed lake bed in consternation, "how can this be? When we arrived here several days ago the water level was as it always had been."

"The Lake is drying out," Drago said. "The TimeKeepers have seized what they need from Fernbrake, and now all that remains for them is what lies here."

Zared looked intently at Drago. "Will the city remain safe? The gate we left by is hardly fortified. If the swarms of animals outside are able to reach it . . ."

"It will not dry out completely for a while yet," Drago said, and turned for Spiredore. "And we shall return within the day." Spiredore, ever faithful to those who served the craft, took them safely to the Western Ranges. A series of steep and narrow stairs deposited them before a narrow corridor that led into an indiscernible blackness.

"Where are we?" Theod asked. His voice was strained, whether from nervousness inherent in everyone's first experience of Spiredore, or what he thought he might find at the end of the journey, no one knew.

"I imagine we will find out at the end of this passageway," Drago said.

They walked down the corridor in a tight group, their steps slow, their hands groping along the walls so that they might not be surprised by a sudden drop in elevation, or a turn.

Even the feathered lizard, normally so exuberant, slunk directly behind Drago, his talons now and then flaring and lighting the gloom.

Drago paused as his hand slid from the smoothness of dry plaster to the dampness of cave rock. He blinked, and then squinted into the almost impenetrable darkness.

There was a faint, rough oval of light ahead.

A cave mouth.

"We have arrived, I think," Drago said, "in the cave in which you and yours were so cruelly trapped, Theod. Be careful now."

There was a scrape of steel as Zared and Theod drew their swords, but Drago motioned the lizard forward. He would be their best protection.

"It's cold," Leagh murmured, and, like Faraday, hugged her cloak tight about her.

Drago motioned them to remain still as the lizard snuffled about the cave—gradually becoming less featureless as everyone's eyes adjusted to the night gloom—and then, as the lizard's body relaxed, led them toward the mouth of the cave.

"The twenty thousand were scattered throughout the ranges," Theod said. "How will you—"

"They will all be relatively close," Drago said. "This cave was the lodestone, the trap, and they would all have been caught here."

"But wouldn't they have started to move elsewhere?" Zared said. "To Carlon, perhaps?"

"Not enough time," Drago said. "They would have waited until the entire twenty thousand had been turned, and that could only just have been accomplished. Theod . . . how long is it since you left the cave?"

Theod calculated swiftly. "Six or seven days, or thereabouts."

Drago nodded. "A week? Then all groups must have come through, but only just."

"But they still must be scattered—" Theod began.

"Then we must 'unscatter' them," Drago said. "For what I am about to do, I need them all close."

Theod turned away, raising his hands in frustration, but Drago ignored him. He squatted down before Katie, and took her shoulders in his hands, staring into her face.

"Katie?" he asked softly. "Will you do it?"

She nodded silently, her face sober.

"I will protect you," Drago said, and the girl smiled and flung her arms about his neck, planting a kiss on his cheek.

Taken aback, Drago disentangled the girl's arms.

"We will need a large open space," he said. "Theod, was there anywhere near here that can fit a crowd?"

"There is a grassy flat at the foot of this hill." Theod's voice was becoming harder by the moment. "But it will not fit twenty thousand."

"No," Drago said, keeping his own voice even, "but enough for a crowd of some thousands at least? Yes? Good. And there are gullies leading toward this grassy flat?"

"Yes! Gods damn you, Drago, what are you going to do?"

Drago stepped up to Theod and took his shoulders as he had just done Katie's.

"Theod," he said, and gave the man's shoulders a little shake. "Just believe."

Drago wore a gentle smile on his face that lit his eyes with warmth, and far more than the words it was that which relaxed Theod.

He nodded slightly. "I am worried for Gwendylyr," he said. "All this time, running about the hills . . . and in what state?"

"Theod." Now Zared spoke up. "Whatever else we have seen, it has not been corpses lying about. The Demons seize their minds and their souls, but they leave their bodies . . . intact."

Zared had been about to say "alive," but alive did not quite describe the state of those held in the Demons' thrall, did it?

"We will *find* her, Theod," Drago finished, and Theod gave another nod.

"Good." Drago walked over to Katie and held out his hand. She took it, her face once again sober, and together they walked toward the entrance.

The feathered lizard ambled after them, but when the others made also to follow, Drago asked them to stay.

"You can see well enough from the mouth of the cave, and for the moment I would like you to remain there."

Drago and the girl walked carefully down the slope of the hill, occasionally stumbling over a rock hidden in a tussock of grass or night shadow. When they reached the bottom, Drago spent a few minutes studying the terrain.

The grassy flat spread in a rough oval shape perhaps a hundred paces east and west and some sixty paces wide. At the far western end a ravine stretched back from the flat into unseen darkness, and four or five steep-sided and narrow ravines snaked into the flat from the east and west.

"Perfect!" Drago murmured, then he squatted down beside Katie. He was nervous, for this would be not only dangerous for all concerned—and especially Katie if he didn't get the protective enchantment right—but would tax his own skill considerably.

Katie studied him, then reached out and took his hand. "You have come a long way from your pastry magics," she said.

"You know about that?"

"I know everything. *You* know that."

Drago sighed. Katie might only look like a tiny girl, but she was as old as the land itself. "Yes. I know that. But I thought *some* small details might have escaped your attention."

"Do this," Katie said, "for whoever still roams raving when Qeteb is fully resurrected will be beyond all of our help."

Now Drago looked truly startled. "I did not know that! Gods! I should have done more to—"

Katie covered his hand in both of hers. "You wasted too many years in self-recrimination, Drago. For now, you can only do your best."

He nodded, then stood up, hefting the staff in his left hand. He glanced up the hill. Everyone was standing at the top of the slope looking down: both women waited in stillness, the men shifted impatiently.

Drago looked back to Katie, who had now sat herself cross-legged on the grass. He thought of the enchantment he would need, and almost in the same moment Drago felt the movement of the staff under his left hand, and with his right sketched the enchantment in the air.

He opened his mouth to ask the lizard to make it visible, but the lizard also acted almost without conscious thought. He lifted his right foreclaw and re-sketched the symbol in light.

Above, Leagh took Faraday's arm in a tight hand. "Do you know," she whispered, "that symbol almost means something to me."

Faraday frowned . . . what could she . . . ah! She too could somehow feel the symbol reaching out for her, communicating with her in some undefinable way.

"Protection," both women muttered at the same time.

"It is an enchantment of protection," Faraday added, then shook her head slightly. What was going on? It felt as if that enchantment was reaching out fingers into her mind, doing something, or appealing to something, but she couldn't—

"It's the Acharite magic in us!" Leagh said, still keeping her voice low. "We can understand it because we have both seen the field of flowers!"

Faraday's frown deepened, and she placed a hand over Leagh's where it rested on her arm. Was Leagh right? When Drago had included her in the vision, had he somehow forged the final link to her forgotten blood magic? She looked back to Drago.

He had taken the enchantment in both hands, and had now stretched it to over three times its original size.

Then he lowered it gently over Katie so that she was surrounded by it.

It glowed a deep crimson—and then vanished.

"It is still there," Leagh said to her husband and Theod, who had moved in surprise. "But invisible. The child is protected."

The child sat very calmly, her eyes downcast, and Drago sketched another symbol in the air.

This was stunningly complicated, and it seemed to Faraday that it would never end. The five fingers on his right hand seemed to move completely independently of each other, while the hand itself danced and wove through the air.

The feathered lizard watched, a frown of deep concentration on its face. Finally Drago's hand jerked to a halt, and he drew a deep breath.

"My friend," he said to the lizard, and the lizard began the tiring task of retracing the enchantment in light.

When it hovered complete in the air before Drago, it was of a strange light, almost a gray light, and to those watching from above it was very, very hard to see in the night air.

But from what they could see of it, it was composed of hundreds, if not thousands, of intertwining lines.

Drago put down his staff and took the enchantment in both hands.

Then he began to compress it. It took considerable strength, for occasionally he grunted, and his shoulders visibly heaved with the effort, but finally the enchantment, now a small ball of gray light, sat in the palm of his left hand.

With his right, Drago drew an arrow from the quiver, pausing briefly to run his fingers through its beautiful blue-dyed feathers.

Then he placed the enchantment on to the arrowhead, shrugged the Wolven off his shoulder, and fitted the arrow to the bow.

"What is he going to do?" Theod asked.

"He is springing a trap," Leagh said. "That is all I know. A trap."

"I can tell no more," Faraday added at Theod's querying look. "Just trust him, please."

There was a twang, and the arrow shot into the air. Drago must be fitter and stronger than I imagined, Zared thought, for I had heard that only the strongest of Icarii could wield that weapon.

But Drago's lithe body obviously held all the strength the Wolven needed, for the arrow shot straight and true into the air, rising higher and higher until it was lost to sight.

Faraday and Leagh both suddenly shivered.

"We cannot see it," Leagh said. "But that enchantment has risen high into the sky where the arrow released it. It has expanded to a thousand hundred times its former size, and its gray lines of light now hang invisible in the night sky."

"A net?" Zared asked.

"Aye," Faraday replied softly. "A net."

And then all four jumped in surprise, for the arrow plunged down into the earth at their very feet. Faraday leaned down and retrieved it, running her fingers up and down its length before finally stowing it under her belt.

Leagh's eyes widened slightly as she saw what Faraday wore under the cloak. "Faraday!" she whispered.

Faraday looked at her, the cloak falling closed about her form.

Leagh unwrapped her own cloak a little, enough for Faraday to see what *she* wore.

"Why?" Faraday said.

Leagh took her time in replying, and when she did, she looked at Drago rather than Faraday. "We have both walked the field of flowers, Faraday, and are thus sisters.

"And this night I think we shall have a third join us."

Faraday shuddered, clutching cloak tight about her with white fingers. "And Goldman and DareWing, if Drago accepts him?"

Leagh grinned, a wide, disarming smile, and looked Faraday in the eye. "But they are men, Faraday. *Men!* How can they be 'sisters?'"

Faraday stared at her, and then she laughed, and hugged Leagh quickly to her.

"You are not alone anymore," Leagh whispered into Faraday's ear, "for you shall end this night with two sisters closer than any blood sisters can be."

Faraday blinked back tears, overwhelmed with emotion. *Not alone anymore? But she had* always *been alone!*

"Nevermore," Leagh whispered.

"What are you two mumbling about?" Zared asked.

"Nothing," both women replied as one, and straightened, Faraday turning away momentarily to control her emotions.

They looked back to Drago.

He was staring straight at them, and Faraday wondered if somehow he'd heard what she and Leagh had whispered.

"He will one day wish to retrieve his arrow," Leagh said, but Faraday did not reply.

"What do you mean, 'a net'?" Theod asked, having completely missed the emotion and exchanges of the past few moments.

"Drago has constructed a huge net in the sky with his enchantment," Faraday said. "Neither you nor Zared were there to see it, but when Drago brought Leagh back, he enveloped her in an enchantment of light. He will do something similar here, methinks."

She fell silent, and watched Drago bend down to Katie to whisper something in her ear.

"A huge net," Faraday finally said. "I think he means to entice the twenty thousand, or whatever of them remains, to this spot, and the ravines and gullies surrounding them, then trap them under his enchantment."

"How so 'entice'?" Zared asked. He had moved to Leagh's side, and had wrapped his arms about her to keep some of the freezing night air at bay. For her part, Leagh cuddled comfortably against his body, relieved beyond measure that he was not only here, but chose to hold her so close.

"He will entice them with the child," Faraday said, and her

voice hardened to brittleness. "Gods forgive him if he harms her, for *I* shall not do so."

Leagh twisted her face slightly to look at her, but she did not say anything. Beneath them, the child began to sing, and all eyes dropped down to her.

Drago had stepped back a pace or two, and now stood behind the child. With his right hand he set the staff firmly in the grass, and with his left snapped his fingers to call the feathered lizard to his side. It settled down close beside him, keeping its eyes on the child.

Both Leagh and Faraday could *feel* the crimson enchantment about the child, though they did not see it. It throbbed, and they could feel the beat in their blood.

The beat of the Star Dance? They only knew it was a beat that not only they, but the entire land of Tencendor throbbed with, and they closed their eyes, and swayed gently with the rhythm of the beat and of the song Katie sang.

The child sang a lullaby, one that all, save Drago, could remember their mothers singing over their toddling cradles. It was a sweet song, one that was redolent with innocence and the joyous dreams of the sinless. It spoke of all-encompassing motherly love, and of fields waving with grain and the cheerful scarves and smiles of the harvesters in the fields within which children could play from dawn to dusk without fear, and whose golden acres of grain dipped and swayed to the music of their laughter and song. This was a land without tears, a land without fear, and a land where all knew that death was but a short walk through the gate never dared into the next field . . .

. . . *the field of flowers, a field thick with peonies and cornflowers and poppies, and crowned with millions of lilies, perhaps billions of them, white and gold and crimson, waving their joyous throats at the sun.*

"That is not quite the same lullaby that I seem to remember," Theod said softly.

"Nor I," Zared said.

Faraday smiled a little, but it was Leagh who responded, her hand on her belly.

"But it is the lullaby *I* shall sing our child to sleep with, methinks," she said, and smiled at Zared.

Katie sings of the land that will be, Faraday thought, once Drago brings Tencendor through death and into the field of lilies. And again, to her annoyance, she had to blink back tears. *I demand that right to walk among the lilies, too, Drago,* she thought, *and I will not let love for you trap me in a dark world without flowers.*

"Look," said Zared, and the tone of his voice made all raise their heads.

Shapes were creeping through the night toward Katie. Some slithered, some crept, some writhed on their bellies, and some crawled, but none walked upright. There were shapes so small they could only be babes in arms. There were shapes with wings, members of what had once been the Icarii Strike Force.

Zared was cold with horror. Not so much at the bestial nature of what writhed and crept through the night, for he had steeled himself against that sight, but at the thought that among these beasts also crawled the Icarii Strike Force. He had grown up with the tales of their heroism and valor during Axis' battles with Gorgrael, and had grown up with the sight of them dancing in the air above Sigholt.

To think of them now crawling through the ravines and gullies through dirt and brambles toward this child—as the Gryphon had once crawled through the snow and ice of Gorken Pass toward Azhure—was almost too much to bear.

He turned his face away, unable to watch.

"They come drawn by Katie's song," Faraday said quietly. "Toward its innocence and beauty and hope." She paused. "They want to destroy it, and kill the singer, for of all things in their maddened world that they cannot stand, it is innocence and hope."

Zared closed his eyes, took a deep breath, and then forced himself to look back toward the child.

She continued to sing, but her lullaby was now underscored by the whisperings and howlings of those that crawled toward her.

"Gods," Zared said quietly, and that was all that any of them said for a very long time.

All through the night the twenty thousand crept toward the singer, some from over three leagues away. They crept through rocks and ravines, dirt and gullies, leaving trails of their blood and excrement where they went. And as they crept, they whispered and chattered, howled and shrieked, for the visions the songstress conjured in their minds were horrible to them, and all they wanted to do was tear her to shreds, so that the lilies and the field of flowers would fade from their minds forever.

When the first crawlers and creepers had reached within three paces of Katie, Drago stepped about her, hefted his staff, then speared it into the ground before her.

Then he resumed his place just behind her.

The watchers above squinted, and wondered if it was the distance and height from the staff that made it seem so blurry, but Faraday and Leagh came to understand that the staff was quivering, just slightly, but so fast that its outlines were blurred by the movement.

Between the staff and the still-invisible crimson enchantment about the girl, none of the creepers dared move to within two paces of her.

They fell to their bellies, snarling and spitting, reaching out tentative fingers, then snatching them back in pain as they encountered the spreading vibrations (*music*) of the staff. Behind the first ranks an immense sea of creepers and crawlers gathered—what had once been men, women, children, and the Strike Force.

It was a ghastly sight. Zared, as Faraday and Theod, had thought that what they'd seen over past months had inured them to those who'd been taken by the Demons, but never had they seen this mass of undulating madness, and stench, and sores, and the sickening, sickening waste of lives and hopes. But they forced themselves to watch. These were people, subjects, friends, and, in one case, a wife and sons that made up this dark sea.

Leagh watched, not with horror, but with an immense sense of sadness. She could remember something of the dementia that had seized her mind and soul, and to see this many, this twenty thousand . . .

She wept for pity; the others wept with the horror.

It took hours for the twenty thousand to gather. In the lightening sky just before dawn, the watchers at the cave mouth could see that the entire grassy space had filled and, beyond that, ravines and gullies awash with people writhing in the dirt, reaching out hands, rolling eyes, and wailing, wailing, wailing.

During all this time, Katie continued to sing, and Drago to stand immobile behind her.

The feathered lizard, while it had spent the first two hours on the ground by Drago's side, had eventually raised itself to pace back and forth, back and forth before Katie, in case any of the creepers overcame their horror at the vibrating song of the staff.

"Zared," Faraday said, and found her throat was so dry her voice was harsh and almost unintelligible. She cleared her throat. "Zared, Theod. You must now go inside the cave. Dawn draws nigh, and Mot will spread his vaporous hunger within minutes. Go."

"But Leagh—" Zared began.

"She will be well," Faraday said. "Their ravages cannot harm her now. Go!"

Zared looked once more at Leagh, but she gave him an impatient shove, and so Zared took an equally reluctant Theod back inside the cave's shade.

Far to the east, Mot reined in his black mount, tipped back his head, and stretched his mouth wide. Hunger filled the land.

Faraday looked to the east, and saw the pink glow of dawn stain the mountain peaks.

Then, just as the pink intensified into red, the light was clouded by the thickening gray miasma of Mot's hunger. Faraday could feel the familiar foul nibbles of the Demon at the edges of her mind, and she took Leagh's hand to reassure her.

"It is horrible," Leagh whispered. "I can *feel* him poking and prodding."

"He cannot enter, not now," Faraday said, and raised her eyes again to the befouled dawn light, "but he can still corrupt the land easily enough."

Mot had kicked his mount forward once his hunger had gushed forth, but now he pulled it to a halt again.

"Another," he said, his lips curling back from his teeth. "*Another resists!* How? How? How?"

The two magicians, the two *unknown* magicians, were never

far from the Demons' minds. Now another had joined their ranks.

Several paces back, tied at his wrists by a short rope leading from the tail of StarLaughter's mount, WolfStar grinned.

"It is the StarSon," he said, hoping his taunt was truth. Caelum was all they had left now! "Moving against you, Caelum. Remember the name, for it will be your nemesis."

"Fool!" Mot hissed, and WolfStar doubled over in agony, but not before he'd heard the fear in Mot's voice.

It was all that enabled him to survive, for as the Qeteb-man had spent himself inside Niah, so Mot had taken his lengthy pleasure with WolfStar.

Something out the corner of one of Faraday's eyes caught her attention and she turned slightly.

"Drago!" she screamed without thought. *"Drago!"*

Startled, Drago twisted about and looked at Faraday and stared, stunned.

She was pointing to a hilltop in the southeast, but Drago could not tear his eyes away from her. In Faraday's excitement, her crimson cloak had fallen open and now flew back from her shoulders in the wind, tangling with the long tresses of her heavy chestnut hair.

Underneath the crimson cloak Drago saw that Faraday had finally abandoned the rough-woven peasant dress and boots. Instead she wore a white linen robe, startling in its simplicity, that fell in a deep vee from her shoulders to a plain leather belt about her waist (in which, he noted, was stuck the arrow he'd shot earlier), then in thick folds of drapery to her feet, now clad in light leather shoes elegant enough for the most discerning of queens.

Drago slowly ran his eyes back up her body to her face. It was alive with excitement, her green eyes sparkling, her mouth slightly open, tendrils of hair drifting across forehead and cheeks. He had never, *never,* imagined she could be this lovely, this magical.

How could his father have ever treated her as he had?

"Drago!" Faraday shouted again, her finger stabbing impatiently at the hilltop.

Slowly, reluctantly, Drago swung his eyes about . . . and stopped, even more stunned than he had been at the sight of Faraday.

At the top of the hill reared Belaguez. Stars foamed about his head and neck, and streamed in a great banner from his tail. The stallion screamed, reaching for the sky with plunging hooves, and the faintest remnant of pink dawn light caught his body, turning the Star Stallion red, and his mane and tail into raging flames.

"It is time," Drago said, and made a curt, sweeping gesture before him, like a scythe mowing sweet spring meadow grass.

With that motion he cut the supports of the enchantment. A gossamer web fell slowly, inevitably, surely from the sky, trapping the entire twenty thousand under its enchanted light.

Above, the stallion dropped to all four hooves, stared, and then disappeared down the far side of the hill.

63

The Fields of Resurrection . . . and the Streets of Death

Leagh! Faraday! Will you join me? Bring the blankets."

The women picked up the blankets where they'd laid them on the ground, reassured Zared and Theod who paced about agitatedly just inside the cave mouth, and began a careful descent of the hill. Every now and then they would pause and survey the scene before them. It was light now, and the mass of creepers were clearly revealed.

All of them lay still and silent under the enchantment, although eyes still rolled, and occasionally a hand or shoulder twitched. The net lay over them like a glowing silvery haze, its delicate strands barely visible.

As they neared the foot of the hill, Drago held out a hand to aid them the final pace or two.

"Leagh?" he asked, his eyes concerned. "How do you feel?"

"Tired," she said, "but not too tired. What do you need us to do?"

"Would you know Gwendylyr if you saw her?"

"Yes. She and I played as children, and I stood at her side when she married Theod."

Drago nodded. "Good. Faraday, do you know DareWing?"

She hesitated. "It has been many years. I knew him as a Crest-Leader when I was," she dropped her eyes, "with your father at Carlon."

Faraday paused, then looked up at Drago through half-lowered lashes. "But I think I would know him again."

Drago stared at her, then collected himself. "Good. We need to search for the three that I can bring back, and separate them from the others."

"There is no need to 'search,'" Faraday said, "for are they not lost? I will lead you straight to them."

"Then why didn't you say so in the first place?" Drago said, angry that she had allowed the conversation to drift on long enough so that she could again mention the time she'd spent in his father's bed.

"You were too busy organizing!" Faraday snapped, and then took a deep breath as Leagh stared at her incredulously.

"I am sorry," Faraday said. "It has been a bad night."

Drago gave a curt nod, accepting her apology. "Then find them."

Herme stood at a safe distance from the rosy dawn light spilling in the window in his chamber and fidgeted.

Something was not right.

Naturally, little had been "right" for months, but today the "feel" of something *else* not right was very, very strong.

"Ah!" he said, and turned from the view. "Guard!"

The door opened and a well-armed and -armored guard entered.

"Fetch Captain Gustus."

The guard nodded, and closed the door behind him. Within five minutes Gustus, captain of Zared's home guard, entered the room and saluted.

"Gustus." Herme indicated the barely touched breakfast table. "Have you eaten?"

"Hours ago, Sir Earl."

Herme paused. "I like not this quiet, Gustus."

"Aye, sir. I know what you mean. The multitude outside is waiting. And more than waiting. They are ready."

For what?

Herme looked at him, noting that, like the guard outside, Gustus was fully armed. "How many men stand as ready to fight as you?"

"The *city* stands ready to fight," Gustus said quietly.

"They may have to," Herme murmured, then hit his fist on the windowsill in his frustration. "Gods! *Where will they attack?*"

And where was Zared? Where Drago?

Faraday hoped she would never have to repeat this experience again. It took over an hour of walking among twitching, fetid bodies, placing each foot carefully so that she did not slip on soft flesh or glimmering enchantment, before she found the three that Drago wanted.

She found Goldman in only the first few minutes. The Master of the Guilds was curled in a tight ball only four or five ranks back from the now-silent Katie, covered in what appeared to be a self-woven coat of twigs, leaves and the skins of at least four rabbits.

Faraday imagined they had not died well, but at least Goldman looked strong and well-fed.

Gwendylyr was harder to find because she'd crouched under a pile of gorse bushes torn loose by the mass during its crawl toward Katie, but, she, too, looked in good condition, although she had several scratches over one shoulder.

There were no signs of her two sons close to her.

Faraday found DareWing last. Like Goldman, he'd tucked himself into a tight ball, and then wrapped his wings about himself so that he was almost unrecognizable. They were tattered and torn, as were his forearms and chest, and he breathed shallowly and rapidly, as if he'd developed a lung infection.

"Drago!" she called, and he carefully picked his way over.

Drago squatted down by the Strike Leader's head, pushing back the gossamer strands of enchantment until the birdman's face was free.

DareWing snarled weakly, but made no move to bite or snap, or even to raise his head.

Drago put his hand on the birdman's forehead, then ran his hand gently down his cheek to his chin, tipping DareWing's face to his so he could look him in the eye.

"Well?" Faraday asked.

"He has not done well crawling about the ground," Drago murmured. "He has picked up a ground fever, and it has run rampant through his body."

"That was not what I asked," Faraday said sharply.

Drago raised his eyes and stared at her. "Do not blame me for every wrong that has ever been visited on you, Faraday. I am guilty of many things, but of you I am *innocent!*"

Faraday's face flushed and she dropped her eyes and turned her head slightly away from him. Drago continued to stare at her for a few heartbeats, watching the flush on her cheeks and neck deepen, then he relented. "DareWing has had an ancestor somewhere in his not-so-impeccable pedigree who strayed, it seems. He carries Acharite blood.

"But," Drago dropped his eyes back to the birdman. "His fever is very, very bad. He may not live, whatever I do for him."

He fell silent, continuing to stare at DareWing, his fingers digging deep into the birdman's chin.

Eventually, Drago sighed. "I have no choice. DareWing could be the saving of this land if he survives the fever."

"Why?"

Drago looked back to Faraday. "Are you sure you want to get into a conversation with me, Faraday? Wouldn't that be dangerous? Might I not use the opportunity to imprison your soul in the frightful chains of betrayal?"

She said nothing, but her jaw tightened, and her eyes grew hard.

"All I want to offer you is love, Faraday. It is your choice whether or not you ever decide to trust me."

Then he stood up, not giving her the opportunity to answer. He hefted the staff in his hand and whistled to gain the attention of the feathered lizard, which sat by Katie's side.

It looked up, but did not move to join him.

Drago drew a symbol in the air, something far simpler than Faraday expected, and from his spot by Katie the lizard retraced the symbol in the air with light, not once, but three times.

Three visible enchantments of a deep violet light appeared, one hovering over each of the three Drago had selected.

He reached for the one over DareWing and pulled it down, wrapping it over the birdman's hands. Then he gently disentangled the gray gossamer strands of the holding enchantment until DareWing's entire body was freed.

"Help him up," Drago said to Faraday. "The enchantment about his wrists will make him tractable, and he will obey whatever you tell him to do. Walk him through this crowd until you reach the open space just behind Katie, then sit him down."

And before Faraday could answer, he'd turned and walked away, signaling Leagh to join him by Gwendylyr.

Faraday briefly watched him walk away, then bent down and pulled DareWing to his feet. The birdman stumbled, but he stood obediently enough, and responded to Faraday's hand on his arm.

"Come, DareWing," she said, and led him through the twitching mass toward Katie.

As they made their careful way, Faraday saw that Leagh now led Gwendylyr toward the same spot, and Drago was occupied with Goldman. By the time she had pulled DareWing into the open, Leagh and Drago already had their charges waiting.

"Sit him down," Drago said, and pointed to where Goldman and Gwendylyr sat. He turned his back on her, busying himself with the sack at his side.

"Drago," Faraday said, not moving to seat DareWing. "I am sorry."

He slowly turned around. "Do you trust me not to betray you?"

Faraday's face worked, and her eyes filled with tears. She dropped her face.

"Noah told you to be my trust," Drago said quietly. "*I am* sorry you cannot do that."

"Faraday." Now Leagh was beside her. "Come, now, bring DareWing over."

Faraday nodded, and sat the birdman down. "You must wonder what is going on," she said, quietly enough that Drago could not hear.

"I have been through it myself," Leagh said gently. "I do not need to wonder." And she patted Faraday's arm sympathetically.

Once Gwendylyr, Goldman and DareWing were seated in a close group, Drago and the lizard worked the same enchantment they'd executed for Leagh.

This time, both Faraday and Leagh—their cloaks whipping back in the wind to reveal their simple white robes—helped him stretch the single enchantment over the three, and anchor its edges to the ground so that they were enclosed.

Then Drago withdrew the mixing bowl from his sack, and, slowly circling the enchantment, again drew pinch after pinch of what appeared to be dust from the sack which he put in the bowl.

"Do you know what this is?" he asked the two women.

Leagh just shook her head, accepting that whatever Drago did was sorcery beyond her ken, but Faraday thought deeply, her forehead creasing in a tiny frown.

"You have collected all sorts of things that you dropped into that sack," she said. "A piece of bread that you took from Leagh, leaves from Minstrelsea forest, dirt from several different places—"

"A lock of your hair," Drago said, and smiled a little at her.

Faraday ignored his smile. "You have pieces of Tencendor in that sack."

"Yes." Drago's smile widened fractionally. "Good."

"You are using . . . Tencendor's magic, the magic of this land, to work this enchantment." Faraday bit her lip, still thinking. "But why Katie's blood?"

The girl had now moved to Drago's side, a bright crimson drop welling on the tip of her forefinger where the lizard had again obligingly pierced her skin.

"Don't you know?" Katie herself said, pausing to stare at Faraday.

Faraday shook her head, and the girl's face fell and she

turned back to Drago silently, and added her blood to the mixture.

Drago accepted the blood, kissing Katie gently on her forehead, then stirred the mixture with his staff. Faraday opened her mouth, wanting to demand that either Katie or Drago tell her *what* the blood symbolized, but she did not dare interrupt the enchantment, and so she closed her mouth and remained silent.

Drago lifted the staff from the bowl and traced its end over the lines of the enchantment.

Instantly the scene about them flickered and faded, and Faraday found herself standing again in the field of flowers.

Turning, turning, turning as the flowers caught at her robe, turning to see the man who smiled and held out his hand for her.

The Demonic Hour of dawn had passed, and Herme took the opportunity to walk off some of his frustration and sense of impending doom to inspect the city's defenses and state of readiness against . . . against *whatever* it was that that howling horde outside might have planned for them.

Herme sincerely hoped that Drago and Zared would get back before the expectation in the air finally erupted. He was too old and set in his ways to cope with a situation this . . . abnormal, and without Drago's help in evacuating the Carlonese through Spiredore into this Sanctuary, then they were as good as dead if the animals managed to break through the city's defenses.

He checked his wife and family, making sure they were in an easily defensible section of the palace, then joined Gustus and Grawen, another of Zared's men, in an inspection of the defenses down one of the city streets.

Initially, the mood of the Carlonese heartened Herme. These people were not wide-eyed with fear, but narrow-eyed with determination. All the population, save the very young and the bedridden aged, had armed themselves as best they might against any attack.

Women held brooms and pans in white-knuckled grips, men had homemade pikes, clubs and blades. Children, ever inventive, had a variety of slings, stones and, down one street, a complex system of oil-filled barrels set in place.

"Any hoofed creature, or crawler, comes a-running down *this* street," one bright-eyed urchin informed Herme, "he'll get a slippery shock for sure!"

Herme grinned, and tousled the youngster's hair, then followed Gustus and Grawen inside a tavern, inspected the main rooms, then clumped down the cellar stairs. Unlike the atmosphere outside, here the tension and fear were palpable.

"Well?" Herme asked.

Two soldiers and the tavern keeper were crowded inside the cellar, and they glanced among themselves before one of the soldiers answered.

"Sir Earl," he said, hesitated, then simply pointed into a darkened corner of the cellar.

Herme turned and peered, and the soldier thrust a burning brand a little closer to the corner.

There was a cat crouched in a far niche, its head almost buried in an all but invisible crack in the floor.

It was growling softly.

"Gods!" Herme exclaimed. "That's one of Drago's cats!"

Gustus nodded. "We've found them in several of the cellars, sir Earl."

"Then, by the gods! Get extra men in and about those particular cellars!"

Even as he finished speaking, there was a thunder of feet above, and then the cellar stairs were crowded with some thirty heavily armed soldiers.

"Already done, sir Earl."

Herme nodded, and turned back to the cat. "Can any of you hear anything?"

The soldier shook his head. "We've crouched down by the cat, but have heard nothing save her growls. Cats have got better hearing than us, anyhow."

Herme took a deep breath, trying to force from his mind the imagine of hundreds of thousands of rodents crawling through the earth beneath his feet, and turned back to Gustus.

"And then there are the Alaunt," Gustus said, forestalling whatever Herme had been about to say.

* * *

Faraday blinked, overcome by the warmth of the sun and the heady scent of the flowers. The man had disappeared. She looked about her, desperate to find him again despite her resolve. Stately lilies rose to waist height about her, and in between their stems crowded a thousand varieties of poppies and cornflowers and peonies creating a veritable rainbow of color to support the lilies.

"Faraday."

She turned at the sound of the quiet voice, but it did not belong to him she sought.

It was Leagh, standing amid the flowers several paces away. Her cloak had disappeared, and now she wore only the linen robe wrapping itself in the slight breeze about her gently distended figure. Her nut-brown hair tangled over her shoulders and in the lilies at her back and sides.

Faraday moved slightly, and realized that she, too, wore only the linen robe. Even her feet were bare.

She tipped her head back and laughed, feeling the tug of her hair caught amid the flowers.

"Is this the Tencendor that will be?" she cried.

As if in answer, she heard the sharp rapping of Drago's staff, and it summoned her back to the grassy flat in the cold-swept Western Ranges, and the enchantment collapsing over Gwendylyr, DareWing and Goldman, and slowly sinking into their forms.

"What about the Alaunt?" Herme asked.

"It is easier to show you than to tell you," Gustus said, and began to climb the stairs.

Herme managed to suppress, with some difficulty, a frustrated curse, then followed Gustus, taking the stairs three at a time.

Gustus led him silently out into the street, down a block, then turned down a laneway that led them through to the next major street.

There several of the Alaunt were pacing stiff-legged down

the sides of the roadway, their hackles bristling, low snarls filling their throats.

They were staring at the gutters.

One of the hounds raised a head and stared at Herme. It whined, almost as if it were trying to communicate with him. Herme stared at the dog, his fingers twitching with frustration at his sides.

"It is FortHeart," Gustus said quietly. "Sicarius' mate."

Herme wondered how Gustus could tell any of the Alaunt apart, but accepted his words.

"One of my men came to me with words of the hounds just before we left the palace," Gustus continued. "They've been stalking the streets for over two hours now."

FortHeart whined again, her entire body quivering with the strength of whatever she was trying to say.

Herme stared at her, fixated by her golden stare.

She whined yet once more, and suddenly Herme was in a very, very different place.

He stood in the streets of a ruined city. Buildings lay tumbled in great heaps of stones that made the streets almost impassable. He led a tense and nervous force down one of the main boulevards, but toward what Herme did not know. On either side of the boulevard the Alaunt ranged, stiff-legged and hackled, their noses and eyes probing every gutter and hole in the tumbled masonry and—

Someone yelled, and the Alaunt clamored, and something horrible wormed from a crack in the gutter. It was gray and leather-skinned, its head encased in bone-like armor hiding silvery eyes behind narrow slits. Its mouth was huge and hungry, with fangs curving out in every direction. It was a—

"Skraeling!" Herme cried, and suddenly he knew where he was.

Hsingard. Hsingard! Hsingard, where Azhure had led a force that had been cruelly attacked in the streets from Skraelings that had wormed from the—

"Gutters!" Herme cried, and FortHeart yelped. "Gustus, they're coming up through the *sewers*! They're coming up through the cursed *sewers*!"

* * *

"Gwendylyr!" Theod screamed, and suddenly he was hurtling down the slope of the hill so fast Faraday was sure he would fall and break his neck.

Behind him Zared came at a more sedate pace, although still as rapidly as caution would allow him. The sun topped the ridges now, and the dawn danger had passed, although Zared had been forced to hold so tight to Theod during the time Drago had collected the three and worked his enchantment over them he'd wondered if the man would have any unbruised skin left on his upper arms at all.

Below, the three were slowly rising from the ground, their faces uncertain, frightened, and yet full of wonder at the same time.

All had woken in the field of flowers.

"Girls," Drago said softly. "The blankets."

Leagh and Faraday jumped, still lost amid the memories of the flowers themselves, and then hurriedly reached for the blankets, wrapping them about the shoulders of Gwendylyr, DareWing and Goldman. Of the three, Goldman seemed the most oriented. He rose to his feet, struggling with his balance, and gripped the blanket about himself, tearing his rabbit-skin and twig garment to the ground with a few angry jerks.

He drew in a deep breath, then looked about until he saw Drago standing slightly to his left. Goldman stepped over, still careful with his footing, and dropped to one knee before Drago. He took Drago's right hand, kissed it briefly, and stared into Drago's face.

"I am yours," he said, his voice intense. "Tell me what to do."

Drago nodded. "Be patient," he said, "and I will."

He walked over to where Theod sat with his arms tightly wrapped about Gwendylyr. The woman looked up at him, and Drago squatted before her and took her face in his hands.

She was lovely, even under the grime of the week spent roaming the hills as a wild animal, with very pale skin and black eyes framed by equally black hair. She was trembling, but whether from cold or emotion, Drago could not tell.

"What have you made me?" she whispered.

"My handmaiden," Drago replied, and leaned forward and kissed Gwendylyr softly on her mouth.

Theod jerked in surprise and some anger, and Drago

shifted his eyes to the Duke's face. "She is back," he said, "but no longer exclusively yours."

Watching, Faraday felt jealousy so profound sweep her body she shivered violently.

Leagh looked at her. "If you push him away," she said, "you must endure the resultant suffering."

Drago rose and stepped over to DareWing. The birdman had sunk back to the ground, holding the blanket tight about his body. His eyes were bright with fever . . . and rage.

"Will you let me revenge?" he asked.

"Of course," Drago said, and put a hand on DareWing's shoulder.

"Three more!" Mot hissed. "What is happening?"

Sheol did not answer immediately, her eyes scanning the western horizon, but when she did, her voice was very, very cold.

"Something is not right," she said.

Drago rose, his eyes flickering to the east. "What I do now," he said, "will never go unnoticed by the TimeKeepers, even though they still be distant, and this is not their hour. Katie?"

She nodded, and from somewhere, none watching could tell from where, she produced a crimson lily. For an instant she held it before her, then she tossed it high into the air.

It floated for one breathtaking moment, and then it fell.

It struck the gossamer-encrusted mass of crawlers before her, and from the point where it first hit, crimson light radiated out along the strands of the holding enchantment.

Faraday's eyes widened, and she heard Leagh gasp beside her. The grassy flat, as the ravines and gullies, was turning into a sea of red.

A sea of blood.

"They are passing through death," Drago said.

"Where are my sons?" Theod shouted. "At least give me the chance to hug them good-bye!"

Drago did not look at him. "There is no need for good-byes. There never will be again."

Behind him DareWing struggled to his feet and stood by Drago's side. Drago glanced at him.

"Be patient," he murmured. "Not today, but one day . . ."

Suddenly Theod screamed in utter grief and fury. *"They're gone!"*

As he'd watched, the entire mass of people had . . . vanished. The crimson tide had spread to the further reaches of the huge crowd, and the entire twenty thousand had simply vanished.

All that was left was the crimson lily lying in the center of the grassy flat, its petals ruffling slightly in the wind.

Sheol screamed, doubled over, and fell from her mount.

As one, the other three Demons also cried out, and convulsed, all dropping from their mounts and crawling and capering through the dust of the eastern Rhactian Plains. Both WolfStar and StarLaughter stared in amazement, although each was consumed by very different emotions.

WolfStar slowly smiled, but StarLaughter blanched, her eyes wide with concern.

"They do not seem well, my beloved wife," WolfStar said, looking at StarLaughter slyly. "Why is that, do you think?"

She shrieked, and tugged hard on his chain, but even the pain of the choking collar could not wipe the smile from WolfStar's face.

"Do you think this is what the StarSon shall do to them when he inevitably meets your sweet companions?" he gasped, and StarLaughter's mouth hardened and she stabbed into him with her power as well until WolfStar's smile finally faded and he shrieked as loud as the Demons.

But her satisfaction at WolfStar's agony could not dampen her concern at the plight of the Demons, and she almost immediately turned her attention back to them.

"What's wrong," she cried. "What's wrong?"

Sheol was the first to regain some semblance of control, and StarLaughter finally perceived that they were convulsing with rage more than anything else.

"We have lost the souls of a crowd, StarLaughter," Sheol hissed. "A *crowd!* Something, some*one* has snatched them from us! Who? Who? Who?"

"StarSon Caelum," WolfStar managed to say from the dirt. "StarSon Caelum."

Sheol stared at him so viciously WolfStar cringed helplessly, certain she would set one of the other Demons to his rape, but she finally turned aside and howled into the wind.

"Attack! Attack! Attack!"

"They've gone, you misbegotten bastard! They've gone! *Where are my sons?*"

It was Katie rather than Drago who answered. She walked over to the lily, picked it up, then returned to stand before Theod. Very slowly she held it out to him.

Leagh smiled, as did Gwendylyr. Faraday's eyes filled with tears.

Theod stared at the lily, then at Katie.

She regarded him solemnly.

Theod's eyes dropped back to the lily, then he reached out to take it with a trembling hand.

Something unusual, but unutterably sweet, swept through him, and when he raised his eyes he found that he—and all the others still in the same positions about him—stood in an infinite field of flowers. Even the feathered lizard was there, snuffling through the flowers for insects. All the women, Gwendylyr included, wore the low-draped heavy white linen robes, while Goldman and DareWing both wore short tunics of the same material over leather sandals.

DareWing FullHeart very slowly stretched out a wing behind him—now fully healed and glossy black under the bright sun—then the other, and smiled gently.

"Welcome," he said, "to the Fields of Resurrection." At midmorning, in the hour of Barzula, on a frigid spring day in the beautiful pink and cream city of Carlon, the patchy-bald rat launched his attack.

All his life, and all the lives of his ancestors, he had planned and lusted for this moment. Now the two-legs who hunted and poisoned and trapped his kind would die, and they would die more horribly than any of his kind had in choking out their poisoned bellies through bile-stained teeth.

The patchy-bald rat was particularly crippled with loathing

for the small male two-legs. He'd seen every one of his litter brothers and sisters tortured and finally murdered by the loathsome beasts. His litter siblings had been staked out on their backs on the early morning cobbles of Carlon's streets, their legs stretched so that tendons popped and tore. The small male two-legs watched from the safety of the pavements what happened when a heavy cart rumbled around the corner and ran over his vulnerable, squealing brothers and sisters.

The male two-legs had clapped and hooted with enjoyment, especially when one of the rats survived for an extra moment or two of agonized screeching. The patchy-bald rat had never, never forgotten the memory of that screeching filling the early morning.

Now, still mourning, he had his chance for revenge.

Aided with the knowledge of a life spent burrowing amid Carlon's sewers, as with the power given him by the Demons, the patchy-bald rat launched a simultaneous attack into every one of Carlon's streets by almost a billion rodents and sundry crawlers.

Nothing, *nothing,* could ever have prepared the Carlonese for what happened next.

"Papa?"

Theod spun about. Two small black-haired boys were advancing hand-in-hand through the flowers toward him.

They were dressed in short white linen tunics identical to those Goldman and DareWing wore.

"Tomas! Cedrian!" Theod swept them up in his arms, laughing and crying at the same time, and the boys peppered his face with kisses.

"It only takes a small effort, coupled with faith," Drago said, "to walk down the passage never dared, and open the door never opened into—"

He stopped, staring unseeing into the distance, and even Theod and the two boys fell silent and looked at him.

"Dear gods," Drago whispered. "We have lingered here far too long."

* * *

This was the hour of Tempest, and the haze of storm swept the land. The streets and the open spaces of Carlon were empty . . . save for the Alaunt.

As a gray tide of fur and claws and over-bright beady eyes erupted from every conceivable drain and crack, the hounds went berserk.

They wanted to hunt, but they had no one to hunt with.

They wanted to track and kill, for the city was alive with prey, but there was no one to tell them which were more important.

They snapped and savaged, and they killed many, but within heartbeats Carlon's streets had been overrun with millions upon millions of rodents, and even as magical as they were, fifteen Alaunt could do little.

The cats had as little success. They had leaped immediately to the fray, but they were only a dozen, and smaller than the Alaunt, and while they feasted well, they cleared no more than one street corner.

Meanwhile the rats and voles, earthworms grown fat on the rotting land, mice and black millipedes, even the rabbits, hares and foxes that followed in a second wave of destruction, all listened to one voice, and all had one target.

The small male two-legs.

And after they'd all been chewed and nibbled, the small female two-legs would become the next target, and after them the breeders of the small two-legs, the big two-legs, and then maybe, just maybe, the world would be a safer place.

And so, in an attack that left every soldier and guard stunned and confused, the invading rodents targeted every child within the city. Not only did children tend to be in places relatively unprotected by the army and militia—attics, cupboards, pantries, anywhere their parents thought they'd be out of the way—if a soldier or guard *was* there to protect them, then they found that scrambling, tiny-bodied rodents, *tens of thousands of scrambling, tiny rodents,* were virtually impossible to smite and kill with cumbersome pikes, swords or arrows. A man might kill several, maybe a dozen, but then he'd be dead himself, covered in rats or mice, his throat choking with a thousand millipedes.

It made the older among them yearn for the relative certainty of a large-bodied Skraeling.

The youngster who'd impressed Herme with his plan to empty barrels of oil down city streets was among the first to die. The children—and adults, for that matter—had planned as best they could for an invasion of the animals, but nothing had prepared them for this tiny-bodied flood.

The boys, the small male two-legs, died horribly. None of them was granted a quick death. While a score of rats would attack a face, keeping hands occupied, thirty or forty mice would chew into a belly, diving through entrails and tunneling up through diaphragms and lung cavities until the boy began to cough mice and whatever millipedes and centipedes that had scrambled in after the initial invasion.

Then, if circumstances permitted it, the rats and sundry rodents would leap off the dying two-leg's body and sit in a fascinated circle about him, listening to his frenzied screeches and wails, watching his agonized convulsions, their whiskers twitching in anticipation as the blood ran in bright rivulets toward them.

There was little that Herme, or any other captain, lieutenant or even general horse waterer could do, save shout orders for people to climb as high as they could and block exits to floors below.

The streets are awash! To the attic, to the attic!

And when families and army units ran for the attics, and thought of some means whereby to block the gray writhing mass on the stairs behind them, not a few instinctively grabbed at lamps and candles, and threw them down to erect a moat of flame between themselves and the rodents.

But it was not only the rodents that went up in flames.

Within a quarter hour of the initial attack, Carlon was on fire.

Beyond the walls the bestial army howled and shrieked, scrabbling at the gates in the hope that soon guards would be dead and bolts chewed through.

Beyond both walls and demonic force, and totally unnoticed by any, the waters of Grail Lake began to quiver . . . almost as if something within their depths was moving.

Upward.

64

The Doorways

"We have lingered here far too long," Drago said again, and the others looked at each other, wondering at the fear in his voice.

"What is wrong?" Zared said.

"Carlon is under attack," Drago said. "Desperate attack."

"Then what are we doing here?" Zared said, waving an arm at the gently waving flowers. "Get us back to the Ranges, and then to—"

"No," Drago said. "We cannot go back to the grassy flat. It is the mid-morning hour of Tempest, and you and Theod would lose your minds the instant we transferred back there."

He opened and closed his hand about the staff, and the next instant sketched a symbol in the air. Again, without being asked, the feathered lizard poked his head out of the flowers, then raised a claw and retraced the symbol in light.

This was pure white light, and the symbol was the least complex Faraday had yet seen Drago draw.

It was a simple rectangle of light, slightly taller than the height of a man, and half as wide.

Through the rectangle she could see the dizzying balconies and stairwells of Spiredore.

"A fortunately uncomplicated enchantment," Drago said, and Faraday looked at him sharply, hearing for the first time the weariness in his voice. She remembered how Axis, as all Enchanters, had sometimes pushed themselves close to death by wielding enchantments that required them to manipulate a frightening amount of the Star Dance.

"Are you all right?" Leagh asked, moving close to Drago and taking his arm.

Faraday watched Leagh and wished she'd thought to ask first.

Drago nodded. "Quick. Through the door. Theod, say good-bye to your sons. They cannot follow for the moment."

For the moment? Faraday locked eyes with Leagh, but she shrugged slightly, and no one else seemed to take any note of Drago's words. Theod bent close to his sons, kissed each one on the cheek, then stood back as they drifted off through the flowers.

"Thank you," he said to Drago.

"Time enough for thanks later," Drago said. "Through the doorway. Now!"

They walked through, a not unpleasant buzz passing through their bodies as they did so, and on the other side grouped on a balcony within Spiredore. Once the lizard had ambled through after them, Drago turned to the rectangle of light, the field of flowers clearly visible, and literally folded the rectangle up into a tiny box of light which he slipped into a pocket.

Curious, Faraday was about to ask what he was doing when he turned to her.

"Faraday, take Katie and DareWing back to Sanctuary—"

"I come with you!" DareWing said, then bent double coughing.

"—and hand DareWing to one of the Icarii Healers," Drago said. "Tell StarDrifter to expect the people of Carlon to start arriving—and tell him to expect that many of them may be injured. Burned. Then get WingRidge, as many of the Lake Guard as are present, and bring them back to me. *Fast!*"

"How will I find you?" Faraday asked, her eyes and voice steady.

"The bridge leading to Sanctuary can reconnect you with Spiredore, and ask Spiredore to bring you to me."

Faraday nodded. "Katie, DareWing . . . come." She held out her hands, and Katie took one.

DareWing looked at the other, then looked silently back to Drago.

"I need you well," Drago said softly. "Now . . . *go!*"

DareWing continued to stare at Drago for an instant longer, then he jerked his head in assent, and turned to Faraday.

"I can walk," he said, ignoring her hand.

"Spiredore, I ask that you take myself, Katie and Dare-Wing FullHeart to Sanctuary," Faraday said softly, and walked down the stairs before her, DareWing following, leaning heavily on the balustrade.

Drago watched them disappear, then looked at Goldman and Gwendylyr. "I will need your help, as yours, Leagh. Are you strong enough?"

"Yes," Gwendylyr and Goldman said together, and Leagh just nodded.

"But—" Zared said.

"Zared," Drago said. "Swords and fighting skills are not going to save Carlon, not now. These three can. Will you deny me their company?"

Zared shot one desperate look at Leagh—how could he put her straight back into danger after having almost lost her?—then made a helpless gesture. "What can *I* do?"

"Both you and Theod can join us," Drago said, "for your wives will need your support. Spiredore, take us to . . . to Herme, Earl of Avonsdale."

StarDrifter, standing in the meadowlands that lay between the bridge and the valley entrance to Sanctuary, could hardly believe what he was seeing. Faraday and the girl? The Strike Leader? Wearing that . . . that *tunic?* And he looked ill. "Faraday? DareWing . . . What are you doing wearing that—"

"StarDrifter, we have no time for pleasantries. Here, take Katie's hand and look after her well. Is WingRidge close by?"

StarDrifter tore his eyes away from DareWing, taking Katie's hand. "He's still at the top of the stairwell. Some of the Avar Clans are coming in. Some . . . Isfrael has made no effort to order the lot in."

"Get DareWing to a Healer. I have to—"

"Faraday, whatever is wrong can wait just one more moment."

"No, it *can't,* StarDrifter. Carlon is under attack, and Drago needs me back there. Very soon there are going to be tens of thousands of Acharites coming over that bridge, and they are going to be frightened and many injured. You are going to need help here to get them into Sanctuary."

"Yes, but, dammit, *listen* to me Faraday. The Demons have come and gone from Fernbrake. And—"

"Why tell me this?" Faraday almost shouted, desperate to get WingRidge and the Lake Guard and get back to Drago. "We always knew that they would go to Fernbrake! I do not need to hear the details of what desecration they committed there. I just don't want to hear it!"

StarDrifter, angry himself now, seized her arm. "Yes, you *do* need to hear it! They have seized WolfStar, and the damned undead Niah thing he had with him. Whatever else, you cursed *impatient* woman, Drago needs to know that!"

And the details of exactly what desecration had been committed in that dead rose garden, StarDrifter certainly knew Faraday did not need to hear.

She stared at him. "Very well. I will tell Drago. Now, will you let go *my* arm and take DareWing's? He needs your support and help far more than I!"

"Faraday . . . be careful."

"I will, StarDrifter." Impulsively she leaned forward and briefly kissed him. "Take care."

She hugged Katie, and then she was gone. Spiredore sent Drago and his companions into a living nightmare that must have sprung straight from the firepits of the AfterLife.

They walked into a room thick with smoke and heat.

Drago took one breath and choked. He pulled a section of his cloak over his mouth and blinked away the stinging tears in his eyes. "Herme? Herme?"

"Who . . . ?" There came the sound of coughing, and then Herme materialized out of the smoke. His face was smudged and lined with sweat. His scabbard was empty, but his hands were swordless. "Drago? Is that you?"

"Yes. What is happening?"

Herme opened his mouth, waved a hand helplessly, and had to obviously battle tears before he found the strength to speak. "Rodents swarmed from the sewers. Gods, *millions* of them. They attacked nothing but *children*, for the gods' sakes! Our weapons were useless against them. Too many. Too small. People fled to attics and high rooms, and some set fire to their stairwells to prevent the rodents following . . . soon . . . soon . . ."

"Where are we?"

"Where?" Herme looked puzzled, then his face cleared as

he realized no one could see where they were. "We're in the guard room of the palace. *Your* palace, sire," Herme added, belatedly catching sight of Zared and the others. "Gwendy-lyr, is that you? And Goldman?"

They nodded, but did not speak as Drago carried on. "How bad are the fires?"

Herme smiled darkly. "*Bad.* The palace, and the two or three streets surrounding it, has not yet caught afire. This heat and smoke is from the rest of the city."

"And the people?"

"Burning."

Drago stared at him, then he spun on his heel, stared into the dense smoke, and gave a piercing whistle.

He waited.

Herme shifted from foot to foot, looked at Zared, who, while he was tense, just indicated Drago with his head and gave a small reassuring nod. He had his arm about Leagh, making sure she kept the hood of her cloak tight about her face to block out as much smoke as possible.

There was a sharp bark in the distance, then another much closer, and the next instant ivory shapes materialized out of the smoke. Sicarius rushed forward and greeted Drago ecstatically, his paws on the man's shoulders, licking his face.

Drago quickly pushed him down, but he had to restrain a grin.

As the hounds milled about, one of the cats appeared, two mice hanging lifeless from its mouth. Another cat loomed from the haze, and then soon the room was milling with Alaunt and cats, pushing through and rubbing up against legs indiscriminately in their joy at seeing Drago back.

Drago started to say something, then choked on the thick smoke. "Enough!" he muttered, and reached into his pocket, withdrawing the small box of light.

While the others watched, Herme in utter amazement, Drago stretched it out into its full size again.

"Spiredore!" he shouted, "take this smoke and smother the damn Demons with it!"

Leagh stared at him. "Drago . . . are you sure? They will know that—"

"They will know anyway," he said. "And I might as well make the knowing uncomfortable for them."

And pray to every god in creation, he thought, that they do not know the *who* behind the doing!

Within moments the room cleared of smoke, save for a thick tendril that the enchanted doorway pulled from a nearby window into its depths.

Herme gave a final cough, and wiped the tears from his eyes. Behind him, Gustus and Gwain, silent and unnoticed until now, stared in amazement at Drago.

"Do you have a map of the city handy?" Drago asked. The TimeKeeper Demons were running their mounts at full speed across the northern Plains of Tare. WolfStar was tied across the back of Rox's former mount, his hands and ankles tied under its belly, his face dragging through the thick dust kicked up by passage of the black beasts. The Qeteb-man sat his own mount easily, the Niah-woman before him. His thick hands held on to her, running automatically up and down her body, kneading her soft flesh as they went.

The smoke enveloped them without warning.

WolfStar did not immediately know what had gone wrong, for the presence of the smoke made relatively little impact on his own problems breathing through the thick dust, but he jerked as his mount faltered, and the Demons and StarLaughter cried out.

The Demons' cries were unintelligible, animalistic shrieks of rage and frustration, and soon the black mounts were milling about in confusion.

Magic!

Enchantment!

Carlon!

Magicians! Magicians!

"What?" WolfStar heard StarLaughter cry out. "What is *happening*?"

There was a continuation of the enraged shrieks for a moment, then Mot roared an answer.

"It is the StarSon! He thinks to frustrate us! Fool!"

WolfStar, even consumed with his own struggle to find air to breathe, nevertheless managed a triumphant—and relieved—grin to himself. He *has* frustrated you, you imp! he thought.

But the next moment a tunnel of clear air appeared through the smoke, and the mounts began their run southward again.

"To Carlon!" Sheol shrieked. "To Carlon!"

And Qeteb. Faraday ran across the bridge, ignoring its polite greeting, and started up the stairs to the Overworld. Damn, how long was this going to take? It seemed that within minutes she was out of breath, her legs and chest screaming in pain, but she gritted her teeth, clung to the railing and literally hauled herself upward. She had hours of this climb to look forward to.

What was happening in Carlon?

She paused, out of breath, and stood with her hands resting on her thighs, her head hanging down, heaving in as much air as she could. Finally, she took a great breath, shook the hair out of her eyes, and started back on the long climb.

"Damn you," she whispered, and hit the railing in frustration. "I need to get to the top!"

And the next instant a breath of cold air ruffled her robe, and a shaft of weak sunlight bathed her face.

She blinked, utterly astonished. How had she done that?

But there was no time for further thought, for here was WingRidge walking across the grass toward her.

"My Lady Faraday?" he said. "What do you here?"

"Come to fetch you," Faraday said. She looked about, paling a little as she saw what had become of Fernbrake Lake, then noted that only a few Icarii were moving down the path toward the stairwell.

"The Icarii have evacuated?" she asked.

WingRidge nodded.

"And the Avar?"

"Isfrael claims he can protect them better."

Faraday's patience snapped and the words were out before she even thought. *"Has he muddled his mind fucking deer arse?* What does he think to *do* against the cursed Demons?"

WingRidge stared, speechless. His perception of Faraday had just been stood on its head.

"Qeteb is only a soul away from seizing their minds forever," Faraday said, still furiously angry. "And Isfrael just says he can protect them better? Ah!"

She made a curt gesture of utter impatience and frustration, and WingRidge thought it prudent to steer the conversation back to her original statement. "You said you had come to fetch me?"

Faraday took a deep breath and calmed herself. Isfrael would have to wait . . . but what would that wait cost the Avar?

"Drago needs you," she said. "In Carlon. Now. With as many of the Lake Guard as you can muster."

"I have only a few score with me here," WingRidge said. "The rest are . . . are at the Maze Gate."

"What are they doing *there?*" Faraday asked.

"Attending to its needs," WingRidge said, ignoring Faraday's exasperated look. "What are we waiting for? How do we get to Carlon?"

"First," Faraday said, "we have to get down those stairs again."

The floor of the room vibrated gently, and Drago strode over to the window as Gustus rummaged about in a drawer for a map.

What he saw through the flames and smoke rising from the city made him grip the windowsill in support. The waters of Grail Lake were now so shallow that he could clearly see the Maze in their depths.

And the Maze was rising. Slowly, but inevitably. It had been waiting tens of thousands of years for this moment.

Drago raised his eyes slightly. Spiredore stood apparently serene and unconcerned by the growing conflagration over the Lake.

And unapproachable.

There was no way anyone could cross the Lake now, and time had run out for the people of Carlon to be gathered in some square for a dash through the army outside.

Drago turned back into the room, and glanced at the rectangle of light. Smoke was still filtering through a far window and through the doorway. Not only had the room cleared of smoke, but a large portion of Carlon as well.

It was time to give the doorway something else to do.

"What we will do," he said, "is to get the people of Carlon through this doorway. It will take them via Spiredore to Sanctuary."

"So all we have to do," Herme said in a voice heavy with sarcasm, "is get all the people of Carlon *out* of their burning homes and *into* this room, and then everything will just be wonderful."

"Herme," Zared said warningly, but he, too, looked at Drago with raised eyebrows.

"Do you have that map, Gustus?" Drago asked.

"Aye, sir. Here."

Drago took the proffered map and calmly spread it out on a table. He leaned over the table, staring intently at it, the fingers of one hand gently tapping as he thought.

"For the gods' sakes!" Herme yelled, hitting the table with his fist. *"Carlon is burning!"*

"Then to you I give the task of finding as many people in the palace, and the blocks surrounding the palace, as you can," Drago said, straightening up. "You will bring them into this room, and you will send them through the doorway."

He waved at the rectangle of light. "Everything that goes through that doorway will end up at the bridge before Sanctuary, so, Herme, make sure that only *people* go through that doorway. Do you understand me?"

Herme nodded.

"Good. Then *move!*"

Herme grabbed Gustus and began giving him orders in an urgent monotone as they walked through the chamber doorway into the outside doorway.

"And us?" Zared asked.

"*And* the people beyond this palace and its immediate environs?" Theod put in.

"Well," Drago began, but before he could go any further, Faraday, WingRidge and some sixty members of the Lake Guard tumbled through the rectangle of light.

"How did we get down that stairwell so fast?" WingRidge was saying to Faraday as he came through, and then he stared about in amazement as he realized where he was.

Lake Guardsmen and -women tumbled through after him, and soon the room was filled with bodies and voices.

"WingRidge," Drago said, "send twenty of your command through that doorway," he indicated the chamber doorway. "Outside they will find Earl Herme and some members of

Zared's army. They are trying to evacuate as many people as they can find in the immediate vicinity into this room and then through that door. The Lake Guard can help. Do it!"

WingRidge quickly sent twenty of the Guard running through the door.

As they ran, Drago bent down to Sicarius and whispered something to him. The hound whined briefly, and then four of the Alaunt had dashed after the twenty Lake Guard.

"They will help find those trapped," Drago said, and then smiled a little at Faraday. "Thank you for getting back here so fast."

He looked about the room. "Now listen. We have little time."

He cocked his head slightly again toward one of the windows. "The hour of Tempest has passed," he said. "And that will make things slightly easier for us."

He lifted a hand and drew four separate symbols in the air before him. When the lizard had completed retracing them in light, four more doorways stood glowing in the center of the room.

WingRidge stared at the doorways, then stared at Drago, nodding slightly to himself.

"Faraday, Leagh, Gwendylyr, and Goldman," Drago said, "you will each take one of these doorways and go to," he named four sections of the city, "where, as Herme does here, you will gather as many people as you can and send them through the door. I say to you what I said to Herme. Make sure *only* people go through those doorways, because *anything* can go through, and I do not want a tide of rodents, or anything worse, to descend on Sanctuary."

"*I* can manipulate that enchantment?" Goldman said wonderingly.

Drago spared the time to smile gently at him, including both Goldman and Gwendylyr in his next remark. "You can feel the changes within you since . . . since the field of flowers?"

They nodded.

"You have been reborn in the fullness of Acharite blood," Drago said. "As have I, Faraday and Leagh."

His mouth twitched. "I think you will find yourselves somewhat amazed at what implications that will have for your lives. But for now, will you just trust me when I say, this enchantment you will be able to manipulate with ease?"

"Aye," Goldman said. "After what you did for us this morning, I could trust you if you said I could survive the Demons themselves."

"Pray it does not come to that!" Drago said hurriedly. "Each of you can take two of the Alaunt with you to help find those trapped—"

"May I take the cats rather than the hounds?" Goldman said.

Drago nodded. "If you wish. Why?"

Goldman squatted down and picked up one of the cats. "I've ever had an affinity for cats, my Lord."

"Don't call me that," Drago said sharply, then turned to WingRidge. "Send some of your guard with each of them. Zared, Theod, go with your wives. They will need your aid."

As WingRidge sorted his guard into groups, Faraday spoke. "How do we use the doorways?"

"Walk through, and you will find yourself in Spiredore. Once there . . . do you remember how I folded the door and pocketed it when we left the field of flowers?"

Faraday, as Goldman and the other two women, nodded.

"Do the same. You will find it easy. Ask Spiredore to take you to your particular section of the city and, when you get there, simply unpocket the doorway and unfold it."

"And when we have found all the people we can?" Gwendylyr asked.

"Then go back through yourselves. Refold the doorway, and ask Spiredore to return you to me."

"And you?" Faraday asked.

Drago looked carefully at her, not sure if the question was asked because she felt he'd given himself nothing to do, or because she was concerned for him.

"WingRidge and I have something else to attend to," he said softly. "Now, go."

The three women and Goldman collected their respective groups of members of the Lake Guard, Alaunt and cats, and moved through their doorways.

When the room was empty save for himself and WingRidge and the single remaining glowing door, Drago reworked the enchantment surrounding the door so that it would again take people directly to Spiredore, then turned to speak to WingRidge.

"The Maze is rising," he said.

"Aye," WingRidge answered. "It needs to speak with you."

65

Evacuation

Faraday led her group of Lake Guard and several of the Alaunt into horror.

Faraday stopped dead just inside the room where Spiredore had deposited her. It was not the heat that had riveted her attention, even though it was close to being overwhelming, nor the smoke which had thickened enough to be irritating if not choking, but the sight directly across the room.

A crowd of rodents ringed a small boy seated against the far wall. The rodents had originally been facing the boy, but when Faraday and her companions had abruptly appeared in the center of the room, they'd turned as one to face the intruders.

Faraday had no eye for the rodents. All she could see was the boy. At first sight he reminded her of Isfrael when he was about five or six, for he had the same green eyes, pale skin and blond hair, although his features were very different.

But as Faraday's vision adjusted to the smoke and heat, she realized that normally the boy had a ruddy complexion, and if he was pale now, it was only because he sat in a pool of his own blood. His green eyes were as wide as Isfrael's had been, but they were widened with horror and agony, rather than curiosity and wonder.

Faraday began to step forward, then halted, appalled.

A mouse, covered in clotting blood, wriggled out of the boy's half-open mouth and dropped down over his ragged belly into his lap.

Another mouse emerged, as bloody as the first, and then a veritable swarm of the creatures wriggled out of the boy's mouth.

"No," Faraday said flatly, trying to deny what she was seeing. "No!"

But it was too late. The boy gave a single hiccup, choked, then died.

There was a movement among the rodents, and Faraday refocused on the rat that walked several paces toward her. It was twice the size of a normal rat, its pelt patchy-bald in places, and its black eyes bright with pure venom and, appallingly, intelligence as keen as Faraday's own.

Somehow, horribly, Faraday could see inside its mind.

It was a warren of dark tunnels and mazes. The rat's consciousness seized hers, and Faraday found herself being pulled along one of the tunnels at breakneck speed, toward some horror that awaited her at the heart of the maze.

She could hear, *feel*, that heart beating with pure malevolence.

No, she thought. *No!* She *knew* what existed in the heart of that Maze!

Get you gone, breeder of small two-legs, the rat said in her mind, *or I shall deliver you into the hands of—*

In the extremity of her fear, Faraday reacted with pure instinct.

In her mind she drew an image of a rat trap, drew it with glowing lines of light, and with all the strength she possessed she threw it toward the patchy-bald rat.

"Get you *snapped*, you filthy disease-monger!"

The rat screeched, and then suddenly its head caved in and its ribs blew apart.

The maze disintegrated, and Faraday's mind was freed.

She smiled, an expression of pure coldness.

Every rodent, worm and burrower and crawler within Carlon suddenly stopped what it was doing and turned itself toward the building where Faraday had just killed their leader.

Then, as a single entity, every one of them screamed (or screeched or moaned or rasped), then scuttled for the nearest dank hole leading back to the sewers.

The brown and cream badger grunted in fury. He quivered, and then gave the order his furred comrades had been waiting to hear for a long, long time.

Faraday blinked, and realized that the room was full, not

only of those who'd come through Spiredore with her, but
with five or six terrified men and women, huddled in a far
corner.

Faraday walked over to them, touched the cheek of the
nearest woman, and smiled, with warmth this time.

"Do you see that door?" she said softly, indicating the
glowing rectangle of light. "It leads to escape and to wonder.
Take the hand of this Icarii man behind me, and he will guide
you through."

One of the men huddled at the back of the group was wrin-
kled with age, and the joints on the trembling hand he now
raised were swollen and painful.

"Queen Faraday?" he whispered. "Is that you?"

"My name is Faraday, indeed," she said, taking his hand,
"but I am queen of nothing but my own destiny. Now, will you
come?"

Even though Faraday, Leagh, Gwendylyr and Goldman had
all moved to different parts of the city, the business of evacuating two hundred thousand people from a burning and fear-
filled city through five small doorways was a mammoth and
well-nigh impossible task.

Nevertheless, several things worked in their favor.

Sheer luck—or Spiredore's good sense—had placed Faraday in the very room the patchy-bald rat inhabited, and her
ability to trust in, and use, pure instinct, together with a long
familiarity with the processes of power, had witnessed the
patchy-bald rat's demise and the subsequent panic and flight
of all his comrades within Carlon.

Suddenly, the creatures that had panicked the entire city
were gone.

The Alaunt and the members of the Lake Guard moved almost as one, hunting out pockets of terrified humanity and
directing them toward the rooms where the women and
Drago had erected their doorways of light.

Goldman, of course, relied on the cats.

Faraday, Leagh and Gwendylyr induced calm by their very
presence. People huddled choking and close to death in a
corner of an attic or kitchen or on a landing of their stair-

wells, would look up to see the smiling face of what they first thought was an apparition of one of the spirits who guided souls in their journey through to the Gate of the AfterLife. Lovely, serene, dressed in flowing white robes, the apparition would bend down with an extended hand, and people would suddenly, startlingly, realize that they looked into the face of Queen Leagh, or the Duchess Gwendylyr or, for some of the older people, the face of the mythical, enchanted Faraday.

There were no questions, no panic. They took the hand offered them, and followed the Icarii who guided them, and they stepped through glowing rectangles of light into a maze of twisting stairs and crazily canted balconies, then onto a bridge—who spoiled the dreamlike quality of their journey thus far with some persistent questioning—and then found themselves on a flower-lined road that led to a magical valley.

Goldman had as much success as his three female companions, but with a slightly different method. Like Gwendylyr, Goldman was still absorbing the full impact of his journey from crazed psychotic to a man not only restored in body and soul, but also augmented with something . . . more. A depth that he'd never realized he'd possessed. Whatever this "depth" was, it did not feel in the least foreign, but very much a part of him, and Goldman realized that he'd been living a half-life to this point.

Now he felt more the priest than the guild master, more the mystic than the hard-talking and scheming Master of Guilds.

He felt as if his spirit had come home.

Goldman was certainly home in body. He knew Carlon better than he knew the contours of his favorite pillow. He'd been born in this city, had spent his childhood scrambling about its roofs and creeping through its cellars, had spent his youth learning its idiosyncrasies in the city workshops, and had spent his adulthood exploiting those idiosyncrasies for the gain of the city's guildsmen and traders.

Now he put a lifetime of knowledge, plus his newfound "depth," to good use. The cats helped Goldman, as the Alaunt helped the women. They found the secret places where parents had hidden children, and the cunningly disguised doors that led to smoke-filled closets filled with the hidden.

They also invariably led Goldman through kitchens to get

to where they had to go, but when Goldman clapped his hands and told them to get to the business at hand, they would do so uncomplainingly, even though they flicked their tails in disgust.

But Goldman had far more in mind than going through his section of the city room by room. Already he could hear buildings crashing down as walls and supports burned through. Drago may have cleared the city of much of the choking smoke, but he could do nothing about the spreading flames through tight-packed tenements that shared walls and roofs.

Goldman knew this was no time for a leisurely stroll through the deathtrap his beloved city had become.

"ProudFlight," Goldman said to the Lake Guard Lieutenant who led the group of guardsmen and -women WingRidge had assigned Goldman. "We are within two blocks of the Wool Weavers Guild Hall. Get me there."

"But—"

"Get me there, and then get on with your task of getting people into the doorway."

"And you?"

Goldman would have grinned, save the situation was getting more desperate by the moment. "Get me to that Hall, and you shall see."

They moved into the street, wrapping spare cloths about their heads as some protection against the thickening fumes. Now that Drago's door was again evacuating people, the smoke was rapidly rebuilding to a point where it was causing serious difficulty in breathing. Burning cinders and ash drifted down from fiery buildings, and ProudFlight spread a wing over Goldman to protect him, disregarding the cinders that burned holes through his feathers.

Fortunately, the streets they took were not badly obstructed by burning debris, and they reached the Wool Weaver's Guild Hall in a relatively short time. Thank the gods, Goldman thought, that the Wool Weavers were a rich enough guild to build with brick rather than wood and shingle!

"Leave me," he said to ProudFlight, gasping for breath. "I will be safe enough here for the moment. Fetch me . . . fetch me when the bells stop."

"The bells?"

"When the bells *stop!* Now, go!"

Goldman gave ProudFlight a shove, and after a glance to make sure the Master of the Guilds had entered the building, the birdman ran back down the street toward the block his command were currently evacuating.

Goldman stumbled inside the building, and stood for a moment to orient himself. The Guild Hall was not yet seriously alight, but its interior was nevertheless filled with the smoke and cinders of the conflagration to either side, and Goldman knew he couldn't waste time by running aimlessly from room to room.

Ah! There! Goldman walked as fast as he could through the shifting, gray-filled gloom, keeping a hand on a wall for direction and support.

He reached a small and almost hidden door, opened it, and climbed the stairway it revealed.

Drago glanced over his shoulder at the group of people that Herme herded into the room. They stared at the glowing door, then walked through without question, glad enough to escape the certain death that awaited them in Carlon.

He returned his gaze to the sight out the window. The Maze was evident as darker smudges of gray under the silvery waters of Grail Lake.

"How long?" he asked WingRidge standing beside him.

"It will take some days, perhaps a week, to fully emerge," WingRidge said. "It will gauge its rising to the approach of the Demons."

Drago nodded absently, his attention now focused on what he could feel of the TimeKeepers. They were still distant, many days travel away . . . but they were very, very angry.

Enraged.

"StarSon!" WingRidge barked, and Drago leaped out of his reverie, surprised not only by the tone in WingRidge's voice, but by the title.

However much Drago had thought he'd accepted it, reminders of his heritage still came as uncomfortable shocks.

"StarSon!" WingRidge said again. "Look!"

Drago stared to where the captain of the Lake Guard pointed, and drew his breath in sharply in shock.

"Dear gods!" he whispered.

The gates of Carlon were rocking back and forth, back and forth, and Drago realized the guards who manned and maintained them were either dead or gone.

As he watched they broke asunder, and a surging tide of maddened animals seethed through into the streets of Carlon.

Then he, as WingRidge, jumped in further surprise.

A peal of bells had sounded over the burning city.

Goldman gritted his teeth and hoped he remembered the correct clarion. The guildsmen of Carlon lived their days according to the dictates of the sundry guildhall bells. The bells rang out the hours, the workday, the holidays, the watches, the curfew, and—unknown to most of the aristocracy of the city—they also rang out coded messages.

Goldman had learned the code and the method of ringing as a child, but he'd not done this for many years, and he hoped that he got the code right.

He rang a clarion of escape, of doorways, and of location. The bells demanded that guild-folk everywhere hark to their message, and move those they were with through the streets and whatever buildings still stood toward the doorways. Into his clarion, Goldman put something a little bit extra. A bit of depth. A degree of compulsion. Anyone hearing the bells, and understanding their message, would be forced to act.

Goldman finished a clarion and paused to heave in some breath. Had any heard? Had they understood? Had—

From somewhere else in the fiery, smoke-filled city, another clarion of bells rang out. Goldman grinned weakly in relief. Someone *had* heard him, and he *had* got the message right, for now a guildsman far distant was repeating the message.

Another set of bells started, slightly closer this time, and Goldman laughed out loud as he saw a man hustle his family and neighbors down a steep ladder from their roof and lead them toward the building where Goldman had erected his doorway.

Another family rushed from a doorway.

Not everyone would understand the bells, but there would be enough guildsmen to interpret.

ProudFlight appeared in the street, glanced up at the window where Goldman's face was framed, and beckoned him down.

"We have trouble," ProudFlight said tersely as Goldman joined him.

"What?"

ProudFlight did not have time to answer, for at that moment a huge pig ran around a corner, its hooves scrabbling for purchase on the cobbles.

In the distance, a woman screamed. The sound was cut off halfway through.

"The gates have fallen," ProudFlight said, and Goldman felt cold fear slither through his belly.

"Gustus!" Drago yelled, "continue with the evacuation! Herme! Follow me!"

"What can we do?" Herme said, running after Drago as he rushed through the door.

Once outside their progress slowed. The hallways of the palace were full of people moving toward the enchanted doorway, and Drago, Herme, and the feathered lizard which had followed its master, had to push bodily though.

Its crest was held high, and it had ruffled out its feathers so that it appeared a third again as large.

"What can we do?" Drago said harshly. "Not much, save protect these people as well as we are able."

WingRidge caught up with them. "Do you want me to take the Lake Guard away from their duties helping those trapped?"

Drago shook his head. "Their only hope is to get through that doorway as fast as they can. WingRidge, if you serve me as you say you do, then *get those people through!*"

WingRidge nodded curtly, then vanished among the crowd.

"And what are *we* going to do, Drago?" Herme asked.

"Against several hundred thousand maddened beasts? Well, I don't intend to hold them off single-handedly, if that's what you thought, Herme. Come on! No time for detailed explanations."

And what *would* he do? Drago thought as he and Herme

jerked to a halt in the courtyard of the palace. Outside the courtyard gates they could see the streets seething with a mass of animals and as they watched several sheep, a goat and a half-grown bitch ran inside the gates, snuffling carefully about the shadows.

He could draw another doorway—but where could he send them? Wherever he chose, he would risk a mass of them escaping into Spiredore . . . and that thought did not bear thinking about, not with thousands of Acharites passing through each minute.

"Drago?" Herme prompted. One of the sheep had spotted them, and stood completely still in the center of the courtyard, staring.

Its lower jaw fell open and it drooled.

Somewhere in a distant street a man screeched in horrified surprise, wailed in agony, and then fell silent.

"Drago?"

The sheep took a step forward, and then another one.

Drago's hand tightened about the staff, but he called forth no enchantment.

What should he do? Gods, but he wished he'd not sent Katie back to Sanctuary!

The sheep suddenly launched an attack. It leaped forward, wailing, its teeth bared, bloody foam frothing from its mouth. Its movement attracted the attention of the other sheep, the goat and the bitch, and they, too, slunk slack-jawed toward where Drago and Herme stood in the doorway.

"For gods' sakes, man!" Herme said, grabbing Drago's arm. *"Get back inside!"*

In answer, Drago seized Herme, pushed him back through the door, and pulled it shut.

In the same instant the sheep reached him, and in one smooth movement Drago brought the staff around and cracked the sheep over the head with it. The lizard sunk its teeth into the wool at the sheep's throat and began to shake the creature.

Drago flinched as bloody foam from the sheep's mouth splattered across his face, then, coming to an instant decision, altered his grip about the staff, and then drew a symbol in the air.

The lizard, still with his jaws locked into the sheep's neck, struggled to raise a foreclaw, but Drago grabbed it.

"No."

The sheep convulsed, and bloody specks flew through the air. Drago ducked his head to try and avoid them, and then fell to the ground as the goat leaped over lizard and sheep, its teeth snapping a bare hand span from Drago's face.

The goat hit the closed door with an audible thud, landing on its side on the stone step and rolling heavily against Drago.

Drago struck it a heavy blow to the head, and had raised the staff again when he—as every other living creature within Carlon, sane or not—halted transfixed.

A heavy voice sounded over the city. It was thick and menacing, and sounded as if it spoke through . . . water.

Attend!

Both sheep and goat stopped struggling, and the other creatures in the courtyard froze.

Attend!

Drago slowly raised himself to his feet. He put a hand on the lizard's head, and it released the sheep, standing itself and looking about. Every creature they could see had stopped in its tracks. Eyes were narrowed, ears cocked, heads tilted to one side.

Listening.

I command you, attend!

No one noticed Drago's lips moving very, very slightly. The pig had been about to attack Goldman and ProudFlight when the voice sounded.

It stopped some three paces from where both men huddled against a wall, ProudFlight with his sword drawn, and turned very slightly toward the Lake side of the city, listening intently.

I command you, attend!

"What is that?" ProudFlight said, shaking his head slightly.

Goldman tilted his head and spoke very, very quietly into ProudFlight's ear. "It is an enchantment."

Faraday had also halted. The room she stood in was packed with people about to move through the doorway, now standing still and confused.

As Goldman, she recognized the voice for what it was.

"Quick, go through!" she said, putting her hand in the small of the back of the person standing next to her and pushing none too gently. "Quick, or the people behind you will die!"

The line began moving again.

The brown and cream badger raised his snout from the remains of the old woman he'd cornered coming out of a doorway, and snuffled the air.

I command you, attend!

Like Goldman, Faraday and the other two women now also herding their charges through the enchanted doorways with renewed urgency, the badger recognized the voice as a sham. An enchantment, although he was not sure of the mechanics or origins of its making.

No! No! he commanded. *Do not attend. This is—*

He got no further. A clutch of cows hurtled about the corner and knocked him against the wall.

They did not stop, nor even look at their commander.

They were attending the voice.

Within moments the majority of the animals and demented humans which had invaded Carlon were dashing back the way they'd come, slipping and sliding in their haste to obey. Some ran straight into burning buildings in their haste, reemerging on fire, and setting fire to their companions thronging the streets leading back to the main city gates.

No! No! the badger cried, but it was too late, they would not listen to him, they were desperate . . . desperate . . . desperate . . . and the voice became more insistent, far more commanding.

They were running for the Lake to attend the Maze which *surely* was about to rise at any moment. There was something in that Maze that the animals knew they would adore, venerate, worship, and which they were sure would adore them in return.

And now it called!

Run! Run! Run to be the first among the ranks lining the Lake!

The badger gave up trying to reason with the mobs fleeing through the streets. He communed with the Demons, letting them see with his eyes what was going on, letting them hear what was ringing through the cinder streets of Carlon.

He struggled to his feet and trotted down an alleyway, thinking to take a shortcut through to the main avenue leading to the gates, when he ran headlong into a man wearing a short white robe and one of the birdmen, a sword in his hand.

"What a nasty mind you have," Goldman said to the badger which had skidded to a halt a bare pace from him.

The badger hissed, and sent everything he saw and heard back to the Demons.

Drago opened the door revealing a disgruntled—and extremely bewildered—Herme.

"What was that voice?" Herme said. "Attend *who?*"

"A sham," Drago said shortly. "And one that will not last for long. Herme, this city has become an oven. Within half an hour no one will be able to survive within its limits. If there is anyone left in this quarter of the city, then get them to the doorway *now!*"

As Herme huried off, Drago spared a moment to look about him. The ancient Icarii palace had thus far survived the flames, and Drago wondered whether, like the hidden city of the Minaret Peaks, it could survive just about any disaster relatively intact.

Well, if it survived this fire, it would find itself sheltering a dark master indeed. The feathered lizard rubbed against his legs, and Drago smiled a little and rubbed its head.

"Did you enjoy the taste of sheep, my friend?"

The lizard grinned.

The badger growled as ProudFlight advanced a step.

"Mind, young man," Goldman said, "this one is particularly nasty."

In truth, Goldman was intrigued. He found that he could see inside the badger's mind, or, at least, understand some of the thoughts that were chasing themselves about the badger's head.

"Wasn't that a clever enchantment?" he said, his tone condescending. "And a clever, clever badger to be able to see through it."

A shifting mass of shadows loomed behind the badger's eyes, and Goldman abruptly realized that there was *more* intelligence and knowledge in those eyes than he'd originally reckoned with.

"Who are you?" a voice hissed from the badger's mouth.

Goldman licked suddenly dry lips. The voice was horribly reminiscent of the voice that Drago had conjured up, and Goldman realized he was speaking to one of the Demons.

Which? he wondered.

"Sheol," the voice hissed, and the badger squatted a little and urinated on the cobbles.

"And a fine good afternoon to you, Mistress Sheol," Goldman said pleasantly. "And now . . . if you'll excuse me . . ."

He began to step about the badger, but then felt *something* reaching out from the animal, something that promised frightful agonies if it reached him. He gasped, stunned, but just as he felt the power touch him ProudFlight plunged his sword into the nape of the badger's neck.

The power dissolved instantly, and Goldman relaxed in relief. He raised his head to thank the birdman but ProudFlight simply grabbed him and hustled him back toward the building—now leaning precariously to one side—where glowed their enchanted doorway. When they finally attained the chamber, Goldman suddenly desperately, remembered the cats, and he turned back to the door leading to the corridor.

"What are you doing?" ProudFlight yelled.

"The cats—"

"The cursed cats can look after themselves. *Get through that door now!*"

Goldman grabbed the birdman's arms, meaning to shove him to one side, but the birdman was much stronger than he, and in the full pride of Icarii youth, and Goldman stood not a hope against him.

The last thing he saw as ProudFlight shoved him through the glowing door was the ceiling collapsing in a shower of sparks and flaming debris.

* * *

The Demons sat their mounts, thinking. What was that, who was that, the badger had spoken to?

There had been a power in him. Something unexpected and, while the man had not been able to use it effectively, the potential was enough to fret at the Demons' minds. They shared their visions and thoughts with StarLaughter, thinking she might be able to explain it.

But StarLaughter shook her head, just as puzzled.

Desperate to solve the riddle, the Demons then allowed WolfStar to share what they'd seen.

"What is it, this power within this man?" Sheol asked.

But WolfStar shook his head. "I do not know," he said, and then grinned. "But I think the StarSon is gathering to his side his lieutenants for the battle."

For that he paid. Dearly.

66

Cats in the Corridor!

The chamber was still crowded as the evacuees Herme and his men had found within nearby tenements filed through the doorway, but even so Drago felt the arrival of Goldman and the Lake Guard who'd been with him.

He turned in time to see them step through air that appeared to ripple slightly, as a still pond that shelters deep secrets. It was the first time Drago had witnessed how Spiredore nonchalantly inserted someone into the spot they'd named.

"Well?" Drago said.

"Everyone we could find in our quarter has been moved through the doorway," Goldman said, patting a pocket in his robe where he'd stored the folded doorway.

"Everyone *alive*," ProudFlight said.

"Except the cats," Goldman muttered.

"The cats?" Drago said.

"They disappeared when we were leading the last of the

Acharites through," ProudFlight said. "Goldman feels he should have saved them."

Drago put a hand on Goldman's shoulder. "They were not your responsibility."

Goldman nodded unhappily, and Drago tightened his hand momentarily.

"Were you responsible for the bells, Goldman?" Goldman managed a small smile, glad of the change in topic. "A good idea, was it not?"

"Yes," Drago said. "But if you'd told me about it sooner it might have saved everyone some trouble."

"I am an aging man, Drago, and the weight of my years has addled my wits."

Drago snorted, then addressed ProudFlight. "Split the Lake Guard you have with you into three and then use Spiredore to go aid Faraday, Gwendylyr and Leagh."

ProudFlight nodded and turned aside.

Drago walked over to the window, and Goldman joined him. His face sobered as he looked outside. Carlon was eating itself up. Most roofs were well alight, and walls and floors crumbled under the heat and the weight of collapsing beams. Many streets were now impassable, or completely inundated with piles of glowing rubble.

Goldman blinked back tears, his distress over the cats exacerbated by the sight before him. Carlon was his home, yet far more than just a "home." It was a place of vibrant life and laughter, of tender love and the exquisite pain that love brings, and the very heart of a realm.

Yet here it was dying, and Goldman could barely tolerate the screams of nails tearing from toppling walls and stone exploding centuries-old constructions.

"We must rebuild," he said. "We cannot let Carlon lie in ruins."

Drago took a moment to answer, and when he did he did not look at Goldman.

"Carlon will never be rebuilt," he said. "This is a final death."

Goldman was about to protest when he realized the depth of sadness on Drago's face. He bowed his head, took a deep breath to bring his emotions under control, then looked out the window again.

He could not bear the agony of the city, and so Goldman looked further out to the tens of thousands of creatures massed about the Lake. For the first time in months all their attention was on the water rather than Carlon itself.

Some were paddling about in the shallows, some swimming over the shadows of the rising Maze, all were concentrating on what they thought was the voice of Qeteb speaking to them from the heart of the Maze.

Even as he watched, the voice sounded again.

Obey me, and I will give you all you desire.

Goldman glanced at Drago, noting the very slight movement of his lips.

"That is a deft enchantment," Goldman said.

"It will not work for very much longer," Drago said. "Already some animals are becoming . . . 'disenchanted,'" his lips twitched, "and are turning away from the Lake. Their master is taking his time, it seems, about granting their every wish."

Drago leaned out the window and surveyed the street immediately below the palace. "Nevertheless, it has given my three girls—"

Goldman noted with some humor the proprietorial way Drago said "my three girls."

"—time enough to complete the emptying of their quarters."

"I ran into a badger," Goldman said, "a most ingenious badger. I found . . ."

Goldman paused, again wondering at the depth of experiences that now suffused his being. When would he find the time to fully explore it?

"I found that I could see inside its mind."

Drago looked at Goldman. "Really?"

"Aye. And most disturbing it was, too. This badger *knew* the voice was a trick, but could not persuade his comrades to believe him."

Goldman paused. "He was a special badger, and I spent a moment or two talking with him."

Drago's eyes narrowed. "That was dangerous, my friend."

Goldman nodded. "That badger's mind connected directly to the Demons. One of them, Sheol, spoke to me through the badger's mouth—"

"What! What did you tell her?"

"Nothing! But . . ."

"But?"

"But I think she realized that I was, ah, something 'other' than she, or her companions, had ever expected to encounter."

The Demons must be truly worried by now, Drago thought. When they'd destroyed the Star Gate, they had thought to have destroyed the most powerful well of enchantment in Tencendor—the Star Dance. All the power that remained was that which emanated from earth and trees, and that the Demons knew they could deal with once Qeteb was resurrected.

What they had never known—what *no one* had known—was that the Star Dance lived on within the craft, and literally within the land itself.

Well, very soon they were going to work it out.

But not before . . . gods! not before he had a chance to get into the Maze. Without understanding why, Drago understood that whatever else happened, he had to enter the Maze before the Demons did.

How far away were they? Far enough, he hoped.

"Drago?"

Herme's voice broke into his reverie, and Drago looked at the Earl.

"There are perhaps a score of people to bring up the stairs and send through the doorway," Herme said. "And then we will have done all we can for this section of Carlon. And not before time. Every building surrounding this palace is afire."

Drago put a hand on Herme's shoulder. "I thank you, Herme." He looked beyond Herme to where Gustus and Grawen stood. "And you. Ten thousand at least owe you their lives."

"Nay," Herme said quietly. "They owe *you* their lives, Drago."

"Well . . . Herme, your family?"

"They are among this final score to come through," Herme said.

Drago nodded. "Good. WingRidge? Get everyone through this door as fast as you can. Herme, take the men you have with you, and follow your family through to Sanctuary. Wait for me there."

"And you?" Herme asked.

"Goldman, WingRidge and I will wait in Spiredore for the others to complete their tasks. And then . . ."

"Then?"

Drago shrugged. "Then I will follow what my heart tells me, my friend."

For Faraday, Gwendylyr and Leagh, the situation was growing ever more desperate. Both the fires, and whatever stray animals who had not responded to the enchanted summons, were closing in like a nightmarish net, and yet the people continued to stream toward the houses where the women had erected the doorways.

Faraday, like the other two women, had lost a little of her serenity. Smoke and biting cinders choked corridors, making eyesight difficult, and control almost impossible to enforce. Faraday strode up and down the lines of people in the corridors leading to the doorway chamber, trying to keep them calm, but finding it difficult to keep composed herself when her lungs felt as though they were afire and her voice was lost amid her coughing. She was reduced to simply grabbing people's clothing, urging them along as fast as they could go—and yet trying not to create panic—and patting faces and shoulders in an effort to generate calm.

But no one could retain a convincing facade of calmness in this degree of calamity. Without exception children were screaming their fear and panic; parents were crying and shouting, young men were pushing and shoving, and girls sobbing and collapsing in sorry heaps on the floor and tripping others up.

"What's happening?" Faraday shouted to the Lake Guardsman who suddenly loomed out of the smoke at her shoulder.

"There are thousands more below in the streets!" he yelled, "and more still moving through falling debris and burning buildings to get to us. Ye gods, Lady Faraday! We are never going to get them all out before this goes up completely!"

"Do your best," Faraday shouted. "Do your best!"

Hopelessly inadequate words. *Utterly* inadequate . . . but what else could she say?

A youth close to Faraday suddenly convulsed, screaming in jerky breaths, and everyone within hearing distance dissolved into complete panic—had the fire leaped through the walls? Had the Demons finally arrived to run amok through their midst?

Were the rats back?

"Calm down!" Faraday screamed. "Calm down!"

But the panic in her own voice did nothing to ease the panic of others, and within heartbeats the entire corridor became a mass of pushing, shoving, screaming people, all determined to get to the doorway and achieve their salvation at their neighbors' expense.

Faraday was pushed and pummeled herself. She tried desperately to think of something she could do—surely there was some kind of calming spell her refound Acharite powers could give her? But she could not think in the midst of this frenzy, she could not *breathe* amid this madness, all she could feel and realize was that she was being consumed, sucked into the trampling stampede of elbows and feet and—

Silence.

A shudder ran through the entire corridor, and Faraday swore she could feel it run through the entire building and then sweep through to the crowds in the streets below.

She slowly got to her feet, straightening her robe and rubbing an upper arm where it had been badly bruised.

Drago's cats were kneading their way along the corridor—that was the only verb Faraday's numbed mind could come up with, but it entirely suited the cats' actions. A dozen mongrel courtyard cats were climbing over the mass of people half-sitting, half-lying in the corridor, their paws enthusiastically kneading flesh as they went.

And as they went, people smiled, stroked the cats, and passed them on to their neighbors to be kneaded and loved in return.

Faraday stared, wide-eyed, her lips slightly parted. A cat brushed by her legs, butting his head against her knees, and she bent down to pat him. A deep rumble of purr met her hands, and the cat moved on to the next person.

Faraday remembered something Drago had told her on their long trip north. His childhood spent in utter rejection, totally unloved . . . save by Sigholt's courtyard cats. They'd accepted him and loved him and given him their total friendship, for no price, and without caring that he was the most reviled creature in Tencendor.

And now here they were again, spreading love and friendship, and somehow imparting hope and joy. People rose to their feet and without prompting moved quietly and quickly through the corridors—now miraculously almost cleared of smoke—toward the enchanted doorway.

The Lake Guardsman appeared again at Faraday's elbow. "It's remarkable," he said in a low voice. "A short while ago I would have said we'd never get these crowds through in time. Now, I think we're going to do it with time to spare."

Faraday nodded, but did not speak.

Instead her eyes, bright with tears, followed the progress of the last cat in sight, a rangy ginger tom, as he rubbed his way through the forest of legs surrounding him.

Gwendylyr and Leagh had had similar experiences. No matter the efforts they'd expended trying to keep people calm, as the fires had drawn hotter and closer, and stray, maddened animals attacked those people moving through streets toward doorways, panic spread. Theod and Zared both thought they were about to again lose their wives: Zared was especially worried as Leagh was pregnant. And yet, just as panic erupted into a potentially deadly hysteria, the cats had appeared, happy, loving, utterly relaxed, and within heartbeats their joy and serenity communicated itself to the crowds.

Nevertheless, both Theod and Zared were heartily glad when their wives had shooed through the last refugee, Lake Guard member, whatever Alaunt they had with them, and had stepped through into Spiredore themselves and folded down their doorways.

Leagh was the last one to close her doorway, and just as she reached to fold it down, the cats came bounding through and thundered down the stairs in Spiredore in some mad feline chase until they were lost in its twisting gloom.

Leagh took a deep breath, recovering from the start they'd given her, then folded down the door. Then she stood as if uncertain, holding the glowing cube of light in her hand, a tear running down her face.

"Why so sad?" Zared asked, wiping the tear away. "We have rescued most people."

Leagh held up the cube of light, her face illuminated in its glow. "Beyond this," she looked at the cube, "Carlon lies a-burning. We could save the people, Zared, but we could not save the city."

"A city is only its people," Zared said, his voice gentle.

Leagh shook her head slightly. "Carlon was ever more than that, Zared."

"Leagh . . ." Zared did not know what to say, but Leagh blinked away her tears and pocketed the cube of light.

"Drago," she said, and then led Zared down the stairs before them.

Drago was atop Spiredore. It was close to late afternoon now, the hour of despair well past. He stood at the western parapets, his hands resting on the stone, the wind ruffling his hair and clothes, watching Carlon burn.

It was both a dreadful and an awe-inspiring sight. The entire city was afire. Flames leaped skyward through wreaths of gray and black smoke, and yet, right at the peak of the city, the ancient Icarii palace stood unscarred and unlit.

Drago wondered at its purpose. Why was it being saved?

Directly below was Grail Lake. The Maze was very slightly more visible than it had been earlier in the day, although it was still deep. Creatures continued to line the Lake's shores, but now they were less certain. The voice had not spoken for an hour or more, and both the patchy-bald rat and the brown and cream badger were dead.

Directionless, but still hot for the taste for blood, some of them had surrounded Spiredore, others drifting to join them.

Drago hoped the tower's door was firmly bolted.

A distant rumble of collapsing masonry reached his ears, and he turned back to the rooftop space, unable to watch anymore.

Gwendylyr, Theod, Leagh and Zared stood in a small group to his left, Goldman, WingRidge and the feathered lizard directly in front of him, but against the far parapet, the

Alaunt were curled up in an ivory pile, and Faraday . . . Faraday stood closest to him on his right.

Her eyes were fixed on the burning city.

"It must pain you to watch it destroyed," Drago said.

Faraday's eyes shifted and refocused on Drago's face. "On the contrary," she said, her voice hard. "I experienced nothing but pain and betrayal in that city."

"And now?" Leagh asked, a trifle too brightly.

"We have a bare week before the TimeKeepers reach Grail Lake," Drago said. "Once they have finally reconstituted Qeteb, nothing still walking the surface of Tencendor can be saved. Therefore . . ."

"Therefore?" Zared prompted.

"Therefore we have a week to empty Tencendor of all life into Sanctuary. A week."

"We do it the same way we emptied Carlon," Gwendylyr observed.

"Yes," Drago said. "Each of you will have a region of Tencendor you shall be responsible for. Use Spiredore and your doors. Ask Spiredore to take you to the groups of people left in your region, group by group. Don't waste time moving about the land by foot. Move everyone you can find into Sanctuary. Then, when the Demons have arrived at Grail Lake—you will *know* the moment—step into Sanctuary yourself and wait for me there."

"Do we take the Alaunt?" Leagh asked.

"No. They, as the lizard, go directly into Sanctuary now. Spiredore can hunt out the isolated groups for you."

"And myself and Zared?" Theod asked.

"You go with the hounds into Sanctuary. Your wives will rejoin you there."

"I cannot allow that!" Zared said.

"You must," Drago responded, and his tone was hard and commanding enough to subdue both Zared and Theod. "They can move as fast without you as with you, and neither of you can work through the Demonic Hours. If anything, you will hinder rather than help."

His tone softened. "They can survive without you," he said, and smiled a little to take the sting out of his words.

"Where do we go?" Goldman asked.

"Goldman, you take Nor and the Island of Mist and Memory. Your territory will be the smallest geographically, but Nor is the most heavily populated."

Goldman nodded, bowed, and descended the stairwell into Spiredore. His footsteps disappeared almost instantly.

"Leagh? You shall be responsible for Romsdale, Avonsdale and Aldeni. Leagh . . . be careful."

She nodded, kissed and hugged Zared, then she, too, was gone.

"Gwendylyr, I want you to take Ravensbund, Skarabost—also sparsely populated—and Ichtar."

"And Star Finger?"

"Yes. Empty Star Finger as well. Whatever happens, and whoever remains, make sure they understand the implications of staying in the OverWorld when Qeteb draws breath."

She nodded, farewelled Theod, and was gone.

"And I?" Faraday asked quietly, but her face was ashen. There was only one region left.

Drago did not respond to her immediately. "Zared, Theod? Take the Alaunt and the lizard and go back to Sanctuary. And do not worry too much about your wives."

Zared snapped his fingers at the Alaunt and the lizard, who rose and moved to his side, but Theod hesitated. He stared at Drago, stared at Carlon, then let Zared lead him and their four-legged companions down the stairwell.

Sicarius was the last to go down, and he paused on the top step, stared at Drago and woofed softly.

"Go!" Drago said, but he smiled at the hound, and Sicarius vanished.

Still Faraday stood, staring at Drago.

"WingRidge? Will you wait below for me?" Drago said.

As WingRidge left the rooftop, Faraday stepped up to Drago and slapped his face as hard as she could.

"How dare you send me to—"

"To the forest?" Drago asked softly. "Faraday, the majority of the Avar, and all the wondrous fey creatures of the forests also need to be saved. You know that with Qeteb at their side, the Demons will turn the Avarinheim and Minstrelsea into matchsticks."

"Axis sent me to the forests, and so now you do the same,"

she said, her tone hard and bitter. "And from there it is but one step to the final betrayal, is it not, Drago? How shall Qeteb seize me, do you think? He has no Timozel now to work his . . . ah! But he has WolfStar! Yes, WolfStar shall trick me and seize me and lead me to Qeteb where, in order to save this beloved land," her voice was heavy with sarcasm, "you shall let me die!"

Drago's eyes narrowed. So . . . the Demons had WolfStar, and no doubt the Niah-thing as well. There was something he *knew* should concern him deeply about that, but for the moment it eluded him.

"You have overlooked one minor detail," he said softly. "Did not my father send you pregnant into the forests? Should I now do the same? After all, we must make sure that Faraday does not miss a step on her preordained journey into sacrifice, must we?"

Faraday's face twisted and she raised a hand to hit him again, but Drago seized it in his own before she managed to strike him.

He dragged her closer. "Faraday," he said, and his voice had lost all its anger and was very, very gentle. "Will you never believe me when I say that I will not betray you?"

"You have no choice," she said. "My betrayal is a fated thing."

He gathered her, still stiff and resisting, into his arms. "No," he said, "it never, never is."

And he bent his head and kissed her.

Finally, he raised his head slightly, and stared into her face. "Go fetch your wondrous people and fey creatures into Sanctuary, Tree Friend. Complete the journey that you started so many years ago. Lead the Avar into Sanctuary."

He kissed her softly again. "And go this time knowing that the man who loves you will never, *never*, betray you. Neither I nor Tencendor need your blood."

He lifted one of her hands, and placed it on his chest.

"Faraday, my heart is always your Sanctuary."

67

The Emptying

Of them all, only Goldman thoroughly enjoyed himself. He had always admired the Nors people for their skillful enterprise, and spent many happy hours chatting to old friends as he waved people toward wherever he'd erected his enchanted doorway. The pirates of the Island of Mist and Memory were just as much fun, for they were a colorful lot who never had let morals stand in the way of a profit, and that Goldman fully appreciated. But of all the areas that he cleared, Goldman delighted in the Complex of the Temple of the Stars the most.

Here he could indulge in his newfound fascination with mysticism to the extreme. The priestesses, calm in crisis, were happy enough to indulge him, and Goldman wasted several hours in their company exploring the implications of his newly acquired "depth." The priestesses, in their turn, were equally fascinated by his news of Drago and the power he exhibited.

It would keep them, they declared, in happy contemplation for many a year.

Eventually, it was a five-year-old boy who had to rescue them from the depths of the library and push them toward the doorway set up in the avenue leading to the now-extinct temple.

Both priestesses and Goldman emerged from the library with the most precious of its scrolls stuffed under arms and belts; even the small boy was pressed into carrying an extra armful.

As they paused before the gateway, the First Priestess turned back and stared a final time at her beloved island, then, her face stoic, she stepped into the doorway.

His eyes shining with tears, Goldman stepped after her.

Leagh found her task depressing beyond words. She wished Zared was with her, and yet was glad he was not. He would only have fussed, and in the end made her feel worse. In the end, Leagh found the best remedy to her heavy-heartedness was to keep busy . . . and there was plenty for her to do.

There were still tens of thousands of people huddled away in hidey-holes and secret chambers across western Tencendor. Many of them had hardly ventured out for months, ever since the Demons had first arrived, and Leagh found herself retelling again and again the tale of the Demons, and what was happening, and how Drago had metamorphosed from betrayer to savior (and whenever she said the word "betrayer" she thought of Faraday, and wondered how the woman was coping), and what a wonderful place Sanctuary was.

"And all you have to do," Leagh always concluded, "is step through this enchanted doorway." And she would wave her hand at the glowing rectangle of light that she'd set up in a barn, or a farmyard, or the market square of some small hamlet.

The frightened, thin and often sick people would look at her, look at the doorway, and then exchange glances between themselves.

And then the invariable question. "Can I bring me pigs?" Or cow, or flock of ducks or geese, or whatever they'd managed to secrete away in their barns or under their beds, or deep in their cellars.

Leagh, and she supposed Drago, had never thought that people could have saved so much of their livestock. Somehow she'd thought that every creature in Tencendor had been demonized, but in actuality thousands had been saved.

And so Leagh would smile. "Of course," she would say, and then smile at the thought of StarDrifter's face as a further herd of pigs or cows or dusty mob of poultry cascaded through Spiredore into Sanctuary.

But the secreted herds of domestic livestock were not the largest surprise Leagh encountered.

On the fifth day of her mission, tired and hungry and determined that wherever she found herself next she would beg a meal before she'd provide an escape, she stood in Spiredore and said, "Take me to those who need to be rescued."

And Spiredore deposited her in a cave in the northern cliffs of Murkle Bay.

Leagh spun about as soon as she found herself there, un-nerved by the darkness and the sense of a great many warm bodies surrounding her.

There were snorts, and squeals, and a sense of wave after wave of undulating movement.

And a stench that turned Leagh's stomach.

"Who's there?" she cried, wondering if Spiredore had finally made a mistake and deposited her in the Demons' boudoir itself.

More shuffles and snuffles and the strange sense of great undulating movement.

Leagh realized she was hyperventilating, and tried to calm herself, steadying her breathing with a huge effort. Her stomach heaved again, and at precisely the same moment her baby shifted and jabbed a heel or elbow into the side of her womb.

It was too much, and Leagh bent double and retched.

As she wiped her mouth, she felt something brush or bump against the back of her legs.

Her heart pounding, Leagh spun around, and saw that she stared into the gray-lit dawn beyond the mouth of a massive cave.

She blinked, her eyes adjusting to the dim light . . . and then gasped as she realized what surrounded her.

Ten thousand seals. All with their bodies and eyes directed straight toward her.

Among them crawled crabs and lobsters, and above bats and numerous small birds circled and chatted.

Stunned, Leagh could do little but stare for a long time, then she began to cry as she realized the enormity of the tragedy that enveloped Tencendor. These seals, alone, waiting for help, and gathering to them all the creatures they could.

Hoping that *someone* would come to save them.

Blinking away her tears, Leagh withdrew the cube of light from her pocket and expanded the doorway.

"Sanctuary," she said, and pointed into the door.

Without hesitation, and in the most orderly exodus Leagh had yet seen, the seals, birds, crabs and whatever other creatures had hidden in the cave, made their way through the door.

She stood for hours watching them go through, and as the

final seals passed into the door, and Leagh was about to step through herself, a shape circled down from the very peak of the cave and alighted before her.

It was a very old, and very majestic, speckled blue eagle, and while Leagh had no way of knowing that this was the eagle that had witnessed the final days of the Seneschal, nor even that he was the same eagle that she'd watched spiraling over Grail Lake on the day she'd sat and pined for Zared, Leagh nevertheless understood his dignity and wisdom, and she bowed slightly to him.

"Friend eagle," she said. "Will you accept Sanctuary?"

In answer the eagle cocked his head and stared at her belly with his bright eyes, then he gave a single, sharp nod, and launched himself into the doorway.

With tears still in her eyes, Leagh followed.

In the next two days, she found many similar caches of wildlife.

Gwendylyr ran her evacuation as efficiently as she had run her household, and as efficiently as she'd run Aldeni. Theod may have been the one to attend the Councils, and to wear the glory and the regalia of Duke, but in reality it had been Gwendylyr who'd kept the bureaucratic machinery of Aldeni going, had overseen the courts when Theod was absent (and that had been much of the time), and had supervised the social, political and economic life of Aldeni.

How she'd managed to bear twin sons amid all this activity she'd never known. Well, now her sons were not around to hang on her skirts and slow down her day (and Gwendylyr's eyes always filled with tears when she thought of Tomas and Cedrian), and neither was Theod, dear that he was. Gwendylyr had a task to do, and she did it fabulously.

Like Leagh, she encountered flocks of sanguine livestock among the hordes of frightened peasants, and flocks of wilder life among the shadows of valleys and small woods. To none of them did Gwendylyr deny entry to Sanctuary, and to none of them did she raise so much as an eyebrow.

The day, however, that a battalion of millipedes crawled over her feet to avoid the trampling hooves of some thirty-score red deer, Gwendylyr did permit herself a brief closure of the eyes and a genteel shudder.

A Sanctuary with millipedes would never be quite the same again.

Faraday had the hardest task of all.

When she first stepped into the trees, she asked Spiredore to place her somewhere peaceful, where there were no people. First she needed to walk, and to come to terms with her reacquaintance with the forests. In strict chronological terms, it had only been some eight months since she'd last wandered the trails underneath the trees, but it felt like a lifetime.

Faraday had not realized how much she'd changed since Drago had twirled that damned Scepter about the Chamber of the Star Gate. She encountered memories in the drooping branches of trees, in the cascade of wildflowers in shadowed glades, in the well-remembered paths and the lullaby of the grasses' song.

Here was where she'd fed as a deer, here where she'd been feted by the Avar, here where she'd watched Isfrael being raised without her.

Here where she'd watched Shra seduce him into manhood.

Here, where she trod again.

And yet, even in sorrow and painful memory, the forest was a gladsome place to be. Shy creatures peeked out from shrubs, and tentatively nosed her outstretched hands. Not just the normal timid creatures of the forest, but sapphire and ruby-spined porcupines, orange and blue splotched panthers, beetles that were as transparent and as lovely as crystals.

Finally, after a half-day spent wandering and remembering, Faraday stepped back through her enchanted door into Spiredore.

"Take me to my son," she said.

Spiredore took her, as Faraday had been sure it would, to the Earth Tree Grove.

There, as she had known there would be, virtually the entire populations of the Clans were gathered, save for those who'd had the good sense to make a decision independently of the Mage-King and made their own way to Sanctuary.

Faraday had materialized just inside the surrounding ring of trees, and for a brief moment she knew she could observe while remaining relatively unobserved. The grove was packed. The Avar sat in a great, murmuring crowd before the Earth Tree and her ring of stone.

It was late afternoon, and brands of fire hung about the circle of stone.

Faraday lifted her eyes. The Earth Tree reared into the darkening sky, massive, far larger than Faraday had remembered it, but if it looked larger, then it also looked far less healthy. Its oval, dark green leaves were splotched with mold, and most of its trumpet-shaped flowers had withered. Those that still hung fat and full had lost their jewellike colors, and were now insipid yellows and blues.

Slowly, Faraday dropped her eyes.

Isfrael sat upon his wooden throne under one of the stone arches leading into the inner sanctum of the Earth Tree herself.

He wore only his kirtle of twigs, his hair was uncombed and twisting close to wildness, his arms and hands tense where they gripped the armrests, his eyes narrow, his face— gods, but it reminded Faraday so much of his father!— carefully impassive.

He knew Faraday was there, even though the outer ring of trees still hid her.

She stepped into the grove, and a ripple of awareness passed through the Avar. There was a buzz of excitement and comment, and faces and bodies swiveled toward her.

"Welcome to the Lady Faraday," Isfrael said, his voice clear across the entire gathering. "Welcome to Faraday, my Lady Mother. What do you here, Faraday?"

Why so hostile? Faraday thought. Why? She remembered the conversation they'd had in the Silent Women Woods just before she'd left to go north with Drago . . . if conversation it could be called.

"I might well ask you the same question, Isfrael," Faraday said.

She walked further into the grove, stepping carefully though the ranks of the Avar.

"You are not welcome here," Isfrael said.

Faraday stopped, stunned and angry. Not welcome . . . not welcome *here?*

She was not the only one who heard Isfrael's words with

dismay. A murmur ran through the Avar, and by Faraday's side a woman reached up her hand and took Faraday's briefly in a gesture of support.

"I thank you," Faraday said softly to the woman, and she resumed her walk toward Isfrael.

"I come on behalf of Drago—" she began.

"My mother," Isfrael said, "has an incredible talent for attaching herself to every leading male figure in every crisis this land endures. Do you whore for Drago as you whored for my father?"

Faraday's temper snapped. "It was not *whoring* that made you, but *love,* you arrogant, be-twigged bastard! And love is something I cannot expect you to understand!"

"You are *not* welcome here!" Isfrael repeated, and rose to his feet. "You should never have left the legend to which Fate consigned you."

Suddenly, in a blinding moment of revelation, Faraday understood why he was so hostile. Isfrael, Mage-King of the Avar, Lord of the Forests, loved his legendary mother dearly . . . but only so long as she remained legend. As legend, she embellished and enriched Isfrael's own power and own legend.

As a walking reality, given the Avar's love and loyalty to her and her own history of power, she was a massive threat. Possibly *so* massive, that in Isfrael's own mind, she outweighed even the threat of the TimeKeepers.

No wonder he had not evacuated the forests. Here he was lord. In Sanctuary he only became another chapter in the continuing saga of his mother's legend. Isfrael would rather be lord of a smoking ruin than king of a people in exile.

Faraday felt very, very sorry for him, yet at the same time she was furiously angry. No king could let himself be overwhelmed with such pettiness!

She took a deep breath and addressed the Avar people.

Even though she was dressed simply in her white robe, she was nonetheless an imposing figure with her aura of power and sheer anger.

"My people," she began, and Isfrael stepped down from his throne and began to push through the crowd toward her.

"I once walked among you as Tree Friend. Then, when fate and the Prophecy of the Destroyer meant that I had to leave you and follow the StarMan to Gorgrael's Ice Fortress, I left you in the capable hands of Shra, who in turn was to hand responsibility over to my son.

"That," she pointed at Isfrael, now more than halfway toward her, "is no more my son than Gorgrael was ever my true lover."

"Silence!" Isfrael roared. Fury rippled off him, and made him appear twice his normal size.

Faraday did not back down. "If you were the true son of Faraday Tree Friend," she said quietly, "you would have led these people into Sanctuary long before now."

Isfrael stopped a pace away. His face was flushed, his chest heaving, his fists clenched by his sides. About them the Avar also tensed, ready to leap to Faraday's defense if need be. For days now they'd been uncomfortable with Isfrael's decision to reject Sanctuary, and had met with him this evening to try to change his mind.

"We can survive these TimeKeepers," Isfrael growled. "The trees will protect us. There is no threat!"

Where had she heard these words before? Faraday wondered.

"No threat?" she said, and she turned slightly so she was directly facing the Earth Tree. "Then what is that?"

Isfrael jerked, as if he was going to lunge for her, but before he could move a ghostly apparition appeared under the stone circle and walked forward so it could address the Avar.

It was Barsarbe, once senior Bane of the Avar, and champion of the idea that the Avar could wait out the time of Gorgrael within the safety of their forests without aiding the StarMan.

The apparition opened her mouth, and spoke. "My people, is this our fight? We have the Avarinheim, and now we have Minstrelsea to the south. The Earth Tree sings, and the forests sing with her. We are safe. Gorgrael cannot touch us!"

Barsarbe spread her arms wide, hands and voice entreating. "Don't we have what we wanted? So why help Axis? It will surely only bring further pain to our people, and Mother knows we have endured enough pain. We have what we want," she repeated slowly, lowering her hands, her voice becoming strident. *"I say we have the choice of refusing the StarMan."*

She lowered her arms, and grinned in triumph. "And further I say, why not let Gorgrael have the plains? Why care we? We will be safe here."

Isfrael stared horrified at the shade which, now that she'd finished her piece, slowly faded.

"If I didn't know better, Isfrael," Faraday said softly, "I could swear that you were Barsarbe's son, not mine. What has happened to you? Does absolute power corrupt absolutely?

"My friends." Now Faraday turned to the Avar and spread her arms wide in entreaty as Barsarbe had. She closed her eyes briefly, and prayed for strength.

"My friends. You cannot hide here. When Qeteb rises he will tear these forests apart as a child will tear apart a pastry tart. See."

The entire grove was overwhelmed in vision.

A mighty wind blew in from the west. It billowed with clouds of gray dust and flames of fire, and among the wind strode a giant who reached to the sky. With one step he was over the Nordra, and with another he straddled the Plains of Tare. The next step brought his foot crashing down in the Silent Woman Woods.

Trees splintered and screamed. Fire leaped from grove to grove. The giant roared, and when he roared the entire forest disintegrated.

There was nothing left save splinters of wood littering the bared soil.

Nothing, save the huddled masses of the Avar.

The giant bellowed again, and lifted his foot to bring it roaring down on a hapless Clan group.

It was enough. Faraday ended the vision.

"Qeteb *will* destroy you," she said softly. "I present you with a choice. Take the path I will make for you into Sanctuary, and perhaps have the chance to rebuild. Or die here, and die knowing that everything you love will die with you."

Isfrael stared at her. "You are no longer Tree Friend," he said. "You relinquished that right when you went—"

"She never relinquished that right in our hearts."

A gray-bearded man stood carefully upright, using the shoulder of his daughter to steady himself. "I remember you, Faraday Tree Friend," he said, "although I was but a hot-headed young man when you stood here in this grove and gave us the StarMan. Faraday . . . Faraday . . . then you told us that you would not lead us into the future. Now?"

"Now?" Faraday glanced at Isfrael, then looked back at the old man. "*Then* I said I would provide you with the path. I thought that path was to be Isfrael. I was wrong."

Isfrael went rigid in disbelief. With those words Faraday had effectively disinherited him! Hatred surged through him, but Isfrael did not speak.

"Here," Faraday withdrew the cube of light from her pocket and expanded it into the doorway, "is the beginning of the path. As yet I do not know where it will lead, but I ask you to trust me, and to trust in the future."

The gray-beard looked at the doorway, then he bent, took the hand of his daughter, and raised her up.

Without hesitation, they both stepped through the doorway. A silence, and a moment of decision.

Then, almost as if of the one mind, the entire Avar nation rose to their feet and, one by one, stepped through the door.

"No," Isfrael shouted. "No, this is madness! We can survive, I guarantee it!"

"Isfrael." Faraday's soft voice.

"Isfrael," she repeated, and he raised his eyes to hers.

She opened her arms. "I love you, Isfrael. Do you not remember me saying those words to you?"

"It's too late," he said. "Way too late."

The line of Avar moved rapidly through the door. To one side stood Faraday, to the other, Isfrael. They stared at each other, neither willing to let go the other's eyes, the shifting Avar flickering shadows over their faces.

Why don't you let me love you? Faraday thought, but all she received in reply was a wall of implacable silent hatred from her son. She had abandoned him, and now she had disinherited him, and Faraday knew she had undoubtedly alienated her son forever.

One child, she thought. Fate gave me but one child, and look what I have done to him!

The last Avar clan group stepped into the doorway, hesitating briefly, as if not wanting to leave these two alone.

Then they were gone.

"You should not have done that," Isfrael said quietly, but with malevolence vibrating through his voice. "You should *not* have done that."

And then he, too, was gone.

Gone to nurse his hatred and resentment within Sanctuary.

"Oh, Shra," Faraday whispered into the empty grove. "What have I done?"

Faraday lowered her face and turned it to one side.

When she raised it again she was alone in the grove.

Alone, save for a pleasant-faced woman in late middle age standing just before the circle of stone about the Earth Tree. Her dark brown hair was graying and coiled loosely about Her head. She had cheerful blue eyes and a friendly smile with slightly crooked ivory teeth. She wore a soft pale blue robe, belted about Her waist with a rainbow-striped band.

The Mother.

"Mother?" Faraday said, and suddenly the Mother was before Faraday, and folding her in Her arms. Faraday wept, and clung tighter.

"Daughter," the Mother said, "do not grieve."

Faraday leaned back and made a poor effort at wiping the tears from her face. "Do not grieve? The land is desecrated about us, and worse is to follow. These forests will become wasteland, and you . . . you . . ."

The Mother hugged her again, then took Faraday's face in Her warm hands. "You are a dear girl," She said, "to worry so much about an old woman like Me. Ah."

Her face took on a mock grave expression. "Here you are, lecturing to your son about paths which must be taken, and yet you do not dare the path yourself? You will not open the gate never opened?"

"What do you mean?"

The Mother laid a hand on Faraday's breast. "Follow your own path, Daughter. Follow your heart."

Faraday averted her eyes. "I cannot. If I . . . if I allow myself to love Drago, then he will betray me."

The Mother shook Faraday's face slightly until the woman looked back at her. "Trust," She said.

Faraday did not answer.

"If Tencendor is to be redeemed, and brought through the darkness," the Mother said, "then it will need love to do so."

"As Axis betrayed me, so will Drago—"

"Silence!" The Mother frowned in annoyance. "Have you never thought, you simpleton, what rewards an honest love will bring you?"

"Drago says he will never betray me, but he will . . . for Tencendor. How can you say he won't?"

"I can only say to you . . . trust. Until you learn to dare, you will never learn to live. What is this you exist in now? Some half-life, not daring a single risk? Faraday . . . *take* that risk, and learn to laugh!"

"And death is worth that laughter? Noah told me that by aiding Drago I would either gain complete and lasting happiness and peace, or annihilation. I cannot risk annihilation again, Mother! I cannot!"

The Mother's fingers dug deep into Faraday's cheeks, and Faraday gasped in pain.

"Why are you so determined to seek annihilation then, girl? Drago offers you the path to lasting peace and happiness . . . yet *you* are so preoccupied with annihilation you will accomplish it by sheer strength of will! Curse you, Faraday!"

Faraday was again silent, remembering what Drago had said to her when they'd parted. *Your Sanctuary is in my heart.*

"If you don't risk it," the Mother said, "then you will surely achieve annihilation. And yet you dare to castigate Isfrael for not daring the unknown and instead choosing the safe path to sure destruction. *You* are the agent of your own destruction, my girl, no one else."

Faraday averted her eyes from the Mother.

"Isfrael did not inherit his stubbornness only from his father, methinks," the Mother said softly.

Faraday sighed. "What will happen to you when Qeteb rises? Can he touch you? What about the Earth Tree?"

"The Earth Tree's roots stretch down very, very far . . . down to unknown caverns. Do you understand Me?"

"Yes."

"Good. The Earth Tree will watch her daughters burn and

crumble into ash, and she will be mightily enraged. But you don't truly believe that *everything* about this forest will die. Do you?"

Faraday managed a wan grin. "You are a very wily Mother."

The Mother laughed and finally released Faraday. "I will return to the Sacred Groves, and close the paths behind Me. The Demons, even with Qeteb, cannot bother Me there. I shall sit and drink tea with Ur and we shall chat about babies. But here . . . I want you to have this."

The Mother unwound the rainbow-striped band from Her waist and belted it loosely about Faraday's. "Remember me with it."

She leaned forward, kissed Faraday softly on the lips, and then She was gone.

Faraday blinked, and realized that cold stars circled about her. She'd been standing all night in the Earth Tree Grove and was chilled through. Shivering, she closed her cloak about her, but as she moved she felt something about her waist.

The Mother's band . . . but something more. There was something inside it.

Faraday slowly unwound it.

Nestled inside the band, warm and snug, was the arrow that Drago had shot over the mass of crazed people in the Western Ranges, its shaft now strangely flexible.

But the arrow was not what made her eyes widen in wonder. Around the arrow's shaft was wound a small and fragile sapling. It had a spray of fine roots at one end, and an equally fine spray of tiny oval-shaped leaves at the other.

Faraday raised her face and looked at the Earth Tree.

It was gone.

68

Mountain, Forest and Marsh

Spiredore deposited Gwendylyr on the very peak of Star Finger. Disoriented, for Gwendylyr had never been to Star Finger—or, indeed, the Icescarp Alps—she turned slowly about, studying the view and the flat surfaces about the huge shaft that dropped away into the mountain, then halted abruptly.

A man stood by a doorway leading to a stairwell. Dressed entirely in black, he had the lithe figure of a swordsman, a hint of the slightly alien features of an Icarii, and faded blond hair above equally faded but penetrating blue eyes.

He was tense, and a hand rested on the hilt of a sword that hung from his weapons belt.

"Who are you?" he asked, his voice hard.

His features reminded Gwendylyr of Drago. "You are Axis StarMan," she said, and bowed slightly. "My name is Gwendylyr, Duchess of Aldeni, and I have come here to show you the path to Sanctuary."

Axis stared, trying to take in both the presence of the black-haired woman, and the words she spoke.

"Sanctuary?" he said, stalling for time.

Gwendylyr withdrew the cube of light from the pocket of her robe and expanded it into the glowing doorway.

"Through here, via Spiredore, lies Sanctuary," she said. "Lord Axis, there is only a day or so left before Qeteb rises, and—"

"Caelum will stop him."

Gwendylyr paused and regarded Axis. "Maybe, and maybe not. Will you risk all who inhabit this mountain?"

There was a movement behind Axis, and an extraordinary woman stepped up the stairwell to join him. She had hair so black it was almost blue, and the most beautiful, and powerful, eyes Gwendylyr had seen in any living person.

"My Lady Azhure," she said, further introducing herself, and bowing with just a hint more respect that she'd given Axis. "Sanctuary awaits."

"Lady Gwendylyr," Azhure said, "that is a most spectacular enchantment, and one I cannot fathom. How is it so?"

Another man and woman had now emerged from the stairwell. They may not have radiated power, but they nevertheless radiated such an aura of wisdom and experience that Gwendylyr knew they must be the elder Star Gods, Adamon and Xanon.

"It is hard for me to explain in the necessary few words, Lady Azhure," Gwendylyr said, "but it is a product of the Acharite enchantment revived through death."

"What?" Axis snapped.

With admirable patience, Gwendylyr told them all she'd learned from Faraday and Drago, and explained to them the power that Acharites could command once they'd passed through death and returned to walk in life.

"Who else commands this power?" Adamon asked.

"Faraday," Gwendylyr said, "and Leagh, Goldman and DareWing—"

"DareWing?" Xanon said.

"DareWing has Acharite blood flowing through his veins." Azhure's mouth twitched. "He had a roving ancestor, it seems."

"So it seems," Gwendylyr agreed. "Our master and teacher in all this, is—"

"Drago," Azhure interrupted softly. She had slipped a hand through Axis' arm, and now gently pushed his hand from the hilt of his sword.

Gwendylyr stared at her, seeing the understanding in Azhure's eyes. "Yes. Drago. He has made this doorway for me."

Axis' face lost its tenseness and grew instead tired. "And Caelum?" he asked. "Where does Caelum fit into all this?"

"My Lord Axis," Gwendylyr said, "will you believe me when I say that *everything* and *everyone* works only to aid the StarSon?"

Of those listening, only Azhure understood what Gwendylyr really meant. The others only comprehended what they wanted to understand.

She nodded very slightly at Gwendylyr, but it was Adamon who answered.

"Yes, we believe you, Gwendylyr. One of the few skills that remain to me is the power to discern truth. What is this Sanctuary?"

"A very beautiful place," Gwendylyr said, although she'd not yet seen Sanctuary herself.

"And who currently has sought Sanctuary?" Xanon asked.

"All of Tencendor we can save," Gwendylyr said. "The people . . . and whatever creatures accepted our offer."

The image of the thousands of millipedes that had crawled over her feet suddenly filled Gwendylyr's mind, and Azhure, who caught just a little of Gwendylyr's instinctive abhorrence, stifled a grin. Just about everything that could crawl had taken refuge in Sanctuary, it seemed.

"There are relatively few of us here," Azhure said. "It will not take long for us to collect what we need."

Axis hesitated. He did not know what to make of this woman, and there was *something* that had passed between her and Azhure that he could not understand.

But if Azhure trusted her . . . and if Adamon and Xanon were nodding and moving back down the stairwell as if to gather those below . . .

"It is a tragic thing," he said softly, "that this mountain must once again be emptied."

"It survived foulness before," Gwendylyr said, "and so we must hope it will again."

"Come, Axis," Azhure murmured, and tugged lightly at his arm. "There is one thing that must not be left behind."

After the Mother had left her, Faraday went to her childhood home of Ilfracombe in the southern Skarabost Plains. This area was not her territory—by this time Gwendylyr had already emptied it—but Faraday had to say good-bye to her home.

It was abandoned, and Faraday hoped it was because Gwendylyr had moved its inhabitants into Sanctuary and not because whoever had lived here had been captured body and soul by the Demons.

Who *had* lived here? Were her two elder sisters still alive?

Did they have children? Faraday suddenly found herself desperate to know what had happened to whatever remained of her family, and she moved through the house room by room, running fingers over remembered furniture, and studying the miniature portraits that hung in the audience room.

There, her two sisters and their husbands, portraits drawn recently, to tell from the wrinkles and aged eyes.

Faraday stared at them a long time, trying to come to grips with the aging of her sisters. Here she stood, in physical form not a whit older than twenty-one or -two, and here their likenesses hung, older than Faraday remembered their mother when she'd died.

Unnerved, she turned away.

Children had lived here—perhaps her sisters' grandchildren—for all the bedrooms had been occupied, and in many of them toys lay scattered as if thrown about in the ruckus of a hasty departure.

Faraday hoped that meant Gwendylyr had taken them, and the children had grabbed what toys they could in the time they'd been given.

But what moved Faraday the most was that her own bedroom had been left exactly as she'd left it . . . what? Forty-five years ago? Her bed, dresser, and drawings lay as last she'd placed them. Even her favorite rag doll sat on a chair where she'd always put it as a child.

Faraday stared at the doll a long time, then impulsively she snatched it up, and fled back through the house to where the glowing doorway waited outside.

From Ilfracombe she went to Arcen, packed with frightened and increasingly desperate people.

They needed no persuasion to empty into her doorway. Once Arcen was bare, Faraday moved to the few communities remaining in Tarantaise—the hamlets in the northern Plains of Tare had been lost to the Demons—and from Tarantaise Faraday went to the one place she'd not had time to study when she'd passed through here forty years ago as she'd planted out the forests.

Bogle Marsh.

It bubbled and seethed happily under a gray and low-slung sky.

Did anything save dragonflies and insects live in this pestilent marsh? In her childhood Faraday had heard of strange creatures that lived here, but were they tales meant to scare children or versions of reality?

She clutched her rag doll and stared uncertainly at the marsh.

"Sanctuary?" she asked with some considerable hesitation.

Instantly a number of the strangest creatures Faraday could ever have imagined—and she had seen some strange things in her lifetime—emerged from the marsh in a series of loud sucking sounds as the mud reluctantly let them go.

The creatures were covered in gray mud so thickly the true lines of their forms could not be discerned, but what Faraday could see made her take an instinctive step back.

The creatures were large and bulky, larger than a horse and twice as heavy, but with cumbersome flippers rather than legs, and lumpish faces with wriggling snouts for noses. Behind them they carried wide, flat muscular tails which they used to propel themselves forward.

Bright brown eyes regarded her happily as they humped and lurched past Faraday into the doorway, and she could hear them snorting and thumping as they negotiated the stairs within Spiredore.

"Goodness," she said quietly as the last one managed to get itself through the doorway, and, picking up her skirts very carefully in one hand, she followed them through.

And after Bogle Marsh there was only one thing left for Faraday to do, and something she had purposely left to last.

The fey creatures of the forests.

And Raum.

She met him the instant she reentered the forest of Minstrelsea. He waited for her in a glade, his white coat luminescent even though there was no sunshine, his skin trembling even though there was no obvious danger.

He held his head high, and slightly to one side, and his eyes great and dark and staring.

The Sacred White Stag of the forests.

She stood and stared at him, then moved slowly forward, lovely herself in her white robe with her chestnut hair cascading down her back.

He trembled anew as she neared, but he let her stroke his coat.

Do you remember that night you bonded me with the Mother, Raum?

The White Stag thought, a dim memory of himself as Raum stirring in his mind. Faraday's mouth jerked in a tiny movement that may have been a smile.

That night was the first time a man had ever seen me naked.

The White Stag regarded her anew, wondering that nakedness was something to be remembered and noted.

Now, too many men have seen me naked, and seeing, attacked my vulnerability.

The Stag understood now that the woman was talking in metaphors, and metaphors he understood very well.

The forests lie naked before the rape that would be inflicted on it. They are vulnerable, lovely woman.

Do you remember the years I ran at your side?

I had a mate, but she disappeared.

Aye, she disappeared. The woman's mind grew sadder. *Wild one, these forests will soon die. Will you now step through the door into Sanctuary?*

And my brethren?

Take them with you.

Will you join me?

Yes, but I will never run by your side again.

The White Stag shifted in sorrow, then he moved away from the woman's hand. She withdrew a cube of light from her pocket and extended it into a doorway. She stood still, regarding it silently, then she stretched it even further, making it at least the height of two men and three times as wide.

She stepped back. *Run, my friend. Run!*

The Stag snorted, and with a wild bell-like cry he leaped through the doorway.

Faraday waited, her heart thudding, and then suddenly there was a movement above her, and a Gray Guardian owl fluttered down from a tree and flew straight through the door.

And then, as when they'd first entered Minstrelsea, there was a massive onslaught of hundreds of thousands of fey creatures, rushing from trees to doorway, a euphony of feather and fur and flashing eye. Faraday stood by a tree, well out of the way of the enchanted stampede, wondering at the curiosity and mysteriousness of the creatures that flashed briefly before her eyes.

When the tide had ceased, Faraday raised her eyes and contemplated the forests. The trees sang to her, strangely offering her comfort when they, as she, knew that they would be the ones to die.

Faraday touched the band about her waist where lay secreted the arrow and the sapling, but tears still sprung in her eyes. For Faraday, this would be a death as painful as that of a child.

"Good-bye," she whispered, and stepped into the doorway.

69

The Dark Tower

It took the Maze five days to rise, and all that time Drago stood atop Spiredore and witnessed.

WingRidge watched with him, and talked to Drago of many things, but mostly of what he and his fellow Lake Guard knew of the Maze and what they knew of its needs.

"It is a gigantic city," Drago murmured on the fourth day, and WingRidge nodded.

"Fifty times the size of Carlon," he said, and both men glanced toward the blackened and still smoking ruin across the rising Maze.

"And infinitely more complicated," WingRidge continued. "See how each street, each tenement contributes to the Maze?"

Drago nodded. The extent and complexity of the Maze astounded and frightened him. How would he ever find his way to its center?

"The heart will call to you," WingRidge said.

The waters had vanished, consumed or absorbed by the rising Maze. It was evident where the heart lay. There was an all-consuming darkness at the core of the Maze. All twists and conundrums of the Maze led to a central circular space, and in the center of this space was a great dark tower rising to the height of the encircling walls.

It was the exact duplicate of Spiredore, but as Spiredore was white and filled with light, so this tower was its darker twin. Its open windows absorbed all light about the circular space, *ate* all light, and still it seemed hungry for more.

"This dark tower is the heart of all Tencendor," Drago said.

WingRidge nodded. "This tower will become the heart of everything once Qeteb rises."

"His palace," Drago murmured. "WingRidge, where is the Maze Gate?"

WingRidge pointed to a section of the external wall slightly to the south of Spiredore. "There."

Drago looked, then nodded. "Facing east to the dawning sun." He gave a small smile. "A positive sign . . . I hope."

WingRidge turned from the Maze and looked at Drago. "It is almost time."

"Yes. And time you were gone to Sanctuary. Here. Take the Wolven and quiver with you."

WingRidge hesitated before he did as Drago requested, then leaned forward and embraced Drago. "Will you say farewell to Caelum for me?"

Nothing WingRidge could have said could have more deeply touched Drago. He could not speak, and merely nodded again, his eyes filled with tears.

"Then good-bye, StarSon," WingRidge said softly. "I wish you good . . . journeying."

He snapped a formal salute, and then stepped down into Spiredore.

During that night the Maze completed its journey into the open air. It soared into the sky, its walls so tall that even atop Spiredore Drago could no longer see the dark-towered center.

But he could feel it, calling out to him.

Come, come, come, come . . .

Its cry surged through him, making the blood pound in his head, and Drago rubbed at his temples, trying to lessen its force.

Come, come, come, come . . . the pounding got worse and worse, and eventually Drago could stand it no longer.

"Yes! Yes!" he cried, "I *will* come, damn you!"

The call abated somewhat, enough for Drago to straighten and let his hands drop back to his sides, but not enough to enable him to ignore it.

He descended into Spiredore, his staff and sack at his side.

It took Drago until midafternoon to reach the Maze Gate.

The gate had grown. Its stone arch reached forty-five paces into the sky, and the twin wooden doors that hung between them were some forty paces high and twenty-five wide.

It was unbelievably huge.

The symbols WingRidge had told Drago he would see about the arch now numbered in their millions . . . and were no longer static. They wriggled and surged and capered about the stone archway. They moved so fast Drago could not concentrate on any one of them long enough to read it—but read he did not have to do, for the shifting symbols formed moving pictures.

Pictures of death and destruction, of a world gone mad, a landscape barren and desecrated.

Tencendor, as it would be within days.

It showed an aerial view of the Maze itself, and a poor desolate figure desperately scurrying through it, harried by a macabre and demonic hunting party. There was no escape. The figure was cornered, and impaled, and the hunters raised their lances and swords in triumph and the darkness in the world intensified twofold. Drago had to turn away, unable to bear the horror.

When he looked back again the stone was bare of symbols save for one in the right-hand side of the archway.

A sword, a lily wound about its blade.

Drago stared at it, his right hand dropping his staff and slowly rising as if of its own volition.

Slowly, slowly, he reached out to the sword, but just as he was about to lay a hand on it there was a sudden movement behind him.

Drago spun about, grabbing his staff again as he did so.

Five or six paces behind him stood the Star Stallion. Belaguez snorted, and tossed his wild mane of stars. He half-reared, his fore hooves raising dust from the arid plain as he landed.

Then he stepped forward, trembling.

Drago switched his staff to his left hand and held out his right to the stallion.

The horse tentatively reached forward with his creamy nose, snorting hot breath over Drago's palm, then he took a step closer, and Drago was able to run his hand over the horse's cheek and neck.

"Welcome, Belaguez," he murmured, feeling the stallion relax under his caressing hand. "Has the Maze called you, too?"

Belaguez snorted, and again tossed his head.

Drago grinned, and without thinking, vaulted on to the stallion's back.

Belaguez skitted about, but did not attempt to throw Drago off, and after a moment Drago lightly touched his heels to the stallion's flanks, and guided him to the wooden doors.

There Drago again took the staff in his right hand, and tapped the doors gently with it. Thrice, then twice again.

"I come to claim my heritage," he said without any thought as to why he spoke the words.

The doors swung open and Belaguez sprang forward . . .

. . . into a cataclysm of wind and sound and light and pain.

Drago felt as if he had again stepped through the Star Gate. His entire being exploded in agony, scraps of flesh and blood and breath mingling into a spray of bloodied moisture about the void into which he'd been propelled.

He screamed, or thought he screamed, but how could he cry out with no throat and lungs with which to form sound?

And then he blinked, and all pain was gone, and his body was whole and the stallion moved smoothly beneath him.

He was naked, save for the irritating rasp of the sack hanging from a rope belt about his waist, and a sword in his right hand.

It was the same sword he'd seen carved into the stone of the archway, except that the emerald stem of the lily now wound about the golden hilt, the spaces between its leaves providing snug purchase for his fingers, and the bright-mirrored blade sprang from the creamy throat of the flower itself.

DragonStar grinned, and wound his left hand amid the

stars of the stallion's mane, and with his right brandished the sword above his head.

"To the Dark Tower!" he cried, and the stallion sprang forward.

DragonStar rode through a maze of mystery and enchantment, and it felt like a home to him.

He hesitated at no turn, nor questioned no path.

He knew the path, and he knew what he rode toward.

Sometimes the Star Rider and Stallion galloped between confining walls of stone, and sometimes they ran through infinite fields of flowers. Sometimes the stallion splashed through shallow lakes of silver, and sometimes descended stairwells that wormed into the depths of creation itself.

Sometimes they passed between confining walls colored gray and grim, and sometimes through gloomy halls filled with the rusting ruins of giant machinery.

And always they ran toward the Dark Tower, and always the Dark Tower called—

—*screamed*—

—to them, begging, pleading, crying that they should waste no time in attending . . .

. . . *for close ride the Demons* . . .

. . . and it wanted to touch them, embrace them, speak with them.

DragonStar tore the sack from his side, for the rub of its hessian against his bare skin had become unbearable. He held it aloft before him.

"Does DragonStar wear a *sack* at his hip? Nay, I think not!"

And the sack transformed, and became a beautiful jeweled purse of gold links and diamonds and rubies, and DragonStar smiled; and hung the purse on the matching belt that now encircled his hips.

He dug his heels into the stallion's flanks, grabbing once again at his mane, and he brandished the sword aloft.

"*To this I was born!*" he screamed, and the stallion reared, and screamed with him.

And the Dark Tower smiled, and thought:

To this were you made.

* * *

They galloped into the circle of flagstones surrounding the Dark Tower, and the Star Stallion skidded to a halt before its open door.

DragonStar sat his mount and studied the tower.

It was the precise twin of Spiredore in height and construction, save for its blackness. DragonStar knew what it would contain. He slid from the stallion's back and walked over to the door, housing his sword in the jeweled scabbard that hung from his belt.

Just before he stepped through the open chasm of the door, DragonStar stood momentarily, reveling in the strength, and the strength of enchantment, that infused him.

Finally. Finally!

He smiled, and entered the Dark Tower.

If the Dark Tower was Spiredore's twin on the outside, then on the inside it was its opposite. No stairways and crazily canted balconies cluttered this interior. Instead a great dome of black marble reared a hundred and twenty paces into the air. Below the dome, similarly dark and desolate marble columns crowded close as if they wanted nothing or no one to escape. They encircled a space some forty paces in diameter. The floor was of black marble.

This dark tower was a mausoleum, and empty save for a chest-high tomb that lay centered under the dome. On the tomb rested a suit of black armor, and a frightful lance and a sword lay over the armor, gripped in the as yet empty gloves.

The visor of the black, horned helmet was down, and over it lay a length of white linen.

DragonStar walked slowly over to the tomb and stopped by the visor. Slowly he reached over the armor, taking care not to touch it, and lifted the length of linen from the visor.

It fluttered in a nonexistent breeze, and the entire tower tensed in a deep, anticipatory breath.

DragonStar smiled at the beautiful soft ripples of linen as they floated before him, and, stepping back from the tomb, shook the cloth out and regarded it thoughtfully.

Then, in swift, economical movements, he girded it about his loins and between his legs, hiding his nakedness.

Thus armored, he whistled the Star Stallion to his side,

took his sword in hand, and with its blade of light, drew a doorway in the space before him and stepped through.

Without hesitation, the Star Stallion followed.

Urbeth and Caelum sat in the snowy, frozen wastes of Gorken Pass and talked of many things. Urbeth had just reached into a tub of fish for a snack when a glowing rectangle of light appeared in the snow before their fire.

From it stepped a man that Caelum had only ever dreamed about.

"DragonStar," Caelum said, and stepped forward and embraced his brother.

"It is time," DragonStar said. "Are you ready?"

70

The Rape of Tencendor

The Demons pushed their mounts until the black beasts' breathing rasped through their throats and their flanks heaved in hungry effort for air. The Demons pounded their heels into flanks, their fists into shoulders, and every so often they would lean down and bite as deeply as they could into the snake-like necks jerking and weaving before them.

The StarSon was at the Maze! They could feel him!

The Demons growled and hissed and spat. The StarSon thought to destroy them, but it was he who would be destroyed.

Nothing would stop them now!

At least nothing once the StarSon had been destroyed.

They'd not thought him this powerful, nor this resourceful. From where had he drawn his power? He'd emptied not only Carlon, but the entire land of good feeding, and taken the prey into a cunning hiding place that the Demons could not yet espy.

The StarSon must be destroyed! The StarSon must be destroyed!

He must die . . . die . . . die!

It was all they could think of. Kill the StarSon before he discovered too many of the Enemy's secrets. Kill him, and then *nothing* could ever seize this land from them. For a million years the TimeKeepers had been seeking a haven, a land they could truly call a home, and this was it. This was home. This was *their* home, and no petty Icarii prince was going to deny them.

And so they rode, desperately, hatefully, and faster and faster until they were only a blur over the landscape. With every stride they drew closer to the Maze, with every stride they drew closer to the Dark Tower, and there lay their salvation, there lay Qeteb's soul, there lay their destiny.

They were now so close to the Maze—a few leagues, no more—that they could draw power to themselves, power to pull themselves forward, faster, faster, faster . . .

And all the time the Dark Tower sang to them.

Come to me! Come to me! Come to me!

The dark Demons came.

WolfStar thought this wild demonic ride would kill him. His internal injuries, constantly worsened by successive rapes, were being pounded into a desperate state by the bounding and jouncing of his mount. He was still slung on his belly over the beast's back, his wrists and ankles tied underneath the beast's own belly, his wings bouncing and trailing through the air.

Blood dribbled from his mouth, staining both the beast's flank and the landscape through which they passed.

StarLaughter rode her beast as a maniac. Excitement consumed her to the point where she'd lost all coherent thought. She sat bolt upright, her tattered and filthy gown snapping in the wind of her passing, her hair tangling in her wings behind her, one hand buried in her beast's mane, the other raised aloft as if in triumph.

A constant thin wail trailed from her open mouth.

StarLaughter was riding home.

The Qeteb-man and the Niah-woman sat their beast passively, although they swayed rhythmically to the surge of its gait. The Qeteb-man's fingers still groped up and down the body of the woman he held before him, and even though his thick tongue trailed wetly from a corner of his mouth, his eyes were blank and, as yet, purposeless.

The Maze, now inextricably married to the blackened twisted streets and tenements of Carlon, hove into view, and as one the Demons shrieked and screamed, beating their mounts into further efforts until the foam that flew from the snake-headed mouths became thickened with blood.

The Resurrection was nigh.

Nothing would stop them now!

Caelum and DragonStar stood atop Spiredore and watched the dreadful cloud roll closer.

Caelum felt ill, not only at the approaching horror, but also at the destruction about him. Carlon—gone! And the land . . . the land was a desecration.

He dropped his eyes to the seething mass of animals about the Maze.

"Is there *anything* left?" he asked softly.

DragonStar shook his head. "Tencendor is empty of coherent and cogent life, Caelum. We," his mouth smiled very slightly, "are the only two left."

"Qeteb will destroy this land," Caelum said. "He will murder it!"

"Yes," DragonStar said. "But you understand why that is necessary?"

Caelum was quiet a long while before he finally nodded. "And after I . . . after I . . ."

He could not bring himself to complete the question.

"Then," DragonStar said, "satisfied the StarSon can no longer irritate their plans for utter hegemony, Qeteb and his companions will rape and destroy this land until nothing remains. Not even hope. They will make for themselves a world fit for their society. Caelum . . . *do* you understand?"

"Yes." Caelum looked his brother full in the eye. "They will not do that if they think you are still alive. They need to think you dead."

Caelum's face took on an expression of utter despair. "There are no words that can be said at this moment, brother, but so many words that need to be said. I—"

DragonStar took Caelum's face between his hands and

smiled with exquisite loveliness and gentleness. "There are no words that need to be said, Caelum."

Caelum stared into DragonStar's deep violet eyes, and saw in their depths not only power and surety, but something far, far lovelier.

The rich field of flowers.

"Will I—?" he began, and DragonStar leaned forward and kissed him softly on the mouth.

"Yes," he said. "Yes, you will."

Caelum gripped DragonStar in a fierce hug, and tears flowed freely down both the brothers' faces.

"I am glad," Caelum whispered, "that I have finally known my brother, DragonStar."

The cloud rolled closer.

"Where must I go?" Caelum asked.

"I will show you."

The Demons screamed and shrieked and wept in their overweening hysteria. For so long, so very, *very* long they had been riding toward this . . .

And now it lay before them.

As the Demons rode to within a half-league of the Maze Gate they began to change. All resemblance of human bodies vanished, and they took on shifting, lumpish forms that one moment resembled eels, the next grossly deformed frogs or dogs. Appendages wove forth from all aspects and every shifting plane of their bodies, some tentacle-like with pop-eyes at their extremities, others like grasping many-fingered hands. They barked and howled and slurped, slipping in and out of one grotesque transformation after the other.

WolfStar retched, but StarLaughter whooped and screamed with joy.

Such power! Such revenge!

And soon her son would come into what was rightly his!

Above wheeled a cloud of Hawkchilds, screeching with the Demons. They swept over Spiredore and saw—

The StarSon! The StarSon atop the white, white tower!

What does he do? Sheol asked of them.

Nothing. He stands, his hands on the parapet, and waits.
Fool! He but waits for his death!

And all the time the Dark Tower wept and wailed and sobbed: *Come! Come! Come!*

The Demons swept under the Maze Gate and it did not hinder them.

They swept through the Maze, and neither did its conundrums impede them. Indeed, their way was as an avenue, wide and smooth and kind, leading them directly to the Dark Tower. Behind them swept the vast army of slavish animals and lost souls, finally free to join their master.

The Maze filled with the demonically insane, a great sweeping tide of fury and darkness.

The Demons paid the horde no attention. They were almost out of control. They gibbered and slobbered, scratching deep gouges of joy into their mounts' necks, and still the black beasts ran, ran straight for the Dark Tower.

The door to the mausoleum swung open, and Demons and mounts and their companions together swept in.

On his tower, Caelum sighed and stepped into the stairwell. "Take me to the Maze Gate," he requested.

The Demons sat their mounts still and silent.

They stared at the tomb with the black armor spread out atop it.

The Demons had once again regained their humanoid forms. Tears trickled down their faces.

It was very hard to believe that, after all they'd been through, the time and the trouble and the trials, they were finally here.

Silently, reverently, they climbed down from their mounts.

StarLaughter also slid down, and strode over to WolfStar. "Watch," she murmured as she cut his bonds and pulled him down from his beast into a heap on the black marble floor. "Watch as your son gains his heritage!"

The Demons helped the Niah-woman and the Qeteb-man to dismount. The Niah-woman they took over to the side, out of the way, and indicated that StarLaughter stand with her.

StarLaughter obeyed, dragging WolfStar over at her heels,

and smiled cruelly at her husband. "See," she said, "what will become of our son."

The Demons grouped reverently about the Qeteb-man and guided him toward the tomb. Once there they patted and fondled him, and then each Demon picked up a piece of the armor and, mumbling strange words in an even stranger tone, laid it against Qeteb's flesh and tied it to his body.

It fit perfectly—but not because the armor fit Qeteb. Instead, as successive plates were fitted against his body, the Midday Demon's flesh swelled to horrible proportions to fill every space inside the armor.

The air grew heavy, and WolfStar could not stop a dreadful sense of oppression sweep over him.

StarLaughter, intent on watching her son, let the chain tethered to WolfStar's collar drift unheeded to the floor.

Slowly, very, very slowly, WolfStar backed away, his fingers fumbling at the loathed collar until it fell to the floor.

He backed into the shadows of the pillars, and wondered: Should I escape? Or attempt some rescue of Niah?

Completely unaware of WolfStar's slow drift away, one of the Demons fitted another piece of armor to Qeteb's body, and again flesh swelled to meet metal for a perfect fit.

Now there was only the visor to go.

Sheol lifted it from the tomb, aided by Mot, and raised it over Qeteb's head.

WolfStar stared from the shadows. Qeteb's face was transforming into something hideous as the Demons slowly lowered the visor.

Gods! WolfStar could not bear to look any further, and pushed his face against the cold floor.

Silence, and then a faint clunk as the visor was secured into the neck and shoulder fittings of the armor.

Everything left above in the land of Tencendor paused, and then turned in the direction of the Maze.

The forests fell silent, the waves ceased to batter the rocky shoreline of the Icebear coast, the animals crowding the Maze outside the Dark Tower fell to their bellies, the Hawkchilds settled on the top of the Maze's walls and folded their wings.

Seated atop his white stallion, the StarSon lifted his eyes and wept.

Underneath the stallion's hooves, the great bridge of Sigholt groaned and fell silent.

A great roar pounded forth from the heart of the Maze.

I am reborn!

Qeteb raised his black-metaled fists and thrust them above his head.

I am reborn!

WolfStar dug his fingers into his ears and screwed his eyes tight shut, *praying* for death!

"I am reborn," Qeteb whispered in a voice hoarse with disuse, and his visored head slowly turned about the circle of the mausoleum.

It stilled each time as Qeteb locked eyes with each of his companion Demons.

"Where is Rox?" he whispered harshly.

"Great Father," Sheol said, her eyes downcast lest Qeteb think her presumptuous, "the Enemy laid a trap, and he was destroyed."

Qeteb growled. The noise was so low it could not be heard, but its vibrations rippled out across the floor. Qeteb's hands lowered to his sides, and they slowly clenched.

"Then I shall destroy!" he cried, and he flung out his arms and splayed open his hands, bending back so far the face of his visor looked directly into the dome of the mausoleum.

Hate rippled forth over the land of Tencendor.

Caelum, standing outside the Maze Gate, felt it coming, and huddled behind the protective wall of the archway so it fled by without touching him.

The forests felt it coming, and screamed—and the next instant their leaves exploded from them in a great, rising cloud of pain.

Star Finger felt it coming and shuddered, and the next instant it exploded as well and crumbled into the glacier surrounding its eastern and northern walls.

Urbeth and her daughters felt it coming, and buried their noses deep into the snow and it did not touch them.

DragonStar felt it coming, and he gripped the mane of his stallion. "Steady," he said, and, protected by the bridge, the hate rushed over without harming them.

"Who?" Qeteb demanded, pointing at the two female figures to one side.

WolfStar crouched as close to the floor as he could. Niah was lost now, lost, all his dreams and plans were dust, and the only thought that crowded WolfStar's head was escape. Escape, and somehow regroup. And Caelum. Somehow . . . somehow . . .

As Qeteb walked toward Niah and StarLaughter, WolfStar slithered carefully ever further into the shadows.

Qeteb stopped before the two females. His visored face turned slowly toward StarLaughter. "Who?" the Midday Demon demanded.

"I am your mother!" StarLaughter said, her voice proud. "I have loved you and protected you and nourished you and—"

"Who?" Qeteb said yet again, and raised one mailed fist.

"I am your mother," StarLaughter repeated, "and you are—"

"I have no mother!" Qeteb screamed abruptly. "I am whole within myself!"

StarLaughter went rigid with shock—and with pure terror. She cast her eyes frantically about, seeking escape, but Qeteb had already forgotten her.

"Who?" he said, indicating Niah.

"Your wife," Sheol said.

Now secreted in darkness a dozen columns away, WolfStar lowered his head and wept silent tears.

"Wife?" Qeteb said, and stroked Niah's cheek with surprisingly gentle fingers.

Niah showed no response.

"Wife," Qeteb said yet again. He paused. "A wife." A rasp of laughter came from behind the visor. "A wife who neither talks nor thinks?"

He turned back to the other Demons. "She will do *well!*"

The Demons, particularly Sheol, visibly relaxed.

For her part, StarLaughter had regained a little of her equilibrium. He will accept a wife but not a mother? she thought. What kind of son is that?

Qeteb, thinking to explore this wife further, turned back toward Niah when he spotted WolfStar amid the shadows and stopped. "Who—" he began, but a voice drifted in the doorway, interrupting him.

"I am Caelum StarSon," it said, "and I dare you to butcher *me,* Qeteb!"

"He thinks to destroy us!" Sheol said, moving to stand by Qeteb's dull metaled shoulder. "In the past few weeks his power has grown to be . . . irritating. It would be best, perhaps, to remove him now."

"No one can best me!" Qeteb roared, WolfStar completely forgotten. "He is no threat!"

"Of course not," Barzula and Mot said as one.

"But it *would* be best to remove him now," Barzula added. "He has, as Sheol said, grown to be an irritating nuisance. He has prevented us feeding."

"He has *hidden* our food!" Sheol said.

"No one prevents us feeding," Qeteb whispered, and strode to the door. As he passed close to the column behind which WolfStar hid, the Enchanter risked another glance.

Qeteb's black armor rippled and moved as skin would, and his wings . . . his wings had changed completely from golden to black, their feathers now dull metal plates.

The Midday Demon was made entirely of metal. No flesh, no feather—and certainly no mortal weakness—remained.

The Demons hurried after their Great Father, Sheol seizing Niah by an arm as she passed. Best to keep the automaton safe now that Qeteb had approved her.

For an instant, StarLaughter stared after the Demons, then she strode after them. "Think not to abandon me *now,*" she said.

Very carefully, WolfStar raised his head and looked about. Then, grimacing with pain, he inched forward.

71

The Hunt

Caelum strode through the Maze. He wore no armor, just a simple linen shirt and dark breeches. His black hair curled back from his brow, his face was composed, although pale.

"I hope to every star in the sky," he whispered, "that you make what I am about to do worthwhile, brother."

There was no answer, not in words, but Caelum nevertheless felt DragonStar's presence, and it comforted him.

As with the Demons' voyage, the Maze allowed Caelum a direct route toward the Dark Tower. Walls twenty, sometimes thirty, paces high reared on either side of him, sometimes so close his shoulders brushed against them, sometimes so wide it seemed to Caelum as if he strode through a stone . . . field.

Writhing, wriggling symbols covered all the walls. If Caelum had felt the urge to read them he would have found the task impossible, for they moved too fast, but Caelum had no eyes for anything save the journey before him, and no thought but for what had to be done.

The sky was so low and so dense with dark clouds Caelum could not tell the time of day. The atmosphere was thick, humid and almost warm, despite the time of year.

Caelum began to sweat.

Animals, and occasionally those which had once been human, appeared in greater numbers. They eyed Caelum hungrily, but they hung back, whispering, moaning and growling as he passed.

This prey belonged to their master.

Gradually, as Caelum walked further and further into the Maze, he realized that the animals no longer looked at him, but had turned their eyes toward the center of the Maze.

Something came.

Despite his resolve, despite having accepted his fate a long time previously, Caelum grew nauseous, his palms damp, his muscles weak and trembly. Had Axis felt this way when he'd gone into Gorgrael's Ice Fortress? No. No, he hadn't, because Axis had always been supremely confident. Axis had always known he would *win*.

No, this was the way Faraday had felt when *she'd* walked toward the Ice Fortress.

Caelum walked. After a while he came to a circular space. It had only two exits. One through which he'd entered, the other directly across the circle in the opposite wall.

Caelum's gait faltered, and he stopped.

He knew what would come through the opposite opening.

The Demons, powerful beyond imagining, hungry beyond anything they'd ever experienced previously, and furious beyond compare, rode their mad mounts in a devilish black cloud through the twists and turns of the Maze.

At their head rode Qeteb, his lance secured to his saddle, a massive black sword in his hand, his armored body drawing in all light about it, his arms flung wide, his head back.

I'm coming for you StarSon!

Die, die, die, he must die, for this StarSon had learned too many secrets of the Enemy. What if he learned enough to deny Qeteb a life again? What if he grew strong enough to deny Qeteb his world?

Die, die he *must,* and when he was dead, this world, this wasteland, would be Qeteb's forever, and every beetle that crawled its surface would be his forever, and nothing, nothing, *nothing* would dare breathe or live without Qeteb's gracious consent.

And under Qeteb's terms, of course.

Qeteb began to laugh, a howling litany of madness, that streamed out behind him in a maniacal wake, a rippling cloud of malevolence.

It enveloped WolfStar, crawling as fast as his ruined body would allow him, and he curled into a tight ball, crying with despair.

All he'd done, all he'd planned, come to this . . . to this.

* * *

Caelum stood in the center of the open space and waited. As yet he could hear only distant murmurs, but he could *feel* the Demons' approach.

It felt like a motionless wind, rushing at him from all directions. Trapping him, binding his arms by his side, stripping him of all hope.

Caelum sobbed, and his entire body sagged, but just before he collapsed on the ground, a vision filled his mind with such loveliness that he gasped, and straightened.

A single white lily in a field of blue.

Caelum blinked tears away. "Thank you," he whispered, and the next instant he heard a sound in the Maze, and a pool of darkness drained into the space from the opposite opening.

A diabolical apparition emerged from it.

A dark rider, on a dark mount, a great black sword in his hand. Worse, far, far, worse than any of Caelum's foulest nightmares.

Behind the black rider, his party of hunters, gibbering with delight.

The prey had been sighted.

Caelum held out his arms wide. "I am StarSon Caelum!" he cried, his voice mercifully clear and strong. "Get you gone from this land, Demon!"

And he began to dance.

He danced the worst dance of all those in the Enchanted Songbook, because he knew that this might be his only chance to . . . impress . . . the Demon. His arms and legs flailed, his head jerked about on his neck like a puppet in the hands of a convulsing child, his breath wailed in fits and starts from his mouth.

It was the Dance of Death.

Qeteb roared, and prepared to dig his heels into his mount. He recognized the dance for what it was—simply another method by which the Enemy had originally trapped him.

This StarSon must be stopped, before he stopped Qeteb.

But just as Qeteb prepared to ride to deal the jerking human death, he paused, stared . . . and roared again, but in laughter this time.

This was a parody of power, a parody of the Dance of Death. The man had access only to a shadow of power—the dance was useless . . . save for the amusement it afforded Qeteb. His laughter became consuming, and soon the entire Maze was laughing: every Demon, every animal, every scrap of existence it contained, save for Caelum consumed in his dance, WolfStar, who had now resumed his painful crawl, toward the Demons, and Niah and StarLaughter, waiting forgotten near the Dark Tower.

Caelum faltered to a halt, hearing the laughter ringing through him even as he struggled to draw breath. He'd done everything he could, every step, every movement had been correct. And yet nothing.

Save for the laughter.

Caelum stood with his hands on his knees, jerking in his breath, staring at the horror waiting across the space, and wondered if death in truth would be as painful and as humiliating as death in dream.

Qeteb finally dug his heels into his mount and raised his sword. "To the hunt!" he roared. *"The hunt!"*

Caelum turned and ran.

It was as terrifying as his dreams. Always Qeteb and his hunting party thundered a bare ten paces behind him, whichever way he twisted, whatever turn he took. The Maze closed in about him, trapping him in a labyrinth of hopelessness.

Above the Hawkchilds dipped and soared, screeching and wailing and giggling, driving him ever forward, ever forward, making sure the quarry gave the Huntmaster a good run for his entertainment. Sometimes they swooped so low their wings beat about his head, and Caelum fell to the ground, screaming in terror, his arms wrapped about his face.

Then he'd struggle to his feet again as he felt the approaching hunt through the trembling ground, and he'd falter forward, his breath rasping through his throat.

And always the hot breath of the hunters behind him.

Once, when he faltered, Qeteb rode close enough that he could prick Caelum in the buttocks with the tip of his sword, and Caelum screamed and darted forward, and Qeteb laughed, and held back the hunt for a few minutes.

"Let him think he has evaded us," he whispered.

But Caelum knew he would never evade the hunt. They

would catch him, as they had always done, and he would die with the tip of the sword or lance, or whatever it was Qeteb chose to drive into him, slicing through breasts and lung and heart until he died with his life bubbling out through his mouth, and Qeteb leaning down harder and harder on the blade until Caelum felt his spine splinter and shatter and . . .

. . . would death ever come?

Or would Qeteb keep him eternally on the point of his sword? Would he spend eternity itself impaled, screaming for merciful oblivion?

Caelum began to cry. Is this how RiverStar had felt? Had death been an eternity for her as well?

He stumbled about another twist in the Maze, and fell over. For a heartbeat he lay there, then he scrambled to his feet again, his hands and face bleeding where he'd scraped them against the rough stone of the Maze, and floundered forward.

"I'm sorry, RiverStar," he muttered between gasps for air. "Forgive me . . ."

And everything about him changed.

The Maze vanished, and in its place Caelum found himself running through a field of flowers.

His strength returned, and he ran freely, joyfully, through this most wondrous of fields. The sun was warm overhead, the scent almost, but not quite, overwhelming, the colors exquisite, the grass and leaves green and damp with freshness.

Behind Caelum, Qeteb grew tired of the chase. He hungered for the pain and horror he would see reflected on the Star-Son's face when he drove his sword through his chest. He would *feed* from the pain and the horror!

Qeteb screamed, and drove his mount forward.

Caelum slowed to a walk the better to savor the sights and scents. He smiled gently, oblivious to everything but the beauty surrounding him.

* * *

WolfStar could crawl no more. He was trapped within the magic of the Maze, and he had no idea where it had taken him. He propped himself up against a wall, holding his belly with one hand, dragging air into his lungs.

Suddenly Caelum walked about the corner and came directly toward him.

He had a beatific smile on his face.

"Caelum StarSon!" Qeteb screamed, and stood in his stirrups and raised his sword.

Caelum, now directly before WolfStar, turned and stared at the horror approaching.

"Caelum?"

Caelum turned and stared.

RiverStar stood there . . . but not the RiverStar he remembered. Her features and loveliness were the same, but her expression was tempered by understanding and gentleness.

"Oh, how I love you," he said.

Caelum turned and stared at the rearing, plunging creature above him, and at the Demon screaming on its back.

"Oh, how I love you," he said.

"No!" Qeteb shrieked, driven beyond the realms of anger, not only by Caelum's words, but by the serene expression on his face.

The Demon drove down his sword.

RiverStar smiled and held out a flower.

A lily.

"For you," she said.

"I thank you," Caelum said, and reached out a hand and took the flower.

* * *

WolfStar could not believe it. As the sword plunged downward, Caelum held out his hand and seized the blade.

It made not a whit of difference.

The sword sliced through Caelum's hand and plunged into his chest, driving Caelum back against WolfStar, who grunted with shock and shifted slightly to one side so the blade would not impale him as well.

Qeteb leaned his entire weight down on the sword, twisting it as deep as he could go, feeling bone and muscle and cartilage tear and rip, seeing the bright blood bubble from the StarSon's mouth.

And still the man smiled.

"Welcome," RiverStar said, "into the field of flowers."

And she leaned forward and kissed him.

"Here," Caelum said, "shall we finally be husband and wife."

She smiled anew, tears glistening in her eyes, and he took her hand, and they walked deeper into the field of flowers.

WolfStar screamed and screamed, unable to believe the horror that Qeteb visited on Caelum's corpse. Again and again the Demon drove his sword into Caelum, time and time again, until all that was left of Caelum was a mass of red-mangled flesh that was barely recognizable.

And still, somehow, unbelievably, his smile and utter serenity continued to shine through.

Qeteb did not even seem to understand that WolfStar was present. All he wanted to do was wipe that smile from Caelum's face, because that smile was what truly hurt, that smile was what cut deeply into him, that smile was what needed to be destroyed before all else.

Finally, Qeteb leaped down from his mount and crushed what remained of Caelum's head between his mailed hands, crushed it until all resemblance to a head had gone, crushed it until bone and blood and brain and teeth enmeshed into one shapeless mess.

The smile had finally gone.

Qeteb stopped, stared—still not seeming to realize Wolf-Star's presence—and then turned back to the crowd of watching Demons and screamed.

"Tencendor is mine! I shall consume it!"

Tencendor died. Rivers dried up, fields crumbled into dust, mountains cracked into jagged, sterile peaks.

The forests were raped and then murdered as they screamed their defiance. Roots were torn from the ground, trunks snapped, leaves were flayed from branches, and entire trees were flung about the landscape as a windstorm throws dried tumbleweeds.

The groves and glades of the Avarinheim and Minstrelsea were exposed first to a hot red sun, a ball of fire, and then to a gale of pure maliciousness.

All magic died.

Everything.

All creatures that had somehow escaped both the Demons' attentions to this point, or the emptying of Tencendor by DragonStar's witches, succumbed to madness.

Every one.

Tencendor, haven of enchantment and of mystery for ten thousand generations, died in a single instant.

Gone.

WolfStar gathered what remained of Caelum's corpse into his arms and wept, caring not if the Demon turned and drove his sword into him as well.

A single object remained in the smoking wasteland that had once been spreading forest.

The enchanted wooden bowl that the silver-backed Horned One had once given Faraday as a means to access the Sacred Groves. It had lain forgotten for forty years after Faraday had completed the planting of the forests. She'd witnessed the rush of the fey creatures into the trees, and had then unharnessed the white donkeys to let them run free. Crippled by her labor pains, Faraday then entered the Sacred Groves to bear Isfrael.

She'd forgotten the bowl.

Everyone had.

Now here it sat.

Waiting for whoever might chance upon it.

Epilogue

He rode his stallion deep into the wasteland.

A man dressed in nothing but a white linen loincloth and clad only with a jeweled sword and purse.

He was sad, but joyous at the same time.

Tencendor was dead, but it could be reborn.

Barren dust swirled about the white stallion's legs, and the man whispered into the wasteland, the whisper reaching across a hundred leagues and deep into the heart of the Maze.

"My name is DragonStar StarSon, Demon, and I am the Enemy reborn. Know that this time I shall not just trap you, but destroy you for all time."

Know that this time I shall not just trap you, but destroy you for all time.

There was a horrible, painful jolt of surprise deep within him, and then Qeteb nodded in recognition.

This pitiful *cursed* mangled wreck had been a decoy, a decoy to allow the true StarSon to grow to maturity.

And to do something else . . . but what?

"No," Qeteb whispered back. "Know that *I* have waited a hundred thousand years planning for this moment, and that this time, *I* shall destroy *you*. Now it will be on *my* terms, in *my* wasteland."

DragonStar smiled at the Demon's ignorance.

No, he thought. On *my* terms, for now that Tencendor has died, the battle will be fought in the field of flowers, and not the wasteland.

This time the Enemy will finish what they started so long ago. Here, on this world, where the Star Dance had always wanted it.

Here, where the Garden would be replanted.

He stared about the wasteland, knowing that the magic only waited, then patted the Star Stallion's neck, pulled his sword from its scabbard, and, drawing a doorway of light before him, rode through into Sanctuary.

Glossary

ACHAR: the realm that once stretched over most of the continent, bounded by the Andeis, Tyrre and Widowmaker Seas, the Avarinheim and the Icescarp Alps. Now integrated into Tencendor, although Zared had claimed back the title of King.

ACHARITES: a term used fairly generally to encompass all humans within Tencendor.

ADAMON: one of the nine Star Gods of the Icarii, Adamon is the eldest and the God of the Firmament.

AFTERLIFE: all three races, the Acharites, the Icarii and the Avar believe in the existence of an AfterLife, although exactly what they believe depends on their particular culture.

ALAUNT: a legendary pack of hounds that now run with Azhure. They are all of the Lesser immortals.

ALDENI: a small province in western Achar, devoted to small crop cultivation. It is administered by Duke Theod.

ANDAKILSA, RIVER: the extreme northern river of Ichtar, dividing Ichtar from Ravensbund. Under normal circumstances, it remains free of ice all year round and flows into the Andeis Sea.

ANDEIS SEA: the often unpredictable sea that washes the western coast of Achar.

ARCEN: the major city of Arcness. It is a free trading city.

ARCNESS: large eastern province in Achar, specializing in pigs.

ARTOR THE PLOWMAN: the now disbanded Brotherhood of the Seneschal taught that Artor was the one true god. Under His sway, the Acharites initiated the ancient Wars of the Ax and drove the Icarii and Avar from the land. Artor was killed by Azhure and her hounds.

ASKAM, PRINCE OF THE WEST: son of Belial and Cazna. Zared's seizure of the title of King of the Acharites and his marriage to Askam's sister, Leagh, has severely disrupted Askam's political and economic power.

AVAR, THE: the ancient race of Tencendor who live in the forests of the Avarinheim and Minstrelsea. The Avar are sometimes referred to as the People of the Horn. Their Mage-King is Isfrael.

AVARINHEIM, THE: the northern forest home of the Avar people.

AVENUE, THE: the processional way of the Temple Complex on the Island of Mist and Memory.

AVONSDALE: province in western Achar. It produces legumes, fruit and flowers. It is administered by Earl Herme.

AXIS: son of the Princess Rivkah of Achar and the Icarii Enchanter, StarDrifter SunSoar. Once BattleAxe of the Ax-Wielders, he assumed the mantle of the StarMan of the Prophecy of the Destroyer. After reforging Tencendor Axis formed his own house, the House of the Stars. He is now the Star God of Song.

AX-WIELDERS, THE: once the elite crusading and military wing of the Seneschal. Once led by Axis as their BattleAxe, the Ax-Wielders are now completely disbanded.

AZHURE: daughter of WolfStar SunSoar and Niah of Nor, and Goddess of the Moon. She is married to Axis. Their children are Caelum, Drago, RiverStar (now dead) and Zenith.

AZLE, RIVER: a major river that divides the provinces of Ichtar and Aldeni. It flows into the Andeis Sea.

BANES: the religious leaders of the Avar people. They wield magic, although it is usually of the minor variety.

BARROWS, THE ANCIENT: the burial places of the ancient Enchanter-Talons of the Icarii people. Located in southern Arcness, the Barrows guard the entrance to the Star Gate.

BATTLEAXE, THE: once the leader of the Ax-Wielders. The post of BattleAxe was last held by Axis. See "Ax-Wielders."

BARZULA: one of the TimeKeeper Demons, Barzula is the Demon of mid-morning, and of tempest.

BEDWYR FORT: a fort that sits on the lower reaches of the River Nordra and guards the entrance to Grail Lake from Nordmuth.

BELIAL: lieutenant and second-in-command in Axis' army during the fight against Gorgrael. Belial is the father of Askam and Cazna. Now dead.

BELTIDE: see "Festivals."

BERIN, BARON: a minor nobleman of Romsdale.

BOGLE MARSH: a large and inhospitable marsh in eastern Arcness. Strange creatures are said to live in the Marsh.

BORNEHELD: Duke of Ichtar and King of Achar. Son of the Princess Rivkah and her husband, Duke Searlas, half-brother to Axis, and husband of Lady Faraday of Skarabost. After murdering his uncle, Priam, Borneheld assumed the throne of Achar. Now dead.

BRACKEN RANGES, THE: the former name of the Minaret Peaks.

BRACKEN, RIVER: the river that rises in the Minaret Peaks and which, dividing the provinces of Skarabost and Arcness, flows into the Widowmaker Sea.

BRANDON: a soldier in Zared's force.

BRIDGE, THE: the bridge that guards the entrance into Sigholt is deeply magical. She will throw out a challenge to any she does not know, but can be easily tricked.

BROTHER-LEADER, THE: the supreme leader of the Brotherhood of the now disbanded Seneschal. The last Brother-Leader of the Seneschal was Jayme.

CAELUM STARSON: eldest son of Axis and Azhure, born at Yuletide. Caelum is an ancient word meaning "Stars in Heaven." Caelum now rules Tencendor.

CARLON: main city of Tencendor and one-time residence of the Kings of Achar. Situated on Grail Lake.

CAULDRON LAKE, THE: the lake at the center of the Silent Woman Woods.

CAZNA: wife to Belial. Now dead.

CHAMBER OF THE MOONS: chief audience and some-time banquet chamber of the ancient royal palace in Carlon. It was the site where Axis battled Borneheld to the death.

CHARONITES: a little-known race of Tencendor, they inhabit the UnderWorld. When Drago killed Orr in the chamber of the Star Gate, it is supposed that the race became extinct.

CIRCLE OF STARS, THE: see "Enchantress' Ring."

CLANS, THE: the Avar tend to segregate into Clan groups, roughly equitable with family groups.

CLOUDBURST SUNSOAR: younger brother and assassin of WolfStar SunSoar.

COHORT: see "Military Terms."

COROLEAS: the great empire to the south of Tencendor. Relations between the two countries are usually cordial.

CREST: Icarii military unit composed of twelve Wings.

CREST-LEADER: commander of an Icarii Crest.

DANCE OF DEATH, THE: dark star music that is the counterpoint to the Star Dance. It is the music made when stars miss their step and crash into each other, or swell up into red giants and implode. Only WolfStar and Azhure can wield this music, although both lost the ability to do so when the TimeKeepers destroyed the Star Gate.

DAREWING FULLHEART: senior Crest-Leader and Strike Leader of the Icarii Strike Force.

DEMONIC HOURS:
Dawn: ruled by Mot, a time of hunger.
Midmorning: ruled by Barzula, a time of tempest.
Midday: currently safe until Qeteb is resurrected.
Midafternoon: ruled by Sheol, a time of despair.
Dusk: ruled by Raspu, a time of pestilence.
Night: ruled by Rox, a time of terror.

DISTANCES:
League: roughly seven kilometers, or four and a half miles.
Pace: roughly one meter or one yard.
Hand span: roughly twenty centimeters or eight inches.

DOME OF THE MOON: a sacred dome dedicated to the Moon on Temple Mount of the Island of Mist and Memory. Only the First Priestess has access to the Dome, and it was in this Dome that Niah conceived Azhure.

DRAGONSTAR SUNSOAR: (Also known as Drago.) Second son of Axis and Azhure. Twin brother to RiverStar. DragonStar is also the name of the son StarLaughter Sun-

Soar was carrying when she was murdered by her husband, WolfStar.

DRIFTSTAR SUNSOAR: grandmother to StarDrifter, mother of MorningStar. An Enchanter and a SunSoar in her own right and wife to the SunSoar Talon. She died three hundred years before the events of this book.

EARTH TREE: a sacred tree to both the Icarii and the Avar. It is situated in the extreme northern groves of the Avarinheim forest, close to the cliffs of the Icescarp Alps.

EARTH TREE GROVE: the grove holding the Earth Tree in the northern Avarinheim where it borders the Icescarp Alps. It is the most important of the Avarinheim groves and is where the Avar (sometimes in concert with the Icarii) hold their gatherings and religious rites.

ENCHANTERS: the magicians of the Icarii people. Many of them are very powerful. All Enchanters have the word "Star" somewhere in their names.

ENCHANTER-TALONS: Talons of the Icarii people who are also Enchanters.

ENCHANTRESS, THE: the founder of the Icarii Enchanters, and the first to discover the way to use the power of the Star Dance. She bore three sons, the eldest of whom founded the Acharite race, the middle founded the Charonite race, and the youngest founded the Icarii race. The Enchantress also gave birth to twin daughters. No one knows the fathers of any of her children. The title of "Enchantress" is now occasionally given to Azhure.

ENCHANTRESS' RING, THE: an ancient ring once in the possession of the Enchantress, now worn by Azhure. Its proper name is the Circle of Stars, and it is intimately connected with the Star Gods.

ENEMY, THE: the name given by the TimeKeepers to the ancient ones who trapped Qeteb and then fled with his life parts through the universe. It was the Enemy who crashed into Tencendor during Fire-Night.

ESCATOR: a kingdom far away to the east over the Widowmaker Sea. There is some intellectual, diplomatic and trade traffic between Escator and Tencendor.

EVENSONG: daughter of Rivkah and StarDrifter SunSoar, sister to Axis and wife to FreeFall SunSoar.

FARADAY: daughter of Earl Isend of Skarabost and his wife, Lady Merlion. Once wife to Borneheld and Queen of Achar, Faraday now aids Drago. She is the mother of Isfrael, who was conceived during her brief and tragic affair with Axis.

FERNBRAKE LAKE, THE: the large lake in the center of the Bracken Ranges. Also known by both the Avar and the Icarii as the Mother.

FERRYMAN, THE: the Charonite who plied the ferry of the UnderWorld. His name was Orr, and was one of the Lesser immortals. Orr is now dead after being struck by the Rainbow Scepter in the chamber of the Star Gate.

FESTIVALS OF THE AVAR AND THE ICARII:
Yuletide: the winter solstice, in the last week of Snowmonth.
Beltide: the spring Festival, the first day of Flower-month.
Fire-Night: the summer solstice, in the last week of Rosemonth.

FIRE-NIGHT, THE: see "Festivals."

FIRST, THE: the First Priestess of the Order of the Stars, the order of nine priestesses on Temple Mount. The First, like all priestesses of the Order, gave up her name on taking her vows. Niah of Nor once held this office.

FIVE FAMILIES, THE FIRST: the leading families of Tencendor, led, in turn, by Prince Askam of the West, King Zared of the North, Prince Yllgaine of Nor, Chief Sa'Domai of the Ravensbund and FreeFall SunSoar, Talon of the Icarii. The delicate balance between these families was greatly upset when Zared seized the throne of Achar.

FLULIA: one of the nine Icarii Star Gods, Flulia is the Goddess of Water.

FLURIA, RIVER: a minor river that flows through Aldeni into the River Nordra.

FORESTFLIGHT EVERSOAR: a member of the Lake Guard.

FORTHEART: one of the Alaunt, and mate to Sicarius.

FORTRESS RANGES: the mountains that run down Achar's eastern boundary from the Icescarp Alps to the Widowmaker Sea.

Pilgrim

"The world Douglass portrays stands with the most inventive creations of fantasy literature . . . Douglass' characters, both good and evil, move beyond stereotypes into flesh and blood."
—*Romantic Times BookClub Magazine* (4½ stars, Top Pick)

Sinner

"Douglass smoothly fills in some backstory about the Sun-Soar dynasty . . . fans of this ambitious epic fantasy should be eager to find out what happens in book five."
—*Publishers Weekly*

Starman

"[*Starman*] should satisfy a fantasy readership hungry for strong female characters."   —*Publishers Weekly*

"Exciting writing with emotional highs and lows! Ms. Douglass has created a mystical world populated with many vividly portrayed races."
—*Romantic Times BookClub Magazine* (4½ stars)

"Heartfelt."   —*Kirkus Review*

"A superior adventure fantasy right to the last."   —*Booklist*

Enchanter

"Douglass holds her own as her characters deepen inventively."
—*Kirkus Review*

"With three races. licit and illicit loves, prophecy, fraternal hatred, and enough battles for several campaigns, Douglass has whipped up enough raw material to avoid shortchanging readers throughout her vast undertaking. Moreover, who has plenty of talent . . . No one who liked its predecessor is likely to complain about Enchanter."   —*Booklist*

"Douglass consistently demonstrates a consistently high standard of storytelling in the epic fantasy tradition."
—*Library Journal*

Pilgrim

— BOOK FIVE OF —

THE WAYFARER REDEMPTION

Sara Douglass

TOR®
fantasy

A TOM DOHERTY ASSOCIATES BOOK
NEW YORK

This is a work of fiction. All the characters and events portrayed in this book are either products of the author's imagination or are used fictitiously.

PILGRIM: BOOK FIVE OF THE WAYFARER REDEMPTION

Copyright © 1997 by Sara Douglass
Teaser copyright © 2006 by Sara Douglass

Originally published in 1997 by Voyager, an imprint of HarperCollins Publishers, Australia.

A Tor Book
Published by Tom Doherty Associates, LLC
175 Fifth Avenue
New York, NY 10010

www.tor.com
Tor® is a registered trademark of Tom Doherty Associates, LLC.

ISBN 0-765-34279-0
EAN 978-0-765-34279-9

First Tor edition: September 2005
First mass market edition: May 2006

Printed in the United States of America

0 9 8 7 6 5 4 3 2 1

Author's Note

I wrote this book while replanting and laying out the century-old gardens of Ashcotte, and their thousands of lilies and cornflowers and peonies and poppies and violets somehow found their way through the open spring windows onto these pages. Thus, *Pilgrim* is in part the re-creation of the field of flowers which surrounds Ashcotte.